PRAISE FOR *SPANDAU PHOENIX*

"AMAZING . . . A MASTERWORK . . .
A TOWERING NOVEL . . . A THRILLER WHOSE
DEPTH AND SCOPE ARE SWEEPING . . .
TWISTING LIKE A SLALOM COURSE
DOWNSHIFTING THROUGH HISTORY."
—*The Tampa Tribune*

"Plot twists, villains, danger . . . compelling writing and thrill-a-minute action."
—*The Clarion-Ledger* (Jackson, MS)

"Compelling and convincing . . . speculating on one of history's most intriguing puzzles . . . and . . . possibilities."
—*The New Orleans Times-Picayune*

"An epic blend of fact and fiction . . . a frightening, fascinating page-turner full of action and suspense."
—*Hattiesburg American*

"Wins the title of 'thriller writers' thriller writer.' "
—Richard Condon

"Intriguing, intricate, tense . . . damn good suspense."
—Victor O'Reilly, author of
The Devil's Footprint

"An auspicious tale!" —*Rocky Mountain News*

"Fascinating historical speculation . . . fueled by dynamic characters and plenty of action."
—*Armed Forces Journal International*

BOOKS BY GREG ILES

Sleep No More
Dead Sleep
24 Hours
The Quiet Game
Mortal Fear
Black Cross

GREG ILES

SPANDAU PHOENIX

New American Library

New American Library
Published by New American Library, a division of
Penguin Putnam Inc., 375 Hudson Street,
New York, New York 10014, U.S.A.
Penguin Books Ltd, 80 Strand,
London WC2R 0RL, England
Penguin Books Australia Ltd, 250 Camberwell Road,
Camberwell, Victoria 3124, Australia
Penguin Books Canada Ltd, 10 Alcorn Avenue,
Toronto, Ontario, Canada M4V 3B2
Penguin Books (N.Z.) Ltd, Cnr Rosedale and Airborne Roads,
Albany, Auckland 1310, New Zealand

Penguin Books Ltd, Registered Offices:
Harmondsworth, Middlesex, England

Published by New American Library, a division of Penguin Putnam Inc.
Previously published in a Dutton hardcover edition and a Signet mass market
edition.

First New American Library Printing, January 2003
10 9 8 7 6 5 4 3 2 1

New American Library Trade Paperback ISBN: 0-451-21026-3

The Library of Congress has catalogued the hardcover edition
of this title as follows:

Iles, Greg.
Spandau Phoenix / Greg Iles.
    p. cm.
  ISBN 0-525-93604-1
  1. Spandau Prison (Berlin, Germany)—History—Fiction. 2. Hess, Rudolf,
1894–1987—Fiction. 3. World War. 1939–1945—Fiction.
I. Title.
PS3559.L47S6   1993
813'.54—dc20

Printed in the United States of America

PUBLISHER'S NOTE
This is a work of fiction. Names, characters, places, and incidents either are the
product of the author's imagination or are used fictitiously, and any
resemblance to actual persons, living or dead, business establishments, events, or
locales, is entirely coincidental.

To Jerry W. Iles, M.D.

ACKNOWLEDGMENTS

Many thanks to Natasha Kern, my literary agent, who proves every day that you don't have to live in New York to play in the big leagues. All authors should be so lucky.

Many thanks to Ed Stackler, my editor, who knew some of my characters better than I did. For effort and enthusiasm far beyond the call of duty.

Many thanks to Hans-Friedrich Müller of the Berliner Rathaus, for expediting my research in Germany; and to Bettina Rauch and Jürgen van der Brock of the Berlin *Polizei,* who had no control over the content of this book, and asked for none. Thanks also to those officers who prefer not to be named.

Special thanks to Betty Iles, my unofficial editor, for a critical eye; to Ken Cumbus, my computer ace; and to Courtney Aldridge, a true friend and a jaded reader, who kept me honest throughout.

Most of all, thanks to my wife, Carrie, for unflagging faith and love.

PROLOGUE

What is history but a fable agreed upon?
—NAPOLEON BONAPARTE

10 May 1941

The North Sea lay serene, unusual for spring, but night would soon fall on a smoking, broken continent reeling from the shock of war. From the bloody dunes of Dunkirk to the bomb-shattered streets of Warsaw, from the frozen tip of Norway to the deserted beaches of the Mediterranean—Europe was enslaved. Only England, beleaguered and alone, stood against the massed armies of Hitler's *Wehrmacht,* and tonight London was scheduled to die.

By *fire.* At 1800 hours Greenwich time the greatest single concentration of *Luftwaffe* bombers ever assembled would unleash their fury upon the unprotected city, and over seven hundred acres of the British capital would cease to exist. Thousands of incendiary bombs would rain down upon civilian and soldier alike, narrowly missing St. Paul's Cathedral, gutting the Houses of Parliament. History would record that strike against London as the worst of the entire war, a holocaust. And yet . . .

. . . all this—the planning, the casualties, the goliathan destruction—was but the puff of smoke from a magician's gloved hand. A spectacular diversion calculated to draw the eyes of the world away from a mission so daring and intricate that it would defy understanding for generations to come. The man behind this ingenious plot was Adolf Hitler, and tonight, unknown to a single member of his General Staff, he would reach out from the Berghof and undertake the most ambitious military feat of his life.

He had worked miracles before—the blitzkrieg of Poland, the penetration of the "impassable" Ardennes—but this would be the crowning achievement of his career. It would raise him at last above Alexander, Caesar, and Napoleon. In one stunning blow, he would twist the balance of world power inside out, transforming his mortal foe into an ally and consigning his present ally to destruction. To succeed he would have to reach into the very heart of Britain, but not with bombs or missiles. Tonight he needed precision, and he had chosen his weapons accordingly: treachery, weakness, envy, fanaticism—the most destructive forces available to man. All were familiar tools in Hitler's hand, and all were in place.

But such forces were unpredictable. Traitors lived in terror of discovery; agents feared capture. Fanatics exploded without warning, and weak men invited betrayal. To effectively utilize such resources, Hitler knew, someone had to be *on the scene*—reassuring the agent, directing the fanatic, holding the hand of the traitor and a gun to the head of the coward. But who could handle such a mission? Who could inspire both trust *and* fear in equal measure? Hitler knew such a man. He was a soldier, a man of forty-eight, a pilot. And he was already in the air.

Two thousand feet above Amsterdam, the Messerschmitt Bf-110 *Zerstörer* plowed through a low ceiling of cumulus clouds and burst into clear sky over the glittering North Sea. The afternoon sun flashed across the fighter's silver wings, setting off the black-painted crosses that struck terror into the stoutest hearts across Europe.

Inside the cockpit, the pilot breathed a sigh of relief. For the last four hundred miles he had flown a tiring, highly restricted route, changing altitude several times to remain within the Luftwaffe's prescribed corridors of safety. Hitler's personal pilot had given him the coded map he carried, and, with it, a warning. Not for amusement were the safety zones changed daily, Hans Bahr had whispered; with British Spitfires regularly penetrating Hermann Göring's "impenetrable" wall of air defense, the danger was real, precautions necessary.

The pilot smiled grimly. Enemy fighters were the least of his worries this afternoon. If he failed to execute the next step of his mission perfectly, it would be a squadron of Messerschmitts, not Spitfires, that shot him into the sea. At any moment the Luftwaffe flight controllers expected him to turn back for Germany, as he had a dozen times before, test flying the fighter lent to him personally by Willi Messerschmitt, then returning home to his wife and child, his privileged life. But this time he would not turn back.

Checking his airspeed against his watch, he estimated the point at which he would fade from the Luftwaffe radar screens based on the Dutch island of Terschelling. He'd reached the Dutch coast at 3:28 P.M. It was now 3:40. At 220 miles per hour, he should have put forty-four miles of the North Sea behind him already. German radar was no match for its British counterpart, he knew, but he would wait another three minutes just to make sure. Nothing could be left to chance tonight. *Nothing.*

The pilot shivered inside his fur-lined leather flying suit. So much depended upon his mission: the fates of England and Germany, very possibly the whole world. It was enough to make any man shiver. And *Russia,* that vast, barbaric land infected by the cancer of communism—his Fatherland's ancient enemy—if he succeeded tonight, Russia would kneel beneath the swastika at last!

The pilot nudged the stick, dipping the Messerschmitt's left wing, and looked down through the thick glass canopy. *Almost time.* He looked at his watch, counting. *Five . . . four . . . three . . . two . . .*

Now! Like a steel falcon he swooped toward the sea, hurtling downward at over four hundred miles per hour. At the last instant he jerked the stick back and leveled out, skimming the wave tops as he stormed north toward Aalborg, the main Luftwaffe fighter base in Denmark. His desperate race had begun.

Fighting through the heavy air at sea level, the Messerschmitt drank fuel like water, but the pilot's main concern now was secrecy. *And finding the landing signal,* he reminded himself. Two dozen training flights had familiarized him with the aircraft, but the detour to Denmark had been unexpected. He had never flown this far north without visual references. He was not afraid, but he would feel much better once he sighted the fjords of Denmark to starboard.

It had been a long time since the pilot had killed. The battles of the Great War seemed so vague now. He had certainly fired hundreds of rounds in anger, but one was never really sure about the killing. Not until the charges came, anyway—the terrible, bloody, heroically insane assaults of flesh against steel. He had almost *been* killed—he remembered that clearly enough—by a bullet in the left lung, one of three wounds he'd taken while fighting in the famous List regiment. But he had survived, that was the important thing. The dead in the enemy trenches . . . who knew, really?

He would kill tonight. He would have no choice. Checking the two compasses strapped to his left thigh, he took a careful bearing, then quickly returned his eyes to the horizon indicator. This close to the surface of the sea, the water played tricks on the mind. Hundreds of expert pilots had plowed into the waves simply by letting their concentration falter for a few moments. *Only six minutes to Aalborg,* he thought nervously. *Why risk it?* He climbed to one thousand feet, then leveled out and craned his neck to survey the sea below. Waveless, it receded before him with the gentle curve of the earth. Except . . . *there* . . . dead ahead. He could see broken coastline . . . Denmark! He had done it!

Feeling a hot surge of adrenaline, he scanned the clouds for fighter patrols. If one spotted him, he decided, he would sit tight, hold his course and pretend to be a straggler from an early raid. The hard, empty northern land flashed beneath him. His destination was a small ancillary strip just short of Aalborg air base. But where was it? The runway . . . his special cargo . . . *where?*

A thousand feet below, the red flash of railway flares suddenly lit up in parallel lines to his left. *The signal!* A lone green flare indicated the proper direction of approach. The pilot circled wide until he had come 180 degrees, then began nursing the Messerschmitt in. The strip was short—no margin for error. Altimeter zero. With bated breath he felt tentatively for the runway. Nothing . . . nothing . . . *whump!*—the wheels dropped hard onto concrete. The plane shuddered from the impact but steadied fast. Cutting his engines, the pilot rolled to a stop thirty meters beyond the last two flares.

Before he could unfasten his harness, two ground crewmen slid the canopy back over his head. Silently, they helped him with his straps and pulled him from the cockpit. Their rough familiarity startled him, but he let it pass. To them he was just another pilot—on a somewhat irregular mission perhaps, operating solo from a practically deserted strip south of the base—but just a pilot, all the same. Had he removed his flying helmet and goggles, the crewmen would have exhibited quite a different attitude, and certainly would not have touched him without permission. The pilot's face was known to every man, woman, and child in Germany—indeed to millions across Europe and the world.

Without a word, he walked a little way off the strip and unzipped his suit to relieve himself. There were only the two crewmen, he saw, and they had been well briefed. From a battered tank truck one pumped fuel into the plane while the other toiled with special fittings beneath the Messerschmitt's left wing. The pilot scanned the small runway. There was an old sock-type wind indicator, a pile of scrap parts left from pre-war days, and, several yards down the strip, a small wooden shack that had probably once housed some Danish mechanic's tools.

It houses something quite different now, I'll wager, he thought. Zipping up, he walked slowly toward the shack, alert for any sign of human occupation. The sleek black bonnet of a Daimler jutted from behind the ramshackle building, gleaming like a funeral hearse. The pilot slipped around the shack and peered through the windshield of the car. Empty. Remembering his instructions, he wound a long flying scarf around the lower half of his face. It made breathing difficult, but combined with his flying helmet, it left only his eyes visible to an observer. He entered the shack without knocking.

Darkness shrouded the interior, but the fetid air was pregnant with human presence. Someone, not the pilot, lit a lantern, and the room slowly revealed itself. A major wearing the smart black uniform of Himmler's SS stood less than a meter from the pilot. Unlike most of his type, this representative of Himmler's "elite corps" was quite fat. He looked more accustomed to the comforts of a soft billet like Paris than a battle zone. Behind him, a thinner man dressed in a leather flying suit sat rigidly in a straight-backed wooden chair. Like the pilot, his face was also draped by a scarf. His eyes darted nervously between the newcomer and the SS man.

"Right on time," the SS major said, looking at his watch. "I'm Major Horst Berger."

The pilot nodded, but offered no name.

"Drink?" A bottle appeared from the shadows. "Schnapps? Cognac?"

My God, the pilot thought. *Does the fool carry a stocked bar about in his car?* He shook his head emphatically, then jerked his thumb toward the half-open door. "I'll see to the preparations."

"Nonsense," Major Berger replied, dismissing the idea with a flick of his bottle. "The crewmen can handle it. They're some of the best from Aalborg. It's a shame, really."

It is, the pilot thought. *But I don't think you're too upset about it. I think you're enjoying all this.* "I'm going back to the plane," he muttered.

The man in the wooden chair stood slowly.

"Where do you think you're going?" Major Berger barked, but the man ignored him. "Oh, all right," Berger complained. He buttoned his collar and followed the pair out of the shack.

"They know about the drop tanks?" the pilot asked, when Berger had caught up.

"*Ja.*"

"The nine-hundred-liter ones?"

"Sure. Look, they're fitting them now."

Berger was right. On the far side of the plane, two ground crewmen attached the first of two egg-shaped auxiliary fuel containers to the Messerschmitt's blunt-tipped wings. When they finished, they moved to the near side of the aircraft.

"Double-check the wet-points!" the pilot called.

The chief mechanic nodded, already working.

The pilot turned to Major Berger. "I had an idea," he said. "Flying up."

The SS man frowned. "What idea?"

"I want them to grease my guns before we take off."

"What do you mean? Lubricate them? I assure you that the weapons are in perfect working order."

"No, I want them to pack the barrels with grease."

Behind Major Berger, the man in the flying suit stepped sideways and looked curiously at the pilot.

"You can't be serious," Berger objected. He turned around. "Tell him," he said. But the man in the flying suit only cocked his head to one side.

"But that's suicide!" Major Berger insisted. "One chance encounter with a British patrol and—" He shook his head. "I simply cannot allow it. If you're shot down, my career could take a very nasty turn!"

Your career is over already, the pilot thought grimly. "Grease the guns!" he shouted to the crewmen, who, having fitted the empty drop tanks, now anxiously pumped fuel into them. The chief mechanic stood at the rear of the fuel truck, trying to decide which of the two men giving orders was really in charge. He knew Major Berger from Aalborg, but something about the tall, masked pilot hinted at a more dangerous authority.

"You can't do that!" Major Berger protested. "Stop that there! I'm in command here!"

The chief mechanic shut off the fuel hose and stared at the three men at the edge of the runway. Slowly, with great purpose, the pilot pointed a long arm toward the crewman under the wing and shouted through his scarf: *"You! Grease my guns! That's a direct order!"*

The chief mechanic recognized the sound of authority now. He climbed onto the fuel truck to get a grease gun from his tool box.

Major Berger laid a quivering hand on a Schmeisser machine pistol at his belt. "You have lost your mind, I believe," he said softly. "Rescind that order immediately or I'll put you under arrest!"

Glancing back toward the crewmen—who were now busy packing the Messerschmitt's twenty-millimeter cannon with heavy black grease—the pilot took hold of his scarf and unwrapped it slowly from his head. When his face became visible, the SS man fell back a step, his eyes wide in shock. Behind him the man in the flying suit swallowed hard and turned away.

The pilot's face was dark, saturnine, with eyes set deep beneath bushy black brows that almost met in the center. His imperious stare radiated command. "Remove your hand from that pistol," he said quietly.

For several moments Major Berger stood still as stone. Then, slowly, he let his hand fall from the Schmeisser's grip. "Jawohl, Herr . . . Herr Reichminister."

"Now, Herr Major! And be about your business! Go!"

Suddenly Major Berger was all action. With a pounding heart he hurried toward the Messerschmitt, his face hot and tingling with fear. Blood roared in his ears. He had just threatened to place the Deputy Führer of the German Reich—*Rudolf Hess*—under arrest! In a daze he ordered the crewmen to speed their packing of the guns. While they complied, he harried them about their earlier maintenance. Were the wet-points clear? Would the wing drop tanks disengage properly when empty?

At the edge of the runway, Hess turned to the man in the flying suit. "Come closer," he murmured.

The man took a tentative step forward and stood at attention. "You understand about the guns?" Hess asked.

Slowly the man nodded assent.

"I know it's dangerous, but it's dangerous for us both. Under certain circumstances it could make all the difference."

Again the man nodded. He was a pilot also, and had in fact flown many more missions than the man who had so suddenly assumed command of this situation. He understood the logic: a plane purported to be on a mission of peace would appear much more convincing with its guns disabled. But even if he hadn't understood, he was in no position to argue.

"It's been a long time, *Hauptmann,*" Hess said, using the rank of captain in place of a name.

The captain nodded. Overhead a pair of Messerschmitts roared by from Aalborg, headed south on patrol.

"It is a great sacrifice you have made for your country, *Hauptmann.* You and men like you have given up all normality so that men like myself could prosecute the war in comparative safety. It's a great burden, is it not?"

The captain thought fleetingly of his wife and child. He had not seen them for over three years; now he wondered if he ever would again. He nodded slowly.

"Once we're in the plane," said Hess, "I won't be able to see your face. Let me see it now. Before."

As the captain reached for the end of his scarf, Major Berger scurried back to tell them the plane was almost ready. The two pilots, enthralled in the strange play they found themselves acting out, heard nothing. What the SS man saw when he reached them struck him like a blow to the stomach. All his breath passed out in a single gasp, and he knew that he stood at the brink of extinction. Before him, two men with the *same face* stood together shaking hands! And *that face!* Major Berger felt as if he had stumbled into a hall of mirrors where only the dangerous people were multiplied.

The pilots gripped hands for a long moment, their eyes heavy with the knowledge that both their lives might end tonight over foreign soil in the cockpit of an unarmed fighter.

"My God," Berger croaked.

Neither pilot acknowledged his presence. "How long has it been, *Hauptmann?*" Hess asked.

"Since Dessau, Herr Reichminister."

"You look thinner." Hess murmured, "I still can't believe it. It's positively unnerving." Then sharply, "Is the plane ready, Berger?"

"I . . . I believe so, Herr—"

"To your work, then!"

"*Jawohl,* Herr Reichminister!" Major Berger turned and marched toward the crewmen, who now stood uncertainly against the fuel truck, waiting for permission to return to Aalborg. Berger unclipped his Schmeisser with one hand as he walked.

"All finished?" he called.

"*Jawohl*, Herr Major," answered the chief mechanic.

"Fine, fine. Step away from the truck, please." Berger raised the stubby barrel of his Schmeisser.

"But . . . Herr Major, what are you doing! What have we *done?*"

"A great service to your Fatherland," the SS man said. "Now—*step away from the truck!*"

The crewmen looked at each other, frozen like terrified game. Finally it dawned on them why Major Berger was hesitating. He obviously knew something about the volatility of aircraft fuel vapor. Backing closer to the truck, the chief mechanic clasped his greasy hands together in supplication. "Please, Herr Major, I have a family—"

The dance was over. Major Berger took three steps backward and fired a sustained burst from the Schmeisser. Hess screamed a warning, but it was too late. Used with skill, the Schmeisser could be a precise weapon, but Major Berger's skill was limited. Of a twelve-round burst, only four rounds struck the crewmen. The remainder tore through the rusted shell of the fuel truck like it was paper.

The explosion knocked Major Berger a dozen feet from where he stood. Hess and the captain had instinctively dived for the concrete. Now they lay prone, shielding their eyes from the flash. When Hess finally looked up, he saw Major Berger silhouetted against the flames, stumbling proudly toward them through a pall of black smoke.

"How about that!" the SS man cried, looking back at the inferno. "No evidence now!"

"Idiot!" Hess shouted. "They'll have a patrol from Aalborg here in five minutes to investigate!"

Berger grinned. "Let me take care of them, Herr Reichminister! The SS knows how to handle the *Luftwaffe!*"

Hess felt relieved; Berger was making it easy. Stupidity was something he had no patience with. "I'm sorry, Major," he said, looking hard into the SS man's face. "I cannot allow that."

Like a cobra hypnotizing a bird, Hess transfixed Berger with his dark, deep-set eyes. Quite naturally, he drew a Walther automatic from the forepouch of his flight suit and pulled back the slide. The fat SS man's mouth opened slowly; his hands hung limp at his sides, the Schmeisser clipped uselessly to his belt.

"But *why?*" he asked quietly. "Why me?"

"Something to do with Reinhard Heydrich, I believe."

Berger's eyes grew wide; then they closed. His head sagged onto his tunic.

"For the Fatherland," Hess said quietly. He pulled the trigger.

The captain jumped at the report of the Walther. Major Berger's body jerked twice on the ground, then lay still.

"Take his Schmeisser and any ammunition you can find," Hess ordered. "Check the Daimler."

"Jawohl, Herr Reichminister!"

The next few minutes were a blur of action that both men would try to remember clearly for the rest of their lives—plundering the corpse for ammunition, searching the car, double-checking the drop tanks of the aircraft, donning their parachutes, firing the twin Daimler-Benz engines, turning the plane on the old cracked concrete—both men instinctively carrying out tasks they had rehearsed a thousand times in their heads, the tension compounded by the knowledge that an armed patrol might arrive from Aalborg at any moment.

Before boarding the plane, they exchanged personal effects. Hess quickly but carefully removed the validating items that had been agreed upon: three compasses, a Leica camera, his wristwatch, some photographs, a box of strange and varied drugs, and finally the fine gold identification chain worn by all members of Hitler's inner circle. He handed them to the captain with a short word of explanation for each: "Mine, my wife's, mine, my wife and son ..." The man receiving these items already knew their history, but he kept silent. *Perhaps,* he thought, *the Reichminister speaks in farewell to all the familiar things he might lose tonight.* The captain understood that feeling well.

Even this strange and poignant ceremony merged into the mind-numbing rush of fear and adrenaline that accompanied takeoff, and neither man spoke again until they found themselves forty miles over the North Sea, arrowing toward their target. As the plan dictated, Hess had yielded the controls to the captain. Hess now sat in the radio operator's seat, facing the twin tail fins of the fighter. The two men used no names—only ranks—and limited their conversation to the mechanics of the mission.

"Range?" the captain asked, tilting his head back toward the rear-facing seat.

"Twelve hundred and fifty miles with the nine-hundred-liter tanks," Hess replied.

"I meant range to target."

"The island or the castle?"

"The island."

"Six hundred and seventy miles."

The captain asked no more questions for the next hour. He stared down at the steadily darkening sea and thought of his family. Hess studied a sheaf of papers in his lap: maps, photographs, and mini-biographies secretly copied from SS files in the basement of the Prinz-Albrechtstrasse. Ceaselessly, he went over each detail, visualizing the contingencies he could face upon landing. A hundred miles off the English coast, he began drilling the pilot in his duties.

"How much did they tell you, *Hauptmann?*"

"A lot. Too much, I think."

"You see the extra radio to your right?"

"Yes."

"You can operate it?"

"Yes."

"If all goes well, you have only a few things to remember. First, the drop tanks. Whatever happens, you ditch them into the sea. Same with the extra radio. *After* my time is up, of course. Forty minutes is the time limit, remember that. *Forty minutes.*"

"Forty minutes I wait."

"If you have not received my message within that time, the mission has failed. In that case—"

There was a sharp intake of breath from the pilot, quiet but audible. Hess knew what caused that sound—the unbanishable fear of death. He felt it too. But for him it was different. He knew the stakes of the mission, the inestimable strategic gain that dwarfed the possible loss of two human lives. Like the man in the pilot's seat, Hess too had a family—a wife and young son. But for a man in his position—a man so close to the Führer—such things were luxuries one knew might be lost at any moment. For *him* death was simply an obstacle to success that must be avoided at all costs. But for the man in the pilot's chair . . .

"*Hauptmann?*" Hess said, almost gently.

"Sir?"

"I know what frightens you now. I really do. But there are worse things than death. Do you understand me? *Far* worse."

The pilot's reply was a hoarse, hollow gurgle. Hearing it, Hess decided that empathy was not the proper motivator for this man. When he next spoke, his voice brimmed with confidence. "Dwelling on that is of no use whatsoever, *Hauptmann*. The plan is flawless. The important thing is, have you been studying?"

"Have I been studying!" The captain was obviously relieved to be talking about something else. "My God, some iron-assed SS *Brigadeführer* grilled me for two days straight."

"Probably Schellenberg."

"Who?"

"Never mind, *Hauptmann*. Better that you don't know."

Silence filled the cockpit as the pilot's mind drifted back to the fate that awaited him should his special passenger fail. "Herr Reichminister?" he asked at length.

"Yes?"

"How do you rate your chances of success?"

"It's not in my hands, *Hauptmann*, so I would be foolish to guess. It's up to the British now." *My advice is to prepare for the worst,* Hess thought bitterly. *The Führer's bankers have been since January.* "Just concentrate on your part of the mission," he said. "And for God's sake, be sure to jump from a high enough altitude to destroy the plane. It's nothing the British haven't seen before, but there's no need to make them a present of it. Once you've gotten my message, just jump and wait until I can get you released. It shouldn't take more than a few days. If you don't get the message—"

Verdammt! Hess cursed silently. *There's just no avoiding it.* His next words cut with the brittle edge of command. "If you don't get my message, *Hauptmann,* you know what must be done."

"Jawohl," the pilot murmured, hoping he sounded more confident than he felt. He was sickeningly aware of the small, sticky cyanide capsule taped against his chest. He wondered if he could possibly go through with this thing that everyone but him seemed to consider simply business as usual.

"Listen to me, *Hauptmann,"* Hess said earnestly. "You know why your participation is necessary. British Intelligence *knows* I am coming to England ..."

Hess kept talking, trying to fill the emptiness that would give the pilot too much time to think. Up here, with Germany falling far behind, the concept of duty seemed much more abstract than it did when one was surrounded by the reinforcing order of the army and the SS. The captain seemed sound—and Heydrich had vouched for him—but given enough time to consider his position, he might do anything. After all, what sane man wanted to die?

"Cut your speed!" Hess ordered, his voice quickening. "Hold at 180."

The miles had melted away before the Messerschmitt's nose. They were a mere sixty miles off the Scottish coast. On a clear evening like this, the RAF radar stations would begin to pick up reflections from the fighter at any moment. Hess tightened his parachute harness, then set aside his maps and leaned backward.

"Stay high and clear!" he shouted to the canopy lid. "Make sure they see us coming in!"

"Where are you going out?"

"We should make landfall over a place called Holy Island. I'll jump there. Stay high over the mainland for a few miles, then dive and run like hell! They'll probably scramble a whole squadron once they realize what you're flying!"

"Jawohl," the pilot acknowledged. "Herr Reichminister?"
"What is it?"

"Have you ever parachuted before?"

"Nein. Never."

An ironic laugh cut through the drone of the twin engines.

"What's so funny, *Hauptmann?*"

"I've never jumped either! That's a pretty significant fact to have overlooked in the planning of this mission, don't you think?"

Hess permitted himself a wry smile. "Perhaps that fact *was* taken into account, *Hauptmann*. Some people might even be counting on it."

"Oh . . . my God."

"It's too late to worry about that now. We don't have the fuel to make it back to Germany even if we wanted to!"

"What?" the pilot exclaimed. "But the drop tanks—"

"Are empty!" Hess finished. "Or soon will be!"

The pilot felt his stomach turn a somersault. But before he could puzzle out his passenger's meaning, he spied land below.

"Herr Reichminister! The island! I see it!"

From sixty-five hundred feet Holy Island was a tiny speck, only distinguishable by the small, bright ribbon separating it from the mainland. "And . . . a flare. I see a flare!"

"Green or red?" Hess asked, his face taut.

"Red!"

"The canopy, *Hauptmann!* Move!"

Together the two men struggled to slide back the heavy glass. Parachuting from a Messerschmitt was not common practice—strictly an emergency measure—and quite a few aviators had died attempting it.

"Push!" the pilot yelled.

With all their strength the two men heaved their bodies against the transparent lid of the cockpit. Their straining muscles quivered in agony until all at once the frame gave way and locked in the open position. The noise in the cockpit was deafening now, the engines roaring, the wind a screaming, living thing that struggled to pluck the men from their tiny tube of steel. Above it all, the pilot shouted, "We're over the gap now, Herr Reichminister! Go! Go!"

Suddenly Hess looked into his lap. *Empty.* He had forgotten to ditch his papers! No sign of them in the cockpit; they must have been sucked out the moment the canopy opened. He prayed they had found their way down to the sea, and not to the island below.

"Jump, Herr Reichminister!"

Hess struggled into a crouch and faced the lethal tail fins

of the *Zerstörer*. The time for niceties had passed. He reached behind him and jerked the pilot's head back.

"Hauptmann!" he shouted. "Heydrich only ordered those drop tanks fitted to make sure you came this far! *They are empty!* No matter what happens, you cannot turn back! You have no choice but to follow orders! If I succeed, your actions really won't matter! But if I *fail,* you cannot! You know the price of failure—*Sippenhaft!* Never forget that! *Sippenhaft* binds us both! Now *climb!* Give me some draft!"

The Messerschmitt's nose pitched up, momentarily creating a small space shielded from the wind. With a defiant yell Hess hurled himself up and backward. A novice, he pulled the ripcord the moment he cleared the plane. The tight-folded silk tore open with a ripping sound, then quickly blossomed into a soft white mushroom that circled lazily down through the mist toward the Scottish earth below.

Cursing, the pilot struggled to secure the canopy. Without help it was twice as difficult, but Hess's final words had chilled him to the core. Only a sheet of curved glass could now separate him from the terrifying destiny he had been ordered to face. With the desperate strength of a condemned man, he slammed it shut.

He dipped his left wing and glanced backward. There was the descending chute, soft and distant and peaceful. Barring a catastrophic landing, the Reichminister would at least begin his mission safely. It heartened the pilot to know that a novice could actually clear the plane, but something deeper in him recoiled in dread.

They had tricked him! The bastards had lured him into a suicidal mission by letting him think he would have a way out! After all his training, they hadn't even trusted him to carry out his orders! Empty auxiliary tanks. The *swine!* They had known he would have sole control of the plane after Hess jumped, and they had made sure he wouldn't have enough fuel to turn back if the mission went bad. And as if that weren't enough ... Hess had threatened him with *Sippenhaft!*

Sippenhaft! The word caused the pilot's breath to come in quick gasps. He had heard tales of the Nazis' ultimate penalty for betrayal, but he hadn't really believed them. *Sippenhaft* dictated that not only a traitor's life but the lives of his entire family became forfeit when judgment was rendered against him. Children, parents, the aged and infirm—

none were spared. There was no appeal, and the sentence, once decreed, was swiftly executed.

With a guttural scream the pilot cursed God for giving him another man's face. In that moment, he felt it was a surer death sentence than a cancer of the brain. Setting his mouth in a grim line, he hurled the plane into a screaming dive, not pulling up until the rocky Scottish earth seemed about to shatter the nose of his aircraft. Then—as Hess had suggested—he ran like hell, opening the *Zerstörer* up to 340 miles per hour over the low stone villages and patchwork fields. In other circumstances, the heart-stopping, ground-level flight might have been an exhilarating experience. Tonight it felt like a race against death.

It was. A patrolling Boulton Paul Defiant had answered a scramble call from the RAF plotting room at Inverness. The Messerschmitt pilot never even saw it. Oblivious, he stormed across the darkening island like a banshee, sixteen feet above the earth. With the twin-engined Messerschmitt's tremendous speed advantage, the pursuing British fighter was outpaced like a sparrow behind a hunting hawk.

Dungavel Hill rose in the distance. *Height: 458 meters:* the information chattered into the pilot's brain like a ticker tape. "There it is," he muttered, spying the silhouette of Dungavel Castle. "My part of this insane mission." The castle flashed beneath his fuselage. With one hand he checked the radio set near his right knee. Working. *Please call,* he thought. *Please . . .*

He heard nothing. Not even static. With shaking hands he touched the stick and hopped over a line of trees bisecting a sheep pasture. He saw fields . . . a road . . . more trees . . . then the town of Kilmarnock, sprawled dark across the road. He swept on. A patch of mist, then fog, the sea!

Like a black arrow he shot out over the western coast of Scotland, climbing fast. To his left he sighted his turning landmark, a giant rock jutting 120 meters into the sky, shining pale in the moonlight. As if drawn by a magnet, his eyes locked onto the tiny face of his newly acquired watch. Thirty minutes gone and no signal. Ten minutes from now his fate would be sealed. *If you receive no signal in forty minutes,* Hauptmann, *you will turn out to sea and swallow your cyanide capsule . . .* He wondered if he would be dead before his plane plowed into the icy depths of the North Atlantic.

Christ in Heaven! his mind screamed. *What mad bastard dreamed this one up?* But he knew—Reinhard Heydrich—the maddest bastard of them all. Steeling himself against panic, he banked wide to the south and flew parallel to the coast, praying that Hess's signal would come. His eyes flicked across the instrument panel. Altimeter, airspeed, compass, fuel—the *tanks!* Without even looking down he jerked a lever next to his seat. Two auxiliary fuel tanks tumbled down through the darkness. One would be recovered from the Clyde estuary the next day by a British drifter, empty.

The radio stayed silent. He checked it again. Still working. His watch showed thirty-nine minutes gone. His throat went dry. Sixty seconds to zero hour. Sixty seconds to suicide. *Here you are, sir, one cyanide cocktail for the glory of the Reich!* For the last time the pilot looked longingly down upon the dark mirror of the sea. His left hand crept into his flying suit and touched the cyanide capsule taped against his breast. Then, with frightening clarity, an image of his wife and daughter came into his mind. "It's not fair!" he shouted in desolation. "It's the fucking nobodies who do the dying!"

In one violent flash of terror and outrage, the pilot jerked the stick to port and headed the roaring fighter back inland. His tear-filled eyes pierced the Scottish mist, searching out the landmarks he had studied so long in Denmark. With a shudder of hope, he spied the first—railroad tracks shining like quicksilver in the night. *Maybe the signal will still come,* he hoped desperately. But he knew it wouldn't. His eyes scoured the earth for his second landmark—a small lake to the south of Dungavel Castle. *There . . .*

The Messerschmitt streaked across the water. Like a mirage the small village of Eaglesham appeared ahead. The fighter thundered across the rooftops, wheeling in a high, climbing circle over Dungavel Castle. He had done it! Like an intravenous blast of morphine, the pilot felt a sudden rush of exhilaration, a wild joy cascading through him. Ignited by the nearness of death, his survival instinct had thrown some switch deep within his brain. He had but one thought now—*survive!*

At sixty-five hundred feet the nightmare began. With no one to fly the plane while he jumped, the pilot decided to kill his engines as a safety measure. Only one engine cooperated. The other, its cylinders red-hot from the long flight from Aalborg, continued to ignite the fuel mixture. He throttled back hard until the engine died, losing precious seconds, then he wrestled the canopy open.

He could not get out of the cockpit! Like an invisible iron hand the wind pinned him to the back panel. Desperately he tried to loop the plane, hoping to drop out as it turned over, but centrifugal force, unforgiving, held him in his seat. When enough blood had rushed out of his brain, he blacked out.

Unaware of anything around him, the pilot roared toward oblivion. By the time he regained consciousness, the aircraft stood on its tail, hanging motionless in space. In a millisecond it would fall like two tons of scrap steel.

With one mighty flex of his knees, he jumped clear.

As he fell, his brain swirled with visions of the Reichminister's chute billowing open in the dying light, floating peacefully toward a mission that by now had failed. His own chute snapped open with a jerk. In the distance he saw a shower of sparks; the Messerschmitt had found the earth.

He broke his left ankle when he hit the ground, but surging adrenaline shielded his mind against the pain. Shouts of alarm echoed from the darkness. Struggling to free himself from the harness, he surveyed by moonlight the small farm at the edge of the field in which he had landed. Before he could see much of anything, a man appeared out of the darkness. It was the head plowman of the farm, a man named David McLean. The Scotsman approached cautiously and asked the pilot his name. Struggling to clear his stunned brain, the pilot searched for his cover name. When it came to him, he almost laughed aloud. Confused, he gave the man his real name instead. *What the hell?* he thought. *I don't even exist anymore in Germany. Heydrich saw to that.*

"Are you German?" the Scotsman asked.

"Yes," the pilot answered in English.

Somewhere among the dark hills the Messerschmitt finally exploded, lighting the sky with a momentary flash.

"Are there any more with you?" the Scotsman asked nervously. "From the plane?"

The pilot blinked, trying to take in the enormity of what he had done—and what he had been ordered to do. The cyanide capsule still lay like a viper against his chest. "No," he said firmly. "I flew alone."

The Scotsman seemed to accept this readily.

"I want to go to Dungavel Castle," the pilot said. Somehow, in his confusion, he could not—or would not—abandon his original mission. "I have an important message for the Duke of Hamilton," he added solemnly.

"Are you armed?" McLean's voice was tentative.

"No. I have no weapon."

The farmer simply stared. A shrill voice from the darkness finally broke the awkward silence. "What's happened? Who's out there?"

"A German's landed!" McLean answered. "Go get some soldiers."

Thus began a strange pageant of uncertain hospitality that would last for nearly thirty hours. From the McLeans' humble living room—where the pilot was offered tea on the family's best china—to the local Home Guard hut at Busby, he continued to give the name he had offered the plowman upon landing—his own. It was obvious that no one knew what to make of him. Somehow, somewhere, something had gone wrong. The pilot had expected to land inside a cordon of intelligence officers; instead he'd been met by one confused farmer. Where were the stern-faced young operatives of MI-5? Several times he repeated his request to be taken to the Duke of Hamilton, but from the bare room at Busby he was taken by army truck to Maryhill Barracks at Glasgow.

At Maryhill, the pain of his broken ankle finally burned through his shock. When he mentioned it to his captors, they transferred him to the military hospital at Buchanan Castle, about twenty miles south of Glasgow. It was there, nearly thirty hours after the unarmed Messerschmitt first crossed the Scottish coast, that the Duke of Hamilton finally arrived to confront the pilot.

Douglas Hamilton looked as young and dashing as the photograph in his SS file. The Premier Peer of Scotland, an RAF wing commander and famous aviator in his own right, Hamilton faced the tall German confidently, awaiting some explanation. The pilot stood nervously, preparing to throw himself on the mercy of the duke. Yet he hesitated. What would happen if he did that? It was possible that there had simply been a radio malfunction, that Hess was even now carrying out his secret mission, whatever it was. Heydrich might blame *him* if Hess's mission failed. And then, of course, his family would die. He could probably save his family by committing suicide as ordered, but then his child would have no father. The pilot studied the duke's face. Hamilton had met Rudolf Hess briefly at the Berlin Olympics, he knew. What did the duke see now? Fully expecting to be thrown into chains, the pilot requested that the officer accompanying the duke withdraw from the room. When he had gone, the pilot took a step toward Hamilton, but said nothing.

The duke stared, stupefied. Though his rational mind resisted it, the first seeds of recognition had been planted in his brain. The haughty bearing . . . the dark, heavy-browed patrician face . . . Hamilton could scarcely believe his eyes. And despite the duke's attempt to conceal his astonishment, the pilot saw everything in an instant. The dizzying hope of a condemned man who has glimpsed deliverance surged through him. *My God!* he thought. *It could still work! And why not? It's what I have trained to do for five years!*

The duke was waiting. Without further hesitation—and out of courage or cowardice, he would never know—the pilot stepped away from the iron discipline of a decade.

"I am Reichminister Rudolf Hess," he said stiffly. "Deputy Führer of the German Reich, leader of the Nazi Party."

With classic British reserve, the duke remained impassive. "I cannot be sure if that is true," he said finally.

Hamilton had strained for skepticism, but in his eyes the pilot discerned a different reaction altogether—not disbelief, but shock. Shock that Adolf Hitler's deputy—arguably the second most powerful man in Nazi Germany—stood before him now in a military hospital in the heart of Britain! That shock was the very sign of Hamilton's acceptance!

I am Reichminister Rudolf Hess! With a single lungful of air the frightened pilot had transformed himself into the most important prisoner of war in England. His mind reeled, drunk with the reprieve. He no longer thought of the man who had parachuted from the Messerschmitt before him. Hess's signal had not come, but no one else knew that. No one but Hess, and he was probably dead by now. The pilot could always claim he had received a garbled signal, then simply proceeded with his mission as ordered. No one could lay the failure of Hess's mission at his door. The pilot closed his eyes in relief. *Sippenhaft* be damned! No one would kill his family without giving him a chance to explain.

By taking this gamble—the only chance he could see of survival—the desperate captain unknowingly precipitated the most bizarre conspiracy of the Second World War. And a hundred miles to the east, alive or dead, the real Rudolf Hess—a man with enough secrets in his head to unleash catastrophic civil war in England—disappeared from the face of the earth.

The Duke of Hamilton maintained his attitude of skepticism throughout the brief interview, but before he left the hospital, he issued orders that the prisoner be moved to a secret location and held under double guard.

BOOK ONE
WEST BERLIN, 1987

*A talebearer revealeth secrets:
but he that is of a faithful spirit
concealeth the matter.*

PROVERBS 11.13

CHAPTER ONE

The wrecking ball arced slowly across the snow-carpeted courtyard and smashed into the last building left on the prison grounds, launching bricks through the air like moss-covered mortar rounds. Spandau Prison, the brooding red-brick fortress that had stood for over a century and housed the most notorious Nazi war criminals for the past forty years, was being leveled in a single day.

The last inmate of Spandau, Rudolf Hess, was dead. He had committed suicide just four weeks ago, relieving the West German government of the burden of one million pounds sterling it paid each year to maintain the aged Nazi's isolated captivity. In a rare display of solidarity, France, Great Britain, the United States, and the Soviet Union—the former Allies who guarded Spandau by monthly turns—had agreed that the prison should be destroyed as quickly as possible, to prevent its becoming a shrine to neo-Nazi fanatics.

Throughout the day, crowds had gathered in the cold to watch the demolition. Because Spandau stood in the British sector of Berlin, it fell to the Royal Engineers to carry out this formidable job. At first light an explosives team brought down the main structure like a collapsing house of cards. Then, after the dust settled into the snow, bulldozers and wrecking cranes moved in. They pulverized the prison's masonry, dismembered its iron skeleton, and piled the remains into huge mounds that looked all too familiar to Berliners of a certain age.

This year Berlin was 750 years old. All across the city massive construction and restoration projects had been proceeding apace in celebration of the historic anniversary. Yet this grim fortress, the Berliners knew, would never rise again. For years they had passed this way as they went about their business, rarely giving a thought to this last stubborn symbol of what, in the glow of *glasnost,* seemed ancient history. But now that Spandau's forbidding battlements no longer darkened the Wilhelmstrasse skyline, they stopped to ponder its ghosts.

By dusk, only the prison heating plant still stood, its smokestack painted in stark relief against the gunmetal clouds. A wrecking-crane drew back its mammoth concrete ball. The stack trembled, as if waiting for the final blow. The ball swung slowly through its arc, then struck like a bomb. The smokestack exploded into a cloud of brick and dust, showering what had been the prison kitchen only minutes before.

A sharp cheer cut through the din of heavy diesel motors. It came from beyond the cordoned perimeter. The cheer was not for the eradication of Spandau particularly, but rather a spontaneous human expression of awe at the sight of large-scale destruction. Irritated by the spectators, a French corporal gestured for some German policemen to help him disperse the crowd. Excellent hand signals quickly bridged the language barrier, and with trademark efficiency the Berlin Polizei went to work.

"Achtung!" they bellowed. "Go home! *Haue ab!* This area is clearly marked as dangerous! Move on! It's too cold for gawking! Nothing here but brick and stone!"

These efforts convinced the casually curious, who continued home with a story of minor interest to tell over dinner. But others were not so easily diverted. Several old men lingered across the busy street, their breath steaming in the cold. Some feigned boredom, others stared openly at the wrecked prison or glanced furtively at the others who had stayed behind. A stubborn knot of young toughs—dubbed "skinheads" because of their ritually shaven scalps—swaggered up to the floodlit prison gate to shout Nazi slogans at the British troops.

They did not go unnoticed. Every passerby who had shown more than a casual interest in the wrecking operation had been photographed today. Inside the trailer being used to coordinate the demolition, a Russian corporal carefully clicked off two telephoto exposures of every person who remained on the block after the German police moved in. Within the hour these photographs would find their way into KGB caserooms in East Berlin, where they would be digitized, fed into a massive database, and run through a formidable electronic gauntlet. Intelligence agents, Jewish fanatics, radical journalists, surviving Nazis: each exotic species would be painstakingly identified and catalogued, and any unknowns handed over to the East German secret police—the notorious Stasi—to be manually compared against their files.

These steps would consume priceless computer time and many man-hours of work by the East Germans, but Moscow didn't mind asking. The destruction of Spandau was anything but routine to the KGB. Lavrenti Beria himself, chief of the brutal NKVD under Stalin, had passed a special directive down through the successive heads of the *cheka,* defining the importance of Spandau's inmates to unsolved cases. And on this evening—thirty-four years after Beria's death by firing squad—only one of those cases remained open. Rudolf Hess. The current chief of the KGB did not intend to leave it that way.

A little way up the Wilhelmstrasse, perched motionless on a low brick wall, a sentinel even more vigilant than the Russians watched the Germans clear the street. Dressed as a laborer and almost seventy years old, the watcher had the chiseled face of a hawk, and he stared with bright, unblinking eyes. He needed no camera. His brain instantaneously recorded each face that appeared in the street, making associations and judgments no computer ever could.

His name was Jonas Stern. For twelve years Stern had not left the State of Israel; indeed, no one knew that he was in Germany now. But yesterday he had paid out of his own pocket to travel to this country he hated beyond all thought. He had known about Spandau's destruction, of course, they all did. But something deeper had drawn him here. Three days ago—as he carried water from the *kibbutz* well to his small shack on the edge of the Negev desert—something bilious had risen from his core and driven him to this place. Stern had not resisted. Such premonitions came infrequently, and experience had taught him they were not to be ignored.

Watching the bulwarked prison being crushed into powder, he felt opposing waves of triumph and guilt roll through his chest. He had known—he *knew*—men and women who had passed through Spandau on their way to the death factories of Mauthausen and Birkenau. Part of him wished the prison could remain standing, as a monument to those souls, and to the punishment meted out to their murderers.

Punishment, he thought, *but not justice. Never justice.*

Stern reached into a worn leather bag at his side and withdrew an orange. He peeled it while he watched the demolition. The light was almost gone. In the distance a huge yellow crane backed too quickly across the prison courtyard. Stern tensed as the flagstones cracked like brittle bones.

Ten minutes later the mechanical monsters ground to a screeching halt. While the senior British officer issued his dismissal orders, a pale yellow Berlin city bus rumbled up to the prison, headlights cutting through the lightly falling snow. The moment it stopped, twenty-four soldiers dressed in a potpourri of uniforms spilled into the darkening prison yard and broke into four groups of six. These soldiers represented a compromise typical of the farcical Four Power administration of Spandau. The normal month-long guard tours were handled by rota, and went off with a minimum of friction. But the destruction of the prison, like every previous disruption of routine, had brought chaos. First the Russians had refused to accept German police security at the prison. Then—because no Allied nation trusted any of its "allies" to guard Spandau's ruins alone—they decided they would *all* do it, with a token detachment of West Berlin police along to keep up appearances. While the Royal Engineers boarded the idling bus, the NCO's of the four guard details deployed their men throughout the compound.

Near the shattered prison gate, a black American master sergeant gave his squad a final brief: "Okay, ladies. Everybody's got his sector map, right?"

"Sir!" barked his troops in unison.

"Then listen up. This ain't gate duty at the base, got it? The Germs have the perimeter—we got the interior. Our orders are to guard this wreckage. That's *os*tensibly, as the captain says. We are *here* to watch the Russians. They watch us; we watch them. Same old same old, right? Only these Ivans probably ain't grunts, dig? Probably GRU—maybe even KGB. So keep your pots on and your slits open. Questions?"

"How long's the gig, Sarge?"

"This pa*trol* lasts twelve hours, Chapman, six to six. If you're still awake then—and you'd better be—then you can get back to your hot little pastry on the Bendlerstrasse."

When the laughter died, the sergeant grinned and barked, "Spread out, gentlemen! The enemy is already in place."

As the six Americans fanned out into the yard, a green-and-white Volkswagen van marked POLIZEI stopped in the street before the prison. It waited for a break in traffic, then jounced over the curb and came to rest before the command trailer steps. Instantly, six men wearing the dusty green uniform of the West Berlin police trundled out of its cargo door and lined up between the van and the trailer.

Dieter Hauer, the captain in charge of the police contingent, climbed down from the driver's seat and stepped around the van. He had an arresting face, with a strong jaw and a full military mustache. His clear gray eyes swept once across the wrecked prison lot. In the dusk he noticed that the foul-weather ponchos of the Allied soldiers gave the impression that they all served the same army. Hauer knew better. Those young men were a fragmented muster of jangling nerves and suspicion—two dozen accidents waiting to happen.

The Germans call their police *bullen*—"bulls"—and Hauer personified the nickname. Even at fifty-five, his powerful, barrel-chested body radiated enough authority to intimidate men thirty years his junior. He wore neither gloves, helmet, nor cap against the cold, and contrary to what the recruits in his unit suspected, this was no affectation meant to impress them. Rather, as people who knew him were aware, he possessed an almost inhuman resilience against external annoyances, whether natural or man-made. Hauer called, "Attention!" as he stepped back around the van. His officers formed a tight unit beneath the command trailer's harsh floodlamp.

"I've told anyone who'd listen that we didn't want this assignment," he said. "Naturally no one gives a shit."

There were a few nervous chuckles. Hauer spat onto the snow. A hostage-recovery specialist, he plainly considered this token guard detail an affront to his dignity. "You should feel very safe tonight, gentlemen," he continued with heavy sarcasm. "We have the soldiers of France, England, the United States, and Mother Russia with us tonight. They are here to provide the security which we, the West Berlin police, are deemed *unfit* to provide." Hauer clasped his hands behind his back. "I'm sure you men feel as I do about this, but nothing can be done.

"You know your assignments. Four of you will guard the perimeter. Apfel, Weiss—you're designated rovers. You'll patrol at random, watching for improper conduct among the regular troops. What constitutes 'improper conduct' here, I have not been told. I assume it means unsanctioned searches or provocation between forces. Everyone do your best to stay clear of the Russians. Whatever agencies those men out there serve, I doubt it's the Red Army. If you have a problem, sound your whistle and *wait*. I'll come to you. Everyone else hold your position until instructed otherwise."

Hauer paused, staring into the young faces around him. His eyes lingered on a reddish-blond sergeant with gray eyes, then flicked away. "Be cautious," he said evenly, "but don't be timid. We are on German soil, regardless of what any political document may say. Any provocation, verbal or physical, will be reported to me immediately. *Immediately*."

The venom in Hauer's voice made it plain he would brook no insult from the Soviets or anyone else. He spoke as though he might even welcome it. "Check your sector maps carefully," he added. "I want no mistakes tonight. You *will* show these soldier boys the meaning of professionalism and discipline. *Go!*"

Six policemen scattered.

Hans Apfel, the reddish-blond sergeant whom Hauer had designated one of the rovers, trotted about twenty meters, then stopped and looked back at his superior. Hauer was studying a map of the prison, an unlit cigar clamped between his teeth. Hans started to walk back, but the American sergeant suddenly appeared from behind the police van and engaged Hauer in quiet conversation.

Hans turned and struck out across the snow, following the line of the Wilhemstrasse to his left. Angrily, he crushed a loose window pane beneath his boot. With no warning at all this day had become one of the most uncomfortable of his life. One minute he had been on his way out of the Friedrichstrasse police station, headed home to his wife; the next a duty sergeant had tapped him on the shoulder, said he needed a good man for a secret detail, and practically thrust Hans into a van headed for Spandau Prison. That in itself was a pain in the ass. Double shifts were hell, especially those that had to be pulled on foot in the snow.

But that wasn't the real source of Hans's discomfort. The problem was that the commander of the guard detail, Captain Dieter Hauer, was Hans's father. None of the other men on this detail knew that—for which Hans was grateful—but he had a strange feeling that might soon change. During the ride to Spandau, he had stared resolutely out of the van window, refusing to be drawn into conversation. He couldn't understand how it had happened. He and his father had a long-standing arrangement—a simple agreement designed to deal with a complex family situation—and Hauer must have broken it. It was the only explanation. After a few minutes of bitter confusion, Hans resolved to deal with this situation the way he always did. By ignoring it.

He kicked a mound of snow out of his path. So far he had made only two cautious circuits of the perimeter. He felt more than a little tense about strolling into a security zone where soldiers carried loaded assault rifles as casually as their wallets. He panned his eyes across the dark lot, shielding them from the snow with a gloved hand. *God, but the British did their job well,* he thought. Ghostly mountains of jagged brick and iron rose up out of the swirling snow like the bombed-out remnants of Berlin buildings that had never been restored. Drawing a deep breath, he stepped forward into the shadows.

It was a strange journey. For fifteen or twenty steps he would see nothing but the glow of distant street lamps. Then a soldier would materialize, a black mirage against the falling snow. Some challenged him, most did not. When they did, Hans simply said, "Versailles"—the code word printed at the bottom of his sector map—and they let him pass.

He couldn't shake a vague feeling of anxiety that had settled on his shoulders. As he passed the soldiers, he tried to focus on the weapon each carried. In the darkness all the uniforms looked alike, but the guns identified everyone. Each Russian stood statue-still, his sharklike Kalashnikov resting butt-first on the ground like an extension of his arm. The French also stood, though not at attention. They cradled their FAMAS rifles in crooked elbows and tried vainly to smoke in the frigid wind. The British carried no rifles, each having been issued a sidearm in the interest of discretion.

It was the Americans who disturbed Hans. Some leaned casually against broken slabs of concrete, their weapons nowhere in evidence. Others squatted on piles of brick, hunched over their M-16 Armalites as if they could barely stay awake. None of the U.S. soldiers had even bothered to challenge Hans's passage. At first he felt angry that NATO soldiers would take such a casual approach to their duties. But after a while he began to wonder. Their indifference could simply be a ruse, couldn't it? Certainly for an assignment such as this a high-caliber team would have been chosen?

After three hours' patrol, Hans's suspicions were proved correct, when he nearly stumbled over the black American sergeant surveying the prison grounds through a bulbous scope fitted to his M-16. Not wishing to startle him, Hans whispered, "Versailles, Sergeant." When the American didn't respond, he tried again. "What can you see?"

"Everything from the command trailer on the east to that Ivan pissing on a brick pile on the west," the sergeant replied in German, never taking his eyes from the scope.

"I can't see any of that!"

"Image-intensifier," the American murmured. "Well, well ... I didn't know the Red Army let its sentries take a piss-break on guard du—*What*—" The noncom wrenched the rifle away from his face.

"What is it?" Hans asked, alarmed.

"Nothing ... *damn*. This thing works by light magnification, not infrared. That smartass flashed a spotlight toward me and whited out my scope. What an asshole."

Hans grunted in mutual distaste for the Russians. "Nice scope," he said, hoping to get a look through it himself.

"Your outfit doesn't have 'em?"

"Some units do. The drug units, mostly. I used one in training, but they aren't issued for street duty."

"Too bad." The American scanned the ruins. "This is one weird place, isn't it?"

Hans shrugged and tried to look nonchalant.

"Like a graveyard, man. A hundred and fifty cells in this place, and only one occupied—by Hess. Dude must've known some serious shit to keep him locked down that tight." The sergeant cocked his head and squinted at Hans. "Man, you know you look familiar. Yeah ... you look like that guy, that tennis player—"

"Becker," Hans finished, looking at the ground.

"Becker, yeah. Boris Becker. I guess everybody tells you that, huh?"

Hans looked up. "Once a day, at least."

"I'll bet it doesn't hurt you with the *Fräuleins*."

"I'd rather have his income," Hans said, smiling. It was his stock answer, but the American laughed. "Besides," he added, "I'm married."

"Yeah?" The sergeant grinned back. "Me too. Six years and two kids. You?"

Hans shook his head. "We've been trying, but we haven't had any luck."

"That's a bitch," said the American, shaking his head. "I got some buddies with that problem. Man, they gotta check the calendar and their old lady's temperature and every other damn thing before they can even get it on. No thanks."

When the sergeant saw Hans's expression, he said, "Hey, sorry 'bout that, man. Guess you know more about it than you ever wanted to." He raised his rifle again, sighting in on yet another invisible target. *"Bang,"* he said, and lowered the weapon. "We'd better keep moving, Boris." He disappeared into the shadows, taking the scope with him.

For the next six hours, Hans moved through the darkness without speaking to anyone, except to answer the challenges of the Russians. They seemed to be taking the operation much more seriously than anyone else, he noticed. Almost personally.

About four A.M. he decided to have a second look at his map. He approached the command trailer obliquely, walking backward to read by the glow of the single floodlamp. Suddenly he heard voices. Peering around the trailer, he saw the French and British sergeants sitting together on the makeshift steps. The Frenchman was very young, like most of the twenty-seven hundred conscripts who comprised the French garrison in Berlin. The Brit was older, a veteran of England's professional army. He did most of the talking; the Frenchman smoked and listened in silence. Now and then the wind carried distinct words to Hans. "Hess" was one— "*lef*enant" and "bloody Russians" were others. Suddenly the Frenchman stood, flicked his cigarette butt into the darkness, and strode out of the white pool of light. The Englishman followed close on his heels.

Hans turned to go, then froze. One meter behind him stood the imposing silhouette of Captain Dieter Hauer. The fiery eye of a cigar blazed orange in the darkness.

"Hello, Hans," said the deep, burnished voice.

Hans said nothing.

"Damned cold for this time of year, eh?"

"Why am I here?" Hans asked. "You broke our agreement."

"No, I didn't. This was bound to happen sooner or later, even with a twenty-thousand-man police force."

Hans considered this. "I suppose you're right," he said at length. "It doesn't matter. Just another assignment, right?"

Hauer nodded. "You've been doing a hell of a job, I hear. Youngest sergeant in Berlin."

Hans flushed a little, shrugged.

"I lied, Hans," Hauer said suddenly. "I did break our agreement. I requested you for this detail."

Hans's eyes narrowed. *"Why?"*

"Because it was busy work. Killing time. I thought we might get a chance to talk."

Hans studied the slushy ground. "So talk."

Hauer seemed to search for words. "There's a lot that needs saying."

"Or nothing."

Hauer sighed deeply. "I'd really like to know why you came to Berlin. Three years now. You must have wanted some kind of reconciliation . . . or answers, or something."

Hans stiffened. "So why are you asking the questions?"

Hauer looked hard into Hans's eyes. "All right," he said softly. "We'll wait until you're ready."

Before Hans could reply, Hauer vanished into the darkness. Even the glow of his cigar had disappeared. Hans stood still for some moments; then, shaking his head angrily, he hurried into the shadows and resumed his patrol.

Time passed quickly now, the silence broken only by an occasional siren or the roar of a jet from the British military airport at Gatow. With the snow soaking into his uniform, Hans walked faster to take his mind off the cold. He hoped he would be lucky enough to get home before his wife, Ilse, left for work. Sometimes after a particularly rough night shift, she would cook him a breakfast of *Weisswurst* and buns, even if she was in a hurry.

He checked his watch. Almost 6:00 A.M. It would be dawn soon. He felt better as the end of his shift neared. What he really wanted was to get out of the weather for a while and have a smoke. A mountain of shattered concrete near the rear of the lot looked as though it might afford good shelter, so he made for it. The nearest soldier was Russian, but he stood at least thirty meters from the pile. Hans slipped through a narrow opening when the sentry wasn't looking.

He found himself in a comfortable little nook that shielded him completely from the wind. He wiped off a slab of concrete, sat down, and warmed his face by breathing into his cupped gloves. Nestled in this dark burrow, he was invisible to the patrolling soldiers, yet he still commanded a surprisingly wide view of the prison grounds. The snow had finally stopped, and even the wind had fallen off a bit. In the predawn silence, the demolished prison looked like pictures of bombed-out Dresden he had seen as a schoolboy: motionless sentries standing tall against bleak destruction, watching over nothing.

Hans took out his cigarettes. He was trying to quit, but he still carried a pack whenever he went into a potentially stressful situation. Just the knowledge that he *could* light up sometimes calmed his nerves. But not tonight. Removing one glove with his teeth, he fumbled in his jacket for matches. He leaned as far away as he could from the opening to his little cave, scraped a match across the striking pad, then cupped it in his palm to conceal the light. He held it to his cigarette, drawing deeply. His shivering hand made the job difficult, but he soon steadied it and was rewarded with a jagged rush of smoke.

As the match flame neared his fingers, a glint of white flashed against the blackness of the chamber. When he flicked the match away, the glimmer vanished. *Probably only a bit of snow,* he thought. But boredom made him curious. Gauging the risk of discovery by the Russian, he lit a second match. *There.* Near the floor of his cubbyhole he could see the object clearly now—not glass but paper—a small wad stuck to a long narrow brick. He hunched over and held the match nearer.

In the close light he could see that rather than being stuck *to* the brick as he had first thought, the paper actually protruded from the brick itself. He grasped the folded wad and tugged it gently from its receptacle. The paper made a dry, scraping sound. Hans inserted his index finger into the brick. He couldn't feel the bottom. The second match died. He lit another. Quickly spreading open the crinkled wad of onionskin, he surveyed his find in the flickering light. It seemed to be a personal document of some sort, a will or a diary perhaps, hand-printed in heavy blocked letters. In the dying matchlight Hans read as rapidly as he could:

This is the testament of Prisoner #7. I am the last now, and I know that I shall never be granted the freedom that I—more than any of those released before me—deserve. Death is the only freedom I will know. I hear His black wings beating about me! While my child lives I cannot speak, but here I shall write. I only pray that I can be coherent. Between the drugs, the questions, the promises and the threats, I sometimes wonder if I am not already mad. I only hope that long after these events cease to have immediate consequences in our insane world, someone will find these words and learn the obscene truth, not only of Himmler, Heydrich, and the rest, but of England—of those who would have sold her honor and ultimately her existence for—

The crunch of boot heels on snow jolted Hans back to reality. Someone was coming! Jerking his head to the aperture in the bricks, he closed his hand on the searing match and peered out into an alien world.

Dawn had come. In its unforgiving light, Hans saw a Russian soldier less than ten meters from his hiding place, moving slowly forward with his AK-47 extended. The flare of the third match had drawn him. *"Fool!"* Hans cursed himself. He jammed the sheaf of paper into his boot, then he stepped boldly out of the niche and strode toward the advancing soldier.

"Halt!" cried the Russian, emphasizing the command with a jerk of his Kalashnikov.

"Versailles," Hans countered in the steadiest voice he could muster.

His calm delivery of the password took the Russian aback. "What are you doing in there, Polizei?" asked the soldier in passable German.

"Smoke," Hans replied, extending the pack. "Having a smoke out of the wind." He waved his sector map in a wide arc as if to take in the wind itself.

"No wind," the Russian stated flatly, never taking his eyes from Hans's face.

It was true. Sometime during the last few minutes the wind had died. "Smoke, comrade," Hans repeated. "Versailles! Smoke, *tovarich!*"

He continued to proffer the pack, but the soldier only cocked his head toward his red-patched collar and spoke quietly. Hans caught his breath when he spied the small transmitter clipped to the sentry's belt. The Russians were in radio contact! In seconds the soldier's zealous comrades would come running. Hans felt a hot wave of panic. A surprisingly strong aversion to letting the Russians discover the papers gripped him. He cursed himself for not leaving them in the little cave rather than stuffing them into his boot like a naive shoplifter. He had almost reached the point of blind flight when a shrill whistle pierced the air in staccato bursts.

Chaos erupted all over the compound. The long, anxious night of surveillance had strained everyone's nerves to the breaking point, and the whistle blast, like a hair trigger, catapulted every man into the almost sexual release of physical action. Contrary to orders, every soldier and policeman on the lot abandoned his post to converge on the alarm. The Russian whipped his head toward the noise, then back to Hans. Shouted commands echoed across the prison yard, rebounding through the broken canyons.

"Versailles!" Hans shouted. "*Versailles,* Comrade! Let's go!"

The Russian seemed confused. He lowered his rifle a little, wavering. "Versailles," he murmured. He looked hard at Hans for a moment more; then he broke and ran.

Rooted to the earth, Hans exhaled slowly. He felt cold sweat pouring across his temples. With quivering hands, he pocketed his cigarettes, then carefully refolded his sector map, realizing as he did so that the paper he held was not his sector map at all, but the first page of the papers he had found in the hollow brick. Like a fool he had been waving under the Russian's nose the very thing he wanted to conceal! *Thank God that idiot didn't check it,* he thought. He pressed the page deep into his left boot, pulled his trouser legs down around his feet, and sprinted toward the sound of confusion.

In the brief moments it took Hans to respond to the whistle, a routine police matter had escalated into a potentially explosive confrontation. Near the blasted prison gate, five Soviet soldiers stood in a tight circle around two fortyish men wearing frayed business suits. They pointed their AK-47s menacingly, while nearby their commander argued vehemently with Erhard Weiss. The Russian was insisting that the trespassers be taken to an East German police station for interrogation.

Weiss was doing his best to calm the shouting Russian, but he was obviously out of his depth. Captain Hauer was nowhere in sight, and while the other policemen stood behind Weiss looking resolute, Hans knew that their Walthers would be no match for the Soviet assault weapons if it came to a showdown.

The sergeants of the NATO detachments kept their men well clear of the argument. They knew political dynamite when they saw it. While the Soviets kept their rifles leveled at the wide-eyed captives—who looked as if they might collapse from shock at any moment—the Russian "sergeant" bellowed louder and louder in broken German, trying to bully the tenacious Weiss into giving up "his" prisoners. To his credit, Weiss stood firm. He refused to allow any action to be taken until Captain Hauer had been apprised of the situation.

Hans stepped forward, hoping to interject some moderation into the dispute. Yet before he could speak, a black BMW screeched up to the curb and Captain Hauer vaulted from its rear door.

"What the hell is this?" he shouted.

The screaming Russian immediately redirected his tirade at Hauer, but the German brusquely raised his hand, breaking the flood of words like a wave against a rock.

"Weiss!" he barked.

"Sir!"

"Explain."

Weiss was so relieved to have the responsibility of the prisoners lifted from his shoulders that his words tumbled over themselves. "Captain, five minutes ago I saw two men moving suspiciously inside the perimeter. They must have slipped in somewhere between Willi and me. I flashed my light on them and shouted, 'Halt!' but they were startled and ran. They charged straight into one of the Russians, and before I could even blow my whistle, every Russian on the lot had surrounded them."

"Radios," Hauer muttered.

"Captain!" the Soviet "sergeant" bellowed. "These men are prisoners of the Soviet government! Any attempt to interfere—"

Without a word, Hauer strode past the Russian and into

the deadly circle of automatic weapons. He began a rapid, professional interrogation of the prisoners, speaking quietly in German.

The black American sergeant whistled low. "That cop's got balls," he observed, loudly enough for all to hear. One of his men giggled nervously.

The terrified civilians were elated to be questioned by a fellow countryman. In less than a minute, Hauer extracted the relevant information from them, and his men relaxed considerably during the exchange. It revealed a familiar situation—distasteful perhaps, but thankfully routine. Even the Russians holding the Kalashnikovs seemed to have picked up on Captain Hauer's casual manner. He patted the smaller of the two trespassers on the shoulder, then slipped out of the circle. A few of the rifles dropped noticeably as he stepped up to the Russian officer.

"They're quite harmless, Comrade," he explained. "A couple of homos, that's all."

Misunderstanding the slang, the Russian continued to scowl at Hauer. "What is their explanation?" he demanded stiffly.

"They're *homosexuals,* Sergeant. Queers, *Schwüle* ... golden boys, I think you call them. Looking for a temporary love nest, that's all. They're all over Berlin."

"No matter!" the Russian snapped, grasping Hauer's meaning at last. "They have trespassed on Soviet territory, and they must be interrogated at our headquarters in East Berlin." He motioned to his men. The rifles jerked back up instantly. He barked an order and started marching toward the parking area.

Hauer had no time to consult his superiors as to legalities, but he knew that allowing Russian soldiers to drag two of his fellow countrymen into the DDR without any semblance of a trial was something no West Berliner with an ounce of pride would do without a fight. Glancing around, he tried to gauge the sympathies of the NATO squads. The Americans looked as if they might be with him, but Hauer knew he couldn't rely on that if it came to a fight. Force would probably be counterproductive in any case, he thought; it usually was. He'd have to try a different tack.

Five steps carried him to the departing Russian. He grasped the burly man by his tunic and spun him around. "Listen, *Sergeant,*" he whispered forcefully, "or Major or

Colonel or whatever the hell you are. These man have committed no serious offense and they certainly pose no threat to the security of this site. I suggest we search them, then book them into one of our stations just like anybody else. That way we keep the press out of it, understand? *Pravda? Izvestia?* If you want to make an international incident out of this, you're quite welcome to do it, but *you* take full responsibility. Am I clear?"

The Russian understood well enough, and for a moment he considered Hauer's suggestion. But the situation was not so simple now. He had gone too far to back down in front of his men. Ignoring Hauer, he turned to his squad.

"These men are suspected enemies of the Soviet Union! They will remain in Soviet custody until the objective of their mission has been determined! Corporal, put them aboard our bus!"

Furious but outgunned, Hauer thought quickly. He had dealt with Russian officers for more than twenty-five years, and all his experience had taught him one lesson: the communist system, inefficient as it was, had grown proficient at breeding one thing out of its citizens—individual initiative. This Russian had to be reminded that his actions could have serious international implications. With two fingers Hauer removed his Walther from its holster and handed it to an astonished Weiss with a theatrical flourish. Again, the Soviet riflemen paused uncertainly, their eyes riveted on the unpredictable policeman.

"We have a stalemate, Comrade!" Hauer declared loudly. "You wish to keep these men in Soviet custody? Very well! You now stand on the only plot of Russian soil in West Berlin—an accident of history that will soon be rectified, I think. You may keep the prisoners *here* for as long as you wish—"

The Russian slowed his march.

"—*however,* crossing into the DDR with two citizens of the Federal Republic is an entirely different matter—a *political* matter—and quite beyond my power *or yours* to authorize. The prisoners must remain here until we have contacted our superior officers! I shall accompany you to the command trailer, where we can make the necessary calls." Hauer looked over his shoulder. "I would also suggest to the British sergeant that he join us, as we are in the British sector of the city."

Hauer started toward the trailer. He didn't intend to give the Russian time to argue. "Apfel!" he shouted. "Weiss! Drive everyone back to the station, then go home! I'll handle the paperwork on this!"

"But Captain!" Weiss protested.

"Go!"

Hans grabbed Weiss's sleeve and pulled him toward the van. The dazed recruits followed, their eyes on Hauer as he marched toward the trailer. The British sergeant, suddenly made aware of his responsibility, conferred with his men, a couple of whom restlessly fingered their Browning Hi-Power pistols.

Bristling with fury, the Russian ordered his men to follow Hauer with the prisoners. It made a strange parade. Hauer, unarmed, strode purposefully toward the command trailer, while the Russians—looking a bit sheepish in spite of being armed to the teeth—herded their rumpled prisoners along behind. The British brought up the rear.

The American master sergeant stood with his hands on his hips, shaking his head in amazement. "That Kraut is one smooth son of a bitch, gentlemen. I hope y'all were paying attention. He may be wearing a cop's uniform, but that man is a *soldier*. Yes, sir, I'd bet my stripes on it!"

The American was right. As Hauer marched toward the trailer, every inch of his ramrod bearing bore the indelible stamp of military discipline. Nothing betrayed the turmoil he felt knowing that the only thing stopping the angry Russian from taking control of the prisoners was the ring of men and steel at the checkpoints leading out of the city—certainly not one headstrong police captain just six weeks from retirement.

Inside the police van Hans calmed down a little. He pulled into the Wilhelmstrasse, then wheeled onto the Heerstrasse, heading east. For a time no one spoke. Hauer's actions had unnerved them all. Finally Weiss broke the silence.

"Did you see that, Hans?"

"Of course," he said tersely. The sheaf of papers felt like a kilo of heroin strapped to his leg.

"Old Hauer stepped in front of those machine guns like they weren't even there," said one of the younger men.

"I kind of got the feeling he'd done it before," mused Weiss.

"He has," Hans said flatly.

"When?" asked a chorus of surprised voices.

"Quite a few times, actually. He works Hostage Recovery for Special Tasks Division."

"How do you know so much about him?"

Hans felt his face flush; he shrugged and looked out the window to cover it.

"I'm glad it happened," Weiss said softly.

"Why?" asked one of the recruits.

"Showed those Russians what for, that's why. Showed them West Berlin's not a doormat for their filthy boots. They'll have quite a little mess on their hands now, won't they, Hans?"

"We all will, Erhard."

"Hauer ought to be prefect," suggested an old hand of twenty-one. "He's twice the man Funk is."

"He can't," Hans said, in spite of himself.

"Why not?"

"Because of Munich."

"Munich?"

Hans sighed and left the question unanswered. How could they understand? Every man in the van but him and Weiss had been toddlers at the time of the Olympic massacre. Turning onto the Friedrichstrasse, he swung the van into a space in front of the colossal police station and switched off the engine. He sensed them all—Weiss especially—watching him for a clue as to what to do next. Without a word he handed Weiss the keys, climbed out of the van, and started for his Volkswagen.

"Where are you going?" Weiss called.

"Exactly where Hauer told me to go, my friend! Home!"

"But shouldn't we report this?"

"Do what you must!" Hans called, still walking. He could feel the papers in his boot, already damp with nervous sweat. The sooner he was inside his own apartment, the better he would feel. Again he prayed silently that Ilse would be home when he got there. After three unsuccessful attempts, he coaxed his old VW to life, and with the careful movements of a policeman who has seen too many traffic fatalities, he eased the car into the morning rush of West Berlin.

The car that fell in behind him—a rental Ford—was just like a thousand others in the city. The man at the wheel was not. Jonas Stern rubbed his tired eyes and pushed his leather bag a little farther toward the passenger door. It simply would not do for a traffic policeman to see what lay on the seat beneath the bag. Not a gun, but a night-vision scope—a third-generation Pilkington, far superior to the one the American sergeant had been toying with. Definitely not standard tourist equipment.

But worth its weight in gold, Stern decided, following Hans's battered VW around a turn. *In gold.*

CHAPTER TWO

5:55 A.M. Soviet Sector: East Berlin, DDR

The KGB's RYAD computer logged the Spandau call at 05:55:32 hours Central European Time. Such exactitude seemed to matter a great deal to the new breed of agent that passed through East Berlin on their training runs these days. They had cut their too-handsome teeth on microchips, and for them a case that could not be reduced to microbits of data to feed their precious machines was no case at all. But to Ivan Kosov—the colonel to whom such calls were still routed—high-tech accuracy without human judgment to exploit it meant nothing. Snorting once to clear his chronically obstructed sinuses, he picked up the receiver of the black phone on his desk.

"Kosov," he growled.

The words that followed were delivered with such hysterical force that Kosov jerked the receiver away from his ear. The man on the other end of the phone was the "sergeant" from the Spandau guard detail. His actual rank was captain in the KGB, Third Chief Directorate—the KGB division responsible for spying on the Soviet Army. Kosov glanced at his watch. He'd expected his man back by now. Whatever the flustered captain was screaming about must explain the delay.

"Sergei," he said finally. "Start again and tell it like a professional. Can you do that?"

Two minutes later, Kosov's hooded eyes opened a bit and his breathing grew labored. He began firing questions at his subordinate, trying to determine if the events at Spandau had been accidental, or if some human will had guided them.

"What did the Polizei on the scene say? Yes, I do see. Lis-

ten to me, Sergei, this is what you will do. Let this policeman do just what he wants. Insist on accompanying him to
the station. Take your men with you. He is with you now?
What is his name?" Kosov scrawled *Hauer, Polizei Captain*
on a notepad. "Ask him which station he intends to go to.
Abschnitt 53?" Kosov wrote that down too, recalling as he
did that Abschnitt 53 was in the American sector of West
Berlin, on the Friedrichstrasse. "I'll meet you there in an
hour. It might be sooner, but these days you never know how
Moscow will react. What? Be discreet, but if force becomes
necessary, use it. *Listen* to me. Between the time the prisoners are formally charged and the time I arrive, you'll probably have a few minutes. *Use* that time. Question each of
your men about anything out of the ordinary they might
have noticed during the night. Don't worry, this is what you
were trained for." Kosov cursed himself for not putting a
more experienced man on the Spandau detail. "And Sergei,
question your men *separately*. Yes, now go. I'll be there as
soon as I can."

Kosov replaced the receiver and searched his pocket for a
cigarette. He felt a stab of incipient angina, but what could
he expect? He had already outfoxed the KGB doctors far
longer than he'd ever hoped to, and no man could live forever. The cigarette calmed him, and before he lifted the
other phone—the red one that ran only east—he decided that
he could afford sixty seconds to think this thing through
properly.

Trespassers at Spandau. After all these years, Moscow's
cryptic warnings had finally come true. Had Centre expected
this particular incident? Obviously they had expected something, or they wouldn't have taken such pains to have their
stukatch on hand when the British leveled the prison. Kosov
knew there was at least one informer on his Spandau team,
and probably others he didn't know about. The East German
Security Service (Stasi) usually managed to bribe at least
one man on almost every KGB operation in Berlin. *So much
for fraternal socialism,* he thought, reaching for a pencil.

He jotted a quick list of the calls he would have to make:
KGB chairman Zemenek at Moscow Centre; the Soviet com-
mandant for East Berlin; and of course the prefect of West
Berlin police. Kosov would enjoy the call to West Berlin. It
wasn't often he could make demands of the arrogant West
Germans and expect to be accommodated, but today would

be one of those days. The Moscow call, on the other hand, he would not enjoy at all. It might mean anything from a medal to expulsion from service without a word of explanation.

This was Kosov's fear. For the past ten years, operationally speaking, Berlin had been a dead city. The husk of its former romance clung to it, but the old Cold War urgency was gone. Pre-eminence had moved to another part of the globe, and Kosov had no Japanese or Arabic. His future held only mountains of paperwork and turf battles with the GRU and the Stasi. Kosov didn't give a damn about Rudolf Hess. Chairman Zemenek might be obsessed with Nazi conspiracies, but what was the point? The Soviet empire was leaking like a sieve, and Moscow was worried about some intrigue left over from the Great Patriotic War?

The Chairman's Obsession. That's what the KGB chiefs in Berlin had called Rudolf Hess ever since the Nuremberg trials, when he was sentenced to life imprisonment in Spandau. Four weeks ago Kosov had thought he had received his last call about Spandau's famous Prisoner Number Seven. That was when the Americans had found the old Nazi dead, a lamp cord wrapped around his neck. *Suicide,* Kosov remembered with a chuckle. That's what the Allied board of inquiry had ruled it. Kosov thought it a damned remarkable suicide for a ninety-three-year-old man. Hess had supposedly hanged himself from a rafter, yet all his doctors agreed that the arthritic old Nazi couldn't lift his arms any higher than his shoulders. The German press had screamed murder, of course. Kosov didn't give a damn if it was murder. One less German in the world made for a better world, in his view. He was just grateful the old man hadn't died during a Soviet guard month.

Another sharp chest pain made Kosov wince. It was thinking about the damned Germans that caused it. He hated them. The fact that both his father and his grandfather had been killed by Germans probably had something to do with it, but that wasn't all. Behind the Germans' arrogance, Kosov knew, lurked a childish insecurity, a desperate desire to be liked. But Kosov never gratified it. Because beneath that insecurity seethed something else, something darker. An ancient, tribal desire—a warlike need to *dominate*. He'd heard the rumors that Gorbachev was softening on the reunification issue, and it made him want to puke. As far as

Kosov was concerned, the day the spineless politicians in Moscow decided to let the Germans reunite was the day the Red Army should roll across both Germanys like a tidal wave, smashing everything in its path.

Thinking about Moscow brought Kosov back to Hess. Because on that subject, Moscow Centre was like a shrewish old woman. The Rudolf Hess case held a security classification unique in Kosov's experience; it dated all the way back to the NKVD. And in a bureaucracy where access to information was the very lifeblood of survival, no one he had ever met had ever seen the Hess file. No one but the chairman. Kosov had no idea why this was so. What he *did* have was a very short list—a list of names and potential events relating to Rudolf Hess which mandated certain responses. One of those events was illegal entry into Spandau Prison; and the response: immediate notification of the chairman. Kosov felt sure that the fact that Spandau now lay in ruins did not affect his orders at all. He glanced one last time at the scrawled letters on his pad: *Hauer, Polizei Captain.* Then he stubbed out his cigarette and lifted the red phone.

6:25 A.M. British Sector: West Berlin

The warm apartment air hit Hans in a wave, flushing his skin, enfolding him like a cocoon. Ilse had already left, he knew it instinctively. There was no movement in the kitchen, no sound of appliances, no running shower, nothing. Still jumpy, and half-starved, he walked hopefully into the kitchen. He found a note on the refrigerator door, written in Ilse's hurried hand: *Wurst in the oven. I love YOU. Back by 18:00.*

Thank you, Liebchen, he thought, catching the pungent aroma of *Weisswurst.* Using one of his gloves as a potholder, he removed the hot dish from the oven and placed it on the counter to cool. Then he took a deep breath, bent over, rolled up his pants leg and dug the sheaf of onionskin out of his boot. His pulse quickened as he unfolded the pages in the light. He backed against the stove for heat, plopped a chunk of white sausage into his mouth, and picked up reading where the Russian soldier had surprised him.

   . . . I only hope that long after these events cease to have immediate consequences in our insane world, someone will

find these words and learn the obscene truth not only of Himmler, Heydrich, and the rest, but of England—of those who would have sold her honor and ultimately her existence for a chance to sit at Hitler's blood-drenched table. The facts are few, but I have had more time to ponder them than most men would in ten lifetimes. I know how *this mission was accomplished, but I do not know* why. *That is for someone else to learn. I can only point the way. You must follow the Eye. The Eye is the key to it all!*

Hans stopped chewing and held the paper closer to his face. Sketched below this exhortation was a single, stylized eye. Gracefully curved, with a lid but no lashes, it stared out from the paper with a strange intensity. It seemed neither masculine nor feminine. It looked mystical somehow. Even a little creepy. He read on: *What follows is my story, as best I can remember it.*

Hans blinked his eyes. At the beginning of the next paragraph, the narrative suddenly switched to a language he could not understand. He didn't even recognize it. He stared in puzzlement at the painstakingly blocked characters. *Portuguese?* he wondered. *Italian maybe?* He couldn't tell. A few words of German were sprinkled through the gibberish—names mostly—but not enough to get any meaning from. Frustrated, he walked into the bedroom, folded the pages, and stuffed them underneath the mattress at the foot of his bed. He switched on the television from habit, then kicked his mud-caked boots into an empty corner and dropped his coat on top of them. Ilse would scold him for being lazy, he knew, but after two straight shifts he was simply too exhausted to care.

He ate his breakfast on the bed. As much as the Spandau papers, the thought of his father weighed on his mind. Captain Hauer had asked him why he'd come to Berlin. Hans often wondered that himself. Three years it had been now. He hardly thought of Munich anymore. He'd married Ilse after just five months here in Berlin. Christ, what a wedding it had been. His mother—still furious at him for becoming a policeman—had refused to attend, and Hauer had not been included in the plans. But he'd shown up anyway, Hans remembered. Hans had spied his rigid, uniformed figure outside the church, standing alone at the end of the block. Hans had pretended not to notice, but Ilse had waved quite deliberately to him as they climbed into the wedding car.

Angry again, Hans wolfed down another sausage and tried to concentrate on the television. A silver-haired windbag of a Frankfurt banker was dispensing financial advice to viewers saddled with the burden of surplus cash. Hans snorted in disgust. At fifteen hundred Deutschemarks per month, a Berlin policeman made barely enough money to pay rent and buy groceries. Without Ilse's income, they would be shivering in a cold-water flat in Kreuzberg. He wanted to switch channels, but the old Siemens black-and-white had been built in the dark ages before remote control. He stayed where he was.

He took another bite of sausage and stared blankly at the screen. Beneath his stockinged feet, the wrinkled sheaf of papers waited, a tantalizing mystery beckoning him to explore. Yet he had already hit a dead end. The strange, staring eye hovered in his mind, taunting him. After breakfast, he decided, he would take a shower and then have another go at the papers.

He never made it off the bed. Exhaustion and the warm air overcame him even before he finished the sausage. He slid down the duvet, the unfinished plate balanced precariously on his lap, the Spandau papers hidden just beneath his feet.

10:15 A.M. French Sector: West Berlin

Ilse hated these visits. No matter how many times she saw her *Gynäkologe,* she never got used to it. Ever. The astringent smell of alcohol, the gleaming stainless steel, the cold table, palpating fingers, the overly solicitous voice of the physician, who sometimes peered directly into her eyes from between her upraised legs: all these combined to produce a primal anxiety that solidified like ice in the hollow of her chest. Ilse knew about the necessity of annual checkups, but until she and Hans had begun trying to have a child, she'd skipped more exams than she would care to admit.

All that had changed eighteen months ago. She had been up in the stirrups so many times now that the stress of the ordeal had almost diminished to that of a visit to the dentist—but not quite. Unlike many German women, Ilse possessed an extreme sense of modesty about her body. She suspected it was because she had never known her mother, but whatever the reason, being forced to expose herself to a stranger, albeit a doctor, for her required a considerable act of will. Only her strong desire to have children allowed her to endure the interminable series of examinations and therapies designed to enhance fertility.

"All done, Frau Apfel," Doctor Grauber said. He handed a slide to his waiting nurse. Ilse heard that hard *snap* as he stripped off his surgical gloves and raised the lid of the waste bin with his foot. It crashed down, sending gooseflesh racing across her neck and shoulders. "I'll see you in my office after you've dressed."

Ilse heard the door open and close. The nurse started to help her out of the stirrups, but she quickly raised herself and reached for her clothes.

Dr. Grauber's office was messy but well-appointed, full of books and old medical instruments and framed degrees and the smell of cigars. Ilse noticed none of this. She was here for one thing—an answer. Was she pregnant or was she sick? The two possibilities wrestled in her mind. Her instinct said pregnant. She and Hans had been trying for so long now, and the other option was too unnatural to think about. Her body was strong and supple, lean and hard. Like the flanks of a lioness, Hans said once (as if he knew what a lioness felt like). How could she be sick? She felt so *well*.

But she knew. Exterior health was no guarantee of immunity. Ilse had seen two friends younger than she stricken with cancer. One had died, the other had lost a breast. She wondered how Hans would react to something like that. Disfigurement. He would never admit to revulsion, of course, but it would matter. Hans loved her body—worshipped it, really. Ever since their first night together, he had slowly encouraged her until she felt comfortable before him naked. Now she could turn gracefully about the room like a ballerina, or sometimes just stand silently, still as alabaster.

"That was quick!" Dr. Grauber boomed, striding in and taking a seat behind his chaotic desk.

Ilse pressed her back into the tufted leather sofa. She wanted to be ready, no matter what the diagnosis. As she met the doctor's eyes, a nurse stepped into the office.

She handed him a slip of paper and went out. Grauber glanced at it, sighed, then looked up.

What he saw startled him. The poise and concentration with which Ilse watched him made him forget the slip of paper in his hand. Her blue eyes shone with frank and disarming curiosity, her skin with luminous vitality. She wore little or no makeup—the luxury of youth, Grauber thought—and her hair had that transparent blondness that makes the hands tingle to touch it. But it wasn't all that, he decided. Ilse Apfel was no film star. He knew a dozen women as striking as she. It was something other than fine features, deeper than the glow of youth. Not elegance, or earthiness, or even a hint of that intangible scent Grauber called *availability*. No, it was, quite simply, *grace*. Ilse possessed that rare beauty made rarer still by apparent unconsciousness of itself. When Grauber caught himself admiring her breasts—high and round, more Gallic than Teutonic, he thought—he flushed and looked quickly back at the slip of paper in his hand.

"Well," he coughed. "That's that."

Ilse waited expectantly, too anxious to ask for the verdict.

"Your urine indicates pregnancy," Grauber announced. "I'd like to draw some blood, of course, confirm the urine with a beta-subunit test, but I'd say that's just a formality. Would you like to bring Hans in? I know he'll be excited."

Ilse colored. "Hans didn't come this time."

Grauber raised his eyebrows in surprise. "That's a first. He's got to be the most concerned husband I've ever met." The smile faded. "Are you all right, Ilse? You look as though I'd just given you three months to live."

Ilse felt wings beating within her chest. After all her anxiety, she found it hard to accept fulfillment of her deepest hope. "I really didn't expect this," she murmured. "I was afraid to hope for it. My mother died when I was born, you know, and it's ... it's just very important to me to have a child of my own."

"Well, you've got one started," said Grauber. "Now our job is to see that he—or she—arrives as ordered. I've got a copy of the standard visiting schedule, and there's the matter of ..."

Ilse heard nothing else. The doctor's news had lifted her spirit to a plane where no mundane detail could intrude. When the lab technician drew her blood, she felt no needle prick, and on her way out of the office the receptionist had to call her name three times to prevent her leaving without scheduling her next visit. At the age of twenty-six, her happiness was complete.

11:27 A.M. *Pretoria, The Republic of South Africa*

Five thousand miles to the south of Germany, two thousand of those below the equator, an old man sentenced to spend half his waking hours in a wheelchair spoke acidly into the intercom recessed into his oaken office desk.

"This is not the time to bother me with business, Pieter."

The man's name was Alfred Horn, and though it was not his native language, he spoke Afrikaans.

"I'm sorry, sir," the intercom replied, "but I believe you might prefer to take this call. It's from Berlin."

Berlin. Horn reached for the intercom button. "Ah . . . I believe you're right, Pieter." The old man let his finger fall from the button, then pressed it again. "Is this call scrambled?"

"Sir, this end as always. I can't say for certain about the other. I doubt it."

"And the room?"

"Swept last night, sir."

"I'm picking up now."

The connection was excellent, almost noiseless. The first voice Horn heard was that of his security chief, Pieter Smuts.

"Are you still on the line, caller?"

"Ja," hissed a male voice, obviously under stress. "And I haven't much time."

"Are you calling from a secure location?"

"Nein."

"Can you move to such a location?"

"Nein! Someone may have missed me already!"

"Calm yourself," Smuts ordered. "You will identify yourself again in five seconds. Answer any questions put to you—"

"You may remain on the line, Guardian," Horn interrupted in perfect German.

"Go ahead, caller," Smuts said.

"This is Berlin-One," said the quavering voice. "There are

developments here of which I feel you should be apprised. Two men were arrested this morning at Spandau Prison. West Berliners."

"On what charge?" Horn asked, his voice neutral.

"Trespassing."

"For that you call this number?"

"There are special circumstances. Russian troops guarding the prison last night have insisted that these men be charged with espionage, or else transferred to East Berlin for such action."

"Surely you are joking."

"Does a man risk his career for a joke?"

Horn paused. "Elaborate."

"I don't know much, but there is still Russian activity at the prison. They're conducting searches or tests of some sort. That's all I—"

"Searches at Spandau?" Horn cut in. "Has this to do with the death of Hess?"

"I don't know. I simply felt you should be made aware."

"Yes," Horn said at length. "Of course. Tell me, why weren't our own men guarding Spandau?"

"The captain of the unit was one of us. It was he who prevented the Russians from taking the prisoners into East Berlin. He doesn't think the trespassers know anything, though."

"He's not supposed to think at all!"

"He—he's very independent," said the timid voice. "A real pain in the neck. His name is Hauer."

Horn heard Smuts's pen scratching. "Was there anything else?"

"Nothing specific, but . . ."

"Yes?"

"The Russians. They're being much more forceful than usual. They seem unworried by any diplomatic concerns. As if whatever they seek is worth upsetting important people. The Americans, for example."

There was a pause. "You were right to call," Horn said finally. "Make sure things do not go too far. Keep us informed. Call this number again tonight. There will be a delay as the call is re-routed north. Wait for our answer."

"But I may not have access to a private phone—"

"That is a direct order!"

"Jawohl!"

"Caller, disconnect," Smuts commanded.

The line went dead. Horn hit the intercom and summoned his security chief into the office. Smuts seated himself opposite Horn on a spartan sofa that typified its owner's martial disdain for excessive comfort.

With his wheelchair almost out of sight behind the desk, Alfred Horn appeared in remarkably good health, despite his advanced years. His strong, mobile face and still-broad shoulders projected an energy and sense of purpose suited to a man thirty years his junior. Only the eyes jarred this impression. They seemed strangely incongruous between the high cheekbones and classical forehead. One hardly moved—being made of glass—yet the other eye seemed doubly and disturbingly alive, as if projecting the entire concentration of the powerful brain behind it. But it wasn't really the eyes, Smuts remembered, it was the eye*brows*. Horn had none. The bullet wound that had taken the left eye had been treated late and badly. Despite several plastic surgeries, the pronounced ridge that surmounted the surviving eye was entirely bare of hair, giving an impression of weakness where in fact none existed. The other eyebrow was shaved to prevent an asymmetrical appearance.

"Comments, Pieter?" Horn said.

"I don't like it, sir, but I don't see what we can do at this point but monitor the situation. We're already pushing our timetable to the limit." Smuts looked thoughtful. "Perhaps Number Seven's killer left some evidence that was overlooked."

"Or perhaps Number Seven himself left some hidden writings which were never found," Horn suggested. "A deathbed confession, perhaps? We can take no chances where Spandau is concerned."

"Do you have any specific requests?"

"Handle this as you see fit, but handle it. I'm much more concerned about the upcoming meeting." Horn tapped his forefinger nervously on the desktop. "Do you feel confident about security, Pieter?"

"Absolutely, sir. Do you really feel you are in immediate danger? Spandau Prison is one thing, but Horn House is five thousand miles from Britain."

"I'm certain," Horn averred. "Something has changed. Our English contacts have cooled. Lines of communication are kept open, but they are too forced. Inquiries have been made into our activities in the South African defense program. Ever since the murder of Number Seven."

"You don't think it could have been suicide?"

Horn snorted in contempt. "The only mystery is who killed him and why. Was it the British, to silence him? Or did the Jews finally kill him, for revenge? My money is on the British. They wanted him silenced for good. As they want *me* silenced." Horn scowled. "I'm tired of waiting, that's all."

Smuts smiled coldly. "Only seventy-two hours to go, sir."

Horn ignored this reassurance. "I want you to call Vorster at the mine. Have him bring his men up to the house tonight."

"But the interim security team doesn't arrive until noon tomorrow," Smuts objected.

"Then the mine will just have to work naked for eighteen hours!"

Horn had wounded his security chief's pride, but Smuts kept silent. His precautions for the historic meeting three nights hence, though unduly rushed, were airtight. He was certain of it. Situated on an isolated plateau in the northern Transvaal, Horn House was a veritable fortress. No one could get within a mile of it without a tank, and Smuts had something that could stop that, too. But Alfred Horn was not a man to be argued with. If he wanted extra men, they would be there. Smuts made a mental note to retain a contract security team to guard Horn's platinum mine during the night.

"Tell me, Pieter, how is the airstrip extension proceeding?"

"As well as we could hope, considering the time pressure we're under. Six hundred feet to go."

"I'll see for myself tonight, if we ever get out of this blasted city. That helicopter of mine spends more time in the service hangar than it does on my rooftop."

"Yes, sir."

"I still don't like those aircraft, Pieter. They look and fly like clumsy insects. Still, I suppose we can't very well put a runway on the roof, can we?"

"Not yet at least."

"We should look into something like the British Harrier. Wonderfully simple idea, vertical takeoff. There must be a commercial variant in development somewhere."

"Surely you're joking, sir?"

Horn looked reprovingly at his aide. "You would never have made an aviator, Pieter. To fight in the skies you must believe all things are possible, bendable to the human will."

"I suppose you're right."

"But you are excellent at what you do, my friend. I am living proof of your skill and dedication. I am the only one left who knows the secret. The *only* one. And that is due in no small part to you."

"You exaggerate, Herr Horn."

"No. Though I have great wealth, my power rests not in money but in fear. And one instrument of the fear I generate is you. Your loyalty is beyond price."

"And beyond doubt, you know that."

Horn's single living eye pierced Smuts's soul. "We can know nothing for certain, Pieter. Least of all about ourselves. But I have to trust someone, don't I?"

"I shall never fail you," Smuts said softly, almost reverently. "Your goal is greater than any temptation."

"Yes," the old man answered. "Yes it is."

Horn backed the wheelchair away from the desk and turned to face the window. The skyline of Pretoria, for the most part beneath him, stretched away across the suburbs to the soot-covered townships, to the great plateau of the northern Transvaal, where three days hence Horn would host a meeting calculated to alter the balance of world power forever. As Smuts closed the door softly, Horn's mind drifted back to the days of his youth . . . the days of power. Gingerly, he touched his glass eye.

"Der Tag kommt," he said aloud. "The day approaches."

CHAPTER THREE

3:31 P.M. *British Sector: West Berlin*

Hans awoke in a sweat. He still cowered inside a dark cave, watching in terror as a Russian soldier came for him with a Kalashnikov rifle. The illusion gripped his mind, difficult to break. He sat upright in bed and rubbed the sleep from his eyes. Still the wrecked compound hovered before him. His soiled uniform still chafed, still smelled of the dank prison yard. He shook his head violently, but the image would not disappear. It was *real* . . .

On the screen of the small Siemens television two meters in front of Hans, a tall reporter clad in the type of topcoat favored by West Berlin pimps stood before a wide shot of the wasteland that yesterday had been Spandau Prison. Hans clambered over the footboard of the bed and turned up the volume on the set.

". . . *Deutsche Welle* broadcasting live from the Wilhelmstrasse. As you can see, the main structure of Spandau Prison was destroyed with little fanfare yesterday by the British military authorities. It was here early this morning that Soviet troops in conjunction with West Berlin police arrested the two West German citizens whom the Russians are now attempting to extradite into East Berlin. There is virtually no precedent for this attempt. The Russians are following no recognized legal procedure, and the story that began here in the predawn hours is rapidly becoming an incident of international proportions. To the best of *Deutsche Welle*'s knowledge, the two Berliners are being held inside Polizei Abschnitt 53, where our own Peter Müller is following developments as they occur. Peter?"

Before switching to the second live feed, the producer

stayed with the Spandau shot for a few silent seconds. What Hans saw brought a sour lump to his throat. A hundred meters behind the reporter, dozens of uniformed men slowly picked their way across the ruined grounds of Spandau. They moved over the icy rubble like ants in search of food, some not far from the very mound where Hans had made his discovery. A few wore white lab coats, but others—Hans's throat tightened—others wore the distinctive red-patched brown uniforms of the Soviet infantry.

Hans scoured the screen for clues that might explain the Soviet presence, but the scene vaporized. Now a slightly better-dressed commentator stood before the great three-arched doorway of the police station where Hans reported to work every morning. He shifted his weight excitedly from one foot to the other as he spoke.

"Thank you, Karl," he said. "Other than the earlier statement by the police press officer that a joint investigation with the USSR is under way, no details are forthcoming. We know that an undetermined number of Soviet soldiers remain inside Abschnitt 53, but we do not know if they are guests here, as is claimed, or if—as has been rumored—they control the station by force of arms.

"While the Spandau incident occurred in the British sector of the city, the German prisoners were taken by a needlessly lengthy route to Abschnitt 53, here in the American sector, just one block from Checkpoint Charlie. Informed sources have speculated that a quick-witted police officer may have realized that the Soviets would be less likely to resort to violence in the American-controlled part of the city. We have received no statements from either the American or the British military commands. However, if Soviet troops are in fact inside this police station without the official sanction of the U.S. Army, the Allied occupational boundaries we have all by familiarity come to ignore may suddenly assume a critical importance. This small incident could well escalate into one of the most volatile crises of the post-*glasnost* era. We will update this story at 18:00 this evening, so please stay tuned to this channel. This is Peter Müller, *Deutsche Welle*, live . . ."

While the reporter solemnly wrapped his segment, he failed to notice the huge station door open behind him. Haggard but erect, Captain Dieter Hauer strode out into the afternoon light. He looked as though he hadn't slept in thirty-six hours. He surveyed the sidewalk like a drill sergeant inspecting a barracks yard; then, apparently satisfied, he gave the reporter a black look, turned back toward the station door, and dissolved into a BMW commercial.

Hans fell back against the footboard of the bed, his mind reeling. Russian troops still in his home station? Who had leaked the Spandau story to the press? And *who* were the men in the white lab coats? What were they searching for? Was it the papers he'd found? It almost *had* to be. No one cared about a couple of homosexuals who happened to trespass public property in their search for a love nest. The realization of what he had done by keeping the papers hit Hans like a wave of fever. But what else could he have done? Surely the police brass would not have wanted the Russians to get hold of the papers. He could have driven straight to Polizei headquarters at Platz der Luftbrücke, of course, but he didn't know a soul there. No, when he turned in the papers, he wanted to do it at his home station. And he couldn't do that yet because the Russians were still inside it! He would simply have to wait.

But he didn't want to wait. He felt like a boy who has stumbled over a locked chest in a basement. He wanted to know what the devil he'd found! Anxiously, he snapped his fingers. *Ilse,* he thought suddenly. She had a gift for languages, just like her arrogant grandfather. Maybe *she* could decipher the rest of the Spandau papers. He lifted the phone and punched in the first four digits of her work number; then he replaced the receiver. The brokerage house where Ilse worked did not allow personal calls during trading hours. Hans would break a rule quicker than most Germans, but he remembered that several employees had been fired for taking this rule lightly.

A reckless thought struck Hans. He wanted information, and he knew where he could get some. After sixty seconds of hard reflection, he picked up the telephone directory and looked up the number of *Der Spiegel.* Several department numbers were listed for the magazine. He wasn't sure which he needed, so he dialed the main switchboard.

"Der Spiegel," answered a female voice.

"I need to speak to Heini Weber," Hans said. "Could you connect me with the proper department, please?"

"One moment."

Thirty seconds passed. "News," said a gruff male voice.

"Heini Weber, please. He's a friend of mine." *A bit of an exaggeration,* Hans thought, *but what the hell?*

"Weber's gone," the man growled, "He was just here, but he left again. Field assignment."

Hans sighed. "If he comes back—"

"Wait, I see him. Weber! Telephone!"

Hans heard a clatter of chairs, then a younger male voice came on the line. "Weber here. Who's this?"

"Hans Apfel."

"Who?"

"Sergeant Hans Apfel. We met at—"

"Right, right," Weber remembered, "that kidnapping thing. Gruesome. Listen, I'm in a hurry, can you make it fast?"

"I need to talk to you," Hans said deliberately. "It's important."

"Hold on—I'm coming already! What's your story, Sergeant?"

"Not over the phone," Hans said, knowing he probably sounded ridiculous.

"Jesus," Weber muttered. "I've got to get over to Hannover. A mob of Greens is disrupting an American missile transport on the E-30 and I need to leave five minutes ago."

"I could ride with you."

"Two-seater," Weber objected. "And I've got to take my photographer. I guess your big scoop will have to wait until tomorrow."

"No!" Hans blurted, surprised by his own vehemence. "It can't wait. I'll just have to call someone else."

A long silence. "All right," Weber said finally, "where do you live?"

"Lützenstrasse, number 30."

"I'll meet you out front. I can give you five minutes."

"Good enough." Hans hung up and took a deep breath. This move carried some risk. In Berlin, all police contact with the press must be officially cleared beforehand. But he intended to get information *from* a reporter, not to give it. Without pausing to shower or shave, he stripped off his dirty uniform and threw on a pair of cotton pants and the old shirt he wore whenever he made repairs on the VW. A light raincoat and navy scarf completed his wardrobe.

The Spandau papers still lay beneath the rumpled mattress. He retrieved them, scanning them again on the off chance that he'd missed something before. At the bottom of the last page he found it: several hastily written passages in German, each apparently a separate entry:

The threats stopped for a time. Foolishly, I let myself hope that the madness had ended. But it started again last month. Can they read my thoughts? No sooner do I toy with the idea of setting down my great burden, than a soldier of Phoenix appears before me. Who is with them? Who is not? They show me pictures of an old woman, but the eyes belong to a stranger. I am certain my wife is dead.

My daughter is alive! She wears a middle-aged face and bears an unknown name, but her eyes are mine. She is a hostage roaming free, with an invisible sword hanging above her head. But safe she has remained. I am strong! The Russians have promised to find my angel, to save her, if I will but speak her name. But I do not know it! It would be useless if I did. Heydrich wiped all trace of me from the face of Germany in 1936. God alone knows what that demon told my family!

My British warders are stern like guard dogs, very stupid ones. But there are other Englanders who are not so stupid. Have you found me out, swine?

And a jagged entry: *Phoenix wields my precious daughter like a sword of fire! If only they knew! Am I even a dim memory to my angel? No. Better that she never knows. I have lived a life of madness, but in the face of death I found courage. In my darkest hours I remember these lines from Ovid: "It is a smaller thing to suffer punishment than to have deserved it. The punishment can be removed, the fault will remain forever." My long punishment shall soon cease. After all the slaughtered millions, the war finally ends for me. May God accept me into His Heaven, for I know that Heydrich and the others await me at the gates of Hell.*

Surely I have paid enough.

Number 7

A car horn blared outside. Strangely shaken, Hans folded the pages into a square and stuffed them back under the mattress. Then he tugged on a pair of old sneakers, locked the front door, and bounded into the stairwell. He bumped into a tall janitor on the third floor landing, but the old man didn't even look up from his work.

Hans found Heini Weber beside a battered red Fiat Spyder, bouncing up and down on his toes like a hyperactive child. A shaggy-haired youth with a Leica slung round his neck peered at Hans from the Fiat's jump seat.

"So what's the big story, Sergeant?" Weber asked.

"Over here," said Hans, motioning toward the foyer of his building. He had seen nothing suspicious in the street, yet he could not shake the feeling that he was being watched—if not by hostile, at least by interested eyes. *It's just the photographer,* he told himself. Weber followed him into the building and immediately resumed his nervous bouncing, this time against the dirty foyer wall.

"The meter's running," said the reporter.

"Before I tell you anything," Hans said carefully, "I want some information."

Weber scowled. "Do I look like a fucking librarian to you? Come on, out with it."

Hans nodded solemnly, then played out his bait. "I may have a story for you, Heini, but . . . to be honest, I'm curious about what it might be worth."

"Well, well," the reporter deadpanned, "the police have joined the club. Listen, Sergeant, I don't *buy* stories, I track them down for pay. That's the news game, you know? If you want money, try one of the American TV networks."

When Hans didn't respond, Weber said, "Okay, I'll bite. What's your story? The mayor consorting with the American commandant's wife? The Wall coming down tomorrow? I've heard them all, Sergeant. Everybody's got a story to sell and ninety-nine percent of them are shit. What's yours?"

Hans looked furtively toward the street. "What if," he murmured, "what if I told you I'd got hold of something important from the war? From the Nazi period?"

"Something," Weber echoed. "Like?"

Hans sighed anxiously. "Like papers, say. Like a diary."

Weber scrutinized him for some moments; then his eyebrows arched cynically. "Like the diary of a Nazi war criminal, maybe?"

Hans's eyes widened in disbelief. "How did you know?"

"Scheisse!" Weber cursed. He slapped the wall. "Is that what you got me over here for? Christ, where do they find you guys? That's the oldest one in the book!"

Hans stared at the reporter as if he were mad. "What do you mean?"

Weber returned Hans's gaze with something akin to pity; then he put a hand on his shoulder. "Whose diary is it, Sergeant? Mengele's? Bormann's?"

"Neither," Hans snapped. He felt strangely defensive about the Spandau papers. "What the hell are you trying to say?"

"I'm saying that you probably just bought the German equivalent of the Brooklyn Bridge."

Hans blinked, then looked away, thinking fast. He clearly wasn't going to get any information without revealing some first. "This diary's genuine," he insisted. "And I can prove it."

"Sure you can," said Weber, glancing at his watch. "When Gerd Heidemann discovered the 'Hitler diaries' back in '83, he even had Hugh Trevor-Roper swearing they were authentic. But they were crap, Sergeant, complete fakes. I don't know where you got your diary, but I hope to God you didn't pay much for it."

The reporter was laughing. Hans forced himself to smile sheepishly, but what he was thinking was that he hadn't paid one *Pfennig* for the Spandau papers. He had found them. And if Heini Weber knew *where* he had found them, the reporter would be begging him for an exclusive story. Hans heard the regular swish of a broom from the first-floor landing.

"Heini," he said forcefully, "just tell me this. Have you heard of any missing Nazi documents or anything like that floating around *recently?*"

Weber shook his head in amazement. "Sergeant, what you're talking about—Nazi diaries and things—people were selling them ten-a-penny after the war. It's a fixed game, a scam." His face softened. "Just cut your losses and run, Hans. Don't embarrass yourself."

Weber turned and grabbed the door handle, but Hans caught him by the sleeve. "But if it *were* authentic?" he said, surprising himself. "What kind of money would we be talking about?"

Weber pulled his arm free, but he paused for a last look at the gullible policeman. The swish of the broom had stopped, but neither man noticed. "For the real thing?" He chuckled. "No limit, Sergeant. *Stern* magazine paid

Heidemann 3.7 million marks for first rights to the 'Hitler diaries.' "

Hans's jaw dropped.

"The London *Sunday Times* went in for 400,000 pounds, and I think both *Time* and *Newsweek* came close to getting stung." Weber smiled with a touch of professional envy. "Heidemann was pretty smart about it, really. He set the hook by leaking a story that the diaries contained Hitler's version of Rudolf Hess's flight to Britain. Of course every rag in the world was panting to print a special edition solving the last big mystery of the war. They shelled out millions. Careers were *ruined* by that fiasco." The reporter laughed harshly. "*Guten Abend,* Sergeant. Call me next time there's a kidnapping, eh?"

Weber trotted to the waiting Spyder, leaving Hans standing dumbfounded in the doorway. He had called the reporter for information, and he had gotten more than he'd bargained for. 3.7 *million* marks? *Jesus!*

"Make way, why don't you!" croaked a high-pitched voice.

Hans grunted as the tall janitor shouldered past him onto the sidewalk and hobbled down the street. His broom was gone; now a worn leather bag swung from his shoulder. Hans followed the man with his eyes for a while, then shook his head. *Paranoia,* he thought.

Looking up at the drab facade of his apartment building, he decided that a walk through the city beat waiting for Ilse in the empty flat. Besides, he always thought more clearly on the move. He started walking. Just over a hundred meters long, the Lützenstrasse was wedged into a rough trapezoid between two main thoroughfares and a convergence of elevated S-Bahn rail tracks. Forty seconds' walking carried Hans from the dirty brown stucco of his apartment building to the polished chrome of the Kurfürstendamm, the showpiece boulevard of Berlin. He headed east toward the center of the city, speaking to no one, hardly looking up at the dazzling window displays, magisterial banks, open-air cafes, art galleries, antique shops, and nightclubs of the Ku'damm.

Bright clusters of shoppers jostled by, gawking and laughing together, but they yielded a wide path to the lone walker whose Aryan good looks were somehow made suspect by his unshaven face and ragged clothing. The tall, spare man gliding purposefully along behind Hans could easily have been walking at his shoulder. The man no longer looked like a janitor, but even if he had, it wouldn't have mattered; Hans was lost in heady dreams of wealth beyond measure.

He paused at a newsstand and bought a pack of American cigarettes. He really needed a smoke. As he sucked in the first potent drag, he suddenly remembered something from the Spandau papers. The writer had said he was the *last* . . . The last what? The last *prisoner?* And then it hit Hans like a bucket of water in the face. *The Spandau papers were signed Prisoner Number Seven . . . and Prisoner Number Seven was Rudolf Hess himself!*

He felt the hand holding the cigarette start to shake. He tried to swallow, but his throat refused to cooperate. Had he actually found the journal of a Nazi war criminal? With Heini Weber's cynical comments echoing in his head, he tried to recall what he could about Hess. All he really knew was that Hess was Hitler's right-hand man, and that he'd flown secretly to Britain sometime early in the war, and had been captured. For the past few weeks the Berlin papers had been full of sensational stories about Hess's death, but Hans had read none of them. He did remember the occasional feature from earlier years, though. They invariably portrayed an infantile old man, a once-powerful soldier reduced to watching episodes of the American soap opera *Dynasty* on television. Why was the pathetic old Nazi so important? Hans wondered. Why should even a hint of information about his mission drive the price of forged diaries into the millions?

Catching his reflection in a shop window, Hans realized that in his work clothes he looked like a bum, even by the Ku'damm's indulgent standards. He stubbed out his cigarette and turned down a side street at the first opportunity. He soon found himself standing before a small art cinema. He gazed up at the colorful posters hawking films imported from a dozen nations. On a whim he stepped up to the ticket window and inquired about the matinee. The ticket girl answered in a sleepy monotone.

"American western film today. John Wayne. *Der Searchers.*"

"In German?"

"*Nein.* English."

"Excellent. One ticket, please."

"Twelve DM," demanded the robot voice.

"Twelve! That's robbery."

"You want the ticket?"

Reluctantly, Hans surrendered his money and entered the theater. He didn't stop for refreshments; at the posted prices he couldn't afford to. *No wonder Ilse and I never go to movies,* he thought. Just before he entered the screening room, he spied a pay phone near the restrooms. He slowed his stride, thinking of calling in to the station, but then he walked on. *There isn't any rush, is there?* he thought. *No one knows about the papers yet.* As he seated himself in the darkness near the screen, he decided that he might well have found the most anonymous place in the city to decide what to do with the Spandau papers.

Six rows behind Hans, a tall, thin shadow slipped noiselessly into a frayed theater seat. The shadow reached into a worn leather bag on its lap and withdrew an orange. While Hans watched the titles roll, the shadow peeled the orange and watched him.

Thirty blocks away in the Lützenstrasse, Ilse Apfel set her market basket down in the uncarpeted hallway and let herself into apartment 40. The operation took three keys—one for the knob and two for the heavy deadbolts Hans insisted upon. She went straight to the kitchen and put away her groceries, singing tunefully all the while. The song was an old one, *Walking on the Moon* by the Police. Ilse always sang when she was happy, and today she was ecstatic. The news about the baby meant far more than fulfillment of her desire to have a family. It meant that Hans might finally agree to settle permanently in Berlin. For the past five months he had talked of little else but his desire to try out for Germany's elite counterterror force, the *Grenzschutzgruppe*-9 (GSG-9), oddly enough, the unit whose marksmen his estranged father coached. Hans claimed he was tired of routine police work, that he wanted something more exciting and meaningful.

Ilse didn't like this idea at all. For one thing, it would seriously disrupt *her* career. Policemen in Berlin made little money; most police wives worked as hairdressers, secretaries, or even housekeepers—low-paying jobs, but jobs that could be done anywhere. Ilse was different. Her parents had died when she was very young, and she had been raised by her grandfather, an eminent history professor and author. She'd practically grown up in the Free University and had taken degrees in both Modern Languages and Finance. She'd even spent a semester in the United States, studying French and teaching German. Her job as interpreter for a prominent brokerage house gave Hans and her a more comfortable life than most police families. They were not rich, but their life was good.

If Hans qualified for GSG-9, however, they would have to move to one of the four towns that housed the active GSG-9 units: Kassel, Munich, Hannover, or Kiel. Not exactly financial meccas. Ilse knew she could adapt to a new city if she had to, but not to the heightened danger. Assignment to a GSG-9 unit virtually guaranteed that Hans would be put into life-threatening situations. GSG-9 teams were Germany's forward weapon in the battle against hijackers, assassins, and God only knew what other madmen. Ilse didn't want that kind of life for the father of her child, and she didn't understand how Hans could either. She despised amateur psychology, but she suspected that Hans's reckless impulse was driven by one of two things: a desire to prove something to his father, or his failure to become a father himself.

No more conversations about stun grenades and storming airplanes, she told herself. Because she was finally pregnant, and because today was just that kind of day. Returning to work from the doctor's office, she'd found that her boss had realized a small fortune for his clients that morning by following a suggestion she had made before leaving. Of course by market close the cretin had convinced himself that the clever bit of arbitrage was entirely his own idea. *And who really cares?* she thought. *When I open my brokerage house, he'll be carrying coffee to my assistants!*

Ilse stepped into the bedroom to change out of her business clothes. The first thing she saw was the half-eaten plate of *Weisswurst* on the unmade bed. Melted ice and dirt from Hans's uniform had left the sheets a muddy mess. Then she saw the uniform itself, draped over the boots in the corner. *That's odd,* she thought. Hans was as human as the next man, but he usually managed to keep his dirty clothes out of sight. In fact, it was odd not to find him sleeping off the fatigue of night duty.

Ilse felt a strange sense of worry. And then suddenly she knew. At work there had been a buzz about a breaking news story—something about Russians arresting two West Berliners at Spandau Prison. Later, in her car, she'd half-heard a radio announcer say something about Russians at one of the downtown police stations. She prayed that Hans hadn't got caught up in that mess. A bureaucratic tangle like that could take all night. She frowned. Telling Hans about the baby while he was in a bad mood wasn't what she had had in mind at all. She would have to think of a way to put him in a good mood first.

One method always worked, and she smiled thinking of it. For the first time in weeks the thought of sex made her feel genuinely excited. It seemed so long since she and Hans had made love with any other goal than pregnancy. But now that she had conceived, they could forget all about charts and graphs and temperatures and rediscover the intensity of those nights when they hardly slept at all.

She had already planned a celebratory dinner—not a health-conscious American style snack like those her yuppie colleagues from the Yorckstrasse called dinner, but a real Berlin feast: *Eisben,* sauerkraut, and Pease pudding. She'd made a special trip to the food floor of the KaDeWe and bought everything ready-made. It was said that anything edible in the world could be purchased at the KaDeWe, and Ilse believed it. She smiled again. She and Hans would share a first-class supper, and for dessert he could have *her*—as healthy a dish as any man could want. *Then* she would tell him about the baby.

Ilse tied her hair back, then she took the pork from the refrigerator and put it in the oven. While it heated, she went into the bedroom to strip the soiled sheets. She laughed softly. A randy German woman might happily make love on a forest floor, but on dirty linens? Never! She knelt beside the bed and gathered the bedclothes into a ball. She was about to rise when she saw something white sticking out from under the mattress. Automatically, she pulled it out and found herself holding a damp sheaf of papers.

What in the world? She certainly didn't remember putting any papers under the mattress. It must have been Hans. But what would he hide from her? Bewildered, she let the bedclothes fall, stood up, and unfolded the onionskin pages. Heavy, hand-printed letters covered the paper. She read the first paragraph cursorily, her mind more on the circumstances of her discovery than on the actual content of the papers. The second paragraph, however, got her attention. It was written in *Latin* of all things. Shivering in the chilly air, she walked into the kitchen and stood by the warm stove.

She concentrated on the word endings, trying to decipher the carefully blocked letters. It was almost painful, like trying to recall formulas from *gymnasium* physics. Her specialty was modern languages; Latin she could hardly remember. Ilse went to the kitchen table and spread out the thin pages, anchoring each corner with a piece of flatware. There were nine. She took a pen and notepad from the telephone stand, went back to the first paragraph of Latin, and began recording her efforts. After ten minutes she had roughed out the first four sentences. When she read straight through what she had written, the pencil slipped from her shaking hand.

"*Mein Gott,*" she breathed. "This cannot be."

Hans exited the cinema into the gathering dusk. He couldn't believe the afternoon had passed so quickly. Huddling against the cold, he considered taking the U-Bahn home, then decided against it. It would mean changing trains at Fehrbelliner-Platz, and he would still have some distance to walk. Better to walk the whole way and use the time to decide how to tell Ilse about the Spandau papers. He started west with a loping stride, moving away from the crowded Ku'damm. He knew he was duty-bound to hand the papers over to his superiors, and he felt sure that the mix-up with the Russians had been straightened out by now. Yet as he walked, he was aware that his mind was not completely clear about turning in the papers. For some irritating reason, when he thought of doing that, his father's face came into his mind. But there was something else in his brain. Something he soon recognized as Heini Weber's voice saying: "Three point seven *million* Deutschemarks . . ."

Hans had already done the calculations. At his salary it would take 150 years to earn that much money, and that represented the offer of a single magazine for the "Hitler diaries." That was a powerful temptation, even for an honest man.

As Hans reached the mouth of the side street, a dark shape disengaged itself from the gloom beneath the cinema awning and fell into step behind him. It neither hurried nor tarried, but moved through the streets as effortlessly as a cloud's shadow.

CHAPTER FOUR

5:50 P.M. American Sector: West Berlin

Colonel Godfrey A. "God" Rose reached into the bottom drawer of his mammoth Victorian desk, withdrew a half-empty bottle of Wild Turkey bourbon, and gazed fondly at the label. For five exhausting hours the U.S. Army's West Berlin chief of intelligence had sifted through the weekly reports of his "snitches"—the highly paid but underzealous army of informers that the U.S. government maintains on its shadow payroll to keep abreast of events in Berlin—and discovered nothing but the usual sordid list of venalities committed by the host of elected officials, bureaucrats, and military officers of the city he had come to regard as the Sodom of Western Europe. The colonel had a single vice—whiskey—and he looked forward to the anesthetic burn of the Kentucky bourbon with sublime anticipation.

Pouring the Turkey into a Lenox shot glass, Rose glanced up and saw his aide, Sergeant Clary, silhouetted against the leaded glass window of his office door. With customary discretion the young NCO paused before knocking, giving his superior time to "straighten his desk." By the time Clary tapped on the glass and stepped smartly into the office, Colonel Rose appeared to be engrossed in an intelligence brief.

Clary cleared his throat. "Colonel?"

Rose looked up slowly. "Yes, Sergeant?"

"Sir, Ambassador Briggs is flying in from Bonn tomorrow morning. State just informed us by courier."

Rose frowned. "That's not on my calendar, is it?"

"No, sir."

"Well?"

"Apparently the Soviets have filed some sort of complaint against us, sir. Through the embassy."

"Us?"

"The Army, sir. It's something to do with last night's detail at Spandau Prison. That's all I could get out of Smitty—I mean the courier, sir."

"Spandau? What about it? Christ, we've watched the damned coverage all day, haven't we? I've already filed my report."

"State didn't elaborate, sir."

Rose snorted. "They never do, do they."

"No, sir. Care to see the message?"

Rose gazed out of his small window at the Berlin dusk and wondered about the possible implications of the ambassador's visit. The American diplomatic corps stayed in Bonn most of the time—well out of Rose's area of operations—and he liked that just fine.

"The message, Colonel?" Sergeant Clary repeated.

"What? No, Sergeant. Dismissed."

"Sir." Clary beat a hasty retreat from the office, certain that his colonel would want to ponder this unpleasant development over a shot of the good stuff.

"Clary!" Rose's bark rattled the door. "Is Major Richardson still down the hall?"

The sergeant poked his head back into the office. "I'll run check, sir."

"Can't you just buzz him?"

"Uh . . . the major doesn't always answer his pages, sir. After five, that is. Says he can't stand to hear the phone while he's working."

"Who the hell can? Don't people just keep on ringing the damned thing when he doesn't answer?"

"Well, sir . . . I think he's rigged some type of switch to his phone or something. He just shuts it off when he doesn't want to hear it."

Rose stuck out his bottom lip. "I see."

"Checking now, sir," said Clary, on the fly.

Since 1945, Berlin has been an island city. It is a political island, quadrisected by foreign conquerors, and a psychological island as insulated from the normal flow of German life as a child kidnapped from its mother. Berlin was an island before the Wall, during the Wall, and it will remain so long

after the Wall has fallen. Kidnapped children can take years
to recover.

The American community in Berlin is an island within
that larger host. It clusters around the U.S. Military Mission
in the affluent district of Dahlem, a giant concrete block
bristling with satellite dishes, radio antennae, and micro-
wave transmitters. In this city of hastily built office towers,
bomb-scarred churches, and drab concrete tenement blocks
whose color accents are provided mostly by graffiti, the
American housing area manages to look neat, midwestern,
suburban, and safe. Known as "Little America," it is home
to the sixty-six hundred servicemen, their wives, and children who comprise the symbolic U.S. presence in Berlin.
These families bustle between the U.S. Mission, the Officer's club, the well-stocked PX, the private Burger King and
McDonald's, and their patio barbecues like suburbanites
from Omaha or Atlanta. Only the razor wire that tops the
fences surrounding the manicured lawns betrays the tension
that underpins this bucolic scene.

Few Americans truly mix with the Berliners. They are
more firmly tied to the United States than to the streets they
walk and the faces they pass each day in Berlin. They are
tied by the great airborne umbilical cord stretching from
Tempelhof Airport to the mammoth military supply bases of
America. Major Harry Richardson—the man Colonel Rose
had sent Sergeant Clary to find—was an exception to this
pattern. Richardson needed no umbilical cord in Berlin, or
anywhere else. He spoke excellent German, as well as
Russian—and not with the stilted State Department cadence
of the middle and upper ranks of the army. He did not live
in Dahlem or Zehlendorf, the ritzy addresses of choice, but
in thoroughly German Wilmersdorf. He came from a mon-
eyed family, had attended both Harvard and Oxford, yet he
had served in Vietnam and remained in the army after the
war. His personal contacts ranged from U.S. senators to supply sergeants at distant Army outposts, from English peers to
Scottish fishing guides, from Berlin senators to *kabob*-cooks
in the Turkish quarter of Kreuzberg. And that, in Colonel
Rose's eyes, made Harry Richardson one hell of an intelligence officer.

Harry saluted as he sauntered into Rose's office and collapsed into the colonel's infamous "hot seat." The chair
dropped most people a head lower than Rose, but Harry

stood six feet three inches without shoes. His gray eyes met the stocky colonel's with the self-assured steadiness of an equal.

"Richardson," Rose said across the desk.

"Colonel."

Rose eyed Harry's uniform doubtfully. It was wrinkled and rather plain for a major. Harry had won the silver star in Vietnam, yet the only decoration he ever wore was his Combat Infantryman's Badge. Rose didn't like the wrinkles, but he liked the modesty. He clucked his tongue against the roof of his mouth.

"Bigwig Briggs is flying in from Bonn tomorrow," he announced.

Harry smiled wryly. "I thought he might."

"You did. Why's that?"

"Stands to reason, doesn't it? With the ham-fisted way the Soviets have handled the Spandau mess so far, I figured the negotiations would have to be bumped up a notch on both sides. Sir."

"Can the 'sir' crap, Harry. Just what do you think *did* happen last night?"

"Do you have anything that wasn't on TV?"

"Nothing substantive. Master Sergeant Jackson pretty much confirmed the press accounts of the incident, and the German police aren't saying squat. Christ, you'd think if the Russians wanted to file a complaint against the Army, they'd give it to us and not the goddamn State Department."

Harry rolled his eyes. "If it's got anything to do with Spandau, the State Department doesn't trust us, and you know why."

"Bird," Rose muttered. He sighed wearily. In 1972 the first U.S. commandant of Spandau Prison, Lieutenant Colonel Eugene Bird, had been relieved of his duties for secretly bringing a tape recorder and camera into Spandau over a period of months and compiling a book on Rudolf Hess, which was published in 1974. The colonel's entrepreneurial spirit hadn't exactly improved the relationship between the Army and the State Department.

"The point," Rose went on, "is that the ambassador will be here in the morning, and he'll want to grill me for breakfast. I want you with me when I talk to him, and I want to know everything he's going to say *before* he says it."

"No problem, Colonel."

"Okay, Harry, what's your read on this thing?"

"I'm not sure yet. I was over at Abschnitt 53 for a few minutes this morning—"

"You *what?*"

"I've got a friend over there," Harry explained.

"Naturally." Rose opened his bottom drawer and set the bottle of Wild Turkey between them on the desk. "Drink?" he asked, already pouring two shots.

Harry accepted the glass, raised it briefly, then drank it off neat and wiped his mouth with the back of his hand. "As I was saying, Colonel, I dropped by there just to get a feel for what was going on. The problem was, I couldn't even get near my guy's office. I got through the reporters okay, but inside the station it was wall-to-wall cops. There was a squad of Russian soldiers guarding the cellblock, and they weren't ceremonial roosters. One guy was wearing a sergeant's uniform, but he was no noncom. Wasn't even regular army. KGB down to his BVDs."

Rose groaned. "Is this the Hess thing again?"

Harry shook his head. "I don't think so, Colonel. They've run Hess into the ground already. Pardon the pun, but it's a dead issue."

"So, what is it?"

"I think this is a Russian territorial thing. Spandau was a Soviet foothold in West Berlin—small maybe, but they don't like giving it up."

"Hmm. What about the Russian accusations that someone murdered Hess?"

Harry sighed. "Colonel, I don't think the Russians ever believed Prisoner Number Seven *was* Hess. But if this is about Hess, I think we should stay out of it. Let the Russians knock themselves out. They've been obsessed with the case for years. But I don't think that's it. I think it's Russian paranoia, plain and simple."

"Jesus," Rose grumbled, "I thought the goddamn Cold War was over."

Harry smiled wryly. "The reports of its death have been greatly exaggerated. Which reminds me, Colonel, I caught a glimpse of Ivan Kosov at that police station this morning."

"Kosov! What the hell was that old bear doing in our sector?"

Harry shrugged. "We'd better find out."

"Okay, what do you need?"

"Do you have a list of all personnel with access to the Spandau site last night? Ours and theirs?"

"I'll have Clary get Ray down here to crack the computer file."

"Don't bother, I'll get it."

"Ray's the only one with the codes, Harry. He buries that stuff deep."

Harry smiled thinly. "Just get me into his office."

Rose cocked an eye at Richardson, then pushed on. "There's something else. I know you're pretty chummy with some of the Brits over here. Been fishing in Scotland with a few ministers and such. But on this thing—the Spandau thing—I'd like to keep the Brits out of it. Just for the time being. It's a matter of—"

"Understood, Colonel. You're not sure they've always played straight with us on the Hess affair."

"Exactly," Rose said, relieved. "Even if you're right about this not having anything to do with Hess, I'd feel better keeping it in-house for a while."

"No problem."

Rose smiled humorlessly. "Right. I'll just—"

"Shit," Harry muttered. "There is one problem. I've got a racquetball date this evening with a girl from the British embassy."

"Cancel it."

Harry looked thoughtful. "Colonel, I understand your thinking on this, but don't you think breaking the date might call more attention—"

"I'll tell you what I think!" Rose cut in with surprising force. "I think the goddamn Brits *killed* Hess! And during our goddamn guard month! How about *that?*" His face flushed. "You think I'm crazy, Major?"

Harry swallowed his surprise. "No, sir. I wouldn't say that scenario was outside the realm of possibility."

"Possibility! Ever since Gorbachev came out with the goddamn *glasnost,* the limeys have been quaking in their boots thinking the Russians would go soft and let Hess out to spill his guts to the world. The Russians were the only ones vetoing his release those last few years, you know. The Brits knew if they ever had to step in and veto it, all the old questions would start again." Rose nodded angrily. "I think those smug sons-of-bitches slipped one of their ex-SAS killers over the wall last month, strangled that old Nazi, and left us holding the goddamn bag! That's what I *think* about the British, Major! And you *will* cancel your racquetball date as of now. Is that clear?"

"Absolutely, Colonel."

"I want your report on my desk by oh-eight-hundred," Rose growled.

Harry stood, saluted, and marched out.

"Clary!" Rose's gruff baritone boomed through the open door.

"Yes, sir?"

"Let Major Richardson into Captain Donovan's office. He's got a little work to do on the computer."

"Yes, sir."

"And Clary?"

"Sir?"

"I want one of those phone gadgets like Richardson's got."

Grinning, Sergeant Clary backed out and pulled the door shut.

Rose looked longingly at the Wild Turkey bottle, then slipped it back into his bottom drawer. He closed his eyes, leaned his chair all the way back and propped his legs up on the huge desk. *That Richardson is one strange bird,* he thought. *Damn near insubordinate sometimes. But he gets the job done.* Rose congratulated himself on a fine piece of human resource management. *Harry can handle the fairies from State,* he thought with satisfaction, *and I'll take care of the friggin' Russians. And if the Brits stick their stuffy noses into it, the devil take the hindmost.*

6:10 P.M. MI-5 Headquarters: Charles Street, London, England

Sir Neville Shaw looked up from the report with anger in his eyes. As director general of MI-5, he had witnessed his share of crises, but the one he now faced was one he had long prayed would remain buried in the ashes of history.

"This cock-up started almost twelve hours ago!" he snapped.

"Yes, Sir Neville," admitted his deputy. "The unit on the scene reported it to General Bishop in Berlin. Bishop informed MI-6 but saw no reason to apprise us. The Russian complaint went to the Foreign Office, and the F.O. apparently felt as the general did. We've got one contact on the West Berlin police force; he's the only reason we got onto this at all. He can't tell us much, though, because he's stationed in our sector. These German trespassers were taken to a police station in the American sector. The thing's been on the telly over there since this afternoon."

"Good *God*," Sir Neville groaned. "One more bloody week and this would have been nothing but a minor flap."

"How do you mean, sir?"

Shaw rubbed his forehead to ease a migraine. "Forget it. This was bound to happen sooner or later. Damned journalists and curiosity hounds poking at the story for years. Matter of time, that's all."

"Yes, sir," the deputy director commiserated.

"Who did we have at Spandau, anyway?"

"Regular military detail. The sergeant in charge said he knew nothing about any papers. He didn't have the foggiest idea of the implications."

"What monumental *stupidity!*" Shaw got to his feet, still staring at the report in his hands. "Can this Russian forensic report be relied upon?"

"Our technical section says the Soviets are quite good at that sort of thing, sir."

Sir Neville snorted indignantly. "Papers at Spandau. Good Christ. Whatever has turned up over there, ten to one it's got something to do with Hess. We've got to get hold of it, Wilson, fast. Who else was at Spandau?"

"The Americans, the Frogs, and the Russians. Plus a contingent of West Berlin police."

Sir Neville wiped his mouth with the back of his hand. "I could hang for this one, that's sure. What do we have in Berlin?"

"Not much. What we do have is mostly on the commercial side. No one who's cleared for this."

"I didn't think anyone was cleared for this rot," Shaw murmured. "All right, you get me four men who *are* cleared for it—men who can *quote* me the bloody Official Secrets Act—and get them here fast. Arrange air transport to West Berlin straightaway. I want those lads airborne as soon as I've briefed them."

"Yes, sir."

After an almost interminable silence, Shaw said, "There is a ship, Wilson. I want you to locate her for me."

"A ship, sir?"

"Yes. A freighter, actually. MV *Casilda,* out of Panama. Get on to Lloyd's, or whoever keeps up with those things. Talk to the satellite people if you have to, just find out where she is."

Perplexed, the deputy director said, "All right, sir," and turned to go. At the door he paused. "Sir Neville," he said hesitantly. "Is there anything I should know about this Hess business? A small brief, perhaps?"

Shaw's face reddened. "If there was, you'd know it already, wouldn't you?" he snapped.

Wilson displayed his irritation by clipping out a regimental "Sir!" before shutting the door.

Shaw didn't even notice. He walked to his well-earned window above the city and pondered the disturbing news. *Spandau,* he thought bitterly. *Hess may stab us in the back yet.* In spite of the ticklishness of his own position, Sir Neville Shaw smiled coldly. *There'll be some royal arses shaking in their beds tonight,* he thought with satisfaction. *Right along with mine.*

He reached for the telephone.

6:25 P.M. #30 Lützenstrasse, West Berlin

Hans reached the apartment building too winded to use the stairs. He wriggled into the elevator, yanked the lever that set the clattering cage in motion, then slumped against the wrought-iron grillwork. Despite his frayed nerves, he was smiling. Heini Weber could joke all he wanted, but in the end the joke would be on him. Because Hans knew something Weber didn't: *where* he had found the papers. And that single fact would make him rich, he was certain of it. He jerked back the metal grille and trotted to the apartment door.

"Ilse!" he called, letting himself in. "I'm home!"

In the kitchen doorway he stopped cold. Wearing a white cotton robe, Ilse sat at the table holding the papers Hans had found at Spandau.

"Where did these come from?" she asked coolly.

Hans searched for words. This was not the way he'd planned to explain the papers.

"Your night duty was at Spandau Prison, wasn't it?"

"Yes, but *Liebchen,* give me a chance to explain. It was a secret detail. That's why I couldn't call you."

She studied him silently. "You haven't told anyone about this, have you?"

Hans remembered his conversation with Heini Weber, but decided that would be best kept private for now. "No," he lied, "I didn't have time to say anything to anyone."

"Hans, you've got to turn these papers in."

"I know."

She nodded slowly. "Then why am I so worried about you?"

He took a deep breath, exhaled. "We have a chance here, Ilse. If you looked at those papers, you know that as well as I do. Finding those papers ... it's like winning the lottery or something. Do you realize what they might be worth?"

Ilse closed her eyes. "Hans, what is going on? You could lose your job for this."

"I'm not going to lose my job. So I found some old papers. What was I supposed to do?"

"Turn them in to the proper authorities."

"The proper authorities?" Hans snorted. "And who are the proper authorities? The Americans? The British? The French? This is Berlin, Ilse. Every person, every company, every *nation* here is looking after its own interests—nobody else's. Why shouldn't I look after ours for once?"

Ilse rubbed her throbbing temples with her fingertips.

"Liebchen," Hans insisted, "no one even knows these papers exist. If you'd just listen for five minutes—if you heard how I found them—you'd see that they're a godsend."

She sighed hopelessly. "All right, tell me."

Four floors below the apartment, in the cold wind of the Lützenstrasse, Jonas Stern accepted a thick stack of files from a young man wearing a West Berlin police uniform.

"Thank you, Baum," he said. "This is everyone?"

"Everyone from the Spandau patrol, yes sir. I couldn't get the file on the prefect. It's classified."

Stern sighed. "I think we know enough about dear Herr Funk, don't we?"

Shivering from the wind, the young policeman nodded

and looked up at the suntanned old man with something near to awe in his eyes.

"You've done well, Baum." Stern flipped through the computer printouts. He stopped at *Apfel, Hans* but saw little of interest. *Hauer, Dieter,* however, told a different story. Stern read softly to himself:

"Attached to Federal Border Police 1959. Promoted sergeant 1964, captain in 1969. Sharpshooter qualification 1963. National Match Champion 1965, '66 . . . Decorated for conspicuous bravery in '64, '66, '70 and '74. All kidnapping cases. Transferred with rank to the West Berlin civil police January 1, 1973. Hmm," Stern mused. "I'd say that's a demotion." He picked up further down. "Sharpshooting coach and hostage recovery adviser to GSG-9 since 1973—" Stern paused again, memorizing silently. Credentials like those made Dieter Hauer a match for any man. Stern read on. "Member of International Fraternal Order of Police since 1960 . . . Ah," he said suddenly, "Member of *Der Bruderschaft* since 1986. Now we learn something."

The Israeli looked up, surprised to see his young informant still standing there. "Something else, Baum?"

"Oh—no, sir."

Stern smiled appreciatively. "You'd better get back to your post. Try to monitor what's going on in Abschnitt 53 if you can."

"Yes, sir. *Shalom.*"

"*Shalom.*"

Stern cradled the files under his arm and stepped back into the apartment building. He reclaimed his broom and dustpan, then started noisily back up to the fourth floor. *This role of custodian isn't half-bad,* he thought. He had certainly known much worse.

Ilse's eyes flickered like camera lenses; they always did when she was deep in thought. Hans had ended his account of the night at Spandau with Captain Hauer's facing down the furious Russian commander. Now he sat opposite Ilse at the kitchen table, staring down at the Spandau papers.

"Your father," she said softly. "Why did he pick last night to try to talk to you, I wonder?"

Hans looked impatient. "Coincidence . . . what does it matter? What matters right now is the papers."

"Yes," she agreed.

"I read what I could," he said breathlessly. "But most of it's written in some strange language. It's like . . ."

"Latin," she finished. "It's Latin."

"You can *read* it?"

"A little."

"What does it say?"

Ilse's lips tightened. "Hans, have you told *anyone* about these papers? Anyone at all?"

"I told you I didn't," he insisted, compounding the lie.

Ilse twisted two strands of hair into a rope. "The papers are about Rudolf Hess," she said finally.

"I knew it! What do they say?"

"Hans, Latin isn't exactly my specialty, okay? It's been years since I read any." She looked down at her notes. "The papers mention Hess's name frequently, and some others—Heydrich, for instance—and something called the SD. They were signed by Prisoner Number Seven. You saw that?"

Hans nodded eagerly.

"The odd thing is that Prisoner Number Seven was Rudolf Hess, yet these papers seem to be talking about Hess as if he were another person." She pushed her notes away. "I've probably got it all wrong. The writer describes a flight to Britain, but mentions a stop somewhere in Denmark. It's crazy. There seem to be *two* men in the plane, not one. And I do know one thing for certain—Rudolf Hess flew to Britain alone."

Hans blinked. "Wait a minute. Are you saying that the man who died in Spandau Prison might not have been Rudolf Hess?"

"No, I'm saying that the *papers* say that. I think. But I don't believe it for a minute."

"Why not?"

Ilse got up, went to a cupboard, and removed a beer, which she placed on the counter but did not open. "Think about it, Hans. For weeks the newspapers have run wild with speculation about Prisoner Number Seven. Was he murdered? Why did he really fly to Britain? Was he really Hess at all? Now you find some papers that seem to indicate that the prisoner wasn't Hess, just as some of the newspapers have been speculating?" She brushed a strand of hair out of her eyes. "It's too convenient. This has to be some kind of press stunt or something."

"My God," he said, coming to his feet. "Don't you *see?*

It doesn't matter if the papers are real or not. The fact that I found them in Spandau is enough. They could be worth millions of marks!"

Ilse sat down carefully and looked up at Hans. When she spoke her voice was grave. "Hans, listen to me. I understand why you didn't turn in the papers immediately. But now is the time for clear thinking. If these papers are fakes, they're worthless and they can only get us into trouble. And if they are *genuine* ..." She trailed off, glanced up at the clock on the kitchen wall. "Hans, I think we should call my grandfather," she said suddenly. "I could only read part of this ... diary, I guess you'd call it, but *Opa* will be able to read it all. He'll know what we should do." She pushed her chair away from the table.

"Wait!" Hans cried. "What business is this of his?"

Ilse reached out and hooked her fingers in Hans's trouser pocket. "Hans, I love you," she said gently. "I love you, but this thing is too deep for us. I heard some of the news bulletins at work today. The Russians have gone crazy over this Spandau incident. Imagine what they might think about these papers. We need some good advice, and *Opa* can give it to us."

Hans felt a hot prickle of resentment. The last thing he wanted was Ilse's arrogant grandfather strutting around and telling him what to do. "We're not calling the professor," he said flatly.

Ilse started to snap back, but she checked herself. "All right," she said. "If you won't call *Opa,* then call your father."

Hans drew back as if struck physically. "I can't believe you said that."

"For God's sake, Hans. Three years without more than a nod to the man. Can't you admit that he's in a position to help you? To help us? He obviously wants to—"

"Three years! He went *twenty* years without talking to me!"

There was a long silence. "I'm sorry," Ilse said finally. "I shouldn't have said that. But you're not acting like yourself."

"And what's so wrong with that? *Liebchen,* people get a chance like this once in their lives, if they're lucky. I *found* these papers, I didn't steal them. The man they belonged to is dead. They're ours now. Imagine ... all the things you've ever wanted. All the things I could never afford to buy you. Your friends from work are always flaunting their fine houses, their clothes, the best of *everything*. You never complain, but I know you miss those things. You grew up with them. And now you can have them again."

"But I don't *care* about those things," Ilse countered. "You know that. You know what's important to me."

"That's what I'm talking about! Children aren't cheap, you know. When you finally get pregnant, we'll need all the money we can get." He snatched up one of the Spandau pages. "And it's right here in our hands!"

For the first time since finding the papers, Ilse remembered the baby. She had been so happy this afternoon, so ready to celebrate their blessing. She'd wanted everything to be perfect. But now . . .

"Hans," she said solemnly, "I wasn't being honest, okay? I probably would prefer driving to work in a Mercedes rather than riding the U-Bahn." Suddenly Ilse laughed, flirting momentarily with the idea of easy money. "I wouldn't turn down a new wardrobe or a mansion in Zehlendorf, either. But if these papers are real, Hans, they are not our ticket to getting those things. Finding these papers *isn't* like finding a lottery ticket. If they are genuine, they are a legacy of the Nazis. Of war criminals. How many times have we talked about the Hitler madness? Even almost fifty years after the war, it's like an invisible weight dragging us backward. When I spent that semester in New York, I made some friends, but I also saw the looks some people gave me— Jews maybe, I don't know—wondering about the blond German girl. 'Does she think she's better than we are? *Racially superior?*' Hans, our whole generation has paid the price for something we had nothing to do with. Do you want to profit from that?"

Hans looked down at the papers on the table. Suddenly they looked very different than they had before. In a span of seconds their spell had been broken. Ilse's laugh had done it, he realized, not her impassioned speech. Her musical, self-mocking laugh. He gathered up the loose sheets and stacked them at the center of the table. "I'll turn them in tonight," he promised. "I'll take them downtown right after supper. Good enough?"

Ilse smiled. "Good enough." She stood slowly and pulled Hans to her. He could feel the swell of her breasts through the cotton robe. She laughed softly. "You see? Doing the right thing sometimes has its rewards." She stood on tiptoe and nuzzled into his neck, at the same time pressing her bare thigh into his groin. Hans laughed into her hair. He wanted her, and his want was obvious, but he sensed something more than desire behind her sudden affection. "What are you up to?" he asked, pulling away a little. Ilse's eyes glowed with happiness. "I've got a secret too," she said. She reached up and touched her forefinger to his lips—then the telephone rang.

With a curious glance, Hans tugged playfully at her robe and walked into the living room. "Hans Apfel," he said into the phone. He looked back toward the kitchen. Standing in the doorway, Ilse opened her robe with a teasing smile. He forced himself to look away. "Yes, *Sergeant* Apfel. Yes, I was at Spandau last night. Right, I've seen the television. What? What kind of questions?" Sensing Ilse behind him, he motioned for her to keep quiet. "I see. Formalities, sure." His face darkened. "You mean now? What's the hurry? Is everyone to be there? What do you mean, you can't say? Who is this?" Hans's jaw tightened. "Yes, sir. Yes, I do realize that, sir. Don't worry, I'll be there. I'm leaving now." Slightly dazed, he returned the phone to its cradle and turned around.

Ilse had retied her robe. "What is it?" she asked, her eyes troubled.

"I'm not sure." He looked at his watch. "That was the prefect's aide on the phone, a Lieutenant Luhr. He said the Russians are still in the station. They're making some kind of trouble, and the prefect wants to satisfy them before the Allied commandants get too involved. He wants to ask everyone from the Spandau detail some questions."

Ilse felt a tremor in her chest. "What do you think?"

He swallowed hard. "I think I don't feel so good about that call." He slipped into the bedroom to change into a fresh uniform.

"Are you going to take the papers with you?"

"Not with the Russians still there," he called. "I'll pull somebody aside when I get a chance and explain what happened. Maybe even the prefect."

"Hans, don't be angry with me," she said. "But I really think you should talk to your father first. He'd cover for you on this, I know he would."

"Just let me handle it, okay?" Hans realized he had spoken much louder than he'd meant to. He buttoned up the jacket of a freshly pressed uniform and went back into the living room. He was reaching for his gloves when the telephone rang again.

Ilse practically pounced on it. "Who is this, please? What? Just a moment." She covered the mouthpiece with her palm. "It's someone named Heini Weber. He says he's a reporter for *Der Spiegel.*"

Hans moved toward the phone, then stopped. "I'm not here," he whispered.

Ilse listened for a few moments, then hung up. Her eyes showed puzzlement and fear. "He said to tell you he made a mistake before," she said slowly. "He wants to meet you as soon as possible. He . . . he said money's no object." Little crimson moons appeared high on Ilse's cheeks. "Hans?" she said uncertainly. "He knows, doesn't he?"

She stepped forward hesitantly, her face flushed with fear and anger. She tried to summon harsh words, but her anger faltered. "Hans, take the papers with you," she said. "The sooner we're rid of them, the better."

He shook his head. "If I let the Russians get those papers, I really could lose my job."

"You could slip them under somebody's door. Nobody would ever have to know they came from you."

He considered this. "That's not a bad idea," he admitted. "But not while the Russians are there. Besides, our forensic lab might still be able to link me to the papers. It's scary what those guys can do."

Ilse reached out, hesitated. The tendons in her neck stood out. "Hans, don't go!" she begged. "There's something we need to talk about."

He kissed the top of her head. Ilse's hair smelled of flowers, a scent he would remember for a long time. "I don't have any choice," he said tenderly. "Everything will be fine, I promise. We're just jumpy because of the papers. Don't worry. I'll be back in an hour." Before Ilse could say anything else, he slipped through the door and was gone.

Ilse sagged against the wood, holding back tears. *Hans, I'm pregnant.* The words had been right on her tongue, yet she'd been unable to force them out. The lie had done it. First Hans's crazy idea about selling the papers—then the lie. She wanted badly to call her grandfather, yet she hesitated. He would probably take an "I told you so" attitude when Ilse admitted that Hans's behavior had shaken even her. He had been against her marrying Hans to begin with. Ilse's doubts made her think back to when she had first met Hans. Three years ago, at a traffic accident. An old Opel had broadsided a gleaming Jaguar right before her eyes on the Leibnizstrasse, smashing the Jaguar's door and trapping its driver. There'd been a police patrol car behind the Opel. Two officers had jumped out to help, but as they tried to free the trapped driver, the Jaguar had burst into flame. All they could do was hold back the crowd and wait for the fire police to arrive. Suddenly a young foot patrolman had bulled his way through the crowd—right past Ilse—and dashed to the Jaguar. Shouting at the driver to get down in the seat, he drew his Walther, fired several shots through the stuck window and kicked out what was left of the glass. He dragged the stunned driver to safety only moments before the gas tank exploded.

The handsome young officer with singed eyebrows had taken Ilse's slightly awestruck statement, then accepted her invitation to go for coffee afterward. Their romance, like the newspaper accounts of Hans's heroism, had been brief and fiery. He was promoted to sergeant, and they were married as his splash of celebrity faded from the picture magazines.

Ilse had always believed she made a good choice, no matter what her snobby friends or her grandfather said. But this madness from Spandau was no traffic accident. Hans couldn't summon a burst of physical courage to stop the danger she felt tightening around them now. The papers lying on her kitchen table were like a magnet drawing death toward them—she *knew* it. She did not believe in premonitions, but as she thought of Hans driving anxiously toward a situation he knew nothing about, her heart began to race. A wave of nausea rolled inside her. The pregnancy . . . ? Afraid she might throw up, she hurried into the kitchen and leaned over the sink. She managed to choke down the nausea, but not her terror. With tears blurring her eyes, Ilse lifted the phone and dialed her grandfather's apartment.

CHAPTER FIVE

7:30 P.M. Polizei Abschnitt 53

A stubborn group of reporters huddled on the sidewalk in the freezing wind, hoping for a break in the Spandau Prison story or the weather. As Hans idled his Volkswagen past the front steps of the police station, he saw klieg lights and cameras leaning against a remote-broadcast truck, evidence of how seriously the Berlin media were taking the incident. He felt a nervous thrill when he realized that even now the press was driving up the asking price of the Spandau papers for him. He accelerated past the journalists before they could get a decent look at him or the car and swung into the rear lot of the station.

The unexpected summons had taken him by surprise, but upon reflection he wasn't really worried. It made sense for the police brass to try to defuse the crisis before the Allied commandants got too involved—if they weren't already. Nobody liked the Four Powers poking about in German affairs, even if Berlin still technically belonged to them.

As he unlocked the rear door of the station, he spied Erhard Weiss's red coupe parked against the wall. A good sign, Hans thought. At least he hadn't been singled out for questioning. He flicked his cigarette onto the snow and walked inside. The back hallway was usually empty, but tonight a pinch-faced young man he didn't know waited behind a rickety wooden table. The unlikely sentry leapt to attention when he saw Hans.

"Identify yourself!" he ordered.

"What?"

"Your identification!"

"I'm Hans Apfel. I work here. Who are you?"

The little policeman shot Hans an exasperated look and reached for a piece of paper on his desk. It was apparently a list of some sort; he ran his finger down it like a prim schoolmaster.

"*Sergeant* Hans Apfel?"

"That's right."

"Report immediately to room six for interrogation."

Under normal circumstances Hans would have challenged the man's authority on general principles alone. Officers from other districts—especially snotty bureaucrats like this one—were treated coolly at Abschnitt 53 until they had proved their competence. Tonight, however, Hans didn't feel quite confident enough to push. He walked on toward the stairs without comment.

The oppressive block of interrogation rooms lay on the second floor, out of the main traffic of the station. *At least they chose number six,* he thought. Slightly larger than the other questioning rooms, "six" held a long table on a dais, some straight-backed chairs and, mercifully, an electric heater. Emerging from the stairwell on the second floor, Hans saw another unfamiliar policeman standing guard between rooms six and seven. A silent alarm sounded in his head, but it was too late to turn back.

Suddenly a door further down the hall burst open. Two uniformed men with heavy beards bustled Erhard Weiss out of the room and down the hall away from Hans. Weiss's feet seemed to be dragging behind him. He turned and gave Hans a dazed look; then he was gone. Hans slowed down. Something odd was happening here.

"Interrogation?" the guard queried, noticing him.

Hans nodded warily.

"Wait in room seven."

Hans looked for a name tag on the man's chest but saw none. "You from Wansee?" he asked. When the man didn't answer, he tried again. "What's going on in there, friend?"

"Room seven," the man repeated.

"Seven," Hans echoed softly. "All right, then."

Taking a deep breath, he stepped through the door. There was only one man inside the smoky room—Kurt Steger, one of the four recruits from the Spandau assignment. Kurt jumped to his feet like a nervous puppy when he saw Hans.

"Thank God!" he cried. "What's going on, Hans?"

Hans shook his head. "I've no idea. It looks like the

whole place has been taken over by strangers. What have you seen?"

"*Nichts,* almost nothing. We started in here together—all of us from Spandau except you. One by one they call us into room six. Nobody comes back."

Hans frowned. "They were practically dragging Weiss down the hall when I walked up. It didn't look right at all." He hated to ask the next question, but he needed the information. "Have you seen Captain Hauer, Kurt?"

"No. I think the prefect's handling this."

Hans considered this in silence.

"I haven't been on the force very long," said Kurt, "but I get the feeling Captain Hauer and the prefect aren't too fond of each other."

Hans nodded thoughtfully. "To say the least. They've been at each other's throats since Funk took over eight years ago."

"What's the problem?"

"The problem is that Funk is an ass-kissing bureaucrat with no real police experience, and Hauer reminds him of it every chance he gets."

"Can't the prefect fire whoever he wants?"

"Firing Hauer isn't worth the controversy it would start." Hans felt himself coloring as he went to the defense of the father he had accused of terrible things in the silence of his own mind. "He's a decorated hero, one of the best cops in the city. He also works with GSG-9, the counterterror unit. Connections like that don't hurt. Plus he's only got one month before retirement. Funk's been waiting for that day a long time. Now he's almost rid of him."

"What a bastard." Kurt snapped his fingers anxiously. "You got any cigarettes? We smoked all we had."

Hans handed over his pack and matches. "Have they said who's handling the questions?"

Kurt's hands shook slightly as he lit up. "They haven't said anything. We've tried to listen through the wall, but it's useless. They could beat a man to death in there and you'd never hear him scream."

"Thanks a lot. I'll remember that while I'm in there. What about the Russians?"

Kurt cut his eyes toward the door. "Weiss said he saw the very same bastard who tried to take the prisoners from us—"

The door banged open, silencing the young recruit. A

bearded man wearing captain's bars stared back and forth between Hans and Kurt, then pointed to Hans. "You," he growled.

"But I've been here for two hours," Kurt protested.

The captain ignored him and motioned for Hans to follow.

In the hall Hans saw another young officer being led around the corner toward the elevators, his arms pinned to his sides by two large policemen. Fighting a growing sense of unreality, Hans stepped into room six.

The scene unnerved him. The sparsely furnished interrogation room had been transformed into a courtroom. A single wooden chair faced a long, raised table from which five men stared solemnly as Hans entered. At the center of the table sat Wilhelm Funk, prefect of West Berlin police. He eyed Hans with the cold detachment of a hanging judge. A young blond man wearing lieutenant's bars hovered at Funk's left shoulder. Hans guessed he was Lieutenant Luhr, the aide who had summoned him by telephone. To the prefect's right sat three men wearing Soviet Army uniforms. Hans recognized one as the "sergeant" who had bullied Weiss at Spandau, but the others—both colonels—he had never seen before. And to Funk's left, a little apart from Lieutenant Luhr, sat Captain Dieter Hauer. Dark sacs hung under his gray eyes, and he regarded Hans with a Buddhalike inscrutability.

"Setzen sie sich," Funk ordered, then looked down at a buff file open before him.

As Hans turned to sit, he saw more men behind him. Six Berlin policemen stood in a line to the left of the door. He knew them all slightly; all were from other districts. On the right side of the door stood the Russian soldiers from the Spandau detail. Their bloodshot eyes gave the lie to their freshly shaven faces, and the mud of the prison yard still caked their boots. Hans looked slowly from face to face. When his eyes met those of the Russian who had caught him in the rubble pile, Hans looked away first. He did not see the Russian nod almost imperceptibly to the "sergeant" at the table, nor did he see the "sergeant" softly touch the sleeve of one of the colonels as Funk began his interrogation.

"You are Sergeant Hans Apfel?" the prefect asked, still looking at the file before him. "Born Munich 1960, *Bundeswehr* service 1978 to 1980, two-year tour Federal

Border Police, attached Munich municipal force 1983, transferred Berlin 1984, promoted sergeant May of '84?"

"Yes, sir."

"Speak up, Sergeant."

Hans cleared his throat. "I am."

"Better. I want you to listen to me, Sergeant. I have convened this informal hearing to save everyone—yourself included—a great deal of unnecessary trouble. Because of the publicity surrounding this morning's events, the Allied commandants have scheduled a formal investigation into this matter, to commence at seven o'clock tomorrow morning. I want this matter cleared up *long* before then. The problem is that our Soviet friends"—Funk nodded deferentially to his right—"*Oberst* Zotin and *Oberst* Kosov, claim to have uncovered something rather disturbing at Spandau today. Their forensic people say they have evidence that something was removed from the area of the cellblocks last occupied by the Nuremberg war criminals."

Hans's stomach rolled. For a moment the room seemed to spin wildly. It righted itself when he focused on the immobile mask of Captain Hauer.

"Of course I denied their request to question our officers *directly*," Funk went on, "but for the sake of expediency I've agreed to act as the Soviets' proxy. That way they can be quickly satisfied as to our lack of complicity in this matter. Thus, the whole mess is over before it really begins, you see, Sergeant? It's really better all around."

For the first time Hans noticed another man in the room. He had been hunched out of sight behind Hauer, but when Funk spoke again he moved.

"By the way, Sergeant," Funk said casually, "in the interest of veracity I've agreed to monitor all responses by polygraph."

Hans felt a jolt of confusion. Polygraph test results were inadmissible as evidence in a German court. The Berlin Polizei were not even permitted to use the polygraph as an investigative tool. Or almost never, anyway. Buried in the budget of the Experimental Section of the Forensics Division was a small cadre of technicians devoted to the subtle art of lie detection. They were used only in crisis situations, where lives were at stake. The only explanation Hans could come up with for the use of a polygraph tonight was that the Russians had requested it.

"We'll be using our own man, of course," Funk said. "Perhaps you know Heinz Schmidt?"

Hans knew *of* Schmidt, and what he knew made his heart race. The ferretlike little polygrapher took perverse pleasure in wringing secrets out of people—criminals or not—no matter how trivial. He even moonlighted to sate his fetish, screening employees for industrial firms. Funk's inquisitor padded around Hauer's corner of the table, pushing his precious polygraph before him on a wheeled cart like the head of a heretic. Ilse had been right, Hans realized. He should never have come here.

"I said is that all right with you, Sergeant?" Funk repeated testily.

Hans could see that both Hauer and Lieutenant Luhr had suddenly taken a keen interest in him. It took all his concentration to keep his facial muscles still. He cleared his throat again. "Yes, sir. No problem."

"Good. The procedure is simple: Schmidt asks you a few calibration questions, then we get to it." Funk sounded bored. "Hurry it up, Schmidt."

As the polygrapher attached the electrodes to his fingers, Hans felt his earlier bravado draining away. Then came the blood-pressure cuff, fastened around his upper arm and pumped until he could feel his arterial blood throbbing against it like a tourniquet. Last came the chest bands—rubber straps stretched around his torso beneath his shirt—to monitor his respiration. Three separate sensing systems, cold and inhuman, now silently awaited the slightest signals of deception.

Hans wondered which vital sign would give him away: a trace of sweat translated into electrical resistance? His thudding heart? Or just his eyes? *I must be crazy,* he thought wildly. *Why keep it up anyway? They'll find me out in the end.* For one mad moment he considered simply blurting out the truth. He could exonerate himself before Schmidt even asked the first stupid control question. He could—

"Are you Sergeant Hans Apfel?" Schmidt asked in a high, abrasive voice.

"I am."

"Yes or no, please, Sergeant. Is your name Hans Apfel?"

"Yes."

"Do you reside in West Berlin?"

"Yes."

Hans watched Schmidt make some adjustments to his machine. The ferret's shirt was soiled at the collar and armpits, his fingernails were long and grimy, and he smelled of ammonia. Suddenly, Schmidt pulled a red pen from his pocket and held it up for all to see.

"Is this pen red, Sergeant?" he asked.

"Yes."

Schmidt made—or seemed to make—still more adjustments to his machine.

Nervously, Hans wondered how much Schmidt knew *he* knew about the polygraph test. Because Hans knew a good deal. The concept of the "lie detector" had always fascinated him. He had taken the Experimental Interrogation course at the police school at Hiltrup, and a close look at his personnel file would reveal that. As Schmidt tinkered with his machine, Hans marshaled what he remembered from the Hiltrup course. The first tenet of the polygrapher was that for test results to be accurate, the subject needed to believe the machine infallible. Polygraphers used various methods to create this illusion, but Hans knew that Schmidt favored the "card trick." Schmidt would ask his subject to pick a playing card at random from a deck, then to lay it facedown on a table. Schmidt's ability to name the hidden card after a few "yes or no" questions seemed to prove his polygraph infallible. Of course the subject always chose his card from a deck in which every card was identical, but he had no way of knowing that. Many skilled criminals had confessed their crimes immediately after Schmidt's little parlor show, certain that his machine would eventually find them out.

Hans saw no deck of cards tonight. *Maybe Schmidt thinks his reputation is enough to intimidate me,* he thought nervously. *And maybe he's right.* Already perspiring, Hans tried to think of a way to beat the little weasel's machine. Some people had beaten the polygraph by learning to suppress their physiological stress reactions, but Hans knew he had no hope of this. The suppression technique took months to master, and right now he could barely hold himself in his chair.

He did have one hope, if he could keep a cool head: picking out the "control" questions. Most people thought questions like "Is this pen red?" were the controls. But Hans knew better. The real control questions were ones which would cause almost anyone asked them to lie. "Have you ever failed to report income on your federal tax return?" was a common control. Most people denied this almost universal crime, and by doing so provided Schmidt with their baseline "lie." Later, when asked, "Did you cut your wife's throat with a kitchen knife?" a guilty person's lie would register far stronger than his baseline or "control" reference. Questions like "Is this pen red?" were asked simply to give a person's vital signs time to return to normal between the relevant questions.

Hans knew if he could produce a strong enough emotional response to a control question, then an actual lie would appear no different to the polygraph than his faked control responses. Schmidt would be forced to declare him "innocent." The best method to do this was to hide a thumbtack in your shoe, but Hans knew that an exaggerated response could also be triggered by holding your breath or biting your tongue. He decided to worry about method later. If he couldn't pick out the control questions, method wouldn't matter.

Schmidt's voice jolted him back to reality.

"Sergeant Apfel, prior to discharging your Spandau assignment, did you communicate with any person other than the duty sergeant regarding that assignment?"

"No," Hans replied. That was true. He hadn't had time to discuss it with anyone.

"Is Captain Hauer a married man?"

Irrelevant question, Hans thought bitterly. *To anyone except me.* "No," he answered.

Schmidt looked down at the notepad from which he chose his questions. "Have you ever stopped a friend or public official for a traffic violation and let them go without issuing a citation?"

Control question, Hans thought. Almost any cop who denied this would be lying. Keeping a straight face, he bit down on the tip of his tongue hard enough to draw blood. He felt a brief flush of perspiration pass through his skin. "No," he said.

When Schmidt glanced up from the polygraph, Hans knew he had produced an exaggerated response. "Am I holding up two fingers?" Schmidt asked.

Irrelevant, thought Hans. "Yes," he answered truthfully.

Schmidt came a step closer. "Sergeant Apfel, you've made several arrests for drug possession in the past year.

Have you ever failed to turn the entire quantity of confiscated drugs over to the evidence officer?"

Control ques—Hans started to bite his tongue again; then he hesitated. If this was a control question, Schmidt had upped the stakes of the game. Giving an exaggerated response here would not be without serious consequences. Police corruption involving drugs was an epidemic problem, with accordingly severe punishment for those caught. The men at the table gave no indication that they saw this question as anything but routine, but Hans thought he detected a feral gleam in Schmidt's eyes. The dirty little man knew his business.

"Sergeant?" Schmidt prodded.

Hans fidgeted. He did not want to appear guilty of a drug crime, but the Spandau questions still awaited. If he intended to keep the papers secret, he would have to give at least a partially exaggerated response to this question. In silent desperation he held his breath, counted to four, then answered, "No," and exhaled slowly.

"Is your wife's maiden name Natterman, Sergeant?"

Irrelevant. "Yes," Hans replied.

Schmidt wiped his upper lip. "Were you the last man to arrive at the scene of the argument over custody of the trespassers at Spandau Prison?"

Relevant question. Hans glanced up at the panel. All eyes were on him now. *Stay calm* ... "I don't remember," he said. "Things were so confused then. I really didn't notice."

"Yes or no, Sergeant!"

"I suppose I could have been."

Exasperated, Schmidt looked to Funk for guidance. The prefect fixed Hans with his imperious stare. "Sergeant," he said curtly, "one of your fellow officers told us you were the last man there. Would you care to answer the question again?"

"I'm sorry," Hans said sheepishly, "I just don't remember." He looked at the floor. The Russian soldier who had caught him in the rubble pile could call him a liar right now, he knew, but for some reason the man hadn't spoken up. Funk appeared satisfied with Hans's answer, and told Schmidt to move along. *There can't be many more questions,* Hans thought. *Just a little longer—*

"Sergeant Apfel?" Schmidt's voice cut like slivers of glass. "Did you remove any documents from a hollow brick in the area of the cellblocks last occupied by the Nuremberg war criminals?"

Holy Mother of God! Hans choked down a scream. Every eye in the room burned upon his face. For the first time Hauer's steely mask cracked. His probing eyes fixed Hans motionless in his chair, stripping away the pathetic layers of deception. But it was too late to come clean.

"No," Hans said lamely.

"Specifically," Schmidt bored in, "did you discover, re-move, see, or even hear of documents pertaining to or writ-ten by Prisoner Number Seven—Rudolf Hess?"

Hans felt cold sweat running down his spine. His heart be-came an enemy within his chest, thumping out the tattoo of his guilt. And there stood Schmidt, lie-hungry, watching each centimeter of paper unspool from his precious machine. Looking at him now, Hans fancied he saw a mad doctor reading an electrocardiograph, a diabolical quack watching each fateful squiggle in the hope of witnessing a fatal heart attack. Hans felt his willpower ebbing away. The truth welled up in his throat, beyond his control. *Just tell the truth,* urged a voice in his head, *tell it all and take whatever consequences come. Then this insanity will focus elsewhere.* Yet as Hans started to do just that, Schmidt said:

"Sergeant, have you ever omitted an important piece of information from a job application?"

Hans felt like a spacewalker cut loose from his tether. Schmidt had asked another control question! *Hadn't he?* But why hadn't he triumphantly proclaimed Hans's guilt to the tribunal? Hans had expected the little demon to dance a jig and scream: *Him! Him! There is the liar!*

"No—no, I haven't," Hans stammered.

"Thank you, Sergeant."

While Hans sat stunned, Schmidt turned to Funk and shook his head. The prefect closed the file before him, then turned to the Soviet colonels and shrugged. "Any ques-tions?" he asked.

The Russians looked like sleeping bears. When one finally shook his head to indicate the negative, the gesture seemed the result of a massive effort. Hans even sensed the soldiers in the back of the room relaxing. Only Captain Hauer and Lieutenant Luhr remained tense. For some reason it struck Hans just then that Jürgen Luhr was the kind of German who made Jews nervous. He was a racial *type*—the proto-

Germanic man, tall and broad-shouldered, thin-lipped and square-headed—a mythical Aryan fiend passed down in whispered tales from mother to daughter and father to son.

"Thank you for your cooperation, Sergeant," Funk said wearily. "We'll contact you if we need any further details." Then over Hans's shoulder, "Bring in the last officer."

Hans floundered. They had drawn him into the trap, yet failed to pounce for the kill. "Am I free to go?" he asked uncertainly.

"Unless you wish to stay with us all night," Funk snapped.

"Excuse me, Prefect," Lieutenant Luhr cut in. All eyes turned to him. "I'd like to ask the sergeant a question."

Funk nodded.

"Tell me, Sergeant, did you notice Officer Weiss acting in a suspicious manner at any time during the Spandau assignment?"

Hans shook his head, remembering Weiss being dragged down the hall. "No, sir. No, I didn't."

Luhr smiled with understanding, but he had the watchful eyes of a police dog. "Officer Weiss is a Jew, isn't he, Sergeant?"

One of the Russian colonels stirred, but his comrade laid a restraining hand on his shoulder.

"I believe that's right," Hans said tentatively. "Yes, he's Jewish."

Luhr gave a curt nod of the head, as if this new fact somehow explained everything.

"You may go, Sergeant," Funk said.

Hans stood. They were telling him to go, yet he sensed that some unspoken understanding had passed between the men in the room. It was as if several decisions had been taken at once in some language unknown to him. He turned toward the soldiers and police at the back of the room and shuffled toward the door. No one moved to stop him. Why hadn't Schmidt called him a liar? Why hadn't the Russian who'd caught him searching called him a liar? And why did he feel compelled to keep lying, anyway?

Because of the Russians, he realized. If the prefect—or even Hauer—had only questioned him alone, he could have told them. Just as Ilse wanted him to. He *would* have told them . . .

A burly policeman held open the door. Hans walked

through, hearing Funk's tired voice resume behind him. He quickened his pace. He wanted to get out of the building as soon as possible. He entered the stairwell at a near trot, but slowed when he saw two beefy patrolmen ascending from the first floor. Nodding a perfunctory greeting, he slipped between the two men—

Then they took him.

Hans had no chance at all. The men used no weapons because they needed none. His arms were immobilized as if by steel bands; then the men reversed direction and began dragging him down the stairs.

"What is this!" Hans shouted. "I'm a police officer! *Let me go!*"

One of the men chuckled quietly. They reached the bottom of the stairs and turned down a disused hallway, a repository of ancient files and broken furniture. When the initial shock and disorientation wore off, Hans realized that he had to fight back somehow. But *how?* In the darkest part of the corridor he suddenly let his body go limp, appearing to lose his will to resist.

"Scheisse!" one man cursed. "Dead weight."

"He soon will be," commented his partner.

Dead weight? With speed born of desperation Hans fired his elbow into a rib cage. He heard bone crack.

"Arrghh!" The man let go.

With his free hand Hans pummeled the other attacker's head, aiming for his temple. The policeman held him fast.

"You bastard . . ." from the darkness.

Hans kept pounding the man's skull. The grip on his arm was loosening—

An explosion that seemed to detonate behind his right eye paralyzed him.

Darkness.

Less than sixty feet away from Hans, Colonels Ivan Kosov and Grigori Zotin stood outside an idling East German transit bus in the central parking lot of the police station. Inside the bus, the Soviet soldiers from the Spandau patrol waited for their long-delayed return to East Berlin. Most were already fast asleep.

Zotin, a GRU colonel, did not particularly like Kosov, and he was deeply offended at the KGB colonel's effrontery in donning the uniform of the Red Army. But what could he do? One couldn't keep the KGB out of something this big, especially when higher powers wanted Kosov involved. Rubbing his hands together against the cold, Zotin tested the KGB man's perception.

"Can you believe it, Ivan? They gave them *all* clean reports."

"Of course," Kosov growled. "What did you expect?"

"But one of them was certainly lying!"

"Certainly."

"But how did they fake the polygraph readouts?"

Kosov looked bored. "We were six meters from the machine. They could have shown us anything."

Grigori Zotin knew exactly which policeman had lied, but he wanted to keep the information from Kosov long enough to initiate inquiries of his own. He was aware of the Kremlin's interest in the Hess case, and he knew his career could take a giant leap forward if he cracked it. He made a mental note to decorate the young GRU officer who had caught the German policeman searching and showed enough sense to tell only his immediate superior. "You're right, of course," Zotin agreed.

Kosov grunted.

"What, exactly, do you think was discovered? A journal perhaps? Do you think they found some proof of—"

"They found a hollow brick," Kosov snapped. "Our forensic technicians say their tests indicate the brick held some type of paper for an unknown period of time. It could have been some kind of journal. It could also have been pages from a pornographic magazine. It could have been toilet paper! Never trust experts too much, Zotin."

The GRU colonel sucked his teeth nervously. "Don't you think we should have at least *mentioned* Zinoviev during the interrogation? We could have—"

"*Idiot!*" Kosov bellowed. "That name isn't to be mentioned outside KGB! How do you even know it?"

Zotin stepped back defensively. "One hears things in Moscow."

"Things that could get you a bullet in the neck," Kosov warned.

Zotin tried to look unworried. "I suppose we should tell the general to turn up the pressure at the commandants' meeting tomorrow."

"Don't be ridiculous," scoffed Kosov. "Too little, too late."

"What about the trespassers, then? Why are you letting the Germans keep them?"

"Because they don't know anything."

"What do you suggest we do, then?" Zotin ventured warily.

Kosov snorted. "Are you serious? It was the second to last man—Apfel. He was lying through his Bosche teeth. Those idiots did exactly what we wanted. If they'd admitted Apfel was lying, he'd be in a jail cell now, beyond our reach. As it is, he's at our mercy. The fool is bound to return home, and when he does"—Kosov smiled coldly—"I'll have a team waiting for him."

Zotin was aghast. "But how—?" He stifled his imprudent outburst with a cough. "How can you get a team over soon enough?" he covered.

"I have *two* teams here *now*," Kosov snapped. "Get me to a damned telephone!"

Startled, the GRU colonel clambered aboard the bus and found a seat.

"And Zotin?" Kosov said, leaning over his rival.

"Yes?"

"Keep nothing from me again. It could be very dangerous for you."

Zotin blanched.

"I want everything there is on this man Apfel. *Everything.* I suggest you ride your staff very hard on this. Powerful eyes are watching us."

"How will you approach this policeman?"

"Approach him?" Kosov cracked a wolfish smile. "Break him, you mean. By morning I'll know how many times that poor bastard peeked up his mother's skirts."

Hans awoke in a cell. There was no window. He'd been thrown onto a stack of damp cardboard boxes. One pale ray of light filtered down from somewhere high above. When he had focused his eyes, he sat up and gripped one of the steel bars. His face felt sticky. He put his fingers to his temple. *Blood.* The familiar slickness brought back the earlier events in a throbbing rush of confusion. The interrogation . . . his father's stony silence . . . the struggle in the hallway. Where *was* he?

He tried to rise, but he collapsed into a narrow space between two boxes. Rotting cardboard covered almost the entire concrete floor. A cell full of boxes? Puzzled, Hans reached into one and pulled out a damp folder. He held it in the shaft of light. *Traffic accident report,* he thought. *Typed on the standard police form.* He found the date—1973. Flipping through the yellow sheaf of papers, he saw they were all the same, all traffic accident reports from 1973. He checked the station listed on several forms: Abschnitt 53 every case. Suddenly he realized where he was.

In the early 1970s, Abschnitt 53 had been partially renovated during a citywide wave of reform that lasted about eighteen months. There had been enough money to refurbish the reception area and overhaul the main cellblock, but the third floor, the basement, and the rear of the building went largely untouched. Hans was sure he'd been locked in the basement.

But *why?* No one had accused him of anything. Not openly, at least. Who were the policemen who had attacked him? Funk's men? Were they even police officers at all? They had said he would soon be *dead weight.* It was crazy. Maybe they were protecting him from the Russians. Maybe this was the only way the prefect could keep him safe from them. *That's it!* he thought with relief. *It has to be.*

A door slammed somewhere in the darkness above. Someone was coming—several people by the sound—and making no effort to hide it. Hans heard clattering and cursing on the stairs; then he saw who was making the noise. Outlined in the fluorescent light streaming down from the basement door, two husky uniformed men were wrestling a gurney off the stairs. Slowly they cleared a path to the cell through the heaps of junk covering the basement floor. Hans closed his eyes and lay motionless on the boxes where he'd been thrown.

"Looks like he's still out," said one man.

"I hope I killed the son of a bitch," growled the other.

"That wouldn't go over too well upstairs, Rolf."

"Who gives a shit? The bastard broke my ribs."

Hans heard a low chuckle. "Be more careful the next time. Come on, we've got to clear a space in there for this thing."

"Fuck it. Just throw this filthy Jew in on top of that one. Not much left of him, anyway."

"Apfel isn't a Jew."

"Jew-lover, then."

"The doctor said leave this one on the gurney."

"Make *him* clear a space," said Rolf, pointing in at Hans.

"Sure. If you can wake him up."

Rolf picked up a rusted joint of pipe from the floor and rankled the bars with it. "Wake up, asshole!"

Hans ignored him.

"Get up or we'll kill you."

Hans heard the metallic click of a pistol slide being jerked back. *Christ* . . . Slowly he rose to his feet.

"See," said Rolf, "he's not dead. Clear out a space in there, you. And be quick about it."

Hans tried to see who lay on the gurney, but Rolf smashed the pipe against the bars near his face. It took him forty seconds to clear a space wide enough to accept the gurney.

"Get back against the wall," Rolf ordered. "Go on!"

Hans watched the strange policemen roll the man on the gurney feet-first into the cleared space, then slam the door behind him.

"You stay away from this Jew-boy, Sergeant," Rolf warned. "Anything happens to him, it's on your head."

The pair hurried up the stairs, taking the shaft of light with them. Hans couldn't make out the face of his new cellmate. He felt in his pocket for a match, then remembered he'd given them to Kurt in the waiting room upstairs. He put his hands on the unconscious man's shoulders and stared downward, waiting for his eyes to adjust to the blackness, but they didn't. Moving his hand tentatively, he felt something familiar. *Shoulder patches.* Surprised and a little afraid, Hans felt his way across the man's chest like a blind man. *Brass buttons . . . patch . . . collar pins . . .* Hans felt his left hand brush an empty leather holster. *A police officer!* Shutting his eyes tight, he put his right hand on the man's face and waited. When he opened his eyes again, he could just make out the lines of the face.

My God, he thought, feeling a lump in his throat. *Weiss! Erhard Weiss!* For the second time tonight Hans felt cut loose from reality. Gripping his friend's body like a life raft, he began trying to revive him. He spoke into Weiss's ear, but heard no answer. He slapped the slack face hard several times. No response. Groping around in desperation, Hans crashed into the back wall of the cell. His palms touched something moist and cold. Foundation stones. *Condensation.* Rubbing his hands across the stones until they were sufficiently wet, he returned to Weiss and laved the cool liquid over his forehead. Still Weiss lay silent.

Alarmed, Hans pressed both forefingers against Weiss's carotid arteries. He felt pulse beats, but very faint and unbelievably far apart. Weiss was alive, but just. The jailers had mentioned a doctor, Hans remembered. What kind of doctor would send a man to a cell in this condition? The obscenity of the situation drove him into a rage as he stood by the cadaverous body of his friend. Someone would answer for this outrage! Lurching to the front of the cell, Hans began screaming at the top of his lungs. He screamed until he had no voice left, but no one came. Slipping to the floor in exhaustion, he realized that the stacks of boxes in the basement must be deadening the sound of his voice. He doubted anyone upstairs had heard even a whimper.

Suddenly Hans bolted to his feet in terror. Someone had screamed! It took him a moment to realize that the scream had come from inside the cell. He shivered as it came again, an animal shriek of agony and terror. Erhard Weiss—who had lain like a corpse through all Hans's attempts to revive him—now fought the straps that held him as if the gurney were on fire. As Hans tried to restrain the convulsing body, the screaming suddenly ceased. It was as if a great stone had been set upon Weiss's chest. The young policeman's right arm shot up and gripped Hans's shoulder like a claw, quivered desperately, then, after a long moment, relaxed.

Hans checked for a pulse. Nothing. He hadn't expected one. Erhard Weiss was dead. Hans had seen this death before—a heart attack, almost certainly. He had seen several similar cases during the last few years—young, apparently healthy men whose hearts had suddenly stopped, exploded, or fibrillated wildly and fatally out of control. In each case there had been a common factor—drugs. Cocaine usually, but other narcotics too. This case appeared no different. Except that Weiss never used drugs. He was a fitness enthusiast, a swimmer. On several occasions he and his fiancée had dined with Hans and Ilse at a restaurant, Hans remembered, and once in their apartment. In their *home*. And now Weiss was dead. *Dead.* The young man who had argued so tenaciously to keep two fellow Berliners—strangers, at that—out of the clutches of the Russians.

In one anguished second Hans's exhaustion left him. He sprang to the front of the cell and stuck his arm through the bars, frantically searching the floor with his right hand. *There*—the iron pipe Rolf had brandished! Steadily Hans began pounding the pipe against the steel bars. The shock of the blows rattled his entire body, but he ignored the pain. He would hammer the bars until they came for Weiss—until they came for his friend or he dropped dead. At that moment he did not care.

CHAPTER SIX

Seated at the kitchen table in apartment 40, Professor Emeritus of History Georg Natterman hunched over the Spandau papers like a gnome over a treasure map. His thick reading glasses shone like silver pools in the lamplight as he ran his hand through his thinning hair and silver beard.

"What is it, *Opa?*" Ilse asked. "Is it dangerous?"

"Patience, child," the professor mumbled without looking up.

Knowing that further questions were useless until her grandfather was ready to speak, she opened a cupboard and began preparing tea. Perhaps Hans would get back in time to have some, she hoped; he'd been gone too long already. Ilse had told her grandfather as little as possible on the telephone, and by doing so she had failed to communicate the depth of her anxiety. Professor Natterman lived only twelve blocks away, but it had taken him over an hour to arrive. He understood the gravity of the situation now. He hadn't spoken a word since first seeing the Spandau papers and brusquely questioning Ilse as to how they came into her possession. As she poured the tea, he stood suddenly, pulled off his reading glasses, and locked the nine pages into his ancient briefcase.

"My dear," he said, "this is simply unbelievable. That this . . . this *document* should have come into my hands after all these years. It's a miracle." He wiped his spectacles with a handkerchief. "You were quite right to call me. 'Dangerous' does not even begin to describe this find."

"But what is it, *Opa?* What is it really?"

Natterman shook his head. "In terms of World War Two history, it's the Rosetta stone."

Ilse's eyes widened. "What? Are you saying that the papers are real?"

"Given what I've seen so far, I would have to say yes."

Ilse looked incredulous. "What did you mean, the papers are like the Rosetta stone?"

"I mean," Natterman sniffed, "that they are likely to change profoundly the way we view the world." He squinted his eyes, and a road map of lines crinkled his forehead. "How much do you know about Rudolf Hess, Ilse?"

She shrugged. "I've read the recent newspaper stories. I looked him up in your book, but you hardly even mentioned his flight."

The professor glanced over to the countertop, where a copy of his acclaimed *Germany: From Bismarck to the Bunker* lay open. "I didn't feel the facts were complete," he explained, "so I omitted that part of the story altogether."

"Was I right about the papers? Do they claim that Prisoner Number Seven was not really Hess?"

"Oh, yes, yes indeed. Very little doubt about that now. It looks as though the newspapers have got it right for once. The wrong man in prison for nearly fifty years . . . very embarrassing for a lot of people."

Ilse watched her grandfather for any hint of a smile, but she saw none. "You're joking with me, aren't you? How could that even be possible?"

"Oh, it's quite possible. The use of look-alikes was standard procedure during the war, on both sides. Patton had one. Erwin Rommel also. Field Marshal Montgomery used an actor who could even imitate his voice to perfection. That's the easiest part of this story to accept."

Ilse looked skeptical. "Maybe during the war," she conceded. "From a distance. But what about the years in Spandau? What about Hess's family?"

Natterman smiled impishly. "What about them? Prisoner Number Seven refused to see Hess's wife and son for the first *twenty-eight years* of his captivity." He savored Ilse's perplexed expression. "The factual discrepancies go on and on. Hess was a fastidious vegetarian, Prisoner Number Seven devoured meat like a tiger. Number Seven failed to recognize Hess's secretaries at Nuremberg. He twice gave the British wrong birth dates for Hess, and he missed by two *years.* And on and on ad nauseam."

Ilse sat quietly, trying to take it all in. Beneath her thoughts, her anxiety for Hans buzzed like a low-grade fever.

"Why don't I let Number Seven speak for himself?" Natterman suggested. "Would you like to hear my translation?"

Ilse forced herself not to look at the kitchen clock. *He's all right,* she told herself. *Just wait a little longer.* "Yes, please," she said.

Putting his reading glasses back on, the professor opened his briefcase, cleared his throat, and began to read in the resonant tones of the born teacher:

I, Prisoner Number Seven, write this testament in the language of the Caesars for one reason: I know with certainty that Rudolf Hess could not do so. I learned Latin and Greek at university in Munich from 1920 to 1923, but I learned that Hess did not know Latin at the most exclusive "school" in the world—Reinhard Heydrich's Institute for Practical Deception—in 1936. At this "institute"—an isolated barracks compound outside Dessau—I also learned every other known fact about Hess: his childhood; military service; Party record; relationship with the Führer; and, most importantly, his personal idiosyncrasies. Ironically, one of the first facts I learned was that Hess had attended university in Munich at the same time I had, though I do not remember meeting him.

I did not serve as a pilot in the First World War, but I joined one of Hermann Göring's "flying clubs" between the wars. It was during an aerial demonstration in 1935 that the Reichsmarschall first noticed my remarkable resemblance to Deputy-Führer Hess. At the time I did not make much of the encounter—comrades had often remarked on this resemblance—but seven months later I was visited at the factory where I worked by two officers of Heydrich's SD. They requested me to accompany them on a mission of special importance to the Reich. From Munich I was flown to the "Practical School" building outside Dessau. I never saw my wife and daughter again.

During the first week at the school I was completely isolated from my fellow students. I received my "orientation" from Standartenführer Ritter Graf, headmaster of the Institute. He informed me that I had been selected to fulfill a mission of the highest importance to the Führer. My period of training—which would be lengthy and arduous, he said—was to be carried out in total secrecy. I soon learned that this meant total separation from my family. To alleviate the stress of this separation, Graf showed me proof that my salary from the factory had been doubled, and that the money was being forwarded to my wife.

After one week I met the other students. I cannot express the shock I felt. In one room in one night I saw the faces of not only famous Party Gauleiters and Wehrmacht generals, but also the most celebrated personalities of the Reich. At last I knew what my mission was. Hermann Göring had not forgotten my resemblance to Rudolf Hess; it was Göring who had given my name to Reinhard Heydrich, the SD commander responsible for the program.

There were many students at the Institute. Some completed the program, others did not. The unlucky ones paid for their failure in blood. We were constantly reminded of this "incentive." One of the most common causes for "dismissal" from the school was the use of one's real name. Two slip-ups were forgiven. The third guaranteed erschiessen (execution). We were known by our "role" names, or, in situations where these were not practical, by our former ranks—in my case Hauptmann.

I trained in an elite group. There were eight of us: "Hitler" (3 "students" studied him); "Göring"; "Himmler"; "Goebbels"; "Streicher"; and myself—"Hess." The training for our group lasted one year. During that year I had four personal interviews with Deputy-Führer Hess. The rest of my training was accomplished through study of newsreels and written records. During our training, several of the "doubles" for the Party Gauleiters left the school to begin their duties. Apparently their roles did not require so much preparation as ours.

At the end of the training period my group was broken up and sent to various locations to await duty. I was sent first to Gronau, where I was kept in isolation, then later to a remote airfield at Aalborg, Denmark. I repeatedly requested to be allowed to see my wife and daughter, but by this time Germany was at war and my requests were summarily rejected. I spent my time in solitude, reviewing my Hess mate-

*rials and occasionally being visited by an SD officer. I did
have access to newspapers, and from them I deduced that
Hess's position in the Nazi hierarchy seemed to have declined somewhat in favor of the generals since the outbreak
of war. I took this to be the reason I had not yet been assigned a mission.*

*I must admit that, in spite of the hardship of the duty, I
was very proud of the degree to which I could impersonate
the Deputy Führer. During my final interview with Hess at
the school, he was so shocked by my proficiency that his reaction verged on disorientation. Actually, a few of the other
"students" had honed their skills to a finer edge than my
own, but what happened to them I have no idea . . .*

Natterman removed his spectacles, put the papers back
into his briefcase, then closed and locked it. "A rather detailed story to be made up out of thin air, wouldn't you say?
And that's only the first two pages."

Ilse was smiling with satisfaction. "Very detailed," she
agreed. "So detailed that it destroys your earlier argument. If
this 'double' was so meticulously trained to imitate Hess, he
certainly wouldn't make factual mistakes as obvious as
missing Hess's birthday, or eating meat when Hess was a
vegetarian. Would he?"

Natterman met his granddaughter's triumphant smile with
one of his own. "Actually, I've been thinking about that
since I first translated the papers. You're quite right: a
trained double *wouldn't* make factual mistakes like that—not
unless he did so *on purpose.*"

Ilse's eyes narrowed. "What do you mean?"

"Just this. Since the double remained silent for all these
years, he could only have done so for one of two reasons: either he was a fanatical Nazi right up until the end, which I
don't accept, *or*—and this is supported by the papers—the
fear of some terrible retribution kept him from speaking out.
If we accept that scenario, Number Seven's 'mistakes' appear to me to be a cry for help—a quiet but desperate attempt to provoke skeptics to investigate his case and thus
uncover the truth. And believe me, that cry was heard. Hundreds of scholars and authors have investigated the case.
Dozens of books have been written, more every year."
Natterman held up an admonishing finger. "The more rele-

vant question is this: Why would the *real* Hess make such mistakes?"

"Because he was crazy!" Ilse retorted. "Everyone's known that for years."

"Everyone has *said* that for years," Natterman corrected. "Hitler and Churchill started that rumor, yet there's not one scrap of evidence suggesting that Hess was unbalanced right up until the day he flew to Britain. He trained *months* for that mission. Can you seriously believe Hitler didn't know that? Hess was eccentric, yes. But mad? It was the men he left *behind* who were mad!"

"Hess could have written those papers himself," she argued. "If Hess didn't know Latin when he went into Spandau, he certainly could have learned it during his years of imprisonment."

"True," Natterman admitted. "But unlikely. Did you note the quote from Ovid? High-flying language for a self-taught student. But that's verifiable, in any case."

Ilse tasted her tea. It had gone cold. "*Opa,* you can't really believe that the Allies kept the wrong man in prison all these years."

"Why not? Ilse, you should understand something. These papers do not exist in a vacuum. They merely confirm a body of evidence which has been accumulating for decades. Circumstantial evidence, testimonial evidence, medical evidence—"

"What medical evidence?"

The professor smiled; he loved nothing more than a willing student. "Evidence unearthed by a British army surgeon who examined Number Seven while he was in Spandau. He's the man who really cracked this case open. My God, he'll be ecstatic when he finds out about these papers."

"What evidence did he discover?"

"A war wound. Or a *lack* of one, I should say. This surgeon was one of Hess's doctors in Spandau, and in the course of his duties he came across Hess's First World War record. Hess was wounded three times in that war—the worst wound being a rifle bullet through the lung. Yet when the surgeon examined Number Seven, he found no scars on the chest or back where that wound should have been. And after looking into the matter further—examining the prisoner's X rays—he found no radiographic evidence of such a wound. There should have been scarring of the lung, caused by the force of the bullet and other organic particles tearing through it. But the surgeon found none. He had quite a bit of experience with gunshot wounds, too. He'd done a tour of duty in Northern Ireland."

Natterman chuckled at Ilse's bewildered expression. "You're surprised by my knowledge? You shouldn't be. Any German or British historian could tell you as much." He laughed. "I could give you twice as much speculation on who started the Reichstag fire!"

"But the details," she said suspiciously. "Dates, medical evidence ... It's almost as if you were studying the case when I called you."

The professor's face grew grave. "My dear, you have obviously failed to grasp the monumental importance of this find. These papers could *shake the world*. The time period they describe—the forty-four days beginning with Rudolf Hess's flight to Britain and ending with Hitler's invasion of Russia—represents the turning point of the entire Second World War, of the entire *twentieth century*. In the spring of 1941, Adolf Hitler held the future of the world *in his hands*. Of all Europe, only England still held out against him. The Americans were still a year from entering the war. German U-boats ruled the seas. If Hitler had pressed home the attack against England with all his forces, the British wouldn't have stood a chance. The Americans would have been denied their staging post for a European invasion, and Hitler could have turned his full might against Russia with his flanks protected." Natterman held up a long, crooked finger. "But he *didn't* invade England. And *no one knows why*."

The professor began pacing the kitchen, punctuating his questions by stabbing the air with his right forefinger. "In 1940 Hitler let the British Army escape at Dunkirk. *Why?* All through the fall of 1940 and the spring of '41 he delayed invading Britain. *Why?* Operation Sea-Lion—the planned invasion of Britain—was a joke. Hitler's best generals have admitted this. Churchill publicly taunted Hitler, yet still he delayed. *Why?* And then the core of the whole mad puzzle: On May tenth, Rudolf Hess flew to Britain on a secret mission. Scarcely a month later"—Natterman clapped his hands together with a crack—"Hitler threw his armies into the icy depths of Russia to be slaughtered. Ilse, that single decision *doomed* Nazi Germany. It gave Churchill the time he needed to rearm England and to draw Roosevelt into the war. It was military suicide, and *Hitler knew it!* For twenty years he had sworn he would never fight a two-front war. He had publicly proclaimed such a war unwinnable. *So why did he do it?*"

Ilse blinked. "Do you know?"

Natterman nodded sagely. "I think I do. There are dozens of complex theories, but I think the answer is painfully simple: Hitler had no choice. I don't believe he ever intended to invade England. Russia was his target all along; his own writings confirm this. Hitler hated Churchill, but he had tremendous respect for the English as a people—fellow Nordics and all that. I think Hitler put off invading Britain because he believed—right up until it was too late—that England could be neutralized *without firing a shot.* I think certain elements of the British government were prepared to sign a peace treaty with Hitler, so that he would be free to destroy Communist Russia. *And* I believe Rudolf Hess was Hitler's secret envoy to those Englishmen. The moment Hess's presence in England was made public, Joseph Stalin accused the British of conspiring with Hitler. I think Stalin was right."

The professor's eyes blazed with fanatical conviction. "But neither Stalin, nor all his spies, nor a thousand scholars, nor I have ever been able to prove that! For nearly fifty years the truth has lain buried in the secret vaults of the British government. By law the relevant Hess files are to remain sealed until the year 2016. Some will *never* be opened. What are the British hiding? Whom are they protecting? A secret cabal of highly placed British Nazis? Were there powerful Englishmen—even members of the royal family—who were so afraid of communism that they were ready to climb into Hitler's bed for protection, no matter how many Jews he slaughtered?" Natterman punched a fist into his palm. "By God, if these Spandau papers end up proving *that,* the walls of Parliament will be hard put to withstand the firestorm that follows!"

Ilse stared at her grandfather with astonishment. His passion had infected her, but it could not blot out the worry she felt for Hans. Yet somehow she couldn't bring herself to confess her fears to the old man. At least debating the fine points of conspiracy theories helped to pass the time quickly.

"But if the prisoner *was* a double," she said, "how could he fool his Allied captors? Even an actor couldn't hold out under interrogation."

Natterman snorted scornfully. "The British claim they never professionally interrogated him. And why should they? They knew Hess was a double from the beginning. They held him incommunicado in England for the first four years of his captivity, and they've been playing this ridiculous game ever since to cover up the real Hess's mission. The American government supports Britain's policy right down the line. And the French have never made a fuss about it. They have their own skeletons to hide."

"But the Russians," Ilse reminded him. "You said Stalin suspected a plot from the beginning."

"Perhaps the double *didn't* fool them," Natterman suggested.

"Then why wouldn't they expose him!"

Natterman frowned. "I don't know. That's the conundrum, isn't it? It's the key to this whole mystery. There are reasons that the Russians wouldn't have talked in the early years. One is that certain alleged Anglo-Nazi intrigues—between Hess and the Duke of Windsor, for example—took place on Spanish and Portuguese soil. If such meetings did actually occur, Moscow would have known all about them"—Natterman grinned with glee—"because the MI-6 officer responsible for the Spanish desk at that time was none other than *Kim Philby.* What irony! The Russians couldn't reveal the Windsor-Hess connection without exposing the Philby-KGB connection! Of course that only explains the Russian silence up until 1963, the year Philby fled England. The real mystery is what kept the Russians quiet during the remaining years."

Ilse was shaking her head. "You make it sound so plausible, but it's like a huge house of cards.... It's just too complex."

"I'll give you something simple, then. Why did the British never use 'Hess' for propaganda during the war? They locked him away from the world and refused even to allow him to be photographed. Think about that. England and Germany were locked in a death struggle. Even if 'Hess' had refused to cooperate, the British could easily have released statements criticizing Hitler that were supposedly made by Hess. Think of the boost that would have given English morale. And the negative effect on the German people! Yet the British *never* tried it. The only possible reason I can see for that is that the British knew they didn't have the real Hess.

They knew if they tried to use 'Hess' against the Nazis, Joseph Goebbels could jump up and say, *'Fools! You've got a bloody corporal in your jail!'* or something similar."

"If that's true, why wouldn't the Nazis have said that from the beginning?"

Natterman smiled enigmatically. "Hitler's reasons I cannot divine. But as for the other top Nazis—Göring, Himmler—they were only too glad to be rid of Hess. He was their chief rival for Hitler's favors. If the Führer, for his own reasons, was content to let the world believe that his lifelong friend and confidant had gone insane, and was a prisoner of the British, Hess's chief rivals would have been only too glad to go along." Natterman rubbed his hands together. "Yes, it all ties up rather neatly."

"So says the great professor," Ilse said dryly. "But you've missed one thing. Even if the Allies had reasons to keep quiet, why in God's name would the *double*—even if he had *agreed* to such a mission—keep silent for nearly fifty years? What could anyone threaten him with? Solitary confinement in Spandau Prison must have been a living death."

Natterman shook his head. "You're a clever girl, Ilse, but in some ways frighteningly naive. Soldiers aren't asked to *agree* to missions; they're ordered. In Hitler's Reich refusal meant instant death. You saw the word *Sippenhaft* in the papers?"

She nodded. "What does it mean? 'Clan punishment'?"

"That's close enough. *Sippenhaft* was a barbaric custom that Himmler borrowed from the ancient Teutonic tribes. It mandated that punishment be visited not only upon a traitor, but upon his 'clan.' After Graf von Stauffenberg's abortive attempt on Hitler's life, not only the count but his *entire family* was executed. Six of the victims were over seventy years old! That is *Sippenhaft,* Ilse, and a more effective tool for ensuring the silence of living men has yet to be devised."

"But after five decades . . . who would be left to carry out such a sentence?"

Natterman rolled his eyes. "How about one of those bald neo-Nazi psychopaths who roam our streets at night with brickbats? No? Then how about these 'soldiers of Phoenix' that Number Seven mentions? He certainly seems terrified of them. And don't forget this: at the end of the war, close to forty divisions of *Waffen* SS remained under arms throughout the world. That's more than a quarter of a million men! I don't know how many Death's-Head SS survived, but what if it were only a few hundred? Just one of those fanatics could wipe out a man's family, even today. I fought in the war, and I could easily shoot someone down in the street tonight." Natterman glanced at his watch. "And *that* is my final word on the subject," he announced. "I must go."

"Go?" Ilse said uneasily. "Where are you going?"

Natterman picked up his briefcase. "To do what must be done. To show the arrogant, self-righteous British for what they were during the war—no better than we Germans." His eyes sparkled with youthful excitement. "Ilse, this could be the academic coup of the century!"

"*Opa,* what are you saying? Those papers are affecting you just like they did Hans!"

Natterman looked sharply at his granddaughter. "Where *is* Hans, by the way?"

"At the police station ... I guess." Ilse tried to summon a brave face, but her mask cracked. Hans had been gone far too long. "*Opa,* what if they know what Hans did ... what he found? What would they do?"

"I don't know," he answered frankly. "Why don't you call the station? If Hans's superiors don't know about the papers, it can't hurt. And if they do, well ... they'll be expecting your call anyway, won't they?"

Ilse moved uncertainly toward the phone in the living room, then snatched it up.

"Listen very closely," Natterman cautioned. "Background voices, everything."

"Yes, yes ... Hello? May I speak to Sergeant Hans Apfel, please? This is his wife. Oh. Do you know where he is now?" She covered the mouthpiece with her palm. "The desk sergeant says he knows Hans but hasn't seen him tonight. He's checking." She pulled her hand away. "I beg your pardon? Is this the same man I spoke to earlier? Yes, I'll be home all evening." Natterman shook his head violently. "I'm sorry," Ilse said quickly, "I have to go." She dropped the phone into its cradle.

"What did he tell you?" Natterman asked.

"Hans stopped in to answer a few questions, but left soon after. The sergeant said he wasn't there longer than twenty minutes. *Opa?*"

Natterman touched his granddaughter's quivering cheek.

"Ilse, is there some place in particular Hans goes when he is under stress?"

Ilse held out for a moment more, then the words poured out of her. "He talked about showing the papers to a journalist! About trying to sell them!"

"My God," said Natterman, his face white. "He wouldn't!"

"He said he wouldn't. But—"

"Ilse, he *can't* do that! It's crazy! And far too dangerous!"

"I know that . . . but he's been gone so long. Maybe that's where he is, meeting a reporter somewhere."

Natterman shook his head. "God forgive me, I hope that's it. He'll probably turn up any minute. But I'm afraid I can't wait." He held up his hand. "Please, Ilse, no more questions. I'm going to the university to get some things, then I'm leaving the city."

"Leaving the city! Why?"

Natterman donned his long overcoat, then picked up his briefcase and took his umbrella from the stand by the front door. "Because anyone could find me in Berlin, and eventually they would. People are searching for these papers *now*—I can feel it." He laid a hand on Ilse's shoulder. "We have stumbled into a storm, my child. I'm trying to do what is best. It's nine o'clock now. You wait here until midnight. If Hans hasn't returned by then, I want you to leave. I'll be at the old cabin."

"On the canal? But that's two hundred kilometers from here!"

"I just hope it's far enough. I'm serious, Ilse, if Hans hasn't arrived by midnight, leave. The cabin telephone's still connected. I always pay the bill. You have the number?"

She nodded. "But what about *Hans*?" she asked, her voice trembling.

The professor set down his briefcase and hugged his granddaughter. "Hans is a grown man," he said gently. "A policeman. He knows how to take care of himself. He'll find us when he's ready. Now I must go. You do exactly as I said." He patted his briefcase. "This little discovery is going to make a lot of people very nervous."

Too dazed to argue, Ilse kissed him on the cheek. "*You* be careful," she said. "You're not a young bull anymore, you know."

"No," said Natterman softly, his eyes glittering. "I'm a

wise old serpent." He grinned. "You haven't forgotten your patronymic, have you? 'Natter' still means snake. Don't worry about me."

With that the professor kissed Ilse's forehead and slipped outside the door. He looked disdainfully at the old elevator; then he stepped into the stairwell and, despite his excitement, started down with an old man's careful tread. He did not hear the stairwell door open again behind him, or the whisper of Jonas Stern's stockinged feet descending the concrete steps.

Stern knew the game now. It was a simple one. *Follow the papers.* Strange how the peaceful present could be shattered by a few strokes from an old pen, he reflected. Cryptic telegrams from an unquiet past. For in the Israeli's pocket nestled another scrap of paper—the seed of the premonition that had brought him to Germany after so many years. One hour before he'd driven out of the Negev desert headed for Ben-Gurion Airport, Stern had dug it out of the little chest he'd saved from Jerusalem—his unfinished-business chest, an old cherry box containing the musty collection of loose ends that would not leave a man in peace. On this scrap of paper was a brief note written in Cyrillic script, unsigned. A Russian Jew had translated it for Stern on the day it arrived in his office, June 3, 1967.

People of Zion Beware! The Unholy Fire of Armageddon may soon be unleashed upon you! I speak not from hatred or from love, but from conscience. Fear of death stays my hand from revealing the secret of your peril, but the key awaits you in Spandau. God is the final judge of all peoples!

Stern's colleagues had not been impressed. In Israel, such warnings were common as dust. Each was routinely investigated, but rarely did any prophesy real danger. But Stern had had a feeling about that particular note. It was vague, yes. Was the author referring to Spandau Prison in West Berlin? Or the *district* of Spandau, which covered over five square miles of the city? Stern never found out. Two days after the "Spandau note" arrived, the '67 war erupted. Shells were falling on Jerusalem, and the note was brushed aside like junk mail. Israel was in peril, but from Egyptian tanks and planes, not the "Unholy Fire of Armageddon," whatever that meant.

Later, when the smoke had cleared and the dead were buried, Stern's superiors decided the note had merely been a warning of Egypt's imminent war plans. After all, the note was in Russian, and it was the Russians who had been supplying Egypt with weapons. "A communist with a religious conscience," they'd said, "a common enough breed." But Stern had never accepted that. Why would the note have mentioned Spandau, of all things? And so he'd kept the note.

At the foot of the stairs, he slipped his shoes back on and glided out into the frigid darkness. Forty meters up the Lützenstrasse stood Professor Natterman, clinging to his briefcase like a diamond courier. He flagged down a speeding yellow taxi and climbed inside. Stern smiled and climbed into his rental car.

Four floors above the street, Ilse sat cross-legged on the floor behind her triple-bolted door, fixed her eyes on the wall clock, and waited with both hands on the telephone.

9:40 P.M. Polizei Abschnitt 53

The clang of the pipe apparently carried much farther than a human voice. Hans had been smashing it against the bars for less than a minute when the basement door crashed open and a powerful flashlight beam sliced down through the darkness.

"Stop that goddamn banging!" shouted a guttural voice.

Rolf again, Hans thought. The profanity was a dead giveaway. The same bearded man trailed behind him, but this time the pair stayed well back from the cell and aimed the flashlight in.

"Well?" said Rolf from behind the glare. "What the hell do you want? The facilities not up to your high standards?"

Hans flexed his fists in rage. If he could only lure one of them into the cell ... "This man's dead," he said, pointing to the gurney.

Neither guard responded.

"Come in here and check his pulse, if you don't believe me."

"If he's dead, what can we do?" said Rolf, chuckling at his logic.

"Get him out of here!" Hans cried.

"Sorry," said the other guard, with a trace of sympathy. "We can't come in. Orders."

In desperation Hans shoved the gurney to the front of the cell and thrust his friend's lifeless arm through the bars. "Feel it, damn you!"

"Take it easy," said the second man. "I'll do it." He pinched Weiss's wrist expertly between his thumb and middle finger and counted to thirty. "The man's dead, all right."

Rolf checked Weiss's pulse himself. "So he is. Well, you just stay right here with him, Sergeant. We'll send somebody down for him. Eventually."

Hans turned to the wall in despair. Obviously these two thugs weren't going to be lured into the cell. When he finally turned back around, they had gone. He picked his way to the rear of the cell and sat down on a box of files. *I can wait,* he told himself. *Someone's got to come in here eventually, and when they do . . .*

Fifteen minutes later the basement door crashed open again. This time Hans heard no cursing or stumbling from the stairs. The tread of boots was loud and regular. Whoever was coming knew his way around down here.

"This way, idiot," muttered a disembodied voice.

Nothing could have prepared Hans for the next few seconds. When the boots stopped in front of his cell, the flashlight beam arced in and blinded him completely. He squinted in pain. Then, out of the blackness behind the dazzling light came a voice that froze his heart.

"Hans? Are you okay?"

Oh God . . . Slowly his contracting pupils filtered out the glare. He saw the hand gripping the flashlight through the bars. Then, just above it, Captain Dieter Hauer's mustached face coalesced in the darkness. The leering grin of Rolf floated above and behind him.

Hans felt a caustic wave of bile rising into his throat. Whatever was going on, Hauer was *part* of it! His mind reeled, fighting the realization that his own father had helped murder his friend. He felt a knifelike pain in his chest, as if his very heart had cracked. *Come in here, you bastard!* he thought savagely. *Just come right in . . .*

Apparently, Hauer intended to do just that. He turned to Rolf. "Give me the key," he said.

"But we're not supposed to go in," Rolf objected. "Lieutenant Luhr said—"

Hauer snatched the key from Rolf's hand and opened the cell door. "Hans, listen," he said softly, "I need to ask—"

"Aaaaaarrgh!" With every ounce of strength in his body, Hans drove himself off the back wall and into Hauer's midsection. The flying tackle crushed Hauer against the steel bars, driving the breath from his lungs. He collapsed in a heap on the floor, sucking for air. Hans grabbed his neck and began throttling him in blind hatred. Here was the man to pay for Weiss's life, and so much more . . .

It was a simple matter for Rolf to pick up the lead pipe and knock Hans unconscious. Having done so, he viciously kicked the limp body off of Hauer and revived the captain by taking hold of his belt and lifting him repeatedly off the floor. Slowly Hauer sat up and looked at Hans lying motionless on the cell floor.

"Thanks," he coughed.

"You owe me for that," said Rolf. "That prick meant to kill you!"

"I don't blame him," Hauer muttered.

"What?" Rolf's eyes narrowed. "What were you trying to say to him, anyway?"

Hans moaned and rolled over. His head banged against the bars.

"Shit," Rolf grumbled, "why don't we just kill this *Klugscheisser*?"

"We need him. Help me get him up on one of these boxes."

Focusing his eyes slowly, Hans sat up. He'd vomited a little on his shirt front. "Fa . . ." he moaned. "Father? You can't be part of this—"

"What did he say?" Rolf asked.

"He's delirious."

"Weiss is dead!" Hans screamed suddenly.

"So are you," Rolf spat. "You pathetic fuck."

The next four seconds were a blur of motion. Hauer's lips flattened to a thin line. Quicker than thought he whirled on Rolf and shattered his jaw with a killing blow from his right fist. Almost simultaneously he snatched the pipe away with his left hand and brought it down on Rolf's skull, fracturing his cranium with a sickening crunch. Rolf died before he hit the floor.

Hans had been stunned by the blow to his head, but even more by this sudden reversal. But there was no time to think. Hauer knelt over him. "Don't ask me anything!" he snarled. "Don't *say* anything! I don't know how you got involved in this, but you're in way over your empty head. I don't know if Weiss was in it, but he paid the price tonight. You're hiding *something*—I saw that at Funk's little hearing, and so did anyone else who was paying attention. You can't lie for shit, Hans, you're too honest for it."

"Wait—I don't understand," Hans stammered. *"Why?"*

"Quiet! We're about to take the most dangerous walk of our lives. If someone finds this shitbag before we get out of the station, we're dead. Can you move?"

Hans tried to rise, but his legs buckled.

"Get up!"

"I can't. It's my head . . . my balance."

"Christ!" With a sudden violence Hauer shoved Weiss's corpse off the gurney and onto the floor.

"Captain!"

"Listen, Hans, he's gone! We're alive. You just be ready when I get back."

With startling speed Hauer battled the gurney through the dark basement, then collapsed its legs and dragged it up the stairs. In two minutes he was back in the cell, leaning over Hans.

"I'm going to carry you up to that gurney and wheel you out the back door. Can you hang on?"

Hans nodded dully.

"I want you to see something before we go."

Hauer picked up the flashlight and held it to the right side of Rolf's smashed skull. He dug in the blond hair until he found what he wanted, then lifted the head slightly and leaned back to make room for Hans. "First this," he said. "Look."

Hans looked. At first he saw nothing. Only the bloody roots of Rolf's flaxen hair. Then Hauer's thick fingers scratched against the dead man's scalp, scraping some of the blood away. Hans saw it now, behind the right ear. It was a tattoo. Bloodred ink had been injected into Rolf's scalp by a very talented needle. The design itself was less than two centimeters long, but very detailed. It was an eye. A single, gracefully curved red eye. With a lid but no lashes. Hans felt his stomach turn a slow somersault. The eye was identical to the one sketched on the opening page of the Spandau papers! *You must follow the Eye . . . The Eye is the key to it all!*

"See it?" Hauer grunted.

Hans nodded dumbly.

Rolf's head thudded against the cement floor. Hauer stepped across the cell and dragged Weiss's corpse over to where Hans sat against the wall. "You won't forget this for a while," he said. He put his hands into Weiss's shirt and ripped it open down the front. Then he pulled up the undershirt.

"What are you *doing*?" Hans asked, offended by this further indignity visited upon the dead.

Hauer picked up the flashlight and shone it onto Weiss's almost hairless chest. Hans leaned over, straining his eyes, then he froze. Weiss's chest was awash in blood.

"Take a deep breath," Hauer advised. He wiped away most of the blood with Weiss's undershirt. "Now," he said. "See it?"

Hans felt dizzy with horror. Gouged deep into Erhard Weiss's flesh by some unspeakable instrument was a large, six-pointed star. The Star of David. The edges of the linear wounds looked so ragged that whoever had inflicted them must have done it with a screwdriver, or a long nail. Hans felt vomit coming up like a geyser. He gagged and turned away.

"No!" Hauer snapped, grabbing his shoulder. "Get up!"

Choking down bile, Hans tried to stand. With a stifled groan, Hauer caught hold of him, slung him over his shoulder like a sack, and plodded out of the cell. Twice Hauer stumbled as they crossed the cluttered basement floor, but both times he regained his balance. The stairs took longer. Each successive step required increasing amounts of time and energy from Hauer's sleep-deprived body.

"Stop!" Hans begged, fearing they would both fall. "Put me down. I can make it."

Just as he felt Hauer's broad back sag under the strain, he saw a crack of light in the darkness. The basement door. They had made it. Grunting, Hauer kicked open the door and heaved Hans onto the gurney. "Don't even breathe," he said, wheezing like a draft horse. "If anyone stops us, I take him out. You *stay on this cart!* As far as anyone knows, you killed Rolf, then I killed you. Period."

Hauer shoved the gurney into motion and veered right, rolling his human contraband toward the rear entrance Hans had used when he arrived. Hans opened one eye to orient himself, but Hauer promptly struck him on the head. Rounding the last corner, Hauer saw the pinch-faced young policeman who had questioned Hans earlier. The guard rose from his desk before Hauer reached him.

"Where are you taking this man?" he challenged. "No one leaves the building without written orders from the prefect."

"This man's dead," Hauer said, slowing to a stop. "He was alive when he walked in here. The prefect doesn't write orders that tie him to embarrassing corpses. Now, let me pass."

For a moment the officer looked uncertain. Then he cocked his chin up and resumed his arrogant tone. "There's no one back here but us. It won't hurt to ring Lieutenant Luhr upstairs."

He lifted the phone from its cradle, then leaned over Hans's face and stared. Hans lay completely still, but it would not have saved them. Hauer could see what was coming. The policeman's left hand was moving up to Hans's wrist, searching for a pulse . . .

Hauer brought his right fist down like a hammer on the man's temple. Hans's eyes shot open when the body landed on him, but he stayed on the gurney. Hauer quickly wrapped the telephone cord several times around the stunned guard's wrists, then, spying a cloth napkin on the desk, stuffed it into his mouth and let him fall to the floor. "Hang on!" he bellowed. He slammed the gurney through the heavy door that led to the rear parking lot.

The cold hit them like a wall of ice.

"Get up!" Hauer said. "We've got to steal a car. Mine's parked in front of the station."

"Mine's back here," Hans groaned, trying to rise.

"You've still got your keys?"

"No one took them."

"Idiots! Give them to me!"

Hans fished the keys out of his pocket and handed them over. Hauer helped him off the gurney and into the car, then climbed into the driver's seat and fired the engine. Incredibly, the Volkswagen kicked over without grumbling.

"This is our lucky day," Hans croaked, still a bit silly from the blow to his head.

Hauer drove slowly out of the lot, turning south on the Friedrichstrasse to avoid the reporters, then shot down the first side street he came to. He had to make some decisions very fast, but he could think of nowhere safe to make them. *Just drive,* he thought. *Head for the seedy section of the city and let my mind clear.* Instinct would guide him. It always had. Maybe Hans could give him a direction. He reached over and jerked Hans's chin up.

"Wake up! It's time to talk."

"My God," Hans mumbled. "Weiss ... what did they *do* to him?"

Hauer cruised past the Anhalter Banhof, then wrenched the VW into another side street. "That was play time," he growled, "compared to what they'll do if they find us. You'd better have some answers, Hans. I just threw away my badge, my reputation, my pension, and probably my life. If you mention our stupid agreement now, I'll brain you myself. Now make yourself useful. Start watching for patrol cars."

Praying that he would awaken from this nightmare, Hans slid up in his seat, put a hand to his throbbing head, and peered out into the icebound Berlin darkness.

CHAPTER SEVEN

9:55 P.M. British Sector: West Berlin

As Captain Hauer wheeled Hans's Volkswagen out of Polizei Abschnitt 53, Professor Natterman stepped out of a taxi thirty blocks away, paid his cabbie, and hurried into the milling throngs of Zoo Station. He tried to walk slowly, but found it difficult. Missing his train would mean standing around the station for hours with nothing to do but worry about the nine sheets of onionskin taped into the small of his back. Sighting a ticket window with a short queue, he got into line and set down his heavy suitcase.

Ten minutes later Professor Natterman was safely berthed in a first-class car, poring over a short volume by Dr. J. R. Rees, the British Army psychiatrist who had supervised the first extensive examinations of "Rudolf Hess" after his famous flight. It made for tedious reading, and Natterman had trouble concentrating. His mind kept returning to the Spandau papers. He had no doubt that Prisoner Number Seven had told the truth—if only because, to date, the man had provided the only possible version of events that fit all the known facts.

The Rudolf Hess case, Natterman believed, shared one major similarity with the assassination of the American president John F. Kennedy. There was simply *too much information*. A surfeit of facts, inconsistencies, myth, and conjecture. Everyone had his pet conspiracy theory. If one accepted the medical evidence that "Number Seven" was not Hess, then two general theories held popular sway. Natterman dismissed them both out of hand, but like most farfetched theories, each was based upon a tantalizing grain of truth.

The primary theory—put forward by the British surgeon who first uncovered the medical evidence—held that one of the top Nazis (either Heinrich Himmler or Hermann Göring) had wanted to supplant Hitler and had decided to use Hess's wartime double to do it. To accomplish this, either Göring or Himmler (or both) would have to have ordered the real Hess shot down over the North Sea, then sent his double rushing on to England. There the double would supposedly have asked the British government if it might accept peace with Germany, if someone other than Hitler reigned in Berlin. Natterman considered this pure fantasy. Both Nazi chieftains had possessed the power to give such orders, of course. And there was quite a body of evidence suggesting that both men had prior knowledge of Hess's plan to fly to Britain. But the question Natterman could not ignore was *why* Himmler or Göring should have elected to murder Hess, then use his double for such a sensitive mission in the first place. It was a harebrained scheme that would have carried tremendous risk of discovery by Hitler, and thus was totally out of character for both the prudent SS chief and the flamboyant but wily Luftwaffe commander. Only a week before Hess's flight, Himmler had sent a secret envoy to Switzerland to discuss the possibility of an Anglo-German peace, with himself as chancellor of the Reich. That might not be so exciting as murder in the skies, but it was Himmler's true style.

The other popular theory held that the real Hess had reached England alive, but that the British government—for reasons of its own—had wanted him silenced. They supposedly killed Hess, then searched among German prisoners of war for a likely double, whom they brainwashed, bribed, or blackmailed into impersonating the Deputy Führer. Natterman considered this tripe of the lowest order. His researches indicated that a "brainwashed" man was little more than a zombie—certainly not capable of impersonating Hess for more than a few hours, much less for forty-six years. And as far as British bribes or blackmail, Natterman didn't believe any German impersonator would sacrifice fifty years of his life for British money or even British threats.

Yet this theory, too, was partially based on fact. No informed historian doubted that the British government wanted the Hess affair buried. They had proved it time and again throughout the years, and Professor Natterman did not discount the possibility that the British had murdered Hess's double just four weeks ago. It was also true that only a native German could have successfully impersonated Hess for so long. Not just any German, however, it would have to have been a German trained specifically by Nazis to impersonate Hess, and whose service was either voluntary, or motivated by the threat of some terrible penalty. A penalty like *Sippenhaft.*

Natterman felt a shiver of excitement. The author of the Spandau papers had satisfied all those requirements, and more. For the first time, someone had offered a credible—probably the *only*—answer to when and how the double had been substituted for the real Hess. If the papers were correct, *he never had been.* Hess and his double had flown to Britain *in the same plane.* It had been the double in British hands from the very first moment! Natterman recalled that a prominent British journalist had written a novel suggesting that, since the Messerschmitt 110 could carry two men, Hess might not have flown to Britain alone. But *no one* had ever suggested that Hess's double could have been that passenger!

Natterman drummed his fingers compulsively as his brain shifted up to a higher plane of analysis. Facts were the province of history professors; *motives* were the province of historians. The ultimate question was not *how* the double had arrived in England, but *why.* Why was it necessary for both the double *and* the real Hess to fly to Britain, as the Spandau papers claimed they had? Whom did they fly there to meet? Why was it necessary for the double to remain in Spandau? Had he been murdered for the same reason? If so, who murdered him? Circumstantial evidence pointed to the British. Yet if the British killed the double, why had they done it *now,* after all these years? Publicly they had joined France and the United States in calling for Number Seven's early release (though they knew full well they could rely on the Russians to veto it, as they had done every year before)—

My God, Natterman thought suddenly. Was that it? Had Mikhail Gorbachev, in the spirit of *glasnost,* proposed to release Hess at last? As Natterman scrawled this question in the margin of Dr. Rees's book, the huge, bright yellow diesel engine disengaged its brakes with a hiss and lurched out of the great glass hall of Zoo Station, accelerating steadily toward the benighted fields of the DDR. In a few minutes the train would enter the narrow, fragile corridor linking the island of West Berlin to the Federal Republic of Germany. Natterman pulled the plastic shade down over his small window. There were ghosts outside—ghosts he had no wish to see. Memories he thought long laid to rest had been violently exhumed by the papers he now smuggled through communist Germany. *God,* he wondered, *does it ever end? The deceit, the casualties?* He touched the thin bundle beneath his sweater. *The casualties* ... More were coming, he could feel it.

Yet he couldn't give up the Spandau papers—not yet. Those nine thin sheets of paper were his last chance at academic resurrection. He had been one of the lions once, an academic demigod. A colleague once told Natterman that he had heard Willy Brandt quote from Natterman's opus on Germany no less than three times during one speech in the Bundestag. Three times! But Natterman had written that book over thirty years ago. During the intervening years, he had managed to stay in print with "distinguished contributor" articles, but no publisher showed real interest in any further Natterman books. The great professor had said all he had to say in *From Bismarck to the Bunker*—or so they thought. *But now,* he thought excitedly, *now the cretins will be hammering down my door!* When he offered his explosive translation of *The Secret Diary of Spandau Prisoner Number Seven*—boasting the solution to the greatest mystery of the Second World War—they would *beg* for the privilege of publishing him!

Startled by a sharp knock at the compartment door, Natterman stuffed Dr. Rees's book under his seat cushion and stood. *Probably just Customs,* he reassured himself. This was the very reason he had chosen this escape route from the city. Trains traveling between West Berlin and the Federal Republic did not stop inside East Germany, so passport control and the issue of visas took place during the journey. Still more important, there were no baggage controls.

"Yes?" he called. "Who is it?"

Someone fumbled at the latch; then the door shot open. A tall, wiry man with a dark complexion and bright eyes stared at the professor in surprise. A worn leather bag dangled from his left hand. "Oh, dear!" he said. "Dreadfully sorry."

An upper-class British accent. Natterman looked the man up and down. *At least my own age,* he thought. *Strong-looking fellow. Thin, tanned, beaked nose. Looks more Jew-*

ish than British, come to think of it. Which is ridiculous because Judaism isn't a nationality and Britishness isn't a religion—although the adherents of both sometimes treat them as such—

"I say there," the intruder said, quickly scanning the room, "Stern's my name. I'm terribly sorry. Can't seem to find my berth."

"What's the number?" Natterman asked warily.

"Sixteen, just like it says on the door here." Stern held out a key.

Natterman examined it. "Right number," he said. "Wrong car, though. You want second class, next car back."

Stern took the key back quickly. "Why, you're right. Thanks, old boy. I'll find it."

"No trouble." Natterman scrutinized the visitor as he backed out of the cabin. "You know, I thought I'd locked that door," he said.

"Don't think it was, really," Stern replied. "Just gave it a shove and it opened right up."

"Your key fit?"

"It went in. Who knows? They always use the oldest trains on the Berlin run. One key probably opens half the doors on the train." Stern laughed. "Sorry again."

For an instant the tanned stranger's face came alive with urgent purpose, so that it matched his eyes, which were bright and intense. It was as if a party mask had accidentally slipped before midnight. Stern seemed on the verge of saying something; then his lips broadened into a sheepish grin and he backed out of the compartment and shut the door.

Puzzled, and more than a little uncomfortable, Natterman sat down again. An accident? That fellow didn't seem like the type to mix up his sleeping arrangements. Not one bit. And something about him looked familiar. Not his face . . . but his *carriage*. The loose, ready stance. He'd been unseasonably tanned for Berlin. Impossibly tanned, in fact. Retrieving Dr. Rees's book from beneath the seat cushion, the professor tapped it nervously against his leg. *A soldier,* he thought suddenly. Natterman would have bet a year's salary that the man who had stumbled into his compartment was an ex-soldier. *And an Englishman,* he thought, feeling his heart race. *Or at least a man who had lived among the English long enough to imitate their accent to perfection.* Natterman didn't like the arithmetic of that "accident" at all if he was right. Not at all.

10:04 *P.M.* MI-5 Headquarters: Charles Street, London, England

Deputy Director Wilson knocked softly at Sir Neville Shaw's door, then opened it and padded onto the deep carpet of the director general's office. Shaw sat at his desk beneath the green glow of a banker's lamp. He took no notice of the intrusion; he continued to pore over a thick, dog-eared file on the desk before him.

"Sir Neville?" Wilson said.

Shaw did not look up. "What is it? Your hard boys arrived?"

"No, sir. It's something else. A bit rum, actually."

Sir Neville looked up at last. "Well?"

"It's Israeli Intelligence, sir. The head of the Mossad, as a matter of fact. He's sent us a letter."

Shaw blinked. "So?"

"Well, it's rather extraordinary, sir."

"Damn it, Wilson, how so?"

"The letter is countersigned by the Israeli prime minister. It was hand-delivered by courier."

"What?" Sir Neville sat up. "What in God's name is it about?" His ruddy face slowly tightened in dread. "Not Hess?"

Wilson quickly shook his head. "No, sir. It's about an old intelligence hand of theirs. Chap named Stern. Seems he's been holed up in the Negev for the past dozen years, but a couple of days ago he quietly slipped his leash."

Shaw looked exasperated. "I don't see what the devil that's got to do with us."

"The Israelis—their prime minister, rather—seem to think we might still hold a grudge against this fellow. That there might be a standing order of some type on him. A *liquidation* order."

"That's preposterous!" Shaw bellowed. "After all this time?"

The deputy director smiled with forbearance. "It's not so preposterous, Sir Neville. Our own Special Forces Club— which the Queen still visits occasionally, I'm proud to say—

still refuses to accept Israeli members. They welcome elite troops from almost every democratic nation in the world, even the bloody Germans. Everyone *but* the Israelis, and they're probably the best of the lot. And all because the older agents still hold a grudge for the murder of an SAS man by Zionists during the Mandate—"

"Just a minute," Shaw interrupted. "Stern, you said?"

"Yes, sir. Jonas Stern. I pulled his file."

"Jonas Stern," Shaw murmured. "By God, the Israelis ought to be concerned. One of our people has been after that old guerilla for better than thirty years."

Wilson looked surprised. "One of our agents, sir?"

"Retired," Shaw explained. "A woman, actually. Code name Swallow. A real harpy. You'd better pull her file, in fact. Just in case she's still got her eye on this fellow." Shaw nodded thoughtfully. "I remember Stern. He was a terrorist during the Mandate, not even twenty at the time, I'll bet. He swallowed his vinegar and fought for us during the war. It was the only way he could get at Hitler, I suppose. Did a spot of sticky business for us in Germany, as I recall."

Wilson looked at Shaw in wonder. "That's exactly what it says in the file!"

"Yes," Shaw remembered, "he worked for LAKAM during the 'sixties and 'seventies, didn't he? Safeguarding Israel's nuclear development program." Shaw smiled at his deputy's astonishment. "No strings or mirrors, Wilson. Stern was a talented agent, but the reason I remember him so clearly is because of this Swallow business. I think she actually tried to assassinate him a couple of times. That's why the Mossad sent that letter."

"Do you really think this woman might pose a danger to him?"

Shaw shook his head. "I doubt Stern's in England. Or even in Europe, for that matter. He's probably sunning himself on Mykonos, or something similar. Which reminds me—did you find that freighter for me?"

"Oh, yes, sir. Lloyd's puts her off Durban; she rounded the cape three days ago."

Shaw rummaged through the stack of papers on his desk until he found a map of southern Africa. "Durban," he murmured, running his finger across the paper. "Twenty knots, twenty-five . . . two days . . . yes. Well."

Shaw brushed the map aside and thumped the stack of papers before him. "This is the Hess file, Wilson. No one's cleared to read it but me—did you know that? I tell you, there's enough rotted meat between these covers to make you ashamed of being an Englishman."

Wilson waited for an explanation, but Shaw provided none. "About the Israeli letter, sir?" he prompted. "It's basically a polite request to leave this Stern alone. How should I reply?"

"What? Oh. The Israeli prime minister is an old terrorist himself, you know." Sir Neville chuckled. "And still looking after his own, after all these years." His smile turned icy. "No reply. Let him sweat for a while, eh?"

"Yes, sir."

"And hurry those hard boys along, would you? I thought I had it tough with the P.M. climbing my back. An hour ago I got a call from the bloody Queen-Mother herself. She makes the Iron Lady sound like a French nanny!"

As Wilson slipped out, Sir Neville huffed and went back to the Hess file. On top lay a very old eight-by-ten glossy photograph. Scarred and faded, it showed a man in his late forties with dark hair, a strong jaw, and a black oval patch tied rakishly across his left eye. Shaw jabbed his heavy forefinger down on the eye patch.

"You started it all, you sneaking bastard," he muttered. He slammed the file closed and leaned back in his chair. "Sometimes I wonder if the damned knighthood's worth the strain," he said. "Protecting skeletons in the royal bloody chest."

10:07 P.M. #30 Lützenstrasse

Outside the apartment another car rattled down the street without slowing. Number twelve. Ilse was counting. *Wait until midnight,* her grandfather had told her. *If Hans isn't home by then, get out.* Sound advice, perhaps, but Ilse couldn't imagine running for safety while Hans remained in danger. She fumed at her own obstinacy. How could she have let a stupid argument keep her from telling Hans about the baby? She had to find him. Find him and bring him to his senses.

But where to start? The police station? The nightclub district? Hans might meet a reporter anywhere. Rising from her

telephone vigil, she went to the bedroom to put on some out-
door clothes. Outside, a long low groan built slowly to a rattling roar as a train passed on the elevated S-Bahn tracks up
the street. During the day trains passed every ten minutes or
so; at night, thank God, the intervals were longer. As Ilse
tied a scarf around her hair, yet another automobile clattered
down the Lützenstrasse, coughing and wheezing in the cold.
Unlike the others, however, this one sputtered to a stop near
the front entrance of the building. *Please,* she prayed, rushing to the window, *please let it be Hans.*

It wasn't. Looking down, she saw a shiny black BMW sedan, not Hans's Volkswagen. She let her forehead fall
against the freezing pane. The cold eased the throb of the
headache that had begun an hour earlier. She half-watched as
the four doors of the BMW opened simultaneously and four
men in dark business suits emerged. They grouped together
near the front of the car. One man pointed toward the apartment building and waved in a circle. Another detached himself from the group and disappeared around the corner.
Curious, Ilse watched the first man turn his face toward the
upper floors and begin counting windows. His bobbing arm
moved slowly closer to her window. *How odd,* she thought.
*Who would be out counting apartment windows at midnight
in—?*

She jumped back from the window. The men below were
looking for *her.* Or for Hans—for what he'd found. She
groped for the light switch to turn it off, then thought better
of it. Instead she ran into the living room, opened the door,
and peered cautiously down the hall. Empty. She dashed
down the corridor and around the corner to a window that
overlooked the building's rear entrance. Three men huddled
there, speaking animatedly. Ilse wondered if they might be
plainclothes police. Suddenly two of them entered the building, while the third took up station in the shadow of some
garbage bins near the exit.

The metallic groan of the ancient elevator jolted Ilse from
the window. *Too late to run.* They would reach her floor in
seconds. With her back to the corridor wall, she inched toward the corner that led back to her apartment. She felt a
tingling numbness in her hands as she peeked around it. A
tall young man in a dark suit stood outside her door. Remembering the fire stairs, she started in the other direction,
but the echo of ascending steps made her thought redundant.

Hopelessly trapped, she decided to try to bluff her way out. Feeling adrenaline suffuse her body, she stepped around the corner as if she owned the building and marched toward the man outside her apartment. She cocked her chin arrogantly upward, intending to walk right past him and into the lift that would take her to the lobby. After all, she had appeared from another part of the floor—she might be anybody. If she could only reach the lobby . . .

The man looked up. He began to stare. First at Ilse's legs, then at her breasts, then her face.

I can't do it! she thought. *I'll never make it past him—*

In a millisecond she saw her chance. *Stay calm,* she told herself. *Steady* . . . Fifteen feet away from her apartment she stopped and withdrew her apartment key from her purse. She smiled coolly at the guard, then turned her back to him and bent over the door handle of apartment 43. *Be here, Eva!* she screamed silently. *For God's sake, be here!* Ilse scratched her key against the knob to imitate the sound of an unlocking door, then she said one last prayer and turned the knob.

It opened! Like a reprieved prisoner, she backed into her friend's apartment, smiling once at the guard before she shut and locked the door. After shooting home the bolt, she sagged against the door, her entire body quivering in terror. For an unsteady moment she thought she might actually collapse, but she forced down her fear and padded up the narrow hall to her friend's bedroom door. A crack of light shone faintly beneath it. Ilse knocked, but heard no answer.

"Eva?" she called softly. "Eva, it's Ilse."

Too anxious to wait, she opened the door and stepped into the room. From behind the door a hand shot out and caught her hair, then jerked her to the floor. She started to struggle, but froze when she felt a cold blade press into the soft flesh of her throat. "Eva!" she rasped. "Eva, it's *me*—Ilse!"

The hand jerked harder on her hair, drawing her head back. The blade did not relent. Then, suddenly, she was free.

"Ilse!" Eva hissed. "What the hell are you doing here? I might have killed you. I would have. I thought you were a rapist. Or worse."

The remark threw Ilse off balance. "What's worse than a rapist?"

"A faggot, dearie," Eva answered, bursting into laughter. She folded the straight razor back into its handle.

Ilse's panic finally overcame her. Tears streamed down her cheeks, and she sobbed as her middle-aged friend hugged her wet face to a considerable bosom and stroked her hair like a mother comforting her child.

"Ilse, darling," Eva murmured. "What's happened? You're beside yourself."

"Eva, I'm sorry I came here, but it was the only place I could go! I don't know what's happening—"

"Shh, be quiet now. Catch your breath and tell Eva all about it. Did Hans do something naughty? He didn't hit you?"

"No . . . nothing like that. This is madness. *Crazy*. You wouldn't believe me if I told you!"

Eva chuckled. "I've seen things in this city that would drive a psychiatrist mad, if you could find one who isn't already. Just tell me what's wrong, child. And if you can't tell me that, tell me what you need. I can at least help you out of trouble."

Ilse wiped her face on her blouse and tried to calm down. Despite the presence of the men outside, she felt better already. Eva Beers had a way of making any problem seem insignificant. A barmaid and tavern singer for most of her fifty-odd years, she had worked the rough-and-tumble circuit in most of the capitals of western Europe. She had returned home to Berlin three years ago, to "live out my days in luxury," as she jokingly put it. Hans sometimes commented that Eva was only semiretired, for the frequent pilgrimage of well-dressed and ever-changing old gentlemen to her door seemed to indicate that something slightly more profitable than conversation went on inside number 43. But that was Eva's business; Hans never asked any questions. She was a cheerful and discreet neighbor who often did favors for the young couple, and Ilse had grown very close to her.

"Eva, we're in trouble," Ilse said. "Hans and I."

"What kind of trouble? Hans is Polizei. What can't he fix?"

Ilse fought the urge to blurt out everything. She didn't want to involve Eva any more than she already had. "I don't know, Eva, I don't *know*. Hans found something. Something dangerous!"

"It's drugs, isn't it?" Eva wrinkled her nose in disgust. "Hashish or something, right?"

"I told you, I don't know. But it's bad. There's a man in

the hall right now and he's waiting for Hans to get home. There are three more men outside by the doors!"

"*What?* Outside here? Who do you mean, child? Police?"

Ilse threw up her hands. "I don't know! All I know is that Hans's station said he left hours ago. I've got to get out of here, Eva. I've got to warn Hans."

"How can you warn him if you don't know where he is?"

Ilse wiped a wet streak of mascara from her cheek. "I don't know," she said, trying to stop her tears. "But first I've got to get past those men outside."

As the old barmaid watched Ilse's mascara run, a hot wave of anger flushed her cheeks. "You dry those tears," she said. "There hasn't been a man born to woman that Mama Eva can't handle."

10:10 P.M. *Europa Center, Breitscheid Platz: West Berlin*

Major Harry Richardson stared curiously at the receding back of Eduard Lenhardt, his contact in Abschnitt 53. In seconds the policeman disappeared into the crush of bodies crowding the bar of the imitation Irish pub in the basement of the Europa Center, West Berlin's answer to the American megamall. This twenty-two-story tower housed dozens of glitzy shops, bars, restaurants, banks, travel agencies, and even a hotel—all of whose goods and services seemed to be priced for the Japanese tourist. Harry had chosen it for its crowds.

He swallowed the last of an excellent Bushmill's and tried to gather his thoughts. Eduard Lenhardt was only the third in a chain of personal contacts Harry had spoken with tonight. Contrary to Colonel Rose's orders, Harry had kept his racquetball date. And by so doing, he had learned that Sir Neville Shaw, director of Britain's MI-5, had ordered British embassy personnel to burn the midnight oil in West Berlin. Shortly after that, Harry had called a State Department contact in Bonn, an old college buddy, who had let it slip that the Russian complaint filed against the U.S. Army specified papers taken from Spandau Prison as the primary object of Soviet concern. The British and the French had received the same complaint. Harry could well imagine the British consternation at such an allegation. After the phone call, Harry had finally gained an audience with his reluctant contact from Abschnitt 53—Lieutenant Eduard Lenhardt.

Lenhardt had revealed information to Harry in three ways: by what he'd said, by what he hadn't said, and simply by how he'd looked. In Harry's professional opinion, the policeman had looked scared shitless. What he had not said was anything about papers found in Spandau Prison. What he had said was this:

That the prefect of police, Wilhelm Funk, had moved out of the Police Presidium and set up a command post in Abschnitt 53, after which the station had taken on the demeanor of an SS barracks after Graf Stauffenberg's briefcase exploded in Hitler's bunker. That two Berlin policemen had been detained in a basement cell, then had either escaped or been killed. And that while the Russians had pulled out of Abschnitt 53 at eight, they had acted as if they might return at any time with T-72 tanks. All this in breathless gasps from a veteran policeman whom Harry had never seen get excited about anything other than the piano quartets of Brahms.

Harry dropped ten marks on the table and hurried out of the pub. Sixty seconds later he was on the Ku'damm, where he flagged down a taxi and gave the driver an address near the Tiergarten. The man who occupied the house there was one of Harry's "private assets," a rather high-strung German trade liaison named Klaus Seeckt. During Harry's first year in Berlin, he had spotted Klaus at the *Philharmonie*, in the company of an arrogant and well-known KGB agent named Yuri Borodin. It hadn't taken Harry long to establish that Klaus was using his semi-official cover to funnel restricted technology to Moscow. That had not interested Harry much; what had interested him—after a thorough investigation of Seeckt—was that while Klaus dealt directly with the KGB, he had no ties, voluntary or otherwise, to the East German secret police, the Stasi. And that was a very rare combination in Berlin.

Rather than arrest Klaus for the high-tech ripoff, Harry had opted to use his leverage whenever he needed a direct line into KGB operations. He never even filed a report on Klaus. Colonel Rose might have insisted that Harry push the German too hard, which would only have spooked him into fleeing the city. Men like Klaus had to be treated delicately. Harry cultivated the man's ego, pretending to share with him the fraternal enjoyment of superior intellect, and applied pressure only when necessary.

Tonight was different. Eduard Lenhardt's apprehensions were worming their way into Harry's gut, and the checks he normally kept on his imagination began to erode as his mind raced through the possible implications of the events at Abschnitt 53. When the taxi reached the Tiergarten house, Harry tipped its driver enough to satisfy, but not enough to draw attention. And as he reached Klaus's door, he decided that his sensitive East German would have to pay the remainder of his debt tonight.

10:10 P.M. The Bismarckstrasse

"Captain!" Hans warned. *"Motorcycle patrol, three cars back!"*

"I see him." Hauer swung the Volkswagen smoothly around a corner just as the traffic signal changed, stranding the police cycle in the line of vehicles stopped at the light. "We've got to get off the street."

"Where do we go? My apartment? Your house?"

"Think, Hans. They'll be covering both places."

"You're right. Maybe—" He grabbed Hauer's sleeve. "Jesus, Ilse's at the apartment alone!"

"Easy, Hans, we'll get her. But we can't walk in there like lambs to the slaughter."

"But Funk could have men there already!"

"Hold your water. Where are we, Bergstrasse? There should be a hotel four blocks south of us. The Steglitz. Just what we need."

"A *hotel?*"

"Get in the backseat," Hauer ordered, and stepped on the accelerator.

"What are you going to do?"

"Do it!"

As Hans climbed into the backseat, Hauer ripped the police insignia from his collar and spurred the VW into the Steglitz garage. The violent turn threw Hans against the side door. They squealed down the curving ramp to the parking sublevels below and into a tiny space between two large sedans.

"All right, Hans," Hauer said. "Out with it. Everything. What really happened at Spandau this morning?"

Hans climbed awkwardly through the narrow gap between the seats. "I'll tell you on the way to my apartment."

Hauer shook his head. "We don't move one meter until you talk."

Hans bridled, but he could see that Hauer would not be swayed. "Look, I would have reported it if it hadn't been for those damned Russians."

"Reported what?"

"The papers. The papers I found at Spandau."

"Christ, you mean the Russians were *right*?"

Hans nodded.

"Where did you find these papers? What did they say?"

Hauer looked strangely hungry. Hans looked out the window. "I found them in a pile of rubble. In a hollow brick, just like Schmidt asked me. What does it matter? I started reading them, but one of the Russians stumbled on me. I hid them without even thinking." He turned to Hauer. "That's it! That's all I did! So why has everyone gone crazy?"

"What did the papers say, Hans?"

"I don't know. Gibberish, mostly. Ilse said it was Latin."

"You showed them to your *wife*?"

"I didn't intend to, but she found them. She understood more of it than I did, anyway. She said the papers had something to do with the Nazis. That they were dangerous." He looked down at his lap. "God, was she right."

"Tell me everything you remember, Hans."

"Look, I hardly remember any of it. The German part sounded bitter, like a revenge letter, but . . . there was fear in it, too. The writer said he had written because he could never speak about what he knew. That others would pay the price for his words."

Hauer hung on every syllable. "What else?"

"Nothing."

"Nothing at all?"

"It was Latin, I told you! I couldn't read it!"

"Latin," Hauer mused, leaning back into his seat. "Who wrote the papers? Were they signed?"

Hans shrugged uncomfortably. "There wasn't any name. Just a number."

"A *number*?" Hauer's eyes grew wide. "What number, Hans?"

"Seven, goddamnit! The lucky number. What a fucking joke. Now can we get out of here?"

Hauer shook his head slowly. "Hess," he murmured. "It's impossible. The restrictions, the endless searches. It can't be."

Hans ground his teeth angrily. "Captain, I know what you're talking about, but right now I don't care! I just want to know my wife is safe!"

Hauer laid a hand on his shoulder. "Where are these papers now?"

"At the apartment."

"No! You made copies?"

"No, damn it! I don't care about the papers anymore! We're going to get Ilse *now*!"

Hauer pinned him against the seat with an arm of iron. "You saw Weiss, didn't you? If you go charging into your apartment, the same thing could happen to you. And to Ilse."

The memory of Weiss's mutilated corpse brought a strange stillness over Hans. "What *did* happen to Weiss?"

Hauer sighed. "Someone got too impatient, pushed the doctor too far. Probably Luhr, Funk's personal stormtrooper." He shook his head. "Later tonight they'll shoot his body full of cocaine and dump him in the Havel."

"My God," Hans breathed. "You *saw* it. You were *there*." He balled his hands into fists.

"Hans! Get hold of yourself! I did *not* see Weiss tortured."

"You knew about his chest!"

Hauer grimaced. "I overheard someone talking about it. It's . . . it's sort of a specialty of theirs. With certain Jews. Why did that boy join the department at all? You'd think a Jew would know better."

Hans's mouth fell open. "You're saying it was Weiss's fault someone mutilated him?"

"I'm saying if you're a lamb you don't run with the wolf pack!"

The memory of Weiss brought back the mark on Rolf's head, the haunting eye from the Spandau papers. "What about the tattoo?" Hans asked quietly. "What does that mean?"

Hauer shook his head. "It's complicated, Hans. The eye is a mark some people use—some very dangerous people. I'm not one of them. I just wanted you to remember the design."

He leaned his head across the seat. "Look behind my right ear. In the hair. If I had the tattoo, it would be there."

Hans studied Hauer's close-cropped scalp, but he saw no tattoo.

"I'm not one of them," said Hauer, straightening up. "But until five minutes ago, they thought I was. We've got to find somewhere safe to hide, Hans, somewhere with a phone. Before we can get your wife, we've got to know what Funk and Luhr are up to. I've got a man inside the station I can call—"

"So let's go upstairs! There are probably a dozen phones up in the lobby. I can call Ilse, warn her to get out!" Hans reached for the door handle, but Hauer stopped him again.

"We can't, Hans. We're in uniform. Everyone will be staring at the two beat-up cops using the pay phones. Funk's men would find us in no time."

Hans jerked his arm free. "Where, then? A friend's house?"

"No. No friends, no family. It's got to be untraceable. An empty house or . . . something."

Slowly, almost mechanically, Hans removed his wallet from his pants pocket and took out a tattered white business card. He stared at it a moment, then handed it to Hauer.

"What's this?" Hauer read aloud: " 'Benjamin Ochs, The Best Tailor in Berlin.' You want to go to your tailor shop?"

"He's not my tailor," Hans said tersely.

"Eleven-fifty Goethestrasse. No one can trace you to this place?"

"Trust me."

Hauer looked skeptical.

Hans turned away. The stress of being treated like an animal, caged and hunted, was congealing into something cold and hard in the pit of his stomach. With a guttural groan he slammed his open hand against the dashboard. "Get this fucking car *moving*!"

Hauer looked hard into Hans's eyes, gauging the mettle there. "Right," he said finally. He fired the engine and roared out of the hotel garage with tires squealing, making for the Goethestrasse.

CHAPTER EIGHT

The men waiting within and without Ilse's apartment building were not police. They were KGB agents sent to the Lützenstrasse by Colonel Ivan Kosov. Kosov himself waited impatiently in a second BMW parked at the end of the block. Kosov hated stakeouts. Long ago he had foolishly thought that once he attained sufficient rank he would be spared the monotony of these endless vigils. And perhaps one day he would. But tonight was one more in an endless series of proofs to the contrary. Exasperated, he reached for the radio microphone mounted on the auto's dash.

"Report, One," he said.

"The lobby's clear," crackled a metallic voice.

"Two?"

"Nothing in the hall. The door's locked, no sound from inside."

"Four?"

"Three's with me. No sign of Apfel or the wife."

"Stay awake," Kosov said gruffly. "Out."

Shit, he thought, how long will it take? Sitting in this ball-freezing cold, chattering over the short-range radios as if simply alternating frequencies could mask the Russian-accented commands ricocheting through the Berlin audio net like lines from a bad movie. He wished there were another way. But he knew there wasn't.

Three floors above Kosov, the door to apartment 43 opened and two garishly made-up redheads stepped into the hallway. One locked the door while her young companion stared invitingly at the man standing at attention outside apartment 40. The young woman nudged her middle-aged companion, who chuckled and led the way over to the silent man.

"*Na, mein Süsser,*" Eva flirted in a husky voice. "All alone up here tonight?"

Taken aback by her directness, the Russian stared back in silence. *She's at least fifty,* he thought, *much too old for my taste. But you're something else altogether,* he thought, hungrily eyeing the younger woman's cleavage. With a flash of surprise, he realized that she was the demure blonde he had seen enter apartment 43 twenty minutes earlier. He barely recognized her beneath the heavy makeup and wig. *She can't be more than twenty-five,* he guessed, *and breasts like a Georgian goddess . . .*

"*Guten Abend, Fräulein,*" he said to the younger woman. "I think you looked much better before."

Ilse felt her throat tighten.

"I think he's set on you, Helga," Eva said, laughing. She patted the Russian on his rear. "Too bad, dearie, little Helga's booked for tonight. But you're in luck. I know a dozen tricks this child's never even heard of. What do you say?"

Abashed by the old tart's boldness, the Russian went temporarily blank.

"Oh, forget it," Eva said, pulling Ilse down the hall. "If you don't know what you want, we don't have time to wait."

Kosov's young agent watched the middle-aged redhead follow her shapely companion into the elevator cage. Eva yanked the lever that started the slow descent and then, still holding eye contact with the guard, pumped her fist lewdly up and down the iron rod. When the Russian colored in embarrassment, she hiked her bright skirt over a well-preserved thigh and burst into laughter.

As soon as the cage sank below the line of the floor, Eva cut her voice to a whisper. "Here comes the hard part. We were lucky that time. The odds just went down."

Ilse clutched her friend's arm. "You shouldn't have come with me!"

"You'd never have made it by yourself, darling."

"But you're in danger too!"

Eva plucked a gob of mascara out of her eye. "I'm glad to do it. If I hadn't had you to talk to for the last three years, I'd have gone mad in that tiny apartment."

"But all your men friends—"

Eva's heavily rouged face wrinkled in disgust. "Don't even mention those bums. Don't act like you don't know what I do. You and Hans have always known, and you've never treated me any different than family. So shut up and take some help. We're not out of this yet."

The elevator screeched to an uncertain stop. Eva yanked open the screen and stormed through the lobby, cursing the elevator and every other mechanical device ever invented. With Ilse struggling along behind on a pair of Eva's four-inch heels, the old barmaid clacked past the two Russians at the building's entrance as if they did not exist.

"Halt!" yelled one of Kosov's men as Ilse hurried past.

Ilse's heart thudded in her chest.

The Russian caught hold of her elbow. "Hey, *Fräulein*," he said, leaning close to her. "Why the hurry?"

Eva paused impatiently at the curb. She looked up and down the street, then walked back to the door. "Next time, sweetie," she snapped, stepping protectively in front of Ilse. "We've got a party to go to."

"It can wait," said the young man, leering at his companion. "Stay here and keep us warm for a while. It's cold out."

"Colder by the minute, *Arschloch*," Eva spat. "If we don't get out of this wind in thirty seconds our tits will snap off."

The Russian shed his smile like a snakeskin. His eyes glazed with a reptilian sheen. He took a step toward Eva.

"Forget it, Misha," urged his companion. "They're just whores."

"Fucking filth," the Russian muttered.

"Misha," said his partner anxiously. "Remember Colonel Kosov."

Misha took a long look at Eva as if to mark her for future retribution, then snorted and walked into the lobby. When he next looked outside, the two women were already across the street and halfway down the block, moving toward Colonel Kosov's BMW.

Kosov had just lifted the microphone from the dash when he spied two prostitutes walking quickly up the Lützenstrasse.

"Report, One," he said, half-watching them.

"Lobby still clear."

"Two?"

"No movement inside the apartment."

"Damn. Three and Four?"

"All clear here. No sign of him."

The prostitutes reached the hood of the BMW, passed it.

"All positions," said Kosov, "I have two women passing me from your direction. Anyone see where they entered the street?"

The radio squawked as three signals competed for reproduction. "Four here, sir. They came from the apartment building. Looked like two whores to us."

Kosov felt a tic in his cheek. He turned away as the headlights of a passing car shone through the BMW. When he looked again he saw one of the women raise an arm and flag the car to a stop. *That's odd,* he thought, *a taxi here at this hour. And picking up a couple of streetwalkers . . .*

"Two here," crackled the radio. "Those prostitutes came from number forty-three, this floor. Opposite my position. One of them even propositioned me."

Kosov struck the dash with his fist. "One of them is the wife! Misha, to the car! Two, enter number forty and proceed!" Kosov looked frantically for an alley in which to turn the BMW around. With cars parked both sides of the street he had no room to make a U.

Inside the taxi, Eva spoke rapidly. "Perfect timing, Ernst darling. Now zoom around the corner and stop as fast as you can." She looked back over her shoulder. "Ilse, when he stops, you jump right out and get into the alley there. If they keep after me, you've made it. If they don't—"

"Who *were* those men, Eva? Police?"

"Stinking Russians, sweetie. Didn't you catch the name Misha?"

The taxi jounced onto the curb. "Eva, how can I thank—"

"Go!" Eva cried, squeezing Ilse's hand. "Jump! *Go!*"

The screech of tires drowned Ilse's reply as the taxi sped down the Gervinusstrasse. Ilse ducked into the alley just as Kosov's BMW careened around the corner and surged after Eva and her cabbie friend. She collapsed against the cold concrete wall of an office building, her heart beating wildly.

Ten seconds later a second BMW raced after the first.

Turning her back to the icy wind, Ilse doffed the sluttish clothes Eva had given her and tossed the wig into an overflowing garbage bin. Now she wore the conservative casuals she'd had on when she first spotted the BMW. Habit made her hang on to one costume accessory Eva had thrust into her hand—a large plastic purse. As she debated whether to keep Eva's flashy coat, Ilse heard the rumble of a heavy automobile engine. Seconds later a pair of headlights nosed into the far end of the alley.

Ilse snatched up the discarded clothes and climbed into the only hiding place she could see—the garbage bin. The smell was terrible, cloyingly sweet. She held her nose with one hand and covered her eyes with the other. The powerful purr of the BMW edged closer, a tiger trying to spook its prey. Ilse knotted herself into a tight ball and prayed. It took little imagination to guess how ruthless the men in the black autos must be. The young man who had propositioned her at the front door—the one called Misha—his eyes had glazed almost to sightlessness when Eva insulted him. Like fish eyes, Ilse thought. She shuddered.

The BMW picked up speed as it approached the garbage bin, weaving occasionally to probe every inch of the alley with its halogen eyes. The walls of the trash bin vibrated from the noise. Ilse shivered from terror and bitter cold. She had no doubt that if the car engine were shut off, the Russians would find her by the chattering of her teeth.

Suddenly, with a scream of protesting rubber, the big black sedan roared out of the alley. Ilse scrambled up out of the garbage and dug into Eva's purse for her shoes. Her hand closed over something soft and familiar. She peered into the bag. Folded into a thick wad at its bottom were three hundred Deutschemarks in small bills. Scrawled across the top banknote in red lipstick were the words: ILSE, USE IT!

Stuffing the bills back into the purse, Ilse climbed out of the bin and edged a little way down the alley. *Damn all of this,* she thought angrily. *If Eva can get me this far, I can do the rest.* In less than fifteen seconds she had analyzed her options and made a decision. She kicked off the stiletto heels Eva had loaned her, pulled on her own flats, and started running toward the hazy glow at the opposite end of the alley.

10:30 P.M. Tiergarten District: West Berlin

The moment Harry Richardson raised his hand to knock on Klaus Seeckt's door, the door jerked open to the length of the chain latch. "Go away, Major!" said a voice from the dark crack.

The door slammed shut. Harry moved to the side of the door, out of the light. "Open the door, Klaus."

"*Please* go away, Harry!"

More puzzled than angry, Harry flattened himself against the wall. Normally he telephoned Klaus before coming over, but tonight he hadn't wanted to give the East German a chance to postpone the meeting. Feeling exposed on the lighted stoop, he pounded his fist against the heavy oak. "I'm not in uniform, for God's sake! Open up! *Now!*"

The bolt shot back with a bang. Klaus pulled the door open but remained out of sight in the dark foyer.

"Take it easy," Harry said. "We'll play it as an official visit. However you want."

Klaus's voice dropped in volume but doubled in urgency. "Harry, get *out* of here! They're watching us!"

As Harry's eyes adjusted to the gloom, he recognized the stubby barrel of a Makarov pistol in Klaus's hand. The East German wore only his bathrobe, but his ashen face and the quivering pistol gave him a frighteningly lethal aspect. Harry glanced back at the street to try to spot watchers. He saw none, but he knew that didn't mean anything.

"I tried to keep you out," Klaus said resignedly. "Remember that."

Writing off Klaus's pistol to paranoia, Harry slipped past the East German and started toward the living room. With a hopeless sigh Klaus shut the door and locked it behind them.

When Harry reached the living room, he saw that Klaus was indeed being watched—but from *inside* the house, not out. Five men wearing dark business suits sat leisurely on sofas and chairs arranged around a glass-topped coffee table. Harry looked back over his shoulder at Klaus. The German hovered ghostlike in the shadows of the foyer, the Makarov slack against his leg. Harry considered bolting, but Klaus hadn't tried it, so perhaps things weren't so bad. *Or perhaps,* Harry thought uneasily, *Klaus didn't run because he knows the front door is covered from the outside.*

Harry turned back to the living room. None of the men around the table looked older than thirty, and no one had said anything yet. Was that good or bad? Suddenly the oldest-looking of the group stood.

"Good evening, Major," he said in heavily accented English. "What can we do for you?"

The young man's accent was unmistakably Russian. There

would be no attempt to pass these men off as other than what they were, Harry realized. A *very* bad sign. He cleared his throat. "And by what rank do I address you, Comrade?" he asked in flawless Russian.

The Russian smiled, seeming to relish the idea of a cat-and-mouse game. "You speak excellent Russian, Major. And I am but a lowly captain, to answer your question. Captain Dmitri Rykov."

"What are you doing so far from home, Captain?"

"Am I so far from home?" Rykov asked gamely. "A debatable point. But I'm protecting the interests of my country, of course."

The young man's candor was an unveiled threat. "I see," Harry said warily. "I also note that we have a mutual friend," he observed, trying to shift the focus away from himself.

In the foyer Klaus turned deathly pale.

"Yes," Rykov agreed, giving Klaus a predatory glance. "This is proving to be an enlightening evening. Take his gun, Andrei. No foolish heroics please, Klaus. It's not your style."

The East German slumped against the foyer wall, his pistol hanging slack. He looked broken, already resigned to the grisly fate that undoubtedly awaited him in Moscow. Corporal Andrei Ivanov moved to disarm him.

"As you can see, Major," Rykov continued, "you've stumbled upon us at a most inopportune time. I'll certainly speak to my superiors about it, but I suspect that your unfortunate timing may cost you your life—"

Before Andrei could reach the unfortunate Klaus, the East German raised the Makarov to his own temple and fired.

The sheer madness of the act stunned everyone, causing a moment of confusion. In desperation Harry bolted for the door. He had his fingers on the brass door handle when someone peppered the wall beside him with a burst from a silenced machine pistol.

"Don't move, Major!" Captain Rykov ordered, his voice strained but even.

Harry let his fingers fall from the handle. He turned around slowly. In the time it had taken him to reach the door, the Russians behind him had been transformed from a quiet group of social acquaintances into a squad of paramilitary soldiers moving in concert to control the unexpected emergency. Two men knelt over Klaus's body, checking for signs of life; two others covered the front and rear windows of the house. Rykov issued orders.

"Yuri, get the car. Major, move back into the room. *Now!*" Rykov tapped the shoulder of a young man leaning over Klaus's corpse. "Leave him, Andrei. Touch nothing. Klaus was a traitor; he deserved a coward's death. Leave the gun in his hand. We couldn't have set this up better ourselves."

"Shouldn't we take him along?" Andrei asked. "The *Kriminalpolizei* aren't stupid."

Rykov's eyes gleamed. "Ideally, I suppose. But we won't have room for him."

"What about the weapons compartment?"

"The major will be in there." Rykov turned to Harry. "You don't want to spend the next hour hugging a corpse, do you, Major?"

Harry's mind raced. If this Russian intended to kidnap an American army officer from the heart of tightly controlled West Berlin, something very big indeed was going on. And to Harry's mind, that something could only be the events at Spandau Prison.

"Kosov won't like this," he said, remembering seeing the Russian colonel at Abschnitt 53 this morning. "You better take some time to think, Captain."

Rykov smiled. "You're very clever, Major."

The sound of an engine rumbled through the front door.

"That's Yuri," said Rykov. "All right, Major, let's go."

Harry didn't move.

"Conscious or unconscious, I don't care. But I must tell you, it's never quite as clean as the movies when you bash someone in the back of the head with a pistol."

Harry moved. He couldn't warn Colonel Rose if he was dead.

It was only a few steps from the front door to the car, a black Mercedes 190. The Russians crowded close around him all the way. *There's got to be a way out,* thought Harry. *Got to be. I've got to warn—*

Dmitri Rykov slammed the butt of his Skorpion machine pistol into the base of Harry's skull. He heard a dull thud but no crunch. "Americans are so gullible," he said, laughing. "Lucky for this one he has a wooden head."

Corporal Ivanov looked distressed. "Are you sure we shouldn't just kill him here?" he said anxiously. "Make it look like some illegal business, perhaps a homosexual tryst?"

"I'm in command here," Rykov snapped, losing a bit of his earlier control. "I'll do the thinking."

"Yes, sir. I was only thinking of Colonel Kosov. If he doesn't approve—"

"*I* know what Kosov wants, Corporal. Did he not choose me for command? We may need this American later as a bargaining chip." Rykov's voice softened. "Andrei, the other team is running down Sergeant Apfel's wife as we speak. Kosov is with them. Do you want us to return to East Berlin empty-handed?"

Ivanov did not look entirely convinced, but he said no more.

Lying half-conscious at their feet, Harry slipped a hand into his inside coat pocket, fished out a white business card, and let it fall. There was no name on it—only a telephone number. As the Russians lifted him into the Mercedes, he glanced down. He saw his own blood, but the white card had already vanished against the snow.

10:31 P.M. Lietzensee Park, British Sector

"Once again," Ivan Kosov said, struggling to keep his voice steady. "Where did the girl get out?"

Pressed into the corner of the taxi's rear seat, Eva Beers scowled and said nothing. Her hands were tied behind her head with her own stockings. The young Russian called Misha had twice smashed her right cheek with his gloved fist, but so far Eva had refused to speak.

"Misha," Kosov growled.

The interior of the taxi echoed with the force of the third blow. A large purplish bruise was already visible beneath the thick patina of makeup Eva wore. In the front seat beside Kosov, Ernst the cabbie slumped unconscious over the wheel of his old Mercedes.

"I have no time for your stupid loyalty, woman," Kosov said. "If you don't answer this time, this zealous young man will have to slit the throat of your sleepy old hero. You don't want that, do you?"

Misha drew a long-bladed stiletto from an ankle sheath and brandished it under Eva's chin.

"I think he's quite eager to use that," observed Kosov. "Aren't you, Misha?"

Eva saw feral eyes glinting in the dark.

"Now, where did Frau Apfel get out?"

Eva struggled to think through the pain of the blows and her growing apprehension that she would not survive the night. How long had Ernst evaded the black sedan? Two minutes? Three? With his taxi finally trapped in the dead-end lane beside the Lietzensee lake, the old cabbie had done his best to fend the Russians off, but the young KGB agents had simply been too agile for him. How far could Ilse have gotten in that time?

Without warning Misha savagely thrust his knee into Eva's left breast, crushing it—

"All *right*!" she gasped.

The pressure eased a little. "You have regained your memory?" Kosov asked.

Perhaps they'll spare Ernst, Eva thought. *Swine*. "We stopped two or three blocks back," she whispered. "When we rounded a corner. Ilse jumped out there."

"Sko'lka?" asked Kosov. "Two blocks or three? Which is it?"

Again Misha jabbed his knee forward. *"Stop!"* Eva begged. "Please!" She could fight no more, but she could fire a last covering shot. "Three blocks," she lied, laboring for breath. "The Seehof Hotel ... by the lake. She ran inside."

Kosov nodded. "That wasn't so difficult, was it?"

Eva gulped air like a landed fish.

Kosov sighed angrily, debating with himself. How in hell was he supposed to find the Spandau papers? Three times Moscow had signaled him, each time telling him just a little more about the Hess case, doling out information like scraps of meat to a dog. Names without physical descriptions, dates of events Kosov had never heard of. And at the center of it all, apparently, a one-eyed man who had no name. Kosov could make no sense of it. And of course that was how Moscow wanted it.

"Now that you're talking," he said amiably, "I have one more question. Did Frau Apfel mention any *names* in connection with what her husband found?"

"No," Eva groaned. "She told me someone was after her, that's all. I didn't ask—"

Unbelievably, Misha's knee buried itself still deeper into Eva's chest. The pain was excruciating. She felt as if she were going to vomit. *"Please!"* she choked.

The pressure relented just enough for her to take a shallow breath. Kosov heaved a bearlike shoulder over the front seat and bellowed, "Names, woman! *Names* are what I want! Did Frau Apfel mention the name Zinoviev to you? Do you hear me? Z-I-N-O-V-I-E-V. It's a Russian name. Did she mention it?"

Eva shook her head violently. She had passed the point of being able to lie, and something in her eyes must have shown it. After several moments Kosov nodded, and Misha removed his knee from her chest. The old colonel's face softened.

"Unlike my young friend," he murmured, "I do not believe in needless killing. However, if you are lying—that is, if we do not find Frau Apfel, or if you feel the sudden urge to speak to the authorities—well, quite obviously we know where to find you. And we *will* find you. I would send Misha personally. Do you understand?"

Eva lay as still as she could. The animals were going to let her live. *"Ja,"* she breathed.

"Good." Kosov climbed out of the old taxi. "Misha, a reminder."

With an expert flick of his stiletto, the young KGB agent opened a two-inch gash along Eva's left cheek. Eva shrieked in pain. Misha grinned, watching her struggle in vain to reach the wound and stop the bleeding. As the young Russian backed out of the taxi, Kosov's hard face appeared in the front window.

"Free her hands," he ordered.

Cursing quietly, Misha slashed the stockings over Eva's head. But instead of getting out of the car, he thrust his hand viciously beneath Eva's skirt and clenched her pubic mound in a clawlike fist. With flashing eyes he leaned close so that Kosov couldn't hear. "When I find your little friend," he snarled, "the pretty one—she's going to bleed, old woman. *Everywhere.*" He wrenched his hand away, tearing hair and skin as he backed out of the taxi.

Shaking like an epileptic, Eva turned away and tried to stanch the flow of blood from her lacerated face. She heard Kosov's BMW skid around and speed down the Lietzensee-Ufer in the direction of the Seehof Hotel. "Screw you," she spat. "*Swine.* You'll never find her." Slowly she leaned forward and put her bloody hand to the old cabbie's forehead. "Ernst, are you all right? Poor darling, you fought well for an old soldier. Wake up for Eva."

The old man didn't move.

If only some of my old friends were here, Eva lamented. *That young pig's balls would be meat for the dogs.*

Ernst groaned and jerked forward in his seat. *"Wo sind sie!"* he cried, flailing his arms.

"They're gone," Eva said, soothing his forehead with a knowing hand. "All gone. You can take me home now, my brave knight. We'll mend our scratches together."

10:33 P.M. South African Airspace: 100 km Northeast of Pretoria

The JetRanger helicopter stormed northward beneath a moonless African sky, startling flocks of black heron, spooking herds of impala and zebra gathered around the waterholes on the *veld* below. Inside the chopper's luxurious cabin, Alfred Horn sat gripping the arms of his wheelchair, which was bolted to the carpeted deck by specially designed fittings. Pieter Smuts, Horn's Afrikaner security chief, leaned closer to his master and spoke above the low beating drone of the rotor blades.

"I wanted to wait until we were airborne to tell you, sir."

The old man nodded slowly. "What is so important that you don't even trust your own security?"

"We've received the new figures from Britain, sir. The American figures. They were delivered by courier just an hour ago."

"The Bikini figures?"

"More than that. Sixty-five percent of American test data from Eniwetok Atoll in 'fifty-two up to the test ban in 'sixty-three." The Afrikaner shook his head. "Sir, you can't imagine what a one megaton surface blast will actually do."

"Yes, I can, Pieter."

"It leaves a crater one mile across and sixteen stories deep. Christ, we've got the design, the plants ... If we had six months, we could probably divert—"

"I'll be dead in six months!" Horn snapped. "What do these figures tell you about our current resources?"

"The blast effects will be greater than we predicted. Using round figures, a forty-kiloton air burst should vaporize everything within three kilometers of ground zero. Intense heat will incinerate anything for a five-kilometer radius beyond that. And the resulting winds and fires will wreak havoc for a considerable distance beyond those already mentioned."

"And the fallout?" Horn asked.

"Twenty percent higher than we predicted."

Horn digested this without emotion. "And these figures . . . you believe they are more reliable than our own?"

"Sir, except for the secret Indian Ocean test, all South African figures are purely theoretical. By definition they are predictions. The American figures represent verified data."

Horn nodded thoughtfully. "Apply them to our scenario."

"Everything depends on the target, sir. Obviously, ground-zero at the center of Tel Aviv or Jerusalem would obliterate either city. But if the weapon were used at the right time, its effects could be greatly enhanced, possibly even doubled, by a collateral factor: the weather."

"How?"

"By the *wind,* sir. At this time of year the prevailing winds in Israel blow southeast. If the weapon were detonated in Jerusalem, the fallout would probably dissipate over Jordan. But if it were detonated in Tel Aviv, not only would it obliterate the city, but it might well spread a lethal blanket of strontium-90 over Jerusalem within one or two hours."

Horn closed his eyes and sighed with satisfaction. "And if we get the cobalt-seeded bomb case in time?"

The Afrikaner turned his palms upward. "We won't, sir. Not sooner than twenty days. The technical problems are formidable."

"But if we *did* get it?"

Smuts pursed his lips. "With a cobalt-seeded bomb case and the revised yield figures, I'd say . . . sixty percent of the Israeli population would be dead within fourteen days, and Palestine would be rendered uninhabitable for at least a decade."

Horn let out a long sigh. "Increase the bounty, Pieter. Five million rand in gold to the team that delivers a cobalt bomb case within seven days."

"Yes, sir."

"Do we have any further information on the Israeli doctrinal response?"

Smuts shook his head. "Our London source dried up after we requested the American satellite photos. Frankly, I don't even trust his initial reports on that subject."

"Why?"

"Do you really think Israel would target Russian cities?"

Horn smiled. "Of course. It's the only way the Jews could win a war against a united Arab force. They must be able to prevent Soviet resupply of the Arabs, and the only way they can do that is to blackmail the Soviets. What do they have to lose by doing so?"

"But the deployment plan for Israel's nuclear arsenal is the most closely guarded secret in the world. How could our London source know what he claims to know?"

Horn smiled. "Not the most closely guarded secret, Pieter. No one has yet proved that South Africa's nuclear arsenal even exists."

"Thanks in no small part to us," Smuts observed. The Afrikaner began cracking his knuckles. "The Russian matter aside, I think we can safely assume that if Tel Aviv or Jerusalem were destroyed, Israel would go beyond a measured response. If they knew the source of the attack, they would respond with a significant portion of their 'black' bomber and missile forces."

"They will know the source of the attack," Horn rasped.

"There is one unpredictable factor," Smuts said carefully. "If our clients were to detonate the weapon at Dimona, Israel's weapons-production plant, there is a slight chance that the rest of the world might believe the explosion to be a genuine Israeli accident. The Americans might coerce the Jews into waiting until an outside investigation was completed. By that time cooler heads might prevail."

Horn made a dismissive gesture with his skeletal arm. "Don't worry. I'm relying on Arab impatience, not stupidity. Hussein, Assad, these men might have the self-control to wait and try to develop a cohesive plan. Not our friend. He will strike swiftly. Consider how quickly he agreed to our meeting. He won't purposefully hit Jerusalem—there are too many sacred Muslim sites there. And the security around Dimona is airtight. We needn't worry on that score. The target will be Tel Aviv."

Horn's one living eye focused on the Afrikaner. "What of the Spandau matter, Pieter? Have they captured the traitor? Have they found the papers?"

"Not yet, sir. Berlin-One assures me it is only a matter of time. However, I received a call from his immediate subordinate, Berlin-Two. He's a lieutenant, I believe. Jürgen Luhr."

"And?"

"Lieutenant Luhr doesn't feel the prefect is up to the job. He's moved some of our German assets into play without the prefect's knowledge. He checked the files on the two missing officers and dispatched men to all locations they might possibly run to. I approved his action. Who knows what those *Bruderschaft* clowns are really doing. A little competition might speed up the capture."

"I'm surprised that these policemen were able to escape at all," Horn remarked.

Smuts shifted uncomfortably. "I did a little checking on my own, sir. The man who betrayed us—Hauer—he's quite an officer, it seems. An ex-soldier. Even the young man with him was decorated for bravery."

Horn raised a long, crooked finger in Smuts's tanned face. "Never underestimate the German soldier, Pieter. He is the toughest in the world. Let this be a lesson to you."

Smuts colored. "Yes, sir."

"Keep me posted hourly. I'm anxious to see how this ex-soldier does."

"You almost sound as if you want them to escape."

"Nonsense, Pieter. By getting hold of the Spandau papers, we might well buy ourselves extra time. At least we can keep the Russians and the Jews out of our business, if not the British. But that's it, you see. At this moment MI-5, the KGB, and the Mossad must be scouring Berlin for our two German policemen, yet so far they have failed to capture them. If these men live up to their racial heritage, I suspect they will manage to evade their pursuers. In the end we will have to find them ourselves."

The Afrikaner nodded. "I'll find them."

Horn smiled coldly. "I know you will, Pieter. If this Hauer but knew you as I do, he would already have given himself up."

CHAPTER NINE

10:35 P.M. *Goethestrasse: West Berlin*

"There," Hauer grunted. He had wedged Hans's Volkswagen so tightly between two parked cars that the one behind would have to be moved to reveal the license plate. "All right, where's the house?"

"I'm not sure," Hans replied, peering through his window. "I've never been here before."

"Are you joking?"

"No."

Hauer stared in disbelief. "So why are we here?"

"Because it's just what you asked for—a place we can't be traced to."

Hans climbed out of the VW and started up the deserted street, skirting the pools of light from the street lamps. "That's it," he said, glancing back over his shoulder. Hauer followed a few paces behind. "See it? Eleven-fifty."

"Quiet!" said Hauer. "You'll wake the whole block."

Hans was already halfway up the walk. He rapped loudly on the front door, waited half a minute, then knocked again. Finally, a muffled voice came from behind the wood.

"I'm coming already!"

Someone fumbled with the latch, then the door opened wide. Standing in a pair of blue silk pajamas, a tiny man with silver hair and a tuft of beard squinted through the darkness. He reached for a light switch.

"Please leave the light off, Herr Ochs," Hans said.

"What? Who are you?" Finally the uniform registered in the old man's brain. "Polizei," he murmured. "Is there some problem?"

Hans stepped closer. He took the tattered business card

from his pocket and handed it to the old man. "I don't know if you remember me, Herr Ochs, but you said that if I ever needed a favor—"

"*Gott im Himmel!*" Ochs cried, his eyes wide. "Sergeant Apfel!"

Hans nodded. "That's right. I'm sorry to disturb you at this hour, but there's an emergency. My captain and I need to make some telephone calls. We can't use the station just now—"

"Say no more, Sergeant. Come inside. Did I not tell you? Ben Ochs knows how to return a favor. And what a favor! Bernice!"

An even tinier gray-haired woman appeared behind Ochs. She stared at the uniforms with trepidation. "What is it, Benjamin?"

"It's young Hans Apfel! He needs our help. Get your slippers, Bernice. We'll need some tea and . . ." Ochs trailed off, noticing the large bruise at the base of Hans's skull, a souvenir of Rolf's lead pipe. "Something stronger, I think."

"Please," said Hans, following the old man inside, "all we need is a telephone."

"Nonsense, you look terrible. You need food, and something to calm your nerves. Bernice?"

Frau Ochs bustled into the kitchen, talking all the way. "There's chicken in the refrigerator, boys, and cabbage too. It's no feast, but this is very short notice."

The old tailor pulled two chairs from beneath the kitchen table; Hans immediately collapsed into one. The Ochses' kindness seemed otherworldly after the events of the past four hours. Hans felt as if he'd been running for days.

Hauer had been too amazed by the warm reception to say anything. Summoning a smile, he extended his hand to Ochs. "*Guten Abend*, Herr Ochs. I'm Captain Dieter Hauer."

Ochs nodded respectfully.

"I'm afraid Hans is right. A rather special situation has arisen. I myself believe it's just another of the endless exercises they put us through, but of course we never know for sure. If we could just use your telephone for a few minutes, we would be gone before you know it."

Ochs nodded again, slower this time. "You are a poor liar, Captain. But I count that in your favor. Most honest men make poor liars. If you're anything like your young friend, you are always welcome in my house. This boy"—Ochs grinned and patted Hans on the shoulder—"this boy saved my life. Three years ago I was trapped in a burning car, and Hans was the only man who had the nerve to get me out."

The light of realization dawned on Hauer's face. Only now did he notice the old man's left hand; it was withered and covered with scar tissue from a deep burn.

Ochs shook his head in wonder. "I thought he was trying to kill me! He blasted out the window right over my head!" The old man laughed and stepped over to the counter. "Here is the chicken," he said. Then he held up a dark bottle his wife had pulled from a high cabinet. "And here is some *bromfn*—brandy—for the nerves. We'll leave you to your business now. Come along, Bernice." Taking his wife under his silk-covered arm, Benjamin Ochs left the kitchen without looking back.

"Unbelievable," said Hauer, shaking his head.

Hans snatched up the telephone and dialed the apartment. He heard three rings . . . four . . . then someone picked up. He waited for Ilse's voice, but heard only silence. "Ilse?" he said finally. "*Liebchen?* Are you there?"

A brittle male voice chilled him to the bone. "*Guten Abend*, Sergeant. I'm afraid your wife is unable to get to the phone just now."

"*Who is this?*" Hans shouted. "Let me speak to my wife!"

Hauer signaled him to keep his voice down, but Hans ignored the warning. "Put my wife on the phone!"

"As I said," the voice continued, "the lovely *Frau* is occupied just now. Indisposed, let us say. If you wish to speak to her, it would be much quicker for you to come here."

"I'm on my way, you bastard! If she's harmed in any way, I'll—" Hans looked at Hauer in a daze. The line had gone dead. He slammed down the phone. "They have her! We've got to get to the apartment!"

He was halfway to the foyer when Hauer barked, "Wait!"

Hans whirled. "*Wait?* Have you lost your mind?"

Hauer's voice went flat. "You won't get far without keys."

Hans groped in his pockets. "Give them to me," he said quietly.

"I can't, Hans. You're making a mistake."

Hans took a step forward. "Give me my keys."

Hauer shook his head. "You don't *know* they have Ilse. You didn't actually speak to her."

"*Give me my goddamn keys!*" Hans sprang forward, ready

to thrash Hauer until he gave up the keys. But when he raised his hands to Hauer's neck, he felt something hard pressing into his stomach. When he looked down, he saw a 9mm Walther P1 pistol, standard issue for the West Berlin police.

"Now," said Hauer, "you're going to sit there quietly while I make a phone call. Then we'll decide what to do about Ilse."

"Don't you understand?" Hans pleaded. "They have my wife! I *have* to go! You ... you ..."—his voice changed suddenly—"you *don't* understand, do you? You never had a wife. You ran out on the one woman who loved you! My mother!"

"That's a lie," Hauer whispered.

Hans's face burned with emotion. "It isn't! You ran out on her when she was pregnant! Pregnant with me! Give me those keys, you son of a bitch!"

Hauer had gone very still. His big fists were clenched— one around the butt of the Walther. "You think you know something about me," he said. "You don't know anything. A file isn't a man, Hans. Yes, I know you went through my personnel file." He worked his left fist angrily. "I don't know if you deserve the truth, but the truth is that I didn't know I had a son until you were twelve years old."

"You're lying!" Hans insisted. But something about that age had sparked a strange light behind his eyes.

"I'm not," Hauer said softly. "Think back. You were twelve years old."

Hans felt his chest tightening. The pain in his eyes told Hauer that he had remembered. "I knew you couldn't have forgotten that," Hauer said. "It was bad. Munich, the day after the Olympic massacre. Did you ever make that connection?"

Hans looked away.

Hauer spoke quickly, as if the words burned his mouth passing through it. "It was the lowest point in my life. Those Jewish athletes died for nothing, Hans. Because of German arrogance and stupidity. Just like in the war. And I was a part of it. I'd been flown into Munich as a sharpshooter ..." Hauer seemed about to continue the story—then he stopped, realizing that one more telling wouldn't change anything. "After the slaughter was over," he murmured, "I went crazy. Went off on my own. I needed something—a human touch, a lifeline. And there I was in the city my old lover had run off to, totally by chance. After a dozen schnapps, though, I started thinking maybe it wasn't by chance. So I went looking for your mother."

"You found her."

"I found *you*. You were the last thing in the world I expected. Your mother called the Munich police on me, of course. My showing up after all those years was her worst nightmare. But the moment I saw you, Hans, I knew you were mine. I *knew* it. She didn't even try to deny it." Hauer's eyes focused on the kitchen floor. "But she had me over a barrel, Hans. Somehow they'd fixed it—her and her rich husband—so that he'd legally adopted you. I paid a lawyer two months' salary to look into it, but in the end he told me to forget it. Your mother had already poisoned you against me, anyway—she let me know that before anything else." Hauer looked up into Hans's eyes. "What did she tell you about that day?"

Hans shrugged. "She told me who you were. That you were my real father. But she said you'd only come back to ask for money. To beg for a loan."

Hauer looked stunned.

"I don't think I believed her, though," Hans said softly, "even then. Not deep down. You know what I remember about that day?"

Hauer shook his head.

"Your uniform. A perfect green uniform with medals on the chest. I never forgot that. And when the police showed up to take you away, you showed them your badge and they went away instead."

Hauer swallowed hard. "Is that why you became a policeman?"

"Partly, I guess. I really became a cop because it was absolutely the worst thing I could do in Mother's eyes. She'd spent twenty years trying to mold me into a banker, like her first husband. And I guess he wasn't so bad, really, looking back. But when she married that goddamn lawyer, I started to hate her. She was so transparent ... always trying to buy respect. And I hated her more because I knew that in some twisted way she was doing it all for me. After she married the lawyer, I wanted to hurt her as much as she'd hurt me. And the best way to do that was to become everything she had run away from when she was young. To become a working-class slave, just like you." Hans laughed. "Then I found out I liked the job. What would Freud say about that, I wonder?"

Hauer forced a smile.

"I believe what you've told me," Hans said. "But when I showed up in Berlin wearing this uniform, why didn't you tell me your side of it?"

"That was ten years after Munich," Hauer explained. "Long before then I'd resigned myself to the fact that I'd have to live the rest of my life without you, or any family. When you came marching up to me outside that police station, with a hundred-pound chip on your shoulder and reciting that stupid agreement you'd worked out, I didn't know what to think. You'd already come that far back to me on your own . . . I wasn't going to rush anything."

Hans nodded. "I wanted to make it on my own. I didn't want any help from you. And no matter how much I hated Mother then, I wasn't ready to find out the truth about you. Not if the truth was that you really had run out on us."

"She never told me she was pregnant, Hans. It's an old story. I was good enough to fall in love with, but not to marry. It's sad, really. She hadn't grown up any better than I had, but she'd set her sights on marrying rich. Fear of poverty, I guess. She did love me, I still believe that. But there was no way her kid was going to be raised by a cop. She wanted it all for you, Hans, *gymnasium*, university—"

"You don't have to tell me," Hans cut in. "I know it all by heart."

"But what I can't forgive is her putting it all on me. Making me out to be . . . Christ, I don't know."

"It's okay. It is. How could she tell me it was her fault I didn't have a father?" Hans's eyes fell on the face of his watch. He looked up quickly. Hauer was still pointing the Walther at him.

"I know what you're thinking," Hauer said. "Don't try it. Look, if whoever was in your apartment really had Ilse, they would have put her on the phone. They'd have made *her* draw you. It's you they want—or what you found."

"But you can't *know* that. What if she's hurt? What if she couldn't speak? What if she's *dead*?"

Hauer lowered the pistol a few centimeters. "I concede those possibilities. But we're *not* going to charge into a situation we know nothing about to die like romantic fools.

First we must know if we are being hunted officially." He picked up the telephone with his left hand and punched in a number. "I want you to think of any possible places Ilse might have run to, or even gone innocently. And Hans— think like a policeman, *not* a husband. That, if anything, will save your wife." With a last look at Hans, he stuck the Walther into his belt.

Hans felt his fists quivering. A wild voice told him to bash Hauer's skull and take the car keys, that quick action was Ilse's only chance. But his police experience told him that Hauer—that his *father*—was right.

"Communications desk," Hauer said curtly.

"Who's calling?"

"*Telefon.* There's a line problem."

"Hold, *bitte.*"

Hauer put his hand over the mouthpiece. "Pray Steuben's still on duty," he whispered.

"This is Sergeant Steuben," said a deep voice. "We have no line problem."

"Steuben—"

"*Dieter?* My God! Where are you?"

"Let's just say I'm still under my own recognizance."

Steuben's voice dropped to a whisper. "You're damned lucky. Funk has an army out looking for you and that young sergeant. They're watching all the checkpoints— everywhere."

"I knew they'd come after us, but I didn't think they'd make such a fuss about it. Shine too much light on us, and some inevitably shines on them."

"No, Dieter, listen. They're saying that you and—"

"Apfel."

"Yes, they're saying that you and Apfel killed Erhard Weiss. They're playing it like a simple murder. They brought Weiss's body up from the basement and paraded a few lieutenants and pressmen through. I'll tell you, Dieter, some of the boys were pretty upset. The story is that you and Apfel were tied into organized crime and Weiss found out. Most don't quite believe you did it, but everyone's damned angry. You'd better walk softly if you come up on any old friends."

"I understand, Josef. What about that other matter?"

"Another call went out from an empty office about 16:30 this afternoon—same destination."

"Pretoria?"

"Right." Steuben's voice dropped lower. "Dieter," he said hesitantly, "you didn't really kill young Weiss, did you?"

"My God, Josef, you know better than that!"

Steuben hesitated. "What about Apfel? I don't know him."

"He tried to save the boy! They were comrades. *Think*, Josef. Weiss was Jewish—that doesn't lead you anywhere?"

Steuben's reply was almost inaudible. "Phoenix."

"Yes. I've got to go now. I want you to stay on duty as long as you can, Josef. You're my last link to that place. Someone's *got* to watch them. And watch yourself, too. Now that I've shown my true colors, they'll start looking for others. They know we were friends. I'll use the same story when I call back—*Telefon.*"

"Don't worry," Steuben whispered. "I'm here for the duration. But ... I'm worried about my family, Dieter. My wife, my little girls. Did you cover them?"

"Just as I promised. There are two men with them now, good friends of mine. GSG-9 veterans. No worries there. Funk couldn't get into your house with anything less than a full-scale military assault."

"Thank you, my friend."

"*Auf Wiedersehen,* Josef."

Before Hauer could set the phone in its cradle, Hans broke the connection and punched in a new number.

"Who are you calling?" Hauer asked.

"None of your goddamn business," Hans snapped. "You can cover your friends with GSG-9 men, but you can't take twenty minutes to save Ilse?"

"Hans, you don't understand—"

"Eva?" he said loudly.

"Hans!"

"Yes. Eva, I want you to look outside your door and—"

"*Listen to me, Hans!* Someone is tearing your apartment to pieces right now! That tells me they haven't found her yet!"

"What? You've seen Ilse?"

"*Seen* her? I sneaked her out of the apartment tonight just before the stinking Russians got her! What the hell have you done?"

"Russians!"

Hans's exclamation brought Hauer out of his chair like a cannon shot.

"Tell me, Eva, hurry!"

Eva related the story of their escape from Kosov's team, ending with Ilse fleeing into the dark alley. Hans slammed his fist against the table. "But you don't know where she is now?"

"No, but she told me to give you a message."

"What message?"

"Mittelland."

"That's it? One word?"

"That's it. Mittelland, like the canal. I guess she didn't want me to know anything."

Hans shook his fist in exultation. "Eva, that's it! I know where she's gone."

"So get her, you damned fool! And you'd better get some serious help. I don't think your Polizei friends are up to it." She paused. "And if you come up on a young fellow called Misha . . ."

"Yes?"

"Kill the bastard. Send him to hell. He cut my face."

Hans felt his heart thump. "What happened?"

"Just find Ilse, Hans. If anything happens to that girl, you're going to answer to me. And stay the hell away from here. Your apartment sounds like a Bremen bar fight." Eva hung up.

Hauer grabbed Hans's shoulder. "You said Russians."

"Eva said Russians came to the apartment looking for me."

"How does she know they were Russian?"

Hans shrugged. "She's been around, you know? She's an old barmaid who turns a few tricks for rent money. She got Ilse out of the building, but that's all she could tell me."

"It must be Kosov," Hauer muttered. "The quiet colonel from Funk's polygraph session. He knew that test was rigged from the start. Did Ilse have the papers with her?"

"I don't know."

"For God's sake, Hans, you've got to start thinking like a policeman."

"I don't give a *damn* about those papers!"

"Quiet! You'll bring Ochs in here. And you'd better give a damn about those papers. They may be the only thing that can keep us or Ilse alive now." He held up a forefinger. "You said you knew where Ilse had gone. Where?"

Hans's eyes narrowed. "Why should I tell you?" he asked, suddenly suspicious. "Christ, you might have brought me here just to find out where she is. Where the *papers* are! God, you might—"

Hauer slapped him, hard. "Get hold of yourself, Hans! You brought me here, remember? You've got to trust somebody, and I'm all you have."

Hans scowled. "Wolfsburg," he said quietly.

"What?"

"Ilse's grandfather has a small cabin on the Mittelland Canal, near Wolfsburg. It's an old family retreat. The professor must have been working there and Ilse found out. God, I hope she's made it." His face clouded. "But how could she? I've got the car!"

"Train?" Hauer suggested.

"She didn't have any money at home."

"All women have money at home, Hans, believe me. They hide it for emergencies we never think about."

"Captain, I've got to get to Wolfsburg!"

"I agree. But before I give you the keys, you're going to listen to me for ten minutes. Then I'll figure out a way for us to get out of Berlin. You know you'd never make it without my help."

Hans knew Hauer was right. He could never evade Funk's dragnet on his own. "Ten minutes," he agreed.

Hauer sat down and leaned forward. "You've got to understand something, Hans. Early this morning you stumbled into a case that I've been working on for over a year. That's what I meant about Steuben. There's more that needs protecting at his house than his wife and children. There's a fireproof safe full of evidence that he and I have compiled over the past year. Until a couple of hours ago, I had no idea that Spandau Prison had anything to do with this case, but now I'm almost certain that it does."

"What the hell are you talking about?"

"Those papers you found at Spandau aren't just some relic from the past, Hans. The Russians haven't gone crazy searching for a museum piece. Those papers pose a very serious threat to someone *now*—in the *present*."

Hauer took a cigar from his pocket and bit off the tip. "Before I tell you anything else, you must understand some-

thing very important. Right now, as we speak, Germany—
the two Germanys—are very close to reunification."

"*What?*"

"I don't mean it's going to happen tomorrow, or next
week. But six months from now ... a year ... maybe."

"Are you mad?"

Hauer paused to light his cigar. "Most Germans would say
so," he said. "And they would be as wrong as you are. Tell
me, as you grew up, didn't you notice all the societies who
clamor for the reunification of the Fatherland? I don't mean
administrative committees plodding through mountains of
paper; I mean the hard-core groups, the ones that exist only
to restore Germany's lost might."

Hans shrugged. "Sure. So what? What's wrong with
working to make Germany strong? I agree with them. Not
some of the crazier factions, maybe, but I want Germany to
be united again. One nation, without the Wall."

Hauer raised an eyebrow.

Hans colored. "It's my country, isn't it? I want it to be
strong!"

"Of course you do, boy. So do I. But there are different
kinds of strength. Some of these groups have some very
strange ideals. Old ideals. Old *agendas.*"

"What do you mean? How do you know?"

Hauer studied his cigar. "Because we've been to their
meetings—Steuben and I. I stumbled into this whole thing
by accident. About two years ago, I got drawn into a Special
Tasks drug case. The money trail led me to two police officers. In short order I became aware that quite a few cops
were involved in the drug traffic flowing into and through
Germany. And in spite of orders to the contrary, I began to
compile evidence on these officers. Steuben helped me all
the way. It didn't take us long to realize that their drug operation extended into the highest ranks of the force."

"Prefect Funk?"

"Excellent example. But then things got strange. Pretty
soon we discerned a pattern. Every officer involved in the
drug traffic was also a member of a semisecret society called
Der Bruderschaft."

"The Brotherhood? I've heard of that."

Hauer exhaled a cloud of blue smoke. "I'm not surprised.
I joined it myself last year. That's what the tattoo is about.
The eye is their symbol. Ever see a policeman with a band-

age behind his right ear? That means he's gotten the mark. They wear the bandage till the hair grows back. I don't know what the eye means, but I was only a month away from getting it myself. You get marked after a year in the group." Hauer stood up and flicked some cigar ash into Ochs's sink. "The real name of the organization is not *Der Bruderschaft*, however; it's *Bruderschaft der Phoenix*. Have you heard of that?"

Hans's eyes widened. "I have! It was in the Spandau papers. Something about the 'soldiers of Phoenix' appearing before Prisoner Number Seven."

"Christ, what else do you remember?"

Hans shook his head. "I only remembered that because it was in German, not Latin."

Hauer began pacing the kitchen. "God, it's so easy to see now. *Der Bruderschaft* is neo-Nazi. It would only be natural for them to try to contact Hess in prison, to try to use him as some kind of mascot. But maybe Hess didn't like the idea, eh? Maybe—my God," Hauer said suddenly. "They might well be the ones who killed him! Hess would be much more valuable to them as a martyr than a pathetic prisoner!"

"Who comes to these *Bruderschaft* meetings?" Hans asked.

"A bunch of malcontents and young toughs, mostly. You know the type—cops who won't answer a call to help a Turkish woman who's being beaten in the street. Most weren't even born until fifteen or twenty years after the war." Hauer shook his head in disgust. "They get drunk, argue, make speeches about throwing the traitors out of Bonn and making Berlin the capital again. Then they sing *Deutschland über Alles.* If they're really tanked they sing the *Horst Wessel.* At first the whole thing seemed comical. But after a while I realized something. These clowns were bringing in millions of marks through their drug operations, yet they didn't seem to be *keeping* any of it. No Ferraris, no new houses. Where was all the money going? I traced the command chain all the way up to Prefect Funk, but after six months of investigation I hit a dead end."

Hauer's eyes flickered. "Then I had my revelation. It had been right in front of me all the time. Their money came from drugs, right? Well, where do the drugs flow in from?"

"The East," Hans said softly.

"Right. So I asked myself, What if their organization extended *laterally,* not vertically? You see? How were the drugs getting through East Germany? Were the Vopos blind? Hell no. They were *allowing* the drugs to get through. The East German police have their own *Bruderschaft* members."

Hans blinked in astonishment. "The *Volkspolizei?*"

Hauer nodded. "And the Stasi."

Hans drew back at the mention of the hated East German secret police. "But why would the Stasi smuggle drugs? For hard currency?"

Hauer shook his head. "Think about being a Stasi agent for a minute, Hans. What it's really like."

"No thanks."

Hauer waved his cigar. "Sure, a lot of them are scum. But they're *German* scum. You see? All day and night they have the Russians leaning over their shoulders telling them what to do. They hate the Russians more than we ever could. They're communists, sure, but what choice do they have? They've been under the Russian boot since 1945. So, what do you think they do? Lie down and take Moscow's crap? Most of them do." Hauer's eyes gleamed. "But some of them *don't.* The HVA—East German intelligence—sucks Moscow's shitpipe. They're like a German arm of the KGB. But the Stasi? Forget it. They go their own way. They can beat the KGB at their own game and the KGB knows it. If Moscow complains about the Stasi, Honecker himself tells the Kremlin to mind its own business."

"You sound like you admire the bastards."

Hauer shook his head. "This isn't a case of absolutes, Hans. The point is that some elements of the Stasi want re-unification even more than we in the West do, and they're willing to fight for it. They want their slice of the European economic pie, and they know that so long as they're separate from us, they'll never get it. And *that* brings us to the drugs."

"How? Drugs are their slice of the pie?"

"No. Drugs are part of the strategy. I think their theory runs something like this: the more rapidly the social situation in West Germany breaks down, the more rapidly the right-wing and nationalist factions in the West consolidate their power. Think about it. For twenty years the Stasi supplied the Red Army Faction and other left-wing terrorists with guns and plastique. Why? Just to create chaos? *No.* Because every time those misguided hotheads blew up a bank or an airport lounge, the right wing in the West hit back a little bit harder. The public reaction got a little stiffer. I'm telling you, Hans, it's a sound strategy. Moscow has never been more lenient than it is *right now*. The entire Eastern Bloc is restless. Trouble and sedition are brewing everywhere. And East Germany is the most independent satellite of all. The Stasi monitors everything there: student unrest, political volatility, economic stress, plus they have that rarest of all commodities, direct intelligence lines into Russia. I think *Der Bruderschaft*—and whoever controls it—believes that a strong enough chancellor in West Germany could seize the right opportunity and wrench the two Germanys back together." Hauer was breathing hard. "And by God, they may be right."

Hans stared, fascinated. "Is the Stasi really as powerful as people say? I've heard they have hundreds of informers here and in Bonn."

Hauer chuckled. "Hundreds? Try thousands. If I had the files from Stasi headquarters, I could break half the political careers in West Germany and a good many in Moscow. I mean that. Some of our most powerful senators are actually on the Stasi payroll. Funk is just small beer."

Hans was shaking his head. "Do you really believe all this?"

Hauer shrugged. "I don't know. One minute I believe every word of it, the next I wonder if schnapps has pickled my brain. When I stand in those *Bruderschaft* meetings, I want to laugh. Funk and his rabble are just grown-up children fantasizing about a Fourth Reich. It's classic infantile bullshit. Germany will be united again, don't doubt it. But not by drunk policemen or skinheads. It's the bankers and board chairmen who'll bring it off. Men from the world your mother worshipped. We're the richest country in Europe now, Hans, and *anything* can be bought for a price. Even a united Germany."

Hauer tugged at his mustache. "The question is this: Is there a connection between *Der Bruderschaft* and those bankers and board chairmen? And if so, what is it? How much power does Phoenix exert over the *institutions* in Germany? The Stasi's potential for blackmail is formidable. Funk's group may seem like clowns, but no matter how you look at it, the Polizei are an arm of the state."

Hans look confused. "But how could all this tie in with the Spandau papers? With Ilse?"

"*Bruderschaft der Phoenix*, remember? Phoenix was mentioned in the Spandau papers, therefore it ties Funk and the Stasi to the papers. Your hooker friend said Russians came looking for you and chased Ilse. The Russians went on the rampage when you discovered the Spandau papers. Do the Russians know about Phoenix? Maybe they've infiltrated *Der Bruderschaft* through the Stasi. Maybe they suspect the Stasi's role in a grab for reunification. What the hell *is* Phoenix? A man? A group of men? At one *Bruderschaft* meeting I heard Funk—who was drunk out of his mind—babbling about how Phoenix was going to change the world, make everything right again, clean out the Jews and the Turks once and for all. But when I tried to pump him, Lieutenant Luhr shut him up."

Hauer shifted in the small chair. "Whatever Phoenix is, I'm almost certain it's based outside Germany. About a month ago, Steuben started noticing calls going out from Funk to different towns in South Africa. I assumed it was more drug business, looking for new markets, et cetera. But I don't think that anymore. Hans, I think you have dredged up something so politically hot that we can't even imagine it. I hope Ilse managed to get those papers to Wolfsburg, but whether she did or not, we won't get out of Berlin by driving your VW through Checkpoint Charlie. We've got to take precautions, make arrangements. People owe me—"

"Pardon me," said a soft voice from the shadows.

Hauer turned in his chair. Benjamin Ochs stood silhouetted against the lighted hall door. "Forgive me," he said, "but the shouting alarmed my wife. Could I join you for a moment?" The old man shuffled into the kitchen and took a seat at the table. He poured a brandy into one of the unused tumblers his wife had set down earlier, drank it, then wiped his mouth on his pajama sleeve. "I know what you're thinking, Captain," he said. "How much did the old goat hear, yes? Well, I'll tell you. I didn't hear everything, but I heard enough. I wish I'd heard damned all. What I heard . . . God help us. You never said it, but I know what you were talking about. Are you afraid to say it?"

"I'm not sure what you mean," Hauer said.

"Nazis!" Ochs cried, his wizened head shaking. "That's what you're talking about. Isn't it? And not just a pack of hooligans desecrating Jewish cemeteries. You're talking about *policemen*—professional men, bankers, board chairmen!"

"You misunderstood, Herr Ochs. It's not so bad as that."

"Captain, it's probably *worse* than that. Don't you know what the Phoenix *is?* It's the bird that perishes in the fire only to be reborn from its ashes." The old tailor drew himself up to his full height. "I am a Jew, Captain, a *German* Jew. Before the war there were 160,000 of us here in Berlin. Now we are 7,000. I was not a child during the war. While you hunted scraps in the streets, I existed in a place you cannot imagine. Beyond hope, outside of time. I lost my entire family—parents, brother, two sisters—at this place. While they passed into oblivion, I sewed uniforms for the German Army. I *lived* while my family died. I promise you, Captain, no uniforms were ever more poorly made than those Benjamin Ochs made for the *Wehrmacht*. Every bit of skill I had went into producing a uniform that would last just long enough to get a soldier to the frozen Russian front, then fall into pieces fit only for a shroud." Ochs raised his withered hand. "If you protect such men, Captain, I tell you now to get out of my house. Now! But if you mean to fight them . . . then let me help you. Tell me what you need."

Hans sat speechless, but Hauer lost no time taking advantage of his offer. "We need a car," he said.

"Done," Ochs said simply.

"We need something to wear besides these uniforms. Do you have anything that might fit us well enough not to draw attention?"

Ochs smiled. "Am I not a tailor? I won't be a minute with the clothes. Take whatever food you can find in the refrigerator. If you're going through East Germany tonight, you won't be stopping for coffee." He turned and started for the hall.

"Herr Ochs?" Hauer called.

"Yes?"

"What kind of car do you have?"

Ochs's eyes twinkled. "British Jaguar. She runs like the wind."

"Petrol?"

"Both tanks are full." The old man took a step back toward Hauer. "You stop these men, Captain. Root them out.

Show them what the German people are made of." Ochs turned and scurried down the hall.

"Is he right?" Hans asked. "Are you talking about real Nazis?"

Hauer shook his head. "I don't think so. Germany is the last place fascism could take hold again. We have the strongest democracy in Europe. And even if we didn't, NATO and the Warsaw Pact would vaporize us before they allowed another German dictator. I think we're dealing with accelerated reunification—economic, political, and military. There are massive profits to be made, and Phoenix knows that the nationalist button is the one to push to get the German people behind them. Funk and his clowns are just foot soldiers. Moneymaking drones." Hauer knitted his brow. "Goddamn it, the answer is right in front of me and I can't pin it down! All of this fits together somehow: Phoenix, reunification, the Spandau papers—" Hauer stopped dead. "My God. What if Hess's papers contain something that could be used as leverage against NATO? Against England and the U.S.? Or even Russia? People have always said Hess knew some terrible secret. What if it's something Phoenix could use to pressure the Four Powers on reunification? Even to pressure *one* power?"

Hauer thrust the VW keys into Hans's hand. "Move your car down the block. We don't want to set the dogs on this old fellow. He's been through enough hell for one lifetime."

As Hans disappeared through the front door, Hauer opened the refrigerator. He couldn't remember when he'd last eaten. As he reached for a jar of Polish pickles, an image of Rudolf Hess flashed into his mind. Tall and cadaverous, the solitary specter shuffled silently through the snow-covered Spandau courtyards. *What could that old man have known?* he wondered. *What did he leave behind? Something big enough to blackmail a superpower? Could anything really be that big?*

"If it is," he told himself with a shiver, "I'm not sure I want to know."

Hauer pressed down a wave of guilt. He had lied to Hans earlier—he *had* seen Erhard Weiss tortured. And he could not blot out the memory. Funk and his goons weren't sophisticated enough for chemicals; they used beatings and electricity. On the face, up the anus, clipped to the penis. And they *enjoyed* it. Especially Luhr. Young Weiss had screamed until Hauer thought his jawbone would pop out of its socket. The poor boy would have shot his own mother to make them stop, but Luhr had wanted information, and Weiss hadn't had any. And Hauer—the brave captain—had stood by in rigid silence while it happened. He *could* have tried to stop it, of course, but he would soon have taken Weiss's place in the torture chair.

Weiss is dead, he told himself. *You can't bring him back. Concentrate on the living.* Hauer hoped Hans's wife had made it to Wolfsburg, but he didn't think much of her chances of getting safely out of Berlin tonight. If she *had* been caught, he hoped it was by the Russians. God alone knew what Jürgen Luhr would do to a woman if he got the chance.

CHAPTER TEN

Prefect Wilhelm Funk appeared on the verge of a myocardial infarction. A critical situation he thought admirably under his control had suddenly exploded in his grossly veined face, and he could do precious little about it. A genetic bureaucrat, Funk searched instinctively for scapegoats, but the unfortunate Rolf already lay dead in the basement cell with Weiss's mutilated corpse. Now Funk sat fuming in his office, accompanied by his aide Lieutenant Jürgen Luhr and Captain Otto Groener of the Kreuzberg district.

"They cannot escape, Prefect," Luhr said, trying to calm his enraged superior. "We have men at every checkpoint. Even the smugglers know that taking Hauer out would be fatal. I made the threats myself."

Funk's fury eased a little at this news. Luhr had always been his favorite. The man had almost no human weaknesses, mercy least of all. "Where do you think Hauer might run, Jürgen? And why in God's name would he betray us to save some green sergeant?"

"It doesn't matter. None of that matters. We'll find him. It's only a question of time."

"Well, that's the point, isn't it!" Funk exploded. "Who knows what that traitorous bastard's gotten hold of! He could destroy years of work and planning!" Funk leaned forward and put his face in his plump hands. "At least you got the damned Russians out."

"I'm not sure Kosov bought the lie detector charade," Luhr said thoughtfully.

Funk waved away his concern. "You said it yourself, Jürgen, it's just a matter of time before we run them down.

And when we do, our problem is solved. All *Bruderschaft* men have the shoot-to-kill order, and the rest of the force will probably do the same out of anger. The Spandau papers will be confiscated, and that will be that."

"What if we don't catch them before they leave the city?" Otto Groener cut in.

"We shall!" Funk snapped. "The alternative is impossible to contemplate."

"But you must contemplate it, *Prefect*," Groener insisted, laying smug emphasis on the title. An old rival of Funk's, Groener enjoyed seeing him placed squarely on the hot seat.

"Worry about your own district," Funk grumbled.

"But the problem isn't *in* my district."

Funk slammed his fist down on the desk. "One small setback and already the dogs are yapping at my heels! What would you do in a real crisis, Groener? Loot our accounts and sell out Phoenix?"

"How can I sell out someone I'm not even sure exists?"

Funk sighed. "Shut up, Otto. This problem will soon be resolved, and when it is, I shall turn my attention to you."

The rotund Groener leaned back in his chair and lit a stained pipe. "I hope you're right, Wilhelm," he said amiably. "For your sake. But somehow I don't think you are. My instinct tells me that something unexpected has happened. Unexpected not only here, but in Pretoria." He raised a fat eyebrow. "Perhaps Phoenix is not the omnipotent force we have been led to believe."

"Fool!" Jürgen Luhr spat. "Words like that could cost you your life. You think you're in private here? Because there are four walls around you? I'm starting to believe you think like a cow as well as look like one."

"You insolent swine!" Groener bellowed, coming to his feet.

Luhr stood defiantly, daring the big man to move against him. His psychotic blue eyes and formidable physique made any question of rank irrelevant. "Hauer is loose in the city, and here you two sit, arguing like children! What are you going to *do*?"

Groener searched for a graceful way to reclaim his chair; Funk looked like a dog disciplined for some reason it doesn't understand. "I've done what I can, Jürgen," he fretted. "Haven't I? Every car has the names and pictures. My God, every man out there knows Hauer by sight! I've convinced everyone that he and Apfel murdered one of their own. What more can I do?"

Luhr paced worriedly. "I'm not sure. But I'm not so certain you've convinced everyone. Most officers will get the report only by radio. They won't actually have seen Weiss's body. Hauer and Apfel have friends out there, Hauer especially. Men he's been under fire with. They won't betray him on the basis of a rumor. Particularly one started by you."

Funk reddened. "But a moment ago you told me they couldn't escape!"

Luhr smiled thinly. "I'm afraid that was to make you feel better. I'm really not that confident." His face hardened. "Tell me about Munich," he said. "I know Hauer was demoted because of the Olympic massacre, but what exactly did he do there?"

Funk wiped his forehead with a handkerchief. "I don't see what that has to do with anything."

"Humor me," said Luhr.

Funk sighed. "All right. Hauer was in the Federal Border Police then. He was a sharpshooter or sniper or whatever you want to call it. The Black September *fedayeen* were holding the Jew athletes at the Olympic village. They'd demanded a jet to take them to Cairo. They'd also demanded the release of Andreas Baader and Ulrike Meinhof, whom we'd just captured that year, plus a couple of hundred Arab political prisoners in Israel. The Israeli government asked us to allow one of their commando teams into Germany to attempt a rescue. And that wet rag Willy Brandt wanted to let them in! He'd offered to release Baader and Meinhof from the very beginning! Thank God the final authority was in the hands of the state government."

"And Hauer?" Luhr prodded.

"I'm telling you," Funk said testily. "The *fedayeen* and their hostages were given buses and allowed to drive out to two helicopters which had been brought to the Olympic village. Some people—Hauer among them—thought that was the best time to try a rescue. But the state government said no. The ambush was to be at Fürstenfeldbrück airport, when the terrorists tried to move from the helicopters to the waiting jet. Almost as soon as the choppers touched down at Fürstenfeldbrück, someone gave the order to fire. Hauer was one of five sharpshooters. The light was terrible, the distance prohibitive, and the shooting reflected the conditions. The whole firefight took about an hour. In the end it took an infantry assault to kill all the Arabs, but not before they had blown up the Jews in the helicopters."

Luhr nodded. "And Hauer?"

"I just told you."

"But the *shooting*—Hauer missed his targets?"

"No," said Funk with grudging admiration. "As a matter of fact he killed one of the terrorists with his first shot, and wounded another with his second. The fool might even have held on to his job if he'd kept his mouth shut. But of course he didn't. He had to tell everyone what we had done wrong, why the rescue was doomed from the beginning. He was screaming for reforms in our counterterror capability. He wanted us to copy the damned Israelis."

"So what happened to him?"

Funk chuckled softly. "He paid the bureaucratic price, along with everyone else associated with the massacre. He was transferred to the civil police here, and he's been a thorn in my ass ever since. I *never* wanted that bastard in our group! I never trusted him after Munich! He's carried a chip on his shoulder about those Jews ever since that day." Funk snorted. "Imagine, losing sleep over a few Jewish wrestlers."

Funk toyed with a shell-casing paperweight on the desk. "The irony is that Bonn created the GSG-9 because of Munich. Hauer wanted to join, of course, but by the time his old friends had lobbied successfully for his acceptance, he was too old to pass the physical tests. You have to be practically an Olympic athlete to get in. He coached their sharpshooters for a while, but that's it. I think they still use him occasionally in some kind of consulting capacity."

"*Wunderbar!*" Luhr snapped. "And you think we're going to catch this man with standard tactics? Christ! We've got to do something more."

"What?" Funk asked, almost pleading.

Luhr shook his head angrily. "I don't know yet. But I know this: you'd better inform Pretoria of what's happened, and the sooner the better!"

Funk blanched. Groener heaved himself from his chair and reached for his cap. "I should get back to Kreuzberg."

"Yes, I suppose so, *Otto*," Luhr mocked. "We'll be sure and tell Phoenix you mentioned him."

Groener slammed the door.

Luhr laughed. "What an old woman. How did he ever survive twenty-five years on the force?"

"By doing just what he did then," Funk replied, lifting the phone, "making judicious exits. Besides, nobody wants Kreuzberg. It's the shithole of Berlin. Nothing there but filthy Turks and students—is that you, Steuben? You're still on duty?" Funk cut his eyes at Luhr. "This is the prefect. Get me an international operator again. Same number. Right, Pretoria. I need some advice from an old friend in the NIS. Those fellows down there really know how to handle a problem. Crack a few heads and no more problem. Yes, I'll wait . . ."

In the first-floor communications room, Sergeant Josef Steuben reached under his computer desk and activated a small tape recorder. After surveying the main station room through the window behind him he logged Funk's call into a small notebook he had kept religiously for the past four months. Steuben had no university degree, but Hauer considered him an electronics genius. It had taken him less than a minute to piggyback the signal cable coming from the third-floor office Funk had commandeered. There were no voltage-measuring devices monitoring Abschnitt 53, so he felt reasonably safe.

Besides, he thought, *if this thing ever gets to court, wild charges by a computer technician and an accused murderer will be worthless. We've got to have physical evidence.*

"Dieter will love this," he said aloud. "Catch the buggers in the act—"

A voice like cracking ice froze Steuben in his chair. "Are you the only man on duty in here?" it asked.

Steuben whirled. Lieutenant Jürgen Luhr stood in the doorway of the communications room, his right hand resting on the butt of his Walther.

"Stand back from the console," he ordered.

11:06 P.M. Prinzenstrasse: West Berlin

Blindness, Hans thought. *This must be what blindness is like.* He felt as if he were staring backward into his own skull. He couldn't see his father's face, although he knew it was only centimeters from his own. Cramped and disoriented, he reached out.

"Be still!" Hauer grunted.

"Sorry."

Somehow, he and Hauer had stuffed themselves into the boot of Benjamin Ochs's Jaguar. Ochs had thrown an old blanket on top of them, and luckily they had gone in head first, so that what little heat passed through the rear seat by convection kept their heads reasonably warm. Now they sped across the city, the nattily dressed old couple staring sternly ahead whenever they passed a green police vehicle. In the lightless boot, Hans struggled to keep his limbs awake. One leg was completely numb already, and his left shoulder felt as though it might actually be dislocated.

"Captain?" he said. "I've been thinking about what you said. About Stasi officers working for reunification. It just doesn't make sense to me. If the Wall came down, wouldn't the Stasi be dismantled? Even prosecuted for criminal actions?"

"Yes. And that should tell you something. Someone in the West must be guaranteeing them some kind of immunity in exchange for their assistance. Don't ask me who, because I don't know."

Hans digested this in the rumbling blackness. "Do you really think it could happen?" he asked at length. "Reunification, I mean."

"It's inevitable," Hauer said. "It's just a question of when and how. Mayor Diepgen himself said as much this year: 'this year with the 750th anniversary we begin with the idea of Berlin as the capital of all Germany.' No one outside Germany took any notice, of course. But they will, Hans. You're young. People on the other side of the Wall seem different to you. And they are in some ways. Big things separate us. The Wall, our educational system, ideologies. But little things join us. What we eat ... our old songs. The mothers in the East tell their children the same fairy tales your mother told you at night. The fathers tell the same stories of heroism from the same wars. Little things, maybe. But in my experience, the little things outlast the big things." Hauer shifted position. "We Germans are a tribe, Hans. That's the best and the worst thing about us."

Hans nodded slowly in the darkness. "Where are we crossing?" he asked. "Staaken?"

"No. That's what everyone will expect. They'll assume that if we run, we'll run west. That's where the heaviest security should be."

"So where are we crossing?"

"Heinrich-Heine Strasse. We're going right into the heart of East Berlin, then swinging south around the city. That old Jew has balls, I'll tell you."

"How are we getting out, exactly?" Hans asked above the drone of the Jaguar's engine. "You don't think they're going to let this car through without checking the boot?"

Hauer chuckled softly in the dark. "I'd hoped you wouldn't ask. The truth is, I'm glad the old man demanded to come. Now we've got three things going for us: *glasnost*, the weather, and the reluctance of the border guards to bother two old Jews traveling to a funeral."

"Funeral? What are you talking about? Whose funeral?"

Before Hauer could answer, Benjamin Ochs leaned back and struck the rear seat with his balled fist. Two muted thuds sounded in the boot. "That's it," Hauer whispered. "We're there."

Two more thuds reverberated through the closed space.

"Damn," Hauer muttered. "Extra security. Don't say a word, Hans. And pray the Vopos are lazy tonight."

Benjamin Ochs stared through his spotless windshield at the gauntlet ahead. Thirty meters away, red-and-white steel barriers blocked the road at both checkpoints. On the East German side, a steel-helmeted Vopo stood at the window of a white Volkswagen, checking the driver's papers. The West Berlin border guards had gone into their booth to escape the biting wind.

The border guards weren't the problem. Ten meters in front of Ochs's Jaguar, a black minivan marked POLIZEI had been parked diagonally across the road, partially blocking it. Beside the van, two great-coated police officers were questioning four men in a black Mercedes that sat idling just ahead of Ochs's Jaguar. As casually as he could, Benjamin Ochs rolled down his window.

"Step out of the car, Herr Gritzbach," said a large, surly

police sergeant to the driver of the black Mercedes. "And shut off the engine."

"Certainly, Officer."

KGB Captain Dmitri Rykov smiled and turned the ignition key. The Mercedes' engine sputtered into silence. Rykov climbed slowly out of the car, moving as if he had all night to stand in the cold and chat with his West German comrades. His three passengers soon joined him.

"Why do you travel at this late hour?" the policeman asked sharply.

Rykov smiled. "Our employer wants us back at a construction site in the East. Apparently there's some sort of emergency."

"What was your business in West Berlin?"

Rykov pointed to his papers. "It's all there on the second page. We're architects for the firm of Huber and Röhl. We're building a civic hall near the Muggelsee. We came to West Berlin to consult with some architects here, and also to study the *Philharmonie* building. Magnificent."

"Yes, quite," added Corporal Andrei Ivanov, whose East German passport identified him as one Gunther Burkhalter.

The policeman grunted. He knew about these men. He had seen the black Mercedes with their drivers who spoke not-quite-perfect German too many times before. He also knew that their cover stories would check out. When operating in West Berlin, the KGB carried authentic East German ID documents supplied by the Stasi. Still, the sergeant was in no mood for a silky-voiced Russian who acted as if he expected the West Berlin police to kowtow to him.

"Open the boot, Herr Gritzbach," he said.

Rykov smiled again and reached into the car for the keys. Andrei and the others tensed, but their worries were for nothing. Hidden in the cramped compartment beneath the rear seat of the Mercedes, Harry Richardson remained unconscious. His hands and feet were bound so tightly with duct tape that they received almost no blood at all. Even if he had regained consciousness, he couldn't have moved. Crammed into every inch of space unoccupied by his body were the oiled weapons of the KGB team.

"You see?" said Rykov, gesturing into the Mercedes' trunk. "Nothing but suit bags. Disappointed, Sergeant?"

The burly policeman slammed down the lid and moved back to the side of the car. He had no legal reason to detain these men, however badly he might want to. Brusquely he handed the passport and other papers back to Rykov. "Pass," he said.

Grinning, Rykov slid halfway into the Mercedes and started the engine. While he waited for his comrades to climb in, he stared at the policeman through the open door and laughed. *I love this,* he thought. *The idiot knows, yet he can do noth—*

"Aaarrrgh!" he shrieked.

"Oh, I'm *sorry*, Herr Gritzbach! I didn't realize!"

The police sergeant had slammed the heavy Mercedes door on Rykov's exposed leg. "Are you all right, Herr Gritzbach? Should I call a *doktor*?"

Rykov's ashen face quivered with rage. "No!" he snarled, rubbing his leg furiously.

"But your leg might be *broken*."

Rykov lifted his throbbing leg into the car and slammed the door.

"Very well, then," the policeman said gleefully. "I hope your stay in West Berlin has been a memorable one."

"I'll remember *you*," Rykov vowed, his face twisted in pain. "Depend on that."

The Mercedes screeched away. It stopped perfunctorily at the western checkpoint, then shot beneath the raised barrier on the East German side, accelerating all the way. "Just as I thought," the sergeant muttered. "Precleared." He turned and signaled the next car forward.

Benjamin Ochs swallowed his fear, placed a reassuring hand on his wife's arm and eased the Jaguar toward the roadblock. The sergeant turned his back to the howling wind and lit a cigarette; then he walked back to the police van. A younger officer stepped up to Ochs's window.

"*Guten Abend*, Officer," Ochs said, handing over his passport. "Is there some emergency?"

"I'm afraid so, Herr . . . Ochs. We're looking for two fugitives. I must ask you a few questions. What is the purpose of your visit to East Berlin?"

"Family emergency. My nephew has been killed. We're on our way to Braunschweig."

Frau Ochs gave a little sob, then turned away as if she were crying. The young policeman leaned over and peered in at her, then scrutinized her husband's papers.

Ochs patted his wife's shoulder. "Now, now, Bernice. We'll be there soon."

Inside the dark boot, Hans could hear every word distinctly. "Captain," he whispered. "What do we do if—"

"Shut up," Hauer breathed. "It's all up to the old man now."

"But if they open the boot . . . do we fight? Do you still have your gun?"

"If they open the boot we do *nothing.* If I pulled out a gun this close to the Wall, they'd be hosing us off the street in the morning. The old couple, too. Just be quiet and *don't move.*"

Though every muscle twitched in pain, Hans struggled to remain still. He tried to ignore the voices outside, but it was impossible.

"He died in an auto accident early this evening," Ochs was saying. "My brother called me. A horrible thing. Four-car pileup."

"Why do you exit here?" asked the young officer sharply. "Braunschweig lies due west."

Ochs tried to think of what Hauer had told him to say, but he hesitated a second too long.

"Open the trunk, please," the policeman ordered. "You may remain in the car if you have an automatic release."

With his heart in his throat, Ochs slowly reached for the button.

"Why is this taking so long?" Frau Ochs cried suddenly.

"He's only doing his job, Bernice," Ochs said, his heart pounding.

"The men we're after murdered two policemen," the young man answered stiffly. "They must be brought to justice." He looked over at the van and motioned toward the Jaguar's boot.

The surly sergeant who had smashed Rykov's leg walked to the rear of the Jaguar. He drummed his fingers on the boot lid, waiting for Ochs to release the catch.

Inside, Hans tensed like a coiled spring. Hauer shoved his Walther deep into the spare tire receptacle, praying it wouldn't be spotted until they were safely away from the vehicle. Just as he got the pistol covered, the catch popped open. The lid rose a little, then the sergeant flipped it all the way up. Seeing the old blanket, he took hold of a corner and jerked it aside.

Blinding glare from the checkpoint spotlights struck Hans and Hauer full in the face, illuminating their twisted bodies. The big policeman froze. This tiny compartment was the last place he had expected to find the fugitives. He groped clumsily for his gun.

Squinting into the light, Hauer discerned the outlines of the policeman's face. *"Steiger!"* he hissed through gritted teeth.

The policeman gaped in surprise, then leaned low over the trunk. "Dieter!" he whispered. "What the hell are you doing?"

Hauer shook his head violently.

Sergeant Steiger glanced around the boot lid at his companion, who was still questioning Ochs. Then he leaned lower and looked into Hauer's eyes. "Dieter, was it you?" he whispered. "Did you kill Weiss?"

Hauer shook his head still more violently. *"Funk,"* he spat. "That bastard ordered it."

Steiger straightened up and glanced over the trunk lid, past his partner, to the American checkpoint, and then farther on to where the East German Vopos waited. He made a hard decision very fast. Leaning back over the boot, he shoved down hard on the car frame with his thighs and hands, giving the impression of checking for a false bottom. Then he stood up, glanced once at Hauer, and slammed the lid.

"Nothing here," he called to his partner. "Suitcases."

Steiger sauntered to the police van and picked up his cigarette. His partner was still questioning Ochs.

"This is highly irregular," the young man said officiously.

What's happening? Ochs thought wildly. *Why didn't that policeman jerk them out of the boot?* "My wife is very upset, Officer," he stammered. "There's an old synagogue in East Berlin—in the Kollwitzstrasse, not far from here. She was practically raised in that synagogue. Before the war, of course."

"You are Jewish?" the policeman asked sharply.

Ochs heard blood roaring in his ears. Memories of his youth flooded into his mind. Midnight knocks at his door . . . screams for help ignored—"Yes," he answered quietly. "We are Jewish."

The young man smiled and handed back Ochs's papers. "There is also a very beautiful synagogue in Braunschweig," he said. "You must see it. I spent my summers there as a boy. That's why I asked."

Ochs swallowed the lump in his throat. "Thank you. Yes, we've seen it many times." With a shaking hand he shifted into first gear.

"You have your money ready for the Vopos?" the policeman asked. "You know you must change twenty-five Deutschemarks as you cross over."

"I've got it, thank you. Right here." The old tailor patted his breast pocket. He let out the clutch pedal and moved slowly away from the van.

Crushing out his cigarette, Sergeant Steiger stepped away from the police van and waved to the West German checkpoint guards. They raised the barrier from inside their booth and let the Jaguar pass unmolested.

Ochs rolled to a stop on the East German side. In the boot, Hans held his breath and listened for the voices of the Vopos. He heard Ochs inquire about the exchange rate, complaining a little but not too much. The wait seemed interminable to Hans, but at last the red-and-white post lifted and the Jaguar glided slowly past the dragon's teeth, barbed wire, minefields, and machine gun towers that fortified the eastern side of the Wall.

"Where are we now?" Hans whispered.

"Swinging south around the city, I hope," Hauer replied. "Would you mind getting your knee out of my balls?"

Hans squirmed in the darkness. His heart was still racing. "Why didn't that sergeant arrest us?"

"Steiger and I go back a long way. He was with me on the Baader-Meinhof case that got me my captain's bars. Stormed a house with me."

"But if there's a warrant for our arrest—"

"He could be arrested too. He knows that. But he also knows Funk and his kind. Mealy-mouthed bureaucrats who've never seen the real Berlin, never had to face down a crazy kid with a gun. Steiger asked me if I killed Weiss, I said no. That was enough for him."

"How long will it take us to cross the DDR?"

"*If* we get out of East Berlin, you mean? Depends on the old man. We're taking the long way around, but it shouldn't take over two hours to reach the Marienborn-Helmstedt crossing. If we make it, we'll leave the Ochses at Helmstedt and you can drive us from there."

Hans made an uncertain sound of acknowledgment.

"Don't tell me," Hauer said. "You've never been to this cabin."

"Actually, I haven't. But I'll recognize it when we get there. I've seen dozens of pictures."

Hauer didn't bother berating Hans; it was difficult to speak for long in the boot. There didn't seem to be much oxygen.

CHAPTER ELEVEN

11:15 P.M. Polizei Abschnitt 53: West Berlin

Funk set the phone back in its cradle and reached for the bottle of soda water on his desk. His hand quivered as he poured.

"I gather Pretoria was not amused?" Luhr said softly.

Funk swallowed a huge gulp of soda. "Outraged," he gargled. "Said we were a disgrace to the German people."

"Was it Phoenix himself?"

"Are you joking? His aide or security chief or whatever that diabolical Afrikaner calls himself."

"I believe Herr Smuts is half-German, Prefect."

"And how would you know that?"

"That one time he came here in person, to our plenary meeting. One of his men told me that he was such an efficient security chief because he'd got the toughest qualities of both races from his parents."

"The worst qualities, if you ask me," Funk complained. "The man doesn't have much tact."

"I don't think tact is a major asset in his business," Luhr said dryly, hoping he didn't sound too sarcastic. For the time being Funk was still his superior in both the police and Phoenix's hierarchies. And until that changed . . .

A brisk knock at the door startled Luhr.

"*Komm!*" Funk barked.

An impeccably uniformed patrolman marched into the office and saluted. "There's been a murder, Prefect," he announced. "Near the Tiergarten."

Funk looked unimpressed. "So?"

"The murdered man, sir. He was an East German trade liaison. He'd lived here just four years. And the way he was killed, sir. Shot in the head at close range by a Makarov pistol. The gun was in his own hand like a suicide, but—"

"A Makarov?" Luhr interrupted.

"Yes, but there were other shots fired at the scene. A burst of automatic-weapons fire."

"*What?* What was the victim's name?"

"Klaus Seeckt, Herr Oberleutnant."

"Who do we have on the scene?" Funk interjected.

"A Kripo homicide team, sir. But they're from the Tiergarten district. The photographer's ours, but he didn't get a chance to call until just now."

"Leave us," Funk ordered.

The officer clicked his boot heels together and marched out.

"What do you make of this?" Funk asked anxiously.

Luhr looked thoughtful. "I don't know, but I'd better get over there. We can't let anything slip until we run Hauer down. I don't like any of this. First the Russians barge in here like an invasion force, then Hauer betrays us, then I find Steuben taping our calls at the switchboard. And now some East German is murdered with a Russian-made pistol? What did Apfel *find* at Spandau?"

Funk frowned worriedly. "If the Russian forensic people are right, some type of paper. A journal, perhaps? Whatever it is, Jürgen, Phoenix isn't amused. Do you think Steuben could be part of an official investigation? One I don't know about? Something Hauer initiated, perhaps?"

Luhr shook his head. "Steuben was working with Hauer, but I don't think it went any farther up than that. We'd have been warned if it did. As soon as I get back, I'll make the bastard own up to the whole thing. Don't worry, we're going to bag Hauer, send Phoenix his papers, and end up better off than we were before."

"You're probably right," Funk said wearily. He stood. "I'll be at home if you find anything I should know about."

Luhr pulled on his coat and strode into the hall, smiling confidently until he closed the door. *You bumbling fool,* he thought. *All you care about is collecting your filthy drug percentages and keeping your mistress happy.* Luhr felt a thrill of secret satisfaction. As soon as he had learned of Hauer's treason and escape, he had dispatched some of Phoenix's deadliest assets to every possible place Hauer or Apfel might go to ground—from the apartment of a woman

Hauer spent his weekends with, to a remote cabin on the Mittelland Canal near the East German border. And as soon as one of Phoenix's killers recovered the Spandau papers, Luhr would step forward and take the credit. *By tomorrow morning,* he thought, *I'll have enough to break that fool with Phoenix, and then Berlin-One will pass to me. To a true German!*

He shoved open the main station door and bulled through the crowd of reporters. Ignoring all questions, he climbed into an unmarked Audi and slammed the door in a journalist's face. "Those South Africans had better be good," he muttered, as he revved the cold engine. "Because Dieter Hauer isn't going to die easily."

Ten minutes after Luhr pulled away from the curb, Ilse Apfel trudged through the huge doors of Abschnitt 53 and presented herself to the desk sergeant. Like the reporters outside, he mistook her for a prostitute and so ignored her for as long as he could. While she waited for him to finish a telephone conversation, Ilse tried to wipe off the remainder of Eva's garish makeup with a tissue.

She did not feel comfortable coming into the station, but her choices were limited: she could talk either to Hans's superiors or to the men in the black BMWs. Twice during her journey here she had spotted the big sedans combing the streets for her, but she'd managed to evade them. At an all-night U-Bahn cafe she had changed some of Eva's paper Deutschemarks for coins, which she used to phone the Wolfsburg cabin. She had tried every ten minutes for an hour, but her grandfather never answered. The proprietor had started to frown after her third cup of coffee, and Ilse decided to get out before he called someone to remove her.

"What can I do for you, Fräulein?"

The sergeant's booming voice startled Ilse, but she stepped up to his high desk and spoke in her clearest voice. "I'm looking for my husband, Sergeant Hans Apfel. Earlier tonight someone told me that he had come here and gone, but I think he may have returned. Could you check for me, please?"

The sergeant's demeanor changed instantly. He jumped from his chair and escorted Ilse to an unoccupied desk. "Frau Apfel, I'm terribly sorry I kept you waiting! Please sit down. I know your husband personally. Let me call upstairs. I'm sure someone will know where he is."

For the first time since seeing the Spandau papers—over six hours ago—Ilse began to relax. She watched the desk sergeant at the telephone, drumming his fingers as he waited to speak to someone. He smiled back. *Hans has probably straightened everything out already,* she told herself.

"But he can't be gone," the sergeant insisted quietly. "He—" The sergeant fell silent as Wilhelm Funk emerged from a first floor office. He dropped the phone so loudly that Funk looked his way.

"What is it, Ross?" Funk barked. "I'm in a hurry."

The desk sergeant cut his eyes toward Ilse, then crossed the room and interposed Funk's corpulent body between Ilse and himself. "Prefect," he whispered, "the woman sitting behind you is Sergeant Apfel's wife. She's come here to find him."

Funk's mouth fell open. It took all his willpower not to whirl and snatch the woman up by her hair. "Go back to your desk," he whispered.

The sergeant obeyed without a word.

Funk glanced at his watch, gauging Luhr's probable time of return. Then he summoned his warmest smile, turned, and extended his plump hand. "Frau Apfel? I am Wilhelm Funk, prefect of police. I believe your husband was on the Spandau Prison security detail?"

Thrown off-balance by Funk's lofty rank and his apparent knowledge of her plight, Ilse stood and put her small hand into his pink paw. "Yes," she said. "Yes, Hans was at Spandau. Have you seen him tonight?"

Funk's smile broadened. "I have indeed. I questioned him earlier this evening. In fact, I've been trying to locate him ever since. Just after Hans left the station, I remembered something I neglected to ask him. Simply a formality, of course, but I try to keep everything proper. You understand. Every thing in its place, every paper signed and all that."

"You're looking for Hans now?"

"Yes, my dear. When Sergeant Ross told me who you were, I hoped you might be able to help us find him. But I see that you're as perplexed as we are. Please, let me escort you upstairs. I have a temporary office there. I'll have coffee sent up and perhaps together we can deduce where your husband has gone."

This is too much to ask! Funk thought gleefully as he whisked Ilse up the stairs. *The instrument of my deliverance walks straight through my front door!* With a lecherous look at Ilse's backside, he closed his office door and seated her before his desk. "Frau Apfel, I wanted to get you in private before I spoke frankly about this. *May* I speak frankly to you?"

In spite of her fatigue, Ilse's adrenaline began to course again. Facing the supreme police officer of West Berlin was a little unnerving. "About Hans?" she asked warily.

Funk paused, appraising the woman before him. What did she know? And more importantly, what did she suspect? Remembering his unpleasant call to Pretoria, Funk decided to gamble. "My dear, I'm afraid our Hans may be in some trouble."

"What do you mean?" she asked quickly. "What kind of trouble?"

"When we questioned the officers from the Spandau patrol this evening, we conducted the proceedings with the aid of a polygraph. You know, a lie detector?"

"I know what they are. You have to pass a polygraph test to work at my company."

"Ah. You're a career woman, then?"

"Yes—please, just tell me what's going on. Why did you use a polygraph?"

Funk smiled condescendingly. "This is a complex matter, my dear. There are . . . other parties involved." Funk lowered his voice. "The Russians, for instance. They were present at this polygraph session. I'm afraid all of our men passed this examination except your husband and a young officer named Erhard Weiss."

"I know Erhard."

Funk thrust out his lower lip. "I see." He glanced at his watch; Luhr might return any minute. "Naturally," he said in a confiding tone, "I instructed our polygraph operator to make no sign if any of our men failed. We even took the precaution of preparing clean reports from several men before the interrogation began. *Glasnost* may be the flavor of the month, but we can't have a pack of Russians barging in here and demanding access to German officers. I'm sure you understand."

Ilse nodded uncertainly.

Funk took a deep breath. *Now for the gamble.* "As soon

as we'd cleared the Russians out, I questioned Weiss and your husband alone. Weiss had nothing to tell. I believe simple nervousness caused him to fail the test. But Hans"—Funk paused—"Hans told me that he had discovered something at Spandau, just as the Russians claimed. He said that he had removed it to a safe place."

Ilse buried her face in her hands. The insane events of this night had become too much to bear. If she had been less tired, perhaps, she might have been more suspicious. But the prefect seemed to know everything already, and he wanted to help her find Hans. Raising her head, she looked Funk in the eye and posed a single test question.

"What did Hans tell you he found?" she asked, her red-rimmed eyes locked on his bluff face.

Funk didn't hesitate. He assumed the Soviet forensic people knew their business. "Why, papers, my dear," he said nonchalantly. "When Hans left the station, he assured me he was going to retrieve them, but as you can see"—Funk flicked his palms toward the ceiling—"he has yet to return."

Ilse stifled a sob. It was no use, she had to trust someone. Try as she might to control herself, the tears came. "Are the Russians looking for Hans too?" she asked. "For the papers?"

Gott im Himmel! Funk felt his heart thud in triumph. *It was papers!* "I'm not sure," he replied, trying to hold his voice steady. "It's possible. Why do you ask?"

"Because they came to my apartment!" she blurted. "They were looking for Hans, I know it! I almost didn't get away!"

My God, I've done it! Funk thought wildly. *I have her!* Rising to his feet, he hurried around the desk and sat beside Ilse. Like a concerned father he clasped both her hands in his and patted them reassuringly.

"Now, now, child," he consoled her. "We'll find Hans, don't worry. We have thousands of men at our disposal. Just calm down and tell me everything. Everything from the very beginning."

Ilse did.

12:01 A.M. British Sector: West Berlin

By the time Jürgen Luhr arrived at the murder scene, the forensic team had repacked its equipment and stacked it beside the front door. A uniformed patrolman guarded the door against any prowling pressmen who might arrive. Chain-smoking technicians rubbed the sleep from their eyes and cursed the man who had the nerve to be killed in the middle of the night. The man of the hour lay wrapped in the polyurethane bag that would be his sole vestment until someone came forward to claim him. For it *was* murder—anyone could see that. The attempt to disguise the shooting as a suicide had been clumsy at best, everyone agreed. Or almost everyone. Detective Schneider hadn't said anything yet. Naturally.

Luhr approached a thin man who sat on a sofa, fiddling with a camera. "Who's in charge here?" he asked in a clipped tone.

"Detective Schneider," said the man without looking up from his camera. "He's in the back."

"I'm Lieutenant Luhr. The prefect sent me to inquire into this matter."

Funk's title brought the photographer to his feet. "It's about time you got here," he whispered.

"Who is the dead man?" Luhr asked.

"His passport says Klaus Seeckt."

"Occupation?"

"He worked in some kind of liaison capacity for the West Berlin government—something to do with trade. From the looks of this place, he didn't do much but cash his checks and stay around the house. There's a three-quarter-inch video camera in the back bedroom. I'll bet this guy made some interesting movies back there—"

"Who discovered the body?" Luhr broke in, annoyed by the photographer's prurient speculation.

"A patrolman. He's gone already, though. An old couple next door heard the shooting and called it in. They didn't see anything."

"They never do, do they?" said Luhr, trying to foster some comradely spirit. "Have you found anything significant?"

Flattered to be asked his opinion, the photographer drew himself to his full height. "Well, it's pretty clear this was no suicide. At least to me. We dug eight slugs out of the front wall. They came from some kind of automatic weapon. Fresh prints everywhere, too. At least three people besides the victim were here tonight. We can't know exactly what happened, of course, but I don't see this fellow deciding to commit suicide just because someone broke into his house. I think he surprised a gang of thieves—pros—and they killed him with his own gun. Then they panicked, put the gun in his hand, and ran."

"Any sign of forced entry?"

"No. Like I said, pros."

Luhr cracked a knuckle joint. "Yes, that's what you said. What type of bullets were fired from the automatic weapon?"

"7.65 millimeter, brand unknown. Didn't find any shell casings."

Luhr smiled skeptically. "Let's summarize your theory, shall we? Your 'burglars' break in without leaving a trace. When the owner surprises them, they panic and kill him—leaving fingerprints everywhere—yet in their panic they stop to hunt down eight shell casings ejected from an automatic weapon fired in the heat of the moment. Rather contradictory actions, wouldn't you say?"

The photographer frowned and rubbed his chin. "I don't know. They make those attachments now that fit right onto your weapon. They catch every shell you can pump out."

"A bit exotic for housebreakers, don't you think?" Luhr glanced around the room. "Anything else?"

"Well, there was, in fact. Detective Schneider found a card outside. In the snow near the walkway. It didn't have anything on it but a number. A telephone number."

Luhr's eyes narrowed. "Where is this card now?"

"I don't know. If it's still here, Schneider would have it. He's in the back."

As Luhr stepped down onto the small stone *terrasse,* a bearish man wearing a hat and a rumpled raincoat waded into the pool of yellow light thrown off by a dim spotlight above the glass doors. The man stopped when he saw Luhr, taking in the silver lieutenant's bars, starched-flat uniform, and gleaming boots.

"What can I do for you, Lieutenant?" he asked warily.

"Detective Schneider, I presume?"

The big man nodded.

"I am here as the unofficial representative of the prefect. He has expressed an interest in this case As the murdered man apparently has some tie to the East German government, the prefect fears that there might be . . . repercussions. You understand?"

Detective Schneider waited for the lieutenant to ask what he had come outside to ask. He didn't like the way Luhr's arrogant little mouth softened his classic Nordic face. *Or the eyes,* he thought. *Rapist's eyes.*

"The photographer tells me that you discovered a card on the premises. A card with only a telephone number. Where is this card now?"

"I didn't actually find it," Schneider said, slipping his right hand into his trouser pocket. "Patrolman Ebert did." Schneider fingered the white card and watched Luhr's face. "I'm not sure where it is now. I had it, but I think Officer Beck asked me for it. He's still here, I believe."

"What have you got in your pocket?" Luhr asked sharply.

Schneider slowly withdrew his hand. He held the brass gorget plate and chain that identified him as a Kripo detective.

With a hiss of frustration Luhr went in search of Officer Beck. As soon as he disappeared, Schneider pulled a ballpoint pen from his shirt pocket and copied the number from the card onto the palm of his hand. Then he followed Luhr into the house.

"Lieutenant?" he called. "Herr Lieutenant!"

Luhr barrelled back through the front door, his face flushed with anger.

"I'm sorry, Lieutenant." Schneider shook his head as if he were a fool and knew it. "That card was in my coat pocket all the time. I could have sworn I gave it to Beck. Here you are."

Luhr snatched the card. "Officer Beck says he never asked you for the card!"

Schneider continued shaking his head. "Must have been somebody else. I tell you, past midnight and my mind just goes."

"I suggest, Detective," Luhr said acidly, "that you either get more sleep or look for a new line of work. Have you had anyone trace this number yet?"

"No, sir. Not yet."

"I'll handle it, then."

While Luhr stalked out to his unmarked Audi, Schneider stood in the foyer and scratched his large head. Something had felt wrong about this case from the moment he walked in the door. While everyone else had gone on about the sloppiness of the murder, Schneider had kept silent. Twenty minutes later the nameless card had turned up. And now this Nazi-looking lieutenant had appeared—the prefect's aide, no less—to spirit that card away. Schneider couldn't remember ever having seen Luhr at a crime scene before. That bothered him. He hurried past the few technicians left outside the house and climbed into his battered Opel Kadett.

"Telephone," he murmured as he cranked the old car.

Jürgen Luhr had beat him to it. As Schneider rounded the corner of Levetzow and Bachstrasse, he spied the prefect's aide standing at a corner call box. Schneider slowed, then drove on, maddeningly shut out of the conversation passing through the wires just over his head.

"Frau Funk?" Luhr asked, when a woman answered. "I'm sorry to disturb you so late. This is Jürgen Luhr. Could I speak with the prefect, please? . . . But he was leaving the station—" Luhr broke the connection and punched in the number of Abschnitt 53. "Berlin-Two," he snapped. "The prefect, immediately."

A full minute passed before Funk came on the line, his voice smug and unruffled in contrast to its earlier panic. "Yes, Jürgen?"

"I've found something odd at the Tiergarten house. A card with nothing but a phone number on it. We should trace it immediately. The crime looked very suspicious. Evidence of automatic weapons fire, conflicting signs of amateurishness and professionalism. I think our brothers in uniform may have been there."

"How interesting," said Funk. "Why don't you come back to the station and we'll discuss your theory."

"What's the matter? Is someone with you?"

A pause. "There *was* someone here, Jürgen. Sergeant Ross just took her downstairs to her new accommodations."

"*Her?* Who are you talking about?"

"The wife of one of our 'brothers in uniform,' as you put it. A Frau Ilse Apfel. She walked into the station just after you left. She had a most interesting story to tell."

"*What?* The sergeant's wife?"

"That's right. I understand the situation much better after talking to her. I suggest you get back here, Jürgen, if you want to be in on this at all. I've already spoken to Pretoria.

I received some very interesting orders, and they involve you."

Luhr left the receiver dangling from the call box and dashed to his car. He squealed down the Bachstrasse in a rage. "Damn that imbecile! How could he be so lucky?" He screeched around a curve. "It's all right," he assured himself, calming a little. "He hasn't found Hauer or Apfel yet. *Or* the Spandau papers. And that's what Phoenix wants— what he's frightened of. And that distinction will be *mine*."

In his fury, Luhr failed to notice the burly figure of Detective Julius Schneider standing at a yellow call box four blocks from the one he had used to place his own call. Unlike Luhr, Schneider wasn't about to try to trace the mysterious phone number through normal channels. An inquiry in his own name might draw unpleasant attention, possibly even the prefect's, and Schneider didn't need that. Besides, he had always believed in taking the shortest route between two points. Reading the telephone number off the palm of his hand, he lifted the receiver and punched in the digits. He heard five rings, then a click followed by the familiar hiss and crackle of an automated answering machine.

"This is Harry Richardson," said a metallic voice. "I'm out. Friends can leave a message at the tone. If you're a salesperson, don't call back. If it's a military matter, call my office. The previous message will be repeated in German. Thank you."

Schneider waited until the German version of the message had finished, then hung up. His pulse, normally as steady as a hibernating bear's, was racing. Schneider knew who Harry Richardson was. He'd even met him once. American intelligence officers who took the time to cultivate investigators of the *Kriminalpolizei* were rare enough to remember. Schneider doubted if Richardson would remember him, but that didn't matter. What mattered was that an American army officer was somehow involved in what was fast shaping up to be an explosive murder case. Schneider took several deep breaths and forced himself to think slowly. He'd found Richardson's card outside the victim's house, but there had been blood all around it. What did that mean? And what should he do? He thought of the prefect's insolent aide, and the overly officious manner that in Schneider's experience spelled *coverup*.

With sudden insight Schneider realized that he now stood

at one of those crossroads that can change a man's life forever. He could get into his car and go home to his wife and his warm bed—a course of action almost any sane German would choose—or he could make the call that he suspected would pluck him from his old life like the wind sweeps a seed from the ground.

"God," he murmured. "Godfrey Rose."

Schneider jumped into his car and fired the engine. Thirty minutes ago he had been mildly intrigued by the night's events. Now his mind ran wild with speculation, electrified by the smell of the kind of chase he had become a detective for in the first place. Squealing away from the curb, he made an illegal U-turn and headed east on the Budapester Strasse, making for the Tiergarten station. He hoped his English was up to the task.

CHAPTER TWELVE

12:30 A.M. Velpke, FRG: Near the East German Border

Professor Natterman swung the rattling Audi back toward the frontier and pushed the old sedan to 130 kilometers per hour. Now that the end of his harrowing journey approached, he could not keep from rushing. The speed was exhilarating; the protesting whine of the tires as he leaned the car into the curves kept his fatigued mind alert. *Thank God for old friends,* he thought. A boyhood chum had come through for him tonight, providing the Audi with no questions asked.

Thankfully, the mysterious Englishman who had "accidentally" stumbled into his compartment had disappeared. Natterman hadn't seen him again on the train, nor at Helmstedt when the few passengers disembarked. A few times during the last hour he had caught sight of headlights in the blackness far behind him, but they came and went so frequently that he wrote them off to nervousness.

As the Audi jounced over the railroad linking Gardelegan to Wolfsburg, the professor spied the eerie, never-dimming glow of the sprawling factory city to the west. The sight startled him still. When he was a boy, Wolfsburg had been a tiny village of less than a hundred, its few houses scattered hodgepodge around the old feudal castle. But when the Volkswagen works came there in 1938, the village had been transformed almost overnight into an industrial metropolis. He could scarcely believe his father's tiny cabin still remained in the quiet forest northeast of the city.

It had been eleven months since he last visited the cabin, but he knew that Karl Riemeck, a local laborer and old family retainer, would have both the grounds and the house in fine shape. The thought of spending some time in the old place had almost blotted out the wild theories whirling through Natterman's weary brain. Almost. As he roared down the narrow road cut through the deep forest, visions of notorious and celebrated faces from the past flickered in his mind like pitted newsreels. *Hitler and Churchill . . . the Duke of Windsor . . . Stalin . . . Joseph P. Kennedy, the American ambassador to wartorn Britain, a Nazi appeaser and father of a future U.S. President . . . Lord Halifax, the nerveless British foreign secretary and secret foe of Churchill . . .* Those smiling faces now seemed to conceal uncharted worlds of deception, worlds waiting to be mapped by an intrepid explorer. The thrill of impending discovery coursed through the old historian's veins like a powerful narcotic, infusing him with youthful vigor.

He eased off the gas as he crossed the Mittelland Canal bridge. Again he had arrived at the impenetrable core of the mystery: what were the British hiding? If Hess's double had flown to Britain to play a diversionary role, what was he diverting attention *from?* Why had the real Hess flown to Britain? *To meet Englishmen, of course,* his mind answered. But *which* Englishmen? With a pang of professional jealousy Natterman thought of the Oxford historians who were documenting the pro-Nazi sympathies of over thirty members of the wartime British Parliament whom they believed had known about Hess's flight beforehand. The gossip in academic circles was that the Oxford men believed these MPs were Nazi appeasers, enemies of Churchill whom Hess had flown secretly to Britain to meet. Natterman wasn't so sure. He had no doubt that an *apparently* pro-Hitler clique of upper-class Englishmen existed in 1941. The real question was, did those men *really* intend to betray their country by forging an unholy alliance with Adolf Hitler? Or was there a deeper, more noble motive for their behavior?

The answer to this lay in Hitler's war plans. The Führer's ultimate goal had always been the conquest of Russia—the acquisition of *Lebensraum* for the German people—which made him very popular with certain elements of British society. For despite being at war with Germany, many Englishmen saw the Nazi state as an ideal buffer against the spread of communism. Similarly, the Führer had visions of Germany and England united in an Aryan front against communist Russia. Hitler had never really believed that the English would fight him. Yet when Winston Churchill refused to accept the inevitable surrender to and alliance with Germany, the Führer got angry.

And there, Natterman believed, lay the basis of Rudolf Hess's mission. Hitler had assigned himself a very strict timetable for *Barbarossa*—his invasion of the Soviet Union. He believed that if he did not invade Russia by 1941, Stalin's Red Army would gain an overwhelming superiority over him in men and matériel. That meant that to be successful, his invasion armies had to jump off eastward by May of 1941 *at the latest,* before the snows melted and made the effective use of tanks impossible. And the British, Natterman remembered, had known this. An RAF group captain named F. W. Winterbotham had worked it out in 1938. And this knowledge—correctly exploited—could have given the British a peculiar kind of advantage. For the longer they could fool Hitler into believing they wanted a negotiated peace, the longer they could stave off an invasion of Britain. And the nearer would draw the date when Hitler would have to redeploy the bulk of his armies eastward. If Hitler could be fooled *long enough,* England would be spared.

But had those "pro-Nazi" Englishmen understood that in 1941? Natterman wondered. Were they altruistic patriots who had lured Rudolf Hess to Britain on a fool's errand, and thus saved their homeland from the Nazis? Or were they traitors who had decided Adolf Hitler was a man they could deal with—a bit of a boor, perhaps, but with sound policies vis-à-vis the communists and Jews? The answer seemed simple enough: If a group of powerful Englishmen had merely *pretended* to treat with Hitler in order to save Britain, they would be heroes and would require no protection from public scrutiny, especially fifty years after the fact. However, the well-documented efforts of the British government to suppress the details of the Hess case tended to reinforce the opposite theory: that those Englishmen *really had been* admirers of Hitler and fascism.

The variable that confused this logic was a human wild card—Edward VIII, Duke of Windsor, former Prince of Wales and abdicated King of England. The duke's pro-German sympathies and contact with the Nazis—both before and *during* the war—were documented and very embarrassing facts. At the very least Windsor had made a fool of himself by visiting Hitler and all the top Nazis in Germany, then trumpeting the Führer's "achievements" to a shocked world.

At worst he had committed treason against the country he was born to rule. After his stormy abdication, the duke, living in neutral Spain, had pined away for the throne he had so lightly abandoned. Startling evidence unearthed in 1983 indicated that in July of 1940 Windsor had slipped secretly into neutral Lisbon to meet a top Nazi, where they explored the option of Windsor's return to the English throne. And *that,* Natterman thought excitedly, was the core of it all! Because according to British historian Peter Allen, the Nazi whom Windsor had sneaked into Portugal to meet had been none other than *Rudolf Hess!*

Natterman gripped the wheel tighter. A clear picture had begun to emerge from the blurred background of speculation. He could see it now: while Hitler's "British sympathizers" may have been feigning sympathy for the Nazis in order to save England, the Duke of Windsor most definitely was not. And if Windsor had committed treason—*or even come close*—that was the kind of royal "peccadillo" that the British secret service would be *forced* to conceal, suppressing the entire Hess story, *the heroism as well as the treason.*

Natterman felt his heart thump. A fourth and stunning possibility had just occurred to him. What if the British "traitors" really *were* pro-Nazi, but had been *allowed* to pursue their treachery by an even more devious British Intelligence? That way the Nazis could not possibly have picked up on any deception, because the conspirators themselves would not have been aware that they were part of one! Natterman's mind reeled at the implications. He tried to focus on that uncertain time—the spring of 1941—but his memories seemed foggy, misted at the edges somehow. His brain contained so many fragments of history that he was no longer sure what he had merely read about and what he had actually lived through. He had lived through so much.

More books, he thought. *That's what I need now. Documentation. I'll have Ilse stop at the university library on her way here. I'll make a list as soon as I get to the house. Churchill's memoirs, Speer's book, copies of Reich documents, a sample of Hess's handwriting ... I'll need all that for even a preliminary study of the document. And eventually the ink, the paper itself—*

Natterman hit the brakes, bringing the Audi to a sliding stop. He had reached the cabin. He turned slowly onto the narrow, snow-packed lane that wound through the forest to the cabin. When the familiar flicker of a lantern appeared in the darkness ahead, he smiled and watched it wink in and out of sight as he negotiated the last few curves.

As he pulled the car into the small turnaround beside the cabin, he decided to invite Karl Riemeck up for a schnapps tomorrow. The old caretaker had obviously taken the trouble to drive out here and light a lamp for him, and Natterman suspected he would also find a good supply of firewood laid by for his convenience. Deciding to retrieve his suitcase later, he hefted his heavy book satchel over his shoulder and climbed out of the Audi. The cold practically pushed him up onto the cabin porch, where he found a week's supply of oak logs stacked on a low iron rack.

"Thank you, Karl," he murmured. "This is no night for old men like us to go without heat." On impulse he tried the knob; the door swung open soundlessly. "You think of everything, old friend," he said, shivering. "I come to the door with a burden, and must I search for my key? No. All is prepared for me."

Switching on the electric lights—which the cabin had done without until 1982—he saw that the main room looked just as it always had. Not too small, but cozy, lived in. Natterman's father had liked it that way. No false opulence, just rough comfort in the old ways. Built of birch and native oak, the cabin felt more solid today than it had when Natterman was a boy. He tossed his satchel on a worn leather chair and walked back out to the porch. Adjusting his eyes to the darkness, he stared out through the forest, up the dark access road, searching for the glimmer of headlights, but he saw none.

He gathered as much wood as he could hold, carried it into the cabin, and stacked it carefully in the rack beside the fireplace. Then he placed two well-split logs on the cast-iron rack, dropped to his knees, and began to build a small pyramid of twigs beneath them, just as his father had taught him to do six decades before. Though his brain still simmered in anticipation of uninterrupted study of the Spandau papers, the familiar ritual calmed him.

When his pyramid stood ready to be lit, he searched the hearth for matches, but found none. Rising with a groan, he padded over to the woodstove that occupied an entire alcove in the rear of the front room. Along with a walk-in pantry, this antique constituted the cabin's kitchen. Here also the professor had no luck. Muttering quietly, he recrossed the room and opened the bedroom door.

When he saw what lay beyond, his chest muscles contracted with a force he thought would burst his heart. On the bed directly before him, bound to the brass bedframe with a thick leather belt, Karl Riemeck stared sightlessly ahead, his face contorted in a mask of rage, incomprehension, and pain. A huge freshly clotted stain of blood blossomed on the caretaker's chest like an obscene flower.

Natterman became as a child. His bowels boiled; urine dribbled into his trousers. He desperately wanted to run, but he had no idea where safety lay. He whirled back toward the main room. Empty and pristine as a magazine photograph. Unable to focus on Karl, he stumbled to the front door and locked it. "My God, my God, my God," he muttered, bending over and putting his hands on his knees. "My *God!*" His chant was a mantra. An incantation. A way to begin thinking. A way back to reality.

Forcing down the wave of bile that struggled to erupt from his throat, the old professor stood erect and strode back into the bedroom to see if he could do anything for his friend. He ignored the gore that matted the shirt, and placed his hand directly over Karl's heart. Still. Natterman had expected nothing. He knew death when he saw it.

Perhaps it was the shock of Karl's death that dulled Natterman's instincts, blinding him to further danger. Perhaps it was fatigue. But when the cold hand reached from beneath the bed and locked itself around his spindly ankle, he froze. He opened his mouth to scream, but no sound came. Again his brain shut itself off against reality. The iron claw jerked his feet from under him; he crashed to the floor like a sack of kindling, certain that his hip was broken.

Moaning in pain and terror, he tried to crawl toward the doorway, but strong arms caught his shoulders and spun him onto his back. When his eyes focused, a flashing silver blade filled almost his entire field of vision. Beyond it he saw only a mane of blond hair. He tried to breathe, but an anvil seemed to have settled on his chest. When the pressure eased slightly, then moved higher, he realized the anvil was a man's knee.

"You have something I want, old man!"

The words were quick and angry, the voice flint against

stone. The knee pressed down so hard into Natterman's chest that he could not have spoken if he wanted to.

"Answer me!" the man screamed.

That's not a British accent, Natterman thought with relief, his mind on the safety of the Spandau papers. *Thank God! It's only a robber—a robber who has killed Karl.* The professor's brain raced through its knowledge of languages, trying to place the unfamiliar accent, but to no avail. *Dutch maybe?*

The blond man flicked the blade back and forth in a lethal dance, then inserted the point deep into Natterman's left nostril.

"Don't be stubborn like your friend, old man. It cost him what little life he had left. Now, *talk.*"

The pressure eased a little. "Take whatever you want!" Natterman rasped. "My God, poor Karl—"

"Pool *Karl?* You idiot! You know what I want! *Speak!* Where is it!"

For another moment Natterman's mind resisted, then he knew. As impossible as it seemed, this murderer knew his secret. He knew about the Spandau papers, and he had managed to beat Natterman here—to his father's house—to *steal* them!

"Oh God," Natterman whispered. "Oh no."

"No?" the blond man sneered.

"But I don't know what—"

"Liar!" In a rage the killer jerked his knife up and outward, severing the old man's left nostril in a spray of blood. Tears filled Natterman's eyes, temporarily blinding him. A warm rush of blood flooded over his lips and chin. He coughed and gurgled, struggling for air.

"Listen, you Jew maggot! You're *nothing* to me!" The killer put his lips to Natterman's ear and lowered his voice to a deadly whisper. "If you don't signal your agreement to cooperate in five seconds, I'm going to sever your carotid artery. Do you understand? That's the pipeline to your addled brain."

To validate his threat the killer jabbed the point of his knife into the soft skin beneath Natterman's left ear. Choking horribly on his own blood, Natterman tried to nod.

"You'll show me where it's hidden?"

Natterman nodded again, spitting up frothy red foam.

The killer hauled him to his feet as easily as he would a

dead branch. He took out a white handkerchief and thrust it toward the professor's streaming wound. "Direct pressure," he muttered.

Natterman nodded, stanching the flow, surprised at even this small gesture of humanity. The man before him looked scarcely thirty. The long mane of blond hair gave him a starving-student look that the professor knew well. A handsome face lit by zealot's eyes.

"Now," the killer said softly, "show it to me."

Natterman turned back to the bed where Karl's body lay. He began to sob as the enormity of what had happened struck him.

"For God's sake, old man, don't fall apart on me! Your friend stuck himself into this business and wouldn't clear off. He forced me. Come into the other room."

Like a drone Natterman followed the killer into the front room. With his face partially masked by the bloody handkerchief, he tried frantically to think of a way out of his predicament. *Chess,* he thought suddenly. *It's just like a game of chess. But played to the death.*

"Don't think, you idiot! Show me where it is! *Now!*"

The blond killer stood two meters from Natterman, but when he thrust the knife forward he halved the distance with fearful effect. Natterman dropped the blood-soaked handkerchief on the floor and began to fumble with the buttons of his shirt.

"What are you doing, fool!"

"It's taped to my back," Natterman explained.

For a moment the man looked confused; then his face resumed its tight grimace. "Well, then," he said uncertainly, "be quick about it."

My God, thought Natterman, *he doesn't know what he's looking for. He was sent . . . by someone else. Who? How did they connect me with Hans and the papers?* Shaking with terror, the professor stripped the foil-wrapped bundle from his back. He felt as if three layers of skin had come up with the tape. *I must survive,* he told himself. *Survive to learn the truth. I must distract him. . .*

"Now," said the killer, "walk forward slowly and hand it to me."

Natterman tossed the taped bundle across the room. It landed on the floor and slid partially under a heavy cabinet that stood in the corner.

"You cracked bastard! Pick it up and bring it here!"

Natterman hesitated for a moment, then slowly walked to the cabinet, bent over, retrieved the bundle. *Just like chess,* he thought. *I move—he moves.*

"Hand it to me."

Natterman extended the packet, watching curiously as several drops of blood fell from his nose onto his twitching biceps. *I must be in shock,* he realized. *I'm watching someone else...*

Keeping his eyes on Natterman, the killer stripped the tape from the foil that the professor had used to protect the papers.

"Carefully," Natterman pleaded. "They're very delicate."

"Is this all there is?"

Natterman shrugged. "That's it."

"Is this *all,* you filthy Yid?" The killer shook the papers in the air.

Afrikaans, blurted a voice in Natterman's brain. *The accent is Afrikaner. But ... why does the animal think I'm Jewish?* "I swear that's all there is," he said. "Please be careful. That's a very important document." As Natterman spoke, he let his eyes wander toward his book satchel. It lay exactly where he had tossed it when he came in—on the leather chair by the door. He stared for a moment, then looked quickly back at the intruder.

"Again you lie!" the Afrikaner cried. "If I find something else in that bag, old man, you're dead."

Natterman stood by the corner cabinet. Silently he willed the killer toward the satchel. Toward the chair. Holding his knife out in front of him, the Afrikaner backed slowly toward the satchel. *Just a little further,* Natterman thought, *a little further ...*

The killer averted his eyes as he reached for the satchel—

Now! Natterman groped in the space between the cabinet and the wall and closed his hand around the big Mannlicher shotgun that had stood there for over sixty years. The shotgun his father had always kept out of the way, yet within easy reach if a deer wandered into the clearing or poachers encroached on his land. The professor cocked both hammers as he brought the weapon up, and fired the moment the barrels cleared the back of the couch.

The killer dived for cover behind the leather chair, but not quickly enough. Twenty-four pellets of double-aught buckshot tore through his right shoulder, leaving his upper arm a mass of pulp and bone that hung from his torso by sinew alone. The bloody knife that had butchered Karl Riemeck clattered to the floor, its owner blown out of sight behind the chair.

"Bastard!" Natterman screamed. Never in his life had he wanted to kill another human being—not even in the war. But now a rage of terrifying power surged through him as his stinging eyes probed the outline of the chair for a clear shot.

The Afrikaner knelt motionless behind the chair, thinking. He had known pain before, and he knew that to give in to it meant death. Silently he seized the door handle with his good arm and jerked inward. His shattered shoulder seared with pain; his agonized scream filled the small cabin as he fought to stay conscious. An almost-forgotten voice shouted from the depths of his brain: *Move soldier! Move!* And move he did. In seconds he had scrambled alligator-style through the doorway, dragging his useless arm behind, pulling the door shut with his foot as he passed through. He flopped off the porch into the snow just as the second blast from Natterman's shotgun splintered the lower quarter of the oak door.

I should have known! the Afrikaner thought furiously. *Should have anticipated. I underestimated the old bastard.* He had a 9mm automatic in his car, but he'd parked his car in the woods beyond the clearing. He'd never make it, not if the old man could see at all. In desperation he swept away a hummock of snow and rolled beneath the cabin into icy blackness.

Above him, Professor Natterman rooted hysterically through the cabinet in search of extra shotgun shells. *There!* Beneath an overturned wicker basket he found a full box of twelve-gauge shells. He broke the breech of the antique weapon, removed the empties, chambered two shells, jammed the gun closed, and cocked both hammers. Then he bolted the splintered oak door.

The papers! he thought suddenly. *The Afrikaner had them!* In a panic he searched the cabin for the onionskin pages, but saw none. *No!* his mind screamed. *He cannot have them!* Crazed with rage, he blasted another hole in the door, then unbolted it and shoved it open. Just outside, crumpled and matted in a huge smear of blood, lay six of the nine Spandau pages. Natterman darted outside and frantically gathered them up, then scanned the snow for the other pages. He saw none. Furious, he staggered back into the cabin and snatched up the tinfoil that had protected the papers. He wrapped it carefully back around the bloodstained pages, then stuffed the foil packet deep into his pocket.

The exertion had broken loose the clot in his nose. Blood poured down his bare chest. *The animal must have a gun,* he thought wildly. *He must. He wouldn't have come with just the knife.* Natterman seized his shirt and jacket from the floor and stumbled into the bedroom, where Karl still stared sightless at the door.

"Aaarrrgh!" he roared in anguish. It took almost all his remaining strength to drag the linen chest from the foot of the bed and wedge it against the bedroom door. When he had blocked it as well as he could, he picked up the telephone beside the bed.

Dead as Karl, he thought bitterly. Pinching his bloody nostrils closed, he surveyed the room. A washstand. A chair. An old pine armoire. His father's bed beside the window. *The window!*

Even as Natterman realized his vulnerability, he saw a pale hand working just over the sill, trying to force the glass upward. He obliterated the window with a double-barreled blast, gibbering like a madman as he did. The stress had finally overcome him. Like a drunkard he staggered over to the armoire and heaved and pushed until finally it slid across the gaping window. Then he collapsed in a heap against it, not even trying to stop the blood that continued to plop onto his heaving chest.

His last act before he fainted was to chamber two more rounds into the Mannlicher.

1:42 A.M. *The Northern Transvaal, Republic of South Africa*

Alfred Horn sat hunched in his motorized wheelchair, his prehensile forearms pressing a leopardskin rug against his arthritic knees, and stared into the fire. As always, his mind raced back and forth between past and present, searching for causes and connections, cataloguing injustices to be avenged. Perhaps it was his advanced years, but to Horn the present seemed merely a small space between two doors—one leading back into a past he could not change—the other opening onto a future that, after five decades of planning and struggle and living with defeat, promised the fulfillment of ultimate destiny. Time was short, he knew, and growing shorter. Did he have a week or a month before his ability to leave his imprint upon the world was stolen from him? He needed a month. How ironic, he reflected, that his knowledge of the past posed the greatest threat to his plans for the future. But he was nearly ready. A soft knock sounded behind him. He answered without turning his gaze from the fire.

"Yes?"

The door opened soundlessly. Smuts stood silently at attention.

"What news from Berlin, Pieter?"

"There's a flurry of British and Russian intelligence activity, sir. I'm almost certain they have not located the papers. No sign so far of Israeli involvement."

"But what of our two policemen, Pieter? *They* have the papers."

"Sir, Berlin-One informs me that while he has not yet captured the young man whom he believes found the papers, he does have custody of the man's wife."

Horn pondered this intelligence. At length he said, "We shall have them all here. Bring the woman, the man will follow. Send a jet tonight."

"I've already ordered it done, sir."

"Good. Can the husband be reached by phone?"

Smuts cleared his throat. "We haven't located him yet, sir."

While Horn's glass eye remained immobile, his good eye flickered with birdlike suspicion over his security chief's lanky frame, finally settling on his craggy face. Under its unrelenting gaze, Smuts shifted his weight uncomfortably from one foot to the other.

"Pieter?" Horn asked finally.

"Yes, sir?"

"Our two policemen have escaped from West Berlin, haven't they?"

To Smuts's credit, he did not dissimulate. "That appears likely, sir. The older man—Hauer—apparently has a great deal of influence in Berlin. We have a man waiting at their last known destination—a cabin near Wolfsburg—but he hasn't reported in."

Horn toyed with a poker in the stand. "These policemen are proving to be a credit to their race, Pieter. After you've drawn them here, we must see what our young friend has dug from the rubble of Spandau."

"It will be done."

"Tell me, how will you convince the young husband that you have his wife if you haven't reached him by the time she's airborne?"

Smuts suppressed a smile. Horn's attention to the smallest details of an operation constantly surprised him. "A simple matter really, sir," he explained. "Audio recordings on two separate tape machines. Prerecorded affirmatives and negatives to be used as needed, with a short statement to open the exchange. With adequate noise reduction the results are quite convincing."

"Excellent, Pieter. I'm pleased."

Smuts's boot heels cracked like a muffled pistol shot.

Horn unconsciously picked at the stippled scar tissue around his glass eye. "I've been thinking, Pieter. I want you to shut down all our drug and weapons trading for the time being. I want no roads leading from the outside world to here."

Smuts nodded. "Very good, sir. We do have that shipment of gold coming from Colombia, though, payment for our ether. Two million dollars in bullion. It's coming by ship, and the ship is almost here."

Horn considered this. "We'll let her land, then. But everything else shuts down."

"Yes, sir."

"When the policeman's wife arrives, bring her directly to me. It's so seldom I get a chance to meet young Germans anymore. I should like very much to speak with her."

"Meet her? But, sir, the risks—"

"Nonsense, Pieter. If you are present, what are the risks?"

Smuts nodded. "As you command."

Horn eyed Smuts appraisingly. "Anything else?"

"Beg your pardon, sir?"

Horn frowned. "The radiation leak. You failed to update me on your progress."

Smuts colored. "I'm sorry, sir. I've been meeting with the engineers about the runway extension." He raised his forearm and read the time from the inside of his wrist. "The leak was contained as of two hours ago. Minimal exposure to personnel, the basement lab is clean."

"Any word on our cobalt case?"

"No, sir. I'm sorry."

"All right, Pieter. Dismissed."

"Sir!" Again the boots fired, and Smuts disappeared.

In spite of his frustration, Horn smiled wistfully. *A jungfrau, he thought, a true daughter of the Fatherland. My God, how long has it been since I spoke with a German woman who wasn't raised in this savage country?*

"Pieter!" he called suddenly.

Smuts raced back into the room, a Beretta pistol in his hand.

"I'm sorry," Horn apologized, "I spoke too loudly. More wood for the fire, that's all. My joints are driving me mad."

Smuts holstered his weapon. "Yes, sir."

Without hesitation, a man who had commanded troops with distinction across half the African continent marched to a woodpile less than a yard from his employer's chair, added a fresh log to the fire, and stoked the flames beneath it. "How's that, sir?"

"Fine, Pieter. Fine." Horn slumped back into his padded wheelchair and there, motionless until dawn, slept the sleep of the saved.

1:50 A.M. Tegel Airfield, West Berlin

"Wing tanks full," the pump jockey said, screwing down the tank cap. He scurried down the hydraulic ladder and onto the tarmac of the fueling area. "On account?" he asked.

Handsomely dressed in a tailored gray suit, Lieutenant Jürgen Luhr nodded curtly, then marched up the ramp that fed into the belly of the sleek Lear turbojet. On the plush carpeted floor of the passenger cabin, trussed from head to toe with industrial tape, Ilse Apfel struggled desperately to breathe.

"Try to relax, Frau Apfel," Luhr said. "The trip will be much more comfortable for us both."

With great difficulty Ilse inclined her head toward the blond policeman and glared. She hoped defiance would mask the abject terror squirming in her stomach. One hour ago she had been forced to watch this insane lieutenant drag a knife across the throat of Sergeant Josef Steuben. Ilse had never met Steuben, but she had vomited from sheer horror. And beneath the horror, she cursed herself for her stupidity. How could she have walked right into the arms of these ruthless animals?

"It's useless to struggle," Luhr advised. "I would have preferred more subtle measures myself, but I'm told that our host is opposed to the use of drugs. Quite ironic, considering the source of some of his income." Luhr tapped a small syringe against his armrest. "I'm sure this has all been a shock to you," he said, "but it's only the result of your husband's stupidity. However, in spite of that—and for reasons quite beyond my understanding—you, as well as I, are to be granted a great opportunity. Tomorrow we're going to meet the man who owns this jet. It is a great honor." Luhr chuckled to himself. "Or so I've been led to believe."

The walls of the Lear thrummed as the engines spooled up for the taxi run.

"Still," he said, "I don't think we need all that constricting tape." Ilse struggled harder. Luhr grinned. "You're sure you wouldn't like a little sedative? We have a long flight ahead." He stood carefully, holding his head sideways beneath the low cabin ceiling. He towered over Ilse on the floor. "Although," he said heavily, "I think we might arrange some interesting inflight diversions."

As if about to relieve himself, Luhr unzipped his trousers and withdrew a large, uncircumcised penis. While Ilse stared in disgust, he tugged himself eagerly, watching her reaction. She wasn't frightened by the sight of his organ—most Berlin girls have seen their share of male anatomy—it was his *eyes*. In a single instant all humanity had gone out of them. As the grunting lieutenant pulled at himself, his blue eyes burned not with lust, but with blind, furious hatred. Jürgen Luhr wanted to do more than rape Ilse—he wanted to kill her—to rape her to death if he could.

She shut her eyes tight and forced her mind away from this place, back to a time just after she and Hans were married. They had gone to Munich to visit Hans's mother, at a small *Pfahlbauten* on the long silver lake outside the city. Frau Jaspers, née Apfel, had been bitchy, but Hans and Ilse had spent hours together on the water, paddling a small boat and—

"You think you can handle this?" Luhr rasped, brandishing his organ. "You're going to get it ways you never even dreamed about—"

Suddenly the plane lurched forward. Luhr lost his balance and fell back into his seat, laughing wildly. Ilse struggled in vain against the tape, trapped like a living mummy. Putting himself back into his trousers, Luhr leaned back in his seat and sighed deeply. "Plenty of time for that," he muttered. The madness had faded from his eyes. He leisurely raised a gleaming boot and prodded Ilse's bottom, then laughed again.

The Learjet reached its assigned runway and paused, engines shuddering, pointed east like a porcelain arrow. The legend on its tail read LASERTEK, but this company was merely a tiny division in the labyrinthine network of subsidiaries owned by Horn Intercomm, a holding company on the outer edges of a vast but nebulous corporate entity known as Phoenix AG. This familial relationship was symbolized by a small design painted on the nosecone of the Lear. The single, gracefully curved, bloodred eye stared down the runway from the port side of the Lear with a strange awareness, as if it, and not the pilot, would guide the plane on its long journey south.

Inside the pressurized cabin, Luhr held Ilse in place with his boot as the jet screamed into the night sky. The flight plan filed in the Tegel tower designated the Lear as Flight 116, destination London. But as soon as the sleek jet faded from Tegel's main radar screen, it would dive and race southward to a remote airfield in Turkey. Another subsidiary of Phoenix AG maintained extensive holdings in the Antalya province, among them a surprisingly well-equipped airstrip on a farm near Dashar. This company fostered extremely cordial relations with the provincial government officials, who often made use of Phoenix jets to take "fact-finding" excursions to the pleasure capitals of Europe. After the Lear left Dashar, it would no longer have a flight number or plan, and its destination would be a matter into which only the most uninformed would inquire. The grasp of the reclusive president and CEO of Phoenix AG Corporation was known to be very long indeed.

CHAPTER THIRTEEN

1:35 A.M. Near Wolfsburg, FRG

"That's it!" Hans cried, whipping his head around for a better look. "You passed it!"

Hauer hit the brakes. "That's what you said two minutes ago."

"I'm sure this time."

Reluctantly, Hauer shifted the Jaguar into reverse. "Why here? It's just another break in the trees. Another dead-end road in the dark."

"No. This is the place. We're between two hills. And that low bridge back there . . . This is it."

Hauer released the clutch pedal and backed the car into position to turn. The Jaguar shot forward. He accelerated down the winding drive at twice the speed Natterman had, squinting ahead through the darkness for any sign of an occupied dwelling. "I don't see any lights," he said skeptically.

"Maybe they're sleeping.

Hauer looked across at Hans. "Your wife has just escaped from the KGB, she has no idea where you are, and you think she's sleeping—"

"Watch out!"

Hauer slammed his boot down on the brake just as the Jaguar broke into the small clearing around the cabin. The car hit a sheet of ice, spun 360 degrees and skated toward the building. It crashed into the trunk of a plane tree just meters from the porch, crumpling the Jaguar's offside wing. The motor died, but the headlights still shone off into the darkness to the right of the cabin.

"This better be the place," Hauer mumbled, shaking his head to clear the fog of impact.

Hans stuck his head through the shattered passenger window and compared what he saw to his mental image of his wife's family retreat. "This is it," he said quietly. He turned to Hauer. "Why were you driving so goddamn fast!"

Hauer bit back a sharp retort. He half-expected them to find the bloody remains of Ilse and her grandfather inside the cabin. "Just knock on the door," he said evenly.

Hans muttered angrily as he struggled with the unfamiliar door handle, not even trying to conceal his exasperation. "Ilse!" he shouted. "It's me, Hans!"

Just as Hans popped the door open, it hammered him back into the car. He did not even hear the booming explosion that resounded through the forest.

"Get down!" Hauer bellowed. His warning was lost as the front windshield shattered in a storm of flying glass.

"Shotgun, Hans! Down!"

Hans had hunkered down on the floor when a third blast shredded the leather upholstery above his head. The fourth missed the Jaguar altogether. Hauer grabbed his Walther from beneath the seat and jerked back the slide.

"Wait!" Hans pleaded, grabbing his arm. "Ilse wouldn't know this car!" He kicked open the shot-riddled door. "Ilse! Professor! It's Hans!" This time he saw the fire leap from the muzzles. The twin barrels exploded simultaneously, shearing off the frozen branches hanging low over the car. Hans ducked behind the Jag's door. "Professor! Your father Alfred was a blacksmith! He built this house in 1925! You helped him make the nails!"

Silence.

"Now you're thinking," Hauer said.

The splintered cabin door creaked open slightly. "Hans?" rasped a voice almost too weak to hear. "Hans, is that you?"

"Don't shoot, Professor! I'm coming out!"

Gingerly he raised his hands above the car door and waved. Then he put a foot onto the packed snow and slowly raised himself into Natterman's line of sight.

"I can't see you!" Natterman called. "Step into the light!"

Painfully aware of the loaded weapon pointed at his chest, Hans eased forward into the twin beams.

"Hans." The voice was louder now, the relief in it obvious. "Are you alone?"

"No! I have . . ." He looked back at Hauer in the Jag. "I have my captain with me!"

There was a long pause. "Do you trust him?"

For the hundredth time that night, Hans examined his feelings about his father. *Did* he trust him? Hauer could just as easily be a *member* of the fanatical societies whose meetings he described as— *No!* Hans slammed that door shut in his mind. If Dieter Hauer could contemplate killing a brother officer and kidnapping his own son's wife, the whole world had turned upside down.

"I trust him!" he called.

Hinges screeched as Natterman pushed open the cabin door. He slumped to his knees. "All right," he croaked, "that's . . ." The old man fell flat on his face, his empty shotgun beside him.

Hans sprinted up onto the porch and bent over him. Hauer stayed in the Jaguar, his Walther extended, covering the porch and the clearing as best he could.

"Professor!" Hans cried, shaking him roughly. "Where is Ilse?"

"I got him," the old man mumbled. "I think . . ."

Hans slapped him. Then again, harder. He saw crusted blood around Natterman's disfigured nose, but he had too much at stake to wait. "*Where is Ilse, Professor?* Where is *Ilse?* Did the people who attacked you take her?" Hans turned to the open door. "*Ilse!*"

"Not . . . not here," Natterman mumbled. "Home, I think. Yes." His voice gained strength. "She's at the apartment, Hans. Coming here later. Tried to call, but . . ."

"Oh God." Hans shivered as the implication of Natterman's ramblings struck him. "Oh no. Captain! Help me get him into the house!"

Hauer scrambled out of the car. He backed up onto the porch, keeping the pistol pointed at the woods as he moved.

"She's not here," Hans told him. "She's not *here* . . ."

"Take his legs!" Hauer ordered, grabbing the old man under the arms. He had to keep Hans moving, keep his mind on something besides his wife until there was time to analyze the situation.

They laid Natterman on the sofa in the front room. Hauer sent Hans to fill a sock with snow, then tried his best to determine the seriousness of the professor's wound. Cleaning it started the bleeding again—which seemed incredible given the amount of blood splattered throughout the cabin—but the frozen compress stanched the flow nicely. Hauer substituted adhesive tape for sutures, fastening the edges of the severed nostril together with surprising skill. He leaned back to survey his work. "Wouldn't pass inspection at a *Bundeswehr* hospital, but not bad for a field dressing. Let's get a blanket on him." He looked around. "Hans?"

Standing rigid at the bedroom door, Hans gasped and staggered backward. Hauer darted to the door, saw Karl Riemeck's body, then returned to Natterman's side.

"Who's the man in the bedroom?" he asked, his mouth an inch from the old man's ear. "A friend of yours?"

Natterman nodded.

"Who killed him? Did you see him killed?"

The professor shook his head, then opened his eyes slowly. "Karl was my caretaker," he whispered. "The *animal* killed him."

"Animal? What animal?" Hauer groaned as the old man's eyes closed. He was out again. "Hans! Get over here and help me!"

Hans didn't move. His eyes seemed to be fixed on some undefined point in space. Hauer had seen the look before: American army officers called it the thousand-yard stare. It was the Vietnam variant of shell shock, but Hauer knew that neither bullets nor blood had caused Hans's torpor. What had overloaded his mind was the justified fear of losing his wife forever. Giving Hans hope became Hauer's primary objective, for he knew that Hans's unearthly calm was merely the silence before the storm, the moment when all his fear and impotent rage would explode through his self-control like a hurricane.

"Ilse must still be on her way," Hauer said confidently, preparing to restrain Hans physically if necessary.

Hans's jaw muscles flexed steadily. "I would have seen her," he mumbled.

"You *wouldn't* have seen her. We crossed East Germany in the trunk of a car, for God's sake. Maybe she took a late train like the professor. Maybe she hitched a ride in a truck. She could still be waiting for a train right now." Keeping his eyes on Hans, Hauer shook Natterman gently. "Is there a telephone, Professor?"

"Dead . . . I think the man who attacked me cut the line."

"Repair it, Hans," Hauer ordered. "Check the unit, then trace the wire."

Hans finally focused on Hauer's face. "No," he said quietly. "I'm going back to Berlin." He was trying to rebutton his coat, but his shaking fingers seemed unable to keep hold of the small buttons.

"You can't get back in," Hauer told him.

"It's Ilse's only chance ... She could be—"

"*No!*" Professor Natterman's stentorian voice boomed through the small room like a thunderclap. Hauer stared as the old man slowly raised himself and leveled a long finger at Hans. "You will *not* go back. To return now would be suicide. Can you help Ilse if you're dead? The telephone must be our lifeline now."

The professor's rebuke left him winded, but it had a dramatic effect on Hans. He rubbed his forehead furiously with both hands as he walked away from the two older men. "If only I hadn't tried to keep those goddamn papers," he muttered.

"You did the right thing," Hauer said firmly. "If you had turned the papers in, Funk would have them now, and you'd be as dead as your friend Weiss."

Hans looked up with red-rimmed eyes.

"Trace the wire," Hauer said softly, looking to Natterman for support.

"It runs out of a hole in back of the cabin," said the professor.

Hans still looked uncertain.

Hauer drew his Walther. "And take this. Whoever attacked the professor may still be out there."

Hans snatched the pistol and disappeared through the front door.

Natterman turned to Hauer. "Will he try to leave?"

"He can't. I've got the keys."

Natterman studied Hauer's face. "You're Hans's father," he said after some moments. "Aren't you? I can see the resemblance."

Hauer took a slow, deep breath, then he nodded curtly.

Natterman made a sound that was almost a chuckle. "Ilse told me you had been at Spandau. So, you've acknowledged your son at last, eh?"

"I acknowledged him the first moment I saw him," Hauer said in a clipped tone.

Natterman looked skeptical. "Tell me, Captain, you're the expert. Do you believe I will ever see my granddaughter again?"

Hauer pursed his lips. "Who has the papers Hans found at Spandau?"

Natterman hesitated, thinking of the three pages that had disappeared with Karl Riemeck's murderer. "I do," he confessed. "They're safe."

Hauer wondered if the old man had the papers on him. "Then I'll give you sixty-forty odds that she's still alive. Frankly, I'd expect a ransom demand any time now. And you know what they'll be asking for." He walked over to the cabinet that had concealed the shotgun. He touched it softly, appearing to examine the grain of the wood. "So," he said. "Exactly what is in these papers Hans discovered?"

Natterman propped himself up on the arm of the sofa. It made him dizzy, but he felt better able to deal with questions from an upright position.

"You must realize that you'll need assistance to do anything from this point on," Hauer said. "You must also realize that I'm the only man within a great distance who is able to help you."

"On the contrary," Natterman said testily. "There are many nearby who would help me."

Hauer sighed. "Men like the one in the bedroom there?"

Natterman's eyes smoldered. "Why should you help me?" he snapped. "What exactly are you after, Hauer?"

Hauer stiffened. In Germany, the cavalier omission of a man's rank or title is an open insult. He was moving forward when boots clattered loudly on the porch. The splintered door banged open.

"I need a knife," said Hans, his breath steaming as he closed the door. He stamped his icy boots on the floorboards while he searched the kitchen alcove.

"How long will it take?" Hauer asked, his eyes still on Natterman.

"Less than a minute if I didn't have to climb that goddamn pole. It's covered with ice, and the bastard cut the wire at the top." Hans found a sharp paring knife in a drawer and clomped out again.

"I'm waiting," said Hauer.

Natterman sighed. He would have to say something, he knew, but misdirecting a police captain shouldn't be too difficult. "All right, Captain," he said. "What Hans found at Spandau—what *your* son found—is a letter of sorts. A diary, if you will. A diary written in Latin by the man known to the world for almost fifty years as Rudolf Hess."

"Perfect," said Hauer. "A dead language from a dead man."

The professor sniffed indignantly. "This diary happens to prove that that particular dead man was not Rudolf Hess."

Hauer's eyes narrowed. "You believe that?"

Natterman looked sanguine. "It's nothing new. You've heard all the theories, I'm sure. Himmler tricked Hess into becoming a pawn in his quest for Hitler's job; Göring had Hess shot down, then—"

"I've heard the theories," Hauer cut in. "And that's just what they are, theories. Bullshit."

"Your expert opinion notwithstanding," Natterman said, "I believe that the man who died last month in Spandau was never the Deputy Führer of the Third Reich. And from what I saw on television today, I'd say the Russians believe that too."

Hauer snorted. "The Russians would hound a rat right up their backsides if they thought it endangered their precious Motherland. What proof is there that the papers are authentic?"

Natterman bridled. "Why the diary itself, of course."

"You mean that it exists? That Hans found it where he did?"

The professor tugged at his silver beard. "No. Those things are significant, but it's the papers *themselves* that are the proof."

"How?"

"The *language,* Captain. You might think that Prisoner Number Seven wrote in Latin to conceal his words from the prison guards, or something similar. But that's not the case at all. *Think,* man. Here was a man who knew he was near death, who decided to leave a record of the truth. Yet all proof that he ever lived had been wiped out long ago by Reinhard Heydrich. How could he prove who he was? I'll tell you. As Hess's trained double, Number Seven had studied everything about the Deputy Führer. Yet no matter how much like Hess he became, he still possessed certain traits and abilities that Hess did not. And knowing those abilities better than anyone, he *used* one to prove his identity. Thus, he wrote his final record in Latin." Natterman's eyes flashed with triumph. "And so far as I have been able to determine,

Rudolf Hess—though better educated than most of Hitler's inner circle—did not know more than twenty words of Latin, *if any*."

"That proves nothing," Hauer argued. "In fact, that suggests to me that some crank wrote this diary."

"Why do you fight this so hard, Captain? Number Seven was the *only* prisoner."

"At the end. There were others before."

"Yes," Natterman admitted. "A few. But cranks? No. And the searches, Captain, there were thousands of them. The diary *must* have been written near the end."

"It could have been slipped in by a guard," Hauer suggested. But the cold ache in his chest belied his words.

Natterman shrugged. "It's not my job to convince you, Captain. But given what's already occurred, I suggest we work on the assumption that the diary is genuine—at least until I can take further steps to authenticate it."

Hauer rummaged through his borrowed suit for a cigar. "But what's the *point* of all this? The KGB and half the Berlin police force haven't gone mad over some scrap of history. What does the diary mean *now?*"

"Now?" Natterman smiled. "I suppose that depends on who you happen to be. Paradoxically enough, the answer to your question lies in the past. That is why the diary is so important." The old man's voice climbed a semitone with repressed excitement. "It is a veritable tunnel into the past . . . into *history*."

Hauer walked to the front window of the cabin and stared out into the frozen darkness. "Professor," he said finally, "if this diary *were* real, is there any conceivable way it could be embarrassing enough to influence NATO? Possibly even the Soviet Union?"

Natterman raised an eyebrow. "Given the lengths to which certain countries have gone to suppress the Hess story, I would say yes. Of course it would depend on what one wanted to influence those nations to *do*."

Hauer nodded. "Suppose someone wanted to use the diary to make the superpowers more amenable to the idea of German reunification?"

Natterman's face darkened with suspicion. "I think I have answered enough questions, Captain. I think you should—"

The splintered cabin door banged open again. When Hauer turned, he saw Hans hunched over, dragging something into the cabin. It took him a moment to realize that it was a human body. Then he saw the hair—long, blond hair.

"Hans?" he said hoarsely.

Hans grunted and fell backward, breathing hard. The corpse's head thudded to the floor. Hauer walked slowly across the room and looked down at the body. It wasn't Ilse. It was a man. A dead man with long blond hair. The right arm hung from the torso by a single cord of tendon; the shoulder had been blasted into mush by the professor's shotgun. But the most shocking sight was the throat. It had been expertly cut from ear to ear.

"A thorough job, Professor," said Hauer.

"I—I didn't do that," Natterman stammered. "Not the throat."

Hauer glanced furtively at the windows.

"There's someone else out there!" Natterman cried.

Hauer watched in astonishment as the old man flew at the carcass like a grave robber. He rifled every pocket, then began groping beneath the frozen, blood-matted shirt.

"What are you doing, Professor!"

Natterman looked up, his eyes wild. "I—I'm trying to find out who he is."

"Any papers on him?"

Natterman shook his head violently, afraid for a moment that Hauer had asked about the missing diary pages. *But he doesn't know they're missing,* he reassured himself, getting to his feet. *He doesn't know . . .*

Hauer said, "It's a good thing he didn't get hold of the Spandau papers. There's no telling where they might be now."

"You have the papers?" Hans asked in surprise.

My God, Natterman thought wildly. *Where are those pages?* "Ilse gave them to me," he said.

"The question," Hauer mused, "is who finished this bastard off?" With a grunt he crouched over the body and heaved it onto its stomach. The half-severed head flopped over last. Hauer probed the thick blond hair behind the corpse's right ear. "Well, well," he said, "at least we know who sent this one. Look."

Hans and the professor knelt and examined the spot Hauer had exposed with his fingertips. Beneath the roots of the dead man's hair was a mark just under two centimeters long. It was an eye. A single, bloodred eye.

"Phoenix," Hauer muttered.

Natterman jerked as if he had been stunned with electricity. "It's the eye from the Spandau papers! The exact design! The All-Seeing Eye. What does it mean there? On this man's *head?*"

Hauer stood. "It means that Funk's little cabal sent this fellow. Or his masters did."

"You said 'Phoenix.' You haven't read the Spandau papers. What do you know about the word *Phoenix?*"

"Not nearly enough."

"But who *killed* him?" Hans asked. "Whoever it was . . . it's almost as if he's helping us. Maybe he knows something about Ilse."

Hans darted toward the door, but Hauer caught him by the sleeve. "Hans, whoever killed this man did it to get the papers, *not* to help us. You were outside for ten minutes and no one talked to you. Obviously no one wanted to. Whoever's out there could cut your throat as easily as he did this fellow's, so forget it." He kept hold of Hans's sleeve. "Did you fix the telephone?"

Hans looked longingly at the door. "The wire's spliced," he said in a monotone.

"Good. I'll call Steuben at the station. If something's changed in Berlin, we just might be able to slip back in before morning."

Hauer knew it was a lie when he said it. They wouldn't be going back to Berlin. Not until they had followed the Spandau diary wherever it led—until they had traveled the professor's "tunnel into the past" to its bitter end. One look at the mangled carcass at his feet told him it was going to be a bloody journey.

"We'd better stand watches," he said. "Whoever killed our tattooed friend may still be out there. You're up first, Hans."

Thirty meters from the cabin, a tall sentinel stood in the deep snow beneath the dripping trees. In one hand he held three bloodstained sheets of onionskin paper, in the other a knife. By holding the blade at a certain angle, he could illuminate the pages by reflecting light from the cabin windows. But it was no use. He spoke three languages fluently, but he could not read Latin. As he watched the silhouettes moving across the yellow-lit windows, he envied the old man's education. Not that it made any difference. He had known what the papers said ever since he'd stood outside the door of the Apfel apartment and listened to the arguments inside. Stuffing the pages into his coat pocket, he murmured a few words in Hebrew. Then he squatted down on his haunches in the deep snow. He had lived in the burning desert for the past twelve years, but the cold was nothing to him. Jonas Stern knew he could outwait anybody.

Especially Germans.

MI-5 Headquarters: Charles Street, London, England

Sir Neville Shaw jerked his head up from the Hess file; he'd been poring over it so long that he had dropped into a kind of half-sleep. He snapped out of it when Wilson, his deputy, barged into his dim office without knocking, something he was forbidden to do on pain of bloodcurdling punishments.

"What the devil!" Shaw snapped.

"I'm sorry, sir," Wilson panted. "I think we've got a problem."

"Well?"

"We finally got something on Spandau—from a Ukrainian in the technical section of KGB East Berlin. It seems the KGB shot pictures of everyone who gathered to watch the destruction of the prison. He didn't know why they took the pictures, but he slipped us the list of names their computers matched to the photos. They actually turned up a couple of old SS men—"

"Get to the point!" Shaw barked.

"It's *Stern*, sir. Jonas Stern. The Israeli that the Mossad wrote us about. He was at Spandau Prison on the day we tore it down!"

Only a steady whitening of Shaw's knuckles on the desktop revealed how shocked he was. He rocked slowly back and forth for nearly a full minute; then he looked up at Wilson, his eyes bright with purpose. "Did you pull the file on the woman I told you about?"

"Swallow? Yes, sir. Ann Gordon is her real name."

"Is she living in England?"

"In a little hamlet about thirty miles west of London."

Shaw nodded contentedly. "I'll need to speak to her. 1

don't want her coming here, though. Set up a secure line so that I can brief her by phone."

Wilson's brow knit with confusion. "But I don't understand, Sir Neville. Swallow is retired."

"I seriously doubt that. But even if she is, she'll come running when she hears Stern's name."

"Do you mean to reactivate this woman, sir?"

Shaw ignored the question. "I don't know how Jonas Stern is tied into the Hess case, but he can't be allowed to get near those papers. If papers are what's been found."

"But why use Swallow at all? She's ... she's an *old woman*. My lads can handle any situation with twice the reliability."

Shaw laughed quietly. "Wilson, we tread shadowy paths, but there are deeds done in this world that should never see the light of day. Swallow has done more than her share of them. I'll bet your four best men couldn't sandbag that old harridan."

Wilson looked indignant. "Sir Neville, this seems terribly irregular. Going out of school like this—"

"That's exactly the *point*," Shaw snapped. "Swallow is absolutely, totally deniable. If something embarrassing were to happen—if she happened to kill Stern, say—all could be blamed on this old vendetta. Even the Israelis couldn't fault us. Their letter practically exonerates us before the fact. It proves Stern was at risk the moment he left Israel."

Sir Neville folded his hands into a church steeple and studied a Wedgwood paperweight on his desk. Wilson watched his master with growing apprehension. The MI-5 director looked as if he'd aged five years in the brief hours since their last meeting.

"You're to put together a second team," Shaw said slowly. "No brief as yet, but have them ready. More hard boys. The hardest."

Wilson cleared his throat. "May I ask what for, sir?"

Sir Neville ran his hands through his thinning hair, then massaged his high forehead with his fingertips. "I'm afraid, Wilson, that if your other lads are unlucky enough to find those Spandau papers, they'll have cashed in their chips."

Wilson's face went white. "But you ..." He faltered, recognizing the diamond-hard gleam in Shaw's eye. "When you briefed them you gave direct orders not to read the papers if found. They won't."

Sir Neville sighed. "We can't be sure of that."

"But they're my best three men!" Wilson exploded.

Sir Neville raised an eyebrow. "*Your* men? Interesting choice of words, Wilson." His craggy face softened. "Damn it, Robert, it's not my choice, is it? It's the word from on high. Tablets from the bloody mountaintop!"

Wilson's mouth worked in silent, furious incomprehension. "But what does that *mean,* Neville? We are a *constitutional* monarchy, for God's sake!"

Sir Neville cleared his throat. "That's quite enough, old boy. I've been instructed that as regards this case, we're to consider ourselves on a war footing."

"But we're not at war! We can't just *kill our own people!*"

Sir Neville attempted a paternal smile, and it was terrible to see. His eyes had focused into some foggy distance that he alone perceived. "Some wars, Wilson," he murmured, "last a very long time. A war like the last one—the last *real* one—doesn't end on a battlefield. Or on some baize treaty table. There are loose ends, unfinished business. Left uncut, those loose ends tangle and eventually get drawn into the skein of the next war. That's what's happening here. For too long we simply hoped that this Hess business would go away. Well, it hasn't." Sir Neville blinked, then splayed his hands on the mahogany desktop. "It's settled," he said with resignation. "I've got my orders. When those papers are found, everyone down the chain is on borrowed time."

"But that's insane!" Wilson almost shouted. "You sound like a bloody Nazi yourself!"

Sir Neville bit his lip in forbearance. "Wilson," he rasped, "*if* your lads find those papers and bring them to you, you shut your eyes and shove them right in here to me. Because *no one* in that chain will be exempt. Am I clear?" He examined his fingernails. "And I've got a feeling that includes myself."

The deputy director's eyes widened. "What in God's name is in those papers, Sir Neville? What could that moth-eaten old Nazi have *known?*"

Shaw grimaced. "It's not what's in them, Robert, but what *might* be in them. What they could *lead* to. You think the Cold War's over? What a load of tripe. Twenty hours ago it reared its ugly head, and not for the last time, I'll wager. I've heard half a dozen back-corridor versions of the Hess affair in my time, and not one of them is true. There are guilty consciences on high, Wilson. It's evidence we're after. Of what? A bargain with the devil, British-style. A marriage of convenience to the Teutonic Mephistopheles. Enough black ink to smudge out the oldest reputations in banking, government, and manufacturing. Maybe enough heat to crack the bloody Crown itself."

Wilson flexed his fists. "The Crown be damned," he said softly. "We should have killed Hess years ago."

Arctic fire flickered in Sir Neville Shaw's eyes. "We did kill him, Robert," he said. "I suppose it's high time you knew."

Wilson felt cold sweat beading on the back of his neck. "I . . . I beg your pardon, Sir Neville?"

"I said we *killed* Hess." Shaw plucked an errant lash from his eye. "The damned thing of it is, we're going to have to kill him again."

CHAPTER FOURTEEN

2:00 A.M. Tiergarten Kriminalpolizei Division, West Berlin

Detective Julius Schneider lifted the telephone receiver and dialed a number from the special list he kept in his top desk drawer. A very loud voice inside his head was telling him it would be better to drop this matter altogether—better for his marriage, much better for his career. But the adrenaline pulsing through his body kept the phone in his hand.

"What?" growled a tired voice at last.

"Colonel Rose?" he said, concentrating on his English pronunciation.

"Yeah, Rose here. Who's this? Clary? Jesus, it's two A.M."

"Colonel, my name is Julius Schneider. You don't know me. I'm a detective with the West Berlin *Kriminalpolizei*."

"What?"

"Are you *awake*, Colonel? I have something very important to tell you."

"Yeah, yeah, I'm awake. Go ahead."

"This is a very sensitive matter. Perhaps we could meet somewhere."

Rose was definitely awake now. His voice took on a hard edge of suspicion. "Who did you say this is?"

"Detective *Julius Schneider*, Colonel. Eighteen months ago you gave a lecture on NATO intelligence-sharing—November, U.S. Army headquarters in Dahlem. I attended along with nine other Kripo detectives."

"Uh-huh," Rose grunted. "Okay, let's say I'm mildly interested. What's your problem?"

"As I said, Colonel, I don't feel comfortable going into it on the telephone."

"Outline the situation."

"I'd prefer to meet you somewhere."

"It's gonna take more than that to get me out into the cold alone, son. Give me something."

Schneider glanced through his office window at the sluggish activity of the night duty officers. "I think you've got a man over the Wall," he whispered quickly.

"A what?" Rose sounded incredulous. "What do you mean? A defector?"

Schneider spoke still lower. "No, Colonel, I think one of your officers has been taken over the Wall against his will—"

"Don't say another word!" Rose snapped. "Where are you?"

"The Tiergarten Kripo station."

Colonel Rose pulled a map of Berlin from his bedside table. "Okay, Mr. Detective," he said slowly, "you know the Penta Hotel? Should be two blocks from where you are now."

"I know it."

"Be standing in the front service doorway in fifteen minutes. I'll cruise by with my door open—you jump in. Got it?"

"Ja."

"You in uniform?"

"Nein. Kripo don't wear uniforms."

"When you move toward the car have both hands extended. *Empty.* Wait a second . . . what was your name? Full name?"

"Julius K. Schneider, Kripo Detective First Grade."

"Right. Fifteen minutes."

Schneider heard Rose disconnect. Looking at his watch, he decided to wait fourteen minutes in his office, then sprint the two blocks to the Penta. At two-twelve he donned his hat and overcoat, said good night to the duty sergeant and strolled casually out of the station. The wind hit his face like a shrew's slap. Schneider turned into the blast and began running with surprising speed for a man of his bulk. He glanced at his watch as he crossed to the next block. Two-thirteen. *Come on, Colonel . . .* A car moved up from his rear, slowed, passed. Halfway up the second block, he ducked into the front service doorway of the imposing Penta Hotel. His gasps filled the lighted alcove with steam.

Two-fourteen, and still no colonel. Schneider pulled off his left boot and smashed the fluorescent bulb over his head. *No sense in advertising,* he thought, tugging the boot back on. As he straightened up, a battered U.S. Army Ford came roaring up the Nürnberger Strasse. The passenger door swung open thirty meters from the Penta's service door, but the car showed no signs of slowing.

Schneider judged the Ford's speed at sixty kilometers per hour. Like a fullback he charged from the safety of his niche and sprinted alongside the car with both hands extended. He could see the bull-necked American colonel in the driver's seat, scrutinizing him over the barrel of what looked like a .45 caliber pistol. Tiring quickly, Schneider flailed his arms for Rose to stop. The Ford slowed to thirty kilometers per hour. Schneider could hear Rose yelling for him to jump in. Almost out of wind, he managed to catch hold of the door-frame and dive headlong across the front seat. When he tried to rise, he felt the cold metal of a gun barrel pressed to his temple.

"That's a Colt .45 on your noggin, son," Rose growled. "Don't move until I say so. Understand?"

"Ja," Schneider grunted.

With a skillful swing of the steering wheel Rose simultaneously slammed the passenger door and swung onto the six-lane Hohenzollerndamm, heading west. "Full name?" he barked.

"Julius K. Schneider."

"Rank?"

"Detective, First Grade."

"Length of service?"

"Seven—no, eight years."

"Name of spouse?"

"What the hell does it matter? I'm the one—"

Rose jammed the pistol barrel into Schneider's ear. *"Name of spouse!"*

"*Aarrghh!* Liese, damn you!"

Rose withdrew the gun. "Okay, get up."

Rattled and angry, Schneider thrust himself against the passenger door and rubbed his cheek where the gun had scraped it. "What the hell was that for?" he asked in German.

"You ought to have expected it," Rose replied in English.

"You call in the middle of the night to tell me one of my men has been kidnapped, and you expect a cocktail party?"

"Is this the way Americans return favors?" Schneider said stiffly.

"Last I checked, you hadn't done me any favors. We'll see how I return one when you do. Now what the hell's this all about?"

"Major Harry Richardson," Schneider answered, relishing the poorly concealed look of shock that crossed Rose's face. "You know him?"

"Go on," Rose said noncommittally.

"Very well, Colonel. Tonight I was called to the scene of a murder. A house near the Tiergarten. The murdered man was one Klaus Seeckt, an East German trade liaison employed by my government. My colleagues believe Seeckt surprised a gang of professional thieves who murdered him, then tried to make it look like suicide. And they could be right, of course. The Kripo are famous for their skill in solving homicides."

"Get to the point, Detective."

"I believe a real suicide took place, Colonel. Not a *simple* suicide, but a suicide still."

"I'm listening. You can speak German if you like."

Schneider sighed with relief. "Physical evidence, Colonel. First, eight 7.65mm slugs fired into an interior wall beside the front door—burst pattern. We found no shell casings to match these slugs. Second, no fingerprints on the pistol in the corpse's hand except his own. Third, I found something odd outside the house. It was a white business card"— Schneider paused for effect—"with nothing but a telephone number on it."

He saw Rose's jaw tighten. "When I called the number on the card, I got an answering machine with a message from one Harry Richardson. As I'm sure you're aware, Major Richardson makes a rather special effort to know Berlin. Consequently, we Berliners know him."

Rose exited right off the Hohenzollerndamm onto Clay-Allee, then looped under to the Avus autobahn. Solemn ranks of bare trees closed about the car as it rolled into the Grunewald. The colonel seemed to feel more comfortable here, Schneider noticed. Perhaps because from the heart of the Grunewald jutted the Teufelsberg—the Devil's Mountain—a massive hill constructed from the millions of tons of rubble that was Berlin after the war. Schneider thought it depressingly symbolic that the highest peak in Berlin was crowned by the futuristic onion domes of a gargantuan U.S./British radar spying station. Rose slowed and turned to Schneider as they rolled through the darkness.

"And what does all that tell you, Mr. Detective?"

"The 7.65mm slugs tell me Czech vz/61 Skorpion machine pistol. I translate that KGB. I know it would be stupid for them to use one here, but they've made stupid mistakes before. I also happen to know that, in spite of the drawbacks of the 7.65 cartridge, several Berlin-based KGB agents still favor the Skorpion. Granted, burglars could use one, but I haven't seen any pass through the evidence room lately."

Rose eyed the German with increasing interest.

"Then there's the weapon that killed Seeckt. If burglars faked a suicide, they had to shoot Seeckt, wipe the pistol, then press a set of his fingerprints onto it. Leaving what? One good set of Seeckt's prints. But there were dozens. If they used gloves, they'd have smudged many of Seeckt's original prints. But they didn't. So what happened? Burglars forced Seeckt to kill himself? Unlikely. But the KGB? It's possible. If KGB agents had just discovered that Richardson had turned Seeckt, for example, Seeckt might have preferred a quick bullet to what would have been waiting for him in Lubyanka. My *trieb*, Colonel—my instinct—tells me that's what happened. The question is, what was your man doing there in the first place? *Was* Klaus Seeckt working for you?"

Rose said nothing.

"One more thing," Schneider added. "There was blood near the card."

Rose winced.

"A good bit of it, too. Colonel, I think Richardson dropped that card as an SOS. Why else would it be there?"

Without really knowing why, Rose decided to trust the German. He really didn't have much choice. "Harry Richardson's an exceptional officer," he said tersely. "A bit of a loner, maybe, but sound as a K-bar. Especially in tradecraft. But even if he has been kidnapped, what makes you think he's not still in West Berlin?"

Schneider's barrel chest swelled a size; he recognized the respect that came with Rose's decision to trust him. "Because Russians wouldn't have the nerve to keep him here," he explained. "East Germans would—the Stasi has assets all over the city. But this crime scene was too clumsy for the Stasi. They would never, *never* use weapons of Eastern manufacture in the West. Also, burglars-turned-kidnappers would soon recognize their mistake in snatching an American officer. Unless they were part-time terrorists, it would scare them to death. That leaves one option—KGB. It has to be."

"Alert the checkpoints," said Rose, his voice taking on the weight of command. "See if any known agents have passed through tonight—"

"I've already checked," Schneider told him. "It's too late. A border officer at Heinrich-Heine Strasse told me four KGB agents with flawless cover passed through at eleven-fifteen tonight. Richardson was probably inside that car."

"God*damn!*"

"What was Richardson working on, Colonel?"

"Sorry, Schneider. I can't go that far."

"I see," the German said icily. "Well, then. I'll leave you to discover the remaining facts for yourself."

Rose slammed on the brakes and glared at Schneider. "Don't you hold out on me, Schneider! This is still a U.S. military zone of occupation. I can have your ass detained for a year if I need to!"

"That is true," Schneider retorted. "But while you carry out that useless exercise, your man could be dying in a KGB cell. Or worse yet, he could be on the next flight to Moscow. Even the KGB is smart enough to know that in East Berlin, a live American major is more of a liability than an asset."

"You're pushing, Schneider."

The German's voice hardened. "I want this case, Colonel."

Rose pursed his lips and leaned back into his seat. "Okay, Detective," he said finally. "*Quid pro quo*. You give me everything you've got, and I'll see you're included in any developments on this side of the Wall."

Schneider searched out Rose's eyes in the darkness. "You give me your word as an American officer and a gentleman?"

Rose eyed the German strangely. "I didn't think that bought much overseas anymore."

"It does from me," Schneider said solemnly.

Rose felt as if he had somehow stepped back in time. "As an officer and a gentleman, then," he vowed.

"Gut," grunted the German. Quickly he told Rose about Lieutenant Luhr's unusual appearance at the murder scene, and his interest in Richardson's card. When Schneider revealed that Prefect Funk was personally directing the Spandau case from Abschnitt 53, Rose looked very uncomfortable.

"Was Richardson working on something related to the Spandau incident?" Schneider asked.

Rose nodded slowly.

The German shook his large head. "Something very big is happening, Colonel. I can feel it. At 10:20 P.M. the prefect issued an all-district alert for two police officers who allegedly murdered a third in a dispute over drugs. And this murder supposedly took place *in that police station.*"

"What?"

Schneider nodded. "One of the 'fugitives' is a decorated officer, a GSG-9 adviser, no less. And both"—the German smiled thinly—"were on the team assigned to guard Spandau Prison last night."

Rose's eyes widened. "Holy *shit!*"

Schneider smiled with satisfaction. "Stasi agents call you 'God, the All-Knowing,' Colonel. Did you know that?"

"I've heard," Rose answered, barely listening.

"I guess they exaggerate."

Rose grabbed the German's beefy shoulder. "Okay, Schneider, *you* listen. Richardson wasn't due to report until 0800 this morning, so technically he's still on schedule. But I've got a bad feeling about this. My sphincter's twitching, and that ain't good." He paused. "You got any whiskey on you?"

Schneider shook his head, nonplussed by the American's sudden change of demeanor.

"Okay, here's the deal. Harry was looking into the Spandau thing for me. He thought there was a lot more to it than your bosses were letting on, and with the damned State Department and the Brits breathing down my neck, I was all too willing to give him room to maneuver." Rose paused angrily. "If you're right, and the Soviets have taken my boy over that Wall . . ."

He smashed his fist against the Ford's dashboard. With an oath he jerked the car into gear, made a screeching U-turn in the wooded lane, jammed the accelerator to the floor and bored through the ranks of frozen trees, making for the forest's edge.

"You gotta be anywhere, Schneider?" he growled.

"Nein."

"You wanna be temporarily seconded to my command?"

"Jawohl, Herr Oberst!"

"Jesus Christ," Rose snorted. "Will you cut out that Kraut lingo? Makes me nervous. You sound like you're in a goddamn John Wayne movie." He glanced suspiciously at the German. "And on the wrong side."

Schneider choked off an acid reply.

To the German's astonishment, Rose snatched up a radiotelephone and began transmitting *en clair*. Schneider couldn't believe it. Hundreds of listening devices constantly sampled the ether over Berlin and fed the intercepted transmissions into tape recorders in every sector of the city. Rose's call would be heard by at least a hundred people before morning, yet he seemed unconcerned.

"Clary!" he shouted.

"Who's this?" came the sleepy reply.

"Wake up, son!"

"Colonel?"

"Clary, we've got a loose fish tonight, you copy that?"

Schneider heard deep breathing. He imagined the stunned sergeant, wakened from a dead sleep to crazy code words coming from his telephone. "Roger that, sir," Clary mumbled. "Loose fish. Is the fish still in the boat?"

"Probable negative on that, Clary. The fish is out, repeat, *out* of the boat. Copy?"

"That's a roge, sir."

Schneider looked bewildered.

"ETA camp ten minutes," Rose snapped.

"Copy that, sir, I'm outta here."

"Out."

Rose pushed the speed limit all the way through the Grunewald. The American certainly knew his way around, Schneider reflected. Despite the labyrinth of icy lanes winding through the forest, he burst out of the trees less than a mile from U.S. Army headquarters. "Russians," he muttered. "Idiots."

"I beg your pardon, Colonel?"

"The *Russians*, Schneider. The goddamn Russkies, Reds, Commies, whatever."

"What about them?" Schneider bit his lip. He had almost called the American colonel "sir."

"I'll *tell* you what about them," Rose grumbled. "If those sons of bitches have kidnapped my man and taken him over the Wall, that's a goddamn act of war, that's what. And they're gonna find out who really runs this burg, that's what!"

Schneider shifted uncomfortably in his seat. "And that is?"

"The U.S. Army, by God."

The German gave a hollow laugh. "Cut out that American imperialist lingo, would you, Colonel? It makes *me* nervous."

Rose wasn't laughing.

2:05 A.M. *The Natterman Cabin: Wolfsburg, FRG*

"Professor, wake up!" Hauer prodded the old man. "Professor!"

Natterman moaned, then his eyes twitched open and his right arm shot outward. "Karl!" he shouted.

Hans grabbed his outstretched hand. "Professor, it's Hans! We're at your father's house."

The old man's eyes focused at last. He pulled his hand free. "Yes ... Karl is dead?"

"I'm afraid so," said Hauer. He leaned over the sofa where Natterman lay and held up something shiny in his left hand. "What do you make of this, Professor?"

Natterman took the object and examined it briefly. "It's a gold Krugerrand. Standard unit of currency in South Africa."

"Is it common?"

The professor shrugged. "Thousands of Germans own millions of them, I should think. On paper, of course."

"Is the *coin* common?"

"I wouldn't think so. Where did you get it?"

"Hans picked it up outside, standing watch."

Natterman sat up. "My God!"

"What is it?"

"The man who attacked me ... I remember now! I recognized his accent. It was Afrikaans!"

"Afrikaans? What do you make of that?"

Natterman pursed his lips. "I don't know. That man—the

Afrikaner—came here to steal something, but I don't believe he knew exactly what he was after until he actually saw the papers. He didn't seem to believe it, even then."

"An errand boy?"

"That was my impression. What time is it, Hans?"

"A little after two A.M."

"Two! Don't let me fall asleep again. Is the telephone working?"

"Yes," Hauer replied, "but we haven't learned anything." He had tried in vain to reach Josef Steuben at Abschnitt 53. And at Steuben's home he'd got only the men he'd sent to protect Steuben's family. No sign of his friend.

"The apartment's empty," Hans said anxiously.

"Ilse is *all right*," Natterman assured him. "You must believe that. Even if someone has taken her, it's you they want. They need her alive to draw you. They believe you will bring them what they seek."

Hans nodded. "They're right."

Natterman's eyes grew wide. "Have you lost your senses? The Spandau papers are much too important to be surrendered to anyone like that."

Hans glared balefully at the old man. "I don't give a damn about those papers, Professor. You'd better understand that now. I'd give them to the devil himself to have Ilse here with us now." His eyes narrowed suspiciously. "Where *are* the papers?"

Natterman looked hunted. "They're . . . in the bathroom," he said. "I'll get them."

Hauer kept silent. His brain was spinning. *Bruderschaft der Phoenix* . . . The gold Krugerrand and the Afrikaner accent—like the calls from Prefect Funk to Pretoria—had dropped into place like two more tumblers in the lock that protected Phoenix from the outside world. But what did South Africa have to do with Germany? What did Pretoria share with Berlin? Hauer was still puzzling over this when the klaxon ring of the old telephone in the bedroom shattered his concentration. Both he and Hans raced to the phone.

"It's Ilse!" Hans cried, grabbing for the receiver.

Hauer caught his wrist in a grip of steel. "If it is, I'll give the phone straight to you." He lifted the receiver as the raucous bell clanged for the third time.

Two hundred and forty kilometers away, locked in an interrogation room of Abschnitt 53, Prefect Wilhelm Funk nervously eyed a technician who sat before three Marantz PMD-430 tape recorders. Each tape deck was wired directly into the transmitter of Funk's telephone. Two contained recordings of Ilse Apfel's voice, recorded at gunpoint reading a script authored by Pieter Smuts, the Afrikaner known to Funk by the code name *Guardian*. The third deck maintained a constant level of background noise to mask the ON/OFF switching of the primary machines. Praying that the elaborate deception would work, Funk began his performance.

"I wish to speak to Sergeant Hans Apfel," he hissed, trying to mask his distinctive growl.

"I know you, you bastard," said Hauer.

Funk abandoned all pretense. "I know you too, Hauer. Fucking traitor. It's *Sippenhaft* for you, just like your friend Steuben."

Hauer closed his eyes, trying in vain to steel himself against the anguish. He had sent a man to his death. He had made a widow and orphans.

"If Apfel isn't on the phone in ten seconds," Funk warned, "I disconnect. Beginning now. Ten, nine, eight . . ."

Hans snatched the proffered phone. "This is Sergeant Apfel. Where is my wife?"

"Do not speak, Sergeant. In a moment your wife will read a prepared statement. After—"

"Ilse!" Hans shouted. *"Ilse?"*

"One more outburst like that, and this conversation will be terminated. After your wife finishes reading, you may ask questions, but keep them simple. She's a bit under the weather."

Hans swallowed hard.

"Hans, listen to me—"

He clenched the phone with all his strength. Ilse's usually musical voice quavered with fear and confusion, but he knew the sound like his own breathing. He clapped his hand to his forehead in relief, then balled it into a fist as the torment went on:

". . . the men who are holding me require only one thing in exchange for my freedom—the papers you discovered at Spandau. The papers belong to them. You have illegally stolen their property. Restitution is all that they seek. I do not know where I am. If you follow the instructions you are

given exactly, we will be reunited. If you deviate from these instructions in any way, they will kill me. These men possess a machine which can detect whether photocopies of a document have been made. If copies have already been made, inform them now and bring all copies to the rendezvous. If you deny that copies have been made, but their machine proves otherwise, I will be shot. Follow every order exactly. They . . ." At this point Ilse's voice broke. She sobbed and spoke at the same time. *"I saw them kill a man, Hans . . . a policeman. They killed him right in front of me. They cut his throat!"*

In Berlin, the technician stopped the first tape machine. Ilse's sobs seemed to fade into the familiar hiss of a poor long-distance connection.

Hans could restrain himself no longer. "Ilse, they can have whatever they want! Tell them! The papers! Anything! Just tell me where to bring them!"

"Have any copies of the papers been made?" Funk asked.

Hans turned to Professor Natterman, who had appeared in the bedroom door. "Did you make any copies of the papers?"

Natterman saw a mental image of his Xerox machine flashing in his darkened office, but he banished it from his mind. "No," he said, looking straight into Hans's eyes, "I didn't have enough time."

"There are no copies," said Hans, his eyes still on the old man.

"Noted," said Funk. "Now, listen carefully to your instructions. Write them down. Error or delay will not be tolerated."

Hans snatched a pen and notepad from Hauer, who had anticipated the need and procured the items from Professor Natterman's book satchel. Across the top of the pad Hauer had scrawled: *Stay calm. Agree to everything they ask.*

"Drive to Frankfurt tomorrow morning," Funk began. "There you will board the first available flight to Johannesburg, South Africa. Your final destination is Pretoria. It's forty miles north of Johannesburg, but shuttle buses run constantly." Hans scribbled as fast as he could. "Your wife informs us that you have no passport, but this will not be a problem if you use the South African Airways counter. Do you have that?"

"South African Airways," Hans said breathlessly.

"Your flight leaves at two P.M. Once in Pretoria, check into the Burgerspark Hotel. Any taxi driver can take you to it. A suite will be reserved for you. At eight P.M. you will be contacted and issued instructions as to how to exchange the papers for your wife." Funk's voice went cold. "If you are not in your room at the Burgerspark Hotel by eight P.M. on the day after tomorrow—with the Spandau papers—your wife will die. That is all, Sergeant."

"Wait! My questions!"

There was a long silence. "Two questions," Funk said finally.

Hans swallowed. "*Liebchen,* are you all right?" he stammered, not knowing what else to say.

In Berlin Funk held up his index finger. The technician pressed the PLAY button on machine 1. *"Yes,"* came Ilse's quavering reply.

"Have they hurt you in any way?"

This time Funk raised two fingers. *"No,"* Ilse seemed to answer.

"Don't be afraid," Hans implored, trying to keep his voice steady. "No matter what. I'm going to get you back—"

"That is all, Sergeant," Funk said sharply.

"Don't hang up! Please—*please* let me speak to her again. I'm going to do everything you ask!"

While Hans pleaded, Funk held up two fingers. His assistant fast-forwarded to a preset location on tape 2 and depressed PLAY one last time. Ilse's voice burned down the wires, cracking with emotion. Her words were an anguished cry of hope and despair captured during the session at the point of Luhr's Walther. She had screamed them after seeing Josef Steuben murdered, believing that she would be killed herself when her taped statement was completed. Luhr had added it to the programme himself—the perfect diabolical touch.

"Oh God, Hans!" she wailed. *"We did it! I'm going to have a baby!"* She broke into sobs again.

Hans's mouth went dry. For a moment he stood speechless, his face a graven image of horror. Then he howled from the depths of his soul. "You fucking *swine!* I'm coming for her! If she's harmed you'll die like pigs under the knife *so help me God!*"

Funk grinned, pleased by the suffering of the young man

who had caused him so much trouble. "Tell Hauer," he growled, "tell him to remember *Sippenhaft.*"

The line went dead.

With shaking hands Hans set the receiver back in its cradle and turned to Natterman. "They have her," he said hoarsely. "And they want the Spandau papers. Where are they, Professor?"

"Hans," Natterman said uncomfortably, "you can't make such a decision in a fit of anger. You must take time to think."

Hans's eyes had glazed. His mouth worked silently. "Just give me the papers," he said finally.

With a desolate sigh the old historian dug the foil packet from his trouser pocket and turned it slowly in his hand.

"They killed another policeman," Hans said in a robotic voice. "Ilse said they cut his throat right in front of her."

Hauer's big hands were balled into fists.

Hans reached out to Natterman for the papers, but as he did a simple, terrible realization struck him. The men who had kidnapped Ilse were the same men who had gouged the Star of David into Erhard Weiss's chest with a screwdriver. His stomach clenched in agony. Never until this moment had he known true fear.

Hauer's lips had begun to tremble. His jaw muscles flexed furiously. "Wilhelm Funk is a dead man," he vowed. *"I swear that by Steuben's children."*

"I'm afraid that won't solve our problem," Natterman observed, backing up a little. "Hans, please, you've got to try to think this thing through rationally. What do these men want you to do?"

Hans stared unseeing at the old man. A single vision floated behind his eyes, a searing memory of a Berlin dawn, two years before. A kidnapped girl . . . lithe and blond like Ilse . . . the daughter of a Bremerhaven shipping magnate. They'd fished her out of the Havel in the gray morning light, her naked body bloated and lifeless, her sightless eyes wide, her pubic hair matted with river slime. The kidnappers had thrown her alive into the river with her hands tied behind her. The thought that Ilse could end up like the wretched girl . . .

Hans hadn't eaten a full meal for almost twenty hours, but his stomach came up anyway. He bolted for the door, tripped over the dead Afrikaner, and fell retching on the floor. Hauer tensed himself against the smell, hoping Hans would feel better after relieving his nausea. He didn't. He rose slowly, wiped his mouth on the back of his sleeve, and stepped toward Natterman, his hand outstretched.

Natterman looked down at the foil packet, backed away a little. Hauer edged closer. He had seen the flash of hysteria behind Hans's eyes, and he knew that at this moment Hans was capable of anything. He had moved just in time.

"Give me those papers!" Hans screamed. He lunged at the professor with both hands extended, his eyes white with fury. Hauer hesitated, timing his blow. As Hans's head surged past, he fired off a right jab that caught him on the point of the chin, spinning him round. Hauer grabbed him as he fell, easing him stomach-down onto the floor. Before Natterman could speak, Hauer had handcuffed Hans and sat him up against the bedroom wall.

"He went mad!" cried Natterman, his eyes wide. "He'd have killed me for those papers!"

"Do you blame him?" Hauer asked, breathing heavily. He touched Hans's bruised chin softly. Hauer felt a strange tightening in his throat. "He'll come to in a minute," he said, and he coughed to cover the catch in his voice. "Just lay the papers on his lap. You won't have to worry after that."

Natterman obeyed, but he looked unconvinced. "Where did you get those handcuffs?"

"I always keep them with me. They're the most underrated tool in the police arsenal." Hauer looked Natterman dead in the eye. "Now, I'd like you to leave me alone with my son, please."

The professor retreated into the bedroom without a word.

CHAPTER FIFTEEN

2:07 A.M. Soviet Sector: East Berlin, DDR

Harry Richardson woke to the sound of men shouting. His head still throbbed from the Russian's pistol blow. Most of the duct tape had been removed from his body, but his hands and mouth were still bound. Unsure of the position of his captors, he kept his eyes closed. He soon realized that the voices were coming from an adjacent room. There seemed to be three men arguing, possibly four. He opened his eyes. Nothing. Then he discerned a thin horizontal line of dim light—beneath a door, he supposed. He recognized none of the voices, but they all spoke Russian. One man seemed to be having a great deal of difficulty speaking it.

"He can't stay here any longer," said the man with a heavy German accent. "Not an American. And certainly not this one. I know him. He's one of Rose's agents."

"Relax, Goltz," said a Russian voice. "This is the East, isn't it? *Ost*—the heart of friendly territory. What can happen?"

Goltz. Harry recognized the name. *Axel Goltz, East German Stasi . . .*

"If you consider East Berlin friendly territory," Goltz said, "you should spend a day on the street here. The people hate us even more than they hate you."

"You and your Stasi sisters have been letting things slide for too long over here," Rykov said with contempt. "You don't have the balls for anything rougher than blackmail."

"You are a fool," Goltz said with surprising venom. "I command here—in this house at least—and I say the American goes. Take him to Moscow if you wish, just get him out of Berlin. There are too many sharp eyes here for him to stay invisible."

Rykov, thought Harry, finally making the connection. Rykov was the Russian captain from Klaus's house. Suddenly the night's events came rushing back to him. Klaus's suicide, the silenced bullets thwacking into the wall beside the door, the argument between the young KGB officers about what to do with him—

A door had slammed in the next room. The squabble ended instantly. "Where is the American?" asked a gruff voice.

"In the next room, Comrade Colonel. He's unconscious."

"Bring him in."

Behind the wall, Harry tensed. *Colonel,* he thought. *Which colonel?* But as soon as he asked the question, he knew the answer. Who but Ivan Kosov—the colonel he'd seen early this morning at Abschnitt 53? A bright vertical bar of light stabbed his eyes.

"Wake up, Major!"

Harry got to his knees, then made an effort to stand. Rykov helped him.

"You hit me anyway, you bastard," Harry muttered.

"Nothing personal. Just easier."

Rykov seemed to be having difficulty walking. When Harry's eyes sought the floor for balance, he spied a bloody tear below the knee of Rykov's trousers, his souvenir from the checkpoint crossing.

Harry looked up as he passed into the next room, and he immediately recognized four of the five men who awaited him. The gruff-voiced colonel *was* Kosov. He lounged in a comfortable chair opposite a portable television. Between Kosov and a door that Harry hoped led to the street stood a hard-looking young man dressed from head to toe in black. Axel Goltz, the Stasi agent, sat behind a deal table next to Andrei Ivanov, the corporal from Klaus's house. Goltz had restless eyes and dark hair cropped close against his skull.

"The major needs a chair," said Kosov. "Misha?"

The black-clad Russian moved lithely to the table, lifted one of the armless wooden chairs and placed it opposite Kosov. Rykov shoved Harry into the chair, then ripped the tape from his mouth. The sudden pain brought tears to his eyes, but passed quickly. He held out his hands to Misha, who looked questioningly at Kosov.

"No!" Rykov objected. "He doesn't need his hands."

"One gentleman to another," said Harry, his eyes on Kosov.

Kosov chuckled, then nodded to Misha, who brought out his stiletto and cut through the sticky mess like tissue paper. Rykov laid a hand on the Skorpion machine pistol in his belt.

"Now that you're comfortable," said Kosov in heavily accented English, "what have you to tell me?"

"What do you want to know?"

"What you were doing at Klaus Seeckt's house."

"Routine debriefing," Harry said offhandedly. "Twice monthly."

"He's lying!" Rykov snapped in Russian. "He almost broke down the door trying to get in!"

Kosov looked to Corporal Ivanov for corroboration.

"He's right," Andrei admitted grudgingly. "Nothing routine about it. The major also speaks excellent Russian."

"You see, Major?" Kosov said. "There's no point in trying to deceive me. I regret that my men brought you here at all, of course. I asked for a German policeman, I got back an American major. An unfortunate accident. But now that the mistake has been made, I intend to use the opportunity to ask you a few questions. You would do the same, I think."

Harry shrugged.

"I simply wish to know the details of your relationship with Klaus Seeckt. Then I can make arrangements for your safe return to West Berlin."

Harry almost laughed. Mistake or not, the Russians had kidnapped him. To return him now would be admitting it, and they wouldn't do that. Even if Colonel Rose had known he was going to Klaus's house—which Rose hadn't—he would have no way of knowing Harry had been taken into the DDR. He might eventually suspect it, but by then the chances of getting Harry back would be slim. And if the Russians moved him any father east, the odds fell to zero. This situation required desperate measures. Shock tactics. Looking straight at Kosov, Harry crossed his legs and began to speak flawless, aristocratic Russian.

"You'd better write this down, Kosov. If you bungle this, Chairman Zemenek will have you back in the Fifth Chief Directorate so fast you won't have time to pack your shorts. You'll be chasing filthy Tatars for the rest of your life."

Kosov started, both at the perfection of Richardson's Russian and the reference to his old job. "What do you know about me, Major?" he asked warily.

"Only what's necessary. Which isn't much, I'm afraid. Ivan Leonidovich Kosov: Born Moscow 1943, entered service 1962, excelled at repression in the provinces—notably Azerbaijan—for the Second Chief Directorate. That and your father-in-law's influence got you transferred to Directorate 'K' in 1971, stationed Yugoslavia. A little more competent than the average K-man, you obtained a posting to the East Berlin Rezidentura in 1978, where you've performed adequately for the past ten years."

"Leave us," Kosov told his men.

Axel Goltz spoke up angrily. "But Colonel—"

"Now!" bellowed Kosov. "Only Misha remains."

When the others had left the room, Kosov said, "Your Russian is excellent, Major. You have a good memory. So what? You think I don't know as much about you?"

Harry looked over at the predatory Misha standing motionless in the shadows. "No, Colonel, I don't. There is a gap in your ... 'consciousness,' shall we say?"

Kosov grunted. "What kind of gap?"

"The fact that we occasionally work for the same team. Broadly speaking. I went to Klaus Seeckt's house tonight to deliver a message."

"Come now, Major, I would know if you had any connection with KGB."

Harry snorted. "You think you're made aware of everything that happens in Berlin? Perhaps you are a fool, Kosov."

The Russian paled as he held up a hand to restrain Misha. "You speak confidently for a man facing death," he said softly.

"I thought you were sending me back to West Berlin."

Kosov grimaced. "Tell me, do you have any proof of this fantastic story? The rich American who secretly serves the worker's paradise?"

Harry played out a little more bait. "I assume you're familiar with the Twelfth Department of your Directorate?"

Kosov nodded almost imperceptibly.

"My contact is Yuri Borodin. Klaus Seeckt was one of our conduits."

Kosov blinked. "What can this fiction profit you, Major?

An extra hour of confusion? You are going to Moscow regardless of what you say here, and it's there your fate will be decided."

Kosov sounded confident, but Harry had seen the doubt flicker into his eyes at the mention of the Twelfth Department. The Twelfth Department was an elite branch of the KGB—an all-star team recruited from veterans of other KGB departments who had proved themselves expert at moving in international society. Developed under Yuri Andropov, the Twelfth Department had more autonomy than any other branch of the service; its agents were allowed to pursue their chosen quarry anywhere in the world. Harry's personal history of wealth and privilege made him an excellent target for a man like Yuri Borodin; plus he had seen Borodin in the company of Klaus Seeckt. He thought his desperate story might stand up to perhaps an hour's scrutiny.

"Tell me about this mysterious message, Major," said Kosov.

My God, thought Harry. *He's buying it.* "Sorry, Colonel," he said gravely. "The message is for Borodin alone."

"You had better tell me something," Kosov warned. "Or I may see fit to let Misha persuade you. He's most eager to do so."

Harry gave a sardonic smile. "That's about what I'd expect from an old Second Directorate thug."

Kosov came up out of his chair. He moved very fast for a big man. For a moment Harry thought he had carried things too far, but the Russian sat down again, albeit slowly. Harry didn't want to push Kosov over the edge—only up to it.

"I'm waiting," Kosov rasped.

Here goes, Harry thought. In the past two minutes he had pieced together the most plausible story he could from the meager facts he possessed about the Spandau case. *Play out the bait, wait for the strike* ... "I can tell you this much, Colonel," he said, "U.S. Military Intelligence is fully aware of the content of the papers found at Spandau Prison. While your moronic thugs were kidnapping me, our State Department was considering a request from the British government to turn over an abstract of those papers to MI-5. My message for Borodin concerns those papers, and if you don't appreciate the sensitivity of that issue, it's your misfortune. So, why don't you get off your fat ass and verify my story before you sabotage what remains of your less-than-illustrious career."

It was a shot in the dark, but it struck home.

Kosov stood up and studied Harry. "An interesting story, Major. Tell me, how is our one-eyed friend these days?"

Harry felt a jolt of confusion. Kosov had blindsided him. *One-eyed friend?* Did Kosov mean Yuri Borodin? As far as Harry knew, Borodin had two perfectly good eyes. Harry racked his memory for a one-eyed man, but all he could come up with was a black kid from Baltimore who'd lost both his eyes to shrapnel in the DMZ. *Jesus—* "I don't quite get you, Colonel," he said lamely.

Kosov smiled. "Well, then, Major, how about the Spandau papers? Did they mention any names?"

"Several. Hess, for one."

"Naturally. Any others?"

"None I'd care to mention," Harry said tersely, feeling the noose closing around him.

"I'll mention a few, then." The Russian grinned. "Tell me if you recognize any. Chernov? Frolov?" Kosov waited. "No? How about Zinoviev?"

Just the house wine, thanks, Harry thought crazily. He felt cold sweat beading on the back of his neck. *Russian names? What the hell could they have to do with Spandau?*

"Well, Major?"

"Zinoviev," Harry whispered.

Kosov blanched. *"Rykov!"*

The three agents rushed back into the room like hungry Dobermans. Kosov seized his overcoat from a rack by the door and issued orders while he pulled it on.

"Hold the major here until I return from headquarters. I need to call Moscow and I want a line the Stasi can't tap."

"But Herr Oberst!" Axel Goltz objected, venting his anxiety at last. "We can't keep an American here! If Rose finds out, the reaction could be *very* severe. Why—"

"Stop whining!" Kosov snapped. "Act like a German, for God's sake! You can manage without me for an hour. Misha?"

The black-clad killer whipped open the door. Kosov hurried through and crunched down the snowy drive, his silent footpad on his heels. The door banged shut.

Harry sat completely still. He couldn't quite believe that his desperate ploy had worked. One brief glance through the open door had told him what he wanted to know—that the room they now occupied stood at ground level, not on the tenth floor of some human warehouse in Pankow. Quickly he mapped the room in his mind: Andrei and Goltz by the deal table; a sofa with a broken spine against the far wall; a large curtained window at right angles to the sofa; Kosov's empty chair, facing him; one door leading to the room where he had been held earlier, and another—guarded by Rykov—leading outside.

The three agents glowered at each other as if they had been arguing in the other room.

"You fellows find a lot to talk about back there?" Harry asked in Russian, his tone insulting.

Andrei scowled, but Rykov only smiled and leaned against the outside door, resting his injured leg.

Suddenly Axel Goltz spoke up. "What is Kosov doing, Comrades?" When the Russians didn't respond, Goltz scratched thoughtfully behind his right ear. "What did the major tell him that weakened his resolve?"

"Relax," said Rykov. "We have everything under control."

Goltz's nostrils flared. "Under control? You don't even know what's going on! I know this man Richardson, he's a skilled agent. I can't believe Kosov fell for his tricks."

"The colonel knows what he's doing," Rykov said evenly. He curled his lip in distaste. "Stop scratching your head, Goltz. You look like a mangy old hound."

The East German flushed. "It's a wound," he said. He cocked his head to the side, exposing a small white bandage behind his ear. "A skinhead threw a brick in a riot. Four stitches to close it."

Rykov snorted with contempt. "Probably a Jew! They'll revenge themselves on you Germans yet!"

Goltz ground his teeth furiously.

"What tricks of mine were you referring to?" Harry cut in. "Perhaps you, like Kosov, are unaware of certain important facts."

"Find another fool, Major," Goltz snapped. "Be glad I'm not in charge of you."

Harry kept smiling, but inside he shivered. He had always believed the Stasi far superior to the KGB in all areas of intelligence work, and he was glad to see Goltz in the minority tonight. Rykov tacitly admitted this with his next question.

"What would you do with him, Goltz, if you were in command?"

"Kill him. Simplest for all parties concerned."

Harry felt a tremor of fear.

"You're a cold one," Rykov observed.

Goltz shrugged.

"What about his intelligence value?"

The Stasi man pulled a wry face. "I don't think he knows a damned thing about Spandau."

"He might."

"Drug him senseless, then. But he's got to disappear."

"Goltz is right," Harry agreed. "Leave it to the Germans to come up with the most efficient solution."

"What the hell does that mean?" Andrei asked from the table.

Now we're getting somewhere, Harry thought. "Just what it seems to mean, Corporal. That ever since the Second World War, the East Germans have run rings around their Russian masters."

Goltz bowed his head slightly, acknowledging a self-evident truth. Andrei flushed and rose from the table.

"Pay no attention to him, Andrei," Rykov said. "He's only trying to provoke us."

"That's right, Corporal," Harry taunted. "Follow your captain's example. I insult him, and what does he do? Lies back and takes it, like a good Russian."

Andrei charged from the table. Harry darted out of the chair and sidestepped him. "Now, now, Corporal, I advise you to treat me with discretion. When Kosov returns, he'll enlighten you as to my privileged status within your organization."

"My God!" Goltz cried. "He's insufferable! He insults your homeland to your face, then tells you that he secretly serves it? Are you complete fools?"

"It's Kosov's responsibility," Rykov said slowly. "He'll be back soon." The Russian captain squinted at Harry. "And while we wait, Major Richardson is going to tell us exactly what was found at Spandau last night."

Harry caught a sudden, furtive alertness in Axel Goltz's eyes. "I just might do that, Captain," he said lightly, his eye on the East German.

Goltz stiffened.

"Tell you what," Harry went on, "get me something to drink, and I'll tell you boys part of a very interesting story."

Axel Goltz had compressed his muscles like steel springs. Harry sensed it like a hunter senses his dog straining to break cover. He rechecked everyone's position: Goltz stood by the table, Rykov still blocked the door. But Andrei stood only a single step from Harry's chair, his eyes smoldering. He had to be moved.

"I'll take Scotch, if you have it," Harry said.

"Get him a vodka, Andrei," Rykov ordered.

Thank you God! Harry flexed his calf muscles.

Andrei started to obey his captain, but after two steps, the resentment he'd been nursing since the argument at Klaus's house finally surfaced. He stopped and turned back to his commander. "Get it yourself," he said defiantly.

Rykov went pale at this public challenge to his authority. He stood erect and laid a hand on the machine pistol in his belt. "You mutinous bastard!" he said, stepping forward.

Harry's heart pounded. *Jesus, this is it* ... Andrei now stood five feet away from him, facing Rykov in fury. *It's now or never—*

Then Harry saw something so unexpected that it froze him in his chair. Axel Goltz silently brought a Heckler & Koch PSP pistol out of his jacket and aimed it not at Harry, but at Dmitri Rykov's astonished face.

"Back against the wall, you Russian bastard!" he shouted. "Throw your gun on the floor!"

Andrei whirled, then froze. Rykov dropped his Skorpion on the floor. "Have you gone mad?" he asked, an incredulous smile on his face.

Goltz grinned scornfully. "Are you surprised, my little Russian puppies? Surprised that a German is about to blow your puny brains out?"

"You crazy fucking German," said Rykov, still unbelieving. "You're a dead man. No matter what you do now, Kosov will hunt you down. That demon Misha will slice your throat like a bratwurst."

Goltz spoke over his shoulder. "Stand up, Major. You and I are going to take a short ride together. You're about to find out what a real interrogation is like. A *German* interrogation."

"You won't get away with this," Rykov said uselessly.

Goltz laughed coldly. "Of course I will. Corporal Ivanov

has already reasoned out my alibi. I left here to attend to other business, you two quarreled, and Major Richardson managed to kill you both and escape. With two idiots like you, Kosov will be the first to believe it."

"But *why?*" asked Rykov, fascinated by Goltz's apparently suicidal impulse. "Do you work for the Americans?"

I'm afraid he doesn't, Harry thought with a sinking heart.

Raising his chin proudly, Goltz spoke his next words in German. "If I die," he said softly, "I die for Germany. For Phoenix." His voice dropped still lower. *"Der tag kommt."*

"The day approaches," Harry echoed softly. *What the hell?*

At that moment Corporal Andrei Ivanov chose to die a soldier's death. With no weapon but his hands he charged a man who was pointing a semi-automatic pistol at him.

Stunned by this display of courage, Goltz hesitated for a split-instant, then fired. Andrei took a round in the chest, but he kept coming. Rooted to his chair, Harry watched the doomed charge with hypnotic fascination. Goltz's third bullet killed the Russian, but the corporal's furious momentum bowled the Stasi agent over backward. Shaken to the core, Harry wrenched his mind back to reality. He knew he couldn't beat a bullet to the door; with a cry he hurled himself from the chair and crashed headlong through the window, trailing the curtains after him into the darkness.

Axel Goltz heaved Andrei's bleeding body off him and scrambled to his feet. Rykov was nowhere to be seen. Cursing, Goltz darted to the window and hit a switch that flooded the courtyard with light. He saw only a sparkling jigsaw of shattered glass. Taking three steps back, he rushed the jagged window and leaped through. He tumbled across the glass-covered bricks in an expert parachutist's roll and came to his feet at a run. The glass cut him badly, but he uttered no sound as he disappeared into the darkness after Harry.

2:26 A.M. The Natterman Cabin: Near Wolfsburg, FRG

"Stop trying to change my mind!" Hans shouted. He lashed out with his cuffed hands, missing Hauer's face by inches. Hauer didn't flinch. They sat opposite each other on the cabin floor, Hans with his back set against the wall, the foil packet containing the Spandau papers in his lap. Behind

Hans's eyes swirled a thousand currents of rage and confusion.

"Listen," Hauer pressed, "you're reacting just like every relative of every kidnap victim I've ever seen. No one wants police involved—they'll try anything to get their loved one back. Anything but the *right* thing. You *know* better, Hans. You know how many kidnap victims we get back alive: ninety percent of hostages are dead before the ransom call ever comes. You've already been lucky. You can get Ilse back, but you're going to have to *take* her."

Hans glowered at the floor. Statistics meant nothing to him now. All he could see was the nightmare image of the girl dredged from the Havel, leached gray by the oily river . . .

Hauer watched him silently. For the fifteen minutes since Hans regained consciousness, Hauer had tried in vain to convince him that Ilse's only chance lay in rescue. In his mind there was no other option. Bitter experience had taught him that the real hostages in a kidnapping were the family members left behind, not the victim. In thirty years Hauer had seen them all: the shattered mothers who served coffee to the police in zombie-like trances of sedation; the raging fathers who refused to sleep until they collapsed from exhaustion; the wives who could not stop crying, or who could not cry at all; and the husbands, like Hans, who toughed it out in stoic silence until helplessness and despair finally unmanned them. Hans had to be saved from himself.

Hauer watched as, despite the handcuffs, Hans worked open the foil packet containing the Spandau papers. Hans examined the first page—the scrawled German that switched to carefully blocked Latin—and then, apparently satisfied that Natterman had not tried to steal the precious ransom, he closed the packet and stuffed it into his trouser pocket. He refused to meet Hauer's eyes, keeping his own focused on the handcuffs.

Hauer stood up. He started to speak again, to marshal the reasons Hans should set aside his fear and do what he himself would do. But as he stared, he began to see with different eyes. He saw that his son, though like himself in many ways, was profoundly different in others. Hans was not yet thirty, still young enough that he defined himself more by his job and his friends than by his inner self. And with the family situation he had—a mother he despised and a father he had hated until tonight—Hans probably drew more emotional sustenance from his wife than he would ever understand. In the span of eight hours, he had seen his job unmasked as a travesty, his friend brutally murdered, and his wife torn from his side.

Little wonder, Hauer reflected, that he lacked the resolve to punch through the blinding red wall of emotion and *act*. Hauer had seen this type of paralysis before, and inexperience was not always the root of it. Hans's internal compass, like that of so many Germans, gravitated toward a magnetic north—the gilded scaffolding of official authority. With that scaffolding shattered and himself branded a fugitive, he was a man adrift. Hauer felt no such confusion. His internal compass pointed to the true north of his spirit. He had lost his illusions very young, and through the trials of finding his way in the world alone, he had learned to exalt the essence, not the trappings, of his work. He took a most un-German approach to his skill as a marksman: in unexpected moments he found himself viewing the world through his rifle scope—not in a limited, but a profoundly focused way. All existence compressed into the tube of polished lenses, the smallest movement magnified a hundredfold, melding him with the target a thousand yards away: the six-inch red paper circle, the tawny fur beneath the stag's shoulder, the pale forehead of a man. When he led men—in the army, on the GSG-9 firing range, in the streets of Berlin—he led not by virtue of his rank, but by example. In situations like this one, cut off from command, the fire inside Hauer burned all the brighter, spurring him to action, driving him toward resolution.

As he watched Hans now, he felt an awful powerlessness. What Hans needed was a new allegiance, a fixed star that the spinning needle in his soul could lock onto. If Hauer could not provide that, if he could not lead the son who had returned to him like a prodigal, then he would truly have failed as a father, as all that he had believed himself to be.

He started suddenly. Professor Natterman was speaking.

"Your father is right," the old man was saying. "Give in to Nazis and they crush you. Exterminate you. We can't surrender the papers, we've got to take Ilse back."

"Nazis?" Hans groaned. "You're both crazy! Crazy old men! What does that have to do with getting Ilse back? With *today?* It's ancient history!"

"You're right," Hauer said quickly. He squatted down on his haunches, his face a foot from Hans's own. "Forget all that crap. What matters is Ilse. But unless you force yourself to look at this objectively, Hans, your emotion is going to kill her. You have never faced this thing you are facing now. You've seen brutality and you've seen death. But you have never faced pure evil. That is what you are facing now. Call it Nazism or Phoenix or whatever you want, it's all the same. It is a thing as mindless and as ravenous as a cancer. It perceives only what it wants, obstacles to getting what it wants, and threats to its existence. Right now it wants those papers. The papers are a threat. You have them, Ilse has read them, so both of you are also threats. Killing her, killing you—this is less than nothing. Remember Weiss, Hans, think of Steuben. I tried to kid myself about it, but Steuben was a dead man the moment I saved your life."

Hans flinched at that. Already he blamed himself for Weiss, and for so much more. He looked up into his father's face, pleading silently for him to stop, but Hauer would not.

"If you get on that plane with those papers, you will never return to Germany. Phoenix's men can kill you on the plane, in the airport, anywhere. The South African police can murder you in jail. They do it all the time. If we have *Der Bruderschaft* in our department, what do they have there? The moment Phoenix has the papers, you will die. You'll *die*. You'll never see your wife again. You'll never see me again."

Hans scrambled to his feet. He slipped past Hauer to the shattered bedroom window and rested his cuffed hands on a knife-edge of glass. Even in the bitter cold he was sweating. Hauer's words had pierced the fog of dread that surrounded him, yet the rush of nightmare images would not stop. They ripped through him like a ragged strip of film, unspooling from his heart, catching in his throat, flashing behind his eyes. He tried to speak, to express the confusion he felt, but his voice broke. Tears pooled in his eyes as he stared out into the frozen forest.

Hauer couldn't see Hans's face, but he heard the sob and knew that his words had had their effect. He stood up slowly and took something from his pocket. A key. He walked to the window, removed the cuffs from Hans's wrists, and put them in his pocket.

"I don't think you understand," he said. "I *want* you to take the papers to South Africa."

Natterman cleared his throat. "Surely you can't mean that, Captain?"

Hauer snapped his head around and gave the old man a withering glare. "I mean to use the Spandau diary to draw the kidnappers into the open. To force them to expose Ilse."

Hans threw up his hands. "But what can you do then? You don't have one of your GSG-9 teams—no twenty-man unit with state-of-the-art weapons and communications."

Hauer spoke with cold-blooded confidence. "You know what I can do, Hans. You're all the team I need."

"And me," Natterman put in.

Hauer ignored him. He had no intention of taking the professor to South Africa, but now was not the time to tell him that.

Hans walked a few steps away from Hauer. It was almost impossible to argue with the man when he brought the power of his personality to bear. Yet Hans feared so much more than Ilse's death. He sensed her terror like a snake twisted around his spine. Not terror for herself, but for the child she was carrying. Of course he remembered her doctor's appointment now. He'd fallen asleep after the Spandau detail and missed it. But why hadn't she told him about the baby when he got home? Yet he knew the answer to that too. Because he had come home acting like a total lunatic, a money-crazed bastard. And hadn't she tried in spite of him? He could still hear her voice: *I've got a secret too* . . . And then the phone call from Funk's man, Jürgen Luhr. And then Weiss. And Steuben. And Ilse . . .

"Look, I don't have a passport," he said sharply. "The kidnappers were right about that. The only way I can get to South Africa is by the route they've set up."

"I can have a forger here in three hours," Hauer said quickly. "I'm not giving those bastards a shot at you on the plane."

"Damn it, they said *any* deviation from the instructions and they'd kill her."

Sensing Hans's growing resolve, Hauer pressed down his exasperation. "Hans, there are no absolutes in these situations. You're like a doctor who must operate on his own wife. She has terminal cancer. She's going to *die* unless you go in and cut out the tumor. But there are risks. The knife could slip, the gas could kill her, a dozen things. You pick up the scalpel, then you hear a voice in your ear saying, 'Hey, you give me what I want, and I'll make this woman as healthy as the day she was born.' " Hauer shook his head. "It's a fucking lie, Hans. That voice is the devil, and he doesn't play by your rules. He feels *no obligation*. It's your call, but no matter how badly you want to believe that voice, there's only one option. Surgery."

Hans's cheek twitched involuntarily. He searched the depths of his father's eyes, but he saw neither subterfuge nor hope of gain—only the indomitable will of a man ready to die in a quest he had made his own. And from somewhere deep within himself, from a place he never knew existed, a voice edged with steel rose into his throat.

"I'll do it."

CHAPTER SIXTEEN

2:35 A.M. Soviet Sector: East Berlin, DDR

Harry picked himself up out of the shattered glass and sprinted for the courtyard wall. He heard no shooting yet, but that didn't reassure him. The rough stone wall was high. Without breaking stride he planted his right shoe three feet up the face of the wall and leaped. His fingers dug into the rough ledge. He pulled with all his strength, both feet pedaling against the stone, and scrambled over the top.

He found himself in a narrow walking space between two houses. Dashing down the dark corridor, he paused where it opened onto a narrow street. He saw no street signs nor any other landmarks he knew. Unsure of where to run, he flattened his back against the wall outside the alley's mouth, locked his hands together in a deadly double fist, and waited.

Axel Goltz was fast, intelligent, and well-trained, but his desperation made him careless. He came barreling down the narrow alley at top speed, and rather than pause at its mouth as Harry had done, he leaned into his sprint, blindly pursuing the man he thought to be at least a block ahead of him by now. Harry's locked fists struck the East German in the center of the forehead and skidded down the right side of his head. Goltz went down like an ox under the slaughterhouse hammer.

Harry heard the metallic ring of a gun hitting the concrete, but he saw no gun. Goltz must have fallen on it. The Stasi agent lay motionless on his stomach. As Harry stared down, he caught the dark glint of metal protruding from beneath Goltz's waist. Cautiously he leaned down and snatched up the pistol. Goltz didn't move. Seeing no one else on the street, Harry decided to question him. He held the pistol to Goltz's head with his left hand and probed beneath the jaw with his right. There was a pulse—weak, but steady.

As Harry opened his mouth to speak, he caught sight of the strange spot behind Goltz's right ear. Harry's blow had torn the bandage away. He expected to see stitches, but instead he saw a perfectly round moon of white flesh shining under the streetlight, marked at the center by what looked like a spot of blood. Leaning closer, he saw what it was—a small tattoo. A tattoo of an eye. A single, bloodred eye, inked into the scalp by a very talented needle. It reminded him of the eye on the pyramid on the back of a one-dollar bill, but only a little. This eye was less defined somehow, yet more piercing, more mystical.

As Harry stared, Axel Goltz flicked his head up from the pavement like a slingshot and cracked him across the bridge of the nose. The next thing Harry saw through stinging tears was the East German on his feet, moving forward with a gleaming knife extended in his right hand.

Harry fired Goltz's pistol without thinking. The explosion of the unsilenced weapon reverberated through the empty streets like a cannon shot. The bullet blew Goltz off his feet. He landed on his back in the street, sucking for air, a tiny hole in his chest, a gaping hole in his back. Harry knelt quickly beside him and said into his ear, "Why did you shoot the Russian? *Why?*"

Wide-eyed in shock, Goltz made a gurgling noise in his throat.

Harry lifted him roughly by his shirt front. "What is Phoenix?" he asked sharply. "Goltz! What is Phoenix?"

The German couldn't speak. A froth of blood spilled over his lower lip. Harry racked his memory for the Stasi man's rank. Lieutenant? *"Was ist Phoenix, Herr Leutnant?"* he barked in the voice of a sergeant major.

A faint smile touched the corners of Goltz's mouth. *"Der Tag kommt,"* he croaked. "For the Jews . . . for the world."

He sighed once, then went limp.

Harry heard sirens in the distance. *"Damn!"* he cursed. He dropped Goltz to the concrete and forced his head to the side. The bloodred eye stared upward. Harry didn't know what the mark meant, but he knew that it was somehow important. Goltz had obviously been hiding it from Rykov and his men; Harry saw no reason to let them find it now. He laid the pistol barrel against the German's skull, muzzle against the tattoo. He pulled against the trigger, then stopped.

Without pausing to think, he jammed the pistol into his belt and pried the knife from Goltz's clenched fist. He tried to grasp the bald circle of Goltz's scalp between his thumb and forefinger, but it was impossible. There was no hair to pull, and the skin was stretched too tightly around the skull. Ignoring the wailing sirens, Harry braced his knee firmly against the right side of the Stasi man's head. He grasped the hair at the lower edge of the shiny circle and tugged up a little hummock of flesh. Then he jabbed the knifepoint into the scalp beneath the tattoo, deep into the fascia. Goltz's body jerked when the point struck bone—from reflex, Harry hoped. But then the bleeding started: little pulsing waves that shimmered black-red beneath the streetlight. Goltz was unconscious, but alive. Gritting his teeth together, Harry levered the knife blade up, using the point as the fulcrum, and worked his left thumb under the raised scalp. This accomplished, it took only a few seconds of sawing to excise the half-dollar-sized swatch of skin that bore the tattoo.

The sirens were much closer now. Harry stood and shoved the fragment of scalp deep into his trouser pocket. Then he sprinted toward the nearest intersection, wiping the blood from his hands as he ran. There were street signs at the intersection, but he didn't recognize the names. With no better option, he began running toward the brightest lights he could see. He soon saw a sign he knew: Rosenthaler Strasse. High in the sky to his left hovered the shining observation sphere of the great Fernsehturm, the 1,215-foot television tower that rises needle-like from the Alexanderplatz to dominate both East and West Berlin. Using the tower as point zero, Harry visualized East Berlin from the air, estimating distances and comparing the times it would take him to reach different destinations.

Twelve blocks to the west stood the British Embassy. Harry knew the ambassador, but he also knew that his chances of getting through the gate unmolested were nil. If either Goltz or Rykov had reached a telephone, the friendly embassies would be covered already. Twenty blocks to the east was a French SDECE safehouse where Harry knew he could find refuge, but the shortest route to it lay through one of the busiest sections of East Berlin. Even at night it would be risky.

Harry started walking. He crossed two deserted corners, then passed a row of yellow phone boxes where an ill-kempt young man stood shouting into a telephone. On impulse Harry turned and walked back to the phone boxes. He took hold of the boy's jacket with one hand and broke the connection with the other.

"Hey!" the boy snapped. "*Arschloch!* Let go!"

"Coins!" Harry demanded, pointing to the phone. "*Pragen!*"

"*Fick Dich in Knie!*" the German cursed.

Harry grabbed the tangled mane of blond hair and twisted until the boy's eyeball rested against the telephone's coin slot. "*Pragen!*" he hissed.

Snarling, the youth pulled thirty *Pfennig* from his jacket and dropped the jangling coins onto the sidewalk. Harry jerked him out of the phone box and shoved him down the street. "Beat it!" he growled. "*Haue ab!*" The boy backed off cursing, then turned and shuffled on. Harry dialed an East Berlin number from memory and waited. He could still hear the siren, but fainter.

"British Embassy," said a sleepy female voice, after a dozen rings.

"I have an urgent message for Ambassador Brougham," Harry said breathlessly. "The code is *Trafalgar*. Am I being recorded?"

"Yes, sir!" The crisis code had worked its magic.

Harry paused, remembering Colonel Rose's warning not to tell the British anything about the Spandau case. He understood the caution, but under these circumstances he might be captured and silenced long before he got through to Colonel Rose.

"Are you there, sir?" asked the Englishwoman.

"Message to God," Harry said, using Rose's nickname. "Zinoviev, repeat, Zinoviev. Break. Phoenix, repeat, Phoenix. Break. Message to Ambassador Brougham: This is Major Harry Richardson, U.S. Army. I was abducted, repeat, *abducted* into East Berlin tonight. I have escaped and I'm on my way to your embassy for asylum." Harry heard a hiccup of astonishment. "I'm on foot, and I should be there in about seven minutes. Get those gates open!"

Harry slammed down the phone and looked westward toward the British Embassy. Then he started east toward the safehouse.

2:36 A.M. KGB Headquarters: Soviet Sector, Berlin: DDR

Ivan Kosov sat thoughtfully in his Swiss-made office chair and gazed at a four-by-five-inch file photograph of Harry Richardson. It was a telephoto shot, long and grainy, but the expression on the American's face looked as cocksure as it had when he picked the name Zinoviev from the three Kosov had tossed out. Kosov muttered an oath and slid the photo aside.

Now he looked into the piercing eyes of Rudolf Hess. This picture was an eight-by-ten, sharp and clear, of the Deputy Führer during his prime. The heavy-browed Aryan face radiated authority and self-assurance. Beneath this photo lay a smaller shot of Hess as a First World War pilot. His eyes looked younger, brighter somehow—unfreighted with the knowledge of immeasurable death and destruction.

Kosov had stared at these photos of Hess for years, wondering why Moscow was still obsessed with the old Nazi's mission. They had proof that Prisoner Number Seven was an impostor—or so Kosov had heard from several Dzerzhinsky Square old-timers that he trusted. Yet if Centre had such proof, why didn't they expose him long ago? *They're waiting,* the old-timers said. Waiting for what? *Corroboration,* they said. Was Zinoviev that corroboration? Whoever Zinoviev was? Was there really some hidden purpose in Hess's flight, or was this simply one more conspiracy theory spawned in the murky corridors of Moscow Centre? Kosov had the feeling he was about to find out at last.

The computers had tracked Yuri Borodin to London. Kosov had sent a query straight on to the embassy, and while he waited for the reply, he'd ordered a printout of Harry Richardson's file. Kosov envied the freedom Borodin enjoyed. Twelfth Department agents, for all practical purposes, "stationed" themselves. A far cry from the deskbound life Kosov had led for the past decade.

Suddenly Kosov's printer began to chatter. *Not bad,* he thought. *Borodin must have been at the embassy when the message came through.* He read the reply as his printer spat it out, thankful that the days when he had to decode his own messages were long past.

TO KOSOV: 07611457
2:39 A.M. GMT/London
In response to query—YES I know agent in question. NO I have no relationship with him other than ADVERSARIAL. Subject is valuable resource. Hold him there until I arrive. ETA tomorrow. CANCEL—TODAY A.M.

                                                    BORODIN

Kosov slammed a horny hand down on his desk. The American had lied after all! But while this knowledge delighted Kosov, Borodin's intention to come to Berlin did not. "I've caught the golden goose," he said bitterly, "and this prima donna wants to come take the credit. We'll see about that."

While Kosov grumbled, his printer began to chatter again. What emerged this time was not a message, but a digital facsimile photograph, a study in grays and black. It showed four uniformed young men in their early twenties, standing shoulder to shoulder against the famous Borovitsky Gate of the Kremlin. Kosov didn't recognize the uniforms, but the young men were obviously officers. A hand-penciled arrow pointed to the face of the second man from the left. The photo was very grainy, but Kosov recognized the hardness in the eyes and around the mouth of that face. *Those eyes have seen much death,* he thought. At the bottom of the photo was a handwritten caption: *V. V. Zinoviev: Awarded Okhrana Captaincy 1917.* Beneath the photo—typed—were the words: *Message follows by courier—Zemenek.*

Kosov felt a thrill of triumph. Here was the mysterious Zinoviev at last! And sent to him by the chairman himself! Yet Kosov's triumph was tempered by puzzlement and uneasiness. Zinoviev an officer of the *Okhrana?* What in God's name could the *Okhrana* have to do with this case? It was a ghost from an even more distant past than Rudolf Hess. The *Okhrana* was the tsar's dreaded secret police force—the most ruthless enemy the communists had ever known. Kosov scratched his grizzled head. With a sharp sense of frustration, he realized what was eating at him. Without quite knowing it, he had been expecting Zinoviev to turn out to be the mysterious one-eyed man. It only made sense. For years he'd had a name with no face to go with it, and a one-eyed man without a name. Why couldn't they be one and the same?

Maybe they are, he thought suddenly, staring at the photo again. The hard-faced young officer in the photo had two living eyes—of that Kosov had no doubt. They stared out from the picture like smoldering lumps of coal. *You are very young here, little tiger,* Kosov thought. *Plenty of time yet to lose an eye. Especially in your job, eh?* Most *Okhrana* officers had lost more than their eyes after Tsar Nicholas was overthrown.

"Telephone, Comrade Colonel!" interrupted a secretary. "Urgent!"

Startled out of his reverie, Kosov snatched up the receiver. When he heard Captain Rykov explain what had happened at the Stasi safehouse, he felt the blood leave his head in a rush. "My God," he muttered. "*My God!* Get back here any way you can, you idiot!"

Kosov slammed down the phone and charged into the communications room. "Close off the Western embassies!" he shouted. "Use our own people—*no East Germans!*"

Several astonished young faces appeared at the doors.

"The fugitive is an American army major," he said more slowly, his voice barely under control. "He's out of uniform and he speaks perfect Russian. Probably perfect German too. If he's apprehended, I want him brought here immediately." Kosov ground his teeth furiously. "Any East German who attempts to get close to him is to be shot. That is a direct order. *Shoot* any East German who interferes. I want the full staff here in twenty minutes. And get me the chief of the Stasi on the phone! *Now!*"

Sagging against a desk, Kosov tried to ignore the pounding in his head. It seemed inconceivable that Axel Goltz had been working for the Americans. The man was practically a Nazi. Why would he turn on his Russian masters? Especially since he could have no doubt that his action would be suicidal. Kosov sighed hopelessly. He could do little else until his department heads arrived. Slowly he walked back into his office, closed the door, and sat at his desk. *Borodin will throw me to the dogs for this,* he lamented. *But not before I strain Axel Goltz through a razor-wire sieve.* Shoving the grainy photograph of Zinoviev out of his way, he swallowed four aspirin without water, pressed his forehead to the cold desktop, and waited for the phone to ring.

4:35 A.M. The Natterman Cabin: Near Wolfsburg, FRG

The forger arrived two hours after Hauer's call. Professor Natterman's explosion occurred two hours after that. Hauer and Hans had buried the dead caretaker and his Afrikaner killer in the snow behind the cabin, while Natterman stripped the bloody bedclothes and scrubbed away the blood from the cabin's interior. The only remaining signs of trouble were the shattered windows and door, and the Jaguar wrapped around the plane tree out front.

Hauer's forger was astute enough to ignore all these signs. Immensely fat and normally jovial, Hermann Rascher appeared to be in mortal dread of Hauer. He lost no time in setting up his equipment. A white screen and chair placed in front of the shattered window and an assortment of chemicals laid out in the bathroom quickly converted the bedroom into a small photographic studio.

Consistent with his plan of keeping Natterman in the dark until the last minute, Hauer instructed the forger to shoot a passport picture of the professor as if he too were to be given false papers. But this ruse went for nothing. Despite Hauer's injunction against discussing their plans, Natterman badgered him every moment that the forger spent in his temporary darkroom. Before Rascher arrived Hauer had probed the professor for his speculations on what the vital secret of the Spandau papers might be, but Natterman had refused to be drawn out. Now, though, Natterman was vigorously attempting to convince Hauer it would be foolish to bait a rescue trap with the authentic papers.

"The kidnappers have *obviously* never seen the papers," he insisted, "so it would be impossible for them to know they were being fooled. Captain, I simply cannot agree to any plan which needlessly risks losing such an important artifact."

Hauer had had enough. He walked to the bedroom door to make sure the forger was closed inside the bathroom; then he turned back to Natterman. "You don't have to agree, Professor," he said evenly. "Because you're not coming to South Africa."

Natterman looked as if someone had emptied a bedpan in his face. Too stunned to speak, he looked to Hans for support, but found none. Hauer kept the initiative. "You're wounded, you can't move faster than a slow walk, and you're over seventy, for God's sake."

Too angry to marshal logical arguments, Natterman raged like a thwarted child. "You can't keep me out of this, you . . . you *fascist!*"

While he ranted on, Hans walked to the window and tried to shut out the argument. The snow was falling again. He shivered, realizing that somewhere out there beyond the trees, beyond the road and the pristine German fields, beyond the Alps, beyond a great sea and a vast, dark continent, Ilse waited, frightened and alone. With a hollow coldness in his chest, he wondered again about her last, anguished cry. Could she really be pregnant at last? Or had the kidnappers somehow twisted that desperate maternal hope out of her to use as extra leverage? He banished the thought from his mind. That snake could eat its tail forever, and his sanity with it. It had no bearing at all on the rescue plan. He would keep that secret to himself. Whatever had passed between him and his father in the last few hours, Hauer had no claim on that knowledge yet.

"Hans, listen to this!" the professor shrieked. "Hauer said it himself: The police only get *ten percent* of hostages back alive! Remember Munich, Hans? The 'seventy-two Olympics? It was Hauer and his stormtroopers who opened up on the Arabs while the hostages were tied inside the helicopters. The Jews were blown to bits! Have you forgotten that? Two days ago you *hated* this man. He deserted you and your mother! Now you trust him to bring our Ilse back alive?"

At the mention of Munich a strange stillness came over Hauer. It was as if a ghost had touched him with icy fingers. His gray eyes turned opaque as they fixed on Natterman. His voice went cold and flat. "I didn't see you on the airfield that day."

Natterman started to reply, but when he recognized the glacial coldness in Hauer's eyes the sound died in his throat. "I'm sorry," he whispered. "I shouldn't have said that. But you don't *understand,* Captain. The key to this situation isn't guns and tactics, it's the Spandau papers. And you can't even *read* them! We're not dealing with Arab terrorists or crazed students here—we're dealing with the legacy of

Adolf Hitler! The key to this whole mystery is in the *past,* and *I am the only man who can unravel it!*"

Hauer sighed. "Professor, why don't you admit that the reason you want so badly to come is that you can't bear to let those papers out of your sight for one moment."

"Liar!" Natterman exploded.

"You didn't argue against forcible rescue until I said I wasn't including you in the plan. Do you deny that?"

"How *dare* you!" Spittle flew from the old man's lips. "You fool! You're not *qualified* to handle this alone! You think you're chasing a neo-Nazi group called Phoenix? Then how do you explain the tattooed eye? The Phoenix is a bird rising from the flames, not an eye. Phoenix is the Greek name of the Egyptian god *Bennu.* The tattooed Eye is also Egyptian—it's the Guarding Eye, the All-Seeing Eye, the Eye of God from the Egyptian *Book of the Dead.* Explain that to me, Captain!"

Hauer shrugged. "The Nazis used all kinds of rituals and mythology."

"Yes! But Teutonic and Arthurian mythology almost exclusively! So, how do you explain the Egyptian symbols?"

Hauer remained silent while he digested Natterman's revelations. "Professor," he said finally, "if you care about your granddaughter you will write down everything you just told me, and you will stay by the telephone so that you can provide us with any other information we need."

"But I can go *with* you!" Natterman insisted. "I can keep up!"

"Enough!" Hans cried, turning from the window. He stabbed a finger at Natterman. "My decision's made. We're taking Ilse back, and my father is in command from this point forward."

Natterman opened his mouth to continue, but the corpulent forger flung open the bedroom door and waddled into the room. "All done," he announced. "Excellent work, if I do say so myself."

Natterman stared at Hauer in silent fury, then he stormed into the bedroom and slammed the door.

The forger held the fruits of his labor beneath the overhead light for Hauer's inspection. The passport bore two excellent frontal shots of Hans and Hauer, taken against the screen in the bedroom. Both wore fashionable jackets provided by the forger and looked every inch wealthy businessmen. At Hermann's suggestion Hauer had shaved his mustache; it was the first time he had seen himself without it in twenty years. He looked ten years younger. With an artist's eye, Hermann had quickly noted the resemblance between Hans and Hauer and had suggested they travel as father and son. That way, he'd said, they would only have to remember one surname—Weber.

"They *are* good," Hauer agreed.

"The best you'll find, east of Brussels," Hermann assured him. "You're lucky Germans don't need visas for South Africa. I didn't have one to work from."

"Start the car, Hans," Hauer commanded.

Hans was gone in an instant. Hauer picked up the passports and slipped them into his coat pocket. "Aren't you forgetting something?" he said to the forger.

Hermann made a painful grimace. It was bad enough being forced to work for free, but to be *robbed*. The mind simply boggled. The consequences of refusal, however, were unthinkable. Eight years ago Hauer had sent the forger to Berlin's Moabit Prison, where he had endured six years of living hell. Upon release he had resettled in Hamburg to escape Hauer's prying eyes, but it hadn't worked. Hauer had kept abreast of his current activities, and he'd made it painfully clear tonight that one phone call to Hamburg could put Hermann right back into prison for another stretch. *What the hell?* Hermann rationalized. *Ten thousand marks isn't too high a price for freedom.* He could make back the money on just four passports. He walked to the sofa, reached into his leather camera bag, and brought out a stuffed manila envelope.

After counting the banknotes, Hauer slipped them into his pocket. "Nice doing business with you again, Hermann," he said. "Now I want you to wait for me right here."

He slipped into the bedroom and closed the door. Professor Natterman sat fuming on the stripped mattress, holding his hand against his bandaged nose. "Professor," said Hauer, "here is where we make our peace. I'm going to South Africa to bring back your granddaughter. I could simply walk out of here, but I realize that would be stupid. You know things that could help me. The question is, will you?"

Natterman said nothing; Hauer went on anyway. He needed the professor's information, but he also wanted to leave the old man some dignity. "I don't trust that forger," he said. "I need an hour's head start on him. I want you to make sure he stays here at least that long. Once he's gone, shut the cabin, take your things, and drive that Jaguar back to Berlin. The car belongs to a man named Ochs. Here's his card."

"That car's shot to pieces!" Natterman protested.

"You shot it," Hauer reminded him. "Just get it back to him. He's a Jew, he'll understand. After you've delivered the car, stock up on enough food to last a week, then get hold of any research materials you'll need to answer questions about Prisoner Number Seven, the Egyptian god *Bennu,* South Africa, and anything else you think might be relevant. Ten hours from now I want you by your office telephone continuously. Sleep by it. I've got to know I can count on you."

Outside, the borrowed Audi rumbled to life. With a last look at Natterman, Hauer left the old man sitting on the bed. He glared at the forger as he passed through the front room. "Don't get anxious and try to leave too soon, Hermann."

The forger's eyes bulged. Hauer turned. Behind him stood Professor Natterman, the double-barreled Mannlicher in his hands.

Hauer offered his hand. "*Auf Wiedersehen,* Professor. Be careful, eh?"

After a moment's hesitation, the old historian took Hauer's hand and squeezed hard. "You bring my granddaughter back, Captain."

"You have my word."

"And you bring back those papers!"

Hauer nodded once, then he ducked out of the cabin.

Natterman heard a car door slam, then the roar of the Audi as it raced up the access road. Hermann Rascher stared at the old man, mystified by the scene he had just witnessed. "You know, Professor," he said, "there's really no reason for us to hang around here while—"

Natterman jabbed the shotgun into the fat man's belly. "Sit down, swine!"

Hermann sat.

5:00 A.M. U.S. Army Headquarters: West Berlin

Colonel Rose stared into the expectant faces of Sergeant Clary and Detective Schneider. Clary nodded once, indicating that the tape reels were turning. Rose spoke into the telephone.

"This is Colonel Rose. Go ahead."

"Colonel, this is Blueblood calling. Repeat, Blueblood."

Rose gasped. "It's Harry! Where the hell are you?"

"Don't say anything, sir. Nothing. This call will terminate in fifty seconds. In our office computer you'll find a file coded 'East'—that's Echo-Alpha-Sierra-Tango. In that file is a list of safe locations in the DDR. I am now at location four, repeat, *four*. I don't think I can get out on my own, Colonel, it's too tight. I suggest you threaten your opposite number here, and if that doesn't work, roll up network seven, repeat, *seven,* and make a trade. I was dead wrong about Hess. This does have something to do with him. Also with someone or something called Phoenix. But the key name is *Zinoviev,* repeat, *Zulu-India-November-Oscar-Victor-India-Echo-Victor*. Find him and we'll be on track." Harry took a deep breath. "You've got to get me out, Colonel. This is big. If I don't hear from you in twenty-four hours, I'm going to try it on my own. That's all."

"Wait!" Rose shouted.

"He's disconnected, sir," Clary said in a monotone, his eyes on a voltage-measuring device.

Rose stood and pounded his fist on the desk. *"Clary!"*

"Sir!"

"You get a squad of uniformed MPs down here *now!* Make sure every one has a rifle!"

"What are you going to do?" Schneider asked, alarmed by the American's hair-trigger temper.

"You heard the man, Detective! I'm rolling up network seven!"

"But he suggested that you threaten the KGB first—"

Rose's face reddened. "Schneider, I don't make threats unless I can back 'em up. It's a friggin' waste of time. When I tell Ivan Kosov that I'll arrest one of his precious networks if he doesn't let my boy out, those slimy bastards *will be* in a holding cell in my stockade! Clary!"

"MPs on the way, sir!"

"Damn straight!" Rose bellowed, reaching into the bottom drawer for his bottle of Wild Turkey. *"Damn straight."*

He filled his Lenox shot glass and poured the whiskey down his throat, feeling his eyes water when it hit bottom. "Friggin' Rudolf Hess," he muttered. "And Zinoviev. Who the hell is Zinoviev?"

"I beg your pardon, Colonel?" Schneider asked. "Who are you talking about?"

"Nobody," Rose mumbled. "Some commie sonofabitch."

He could not have been further from the truth.

5:10 A.M. MI-5 Headquarters: Charles Street, London, England

The door to Sir Neville Shaw's office shook with the force of Wilson's knock.

"One moment, your lordship," Shaw said into the telephone. "What is it, Wilson?"

The deputy director stuck his head into the office. "It's *that woman,*" he sniffed, meaning Swallow. "She said she'd wait one more minute and then she's leaving."

"Tell her I won't be a moment."

Wilson sighed with exasperation and withdrew.

I'm sorry, your lordship," Shaw apologized. "Where were we?"

"Your career," replied a deep voice with a vintage Oxbridge accent. Shaw was briefly reminded of Alec Guinness. "It is *felt,* Neville, in some quarters, that you have bungled this whole affair from the beginning. It was nearly a year ago that some of us suggested that you act to prevent just this sort of mess."

Sir Neville bridled. "If they'd torn the bloody prison down last year, the very same thing would have happened. I couldn't control what the man *wrote,* for God's sake."

This riposte was met with frosty silence. "Yes," the voice said finally. "Well. What about the African end of the problem?"

"It's being taken care of. Two or three days at the most."

"A lot could happen in three days, Neville. We want every loose end snipped, every trace erased."

"It's *being done,*" Shaw insisted.

"Are there any complications we should know about?"

Shaw thought of Jonas Stern, and of Swallow waiting just outside his door. "No," he lied.

"Keep us posted, then." The caller rang off.

Shaw exhaled a great blast of air and began to massage his temples with his fingertips. He badly needed sleep. He had spent five of the past six hours on the telephone. Across London, in places like the India Club, the House of Lords, and the All-England Lawn Tennis and Croquet Club—and across Britain in the ramshackle palaces and crumbling stone castle outposts of the aristocracy—privileged men and women both young and old were gathering in quiet councils. Like ripples spreading outward from the epicenter of Buckingham Palace, waves of apprehension rolled through this most rarefied level of society; and all, Shaw reflected, because one little stone had dropped far away in the atrophied heart of Berlin. Slowly but surely, those frightened men and women were bringing a great deal of pressure to bear on Sir Neville Shaw. For Shaw, like his predecessors before him, was not only the possessor but also the *protector* of their dark secret. Most of the calls had been like the previous one—a bit of carrot, bags of stick. Shaw was about to rise and go to his liquor cabinet for a medicinal Glenfiddich when his office door opened and Wilson ushered in the woman code-named Swallow.

Sir Neville was stunned. The woman standing before him looked nothing like the photo in the file he'd been studying. "Ah ... Miss Gordon, isn't it?" he stammered as Wilson withdrew from the office.

Swallow did not respond.

"I'm told you insisted on seeing me personally," he tried again. "Mind telling me why?"

Still Swallow held her silence. She obviously felt the burden of explanation lay on the man who had called for her services. Thoroughly discomfited, Shaw looked down at the file. The woman in the photo looked like a grandmother, a blue-rinsed clubwoman who spent her Sundays baking biscuits for the church. The woman who stood before him now looked like ... well, Shaw had never quite seen the analogue that would describe her. Swallow had iron gray hair cropped close against her skull, perfect for wearing wigs. She carried none of the excess fat that weighted most women her age— and there Shaw paused. For looking at Swallow now, he couldn't quite get his mind round the fact that she had been in the war. She'd been practically a child, of course, but still. It was downright eerie. The file put her at sixty-one, but she looked nearer fifty. As he stared, the scent of perfume wafted to him; this single acknowledgment of femininity surprised him. He couldn't name the fragrance, but it smelled expensive and vaguely French. To be honest, Shaw mused, he might have been attracted to Swallow if it wasn't for what he knew about her. No, he decided, even if he'd known nothing of her fiendish work, her eyes would have put him off. They were like stones. Dull, flat stones. Not that they communicated *intellectual* dullness—quite the contrary. They were rather like slate lids on a blast furnace, protecting those outside from the fierce hatred that burned behind them. That hatred had probably served Swallow well through the years, Shaw reflected, for by trade she was an assassin.

"Yes, well," he began again, "did Wilson tell you this regards Jonas Stern?"

Swallow nodded soberly.

"What I'd like is for you to follow him, see what he's up to. His last known location was Berlin, but he's probably on the move. He's traveling under his own name, which seems odd, so he must not feel he's in any danger."

Swallow smiled at that.

"As soon as we pick him up, we'll put you onto him. We think he's trying to get hold of something . . . something that we'd prefer the Jews didn't get hold of. Understood?"

"Perfectly," said Swallow. She had, after all, done her part against the Zionist terrorists of Palestine.

Shaw cleared his throat. "Yes, well, what kind of payment would you want? Would twenty thousand pounds cover it?"

Swallow's eyes hooded over at this. It struck Shaw just then that, from Swallow's perspective, they had come to the point of the meeting. "What I want," she said in a toneless voice, "is Jonas Stern. When your little operation is over, I want a free hand with him."

Shaw had no illusions as to what this meant. Swallow wanted official permission to kill an Israeli citizen. He knew the answer to his next question, but he asked it anyway. "What was it, exactly, that Stern did to you?"

"Killed my brother," she replied in a voice that could have come from a corpse.

"That was quite some time ago, wasn't it?" Shaw commented.

"And every year since, my brother has lain in his grave." The furnace heat behind Swallow's eyes flashed at the edges. "They scarcely found enough of him to bury. *Bloody Jews.*"

Shaw nodded with appropriate solemnity. "Yes, well . . . your condition is accepted." He drummed his fingers on his desk. "Tell me, what's your feeling about Stern as an agent?"

"He's the best I ever saw. If he wasn't, he'd have been dead long ago. He's got the instincts of a bloody clairvoyant."

"Any ideas on his motive? Why he would leave Israel now?"

Swallow considered this. "To protect it," she said at length. "Israel is his weakness. He must believe the country is in imminent danger."

"I see."

"Is Israel in danger?"

"Not that I'm aware of," Shaw replied thoughtfully. "Not any more than usual."

As Swallow stood thinking, Shaw noticed that she stood with a vaguely military bearing—not tensely, but with a relaxed kind of *readiness,* rather like some Special Forces types he had known. They had all been men, of course.

"Is there anything else, then?" she asked.

Shaw flipped through the files on his desk with exaggerated casualness. "There is, as a matter of fact. Another job. A small one. Domestic job, actually. I thought you might take care of it for us. But it's a rush job. It must be done by tonight."

Swallow's eyes narrowed in suspicion. "Who is it?"

"Chap named Burton. Michael Burton. Retired. Lives in a cottage outside Haslemere in Surrey. Raises orchids, I believe. I'm afraid he knows too much for his own good." Sir Neville cleared his throat again. "There is one possible complication. He's only forty-eight. Retired Special Air Service."

At this Swallow seemed to withdraw into herself for consultation with whatever demon sustained her startlingly youthful appearance. At length, she asked, "Does he have any family?"

"Divorced. There's a brother. Why do you ask?"

"Is he SAS also?"

Shaw shook his head. "Regular army. But he's out of the country permanently. He lost his citizenship papers some years ago for mercenary work. He won't be a problem."

"Would you want it to look like an accident?"

"Can you run up an accident in Haslemere by tonight?"

Swallow made a sound in her throat that Shaw heard as a dry chuckle. "I doubt it. SAS men don't have accidents like that, as a rule. They're trained not to. They can drive, swim, run, shoot—"

"I don't care how it's done, then," Shaw flared. "Just do it. What's your price?"

A satisfied smile touched the corners of Swallow's mouth. She liked to see bureaucrats squirm. "My price is protection from the Israelis after Stern is dead."

"Good Christ!" Shaw exploded. "We can't babysit you forever. You kill Stern at your own risk."

Swallow's eyes turned opaque. "Don't play coy with me, little knight. Your hands are bloody too. By killing Stern I'm only doing what you want done. You picked me because you knew if he had to be liquidated, you could blame his death on my vendetta." She raised her chin defiantly. "If you try that, the Israelis will certainly get me, but not before *I kill you.*" Shaw drew back unconsciously. "I'll kill your SAS man for you," she went on, "but you'll cover for me on Stern. Otherwise I might *warn* this Mr. Burton instead."

"Condition accepted," Shaw snapped. "Now get out. All communication from this point forward will be through cut-outs. No further contact between you and this office."

Swallow made a mock curtsey and backed out of the room.

That witch should have been code-named Medusa, Shaw thought angrily. *She makes my bloody skin crawl.* When he closed Swallow's file, his eyes fell on the Hess dossier lying open beneath it. He sighed heavily. There lay the dreaded file, like a modern Domesday Book, a lexicon of heroism and treason, the highest and lowest expression of the English soul. And looking at it, Shaw's anger—an anger that had been building for a very long time—finally boiled to the surface. For if the truth were told, he would prefer to turn Swallow loose on the smug quislings and their moribund broods who for decades had cowered behind the shield of his service. He had no part in their crimes, or their guilt, and he felt no pity for them or their "honor." But what of England? He did have a stake in *her* honor. He had been only a child during the war, but in those heady years after Hitler was crushed, and all the years since, he had allowed himself to feel a part of the grand legend—what one British historian called the "Churchillian myth"—that in the early desperate days of the war England, all alone, had stood united, uncompromising, and unconquerable against the Nazis, and had thus saved Western Civilization from the Hun and the Bolshevik.

But that, Shaw had learned to his eternal sadness, was not quite the truth. *Then the truth be damned!* he thought bitterly. He understood the protective urge of the aristocrats. England had given the world so much; she deserved a little moral charity. Part myth though Churchill's history might be, the craven machinations of a few spineless lords (or, God forbid, a fool of a prince) could not be allowed to tarnish it. If a treacherous shadow dogged the House of Windsor, should it also stain the legacies of Plantagenet and Tudor and Hanover? And what of the *good* people in the war? The women who fought the fires in the Blitz? The callow lads whose shattered Spitfires practically clogged the Channel in 1940? The kids who crouched under the buzz bombs and the V-2s? The martyred population of Coventry?

As he poured himself a large whiskey, Shaw recalled the famous quote Churchill spoke after the Battle of Britain, but he twisted it to his own secret knowledge: *Never in the field of human conflict have so many nearly lost so much because of so few.* Shaw hated them! Hated them all! Appeasers . . . knights without courage . . . nobles without nobility. Because of them good men had died, and more were soon to follow. The man Swallow would kill tonight had but done his duty. It was the familiar chorus of English history: the good men had died while the scoundrels prospered. "Treason doth never prosper, what's the reason?" Shaw muttered, quoting the old epigram, "For if it prosper, none dare call it Treason." Yet in the midst of his furious meditation, Shaw felt a glimmer of satisfaction. Because if all his Machiavellian stratagems failed and the temple came tumbling down around his ears, the Judases would finally be unmasked, and the most heroic chapter in the history of his noble service would be brought to light at last.

Shaw drained his Scotch and fell instantly asleep with his head on his desk blotter.

CHAPTER SEVENTEEN

6:05 A.M. The Natterman Cabin: Near Wolfsburg, FRG

Hermann the forger was gone. After forty nerve-racking minutes under the gaze of Professor Natterman's shotgun, the bearish Hamburger had gathered up his equipment and scampered out of the cabin without a word. The professor sat in his chair, contemplating the night's events as the dawn filtered through the shattered cabin door. He had never felt so impotent in his life. His lifelong friend had been murdered, the Spandau papers had been taken from him, his granddaughter had been kidnapped, and he had been unable to prevent any of it from happening. And now the two men who proposed to stop the madness had refused his help!

Cradling the Mannlicher under one arm, he picked up his book satchel and walked out of the cabin without looking back. His suitcase lay in the slushy rut where the Audi had been parked. In their haste Hans and Hauer had not even taken the time to bring it into the cabin. The shot-riddled Jaguar waited behind the trunk of the old plane tree. Natterman walked over and looked inside to make sure the keys were still in the ignition. Tossing his satchel into the passenger seat, he retrieved his suitcase, then wriggled into the car and turned the key. In spite of the damage, the engine roared responsively.

He left the Jaguar idling and clumped through the snow to the rear of the cabin. In the shade of a tall cedar, a jury-rigged crucifix marked the shallow grave of Karl Riemeck. With bowed head Natterman laid the shotgun against the cross and softly spoke a few lines from Heine over his friend. Then he shuffled back to the rumbling Jaguar, jammed it into first gear, and sped up the access road.

The morning sun had already transformed the twisted lane into a morass of slush and mud that threw the speeding car from one bank to another as it approached the main road. Two curves away from the intersection, the professor saw a black log lying across the lane. When he swerved to avoid it, the Jaguar skidded out of control and slammed nose first into some saplings. It rebounded from their springlike trunks and coughed into silence.

He staggered out of the car and cautiously approached the log. Just as he bent to drag it out of the lane, he heard a crack in the trees behind him. *Ice?* he wondered. *No.* He stumbled back, thinking he would get the Mannlicher from the car. Then he remembered dropping it at Karl's grave. With panic knotting inside his chest, he scrambled toward the Jag, planning to drive around or even over the log to get to the main road. He had one leg inside the car when a voice froze him motionless.

"Herr Professor?"

Natterman whirled, but saw nothing.

"Herr Professor! May I speak with you for a moment?"

Again! Where had the voice come from? The brush on the opposite side of the road? The trees further on? Natterman tried to calm himself. Might a neighbor have come out to investigate last night's shots in the light of morning? These days even country people left such things to the police. Backing against the Jaguar, he called, "Who's out there? What do you want?"

"Only to speak with you!" the voice replied. "I mean you no harm."

"Come out, then! Why do you hide yourself?"

A tall dark-skinned man stepped noiselessly from the trees twenty meters up the road. "One has to be careful," he said, and then he smiled. "I wouldn't want to wind up like your Afrikaner friend."

Natterman stared fearfully at the stranger. He felt he knew the man from somewhere. Suddenly he had it. "You're the man from the train!" he cried. "Stern!"

The Israeli smiled. "You have an excellent memory, Professor."

"My God! Did you follow me here?" Natterman took a step back toward the Jaguar. "Are you in league with the Afrikaner?"

"Yes, I followed you here. No, I'm not in league with the Afrikaner. I'm here to help you, Professor."

Natterman pointed a finger at the Israeli. "What happened to your British accent?"

Stern chuckled. "It comes, it goes."

"You must have been here last night. Why didn't you help me?"

"I did help you. I stopped that Afrikaner from going back inside the cabin and killing you. By the time I'd finished dealing with him, your Polizei friends had arrived."

"Why didn't you come forward then?"

"For all I knew, Professor, you had come here specifically to meet that Afrikaner. The same holds true for your friends. I needed certain assurances about your motives."

"You're mad," Natterman declared. "Who the devil are you?"

Stern seemed to search for words. "Call me a concerned citizen," he said finally. "I'm retired, but I keep myself well-informed in the area that you've stumbled into with such dire consequences for yourself and your family."

"And what area is that?"

"The security of the State of Israel."

"*What?*" Natterman gaped. "Are you a Nazi-hunter?"

"No."

"You're not a historian!"

Stern laughed again. "Professional jealousy, Professor? Don't worry. I'm a historian of sorts, but not like you. You've studied history all your life—I have lived it."

Natterman scowled. "And what have you accomplished, my arrogant friend?"

"Not enough, I'm afraid."

"What do you want from me?"

"Everything you know about the document that Sergeant Apfel discovered in the ruins of Spandau Prison."

Natterman paled. "But—how do you know?"

Stern glanced at his watch. "Professor, I haven't been more than five hundred meters from those papers since they were discovered. I know the British and the Russians are searching like mad for them. I know about Hauer, Apfel, and your granddaughter. I know you made a copy of the papers in your office at the Free University, which you mailed to a friend for safekeeping. I know that Hauer and Apfel have taken away the six pages which were not stolen by the Afrikaner. I know—"

"Stop!" cried Natterman. "Where are the other three pages?"

"In my pocket. Our Afrikaner friend was kind enough to give them to me, after a little friendly persuasion."

Natterman shivered, realizing that Stern meant torture. But ambition overpowered his fear. "Give them back to me," he demanded. "They're mine."

Stern smiled. "I hope you haven't deluded yourself into believing that. These papers belong to no single man. Now, Professor, I'd like to ask you some questions."

Natterman recoiled. "Why should I tell you anything?"

"Because you have no choice."

"That's what everyone keeps telling me," Natterman grumbled.

"I assure you, Professor, if I'd wanted the papers, I could have taken them any time in the last sixteen hours."

Natterman felt a flash of anger, but something told him Stern was telling the truth. The same instinct told him that to resist the Israeli would be pointless, that this man who had materialized out of the snow like a ghost would get the information he wanted, one way or another. "All right," he said grudgingly,

"Prisoner Number Seven," Stern said brusquely. "The papers prove he was not Hess?"

"I believe they do," the old historian said warily.

"Where was the double substituted?"

"Hess picked up the double in Denmark. They flew to Britain together. The double was part of the plan all along. Hess bailed out the moment they reached the Scottish coast, over a place called Holy Island."

Stern digested this quickly. "And his mission?"

"The double didn't know Hess's mission, only his own. After Hess bailed out, the double was to fly on toward Dungavel Castle and await some sort of radio signal from Hess. If he received it, he was to parachute down and impersonate Hess for as long as he could."

Stern's eyes narrowed. "And if he didn't receive the signal?"

Natterman smiled wryly. "He was to fly out to sea, take cyanide, and ditch the plane. Standard SS procedure."

Stern smiled cynically. "Nazi melodrama. Few Occidentals have the nerve or the fanatical loyalty required to sacrifice themselves in cold blood." The Israeli's eyes moved restlessly as he pieced the rest of the story together. "So when the double turned back and jumped, he was disobeying orders. He went ahead and impersonated Hess as if he had received the signal . . . and the British believed him." Natterman listened to these deductions in silence. "Or perhaps they didn't believe him," Stern mused. "It doesn't really matter. What matters is this: Who did the *real* Hess fly there to see? And why in God's name should anyone in South Africa give a damn about it?"

"Now that you know what the papers say," said Natterman, "what do you intend to do?"

"I told you, Professor, my interest is not in the Hess case." Stern's hand slipped into his trouser pocket, fingered something there. "Long before the death of Prisoner Number Seven, I had reason to investigate Spandau. My reason had nothing to do with Hess—everything to do with the safety of Israel. But *until* Number Seven's death, gaining access to Spandau was virtually impossible." Stern paused, apparently conducting some debate with himself. "Tell me, Professor," he said suddenly, "does the Spandau diary mention weapons or scientific materials of any type?"

Natterman blinked in confusion. "*Weapons?* Herr Stern, the Spandau diary has nothing whatsoever to do with any kind of weapons."

"Are you positive?"

"Absolutely. What is it, suddenly? First Hauer badgers me about reunification, now you ask me about weapons—"

"Reunification?" Stern asked sharply.

"Oh, it's nonsense," Natterman said. "These papers deal only with the Hess case. They are going to expose those who share responsibility for the scars on Germany's national pride."

Stern's suspicious face hardened. "I'm afraid there's new infection festering beneath those old scars," he said coldly.

"What the devil do you mean?"

"Professor, I don't care if you're after academic fame, or if you want to ease Germany's national guilt." The Israeli waved away Natterman's protests. "I care about the past only insofar as it impacts the present and the future. The people who are after these papers are worried about a lot more than history books. I tried to interrogate that Afrikaner.

He forced me to kill him. He did that to *protect* someone, Professor. He had the crazy eyes, did you notice? With only one arm he fought like a tiger, and before he died he screamed something very startling at me. It was in Afrikaans—which I don't speak—but I knew enough Dutch to translate it. Roughly, it was 'Death to Israel! Death to Zion!' " Stern paused. "He didn't even know I was Jewish."

Natterman looked thoughtful. "He said something similar to me in the cabin. He called me a 'Jew maggot,' I believe."

Stern raised an eyebrow. "You don't find that curious? Why should a South African have some fixation on Jews? Or on Israel?"

"I never considered it until now."

Stern glanced back toward the main road as the drone of a heavy truck filled the woods. "Tell me," he said, "are Hauer and Apfel flying directly to South Africa?"

Natterman's eyes grew wide. "You know their destination?"

"Answer me!"

Natterman held out but a moment more. "Yes!" he blurted. "My granddaughter is being held prisoner there. The kidnappers instructed Hans by phone to leave today from Frankfurt."

"With the Spandau papers as ransom?"

"Yes, but Hauer has some kind of rescue plan up his sleeve."

Stern looked off into the dark forest. Frozen limbs cracked in the slowly rising sun. Icicles stretched earthward, reaching it one drop at a time. "The diary is incomplete now," he murmured. "Who is aware of that?"

"No one," Natterman confessed. "Only you and I."

Stern turned and eyed the professor appraisingly. "That is good for us, but very dangerous for your granddaughter. Tell me, what kind of man is this Captain Hauer?"

"Tough. Very tough."

"And the boy?"

"Angry . . . frightened to death. Untested."

Stern nodded. "One thing has puzzled me from the beginning, Professor. Why has Captain Hauer—a man nearing retirement, a man whose own personnel file shows him to be a member of a neofascist police organization—sacrificed his pension and possibly his life to help this apparently innocent young sergeant?"

Natterman smiled at the irony. "Hauer is Hans's father. It's a complicated family matter. Very few people know about it."

Stern took a deep, satisfying breath, as if this last bit of information had completed some circle in his mind.

"You must tell me who you are," Natterman demanded. "Are you a spy? Are you really an Israeli?"

To the professor's amazement, Stern turned suddenly on his heel and without a word marched down the lane toward the main road.

"Where are you going?" Natterman cried.

"South Africa, Professor! Get that log out of the road if you want to come!"

Natterman's jaw dropped in astonishment. "But I have no passport!"

"In an hour you shall!" Stern called, then he disappeared around the curve.

As the huffing professor wrestled the rotted tree trunk over a snowdrift at the lane's edge, he heard the sound of an approaching engine. Seconds later, a big blue Mercedes rounded the curve from the direction of the main road and stopped beside him. At the wheel sat Jonas Stern. In the backseat, laid out and trussed like a Christmas turkey, Hermann the forger jerked his head back and forth in impotent rage.

"Get in," said Stern. "I thought this fellow might come in handy, so I invited him to stay for a while."

Too surprised to speak, Natterman climbed into the car and stared back at Hermann as they drove back to the cabin.

"Is the cabin phone still working?" Stern asked.

Natterman nodded.

"I've quite a few calls to make, but soon we shall be on a plane bound for Israel. And from there, South Africa."

"Why Israel? Why not fly straight to South Africa?"

Stern skidded to a stop before the battered cabin. "We have some packages to pick up. Now, untie that fool while I get his equipment. I have much to arrange before we can be on our way."

Like a dazed recruit of eighteen, the old historian followed the Israeli's orders, a little afraid, but grateful to be part of the chase at last.

5:55 P.M. Sonnenallee Checkpoint: American Sector, West Berlin

Harry Richardson walked slowly toward the barrier post on the eastern side of the Berlin Wall. In spite of Kosov's assurances to Colonel Rose, Harry still half-expected to be arrested at the checkpoint. He walked quickly past the East German documents-control booth, then stopped as instructed at the currency-check station. Glancing right, he saw two pale faces peering out of the warmly lit observation window. One hovered above the red shoulder boards of a KGB colonel: Ivan Kosov. The other, angrier face belonged to Captain Dmitri Rykov. A bad week altogether for the young *chekist,* Harry thought. He tipped his head at Rykov, then walked on.

The gray sky had darkened. Harry could just make out the U.S. Army Ford waiting on the American side of the Wall, parked beyond the harsh glow of the checkpoint area, motor running. Beside the Ford, a restless line of cars and lorries waited to pass through the blocked checkpoint. Fifty yards closer, the door to the West Berlin customs booth opened suddenly and a young border policeman stepped out. Behind him emerged Colonel Rose, wearing a long olive-drab greatcoat. Then came two men wearing civilian clothes and handcuffs, followed by Sergeant Clary, who carried a Colt .45 in his right hand.

Harry heard footsteps behind him, then felt Kosov's hand grip his upper arm. Twenty seconds later, seven men stood awkwardly around the white-painted line that marked the absolute boundary between East and West Berlin—five on the American side, two on the Soviet. Tonight protocols were few. With a nod Kosov signaled the two handcuffed Soviet illegals to step over the line. As they did, he released his grip on Harry's arm. Harry stepped across the line. He breathed a heartfelt sigh of relief when Clary clapped him on the back in welcome.

Kosov looked at Rose. "I commend your nerve in negotiating this exchange, Colonel. Your pragmatic style is somewhat surprising in an American. Next time, however—"

Rose turned and marched away without a word. Sergeant Clary and the border policeman followed him. Before Harry could turn, however, Kosov reached out and caught hold of his arm. "Axel Goltz is dead," he growled.

"Does that bother you?"

"What bothers me is that I don't understand why he did what he did. Since you killed him, I doubt very much that he worked for you. And given that, I must begin to take seriously the nationalistic drivel he spouted off before he shot Corporal Ivanov. He mentioned something called Phoenix, I believe? Have you heard of this?"

Harry shrugged. "Sure. It's about a hundred miles south of Tucson, isn't it?"

Kosov smiled coldly. "Have it your way, Major. I would prefer that our two services collaborate on the Hess case. All my country wants is for the truth to be exposed to the world. When Germany begins to stir, even traditional enemies must join forces."

"Someone should have told Stalin that in 1939," Harry observed. "*Guten Abend,* Colonel." He turned and jogged to the waiting Ford.

While Kosov fumed, Rykov emerged from the customs booth, trailed noiselessly by a lean figure dressed from head to toe in black. "Misha," Kosov muttered, his voice hoarse with fury.

The young killer pricked up his ears like a hungry panther.

"I think it's time you paid a visit to the whore who showed us such disrespect. Show her that we keep our promises."

Misha nodded, and then, with a swiftness that astonished Rykov, he melted into the gray dusk of the Sonnenallee.

"What now, Colonel?" asked Rykov.

"We wait," Kosov replied, still staring after the Americans. "I'm expecting a visitor."

Fifty meters away, Harry climbed into the Army Ford and found a bearish man wearing a hat and civilian clothes waiting in the backseat. He looked familiar, but Rose made no introductions.

Sergeant Clary swept across West Berlin with the subtlety of a fire truck. Harry let his head fall back on the seat, intending to savor his newfound freedom, but Rose gave him no respite. The colonel heaved a beefy forearm back over the passenger seat and grinned. "Okay, Harry, what did you find out over there?"

Harry answered with his eyes closed. "I found out that whatever is in those Spandau papers is important enough for a Stasi agent to kill a KGB officer over it."

"Axel Goltz," said Rose. "Did you kill him?"

"He didn't leave me any choice."

The colonel nodded. "Our East German sources said Kosov went berserk when he found out he couldn't interrogate Goltz. He arrested every ranking Stasi officer he could lay his hands on."

Harry shook his head. "Colonel, Goltz was no more afraid of Kosov than a rabid dog would have been. He acted as if he expected Heinz Guderian's tanks to roll out of the Black Forest any minute and chase the Russians right out of Germany."

"It'd take more than that," Rose muttered. "Every T-72 tank in the DDR is on the move. They're running civilian vehicles right off the roads. Someone in Moscow has decided that the Germans need a lesson in humility."

"Maybe they do," Harry said softly. "Did you pick up anything on the names I gave you? Zinoviev or Phoenix?"

"Yes and no." Rose shared a glance with the unidentified passenger in the backseat. "In the office, Harry."

Harry nodded slowly. "Okay."

In the silence that followed, it became impossible for Harry to ignore the man on the seat beside him. Finally, Rose acknowledged the stranger. "Harry, meet Detective Julius Schneider of the Berlin *Kriminalpolizei.* He's gonna be working with us for a while. He's the guy who saved your ass. Says he knows you."

"A pleasure, Detective." Harry shook Schneider's bearlike paw. "I thought you looked familiar. I owe you a very tall drink."

"It is not necessary," said the German.

"Okay, okay," Rose grumbled. "Let's adjourn this mutual admiration society and get up to my office."

The car had arrived in Clay Allee, the thoroughly American boulevard named for the first U.S. commandant of West Berlin. While Sergeant Clary returned the Ford to the motor pool, Rose, Schneider, and Richardson made their way to the fourth floor. Rose took a seat behind his huge desk, poured whiskeys all around, and waited for Clary to take up his post outside the door.

Harry opened the discussion. "So what's the big secret, guys? Who's Comrade Zinoviev? He isn't *Lenin's* Zinoviev, is he?"

Rose gave Schneider a sidelong glance. "Hardly, Harry.

We don't know exactly who Zinoviev is, or was. We don't know if he's dead or alive. But I can guarantee you that 'comrade' wasn't his preferred manner of address."

Harry drummed his fingers impatiently. "Christ, tell me something."

Rose took a pull from his Wild Turkey. "Our computers didn't have squat on Zinoviev, Harry, zero. I was tempted to put in a coded request to Langley—you know, can we run a name through your sacred database, blah, blah? But I never liked using those guys. To me it's kind of like going to the Mafia. They're a little too greasy for my taste. So what I ended up doing was calling an old buddy of mine stateside. Programs computers for the FBI. He ran it through their setup for me, and you wouldn't believe what their machine spit out."

"Surprise me."

Rose smiled, knowing that for once he would. "V.V. Zinoviev was a captain in the *Okhrana*. Ring any bells?"

Harry looked bewildered. "The tsar's secret police?"

"Give the boy an apple," Rose quipped. "The *Okhrana* were the world's o-riginal anti-communists. They make Joe McCarthy and his pals look like a pack of church ladies. The question is, What could a hitman for Tsar Nicholas possibly have in common with Rudolf Hess?"

"Well," Harry reflected, "for one thing, the *Okhrana* carried out massive pogroms against the Jews in Russia."

Both Rose and Schneider looked stunned.

"Look, Colonel," said Harry, "you're way ahead of me on this. Why don't you just back up and give me the *Reader's Digest* version?"

"Okay. My FBI buddy punches Zinoviev into the Bureau computers, right? Well, up comes a file. It gives the *Okhrana* reference, Zinoviev's date of birth, but no death date. It says he disappeared from sight in 1941, which was—"

"The year Hess flew to Scotland," Harry finished.

"Right. Well, in Zinoviev's file was a code—HCO—which I'm told stands for 'Hardcopy Only.' There was also a cross-index to another file."

"Hess?"

"You got it. So my buddy goes for the Hess file, right? And what does he find? A bunch of crap you can get from *Encyclopaedia Britannica*. But he *also* finds a notation showing a special addendum to Hess's file, with what the Bureau calls a *J* classification. Want to guess what the *J* is for?"

Harry's face showed disbelief. "No way."

Rose smiled thinly. "Old J. Edgar himself. And *J* files cannot be accessed by anyone except the director."

"Christ. What does the FBI have to do with Rudolf Hess?"

"You're not gonna believe this, Harry. Remember the big Soviet defections of the sixties and seventies? Nosenko, Penkovsky and the rest? The CIA handled their debriefings, right? Naturally. But if you'll recall, the FBI wasn't always limited to operations within the Continental U.S. During World War Two, Hoover couldn't stand seeing Bill Donovan's OSS get all the glory, and the result—aside from a lot of political head-butting—was that the Bureau got involved in some pretty big espionage cases. *So*—after the CIA finished debriefing those big defectors, the FBI got themselves a little taste. They were given a very limited brief, of course, questions to be confined to KGB recruitment methods on U.S. soil, et cetera."

Harry nodded slowly.

"*However,* when the FBI got their shot at these defectors, they took the chance to clean up some unfinished business. They had quite a few unsolved cases from the war years, and Hoover had left instructions that they be pursued whenever possible. One of those cases happened to involve British collaboration with the Nazis—e.g., the flight of Rudolf Hess."

Harry whistled long and low.

"The FBI questioning turned up a shitload of information, but as you might imagine, the Bureau wasn't anxious to reveal to the CIA how far outside their brief they had strayed. Anything that couldn't be confirmed by collateral evidence was buried in the basement of a file warehouse. 'Hardcopy Only,' get it? Apparently Zinoviev fell into that category." Rose's eyes shone with excitement. "Harry, those files have been sitting in that warehouse for *twenty-five years*. My contact thinks our query is the first thing to turn up Zinoviev's name since it went to disk."

"Jesus. What kind of access do we have?"

"Hess's file is out of the question. A team of MIT hackers couldn't break into a *J* file in a month." Rose suppressed a satisfied smile. "Zinoviev, on the other hand, we may get.

My buddy is constantly updating the Bureau files, and it seems he's got legitimate access to the warehouse where the 'Hardcopy Only' stuff is. He's probably digging through Zinoviev's file right now."

Harry looked skeptical. "Colonel, you realize that there may be nothing on Zinoviev in that warehouse. If Zinoviev is cross-indexed to Hess, his real file probably has a *J* classification too."

"We'll find out soon enough," Rose concluded. "Let's get to the heart of this mess—the Spandau papers."

Harry glanced over at Schneider. "I assume the Berlin police have them?"

"Not exactly," said Rose. "Two Berlin police *officers* have them." Rose consulted a file on his desk. "Hans Apfel, sergeant, age twenty-seven; Dieter Hauer, captain, age fifty-five. Schneider here thinks one of these two must have stumbled over the papers while they were guarding the prison. He says this guy Hauer's a real piece of work—counterterror training, the works. And he must be right. Not only have these two escaped the city, they've escaped Germany. They flew out of Frankfurt two hours ago."

"*What?* How do you know that?"

While Schneider listened in silence, Rose summarized his actions after receiving Harry's call. Rose had wanted to storm Abschnitt 53 with guns blazing, but Schneider had persuaded him to pursue a more discreet course. The colonel's compromise had been a citywide communications blanket of West Berlin, conducted by the Army Signal Corps under the reserve powers held by the Allies since the Second World War. Assets normally dedicated to the Soviet target were reassigned to cover all police communications traffic entering or leaving Berlin. Rose was grinning as he revealed his breakthrough.

"Six hours ago it paid off, Harry. We intercepted a call from the Wolfsburg police to West Berlin police HQ. A traffic unit stopped a man for speeding and reckless driving, and because they'd received reports of shooting in the forest to the south the night before, they made a routine search of the car. They hit the jackpot. The driver was a forger from Hamburg. Right away the guy starts screaming how he's just been blackmailed into manufacturing false passports for two West Berlin cops. Claimed he knew Hauer personally, and he described Apfel to a T."

"Did he have any idea where they were headed?" Harry asked.

Rose grinned. "That ever-popular vacation spot, the Republic of South Africa. Traveling as father and son. The forger also made passports for two older guys who were with Hauer and Apfel, but traveling separately. He didn't know their true identities or their destination, but he gave us the names and numbers on all four fake passports."

"Great. Who else knows that?"

"If our luck is holding, almost nobody. I called the Berlin police presidium and used every authority short of the president to block the relay of that information to Abschnitt 53. I also let them know in no uncertain terms that I'd know if they tried."

Harry sat in silence for nearly a full minute. "South Africa," he said finally. "Is there anything that connects any of what's happened to South Africa in any way?"

"As a matter of fact, there is. My little high-tech offensive included pulling the telephone toll records of certain West Berlin police facilities. We found several calls from the police presidium going out to different numbers in South Africa. Some of those calls were made from the office of the prefect himself."

"Holy shit. Do you have names to go with the numbers?"

"I should have them within twenty-four hours. For once *I* happen to have an exotic contact—a major in the South African secret service."

"That's not soon enough, Colonel."

"That's as soon as we can get it, *Major.* And that's if we're lucky."

Harry stood. "You've got to get me down there, Colonel. Whatever's going down, it's going to happen there."

Rose shook his head. "I can't send you, Harry."

"What?"

"You heard me. That's not our territory—not even close. We can't prove that this thing endangers American interests. Also, we're not too damned popular down there right now, in case you haven't noticed. Not since the sanctions were put into effect and half our industry pulled out of there. The Army's not gonna let me send you down there just because the Soviets are interested."

"Interested! They kidnapped me, for Christ's sake. There's something big going on, Colonel, I can feel it. The reason you can't find out anything about this Phoenix is that it isn't based here. It *must* be in South Africa. This isn't just some legacy from the past ... Can't you feel it?"

"I feel it," Detective Schneider said softly.

Rose drained his second whiskey, stood, and laid his stubby hands flat on the desktop. "I feel it too, Harry, but my hands are tied. I've got half of Bonn and all of Berlin breathing down my neck to prevent any kind of international incident. Officially, I can't do a thing."

Harry stared curiously at Rose. He sensed some implied communication, but he couldn't quite pin it down. Suddenly the answer came clear as ice water. "Grant me two weeks leave, Colonel," he said. "I've got it coming."

Rose grinned. "That you do, Major. That you do."

"Can you get me a military flight?"

"Negative."

"But it's probably a fifteen-hour flight by commercial carrier!"

"Eleven on Lufthansa," Rose corrected. "Fourteen via South African Air."

"That's still too long!"

"You're lucky to get a flight at all, Harry. Most airlines only fly there once a week. Your flight leaves Frankfurt at two P.M. tomorrow."

Harry shook his head in exasperation, then grinned in spite of himself. "By the time I get there, I want some names tied to those telephone numbers."

"You'll have 'em." Abruptly, Rose slammed an open hand down on his desk. His face showed puzzlement, exhaustion, frustration. "Goddamnit Harry, what the hell is going on? Do the Russians really care that much about something that happened fifty years ago?"

Harry looked thoughtful. "I know what you mean. Gorbachev has a hell of a lot bigger things on his plate than fifty-year-old mysteries. I wouldn't think the truth about Hess would help *glasnost* any."

"The Russian memory is long," Schneider said gravely. "And Gorbachev has limited influence over KGB."

Harry glanced at the German. "Maybe. But we're missing the forest here. We're not talking ancient history. The Berlin police wouldn't give two shits about something like that. We're talking about a tie between the past—*Hess's past*—

and the present. The here and now. Maybe Zinoviev is the connection."

"Whatever the connection is," said Rose, "I've got a feeling it's pretty goddamn dirty. I don't have to tell you how many friggin' Nazis our own government shielded from justice."

Harry looked hard at both men for a few moments; then he reached into his pocket, drew something out, and tossed it on Rose's desk. The fragment of Goltz's scalp landed upside-down with a plop, like a wet scab. Black flecks of blood stained the file on Rose's desk. The colonel reached out to pick it up, then jerked back his hand in disgust.

"What the fuck is *that?*"

"Goltz," Harry explained. "That was a shaved spot a little above and behind his right ear. Turn it over, Colonel."

Rose looked up at Harry with an expression that suggested he might be wondering if Harry kept a Viet Cong ear necklace in his dresser at home.

"I didn't have a camera," Harry muttered.

Rose took a ballpoint pen from a stand and flicked the shriveled swatch of skin over, revealing the tattoo it bore. He made no sound as he studied it, but Schneider sucked in his breath so sharply that both men turned to him.

"You've seen this mark before?" Rose asked.

The German nodded. "Yes. It's hard to detect. Once the hair grows back in, the mark is invisible."

Harry looked curiously at the German.

"What the hell's it mean?" Rose demanded.

Schneider shrugged. "Certain members of a semisecret political group wear that mark. The group is called *Der Bruderschaft*—the Brotherhood. Quite a few policemen belong to it. I don't know what the tattoo means. I always thought it was just a badge of membership. Now and then you'll see a policeman with a bandage behind his ear. They always make some excuse, but after a while you realize what it is."

"Sounds like some kind of friggin' cult thing," Rose declared. "Is it like the Aryan Brotherhood in the States?"

Harry shook his head. "The Aryan Brotherhood is made up of convicts, not police. They're cop killers."

"How many Berlin cops have this mark? A dozen? A hundred?"

"More than a hundred," Schneider said thoughtfully. "But

I never realized that it extended into the DDR. That's very disturbing."

"You're goddamn right it is," Rose agreed.

"Detective," Harry said softly, "do all members of *Der Bruderschaft* have the tattoo? Or just a select few? A few who might belong to some truly secret group, for instance."

"Like Phoenix, you mean," mused Schneider. "No, I don't think all the members have the tattoo."

Rose was staring strangely at Schneider. When Harry realized why, he couldn't help staring himself.

The big German scowled back at them. "No, I don't have a tattoo under my hair," he growled. "And the first man who asks to look is going to spend the night in the hospital."

When Rose looked as if he might ask, Harry stood quickly. "Thanks again for saving my life, Detective. If you fellows don't mind, I'm going to crash until takeoff time tomorrow."

Rose finally shifted his attention to Harry. "Just remember," he warned, "you'll be going in blind down there. What I told you about the British still holds: no contact at all, not even with your personal connections. No one's above being manipulated by his government—especially ministers and lords."

"Not even me," said Harry, and smiled wryly. "You worried about James Bond catching up with me, Colonel?"

"No. I'm worried about some goddamn George Smiley type. A fat little guy with glasses who's five steps ahead of us already. Somebody who knows all about whatever happened back in Germany in 1941."

Harry ruminated on this for a moment. "By the way, Colonel, Ivan Kosov told me he'd like to collaborate on the Hess case."

"When hell freezes over," Rose muttered. "We'll get to the bottom of this well ourselves."

Harry grinned. "That's what I told him you'd say."

Schneider stood and offered his prodigious hand. "*Gluck haben,* Major."

"*Danke,*" Harry replied.

"Get the hell out of here," Rose bellowed. "I'll brief you before you fly out."

Harry sauntered out, returning Clary's sharp salute as he passed through the outer office.

"What do you think?" Rose asked, when Harry had gone.

"I think I should go with him," Schneider said bluntly.

"Well, you can't. I need you here. You've got a lot to do before you get any rest, mister."

"Such as?"

"Such as helping me rout out the scum that's holed up in that police station."

Schneider smiled coldly. *"Gut."*

"But first I want you to get over to that police sergeant's apartment. Apfel, right? Talk to the guy's wife. We should've covered it hours ago, but I couldn't spare you."

Schneider stepped to the door and pulled on his heavy wool overcoat.

"And Schneider?"

"Yes, Colonel?"

"Sorry about that tattoo business. I'm on edge. If you stumble into trouble, don't play hero, okay? I know you don't like Americans messing around in your backyard, but solo's no way to fly on something like this. You get me?"

Schneider nodded, but as his broad back disappeared through the office door, Rose wondered how sincere the gesture really was.

CHAPTER EIGHTEEN

6:12 P.M. Soviet Sector: East Berlin, DDR

In a black BMW parked two blocks from the red-and-white border posts of the Sonnenallee checkpoint, Colonel Ivan Kosov sat in silent rage while a man in a two-thousand-dollar Savile Row suit berated him for blatant incompetence. The man was Yuri Borodin, himself a colonel and one of the brightest stars of the Twelfth Department of the First Chief Directorate of the KGB. Kosov hated everything about Borodin—his undisguised arrogance, his hand-tailored clothing, his aristocratic family background and manner of speech, his meteoric rise to high rank—everything. It made the situation all the more difficult to bear.

"So you think your men can handle a simple surveillance job?" Borodin asked coldly.

"*Da,*" Kosov grunted.

Borodin looked out of the car window distractedly. "I'm afraid I do not share your faith. Major Richardson will go to U.S. Army Headquarters for debriefing, then he'll move. Wherever he goes, that is where the missing Polizei officers and your Spandau papers are. *If* indeed papers are what the young German found. If it is papers, I'd bet my career that the Americans have them already."

I hope you do, thought Kosov. "What makes you think the Americans have caught them?" he asked. "And what makes you think Major Richardson was even working on the Spandau case when my men captured him?"

Borodin switched to an upper-class English accent. "Instinct, old boy," he said primly.

Kosov wrinkled his lip in disgust. "You sound like an Oxford professor with a pipe stuck up his ass."

"And how would you know what an Oxford professor sounds like?" Borodin needled. "I'm just practicing the King's English, *Comrade.* I'll probably be needing it in the next few days."

Someone tapped on the smoked-glass window on the driver's side of the BMW. Kosov cranked down the window.

Captain Dmitri Rykov stuck his head into the window. "They've taken him to U.S. headquarters," Rykov informed them, eyeing Borodin with curiosity.

"I'll be off, then," Borodin said lightly.

"Where are you going?" asked Kosov.

"To pick up Major Richardson when he leaves army headquarters. You don't really think I trust your chaps to stay on him, do you? No offense intended, of course."

"But how will you get there?"

Borodin smiled. "In this car, of course."

"But this is my personal car!" Kosov exploded.

"Now, now, Comrade," Borodin said. "Relax. This car belongs to the *people,* doesn't it? I need a car—this one's available. You'll get it back eventually. Now, out of the car. I must be on my way."

Kosov hauled himself out of the vehicle and slammed the door behind him. Borodin didn't even notice. He roared up to the checkpoint, not the slightest bit nervous about his false papers. Borodin was Twelfth Department, and Twelfth Department always got the best.

Dmitri Rykov stared dumbfounded at his superior. He had never seen Ivan Kosov allow someone to run roughshod over him like that.

"Who was that man, Colonel?"

Kosov stared after his receding BMW. "Someone you will get to know very well in the next few days, Dmitri." He turned to Rykov. "You still have your travel papers?"

"Yes, Comrade Colonel."

"Good. I want you to cross into the American sector and go to U.S. Army Headquarters. There you will find the man you just saw steal my BMW. You're to follow him and report his every movement back to me. Do you have any credit cards?"

Rykov nodded with enthusiasm.

"American Express?"

"Gold Card."

Kosov scowled. "Captain Rykov, I am authorizing you to

spend whatever is necessary to follow that man wherever he goes."

"Yes, sir!"

"Anywhere in the world," Kosov added.

Rykov's chest swelled as he absorbed the import of Kosov's words. This had to be something *big*. Something that could make a career.

"His name," said Kosov quietly, "is Yuri Borodin. He's a colonel in the Twelfth Department."

Rykov paled.

"Do you wish me to find someone else, Captain?"

Rykov cleared his throat. "*Nyet,* Comrade Colonel. Dmitri Rykov is your man."

"Then get your ass over to the checkpoint and find out what cover Borodin used to cross. I'll call a car for you."

Kosov laid a hand on Rykov's shoulder. "Keep your eyes open for someone named Zinoviev. He's either a very old man or a very dead one. Call me as often as you can. I'll have more information on Borodin for you."

"Thank you, Comrade Colonel!"

"And Dmitri . . . about that tattoo. The eye on Goltz's head." Kosov lowered his voice. "It is the symbol of a one-eyed man. I don't know his name, but whoever he is, he's at the center of this case. The Americans don't know anything about him, and I don't think Borodin does either. So if you happen to meet a man with one eye—a glass eye, or even a patch—you are to call me immediately. If you even *hear* of a one-eyed man involved with this case, you call me."

Rykov looked confused, but he nodded.

"Now go!"

Ignoring his bruised leg, Rykov sprinted after the BMW.

Kosov lit a Camel cigarette and took a deep drag. He held in the acrid smoke for a long time before he exhaled. He felt better now. Much better. When he smiled, the expression made him look even uglier than he was.

6:30 P.M. #30 Lützenstrasse

Ivan Kosov's black-clad assassin padded softly into Ilse's apartment building and slipped into the stairwell. He was looking forward to paying back the German whore who had taunted him yesterday, and he knew a hundred ways to extract his pound of flesh. He only hoped that the old tart's young companion would be home with her. She could prove very entertaining before she died. It never ceased to amaze Misha how cooperative women became after only the briefest acquaintance with his knife.

Three floors above him, Eva Beers leaned toward her bathroom mirror and pulled a stained bandage away from her cheek. The laceration looked considerably worse than it had twelve hours before. The skin hung slack in spite of her best attempts to smile or grimace. Last night, when she had first got back to her apartment, she'd discovered that the lower half of her left cheek did not seem to be moving normally. It disturbed her, but she put the problem down to shock. Eva had been in her share of bar brawls, and drawing on this experience she did a fair job of patching the deep gash inflicted by the young Russian. But now she worried. The bleeding had long since stopped, but the stubborn flesh to the left of her mouth still hung lifeless, like that of a stroke victim. Replacing the bandage, she decided to ignore Kosov's warning and seek proper medical assistance.

She slipped on a housecoat and walked out to the front room of her modest apartment to check on Ernst. The tough old cabbie lay snoring on the sofa. He had taken a bad beating and needed a doctor almost as badly as Eva did. She leaned over him, listening to his irregular breaths. His bruised and battered face made her furious again. She had expected the Russians to come back for her as soon as they realized she had lied about Ilse, but they hadn't. *Lucky for them, too,* she thought. Because for the remainder of last night and most of today, some of her heavily built friends from her *Ratskeller* days had hung around the apartment just in case the Russians showed up. An hour ago Eva had thanked them and sent them on their way, glad that no further trouble had visited.

Kissing Ernst lightly on his forehead, she went back to her bedroom and pulled the door shut. In her bureau drawer she found the number of an old general practitioner who not so long ago had run a quiet practice catering to smugglers, addicts, and young girls in trouble. *I hope he's still in business,* she thought. She had no patience with emergency rooms— too many forms to fill out, too many questions to answer. She left the doctor's number on the bureau and went into the bathroom to make up her face.

In the hallway outside the apartment, Misha inserted a needle-thin tool into the door lock and picked it with ease. Eva had carelessly left the bolt unshot when her friends left, but she had fastened the chain. Misha put his deceptively narrow shoulder against the door and leaned into it hard, yanking the chain's anchor-plate from the doorjamb.

The noise of the screws pulling loose was minimal, but enough to make the sleeping cabbie shift on the sofa. Misha's ears detected the rustle, and after his eyes adjusted to the darkness, he discerned the supine form. He crossed the room silently and stared down. Bruises and a badly blackened eye distorted Ernst's face, but Misha recognized the old man who had fought so tenaciously outside his taxi on the previous night. As Misha stared, Ernst's eyes fluttered open. With the dreadful clarity of nightmares the old cabbie recognized the Russian above him. He opened his mouth to scream a warning to Eva, but Misha snatched a threadbare pillow from the couch and slammed it over Ernst's contorted face, pressing down with all his strength.

In the bathroom Eva heard nothing. The battle being fought in her front room was desperate but soundless. Just when Misha felt the old man's struggles begin to subside, a hand shot upward and locked around his throat in a maniacal death grip. The Russian struggled to hold the smothering pillow in place, not believing the old man's strength. The bony fingers clutching his throat seemed to be probing for some hollow place where they could gain sufficient purchase to crush his windpipe.

Misha had had enough. The pillow had seemed a good idea at first, but it was obviously too slow for this old lion. Fighting to breathe, he held the pillow in place with his right hand and drew his stiletto from its ankle sheath with his left.

A veteran of the streets, Ernst the cabbie knew what the snick of spring and steel meant, but he could fight no harder than he was already. He felt the cold blade pierce his chest just below the sternum. Misha expertly twisted the blade across the midline marking the passage of the aorta; the old man felt ice turn to fire. He jerked spasmodically, then his wrinkled hands slipped from Misha's throat.

The Russian gulped in huge lungfuls of air and shook his head to clear it. He had not expected this battle. Then suddenly, as the pillow slipped from the old man's livid face, Ernst somehow summoned a last measure of energy and cried out—not loudly, but it was enough. Misha looked up to see Eva's bedroom door slam shut and hear the click of the bolt shooting home. Cursing, he scrambled around the room's baseboards until he found the telephone line running from the bedroom. He severed the black wire two seconds after Eva picked up the receiver in her room.

Sheathing his knife with a grin, he charged the bedroom door. The bolt did not give. He stepped back and examined the door. It had a heavy frame with two solid planks crossing in the middle, but it was paneled with four thinner sheets of wood. Aiming at a spot on the upper right panel—just above the knob—Misha kicked hard, splintering the brittle wood. A second kick opened the hole he wanted. He thrust his left hand through the jagged opening, groping for the bolt.

With the sure eye of a seamstress, Eva drove the point of a brass letter opener through the back of the Russian's exposed hand. The shriek from the other side of the door did not even sound human. Misha's spasming hand jerked back through the splintered door panel, taking the letter opener with it.

"Devil's whore!" he screamed, wrenching the blade from his punctured hand. "You're *dead!*"

Eva did not own a gun, and she was now truly terrified. Her attacker launched his body repeatedly against the door, screaming in animal rage. Still the bolt refused to give. Then, suddenly, the bloody hand reappeared through the hole and probed for the bolt. The circular wound in its center made Eva think of the hand of Christ. Hysterically, she screamed some part of a childhood prayer and smashed a chair down on the bloody fingers. The crack of bones made her shudder, but it renewed her hope for survival.

Unbelievably, the hand tried for the bolt again. Again Eva brought the chair down, this time on the wrist. Misha howled like a madman. Enraged beyond feeling pain, he withdrew his shattered hand, backed up, and took a flying kick at the spot where he judged the bolt to be. This time the door crashed open.

With tears of terror streaming down her bandaged face, Eva backed toward the bedroom wall, holding the small wooden chair in front of her like a lion tamer. When she collided with her cluttered vanity table, she felt her bladder let go. She froze there, transfixed by the predatory gleam in the Russian's eyes. Then he moved toward her, breaking the spell. Eva swung the little chair in desperation, but he parried it easily. Laughing, he snatched the chair from her and tossed it aside.

The killing fever was on him now. He closed on the shivering woman, his blood-slickened knife dancing like a cobra's head. Moaning in mortal terror, Eva lunged blindly, hoping somehow to get past the Russian. She had no chance. Misha expertly channeled her momentum downward and pinned her against the floor, his boot planted solidly between her shoulder blades. He snatched her hair and jerked her head back, pressing the knife blade to her throat. His fractured bones seared with agony, but he thought he could hold the blade steady long enough to drag it across the stubborn woman's throat. He dangled the bright blade before her rolling eyes.

"You know whose blood that is, woman?" he rasped in Russian.

"Go on, you bastard!" she screamed. *"Do it!"*

Misha pressed the blade against her throat, trying for a firmer grip with his wounded hand.

Suddenly, a roar like that of a Black Forest bear filled the room. Misha looked up in surprise. A huge form blocked out the light as it charged toward him. It was Schneider. The big detective had just gotten off the elevator and started toward Ilse's flat when he heard Misha kick down the bedroom door. He raced toward the noise, saw Ernst's blood-soaked corpse on the sofa bed, and continued his headlong charge into the bedroom.

Misha flung his arm up and tried to hold his knife steady, but Schneider's momentum bowled him over like a child. He tumbled back against the vanity and landed in a sitting position. Dazed, he transferred his knife to his good hand and got up onto his knees. Schneider backed off slightly, crouching in a classic knife fighter's stance.

Eva scrambled unsteadily to her feet and stood a few feet behind him. "Run!" she shouted. "Here's the door behind you!"

"Get out!" Schneider ordered.

"I'll call the police!" Eva cried, searching hysterically for her useless phone.

"Don't call anyone!" Schneider snapped. "Go downstairs!"

Having regained some of his faculties, Misha rose into a

low crouch and moved out from the vanity, smiling cruelly. "You should have brought a knife," he taunted in German.

Schneider snatched a sheet from the bed and twisted it quickly around his left arm, as he had been taught to do against an attacking dog. He circled carefully, waiting for the Russian's lunge. He knew it would come soon.

With a cry Misha feinted left, then struck hard, driving the point of the knife upward toward the German's huge chest. More like a mongoose than a bear, Schneider parried the outstretched blade with his sheet-wrapped arm and darted out of danger; in the same movement he rammed his mammoth right fist into Misha's eye socket as the Russian's body followed his knife thrust.

The blow felled Kosov's assassin like a rotted oak.

When Misha regained consciousness four minutes later, his right eye had swollen shut. A distant voice in his brain told him that he would soon have his vision back, but the voice was wrong. Schneider's impacting fist had so suddenly increased the pressure inside the Russian's eyeball that it literally exploded at its weakest point—in Misha's case around the optic nerve—scrambling the delicate contents into jelly.

With his good eye Misha saw the big German speaking into a telephone beyond an open door. He heard the name Rose, but it meant nothing to him. A disheveled blond woman with a white bandage on her face knelt over a sofa, weeping softly. Misha tried to rise, but found that his feet were tightly bound with telephone wire. His hands, too, were tied. That was really unnecessary, he thought distantly, since his mangled left hand and wrist had swollen to twice normal size. He heard the big man speak angrily into the phone, then slam it down.

Schneider strode through the splintered bedroom door and looked down. "You've got some friends coming to see you," he said. Then he walked back to the woman and laid a comforting hand on her shoulder.

The next thing Misha would remember was four men in white medical coats lifting him onto a stretcher. He felt strangely comforted by this, until he spied the olive-drab of American army uniforms beneath the coats. When he tried to rise, a strong hand pressed him firmly back onto the stretcher. The hand belonged to Sergeant Clary. Misha's short, violent career was over.

* * *

Just over a mile to the east of Eva Beers's apartment, Captain Dmitri Rykov sprinted up to a phone box and punched in the number of KGB headquarters in East Berlin. He got an answer after two rings. "Is Colonel Kosov back yet?" he asked breathlessly.

"No. Who is this?"

"Rykov. Shut up and listen. Tell Kosov that Borodin followed Major Richardson to his apartment—not just to it but *into* it! I'm outside now, but I'm going back up. The building's in Wilmersdorf, about three blocks north of the Fehrbelliner Platz. Zahringerstrasse, I think. It's a really expensive building. Kosov can trace it. Sixth floor. Have you got that?"

"I think so," replied a nervous voice. "But could you repeat it on tape? I just got the recorder rolling."

"Christ!" Rykov repeated his message for the tape; then he dashed back into the lobby of Harry Richardson's apartment building.

7:23 P.M. Haslemere, Surrey, England

Swallow arrived at Michael Burton's tile-roofed cottage just as it started to rain. She climbed out of the Ford Fiesta which she'd rented at Gatwick Airport and puttered up the walk carrying a bright blue umbrella. In her other arm was a clipboard and a large tin cup—the bona fides of a charity worker. She rang the bell, but there was no answer. Seeing no lights in the windows, she went round back, and there she spied the yellow-lit hothouse that Burton had constructed from second-hand lumber and thick sheets of clear painter's plastic. The hothouse glowed like an island of summer in the chilly dusk. Swallow walked right up to it and, finding the door open, stepped inside.

It was incongruous somehow: the tall, rangy ex-commando standing among the fragile orchids; the artificial warmth of the hothouse after the bracing evening air. Humidifying heaters hummed somewhere out of sight. Rain pattered on the plastic above their heads. The cloying scent of orchids masked even Swallow's distinctive perfume. Burton looked up suddenly, startled, but he relaxed when he realized that his visitor was a woman, a village matron by the look of her, probably collecting for the orphans or something. He watched her shake off her umbrella and lean it against a two-by-four stud.

"What can I do for you?" he asked in a kindly voice.

Swallow had meant to shoot him through her handbag, but when her hand went into her purse, the ex-SAS man perceived what almost no one else would, an involuntary narrowing of the eyes, a slight tensing of the arm that suggested a shooting posture. Swallow was too far away for Burton to attack her—which his training told him to do—so he spun away toward the double-layered plastic wall of the hothouse. He snatched up a sharp spade in his right hand as Swallow fired, hitting him in the shoulder. He dropped behind the line of a planting table, slashed open the plastic wall with the spade, and plunged through it into the yard.

Swallow darted to the opening and knelt in a textbook shooting stance, preparing to fire again as Burton fled across the lawn. But Burton did not flee. Having judged it too long a run over open ground, the ex-commando stabbed the spade back through the plastic, missing Swallow's throat by inches. Stunned, she aimed at his blurred silhouette and shot him again, this time in the chest. The impact blew Burton backward onto the glistening turf. Swallow stepped through the rent in the plastic wall and stood over him. He was gasping, and she could hear the pitiful wheeze of a sucking chest wound.

The last words Michael Burton spoke were not the names of his ex-wife, his children, his mother, or his brother. In the gathering dusk he raised his head, choked out, "Hess"; then he fell back and gurgled, "Shaw, you bloody bastard." But only Swallow was there to hear him. Four seconds later she shot him in the forehead, turned, and walked calmly back across the lawn toward the cottage, leaving Burton lying in the rain with potting soil on his fingers and the smell of orchids seeping out of the little hothouse like a soul.

As she drove back toward Gatwick—where she had a seat reserved on the next flight to Tel Aviv—it struck Swallow why Sir Neville Shaw had wanted Michael Burton dead. No doubt it had been Burton who four weeks ago had slipped over the wall of Spandau Prison during the American watch month, stuffed a forged suicide note into Rudolf Hess's pocket, and strangled him with an electrical cord. But Swallow had no interest in this, unless at some future date it might give her leverage over Shaw. To her the man who murdered Rudolf Hess was merely a way station on the road that led to Jonas Stern.

CHAPTER NINETEEN

Julius Schneider wished he'd taken the stairs. The elevator was an old hydraulic model, slower than walking. When the doors finally opened, he hurried into the green carpeted hallway and toward the corner that led to apartment 62—the number Colonel Rose had given him over the phone. The colonel had said little—no more than a choked command to appear at this address as soon as humanly possible.

When Schneider rounded the corner, he saw Sergeant Clary standing guard outside the door to apartment 62. Clary's right hand rested on the butt of the .45 in his belt. His taut face revealed nothing. Schneider remembered the young man only an hour before at Eva Beers's flat, grinning with satisfaction at taking a KGB killer into custody. Clary looked like he couldn't grin now if he wanted to.

"Inside, sir," he said as Schneider approached.

"Danke," the German replied, and passed through the door.

Even if the corpse had not been lying in the foyer, Schneider would have felt the presence of death in the apartment. He smelled gunpowder, and worse—burnt flesh. The overheated air hung with that foul stillness that Schneider had long ago learned to breathe only shallowly when exposed to it. Too much of that reek could poison a man's soul. But the corpse was there, lying on its stomach. A small bullet hole—probably an entrance wound—stained a dark spot between the shoulder blades. Without hesitation Schneider rolled the body over. Dmitri Rykov stared up with sightless eyes.

"Well?" said a strained voice.

Schneider looked up at Colonel Godfrey Rose. The American had an unlit cigar clamped between his teeth. His face was gray and haggard.

"Isn't he the Russian from the Sonnenallee checkpoint?" Schneider asked.

"Yeah. Clary got a telephoto shot of him standing outside the customs booth."

Schneider nodded. "Is this why you called me here?"

Rose shook his head, then turned and disappeared down a short dark hallway. The German followed, the familiar weight of mortality in his belly. When he saw what awaited in the bedroom, a cold dread began to seep outward from his heart.

Harry Richardson sat wide-eyed in a wooden chair, facing the bedroom door. He was naked. The chair sat in a pool of blood. Thin nylon ropes bound Harry's arms and legs to the chair. A pair of navy blue dress socks had been stuffed into his mouth. Schneider immediately noticed the cluster of small red circular marks on Richardson's chest. Cigarette burns. Schneider had worked his share of child abuse cases. Just below the burns, three lateral slashes trisected the abdomen, not deep, but bloody and probably unbearably painful. But the head was the worst. Carved into Harry Richardson's high forehead was a jagged red swastika. Rivulets of sticky blood streaked down from the arms of the broken cross, into Harry's open eyes, across his lips. Schneider had to remind himself to start breathing again.

"What happened?" he asked in German.

Colonel Rose stood in the far corner of the room, his legs slightly apart, planted as firmly as trees in the earth. He held his arms folded across his chest. "You tell me," he said, his voice distant, almost nonhuman. "That's why I called you."

"Goddamn it," Schneider muttered, "why haven't you closed his eyes?"

"You're the homicide detective. I wanted you to see the crime scene before we touched him. Maybe you'll see something I don't."

Schneider looked around the room. It had been torn to pieces by someone who knew how to conduct a rapid search. "What about your people?"

Rose's eyes narrowed. "You said you wanted to help me, Schneider. Here's your chance."

The German squinted at Rose, then shook his big head

slowly. "Colonel, a homicide investigation is a team process. I need fingerprint men, photographers, forensic technicians."

"I don't care about all that crap," Rose retorted. "I could have high-tech coming out the wazoo if I wanted it. I'm interested in your gut. Your *trieb,* remember?"

With a surreal sense of dislocation, Schneider walked a slow circle around the room, keeping his eyes on Richardson's naked body all the time. He noted several facts at once—the obvious. But Schneider was a great mistruster of the obvious. Too often plain facts concealed more subtle truths. The cause of death seemed plain enough: a bullet hole in the back of the neck, small caliber, fired into the fragile bones of the cervical spine. An execution. That Harry had resisted death was also plain; his skin had been burned by the ropes that held him fast. Schneider's eyes found Harry's lifeless gray orbs just once, and he looked away quickly. There was nothing to be found there but the frozen moment of stunned horror—more animal than human—that Schneider had seen more times than any man should.

Last came the message—if message it was. Drawn in the pool of blood beneath Harry's right foot, like a child's fingerpainting, was a small but clear capital *B*. Harry's right great toe was stained scarlet, like a blunt pen dipped in a well of blood. After the *B* came a curved line that could have been the start of another letter—perhaps a lower-case *r*—but in the midst of forming it Harry must have been shot, for a tangential line arced sharply outward, as if the foot drawing it had been flung wide in spasm.

Schneider crouched and examined the first letter. There was no mistaking it: it was a *B* or nothing. With a long last look at the second letter, the big German stood, carefully closed Harry's eyelids, and walked back to the front room. The air was breathable there. Rose's marching feet echoed behind him.

"What do you make of it?" Rose asked.

"Dead Russian, dead American," Schneider replied. "None of my business."

"I'm making it your business. Who do you think did it?"

"Someone in a hurry."

"I'm not in the mood for games, Schneider."

The German took a huge breath, exhaled. "All right. Someone broke in here, surprised Richardson, tortured him for information, and was surprised by the Russian in the front. The Russian tried to run; the killer shot him in the back. After getting his information—or not getting it—the killer executed Richardson and left." Schneider sighed. "How did you find out about it?"

"Anonymous call. Guy had a British accent. Clary and I hauled ass over here, found Harry, and sealed the place off."

Schneider digested this in silence.

"What about that swastika?" Rose asked.

Schneider shrugged.

"A bullet in the neck is a Dachau-style execution," Rose pointed out. "SS-style."

"They do it the same way in Lubyanka."

"Yeah," Rose muttered. "So you don't think it's the Germans? Not Phoenix, or the Brotherhood, or whatever neo-Nazi wackos Harry pissed off when he killed Goltz?"

"Why would Germans do this?" Schneider asked. "Even *Der Bruderschaft?* Or if they did, why would they leave a swastika? Why not the red eye? Why leave anything at all? They would know you Americans would go mad with rage. How could that help them? If you implemented one-fourth of your reserve powers, Berlin would become Beirut."

"Why this, why that?" Rose grumbled. "Why would the fucking Stasi kill a KGB officer and bring the whole weight of the KGB down on their heads? Nothing makes sense since yesterday, Schneider. Maybe they *want* us to crack down on Berlin. Maybe they think that would spark big protests against continued occupation." Rose rubbed his forehead anxiously. "The scary thing is, I can't do a damned thing about this. Five minutes before that anonymous call, I received an order to cease and desist all investigations pertaining to Spandau Prison or Rudolf Hess."

A faint smile touched the corners of Schneider's lips. "Who gave you that order, Colonel?"

"It came from on high, my friend. What we call Echelons Beyond Reality. If you ask me, Washington's covering for the goddamn Brits."

"You mean the letters on the floor?"

"Damn right. Harry was obviously trying to tell us who did this. And it seems to me that *B* and *r* are the first two letters of *British.*"

Schneider sucked in his breath. "Colonel, I'm not sure that second letter is an *r.* It could be a *c* or even an *o.* If it is an *r*, Richardson could have been trying to write *Bruderschaft*—the Brotherhood. Phoenix."

"Maybe," Rose admitted. "But you just told me you didn't think Germans did it. Make up your mind, will you?" He paused in thought. "No, that swastika is just too goddamn obvious. This case revolves around Spandau, and Hess. We've got a dead Russian and a dead American. In my book that leaves the Brits, not the Germans."

Schneider raised an eyebrow. "An anonymous caller using a British accent is just as obvious as that swastika. Also, we can't discount the possibility that the murderer himself drew those letters in the blood. To mislead us." The German sighed uncomfortably. "Colonel, is it possible that men from your own government could have done this?"

Rose looked up sharply. "Schneider, I've been in this man's army all my life. But if I believed what you just suggested, I'd take this story straight to the fucking *New York Times*."

Schneider believed him. "So what are you going to do? If your own people won't help you on the Hess case, you're stuck."

"You ought to know me better than that by now," Rose countered. He lifted an arm and pointed back down the hall. "I liked that man back there," he said softly. "He served his country in war, and he served it in what the politicians like to call peace." Rose's cheek twitched with the intensity of his anger. "Whoever did that to him—Brit, German, whoever—he and his bosses are going to pay like they never dreamed in all their worthless goddamn lives. I won't rest until they do."

Just then Clary knocked twice quickly on the door, then opened it. Schneider's mouth fell open. Silhouetted in Harry Richardson's apartment door was the stocky, trenchcoated figure of Colonel Ivan Kosov. The Russian took two steps into the foyer and bent over the body of Dmitri Rykov. When he looked up, Schneider saw points of black fire flickering in his eyes. Fury crackled off him like static electricity. Stunned, Schneider turned to Rose for an explanation.

"I called him," Rose confessed. "If my own people won't help me, by God, I'll take help where I can find it."

Schneider peered into Rose's eyes. "Why am I really here, Colonel?" he asked quietly. And then suddenly he knew. Rose had been forbidden to pursue the Spandau case using his own men, so he had called Schneider here to pick up the torch Harry Richardson had dropped. It made Schneider angry that the American thought he needed cheap theatrics to motivate him. He had wanted to go to South Africa with Richardson all along. Funk, Luhr, Goltz: these men were minions, corrupt servants of an insidious power creeping into Germany from without. Stopping them would be a temporary victory at best. Whoever they served was the true enemy. To unite officers of the Stasi and the Polizei—sworn enemies—would take a truly monstrous power. And to kill a monster, Schneider knew, you cut off its head, not its hand. With a glance back at Kosov's kneeling figure, he caught Rose by the arm and pulled him back into the room where Harry's corpse sat baking in the dry heat.

"I'll go to South Africa, Colonel," he growled. "But I don't like being manipulated. You should have sent me in the first place. You want to find two German cops? Send a German cop." Schneider jerked his thumb toward the front room. "But I report to you, not him. Understood? I trust you alone. Not your government, not Kosov, not his government. Just you."

"Agreed, Detective." Rose pulled Harry's airplane ticket from his pocket and handed it to the German. "From now on, all expenses will be paid out of my personal bank account." He lowered his voice. "Your flight leaves at two P.M. tomorrow. I'll brief you just before you leave. Now, if you don't mind, I need to talk a little shop with my new Russian friend."

Schneider turned. Ivan Kosov stood motionless in the bedroom door, his eyes riveted on Harry Richardson's mutilated head. He made no sound. Schneider stuffed the plane ticket into his coat pocket and moved toward the door. At the last moment, Kosov stepped aside. Schneider paused, looked back at Harry, then looked into the Russian's eyes long enough for Kosov to read the message there. *I hate Russians as much as you hate Germans,* it said. *I blinded your little black assassin, and I haven't ruled you out as a suspect in this either.*

Schneider walked on. He understood Colonel Rose's motives: this was a marriage of expediency, nothing more. Politics, as ever, made strange bedfellows. Rose didn't trust his Russian counterpart any more than Schneider did, but the two professionals had much in common. *They're like a pair of fathers grieving over murdered sons,* Schneider thought as he trudged down the stairs. *A pair of very dangerous fathers.* Kosov had looked even angrier than Rose, if that was possible. Schneider only hoped the two men realized what they—and he—were up against. Eighteen hours ago Harry Richardson had practically scalped a Stasi agent in an East Berlin street. Tonight he was slated for a closed-casket funeral. The man who had done that to him, Schneider reflected, was a man to be taken very seriously indeed.

Six floors below Harry's apartment, Yuri Borodin smiled with satisfaction. His plan had worked after all. Ten minutes ago he'd been furious. Richardson hadn't had the Spandau papers—as Borodin had thought he might—and he had refused to discuss the two German policemen, even under torture. Borodin hadn't intended to kill Richardson, but the American had made him angry. And then Kosov's bumbling footpad had blundered in during the interrogation. Borodin had shot Rykov from reflex, without even knowing who he was. That had sealed Richardson's fate. Borodin couldn't very well leave anyone alive to reveal what he had done. Even a Twelfth Department man could not kill a fellow KGB officer with impunity.

Yet in the midst of adversity, inspiration had struck. Before leaving Harry's apartment Borodin had planted two microtransmitters—one in the front room, one in the bedroom. Then he'd made an anonymous telephone call to Colonel Rose. The harvest had been bountiful. Now he knew not only the location of the two German policemen, but also the identity of Rose's emissary to South Africa. The burly Kripo detective would lead him straight to Hauer and Apfel, and ultimately to the Spandau papers.

And if that wasn't enough, he was now listening to Kosov and Rose hatch a renegade operation that could smash both their careers. The only oversight, Borodin conceded to himself, had been the writing on the floor. The American had sneaked that past him. Richardson had been trying to write *Borodin,* of course, but a bullet through his spinal cord had apparently turned his *o* into something like an *r.* The Anglophobic Rose had already misread the one clue that could help him, though; and Ivan Kosov wasn't likely to disabuse him of his fantasies! As Schneider emerged from the front entrance of Harry's building, Yuri Borodin laughed aloud.

Even in the dog days of *glasnost,* his job was sometimes more fun than work.

7:31 P.M. Lufthansa Flight 417, Corsican Airspace

Dieter Hauer looked down at the shiny, wrinkled ball of aluminum foil in his hand. It had taken four minutes of his best pickpocket technique to remove the Spandau papers from Hans's trousers, but he had finally done it. Hans sat in the airplane seat next to him, sleeping fitfully. Hauer removed the foil wrapping the thin sheets as if it concealed an archaeological treasure. Despite all that had happened, he had yet to actually see the papers.

The first page looked just as Hans had described it: a paragraph written in German, followed by a stream of unintelligible gibberish. Hauer scanned the German, but learned nothing new. Sighing, he pulled the bottom page from the stack and looked for the signature. There it was: *Number 7.* My God, he thought, to have been in prison so long that you didn't even use your name. If the poor bastard remembered it at all ...

On the last page Hauer saw the carefully drawn eye. It looked exactly like those he'd seen tattooed on at least a dozen scalps. Whoever wrote the Spandau papers, he decided, had obviously been visited at least once by someone with more than hair behind his right ear. Hauer didn't realize that three of the pages were blank until he began arranging them to repack them in the foil. He rubbed his eyes vigorously, unwilling to accept what he saw, but the truth was plain to see. Three pages bore no ink at all. The paper wasn't even the same! His first impulse was to shake Hans awake and demand to know what he had done with the missing pages. Yet as soon as he raised his hand, Hauer realized what had happened. The substituted sheets told the story. Professor Natterman had lied. The old man had held back after all ... he'd kept some of the pages for himself! Hauer cringed as he recalled Natterman slipping into the bathroom before laying the foil packet on Hans's lap.

Greedy bastard! he thought furiously. *With your family's lives at stake!* Pulling the bottom page out again, Hauer stared with grim frustration. Angrily, he read the final note in German. The last bit caught his eye:

*Phoenix wields my precious daughter like a sword of fire!
If only they knew! Am I even a dim memory to my angel?
No. Better that she never knows. I have lived a life of mad-
ness, but in the face of death I found courage . . .*

Better that she never knows. Those words resonated in
Hauer's mind. *Better that you don't know, either,* he thought,
looking at Hans's sleeping face. *You'll find out soon enough.*
Hans's lank blond hair hung down across eyelids that quivered in troubled sleep. Carefully, Hauer refolded the aluminum foil around the pages and slipped them back into
Hans's pocket. *And what will you do,* he wondered, *when
you finally learn that your grandfather-in-law has condemned your wife to death?* For without the Spandau papers
to trade to the kidnappers, Hauer knew—*intact*—the chance
of bringing Ilse out of Africa alive dropped by at least 50
percent. *How could that bastard do that to his own flesh and
blood?*

And then Hauer knew. The old man had not stolen the
missing pages—he'd *lost* them! Lost them to the Afrikaner
who attacked him. And the Afrikaner had lost them to whoever had attacked him! *That* was why Natterman had frantically searched the carcass that Hans dragged into the cabin;
he'd been looking for the missing pages. And he had found
nothing! *My God,* Hauer thought, feeling acid flood his
stomach, *someone else has those pages!*

As the DC-10 roared south toward the bottom of the
world, Hauer wondered who could possibly have found
Natterman's cabin before he and Hans. Funk's men? Ilse had
obviously been forced to give the cabin telephone number to
her kidnappers. Had she also given them the cabin's location? How early had she been captured? Who else was hunting for the papers now? Hauer had seen some rather
English-looking young men hovering around the ticket
counters at Frankfurt Airport, but he and Hans had slipped
by them on the strength of their false passports.

If Hauer had only known—really known—who had the
missing pages, he might have felt less like a shepherd leading a lamb to the slaughter. But he didn't know. And as he
closed his eyes to the sound of the roaring turbines, one
word cycled endlessly through his mind.

Who?

7:40 P.M. E-35 Motorway, Frankfurt, FRG

Jonas Stern took his eyes from the motorway long enough to glare at Natterman in the passenger seat. "We're going to Israel to pick up some packages, and that's all I'll bloody say about it!"

"But what *kind* of packages?"

"You'll find out soon enough."

"But you were on the phone for hours," Natterman persisted. "You wasted a whole *day.*"

"*Klap kop in vant!*" Stern snapped in Yiddish. "So the Messiah comes a day later! You don't order these packages like a pizza pie, Professor. You told me yourself that the rendezvous with the kidnappers isn't until tomorrow night. We'll make Pretoria in plenty of time."

Natterman sulked in his seat. "Why were you talking to an air force general?"

Stern exploded. "You were listening to my calls!"

"Only one," Natterman lied. "I just want to know what's going on. Where's the harm in that?"

"You'll know all you need to know," Stern said, scowling. "*When* you need to know it, not before. If you'd put your precious career aside for a moment and tell me all you know about Hess's mission, I might see fit to reciprocate."

Natterman put an age-spotted hand to his mouth and bit his thumbnail. He looked like a gold prospector deciding whether or not to reveal the location of his big strike to a stranger whose help he needs. With sudden gravity, he reached across the seat and took hold of Stern's arm. "I'll tell you what I think about Hess's mission," he said excitedly. "*I think Rudolf Hess is still alive.*"

Stern turned and caught Natterman's eye; then he looked back at the wide motorway. He chuckled softly. "I know you do, Professor. And I wish it were so easy. But you watch too many movies."

"Then you *don't* think Hess is alive?" Natterman asked incredulously.

Stern grinned. "Sure. He's set up housekeeping with Martin Bormann and Josef Mengele. Amelia Earhart is the housemaid and Elvis Presley provides the dinner entertainment."

Natterman ignored the levity. "Then you're really not hunting Hess?" he said suspiciously.

Stern shook his head. "I told you, Professor, I'm no Nazi-hunter. I'm more of a gamekeeper. And the preserve I protect is Israel."

"Hess is alive," Natterman insisted. "I *know* he is. It's completely conceivable. His double died only four weeks ago, and the medical care at Spandau was atrocious." Natterman folded his arms defiantly. "Rudolf Hess is alive and I'm going to find him."

Stern grunted skeptically.

"Since you're not hunting him," Natterman said in a superior tone, "I suppose I can tell you how I know he's alive."

"Enlighten me, O Master," Stern said with mock gravity.

Natterman scowled. "Laugh if you like. I'll bet you don't laugh at this. Remember the tattooed eye that I showed you on the Afrikaner's head? That's the constant in this whole mess, the one unifying symbol. The Spandau papers said the eye was the key, and the fascist members of the Berlin police have the eye tattooed on their scalps beneath the hair. Hauer told me so. But what Hauer *doesn't* know, Stern, is what that symbol means. I do. It's an Egyptian symbol—the All-Seeing Eye, the Guarding Eye of God." Natterman nodded knowingly. "Hauer also told me that the police fascists protect something or someone called Phoenix. Are you familiar with the Phoenix, Stern?"

"Of course. It's the mythological bird of flames that rises from its own ashes every five hundred years."

"Very good. Now, 'Phoenix' is a Greek word, but the Greeks did not invent the Phoenix myth. Phoenix is but the Greek name of the Egyptian god *Bennu*—the bird who rises from the ashes of its own destruction. Do you see?"

"What I see," said Stern irritably, "is a history professor who has lost touch with reality."

Natterman cackled. "That's because you're blind, Stern! Blind like all the rest! Blind to *history!* I told Hauer that the key to this mystery lay in the past, but the arrogant fool didn't believe me!"

"What in God's name are you babbling about?"

"Egypt, Stern, *Egypt.* Don't you see? All these mystical signs and symbols, they lead ultimately to one man: Rudolf Hess!"

"How?" Stern snapped.

"Because," Natterman explained, "Rudolf Hess was born

and raised in Egypt! He went to school in Alexandria until he was fourteen years old!"

Stern sat in stunned silence. "That's true," he murmured finally. "I remember now."

Natterman was nodding with nervous energy. "I'm going to find him, Stern. I'm going to deliver that Nazi bastard into the modern world. It will be the academic coup of the century!"

"Take it easy, Professor. I think you're letting your imagination run away with you. That eye could mean any number of things. And the name Phoenix has been used to name everything from cities to cars to condoms. You're stretching logic too far. So Hess was raised in Egypt ... I'm sure he attended a German school there, and he was still only a boy when he emigrated to Germany."

"He did attend a German school," Natterman admitted. "But fourteen is not so young. And childhood impressions are often the most vivid of our lives. The treasures and mysteries of Egypt's past would have fascinated any European boy. No, Stern, I don't think I'm stretching logic. It's simple deductive reasoning."

Stern looked thoughtful. "Think what you wish, Professor. I will say this: I'm not so sure Hess's original mission is over yet"—he smiled—"I just don't think Hess is running it."

Natterman looked anxious. "What do you mean?"

"I mean that Hess flew to Britain to arrange an Anglo-German peace. I accept that as fact. Whatever delusions Hess may have had, the strongest—correction, the *only*— real foundation for such a peace was the widespread belief in England that Germany represented the last and strongest possible barrier against an expansionist-minded Russia. Against communism."

"That's freshman history," said Natterman. "What's your point?"

"My point is that things may not be so different now. The Soviet Union is disintegrating, Professor. The heart of the military colossus is economic chaos; the great warrior is starving inside his armor. Russia's provinces and satellites seethe with resentment and sedition. One day not so long from now, Professor, the Soviet Union could explode."

"And?"

"And I'm not the only fool who knows that! I'm saying

that some people may *still* believe that Germany represents the best natural barrier against Russia, the unstable colossus."

"Germany? As a barrier to Russia?"

Stern smiled coldly. "Not Germany as you know it. But a Germany reunited. Reunited and armed with nuclear weapons. Its *own* nuclear weapons."

"No," Natterman breathed. "That can't be true. If we Germans wanted nuclear weapons, we could have developed them ourselves long ago. We invented the ballistic missile, for God's sake!"

Stern snorted. "It's no more fantastic than your fairy tale about Rudolf Hess."

"Hess is alive!" Natterman insisted. *"I know it!"*

Stern's face hardened. "Whether he is or he isn't, Professor, I don't want you mentioning his name in front of anyone from this moment forward. You understand? No one. Not friends, not family. Fantasies like yours can produce hysterical responses in some people."

"But not in you," Natterman said, eyeing the Israeli closely.

"Since you think Hess is alive, Professor," Stern said gamely, "tell me this. If Hess survived his mission to England, why didn't he return to Germany? To his beloved Führer?"

Natterman opened his mouth to speak, then realized that he did not have an answer. "I won't know that until I know what Hess's real mission was," he said. "Until we find Hess himself."

Stern swung onto the access road for Frankfurt-Main International Airport. "Professor," he said, "we are after two different things. You're obsessed with the past, I fight in the present. But the Hess case links us. We're on a road we cannot see, and at the end of it, I fear, lies something as evil as human beings can devise. I believe that the danger that exists now came out of the past. But I can't rip away the curtain of time and see what ill-begotten proposition Rudolf Hess carried to England forty-seven years ago." Stern flicked his lights and passed a slow-moving BMW. "So you know what I think? I think maybe having a German history professor along with me is the next best thing. Even if he is an ambitious, close-mouthed *goyim* who thinks he's Simon Wiesenthal."

Stern swung the car into the TICKETING/CHECK-IN lane. When he had parked, Natterman climbed out and looked at him across the car's roof. "I just hope you're not condemning my granddaughter to death by making this stupid side trip to Israel," he growled.

Stern bunched his coat collar higher around his neck. "This mystery has waited half a century to be solved, Professor. It can wait one more day."

He turned and hurried into the terminal.

I wonder, Natterman asked himself, walking toward the huge glass doors. *I wonder if it can.*

THE PLAN
NAZI GERMANY, 1941

He is insane. He is the Dove of Peace.
He is Messiah. He is Hitler's niece.
He is the one clean honest man they've got.
He is the worst assassin of the lot.
He has a mission to preserve mankind.
He's non-alcoholic. He was a "blind."
He has been dotty since the age of ten.
But all the time was top of Hitler's men . . .

"Hess, the Deputy Führer"
BY A.P. HERBERT, 1941
after Hess parachuted into England

CHAPTER TWENTY

January 7, 1941, The Berghof: The Bavarian Alps

Rudolf Hess stood alone before the great picture window of Adolf Hitler's Alpine headquarters and waited for his Führer. Hess was a big man, with an athlete's body—broad across the shoulders and, even at forty-seven, narrow through the waist—yet Hitler's window dwarfed him. Like all things designed by or for the Führer, it was the largest in the world. Silhouetted against its Olympian panorama, Hess looked like a tiny extra in the corner of a movie screen. Deep in the valley below him, the village of Berchtesgaden slept peacefully. Beyond it the magnificent Untersberg rose skyward, covered with fresh January snow. Far to the north Hess could just see the rooftops of Salzburg. He could understand why the Führer retreated to this mountain eyrie when the pressures of the war became too onerous.

This was one of those times. As Hess stared out at the mountain, a stabbing pain pierced his stomach. He bent double, clenching his abdomen with his heavy-muscled forearms until the agony abated. He had endured these attacks for three weeks now, each in stoic silence. For he knew it was no organic toxin that caused the pain, but anxiety—a terrible, withering apprehension. The first attack had struck him on December 18, less than twelve hours after Hitler issued his secret Directive Number 21. In that order the Führer had commanded that all preparations for plan *Barbarossa*—the full-scale invasion of Soviet Russia—be completed by May 15 of this year.

Hess regarded Directive 21 as insanity, and he was not alone. Some of the *Wehrmacht*'s most gifted generals felt the same. Hess felt no moral qualms about betraying Stalin or attacking Russia. If a few million Russians had to die to create new living space for Germans, so be it. But to attempt the invasion *now,* while England remained unbeaten in the west? Madness!

Hess had a single hope. If peace with England could somehow be secured before *Barbarossa* was launched, suicidal tragedy might yet be averted. Just six months ago Hitler had offered peace to the British from the floor of the Reichstag, and Winston Churchill had immediately answered with a resounding "No!" Yet that had not discouraged Hess. With the help of Professor Karl Haushofer, a family friend, he had sent a sub-rosa letter to England proposing a secret meeting in Lisbon between himself and Douglas Hamilton, the Premier Duke of Scotland. The subject to be discussed: Anglo-German peace. The Duke of Hamilton was renowned as the first man to fly over Mount Everest, and Hess liked the idea of dealing with a fellow flyer. He himself had won the dangerous air race around the Zugspitze, Germany's highest peak. Hess had met Hamilton briefly at the 1936 Olympics in Berlin, and the dashing young duke had seemed just the type of fellow who could short-circuit the tedious process of diplomacy and bring Churchill to his senses.

Yet three months had passed since the peace letter began its circuitous journey to England, and still Hess had received no answer. For the first few weeks he hadn't worried too much; Hitler had given tacit consent to the peace feeler, and gratefully he hadn't seemed too disappointed when the effort did not immediately pan out. Even as weeks turned to months—while Hess grew more agitated with each passing day—Hitler seemed unconcerned. Then on December 18, Hess, to his horror, discovered the reason for the Führer's uncharacteristic patience. Hitler meant to invade Russia whether peace with England had been secured or not! From that day forward Hess had prayed desperately that an answer from the Duke of Hamilton might still arrive—that peace negotiations could still be arranged. He hoped that he had been summoned to the Berghof today to discuss that very event.

Wiping the sweat from his brow, he took another long look out at the great mountain across the valley. Legend told that the Emperor Charlemagne slept beneath the Untersberg, that one day he would rise up to restore the lost glory of the German Empire. Hess had often boasted that Adolf Hitler was the fulfillment of that prophecy. Now he was not so sure. No man was more faithful to the Führer than he, but lately he had begun to think back to the old days, to the Great War. Hess had been Hitler's company commander then, and young Hitler only a dispatch runner, one more mustard-gassed soldier betrayed by the Jewish financiers.

Hess caught his breath as another stab of agony twisted his stomach. He shut his eyes against the pain, yet even as he did, a horrifying vision filled his mind. He saw the frozen, limitless steppes of Russia stretching away before him, league after league, drenched in blood. *German* blood. When the pain finally eased, he pressed his sweaty palms to the great sheet of glass, fingers outspread, and looked out at the Untersberg in silent invocation: *If ever there was a time for you to rise, Emperor, it is now! What the Führer plans was beyond even Napoleon, and I fear that without some miracle, the task he set us is too great—*

"Rudi!" Adolf Hitler called across the richly appointed salon. "Come here! Let me see you!"

When Hess turned from the window, he felt a jolt of astonishment. The effusive welcome had not surprised him; Hitler often complained that his senior staff did not visit the Berghof frequently enough. But his *clothes* ... Hess was startled speechless. For some time now Hitler had worn dark business suits during the day, and dressed with particular severity around the time of military conferences. But today— with a major war conference scheduled in a matter of hours—he looked just as he had during the early thirties, wearing a blue linen sport jacket, white shirt, and a yellow tie to top it all off. Hitler strode forward and clapped Hess on the back, then led him away from the window.

"I've had historic news today, Rudi," he said, his voice quavering with excitement. "*Prophetic* news."

Hess braced himself for whatever revelation might follow this ominous preface. "What has happened, my Führer?"

"All in good time," Hitler said cryptically. "Tell me, how are your training flights progressing?"

Hess shrugged. "I've managed one or two a week since October."

"Good, good. Anyone taking an unusual interest in your activities?"

For a moment Hess thought he had seen the Führer wink, but he banished the thought. "I don't believe so."

"Not Göring? Or Himmler?"

Hess frowned. "Not directly, no."

Hitler's eyes flickered. *"Indirectly?"*

"Well ..." Hess looked thoughtful. "Last fall Himmler lent me his personal masseur, to see if he could relieve my stomach pains—"

"Felix Kersten?"

"Kersten, yes. He was a bit more inquisitive than I thought proper at the time. Is he one of Himmler's spies?"

"Notorious!" Hitler cackled.

Hess was perplexed. He had not seen the Führer in such a mood since Compiegne, after the French surrender. He watched Hitler clasp his hands behind his blue-jacketed back, then pace across the room and stop before a magnificent Titian nude.

"I have a destination for you, Rudi," Hitler said to the painting. "At last. Would you like to guess it?"

Hess felt a tightening in his chest. He had played these games before, and he knew Hitler would say nothing more until he had guessed at least twice. "Lisbon?" he tried impatiently.

"No."

"Switzerland?"

"No!"

Hess could hear the laughter in Hitler's voice. This really was intolerable, even from the Führer. Just as Hess started to say something he might regret, Hitler turned to him with an expression that could freeze molten steel. "England," he said softly.

Hess thought he had misheard. "I beg your pardon, my Führer?"

"England," Hitler enunciated, his eyes flashing.

With a sudden surge of elation Hess understood. "We've had an answer from the Duke of Hamilton! Professor Haushofer's letter has done it!"

Hitler waved his hand irritably. "No, no, Rudi, don't be silly. Haushofer and his son are merely decoys—diversions meant to confuse British Intelligence."

Hess opened his mouth to protest, but no words came out.

"I know Haushofer is an old friend of yours, but his dilettante son is a member of the German resistance, for God's sake. But for you, I'd have had him shot months ago."

Hess was dumbfounded. To hear that all his peace efforts to date had been in vain was bad enough, but the revelation that his old friend's son was a traitor . . . It was beyond be-lief!

"And the Duke of Hamilton, my Führer? There is no chance that he might still help us?"

Hitler snorted. "The Duke of Hamilton is as loyal an En-glishman as you could find, Rudi. Of course, that doesn't mean the fool can't prove useful."

"England," Hess murmured, trying to will away another stomach cramp. "Would my visit be in an official capacity?"

"Of course not," Hitler scoffed. "That kind of play-acting I leave to blusterers like Ribbentrop. Your mission will be all substance, Rudi. A master stroke of statesmanship!"

Hess stood silently for some moments. "Do you . . . do you mean that you have a plan to secure peace from the British?"

Hitler beamed with self-satisfaction. "That is *exactly* what I mean. Fate has answered us in our hour of need. Peace with Britain is at hand, Rudi, and Russia is within our grasp."

Apropos of nothing, Hitler launched into a critical assess-ment of Charles XII's campaigns on the Russian steppes, then segued abruptly into a harangue about Mussolini's arro-gant nephew Ciano. From years of practice Hess managed to look attentive while ignoring the entire monologue. His mind was filled by an image of himself flying hell-for-leather over the English Channel on an errand to see God only knew what Englishmen. Finally his anxiety got the bet-ter of him, and, quite out of character, he interrupted Hitler.

"You wish me to fly to *London*, my Führer?"

"I'm not sure of the exact destination yet," Hitler replied, ignoring the interruption. "But certainly not London. My God, they'd throw you in the Tower before you got a chance to speak to anyone!"

"Undoubtedly," Hess agreed.

Hitler frowned. "You seem uneasy, Rudi. What is it?"

"Well . . . England. I mean, it's not *neutral*. We're still at war. If I were to be captured there, the results could be cat-astrophic." Hess saw Hitler's face darken, as it always did at the slightest hint of opposition. "I'm not worried for myself, of course," he said quickly, "but with all that I know . . . the Russian invasion . . . *Barbarossa*."

"I'm well aware of the risks," Hitler snapped. "But there is no alternative, Rudi. We must have peace with England now, no matter what the cost. I have considered every option. I even thought of sending your double in your place. He hasn't done anything but sit on his backside in Denmark since we trained him."

Hess felt a jolt of surprise. He had almost forgotten he had a double. The Führer obviously had not.

"But it would never work," Hitler declared. "The English will be looking for a trick, and they know you too well. A simple check for your war wounds would unmask any impostor." Hitler chuckled. "I'm afraid you're almost as famous now as I am, old friend. And that's what makes you perfect for this mission."

Hess cleared his throat. "What exactly *is* the mission, my Führer?"

Hitler began pacing out the room. "The operation will be called *Mordred*. But for the time being, the less you know the better. I only tell you your destination now because I *must* know you can reach England on the given night. Whatever training or navigational practice you need to ensure success on such a flight, you must do it." Hitler stopped pacing and looked into Hess's deep-set eyes. "Can you fly alone to England, Rudi? Alone in the darkness?"

Hess nodded crisply. "Absolutely, my Führer."

Hitler nodded. "Do you have any parachute training?"

Hess's eyes widened. "No."

Hitler clucked his tongue. "I thought not. You probably won't need it, anyway. I'm told the Duke of Hamilton has a landing strip right beside his castle."

Hess felt more confused than ever. "But you said that the Duke of Hamilton was a loyal Englishman!"

Hitler smiled enigmatically. "That is quite irrelevant." His eyes twinkled. "Do you remember *The Scarlet Pimpernel*, Rudi?"

Hess's heavy black eyebrows bunched in puzzlement. "I . . . I believe you showed the film here at the Berghof, didn't you?"

"That's right, just last year. The Pimpernel was the daring English nobleman who made fools of the French during the Reign of Terror."

"What has that to do with me?"

Hitler's eyes flashed with wicked glee. "Everything, Rudi! You know I have always admired the English. They are fellow Aryans. They are great empire-builders, as we

Germans are. *But*"—Hitler stabbed a stiff finger into the air—"they have allowed themselves to be deluded by Churchill. *Dangerously* deluded. Look what happened when I spared their pathetic Expeditionary Force at Dunkirk! I halted Guderian's tanks, blamed the British escape on Göring and the *Luftwaffe*"—Hitler's face reddened in anger—"and then Churchill had the nerve to call Dunkirk a British victory! The English people must be freed from the influence of that warmonger!"

Utterly adrift, Hess folded his arms across his broad chest. "But this Pimpernel business, my Führer. How does it relate to me?"

"Don't you see, Rudi? *You* are my Scarlet Pimpernel!"

Hess stepped back in disbelief.

Hitler nodded excitedly. "Yes! You are the exact opposite of what you appear to be! Since the war heated up, everyone has written you off as merely a loyal bureaucrat who wastes his time on Party administration. All my officers think I've forgotten you." Hitler shook his head bitterly. "How can they have forgotten, Rudi? From the beginning you fought beside me, took wounds meant for me. And now, you will be the man who receives my most sacred charge, the responsibility of the most sensitive mission in the history of the Reich. Together we shall prove yet again what fools they all are!"

Hitler's eyes went cold. "In such times as these, Rudi, we learn who our real friends are. I'm afraid that some of our oldest and most trusted comrades may have decided that the time has come to explore *alternatives* to the road I have chosen for Germany. They seem to think my decision to invade Russia is a symptom of madness. Imbeciles! To imagine that I—*Adolf Hitler*—would invade Russia without first neutralizing England!"

Hess looked guiltily at the floor. For the past month he had subscribed to the very same heresy. Yet the Führer had obviously had his own peace plan in the works all along. Of course! It was only natural that the Führer should inspire powerful allies in England! So many questions thundered in Hess's brain that he could not decide which to ask first. Before he could say anything, however, Hitler transfixed him with a zealot's stare and began to speak with quiet conviction.

"Every man has his hour, Rudi, his time upon the world's

stage. Your hour has come. Some men—men like myself—play their part in public, like stars flashing across the sky. Others must play their part in shadow. It is to such a role I call you now. Take heed, old friend. There are traitors all around us. From the moment you leave this room you will be in mortal danger. But you are a soldier, Rudi, the embodiment of the true Nazi. I do not exaggerate when I say that the very future of the Reich rests upon your success!"

Hess felt his chest swell with burning pride. He did not yet understand his role in Operation *Mordred*, but if the Führer was ready to gamble the future of the Reich on him, he was ready to lay down his life without question. What German could do less?

Hess started when, after a perfunctory knock, Reichleiter Martin Bormann marched loudly into the salon.

"General Halder has arrived, my Führer," he announced.

As a courtesy, Hitler waited for Hess to dismiss Bormann. The thickset, unctuous Bormann was Hess's deputy, after all.

"Dismissed!" Hess barked.

Bormann saluted and backed reluctantly out of the salon. Hess felt better immediately. Lately he spent most of his time in his Munich office, and he had reluctantly come to depend more and more on Bormann for satisfying the daily whims of the Führer. Bormann was an able assistant, but he possessed many traits Hess detested. He was cruel and merciless to his subordinates, yet fawning and obsequious to his superiors. No one liked him much—except Hitler—but everyone respected his proximity to the epicenter of power.

"A good man," Hitler said with some embarrassment. "But it's not like having you around, Rudi. Not like the old days. Remember Landsberg?"

For a moment Hess thought back to the months in Landsberg Prison, where he had edited the manuscript of *Mein Kampf* while Hitler dictated it. Hess had done his best to force the fevered ideas into intelligible progressions of words. In those days he had been the apple of the Führer's eye. It seemed a thousand years ago now. Or it had until five minutes ago.

"I remember," he said softly.

Hitler crossed to the fireplace, reached up to the mantel, and took down a long manila envelope. He tapped it against the palm of his left hand. "On this envelope, Rudi, is written the name of the man I have chosen to help you carry out your mission."

Hitler extended the envelope. Hess accepted it, and held it at belt level while he read the large blocked letters: REINHARD HEYDRICH: OBERGRUPPENFÜHRER SD.

Hitler had written the words himself; Hess recognized the hand from the endless nights in Landsberg. He also recognized the name. Heydrich was commander of the feared SD—the counterintelligence arm of the SS—and second-in-command to SS Reichsführer Himmler. Hess half-recalled an unpleasant story he had once heard about Heydrich—a man so ruthless that even the brutal SS had christened him the "blond beast"—but the Führer's voice broke his train of thought.

"Himmler is to know nothing of this," he said. "Heydrich keeps an office in the Prinz-Albrechtstrasse, but you're not to deliver it there."

"Deliver it?" Hess said incredulously.

Hitler was pacing again, faster now. He spoke as if dictating to one of his secretaries. "As soon as you get back to Munich, wire Heydrich that you must see him on a matter of Reich security. Include the word *Mordred.* This will prevent him from informing Himmler. Heydrich spends a good deal of time at the SD offices in the Wilhelmstrasse. Deliver it there—*not* Prinz-Albrechtstrasse. You can log the trip as another training flight. Make some small talk for a half hour, then return to Munich." Hitler pursed his lips. "You will have no further contact with Heydrich, Rudi. But rest assured, he will be working with you. Besides myself, he will be your only ally."

Hitler paused by the door, his fingers on the handle. "Any questions?"

Hess cleared his throat. "Only one, my Führer."

One question was more than Hitler liked, but he forced himself to smile. "What is it?"

"When do I leave for England?"

Hitler let his hand drop and walked back to Hess. He reached up, laid a hand on the powerful shoulder, and gazed into Hess's earnest eyes. "From the filthy trenches of France," he said softly, "we have risen up and conquered all Europe. We have avenged the outrage of Versailles. Now we stand poised to invade Russia itself. *Russia itself!"* Hitler paused, his eyes burning. "Such a step is not to be taken without an awareness of destiny, Rudi. On what day did we begin our glorious westward march to the Channel?"

Mystified, Hess groped for the date. "The tenth of May, 1940?"

"Yes! And what day is our *eastward* invasion—*Barbarossa*—to begin?"

"May fifteenth," Hess replied more confidently, recalling the date from Directive 21.

"No! Our tanks will roll on the fifteenth, but the invasion of Soviet Russia begins with your mission, Rudi! On the *tenth* of May! One year *to the day* after we marched on France! *Just as before!*"

Hess felt a wild thrill of foreboding, a tangible sense of destiny, as if Fate herself had materialized in the room.

"It is all *preordained!*" Hitler cried, flinging his arms toward the ceiling. His mesmerizing voice filled the salon, brimming with the conviction of a prophet. "On the tenth of May you will secure our western flank, and on the fifteenth we shall wipe the plague of communism from the planet! By Christmas of this year, Greater Germany will extend from the English Channel to the Ural Mountains and *it will be settled by pure German stock!*"

Hess's ears roared with excitement. Only slowly did he become aware of an insistent knocking at the door. It might have been going on for a full minute. He slipped the manila envelope into his coat pocket as Hitler opened the door.

It was Bormann again, but this time Hess's deputy hesitated in the doorway. Hitler smoothed his black forelock and looked into Hess's eyes. "You will take care of that today, Rudi?"

"Immediately."

"Excuse me, my Führer," Bormann interrupted, "General Halder is waiting."

"Let him wait!" Hitler bellowed. "Escort the Deputy Führer to his car, Bormann."

"Heil Hitler!" Bormann clicked his jackboots together, turned, and marched down the hall.

"I'm going up to change clothes, Rudi," Hitler said softly. "I cannot let my generals see me like this. They'll think they can run right over me in the conference."

Hitler looked embarrassed by the confidence. Hess grinned and waved him out. It had been good to see the old Hitler for a few moments, even if it was just an illusion. Putting on the old spring jacket and tie could not revoke any of the steps they had taken in the intervening years. Those steps were written in blood and fire, and they could only be erased by more of the same.

Bormann waited like a Dachshund at the end of the hall. Hess felt a new and powerful sense of purpose in his tread as he followed his deputy out of the Berghof. "How are the children, Martin?" he asked. Just now Hess could not have cared less, but since Bormann had seen fit to name his offspring after Hess and his wife, he felt obliged to ask.

"Rudi is strong as a bull," Bormann bragged over his shoulder. "And Ilse is the very flower of German womanhood!"

Hess smiled wanly.

Outside, Bormann held open the door of Hess's brown Mercedes. Hess sensed a kind of animal exultance in him now that the interloper—Hess—was leaving. Unreasonably irritated, he cranked his Mercedes and goosed the pedal a few times. The engine roared responsively.

"Is there anything I can do for you, Herr Reichminister?" Bormann asked.

Hess considered ordering his deputy to call ahead and have his Messerschmitt readied, then thought better of it. He shifted into first gear, all the while looking hard into Bormann's eyes. He could see the arrogance lurking just behind the peasant face. Bormann wore power clumsily, like all men unaccustomed to it. But the little rat was learning. By all reports, he was setting himself up as lord of Obersalzburg, strengthening his position by acting as sole conduit between Hitler and the outside world. One of Hess's secretaries had actually heard Frau Goebbels whisper that Bormann's star had eclipsed Hess's in the Nazi firmament.

"I see you still haven't finished the construction up here, Martin," Hess said breezily. He waved his hand toward a half-finished concrete bunker.

"The Führer's needs expand every day," Bormann said proudly. "I can barely keep up with the demand, but I do my best."

Hess forced a smile. "There is something you can do for me, if you get the time."

"Anything," said Bormann, with a nod of false obeisance.

With a casual motion Hess reached out of the car and caught Bormann by the collar. One flex of his thickly muscled arm brought the shocked Reichsleiter to his knees in the snow. Hess could feel the softness in Bormann, the boorish strength dissipated by alcohol and gluttony. Bormann's piggish eyes bulged in terror.

"Never," Hess said harshly, "never forget who you are, Bormann. You are my deputy, and as long as I live, that is all you will ever be."

Hess roared away, leaving his stunned subordinate kneeling in the noon snowmelt. He skidded to a stop at the inner perimeter gate.

"How long to call Munich?" he barked at a surprised SS private.

"We have a direct line, Herr Reichminister!"

Hess reeled off the number of his office telephone.

"And the message, Herr Reichminister?"

Hess said nothing. To the sentry he seemed lost in a world of his own, but the SS man was not about to rush the Deputy Führer of the Reich. Hess's brain was spinning. All the dark misgivings of the past few months were lifting from his mind like bad dreams at the coming of dawn. The road to Moscow would soon be open, and *he* was the man Adolf Hitler had chosen to open it! Yet the vision Hess saw now was no epic scene of conquest, not German legions crossing their Russian Rubicon. He saw a very small section of a shadowy Munich street, in 1919. It was on that street, and a hundred others like it, that the seeds of the Nazi party had battled the communist gangs for control of postwar Germany. It was to that street that a young Rudolf Hess had returned one afternoon, to find that a communist gang had reached his local group headquarters ahead of him. Hess had hidden and watched in horror as heavily armed Red Guard ruffians loaded twenty of his friends into a panel truck. Later that night the communists shot all of Hess's comrades, loyal Germans to a man. A captured communist later claimed the Reds had lined the prisoners up and shot them one by one. Among all the communist crimes, Hess vowed, this was the one for which he would exact revenge in Russian blood—

"Herr Reichminister?" the sentry asked tentatively.

"What?" Hess looked up. "Oh. The message. To Karlheinz Pintsch: Have my Messerschmitt fully fueled and ready for a round-trip flight to Berlin. I want nine-hundred-liter drop tanks fitted and filled. Got that?"

"*Jawohl*, Herr Reichminister!"

Hess kicked the Mercedes into gear and raced down the winding mountain road as fast as the snow would allow. *My God!* he thought with exhilaration. *I am the man who will seal the peace with England . . . and open the road to Moscow!*

With Reinhard Heydrich's help, Hess remembered uneasily. He touched the envelope in his coat pocket. With a shiver he suddenly recalled the story he had heard about Heydrich. Apparently the "blond beast"—after an exhausting night of drinking and whoring—had caught sight of his own reflection in a lavatory mirror. Wild-eyed and sweating, he had screamed, "At last I've got you, scum!" then whipped out his pistol and emptied it through the glass.

Hess felt a cold chill of presentiment, but he quickly shook it off. One could not pick one's allies in the war against the Bolshevik and the Jew. Sometimes it took a beast to slay a beast. If the Führer trusted Heydrich, there was nothing more to be said. Hess had other things to worry about. A night flight to Britain, for example. Englishmen who had survived the hell of Hermann Göring's terror bombing would not mince words if Hess landed alone and unprotected in their country. They would do their talking with bullets. *And that's fine,* Hess thought. *I've faced bullets before; I can do it again.* The mere thought of his destination brought a strange quickening to his blood. *England!*

CHAPTER TWENTY-ONE

January 7, 1941, The Bavarian Alps

Obergruppenführer Reinhard Heydrich, Reich Commissar for the Consolidation of German Stock and chief of the SD, landed at Ainring Airport near Berchtesgaden just two hours after Rudolf Hess delivered Hitler's unexpected message to Berlin. Like Hess, Heydrich piloted himself, and upon landing he commandeered a convertible Porsche from a local Gestapo sergeant. The sergeant professed great pleasure at being able to help the Obergruppenführer, but inside he felt only despair. He knew that even if the beautiful car were returned a burned-out wreck, he could say nothing. Men who angered Reinhard Heydrich had been known to disappear without a trace.

The open Porsche rocketed along the blacked-out highway, half-sliding around curves made deadly by a sudden winter shower. Heydrich drove stonefaced despite the brittle drops that stung his skin and eyes. The frigid wind would have driven any normal man to groan in pain, but the young Obergruppenführer prided himself on his ability to control his human weaknesses. The fact that he was quite mad aided him considerably in this task.

Unlike most of Hitler's chieftains, Heydrich seemed the incarnation of the mythical Aryan superman. Tall and blond, blue-eyed, spare and muscular of frame, he carried himself with the self-assurance of a crown prince. A jarring amalgam of opposites, Heydrich put every man he met off balance. A world-class fencer, he had been asked to join the German Olympic team, yet tales of his homosexual conquests were whispered in SS barracks throughout the Reich. He was an accomplished violinist who not only brought tears to the eyes of his audiences, but sometimes cried himself during particularly beautiful passages. Yet his sadistic rampages through Eastern Europe would eventually cause Czech partisans to christen him the "Butcher of Prague," and British intelligence to order his assassination. And the most telling paradox of all: Reinhard Heydrich—the man who had vowed to "eliminate the strain" of Jewry from the world—had Jewish blood flowing through his veins.

At the outer gate of Obersalzburg, the SS guards eyed the approaching Porsche with suspicion. When they recognized its driver, however, they snapped to attention and waved Heydrich through. The sentries at the inner gate displayed the same deference, and he soon reached the summit of the mountain. The Berghof appeared to be under siege. Most of the High Command had arrived during the afternoon; long black staff cars overflowed the parking lot and encircled the rear of the house. Heydrich picked a path through the cars, made his way around to the front of the house, and opened the door without knocking.

An SS sergeant of the *Liebstandarte Adolf Hitler* had been posted in the entry hall to meet him. After a curt salute, the sergeant whisked Heydrich up the stairs to the bedrooms and indicated the door he wished the SD chief to enter.

"You're to wait here, Herr Obergruppenführer. By order of the Führer."

Heydrich looked mystified. "Am I not to attend the conference downstairs?"

"*Nein*, Herr Obergruppenführer. Reichleiter Bormann instructed me to have you meet the Führer in the teahouse, but I just received word that he won't have time for the walk."

"We could drive," Heydrich suggested.

"The Führer never drives to the teahouse."

The sergeant seemed to think this explanation sufficient. Heydrich dismissed him and reached for the bedroom door handle, then paused as another door opened farther down the hall. A blond woman leaned furtively out; Heydrich registered an ample bosom beneath a rather plain face before she ducked back inside. Only after entering the small bedroom designated for his meeting with the Führer did he realize that the woman he had just seen must be Eva Braun. With an extreme sense of discomfort Heydrich put the incident out of his mind. The Führer in a carnal entanglement with a peasant girl? Preposterous!

Out of habit Heydrich surveyed the Berghof grounds from the small bedroom window. He saw SS guards and dogs silhouetted against the snow at regular intervals all over the compound. Nodding with satisfaction, he sat stiffly on the edge of a narrow bed. An hour passed. When he next heard footsteps in the hall, he knew they belonged to the Führer. Standing deliberately, he straightened his silver-bordered collar and faced the door. As it opened, he cried, *"Heil Hitler!"* and gave a whipcrack Nazi salute.

Adolf Hitler stood blinking in the doorway. He looked like a man suddenly pulled into a quiet alcove from a beer hall where a violent brawl was in progress. "Heydrich," he mumbled.

"My Führer."

"We haven't much time. I have to get back to my generals. They've taken a break for food." With sudden purpose Hitler strode into the room and walked to the window. *"Food!"* he cried, pounding his right fist into his palm. "They think I am a fool, Heydrich! *Adolf Hitler!* My God, if I had listened to my generals we would never even have crossed into the Rhineland. And now that we stand ready to begin the greatest land invasion the world has ever *seen,* they counsel me to be cautious!" Hitler whirled, evangelical fire burning in his eyes. "Would caution have won us Poland, Heydrich?"

"No, my Führer!"

"Would it have won us France?"

"No!"

"Then how can it win us *Russia*?" Spittle flew from Hitler's quivering lips.

"It cannot, my Führer!"

"Exactly! You should hear them ... Halder, Jodl, even Guderian's reports sound like the whining of an old woman. They speak as if we have allies. *We have none!* For hours the fools have gone over and over the North African situation. The situation is *clear!* On January third the British captured thirty-eight thousand Italian soldiers at Sidi Barrani. Did you know that? *That's more prisoners than the British had soldiers!"*

"The Italians are swine," Heydrich declared, watching Hitler wind up again.

"What does Africa matter, I ask you? All my generals proudly display *Mein Kampf* on their mantelpieces. I don't believe one of the idiots has read it! Russia is the key to everything! When Russia falls, Japan will be free to attack the United States. And with Roosevelt's attention turned there, Churchill will be *forced* to sue for peace. It's so simple a child could see it." Hitler's left eye twitched angrily. "Perhaps I should place my armies under the command of the Hitler Youth!"

Heydrich said nothing to this remarkable suggestion. Hitler smoothed his unruly forelock, then clasped his hands behind him and said, "Do you know what my Prussian peacocks are afraid of?"

Heydrich swallowed. "England, my Führer?"

"Precisely! They throw my own words back at me as if I did not write them myself. 'Germany should never again become embroiled in a two-front war. Never will I fight a two-front war.' *Enough!* England lies prostrate beneath our bombs, yet my sniveling generals call her a western front. A front! When we turn east, Heydrich, the cowards *will learn what a front truly is*!"

Heydrich suppressed a sadistic grin.

Hitler squared his shoulders. "Directive Twenty-one commands that all preparations for Plan *Barbarossa* be completed by May fifteenth of this year. Do you know why?"

"So that we may defeat the communists before winter sets in?"

"Exactly. And why this year, Heydrich? Because Stalin is arming Russia even faster than I am arming Germany! The purge of 'thirty-seven slowed him down considerably, yes, but he has a new program in place—a *total reorganization.* If we wait another year it will be too late! All that we have accomplished will be dust! Do you understand?"

"Perfectly, my Führer."

"I believe you do. And that is why you are here." Hitler carefully read his watch, holding it close to his face because of his poor vision. "I have no intention of fighting on two fronts, Heydrich. But can I trust my spineless generals with my plans?" He waved his hand impatiently. "My *brilliant* generals. Imbeciles, every one. England doesn't want war. No matter what your agents tell you, Heydrich, *I know.* Withstanding aerial bombardment is one thing—fighting a land war is another. The English people will do almost anything to keep from sending their sons to die at another Somme or Ypres. Believe me, Heydrich, *I was there.* No, the only obstacle to an Aryan peace is Winston Churchill. Churchill and his warmongering cronies! Do you agree?"

"Absolutely, my Führer."

"Tell me," Hitler said in a confiding tone, "what do you think of our chances of making peace with the British?"

Heydrich tried to guess which answer Hitler wanted today. The Führer did not tolerate equivocation; it had to be one absolute or the other. "As things now stand," he ventured carefully, "we have no chance whatsoever."

Hitler's eyes sparkled. "You seem certain. Yet I suspect that some of your superiors might disagree with you."

Heydrich felt his chest tighten.

Hitler's voice cut like a blade. "What do you know, Herr Obergruppenführer, of attempts by my officers to make clandestine contact with the British?"

Heydrich felt the tingle of opportunity in his palms. "May I speak frankly, my Führer?"

"You had better!"

"My Führer, so far, despite exhaustive efforts, I have not uncovered any proof of treason around you. However, I am aware of efforts on the part of certain individuals to make clandestine contact with British citizens in various neutral countries. I've taken the liberty of compiling dossiers on the activities of each for your review."

Hitler frowned disdainfully. "The Haushofers, for instance? Karl and Albrecht?"

"Yes," said Heydrich, surprised by Hitler's knowledge.

"You know of their communications with Hess?"

Heydrich nodded warily.

"Göring?"

"Surely you don't suspect the Reichsmarschall!"

Hitler dismissed his shock with a wave of the hand. "Who knows? The air war over the Channel came close to breaking him. Göring hasn't the stamina for wars of attrition. He was trained for aerial dogfighting—nothing else. But what of my question? How do you rate the chances of gaining peace by clandestine means?"

Heydrich licked his thin lips. "As long as Churchill rules in London, my Führer, England will fight us."

Hitler nodded. "And the result?"

"England will be crushed."

"No," Hitler said softly. "There will be no war with England."

Heydrich waited for some evidence to back up this optimistic assertion.

"There will be no war with England, because soon Winston Churchill will no longer sit at the head of the British government."

Heydrich's pulse quickened.

"Does that statement surprise you, Heydrich? It shouldn't. Because you are the man who is going to ensure that my prediction becomes fact."

It took all of Heydrich's self-control to hold his facial muscles in check. *Remove Churchill from the government? It was too fantastic . . .*

"Let me ask you another question, Herr Obergruppenführer. You consider yourself a good judge of men. What do you think of the Duke of Windsor?"

Heydrich chose his words carefully. "As you know, my Führer, I handled security on the occasion when the duke secretly met with Reichminister Hess in Lisbon. During my limited time with the duke, I developed an impression of a weak, self-centered man. He behaved like a spoiled child. Having voluntarily relinquished the throne of England, he would like nothing better than to sit upon it again, if only so that his American wife can be called 'Her Royal Highness.' Windsor imagines that he would do anything to attain this end, when in fact he would probably do everything short of what is required."

Hitler smiled. "You are indeed a good judge of men. But none of that matters in the slightest. It is the royal blood that matters, Heydrich. The *blood*. The English pretend to abhor my racial policies, they revile me at every turn. Yet in the final analysis *they revere the blood just as we do!*" Hitler tugged anxiously at his forelock. "How would you rate Windsor as a friend to Germany?"

"There can be no doubt of his sympathies, my Führer. From an intellectual standpoint, he's the most right-thinking Englishman in the Empire. His actions in France proved that. Knowingly or not, he accelerated our invasion timetable by at least a week. But may I ask, my Führer, why this is relevant? The English constitution forbids an abdicated king from ever resuming the throne, even should he wish to."

"Don't worry about the English constitution!" Hitler

snapped contemptuously. "If the English *people* recalled Windsor, would he accept?"

"Undoubtedly. He said as much to Hess in Lisbon."

"Well, the people *are* going to recall him, Heydrich. And soon."

Heydrich blinked.

"If King George were to die suddenly," Hitler postulated, "what would happen? There are two possibilities. Either his eldest daughter, Elizabeth, would assume the throne—a highly dubious prospect, considering that England is engaged in a life-and-death struggle—*or* the English people would remember the Duke of Windsor, their once-adored Prince of Wales and uncrowned king, who now wastes his not-inconsiderable gifts as crown governor of the Bahamas. Which alternative do you think they would choose, Heydrich? Which would *you* choose? An empty-headed child, or the strong hand of a man trained to rule? How important will Windsor's romantic follies seem in the face of England's greatest peril?"

Heydrich shifted uncomfortably. "I ... I'm not sure the English view these things as we do, my Führer."

"*Rubbish!* And what does it matter? Windsor would only be the window dressing! The real power of England is in Downing Street! That is where the change must be made!"

Heydrich sensed that Hitler had finally come to the point of this meeting. "But *how* is this change to be made, my Führer?" he asked softly.

Hitler's eyes flickered. "Ruthlessly, Heydrich, as all acts of war must be. On the tenth of May, Winston Churchill is going to die. And with him King George the Sixth. When that happens, Britain will hold its breath, headless for a few moments of history. And through that brief window, we shall snatch the prize we want—peace in the west. Then Russia will be ours for the taking, and Guderian's panzers will roll!"

Heydrich cracked his boot heels together and stood rigid before his master.

"Have you been struck dumb?" Hitler asked, his very posture a challenge.

"No, my Führer. It's simply that ... the scope and genius of your concept have shocked me."

Hitler nodded. "I understand. Few men think as I do, with a mind unfettered by the restraints of so-called 'civilized' war. Such a concept is ludicrous, a blatant contradiction in terms. But I'm sure you're wondering exactly how the deaths of these two men will gain us peace from the English."

Heydrich nodded, though he was actually wondering how the deaths of those men could be accomplished.

"It's quite simple," Hitler explained. "When the new prime minister takes Churchill's place, his government will be mine. Or at least sympathetic to my ideas. Don't look so surprised. Like Haushofer and others, I too know of certain Englishmen who want peace. However, the men I speak of are men of deeds, not words. They understand my true aims, that my primary goal is to expand *eastward*—not into Britain. They know that Adolf Hitler is the hammer that will crush world communism!"

Heydrich stepped back from the raw force of Hitler's zeal.

"The British Empire was not forged by men who whined at the sight of a little blood, Heydrich. The English understand that to *create*, one must first *destroy*. That out of death comes life!" Hitler wiped his brow. "So you see . . ."

Heydrich did see. He saw that Hitler—from Machiavellian genius or sheer desperation—had decided to extend the tactics of terror, which had served him so well during the Party's early expansion, into the realm of international policy. Heydrich also saw that this decision would immeasurably raise his value to Hitler vis-à-vis purely military officers. Where another man might recognize imminent disaster, Heydrich saw opportunity.

"*So,*" Hitler concluded, bringing his hands together, "beginning now, you will devote all your energies to devising a method by which Winston Churchill and George the Sixth can be liquidated. Three limits must define your plan. First, your mission cannot be accomplished in such a way as to incriminate Germany or the National Socialist Party. Second, you will conduct all inquiries involved in your planning in such a way that neither Reichsführer Himmler, Admiral Canaris, nor any other member of the High Command becomes aware of your mission. And finally, the mission must be carried out on the tenth of May—the glorious anniversary of our historic westward invasion!"

Heydrich blanched. The Führer had just placed restrictions on the operation that would make success all but impossible. Even if a bolt of lightning were to strike down

Churchill and the king in Trafalgar Square, accusing fingers would still point to Germany. Yet despite this grim truth, Heydrich elected to keep silent. He had seen what happened to men who protested to Adolf Hitler that his orders were impossible.

"Am I to understand, my Führer, that I am to *assassinate* these men?"

Hitler exploded. "Were you not listening? The thought of making Winston Churchill a martyr turns my stomach, but alive he hounds me like the devil incarnate. I want him *dead*! The king too!"

Heydrich's mind reeled at the implications of this order. If what the Führer said about Nazi sympathizers in England was true, the plan could actually work. But what were the odds of that? The terror bombing of London and other population centers had hardened Britain's will to adamant; the reports of all his agents confirmed this. Could there really still be Englishmen who feared Stalin more than they feared Hitler? Men to whom profits meant more than national honor? Men to whom a guarantee of safety from Adolf Hitler was worth more than a pre-war Deutschemark?

"Do not think I labor under any illusions," Hitler said, almost telepathically. "The English have no love for me, or for things German. But they *understand* me, Heydrich. I represent absolute power concentrated in the head of the state, and the English respect that. Their industrialists and nobles fear Stalin and his hordes *far* more than my policies. Communism—power seized by millions of fanatical workers who cannot wait to tear down the ivied walls of tradition— that is like the plague to the English, the Black Death come again!"

A sharp knock on the bedroom door halted Hitler in midstream. Martin Bormann opened the door and stood there stubbornly, ignoring Heydrich. "You asked me to inform you when the generals finished their dinner, my Führer."

"So I did, Bormann, thank you. Dismissed."

Bormann reluctantly closed the door. Hitler folded his arms and peered closely at Heydrich. "Do you foresee difficulties, Herr Obergruppenführer?"

"None, my Führer," Heydrich replied automatically.

Hitler raised his chin and smiled. "That is why I selected you for this mission. The word *impossible* is one you never learned. If my generals had the same attitude, we would be in Moscow by now."

Heydrich inclined his head briefly.

"I am going you give you a name, Heydrich. You will never repeat it. You will never write it down. This is the Englishman you may contact if there is vital information you cannot obtain by any other means. Churchill's likely whereabouts, such matters as that. His name is Robert Stanton—"

"Lord Grenville?" Heydrich ejaculated. He reddened. "I apologize for the interruption, my Führer, but . . ."

"But he is the last man you would have guessed to betray his king?" Hitler smiled wickedly. "That is good. Just remember, you will *never* use his name—only his code name. Lord Grenville is Mordred."

While Heydrich's brain raced, Hitler said, "I'll go downstairs first. You follow in a few minutes. I don't want my generals to know of our meeting. On the eleventh of May I shall present them with a *fait accompli*, just as I did with my 1939 pact with Stalin. That should stiffen their resolve when they cross into Russia!"

"It should indeed, my Führer!"

"The operation *must* take place on the tenth of May, Heydrich. Other wheels are already in motion. When your plan is ready, call Bormann and say the word *Mordred*. He'll set up another meeting." Hitler reached for the door handle, then paused. "By the way, about those files you have compiled on potential traitors. Is Hess among them?"

Heydrich nodded solemnly.

"Burn his file."

"The moment I return to Berlin, my Führer."

Hitler saluted smartly. "*Guten Abend*, Herr Obergruppenführer."

Heydrich's "Heil Hitler!" died against the closing door. In spite of his pounding heart, he resumed his cross-legged position on the edge of the bed. He sat absolutely still, and before five minutes passed, his throbbing pulse had returned to a point of equilibrium that most men of eighteen would be hard put to equal at rest. He stood deliberately, passed a slim hand over his blond hair, and walked into the hall.

Halfway down the stairs, he heard a furtive noise behind him. Eva Braun again? *Better to let it pass,* he thought. But he could not. His predatory instincts were too strong. With the stealth of a leopard, Heydrich turned and crept back up the stairs.

He arrived on the second floor just in time to see the round-shouldered back of Martin Bormann disappear into the bedroom opposite the one Eva Braun had leaned out of. Heydrich heard the shallow tinkle of girlish laughter, and as the door closed he glimpsed a swatch of unclad flesh. For a moment he stood still. Then, almost as if pulled against his will, he moved up close against the door.

He heard the laughter again, like cheap crystal. First teasing, then hysterical, it had a lilt of drunkenness in it. Then a sharp cry of pain pierced the door. Dry-throated, Heydrich tried to swallow. He heard another cry. Then a deeper, animal sound began to punctuate the brittle protests of the woman. Heydrich felt his organ move, then stiffen. A nerve tic intermittently closed his left eye. Grinding his teeth, he blocked out the primitive sounds until the spasm ceased.

The grunts grew regular. Heydrich no longer heard the woman. Beads of sweat formed on his brow. He opened and closed his right fist in synchrony with the groans coming from behind the door. The next sound he heard started the tic again. Only slaps at first—almost playful, echoing lightly— but the deadened thump of solid blows soon followed. Heydrich knew that sound as well as any man on earth. Like an arrhythmic heartbeat it drove him through each hour, each new day of conquest.

The woman was protesting again, but her cries were muffled. *A pillow*, Heydrich thought distantly. Conflicting emotions struggled for control of his taut body. Anger, revulsion, arousal. He longed to smash open the door, but whether to flay Bormann in disgust or to plunder his share of the woman, he did not know.

He did neither. He simply stood facing the door, his body rigid as a steel beam, his brow pouring sweat, and listened. Coupled with his earlier proximity to the Führer, the stress of this violently erotic encounter pushed him into a kind of trance. The sound of the blows deepened, the cries grew closer together, and Heydrich, with Adolf Hitler's voice still echoing in his ears, waited for the orgasmic groan that would resolve it all.

It never came.

CHAPTER TWENTY-TWO

Two Months Later

Reinhard Heydrich felt like a god. Seventy days ago, when he first heard Hitler impose his operational restrictions on Plan *Mordred*, Heydrich thought his meteoric rise through the Nazi hierarchy had been stopped dead. To find a way to assassinate not only Winston Churchill but also King George VI, to do it on a specific day, and without leaving a smoking gun in German hands? Ridiculous! Yet even before he landed his Fieseler-Storch back at Berlin-Staaken Airport on that frozen January night, the essential elements of the plan had flashed into his mind as if by divine inspiration. The concept was so ingeniously simple that, if brought off successfully, not only would Britain be neutralized with little more than sporadic small-arms fire, but she would become Germany's strongest ally!

It had taken the Obergruppenführer SD a further sixty-eight days to determine whether his unprecedented plan could actually be put into operation. Sixty-eight nerve-racking days of frantic intelligence work carried out under the lidless gaze of Heinrich Himmler: a dozen trips taken under false pretenses; a hundred agents lied to about the reason for the questions he had asked them; a thousand scraps of information gathered from around the globe and funneled through the sieve of the SS/SD intelligence complex, each tiny piece sucked out of the system without the knowledge of the ruthless little tyrant who controlled it.

Now, driving back to Obersalzburg beneath a cold, starlit sky, Heydrich knew that he was ready. The leather briefcase on the seat beside him contained his ticket to the most exclusive club in the world. Two months ago he had been a mere subaltern—a loyal centurion charged by his Caesar with nailing millions of Jews to the Iron Cross of the Reich. But *now*—now the centurion had glimpsed the keys to the palace! Behind Heydrich's glacier-blue eyes. a seething blast furnace of all-consuming desire fired his brain. Only one man alive possessed the kind of power he craved, and Heydrich was on his way to see that man now. With him he carried the plan that would prove his worthiness to Hitler beyond doubt, and one day—one day very soon—the mantle of dictatorship would pass to *him*!

Passing through the Obersalzburg gates, he noted the almost casual attitude of the SS guards. Desultory fighting on all fronts was taking its toll in efficiency throughout the Reich. *What everyone needs is another good blitzkrieg to wake them up,* he thought. *And they'll get one soon enough.* He reminded himself to give the laggards a good dressing down on his way out.

He parked in the garage beneath the Berghof's enormous picture window and walked around to the front of the house. A sergeant of the *SS Liebstandarte Adolf Hitler* barred the door. Before Heydrich's boot even touched the first step, the guard instructed him to turn around. When he did, he saw the last thing he expected: Adolf Hitler, outfitted in a dark suit, homburg hat, and carrying a walking stick, stood silent in the snow, watching him. Arc lights silhouetted Hitler's harlequin figure. For a moment Heydrich felt as if he were watching a newsreel in a darkened theater. Then the Führer—for all the world like Charlie Chaplin's caricature of him—turned and bobbed off across the snow.

"The teahouse," whispered the SS sergeant.

Heydrich caught up with Hitler forty meters from the Berghof, walking briskly along a deep path cleared through the snow. There was just room for two to walk abreast. Heydrich fell in beside Hitler and waited for a cue to begin his report, but Hitler walked in silence. Heydrich heard dogs barking in the distance—the Führer's German shepherds, he guessed—but when Hitler stopped and called them, they did not come. Unable to restrain himself any longer, Heydrich took a deep breath and announced: "I have finished my report, my Führer."

"In the teahouse," Hitler said tersely, and set off again.

Mystified, Heydrich hurried after him. Another twenty minutes' silent marching brought them to their destination—

the round, rustic building where Hitler liked to hold court after dinner. In contrast to the opulent Berghof, the teahouse
had been furnished for comfort. The circular main room was
about twenty-five feet across, with a round wooden table and
easy chairs. It reminded most people of cozy country holi-
days before the shadow of war fell across their lives.
Heydrich did not even notice the blazing fire. Nothing existed for him in that space save himself and Hitler—two un-
alloyed souls staring at each other across a gulf of limitless
ambition.

"So?" Hitler snapped. "You have brought me my plan?"

"Yes, my Führer," Heydrich said proudly.

"And it took you only two months. Two months! What
were you thinking of?"

Heydrich stepped back in surprise.

"Did I ask you for the *impossible*, Herr Obergruppenführer? *No!* I asked you to plan two simple murders! Surely
that could not be too difficult for you? They tell me you left
Gregor Strasser's brains on the wall of a Gestapo cell for
weeks!"

Stunned by Hitler's fury, Heydrich waited in silence.

"Is it in that briefcase?" Hitler asked sharply.

"Yes, my Führer."

"You *wrote it down?*"

Heydrich nodded uncertainly.

"I am surrounded by fools." Hitler crossed the room and
collapsed into a leather easy chair opposite Heydrich.
"Well?" he said finally. "Report!"

Too shocked to do anything else, Heydrich sat stiffly in
one of the easy chairs and emptied the contents of his briefcase onto the coffee table. His notes, clear and concise. And
a stack of eight-by-ten photographs held neatly together by
a paper clip.

"My Führer," he began, "my orders entailed finding a
way to remove Churchill and George the Sixth from power
on the tenth of May, without leaving any clue that might
possibly point to Germany. While this seems—"

"I am aware of the orders I issued you!" Hitler exploded.
"I want to hear your plan, not a description of the problem!"

Heydrich's notes slipped from his clammy palms. Standing erect, he screwed up his courage and locked his blue
eyes onto Hitler's black ones. "Accountability," he said
slowly. "That, my Führer, is the paramount consideration in

this operation. Even if Churchill and the king could be killed without leaving a trace of their killers, the finger of accusation would still point to Germany. More than anyone, we have the *motive*—and in time of war, motive is the only consideration. To avoid making 'Remember Churchill!' the new rallying cry against us, we must accomplish two things. First, we must leave no German at the scene of the crime. Second—and most important—we must provide the British with a culprit they cannot ignore."

He watched Hitler for a reaction, but the dictator sat sullenly immobile. "So," he continued, "who to blame? My Führer, the solution came to me that first night as if screamed in my ears! Who besides yourself do the English fear most? The *communists*. You've said it yourself a thousand times: 'The communists are the enemy of all civilized nations.' We know the English industrialists share this view. The march of Bolshevism since 1917 has every nation in Europe trembling." Heydrich drew himself to his full height. "And so, my Führer, the men who assassinate Churchill and the king must be *communists*!"

Heydrich sensed a stirring in Hitler's eyes, a heightening of awareness. "If communist agents were to assassinate Churchill and the king," he went on, "England would explode into panic. Instead of being united against Germany, every Englishman would begin to fear his own neighbor— his own brother! Communism would become Britain's new enemy—its new Satan. And what is the source of world communism? Russia! 'Strike back at Russia!' will be the new rallying cry in Britain."

Heydrich raised one delicate finger into the air. "But *can* they? Bombed and beaten almost beyond rising, England is virtually powerless against a nation so distant and strong. But *you* are not, my Führer. Adolf Hitler is the most implacable foe Communism has ever known—the whole world knows it! Your nonaggression pact with Stalin means nothing—a temporary alliance of convenience. One look at *Mein Kampf* will tell the most skeptical Briton that your primary aim has always been Russia. *Lebensraum!* Expansion eastward into Russia over the bodies of the subhuman Slavic barbarians!"

Hitler opened his mouth to speak, but Heydrich rolled on, caught up in the momentum of his emotions. "And most important, my Führer, every word, every warning ever given by your friends in England will be proved true! Germany will finally be recognized as the last bastion shielding England from the fanatical hordes of the East! Isn't that what the Duke of Windsor has argued all along? That another war between England and Germany can only end in common slavery under the communists?"

While Heydrich paused for breath, Hitler rose slowly to his feet and folded his arms. "An interesting plan, Herr Obergruppenführer," he said, his voice edged with excitement. "I myself was thinking along similar lines just the other day. But tell me, who will commit these murders? No Russian communist will attempt such a thing without Stalin behind him. And if a German communist does it, we are lost. To the English, Heydrich, a German is a German. They will not split hairs when they ask America for our blood in revenge."

"I've thought of that, my Führer," Heydrich said smoothly, his cruel lips cracking into a smile. "There is but one way that this thing can be accomplished—*one way* that British fury can be turned away from us and against Russia." He paused like a magician reluctant to reveal his last, best trick. "The communists who assassinate Churchill and the king must be *British subjects.*"

Hitler sat still as stone. "Explain."

Heydrich frowned. "That is all, my Führer. That is the key. The men who carry out the assassinations must be British subjects—of course I mean British *communists.*"

Hitler ground his teeth slowly. "Are you about to tell me, Herr Obergruppenführer, that you have devised a way to get Stalin to order his English cadres to execute Churchill and the king at the time and place of our choosing?"

"No, my Fü—"

"I hope not!" Hitler shook his hand in the air. "It's all I can do to keep Stalin out of my Rumanian oil fields! For a while you were making sense! Now ... we shall see."

Heydrich squinted with a gambler's concentration. "What I propose, my Führer, is not really so far from what you just suggested. But before I can give you the mechanics, I must explain a little recent history."

The idea of playing history pupil did not please Hitler, but he held a fitful silence while Heydrich laid the foundations of his plan.

"Do you recall the communist takeover of Bavaria in 1919, my Führer? Specifically Munich?"

Hitler scowled. "I fought in it, you fool. With Hess at my side I battled in the streets, and Hess with only his tattered old uniform for clothing!"

"Of course, my Führer!" Heydrich said quickly. "Yes . . . well, during the final *Friekorps* assault on the Hauptbanhof—where the communists chose to make their final stand—we had a man inside the building."

"We?" Hitler said disparagingly.

"The *Friekorps*, my Führer."

"I thought the communists in the Hauptbanhof were wiped out to a man."

"The real communists were. It was a massacre. But one *Friekorps* spy—a loyal young German who provided critical information during the crisis—managed to escape. With *Friekorps* help, of course. His name was Helmut Steuer, and he became known among the communists as the 'Survivor of Munich.' "

"And what has this Helmut got to do with your plan?"

"Everything. But these early details are important." Heydrich smoothed his thinning blond hair. "After the Party began to assert itself in Germany under your inspired leadership, it was decided in the interests of security to infiltrate informers into the communist cadres of our past and probable future enemies—England and France. The agents were sent into whatever countries their language abilities suited them for. It was a primitive program, but quite remarkable considering the state of our security services at the time. A few men were sent to Paris, a few to Marseilles. Those who had no second language stayed in Germany. And a very few were sent to England. Four went to Manchester and Leeds to work in the mills, three to the mines around Newcastle. Helmut Steuer, however, was a unique case. He had a fair grasp of French, but his real gift was English. He'd worked the Rhine packets on the English runs for most of his life and spoke the language like a London dockworker. With little else but a prayer, Helmut was sent to London.

"Being something of a communist hero after Munich, Helmut was welcomed into the London cadres with open arms. They considered him a great fugitive—a celebrity of sorts. He worked the docks for a few years, always doing his bit for the Party, selling the *Daily Worker* like a good Bolshevik, but never doing quite enough to bring the British police down on him. He wasn't really much use to us at that point, but he was ordered to stay. He had possibilities."

Heydrich felt himself coming into stride. He clearly had the Führer's attention now.

"Then in 1936, Helmut did something crazy. He packed a suitcase and set out for Spain with the English communists who went to fight in the International Brigades. And strangely enough, my Führer, that's when he became a real asset. He drove an ambulance for the Republican forces, all the while passing information to Franco's fascists and our Condor Legion. No one knew why he was doing it—he hadn't been ordered to—but I believe that he simply acted out of patriotism. He was a loyal German; he saw the Reich supporting Franco; so he did what he could from the position he was in."

"An excellent man!" Hitler cried. "Why have I not heard of him before?"

"I'm not sure, my Führer," Heydrich said smugly. "Perhaps Reichsführer Himmler never considered Helmut's reports important enough to bring to your attention."

"Ridiculous! I need men with *initiative*! Like the English commandos! This Helmut sounds like just that type of man!"

"He is better than that, my Führer. After the Spanish War, Helmut returned to England in disfavor with the British government, but an even greater hero to the British communists. It was then that I suggested the idea which now makes Plan *Mordred* possible."

Hitler's eyes glowed with anticipation.

"I instructed Helmut to organize his own group of communist activists—hard cases—and isolate them from the local Party cadres. You know the standard communist procedure: they organize small groups called *cells*, which are subordinate to various committees and finally the national party executive. Anyway, Helmut did as I asked, and out of genius or by accident he hit upon a remarkable idea. In short order he welded together a small, highly committed group of combat veterans, all rabid communists, all of whom had been wounded either in the Great War or in Spain."

Heydrich tilted his narrow head forward. "Can you imagine the value of this group, my Führer? While they *appeared* to be merely a handful of the thousands of English patriots who'd barely survived the Great War, in reality they were dedicated radicals, men so violently disillusioned with their government that they would strike at its foundations whenever they got the chance!"

Hitler sat spellbound; Heydrich breathed harder.

"Helmut started small. He reported the movements of the British Fleet in and out of port, estimated factory capacities, things like that. But I always believed the time would come when his group could do some real damage." Heydrich held up his arms in admiration. "In Plan *Mordred*, my Führer, you have created the perfect opportunity to exploit their special talents! Remember, these men are combat veterans trained by the British Army!"

"And this Helmut," Hitler said, his voice tremulous, "you believe he can trick these Englishmen into carrying out our will?"

"He already *has*," Heydrich said exuberantly. "In small ways, of course. A bit of sabotage in the munitions factories, improper packing of ships in London. But with the right cover story—"

Hitler silenced Heydrich with a stab of his right hand. "Why haven't these men been recalled to duty in the British Army?"

Heydrich faltered a little. "When I said they were wounded, my Führer, I meant it. In Helmut's signals, he refers to his unit as the *Verwunden* Brigade—the Wounded Brigade. One of the men has only one leg, another has but one hand. One man is internally damaged. Helmut himself has only one eye. He lost the other at Guernica."

Hitler's mouth fell open. "What! You speak of *cripples*? A one-eyed man leading a rabble of cripples against the British security services? How can they possibly do what is necessary to carry out your plan!"

"They can do it," Heydrich said evenly. "Helmut is the most remarkable agent I have ever come across. But you pinpointed the problem with your very first question, my Führer. How do we get Helmut's *Verwunden* Brigade to assassinate Churchill and the king *at the place and time of our choosing*?"

"Just as I said!"

Heydrich's face assumed a surgeon's impassivity. "As I said before, motivation is not a problem. These men believe that Churchill is dragging the English working class into yet another worldwide slaughter for capitalist greed. They've already proved their sympathies by sabotaging the British war effort, albeit in small ways, and they certainly have no moral compunction against killing. No, my Führer, the problem is one of *authority*. These men idolize Helmut, but Helmut alone simply hasn't the authority to order an action on that scale. Not even Britain's National Communist Party executive could order the assassination of a head of state—much less *two*. An order like that must originate"—Heydrich looked Hitler dead in the eye—"from *Moscow*."

"Then we are lost!" Hitler bellowed, leaping to his feet. "I told you about my Rumanian oil fields! How can I possibly persuade Stalin to mount an operation like this? That crafty old bear would immediately guess our true intent!"

"You need not persuade Stalin of anything," said Heydrich. "I've solved the problem already. That is what took me two months, my Führer, solving problems like this. But I have the answers with me tonight. All of them."

"I'm tired of this game, Heydrich! Get to the point!"

The young SD chieftain nodded slowly. "My Führer, do you remember a Russian named Zinoviev?"

Hitler knitted his brow. "The Bolshevik leader of 1917?"

"No." Heydrich cracked a reptilian smile. "A Russian as opposite from a Bolshevik as any man could be. He was captain in the *Okhrana*, the tsar's secret police."

Hitler tugged at his forelock. His eyes darted around the teahouse, looking everywhere but at Heydrich. The fire had died, but neither man noticed. Finally Hitler sat down again, perching on the edge of the leather easy chair. "Proceed," he said.

As trim and hard as a rapier, Reinhard Heydrich stood before the most powerful man on earth and outlined the plan that would place him first in the line of succession to the black throne of the Nazi empire. With each new revelation, his voice rose in excitement, and Hitler, spellbound, followed him up the scale.

"And the genius of the concept," Heydrich exulted, with the thrill of consummation, "the *beauty* of it, is that England will not simply be neutralized, it will *join us in our war against Russia!* Think of it! Paralyzed by grief, the British people will cry out to their new leaders for guidance, and they will be told by those leaders—*your men*—to do exactly what they so desire to do—take revenge on the godless enemy! On Russia, the cradle of assassins! And to do that they must reach out to *you*! *Barbarossa* will become an Aryan crusade!"

Hitler's facial muscles had seized into an almost catatonic spasm. His right hand shook as if from palsy. The genius of Heydrich's plan had burst into his brain with the brilliance of a dying star. All his life Hitler had fed upon the intellects of more timid men, seizing upon their revolutionary ideas and charging forward without looking back. Now—given Heydrich's plan like a gift from heaven itself—he reveled in the knowledge that he would once again beat all the odds, once again prove himself right and all his generals wrong! This certainty coursed through his veins like a blast of morphine. Visions of conquest flashed behind his eyes: the Kremlin, shattered and smoldering in black ashes; tall young Germans tilling the great fields of the Ukraine; German ships sailing forth from Odessa and Archangel . . .

"I see it!" Hitler cried. *"I see it all now!"* He scurried around the table like a human lightning rod attempting to discharge itself. "It can work! *Churchill is going to die!*"

"And the king!" Heydrich added euphorically. "My Führer, Helmut *assures* me that it can be done. Zinoviev is already preparing for the mission!"

"My God," Hitler murmured, suddenly mortified. "How do you communicate with Helmut?"

"I don't. It's always been a one-way conduit. "Because of that—"

"Yes?"

"I had to send a man into England with a message."

"What?"

"I take full responsibility, my Führer. I felt that this mission was simply too important to risk by using radio communications. I trust no one. I never even contacted Lord Grenville."

"And what if your messenger had been captured?"

"He wasn't."

"And what if he read your message, Herr Obergruppenführer? What if he decided to *sell it to the highest bidder!*"

"The message was in code," Heydrich replied evenly. "He simply delivered an envelope and returned with a one-word answer: *Ja.*"

Hitler's voice went shrill with paranoia. "And you think

this courier knows nothing? Can reveal nothing? What if he decides to sell his knowledge *now*?"

"That would be impossible, my Führer. I shot him myself, five minutes after he delivered Helmut's reply."

Hitler said nothing for a long while. Putting his hand to his chin, he looked out through one of the small-paned windows near the fireplace. Outside, the snow had begun to fall again. "Remarkable," he murmured. He took his walking stick from its resting place on the hearth and turned back to Heydrich. "Let's return to the Berghof. We can talk on the way back."

They walked through the darkness without speaking. The crunch of Heydrich's boots on the hard-packed snow punctuated their progress across the mountain. Now and then the howls of German shepherds reverberated across the rocky slope. After twenty minutes they reached the parking area. Hitler fixed Heydrich with his dark gaze.

"Are you confident that Helmut's Englishmen can reach their targets, Herr Obergruppenführer? Can they kill both men on the tenth of May?"

"My Führer," Heydrich said confidently, "any man can be assassinated on any day, if one critical condition is satisfied."

"What condition?"

"That the assassin be prepared to die in the doing of the deed."

Hitler's eyes narrowed. "And you believe these Englishmen will die for Helmut?"

Heydrich blinked against the wind. "No. They will die for their lost ideals. They will die for their gods—Lenin and Marx. For Moscow, perhaps. But most of all, they will die believing they have delivered their country from the clutches of ruthless oppressors who have held England's poor—and half of the rest of the world's—in slavery for a very long time. They will die to become martyrs."

"Remarkable," Hitler said finally. "You seem to have considered every possibility."

Heydrich nodded with formal correctness.

"I shall leave you here, Heydrich. Is there anything further you require from me?"

"Yes," Heydrich answered without hesitation. "A diversion. If you could possibly arrange some type of limited attack on England on May tenth—a small commando attack on a Channel port, perhaps? A U-boat raid near London?"

"I've already taken care of that," Hitler said. "Have no fear, your assassins will have all the confusion they need. On the night of May tenth, I shall unleash the most devastating air attack London has ever known. And it will be the *last* raid against Great Britain. At least until Russia has been conquered. Perhaps then . . ." He trailed off, his voice soft and ruminative.

Heydrich licked his wind-burned lips. Unexpectedly, he had discovered the courage to ask the question which had haunted him since the night Hitler first gave him his assignment. "My Führer?" he said tentatively.

"Yes?"

"With all respect, you have not told me much about the political side of the mission. To be quite frank, it worries me. The success of the entire operation hinges on a single factor, and that factor is beyond my control."

"What are you talking about?"

"My Führer, again with all respect, do you have Englishmen ready to assume control of the government when Churchill dies? When the king is dead? My sources indicate—"

"That does not concern you!" Hitler jabbed a stiff finger into Heydrich's chest. "You have Lord Grenville's name! You know all you need to for now! Just make certain that your *cripples* carry out their orders! Hess has the names. He will handle the political side of the mission."

Too shocked to be afraid, Heydrich raised his eyebrows in surprise. "Reichminister Hess, my Führer? But . . . I was under the impression that your confidence in him was waning. Both Göring and Himmler speak of him as—"

"Göring and Himmler? You should spend less time listening to gossip and more time studying how the Party rose to the position it now holds! Hess has done more for me than . . ." Hitler shook his fist in the air. "Let me tell you something, Heydrich. It took Hess just *one month* to do what you could not do in a year. Hess rooted out the traitor in our midst. And that traitor is your own boss—Himmler! Yes— loyal Heinrich. Already he searches for ways to usurp my power. And you, working right under his nose, you could not see it!" Hitler's face suddenly darkened. "Or *could* you?"

Heydrich blanched. "No, my Führer! I swear to you . . .

What can I do to prove my loyalty? I shall arrest the Reichsführer myself!"

"Don't be ridiculous," Hitler scoffed. "We cannot arrest the head of the SS for treason. No, we shall rely on the safety mechanism already in place."

Heydrich wiped his brow with relief. His hand was shaking. "My Führer, a disturbing thought has occurred to me. It concerns the 'double' program. If Reichsführer Himmler is indeed a traitor, it is all the more frightening. I think you should place all the doubles from the Practical School under my direct command."

Hitler scowled in confusion. "What the devil are you talking about, Heydrich?"

"My Führer, consider this: If, God forbid, a traitor succeeded in having *you* assassinated, the doubles could be of inestimable value to that traitor in gaining the confidence of the people and the army. If the traitor could present a trusted comrade of yours—Reichminister Hess, for example—a true Nazi who would stand at his side like an ally, the people might well accept the traitor's authority. Himmler is certainly devious enough to have worked this out."

This terrifying possibility seemed to shrink Hitler in his very clothes. "I want every double shot immediately!" he cried. "Such a risk cannot be tolerated!"

Heydrich replied very softly. "My Führer, perhaps you might reconsider? Our political doubles represent a tremendous investment of time and resources. I believe they will prove invaluable to us in the coming war with Russia. You could remove the danger simply by placing them under my direct command."

Hitler's black eyes bored relentlessly into Heydrich's face, probing for disloyalty. After a full minute of silence, he said, "Permission granted." Then he added, "For now."

Heydrich stared in surprise as Hitler turned and hurried up the frozen path. "My Führer!" he called, hastening up the slope after him. "Nothing can stop us now! Failure is not a possibility!"

Hitler paused twenty meters from the Berghof. In a flat voice suddenly drained of anger, he said, "I am pleased, Heydrich. When *Barbarossa* is completed, I shall not forget you. Once Russia's vast lands lie under our control, I will need a man of iron to rule her—a Reich-Protector I can trust. Are you that man, Heydrich?"

"As you command, my Führer!"

Without a word Hitler turned and marched up the steps to the Berghof. Heydrich stood motionless in the snow. The promise of a Reich-Protectorship made his heart pound, but a darker dread still ate at his confidence. In the face of Hitler's wrath, he had quailed from voicing his deepest doubt about Plan *Mordred*—his nagging suspicion that the Führer's English "sympathizers"—whoever they might be—were actually English patriots working desperately to lure Germany into a suicidal strategic blunder. The stakes for Britain—national survival—would justify almost any human effort. But what could Heydrich do about it? The game had to be played to its end. He could only make sure that his part ran smoothly.

From this moment forward, Heydrich existed almost without sleep, without food. The Führer had extended the grail of power to him, and he moved through his days like a knight sworn to a holy quest. His allies in that quest were an embittered Russian expatriate, and a one-eyed German agent living in the heart of beleaguered London. All three lived only that a fat English warrior and a shy English king might die.

In Hitler's small study on the second floor of the Berghof, Rudolf Hess anxiously awaited his Führer. Dressed in his gray uniform, he sat behind a desk littered with architectural plans and sketches. Most of the sketches were by Hitler; Hess recognized the cramped, untutored style. The building plans, though, had been drafted by Albert Speer. Strong-lined and well-proportioned, the great avenue of the Führer's new Berlin stretched across the desk like a blueprint of the future. The magnificent Imperial Palace, the Triumphal Arch that would dwarf the one in Paris—all seemed the natural fruit of the labor of the new Reich, a mighty city built to endure for a thousand years. Or so it seemed on those happier occasions when Hess had studied these plans in the past. He would never look at them in quite the same way again.

The Party and the Reich that he had once viewed as a united force—an unstoppable juggernaut destined for immortality—he now saw as a fragile alliance of ambitious men held together only by their common fear of Adolf Hitler. Since Hess's momentous meeting with the Führer in January, both Heinrich Himmler and Hermann Göring had deduced the real reason for Hess's training flights. At Gestapo headquarters in Berlin, Hess had conducted a conversation with Reichsführer Himmler that could only be described as a war of nerves. The smell of treason had hung in the room like cordite. As the two men spoke in measured tones, Hess had realized that Himmler's office was, in every sense of the word, a battlefield. In the narrow confines of four walls, words became bullets, names flashed like tracers, and the silences were mined as lethally as the sands around Tobruk. Himmler had claimed that the British would never make peace with Hitler, but might make peace with Germany if he himself sat in the seat of power. Then—as Hess's rage boiled over—Himmler had disguised his power grab by claiming it would be a mere strategy to trick the British into making peace. Hess had not been fooled. Behind Himmler's bland face and pince-nez glasses, Hess had glimpsed a power lust more sickening than the greed of any Jew. He had left the Prinz-Albrechtstrasse with no doubt that Heinrich Himmler was a traitor.

The conversation with Göring had been very different, if only in terms of style. Himmler had begun his interrogation on an obscure pretext, and arrived at his main point only after circumlocuting a veritable maze of half-truths and theories. Göring charged in with guns blazing, like the fighter ace he was. In substance, however, Göring's assessment of the British position had been remarkably close to Himmler's—no peace with Germany, ever. Unlike Himmler, though, the corpulent *Luftwaffe* chief had not suggested treason. Hess recalled Göring's last words with grudging admiration: *If the Führer wants to invade Russia now, it is our duty to stand by him to the end, whether the reward be ambrosia or cyanide. It's war now, Hess, war to the bloody end!* Yet Göring's opinion of Germany's future had been plain to see. He had pronounced Hess's intended peace mission to England suicidal, then declared that if Hitler attacked Russia before finishing Britain, all was lost. Hess thanked God that the Führer was in good health. If the future depended on men like Himmler and Göring, the Fatherland was indeed lost.

"Rudi?" said a soft voice.

Hess turned quickly. Silhouetted in the doorway of the study, Adolf Hitler stood watching him intently. Hess tried to read the black eyes, but they were, as ever, inscrutable.

Regarding Hess from the door, Hitler felt a strange, almost paternal sadness. Hess's broad shoulders, strong jaw, and high Aryan forehead fanned the flames of pride in his breast. The resolute eyes looked back at him with a frankness that seemed to say, "I am ready for anything! Command and I shall obey!"

But *was* Hess ready for anything? Was he ready for Plan *Mordred*? Explaining the operational details of the mission would be easy. Hess would admire the plan for its boldness and intricacy. Technical details fascinated him. But the rest—

"My Führer," Hess said abruptly, "I am curious about something. It's been two weeks since I informed you of Reichsführer Himmler's seditious conversation, yet nothing seems to have been done. Are you delaying punishment for some reason?"

Hitler smiled wanly. "Remember the old proverb, Rudi? Better the devil you know than the one you don't?"

"But Himmler could betray you at any moment!"

Hitler sighed. "Sooner or later, Rudi, he will probably try. It is a delicate balancing act I perform. It has been from the beginning. It's the same for all men of power. Churchill, Stalin, Mussolini, Roosevelt—no one is immune. Himmler's SS is powerful, old friend, too powerful to alienate or ignore. But it is also corrupt. Himmler fears Heydrich—his subordinate—yet he thinks because Heydrich has a little Jewish blood, he can be controlled by blackmail." Hitler's eyes flickered like black stars. "Don't worry, Rudi, I have my own controls over Reichsführer Himmler. His personal adjutant happens to be Heydrich's man, and Heydrich is *my* man. One word from me, night or day, and Himmler dies. But for the present—while he is useful—he lives."

Hess looked unconvinced.

"I expected it to be Göring," Hitler confided. "I always thought him weaker than Himmler."

Hess nodded. "I must confess that I thought—I *hoped*—the same thing. I never liked Göring. He's a braggart and a libertine. But he is also loyal. For the time being, at least."

You're so straightforward, old friend, Hitler thought. *Perhaps that is why I trust you. Heydrich explained it all so well, made it seem so easy and mechanical. But in truth it isn't. The English fanatics who will die after firing bullets into the brains of their leaders mean nothing. They are ma-*

*chines, like tanks or rockets. But you, Hess, are the closest
thing to a friend I have left. How can I explain to you that
the same rules which apply to five communist fanatics also
apply to you? Yet somehow I must. For England must be
neutralized. Churchill must die. And contrary to what
Heydrich boasts, failure is always a possibility. In the
event—God forbid—that something does go wrong, my personal envoy and confidant cannot be captured on British
soil. For in your head you carry the secrets of Barbarossa.
If the "impossible" happens—if the fanatics miss their targets, if they lose their nerve, if they're caught, if the mission
is blown and the great gamble is all for nothing—my messenger will have to die. You, Hess, will have to die. And,
quite simply, there will be no one there to kill you. No
Reinhard Heydrich—no steely-eyed SS officer sworn to
shoot without question at my order. You will have to do it
yourself. Can you do that, I wonder? You once proclaimed to
a multitude that I, Adolf Hitler, was Germany. Will you die
for Germany, old friend? Will you die for me?*

With his right hand on Hess's powerful shoulder, Hitler
looked deeply into the bright, worshipful eyes. "Rudi," he
said softly, "there are two possibilities . . ."

One hour later Rudolf Hess rose and marched to the door
of the study. He turned and placed his right fist against his
heart. "My Führer," he said, "to die for Germany is no more
than we ask of any soldier. In the most extreme circumstance
I shall sacrifice myself with an unfaltering heart. My only
regret is for my wife and son." Hess paused for a moment,
too full of emotion to speak. "Yes," he said at length, "even
they would understand. *Deutschland über Alles:* these words
are our creed."

Hess took a deep breath and squared his shoulders. "Do
not let this trouble you, my Führer. We were never meant to
fight the English, and this is the solution Fate has provided
us. You, Adolf Hitler, were sent by God to free the world
from the scourge of the Bolshevik and the Jew! I believe that
with all my heart. If my death were to bring our goal one
day closer, my life would not have been wasted. But I *shall
not fail.*" Hess nodded solemnly. "I await your final orders.
Heil Hitler!"

Hitler felt a numbing jolt of profound fulfillment. The
sight of Rudolf Hess, tall and resolute, his hard-muscled

right arm extended in the Nazi salute, moved him almost to tears. This man, born to wear the German uniform, possessed a devotion far deeper than loyalty, deeper than patriotism. As Hess turned and marched through the study door, Adolf Hitler, his hands resting on the plans for the world's youngest imperial city, realized that he had not asked the ultimate sacrifice of his deputy or his friend—but his *disciple*.

BOOK TWO
SOUTH AFRICA, 1987

If ... the Jew conquers the nations of this world, his crown will become the funeral wreath of humanity, and once again this planet, empty of mankind, will move through the ether as it did thousands of years ago.

Eternal Nature inexorably revenges the transgressions of her laws.

Therefore, I believe today that I am acting in the sense of the Almighty Creator: By warding off the Jews I am fighting for the Lord's work.

ADOLF HITLER, *Mein Kampf*

CHAPTER TWENTY-THREE

2:04 A.M. *Lufthansa Flight 417: South African Airspace*

The German airliner shuddered against the increased drag of descent. Hans Apfel took a deep breath and gripped the armrests tighter. The announcement bell rang.

"Attention ladies and gentlemen," said a male voice. "This is your captain speaking. We are now beginning our descent into Jan Smuts International Airport. We expect to arrive on schedule. The temperature is seventy-eight degrees Fahrenheit in Johannesburg. There's been no rain for two weeks, and none expected soon. We hope you enjoy your stay in South Africa, and we appreciate your flying Lufthansa. *Danke Schön.*"

"Nice change," Hauer remarked.

"What?" said Hans.

"The weather."

"What?"

"It's summer here, Hans. No snow. We've hardly had a break for three weeks in Berlin."

"Oh. Sorry. I was thinking about the exchange. Have you settled on the plan yet?"

Hauer nodded. "With our limited resources, there's really only one option. We've got to find some place that's really open, but with plenty of concealment for me. An empty football stadium would be ideal. I can hide in the stands—the high ground—while you make the exchange on the field. You'll have two jobs. The first is acting."

"Acting?"

Hauer nodded. "You're going to be holding a grenade, and you've got to act like you'll blow everyone to hell if they don't hand Ilse over as soon as they touch the papers."

"I won't have to act," Hans said.

"I'm afraid you will. It won't be a live grenade. We won't have access to one. We'll buy an empty one at an army surplus shop. The grenade is just a prop to speed things along. We want Ilse in your hands ten seconds after you hand the papers over."

"And my second job?"

"Running. As soon as you get Ilse, you'll start walking toward preplanned cover. The kidnappers will have no intention of letting you escape alive, of course. When you hear the first shots, you run like hell."

"What's your job?"

Hauer made a pistol with his thumb and forefinger. "Suppressing fire. The second you get Ilse clear of my line of fire, I start knocking people down. The first shot you hear will be mine. I'll take out the men on the field, plus anyone they may have covering the exchange location."

Hans studied Hauer's face. "Can you do that?"

"I won't lie to you. Two snipers would be better. But I'm still one of the best rifle shots in Germany. I can do it."

Hans stared out of the small window at the stars hanging in the African darkness. "Have you used this plan before?"

Hauer smiled faintly. "I've seen it used. Ten years ago I saw terrorists use it successfully against the Cologne police."

"Oh."

The Lufthansa jet leaned sixty-five degrees to starboard, banking for final approach. Hans gripped the armrests of his seat and stared straight ahead. Hauer watched him silently, wishing he could reassure his son more. At least he had spared Hans what he himself knew: that the terrorists who had used his hostage-exchange plan had escaped the Cologne football stadium only to be blown to pieces in a train station an hour later. Escaping an exchange point with Ilse might not be too difficult; escaping from South Africa was another thing altogether. Hauer laid his callused hand over Hans's and squeezed tightly.

"We'll get her, boy," he said softly.

Hans looked over at his father, his jaw resolute. "I'm ready. But there's something I can't get out of my mind. Who cut the throat of that Afrikaner who attacked Professor Natterman? Why did he do it? And where did he go? Did he just disappear?"

Hauer's face darkened. He knew exactly why the unknown killer had cut the Afrikaner's throat, and if Hans opened the foil packet in his inside coat pocket, he would know too. The killer had escaped with three pages of the Spandau diary. At Hauer's orders the packet had remained hidden for the duration of the flight. But sooner or later, Hans would have to be told the truth. Otherwise he would find it out for himself.

"Hans," he said, "I've got a feeling we may meet our elusive killer sooner than you think."

2:20 A.M. El Al Flight 331: Over Tel Aviv, Israel

The El Al 747 flew a lazy racetrack pattern over Ben-Gurion Airport at a comfortable twenty-eight thousand feet, one of a dozen tiny blips on the emerald air-traffic screens below. An equipment malfunction on an Eastern whisperjet on runway 3 had caused a delay, and until the men who monitored the skies over Tel Aviv granted clearance, Professor Natterman and his reticent Jewish companion would have to wait in the sky along with two hundred and seventy other impatient travelers.

"What are these mysterious *things* we need to pick up?" Natterman asked. "Weapons? Explosives?"

Stern looked out at the darkness. "We will need weapons," he murmured. "But we'll have to get them in South Africa, not Israel. I arranged it all from your cabin."

Natterman tried without success to ignore the acid stomach he had developed during the flight from Hamburg. Combined with the stinging pain radiating from his ripped nostril, the indigestion made the unexpected delay almost unbearable. "Do you think they've arrived in Pretoria yet?" he asked.

Stern looked at his watch. "If they took the first flight out of Frankfurt, they should be landing in Johannesburg right about now."

"God help them."

Stern grunted skeptically.

"I've been thinking about what you told me back in Frankfurt," Natterman said. "About that Lord Grenville character. The one who owns the corporation called Phoenix AG. If Grenville is English, and his company is based in South Africa, why did you come to Berlin at all?"

"That's a good question, Professor. But the answer is complicated, and for now at least, private."

"If you're not going to tell me anything," Natterman grumbled, "why did you bring me along in the first place? A man like you doesn't do things without a very good reason."

"That's true, Professor," Stern said. "I brought you with me for two reasons. One is that you may be able to provide historical information that might help me. I know you're bursting at the seams to tell me your theories about Rudolf Hess, and there is some of it I need to hear. But first, let me explain how this is going to work. You want information about what I think is going on in South Africa. Fair enough. But you are going to have to earn it. You will answer my questions about the Hess case now; then I will decide how much information to give you in return. If you tell me things I do not already know, I'll reward you in kind. But this is the only time we will discuss Rudolf Hess. Do you agree?"

Natterman sat without speaking for nearly a minute. Then he cleared his throat and said, "What do you want to know?"

"Tell me about Hess and the British. Was there a pro-Nazi clique high in the British government in 1941?"

Natterman folded his hands together on his lap. "It's very complicated, Stern."

"I think I can stay with you, Herr Einstein."

"All right, then. Yes, there was a group of Nazi appeasers—*very* highly placed—who wanted to make a deal with Hitler. That's been proved. Or at least it's *being* proved, by an Oxford academic. The question is, was that group *sincere*? Do you follow me, Stern? Were the members of this group English fascists who loved the swastika? Or simply war profiteers out for all the gold they could get? Were they paranoid anticommunists who wanted peace at any price so that Hitler would be free to crush Russia? *Or*—and here's the rub—were they patriotic Englishmen leading Hitler by the nose until it was too late for him to invade England? Do you see my point about complexity?"

Stern waved his hand.

"And if they *were* genuinely pro-Nazi," Natterman went on, "were they truly operating in secret? Or was British Intelligence aware of them all along? After all, what better stalling ploy could MI-5 have come up with than to allow *real* traitors to lead Hitler on—letting him think he could neutralize England without an invasion—until he could no longer wait to attack Russia? Remember, these 'traitors' weren't the class of people one likes to arrest for treason. We're talking about the backbone of British government and industry. What if MI-5 decided to use these blue-blooded turncoats while they could, and then slap them on their noble wrists when it was all over? Are you with me, Stern?"

"I'm ahead of you, Professor. What if the top officers of British Intelligence—expecting a few closet Reds from Oxford—were virulent anticommunists? Brothers-in-spirit with your alleged aristocratic, pro-Hitler clique? What if for strictly pragmatic reasons *British Intelligence* wanted to do a deal with Hitler, thereby freeing him to crush Stalin? Or . . . British Intelligence could have been *ordered* to explore such a deal. In that case the impetus to make peace with Hitler would have originated at the highest level of British government. And I mean the very top. Excluding Churchill, of course. But *including* the monarchy." Stern winked at Natterman. "Are you with *me*, Professor?"

Natterman gave him a black look. "You should have been a historian, damn you. You've struck the main pillar of my thesis—the Duke of Windsor. British Intelligence has been helping to conceal Windsor's shadowy past for years. All records of the duke's wartime activities are sealed forever by order of Her Majesty's government. Yet in spite of that, there's a growing body of hard evidence linking Windsor to the Nazis. It's almost certain that in 1940 the duke met Hess secretly in Lisbon to try to reach an accommodation with Hitler that would put him back on the throne. Windsor was the archetype of the privileged, Russophobic, Jew-hating British admirer of Hitler. And I'm sure you're aware of the fact that many informed sources believe British Intelligence murdered Number Seven in Spandau last month."

"Yes. But I have my doubts about that. I'm not sure that in this day and age the British would kill over the reputation of the royal family. It's tarnished enough already."

"If Windsor were merely the tip of an iceberg," Natterman mused, "they might. Many historians believe that Lord Halifax, the British foreign secretary during the war, and possibly as many as forty ranking members of Parliament continued to try to make a deal with Hitler long after

Churchill declared: 'We shall never surrender!' I doubt if the most revered families in England would care to have their names linked to Adolf Hitler after all these years. And no Englishman in his right mind wants Churchill's 'their finest hour' myth stained. Think about it, Stern. Neville Chamberlain is excoriated today, and he was merely an *appeaser*. Men who sought to accommodate Hitler after the Battle of Britain would be branded *collaborators*." Natterman looked thoughtful. "You know, I'd be surprised if some of those noble English family trees haven't spread quite a few branches into South Africa."

"Branches," Stern muttered. "It's *roots* I'm interested in, Professor. And not the roots of the past, either. I mean the roots of conspiracy in the present. The here and now. That's where the threat to Israel is."

Natterman's eyelids lowered in meditation. "I don't know about any threat to Israel," he said, "but I think I've earned some information, Stern."

The Israeli shook his head slowly. "Professor, what you have told me thus far is available in libraries. I want your *analysis*. Amaze me with the fruits of your years of scholarship!"

Natterman looked up at Stern, his lips pale with anger. "If you know so much, why don't you finish this conversation alone?"

When Stern didn't respond, Natterman said, "All right, I'll give you something. But you'd better be prepared to pay me back in kind."

"Ask and it shall be given, Professor."

"That's the New Testament, Stern."

"You were saying?"

Natterman actually blushed as he whispered his next words. "What I am about to tell you, Stern, I learned by . . . by rather dubious means."

Stern's eyes flickered interest.

"As I told you, several historians are currently working on the Hess mystery. Two of them are at Oxford University. You may not know this, Stern, but history is a very competitive field. In the top rank anyway. And it pays to know all you can about your competition."

"Are you telling me that you have your own spies, Professor?"

Natterman averted his eyes. "I prefer to call them 'good friends.'"

The Israeli chuckled. "Naturally."

"One of these friends," said Natterman, "managed to get a very close look at the Hess research going on at Oxford. It seems that there's a very mysterious fellow who figures in the Hess case. A *heretofore unheard of* fellow, who seems to have done some particularly nasty mischief on the night of May tenth 1941. In the Oxford draft papers he is referred to as *Helmut*, but—"

"Helmut?" Stern sat up. "Another German in England on that night?"

Natterman smiled cagily. "The Oxford draft research indicates that. However, I belive that 'Helmut' is simply a code name—a device that the Oxford historians are using to mask this person's real identity. Never in my own research have I found anyone named Helmut associated with the Hess case in any way."

"You're not telling me you think 'Helmut' is a code name for the real Hess?"

Natterman smiled triumphantly. "In the Oxford papers 'Helmut' is referred to as having had one particularly distinguishing characteristic, Stern. I think it will interest you."

"Well?"

"He had only one eye."

Stern looked surprised, then thoughtful. "That might tie in with our tattoo," he allowed. "But I shouldn't think you'd be too happy about it, since Rudolf Hess had two perfectly good eyes."

Natterman raised a long forefinger. "He did as of May tenth 1941. But if Hess survived that night—as I believe he did—he had plenty of time left to lose an eye. He might even have lost it on the very night of his flight!"

"You should be writing movies, Professor. Do you know how many men lost eyes in the Second World War? Do you plan to scour all Africa for a one-eyed man, in the hope he will lead you to your fantasy Nazi?"

"We'll see how fanciful I am," Natterman muttered.

"Why *couldn't* there have been a German named Helmut in England on that night in May?" asked Stern.

"There could have been," Natterman admitted. "But there wasn't. So—have I earned your half of the story?"

"Yes, Professor, I think you have. Just one more question,

though. Were there any Russians involved in the Hess case, as far as you know?"

"Russians?" Natterman was silent. "In Hess's original mission? None that I know of. But I'll certainly think about it."

"Please do that. And please remember our deal when we get on the ground. No fairy stories about Rudolf Hess in front of anyone. Talk like that can make some Jews very upset."

Natterman nodded solemnly.

"Attention ladies and gentlemen," demanded the loudspeaker. "Please take your seats. We have been cleared for approach to Ben-Gurion Airport."

A collective sigh of relief went up throughout the plane. Stern chuckled and touched Natterman's sleeve. "I'm afraid my contribution to this epic will have to wait for the second leg of our journey."

Natterman studied the Israeli's tanned, angular face. "You said information was the first reason you brought me with you, Stern. What was the second?"

Stern looked away from the professor. When he looked back, his eyes were dark and hard. "Phoenix kidnapped your granddaughter, Professor. You are her closest blood relative. That makes you my direct line into Phoenix. I'm not sure how yet, but I think you might just be my best weapon against them."

Natterman leaned thoughtfully back in his seat as the pilot stretched his holding pattern into a smooth approach and made a flawless landing on the main runway. A security gate with metal-detection and X-ray equipment awaited the deplaning passengers at the end of a long passage, but when Stern presented his wallet to the senior security officer, he and Natterman were waved through.

"That's no small trick in this country," Natterman said. "Is it, Stern? What exactly did you do for a living before you retired?"

Stern didn't answer. He was searching the concourse for something or someone he apparently expected to find waiting.

"You must be with the Mossad," Natterman guessed. "That's it, isn't it?"

Stern kept watching the crowd. "I go back a lot further than the Mossad, Professor. You should know that."

"Yes, but it's something similar, I'll bet. Something quite unsavory."

"Gadi!" Stern cried.

Suddenly the Israeli was moving across the concourse at great speed, not running, but taking long strides that seemed to swallow distance effortlessly. Natterman tried to pick out Stern's objective but couldn't, until he reappeared out of the milling crowd with one arm draped affectionately around a dark young man of about twenty-five.

"Professor Natterman," Stern said, "meet Gadi Abrams, my great-nephew."

"My pleasure, Herr Professor," said the young man graciously, extending a sun-browned hand.

"Guten Abend," said Natterman, turning to Stern. "Is this one of the 'packages' we stopped to pick up?"

"Yes, Professor, one of three."

Two smiling young men appeared from behind Gadi Abrams. They extended dark-tanned hands to Natterman, nodded politely, then embraced Stern as if they hadn't seen the older man for many months.

"Aaron," said Stern, "Yosef—this is Professor Natterman of the Free University of Berlin."

The young men nodded courteously, but said nothing. Both appeared to be about Gadi's age, if not younger, and both carried canvas overnight bags. Stern began walking down the concourse toward a row of expensive restaurants, talking quietly to his nephew as he moved. Natterman tried to keep close enough to the pair to overhear their conversation. Aaron and Yosef padded along behind at a discreet distance. Stern finally turned into a restaurant styled after a French cafe—the only one open at this hour. He waved away a bald waiter who started toward them with a sheaf of menus.

"What about the plane, Gadi?" he asked in Hebrew. "How long?"

"You won't believe this, Uncle, but a flight leaves for Johannesburg in ninety minutes."

" *'Siz bashert,'* " Stern breathed. "It is meant to be. Nonstop?"

"One stopover. Athens."

"Good enough."

"You don't seem surprised, Uncle. Lucking into a flight to South Africa on such short notice? I couldn't believe it."

"It wasn't luck, Gadi. I called an old friend of mine in the air force and requested a bit of creative rescheduling."

"You're kidding. They can do that?"

"I really wasn't sure. My faith in mankind is renewed."

Gadi laughed infectiously. "It's very good to see you again, Uncle. Traveling first class, as usual?"

Professor Natterman could contain himself no longer. As far as he was concerned, the conversation had taken a sudden turn into outer space. *"Stern,"* he interrupted. "Would you please tell me why we are sitting here in this godforsaken airport while my granddaughter is in mortal danger in South Africa?"

Stern switched back to German. "Professor, your manners leave quite a bit to be desired. However, I do appreciate your motive. In ninety minutes we board an El Al flight to Johannesburg, from whence we shall begin our search for your granddaughter. We are only one day behind Hauer and Apfel, and we know the time and location of their rendezvous with the kidnappers. The Burgerspark Hotel at eight tomorrow night, remember? And remember this also: that our interests happen to coincide is for you a lucky twist of fate. For me that remains to be seen."

The Israeli's words infuriated Natterman, but since he knew Stern could simply abandon him in the airport, he decided to remain silent.

"Now," said Stern, "I suggest we all have something to eat. I expect everyone to sleep during the flight. Once we land in South Africa, we won't have much time for it." He summoned the waiter with a flick of his eyes. Everyone took one of the flimsy paper menus.

"Cheer up, Professor," Stern said. "You and Gadi should have quite a lot to talk about. He took his degree in history just last year."

"Really?" said Natterman. "He looks more like a soldier than a scholar to me."

Gadi stiffened.

"You have a good eye, Professor," Stern said, gentling his nephew with a quick glance. "You may prove to be more of an asset than I thought."

Four tables away sat an expensively dressed woman with blue-rinsed hair. She looked thin for her age—which could have been anywhere between fifty and sixty—and she was obviously not an Israeli. A Louis Vuitton handbag lay on her table. Beside it stood a glass of orange juice. When the waiter inquired if the woman would like to order some food, she politely declined. Her voice was pitched low, but the waiter thought it very pleasant. In the babel of the Mideast, there was nothing like a crisp British accent to tickle the ear. When the woman smiled, the waiter thought the smile was for him, but he was wrong. It was for Jonas Stern.

Swallow had acquired her target.

2:25 A.M. *Jan Smuts Airport, Johannesburg*

The taxi was a small, clapped-out Ford. It stood out sharply from the short line of Rovers and Mazdas, which were mostly new and owned by the same two taxi companies. Hauer chose a taxi over the shuttle bus because he wanted speed and privacy. The forty-mile taxi ride to Pretoria would be outrageously expensive, but money was the least of their worries. He chose the old Ford because he wanted a driver with some character—an entrepreneur.

"English?" the driver asked with a strong Indian accent.

"Swiss," Hauer replied.

The driver switched to a strange but fluent German. Oddly enough, the Teutonic consonants did not prevent the dark young man from speaking with the singsong inflection of his native country. "And where do you wish to go?" he crooned.

"You speak German?" Hauer said, surprised.

"Most happily, yes. Taught to me by a cousin on my mother's side. His father was a houseboy to the German ambassador in New Delhi. He knew the language well and I picked it up quite easily when they moved back to Calcutta. I pick up all languages easily. A wonderful aid in my humble profession . . ."

Hans sank back into the Ford's rear seat and listened to the Indian's spiel, luxuriating in the stability of the automobile.

"Listen," Hauer said, breaking the Indian's flow, "we need to get to Pretoria. My son and I are stockbrokers. We've come to South Africa to do a little business, but also to have a little fun, you understand?"

"Most certainly, sir," said the driver, sensing the possibility of a generous tip.

"For this reason we'd like you to take us to a somewhat cheaper establishment than you might expect—a fleabag, one might say."

"I understand perfectly, sir," the driver assured him, appraising Hauer in the rearview mirror.

"Then drive," said Hauer. "And keep your eyes on the road."

The Ford jumped to life and joined the stream of taxis moving out of the airport like a line of beetles.

"Salil is my name," the Indian sang out. "At your service."

Hauer said nothing.

"Sir?" Salil tried again.

"What is it?"

"I believe I understand your requirements perfectly. But might I suggest that for gentlemen such as yourselves, a fleabag—as you so accurately call it—might be just the type of place where you are most quickly noticed? Why not one of the higher-priced hotels? If you have the money, of course. You would blend right in, and no one would think of asking questions. Privacy is at a premium in such places."

Hauer considered this. "Any suggestions?" he asked, liking the idea better the more he thought about it.

"The Burgerspark is an excellent hotel."

Hans jumped as if struck physically.

"Where else?" Hauer asked quickly.

"The Protea Hof is also a fine hotel, sir." Salil glanced furtively at his rearview mirror.

"The Protea Hof it is."

While the taxi sped northward, Hauer peered out at the ultramodern skyline of Johannesburg, the City of Gold. Dozens of brightly lit skyscrapers towered above a dense network of elevated freeways. Compared to this futuristic metropolis West Berlin looked like a sooty hand-me-down. South Africa looked nothing like what Hauer had expected. Already he sensed the change in altitude, the huge expanses of space around him.

"Sir?" Salil said, catching Hauer's eye in the rearview mirror.

"Yes?"

"Would you be interested to know that someone is following us?"

Hauer clutched Hans's shoulder to keep him from turning. "Any idea who it might be?" he asked calmly.

"Yes, sir. I believe they are British agents. They've been with us since the airport."

Hauer heard a sharp intake of breath as Hans slid down in his seat. "And how would you know that?" he asked.

"I saw many British agents in India," Salil explained. "I've seen that car at the airport many times before. The young man driving it, though, I have not."

Hauer rubbed his stubbled chin thoughtfully. Hans tried to turn around, but Hauer restrained him. "I've changed my mind, driver," he said. "We'll check into the Burgerspark after all."

"Very good, sir."

Hans opened his mouth to protest, but Hauer whispered: "There's already a room there in your name. We might as well let the kidnappers think you're really staying there.

"Driver?"

"Yes, sir?"

"Could you lose that car after we check into the Burgerspark? I'd make it worth your trouble."

"Certainly, sir!" the Indian replied, foreseeing a very good tip indeed. "You are in most excellent hands!"

The taxi climbed from the airport road onto the northbound side of Highway 21—the left side of the road, Hauer noticed, as in England—where a few lorries rumbled languidly toward Pretoria. Hauer wondered what he and Hans would find in the capital city. Had Ilse Apfel really been brought there? Or did she still wait somewhere back in snowbound Berlin? Was she still alive? The professional in Hauer doubted it, but some deeper part of him still held out hope. For Hans's sake, he supposed. He flattened his palm against the taxi's window and felt the heat. *Strange, this sudden change of seasons,* he thought. But he liked it. He felt good, and he knew he would feel even better once he'd met the enemy face to face.

"Thirty minutes to Pretoria, sir," Salil sang out.

"No hurry," Hauer lied, watching Hans carefully. "No hurry at all."

CHAPTER TWENTY-FOUR

2:45 A.M. The Northern Transvaal:
The Republic of South Africa

Ilse awakened slowly, like a diver fighting to the surface of a deep black lake. Finally aware, she found herself in a bed, tucked beneath cotton bedcovers. She was naked. Tacky residue from the tape that had bound her on the jet made the sheets stick to her skin. She tried to remember how she had lost her clothes, but could not. Her eyes darted around the room. The bedroom was sparsely but expensively furnished: an antique bureau, a chair, an end table, and the bed. No windows, just two doors—one half-open and leading to a bathroom, the other closed. No telephone. Nothing offered any clue as to where she was or what lay beyond the four walls. Wrapping the blanket tight around her, she climbed out of the bed and tried the closed door. It was locked. A moment later she found the note. It lay on the teak bureau, weighted by a silver hand mirror. Written in German on a small white card were the words:

> *Frau Apfel,*
> *Welcome to Horn House. Please make yourself*
> *presentable. All will be made clear at dinner.*
> *Alfred Horn*

When Ilse saw her face reflected in the hand mirror, she put a quivering finger to her cheek. Her fine blond hair hung in lank, dirty strands, and her usually luminous eyes looked gray and opaque beneath swollen lids. The shock of seeing herself in such a state drove her into the adjoining bathroom. Standing before a long mirror, she dropped the blanket from her shoulders and saw the welts left by the tape. Her face, neck, wrists, and ankles bore the angry red marks. Sudden panic wriggled in her chest; gooseflesh rose like quills on her arms and thighs. There were other marks too: deep blue bruises mottling her breasts and thighs. They reminded Ilse of the times when she and Hans had made love too roughly, except . . . this was different somehow. She looked as though she had been *fighting* someone. Had she—?

Oh God, she thought wildly, suddenly remembering. The lieutenant! The arrogant animal who had exposed himself to her on the plane! He had drugged her! Ilse remembered the needle lancing into her immobilized arm. The possibility that she had been raped while unconscious hit her in a hot, nauseous wave. Barely able to keep her balance, she stumbled into the shower and cranked on the hot water until it nearly scalded. She scrubbed her skin raw while the steaming spray obliterated her tears. Where *was* she? She had been airborne for a long time, she knew that. Her entire body ached. She felt as though she had slept thirty hours or more. She vaguely remembered the plane touching down—a jarring bump followed by murmured voices she did not understand—but it had lifted off again and she'd slipped back into a black void.

Rather than feel the hot water drain away slowly, Ilse shut it off altogether and let the frigid spray shock her back to reality. She screamed once, twice, but endured the icy torrent until her head pounded from the cold. Shutting it off at last, she wrapped one towel around her waist and used another to dry her hair.

In the bureau drawer she found some lotion, which she applied liberally to her swollen wrists and ankles. The air in the bedroom felt strangely warm. She let the towel fall and reached for her clothes, then with a start remembered that she had none. As she bent to retrieve her towel, she caught her reflection in a dressing mirror. Straightening up, she stared at her belly, drawn taut and flat from lack of food. With her forefinger she traced a line from her pubic triangle to her navel. *How long?* she wondered. *How long before you begin to show, little one?* A strange serenity slowly warmed Ilse's heart. In spite of the desperate situation, she felt a powerful conviction that she had but one obligation now—to *survive.* Not for herself, but for her child. And with this realization came a resolution: no matter what horrors or indig-

nities she might face in the next hours or days, she would
not act in any way that might cause her harm. Not even if
she wanted to die. Because harm done to her would be harm
done to her baby, and that was simply unacceptable. She still
felt nauseated, which was surprising because so far she had
not experienced any morning sickness. Then with a shiver
she again recalled the needle on the plane. *Oh no,* she
thought dizzily, her mouth suddenly dry. *Could the drug
have hurt my baby—?*

Without warning, the bedroom door banged open. Ilse
froze in terror. Looming in the doorway stood a black
woman who appeared to be at least six feet tall. She could
have been thirty or sixty; her ebony skin was smooth, but
her deep eyes glowed like ancient onyx stones.

"Madam will dress," she said in stilted German. She
stepped forward and set a soft bundle on the edge of the bed.

Ilse recognized the bundle as her clothes. They had been
washed and neatly folded. "Where am I?" she asked. "What
day is this?"

"Madam will dress, please," the woman repeated in a
deep, resonant voice. She pointed to the small end table by
the bed. "It is nearly three of the clock. I come in one quarter of the hour. Dinner then."

Before Ilse could speak again, the giant black woman
slipped out and shut the door. Ilse sprang forward, but the
doorknob would not turn. Alone again, she fought back another wave of tears and reached for her clothes.

Alfred Horn sat in his wheelchair in the study, his
hunched back to a low fire. He watched his Afrikaner security chief put down a red telephone. "Well, Pieter?"

"Linah says Frau Apfel is awake now, sir."

"She slept so long," Horn said worriedly. "I don't mind
waiting dinner, of course, even until three in the morning.
But it seems very odd."

Pieter Smuts sighed wearily. "Sir, do you really think you
have time to dally with this young girl?"

"Pieter, Pieter," Horn admonished. "It's much more than
that. I don't expect you to understand, but it's been so long
since I dined with a real German. And a *Frau* at that. Grant
me this indulgence."

Smuts looked unconvinced.

"What is she like, Pieter? Tell me."

"She's quite young. Early twenties, I'd guess. And beautiful, I must admit. Tall and slender with fair skin."

"Her hair?"

"Blond."

"Eyes?"

Smuts hesitated for an instant. "I didn't see her eyes, sir. She was unconscious when she arrived."

"Unconscious?" Horn asked sharply.

"I'm afraid so."

"But I instructed that no drugs of any kind be used."

"Yes, sir. I'm afraid Frau Apfel arrived in rather poor condition, sir. She had bruises about her legs and torso. I ordered the doctor to examine her. She wasn't sexually molested, but he thinks the police lieutenant who accompanied her from Berlin probably used an intravenous barbiturate to quiet her."

Quivering with rage, Horn wheeled around to face the fire. *"Can no one follow orders!"* he screeched. "Where is the swine?"

Smuts heard the old man wheezing, as if unable to get enough oxygen. "He's in one of the basement cells, sir. Do you have a particular punishment in mind?"

Horn did not reply, but when he finally turned back around, his distorted face had regained its composure. "All in good time," he mumbled. "Help me, Pieter."

Smuts moved behind the wheelchair, but the old man shook his head impatiently. "No, come around front."

"Beg your pardon, sir?"

"Help me up," Horn demanded.

"Up, sir?"

"Do it!"

Smuts bent slightly and with slim but powerful arms drew the old man bodily out of the chair. "Are you sure, sir?" he asked.

"Absolutely," Horn croaked, trying to subdue the pain in his ruined leg joints. "The *Jungfrau* will see me as a natural man before she sees me as . . . an invalid. Even after these past two years, Pieter, I still can't accept it. That I, once a superior athlete, should be reduced to this. It's obscene."

"It comes to all of us, sir," Smuts commiserated.

"That's no comfort. None at all. Is dinner ready?"

"When you are, sir."

Horn's thin legs trembled. "Let's go, then."

"Take my arm, sir."

"Only to the hallway, Pieter. Then I'm on my own."

Smuts nodded. He knew the old man was in great pain, but he also knew that if Alfred Horn meant to walk to the dining room under his own power, nothing would stop him.

Seated in the huge dining room, Ilse tried desperately to conceal the panic that knotted her stomach. She sensed the presence of the tall black woman behind her, watching. Fighting the urge to turn, she concentrated on the spectacular table. She had never seen such splendor gathered in one place before: Hutschenreuther china rimmed with eighteen-karat gold; fine lead crystal from Dresden; antique silver from Augsburg. The fact that each piece was of German manufacture reassured her. On the plane she had worried that her captors might take her out of the country; now she felt Hans could not be too far away. As she stared up into a sparkling chandelier, Alfred Horn appeared in the doorway and strode with slow dignity to the head of the table.

"*Guten Abend*, Frau Apfel," he said, inclining his white-haired head with courtly grace.

Ilse's heart leaped. The moment she saw the frail old man, she knew that he had the power to free her. In spite of Horn's advanced age, his gaze burned with an intensity Ilse had seen in very few men during her life. She started to her feet, but the strong hands of the Bantu woman pressed her firmly back into her seat.

Struggling to silence the screams of his arthritic knees, Alfred Horn seated himself. "Please," he said, "do me the honor of sharing my table before we discuss any details of this awkward situation. There will be no chains or rubber hoses here. You might even find this to be an enjoyable evening, if you but allow yourself to. Sit, Pieter."

Smuts took the nearest chair to Horn's left.

"Allow me to introduce myself," the old man said. "I am Alfred Horn, master of this house. The man across the table from you is my security chief, Pieter Smuts." Horn frowned at a large wooden clock hanging over the buffet to his right. "And any moment now," he added, "we should be joined by a young man who—"

A sudden flurry of footsteps in the hall heralded the arrival of the tardy guest, a young man who hurried in and took the seat next to Ilse without a word. He looked to be about Hans's age, perhaps a couple of years older. His neck was short and thick, his head a size too large—indeed all his features seemed a little oversized—and his sandy hair, though freshly combed, was wet. Beneath his sunburned nose, Ilse noticed something she saw all too often at parties in Berlin, the gleam of clear mucus that often betrayed the recent use of cocaine.

"You're late," Horn complained.

"Sorry," said the young man without a trace of apology. "There's a late rerun of the Open on the telly." He appraised Ilse with undisguised relish. "Who's this little plum, Alfred?"

"Frau Apfel," said Horn, annoyed, "may I introduce Lord Grenville? He's English, if you haven't surmised that already."

"How do you do, m'lady?" the young man asked too courteously, and offered his hand.

Ilse ignored it, keeping her eyes fixed on the white-haired man at the head of the table.

Horn's eyes twinkled. "Frau Apfel is not favorably impressed," he observed. Noticing Ilse's look of uneasiness, he softened his tone. "Linah—the Bantu woman behind you—remains only to bring us anything we require from the kitchen. Ask for whatever you like."

Ilse swallowed. "Do you mean I'm free to leave if I wish?"

Horn looked uncomfortable. "Not exactly, no. But you do have the run of the house and grounds—with certain restrictions. I think you'll find that out here on the veld, there isn't much of anywhere to go. Not without an airplane, in any case."

While Ilse pondered the word *veld*, Horn began to eat his salad. Linah lifted the covers off large dishes of split-pea soup, red cabbage, and dark pumpernickel bread—all classic German fare. A huge roast ham sat at center table, but Horn ignored it. He talked between healthy bites of the cabbage, acting more like a patriarch presiding over a gathering of distant relatives than a kidnapper toying with his hostage.

"You know," he said, his mouth full, "I've tried to adapt myself to African cuisine—if one ventures to call it such— but it simply doesn't compare to German food. Robust enough, of course, but terribly bland. Pieter loves the stuff. But then, he was raised on it."

Africa . . . ? Fighting the urge to bolt from the table, Ilse remembered her vow to behave as unprovocatively as possible. "So you're originally from Germany, then?" she stammered.

"Yes," Horn replied. "I'm something of an expatriate."

"Do you go back often?"

Horn stiffened for an instant, then resumed eating. "No," he said finally. "Never."

My God, she thought, her face hot. *Africa! No wonder it feels so warm here.* As Horn glanced around the table, Ilse realized that only one of the old man's eyes moved. The other remained fixed in whatever direction Horn's head faced. As she stared, she noticed faint scarring around the eye, stippled skin shaped in a rough five-pointed star. With a chill she forced herself to look away, but not before Horn caught her staring. He smiled understandingly.

"An old battle wound," he explained.

Lord Grenville forked a huge slab of ham onto his plate. "And what does a beautiful woman like you do in the Rhineland?" he asked, grinning.

"I believe the young lady works for a brokerage firm," Horn interjected.

Suddenly the double doors behind Horn bumped open. A young black man entered with a wheeled cart and took away the used dishes. A servant girl followed with another cart that bore an antique Russian samovar filled with steaming tea. She poured a brimming cup for Horn; Smuts, Grenville, and Ilse declined.

"I suppose you're wondering exactly where you are," Horn said. "You are now in the Republic of South Africa, and unless you neither watch television nor read the newspapers, I'm sure you know where that is."

Ilse clutched the tablecloth as her stomach rolled. "As a matter of fact," she said hoarsely, "my company maintained close ties with a South African firm before we ceased speculation in the Rand."

"You know something about our country, then?" Smuts asked.

"A little. What one sees on the news paints a pretty bleak picture."

"For some," Smuts said. "Not half as bad as they make out, though."

"I think what Pieter means," Horn said smoothly, "is

that ... *racial problems* in any society are always more complex than they appear to an outsider. Look at the Asian question the White Russians must soon face. In twenty years the Soviet Union will be over forty percent Islam. Think of it! Look at America. For all their bluster about equality, the Americans have seen abuses as bad as those anywhere. In South Africa, Frau Apfel, prejudice does not wear a mask. And no one will forgive us for that. Because South Africa admits something that the rest of the world would prefer to hide, the world hates us."

"Do you think that's an excuse?"

"We're not looking for excuses," Smuts muttered.

"Simply an observation," Horn said, glaring at Smuts.

"Isn't this bloody *marvelous*," Lord Grenville crowed. "Two Germans and a bloody Afrikaner debating the finer points of race relations! It's *really* too much." He poured himself a second brandy from a bottle he had claimed as his own.

"You think England's any better?" Smuts snapped. "All you've ever seen of it is public schools and polo fields, you—"

"Pieter," Horn cut in. He turned to Ilse. "Herr Smuts is what the Americans call a self-made man, my dear. He views the aristocracy as something of an obsolete class."

"That's one view I sympathize with."

The Afrikaner inclined his head respectfully, his smoking gaze still on the Englishman.

"Actually," said Horn, "even the South Africans shrink from truly effective measures in the race question."

"Effective measures?"

"State-sponsored sterilization, my dear. It's the only answer. We can't expect *kaffirs* or Mohammedan savages to regulate their own breeding habits. One might as well expect the same of cattle. No, the government health services should simply sterilize each black female after the birth of her first child. An entire *spectrum* of problems would disappear within a single generation."

While Ilse stared in astonishment, Horn signaled to the stone-faced Linah, who brought him a thick Upmann cigar, clipped and ready to light. He did so without asking if anyone minded, took several puffs, then exhaled the smoke in deep blue clouds that wafted gently above the table.

"Well," he said finally, "I'm sure you have many questions. I'll try to answer what I can."

Ilse had not even touched her salad. Now she set her quivering hands flat on the table and took a deep breath. "Why am I here?" she asked softly.

"Quite simply," Horn replied, "because of your husband. I'm afraid your Hans stumbled upon a document that belonged to a man I knew well—a document he should have turned over to the proper authorities, but did not. Pieter decided that the most expeditious method of recovering the property was through you. That is why you are here. As soon as your husband arrives, the matter will be resolved."

Ilse felt a flutter of hope. "Hans is coming here?"

Horn glanced at his watch. "He should be on his way now."

"Does he know I'm safe?"

Smuts answered. "He heard the tape you made."

Ilse shivered, recalling the gun held to her head by the wild-eyed Lieutenant Luhr.

Horn blew a smoke ring. "I assure you that such unpleasantness will not be repeated. The man who drugged you on the plane is now in a cell a hundred meters beneath your feet." Horn smiled. "Now, if I may, I'd like to ask your opinion of the document your husband discovered in Spandau Prison."

Ilse studied her hands. "What about it? It looked like a hoax to me. Things like that have come up a dozen times since the war—"

"Please," Horn interrupted, his tone harder, "do not try my patience. Your discussion with Prefect Funk indicated that you well understood the importance of the papers."

"I only thought that they might be dangerous! I knew that because Hans found them in Spandau they'd probably been written by a war criminal. Because of that—"

"Excuse me, Frau Apfel." Horn's single eye settled on Ilse's face. "How would you define that term—*war criminal*? I'm curious."

Ilse swallowed. "Well . . . I suppose it means someone who has departed from the laws of morality so radically that it shocks the civilized world, even in time of war."

Horn smiled sadly. "Very articulate, my dear, but completely incorrect. A war criminal is merely a powerful man on the side that happens to lose a war. Nothing more, nothing less. Was Caesar a war criminal? By your definition, yes. By mine? No. Was Alexander? Was Stalin? In 1944, Marshal Zhukov's Red Army raped, murdered, and looted its way across Germany. Was Zhukov a war criminal? No. But Hitler? Of course! The Anti-Christ! You see? The label means nothing in absolute terms. It's simply a relative description."

"That's not true. What the Nazis did in the concentration camps—"

"Maintained the German war economy and furthered medical science for the entire world!" Horn finished. "Of course there were excesses—that's human nature. But does anyone ever mention the advances that were made?"

"You don't believe that. Nothing justifies such cruelty."

Horn shook his head. "I can see that the Zionists have kept a firm grip on our country's schools since the war. DeNazification," he snorted. "My God, you sound just like an Israeli schoolchild. Can you be so *blind*? In 1945 the Allied Air Forces attacked Dresden—an open city—and killed 135,000 German civilians, mostly women and children. President Truman *obliterated* two Japanese cities. That is not criminal?"

"Then why is hiding the Spandau diary so important to you?" Ilse challenged. "Why not let it be known and publicly argue your case, whatever it is?"

Horn looked at the table. "Because some chapters of history are best left closed. The case of Rudolf Hess has had a startling long-lived effect on relations between England, Germany, and Russia. It's in the best interest of all concerned to let sleeping dogs lie."

"But that's what I don't understand. What does it *matter* what happened fifty years ago?"

"Nations have very long memories," Horn said.

"What happened to Rudolf Hess?" Ilse suddenly asked. "The *real* Hess."

"He died," Horn said. "In Resistencia, Paraguay, in 1947. I knew him well, and he died a bitter man, less than two years after his beloved Führer."

"Beloved?" Ilse echoed, horrified. "But the man in Spandau—who was he?"

"No one," Horn said. "Anyone. The poor fool was part of a failed gambit in foreign policy, that's all. But the result of that failure was that he had to remain in prison—*as Hess*—

for the rest of his life. That is all in the past. Unfortunately, your husband reopened this sticky little case, and now it must be closed again. For me it is a small annoyance, but one cannot ignore details. 'For want of a nail ...' "

" 'For want of a nail,' " Ilse said thoughtfully, " 'the kingdom was lost.' What is the 'kingdom' in this case?"

Horn smiled. "My company, of course. Phoenix AG."

Ilse looked thoughtful. "I don't recall seeing that name listed on any stock exchange."

"I'm sure you don't. It's a private holding company. If I were to furnish you with a list of my worldwide subsidiaries, however, I'm sure you would recognize quite a few."

Smuts smiled at Horn's understatement.

Ilse was genuinely curious. "So you're multinational, then. How big are you? Two, three hundred million in revenues?"

The young Englishman snickered.

"Three hundred million in *assets*," Horn corrected softly.

Ilse stared, incredulous. "But that would put your revenues at over a billion dollars."

There was silence until Horn gracefully resumed the conversation. "I see you have a keen interest in business. Why don't we excuse Pieter and Lord Grenville? You and I can continue our discussion without boring them. Gentlemen?"

"But I find this discussion extremely interesting," the Englishman protested.

"Nevertheless," Horn said icily.

"How about some billiards, Smuts?" the Englishman asked gamely, trying to preserve some illusion of free will.

Horn's stare commanded the reluctant Afrikaner to accept the invitation.

"Don't suppose I'd mind taking a few rand off you," Smuts said, chuckling. He had a brittle laugh, like a man who finds humor only at others' expense. He gave Horn a shallow bow as they went out.

"That man seems quite devoted to you," Ilse observed.

"Herr Smuts is my chief of security. His loyalty is absolute."

"Are you in danger?"

Horn smiled. "A man in my position makes enemies, Frau Apfel."

Suddenly Ilse's eyes glistened with moisture. The plea she had pressed down deep in her heart welled up into her throat at last. "Sir, please, isn't there some way that you could forgive my husband? He meant no harm! If you only knew him, you would see—"

"Frau Apfel! Control yourself! We will not discuss the matter again until your husband arrives. At that time I shall decide what is to be done—not before. Is that clear?"

Ilse wiped her eyes with her linen napkin. "Yes ... yes, I'm sorry."

"There's no need to be sorry. Women are at the mercy of their emotions; it's their biological flaw. If it weren't for that regrettable fact, who knows what they might have accomplished throughout history."

Ilse remained silent. She saw nothing to be gained by antagonizing her captor further.

"Frau Apfel," Horn said, "the reason I excused the others was to invite you to attend a business meeting with me tomorrow evening. The gentlemen I'm meeting have a rather medieval attitude toward your sex, I'm afraid, so you would have to pose as my secretary. But I'm certain you would find the negotiations extremely interesting." Horn raised his chin. "It will be the first meeting of its kind in history."

"It sounds ominous," Ilse said, trying to regain her composure.

"Let us say 'momentous' instead. It's only business, after all. I'm sure the experience would prove invaluable to a young woman who plans a career in the world of finance."

In spite of her perilous situation—or perhaps because of it—Ilse accepted the invitation.

"Linah?" Horn called.

The tall Bantu woman appeared instantly.

"Escort Frau Apfel to the billiards room."

Ilse rose to go.

"And Frau Apfel," Horn said, "would you ask Pieter to join me when he has finished his game?"

Ilse nodded.

"You won't see me until tomorrow afternoon, possibly not until tomorrow evening. Pieter will show you around the estate in the morning. Certain rooms are locked, but you have the run of the house and grounds otherwise. Please refrain from using the telephone until the matter of the papers has been resolved."

With the touch of a button Horn wheeled his chair around the table. "May I see your hand?"

Puzzled, Ilse slowly extended her hand. Before she knew what was happening, the wizened old man had bent his head and lightly kissed it. She felt a sudden chill, but whether from physical revulsion or some deeper fear, she could not tell.

"I apologize for the young Englishman's rudeness," Horn said. "I shouldn't tolerate it, but his grandfather and I worked together during the war." Horn smiled wistfully. "His grandfather was a very special man, and I feel some responsibility for his heir. *Gute Nacht*, my dear."

The tall Bantu housekeeper took Ilse's elbow and led her into the hall, where she let Ilse take the lead. Ilse had the feeling that the woman's arm was but a fraction of an inch behind her own, ready to seize her if necessary. The long hall opened into a large gallery, which in turn gave onto two more beyond, each great room joined by means of a wide arch. Ilse gasped. As far as she could see, the walls were lined with paintings. She knew a little about art, but the works she saw in the first room required no training to appreciate. The strokes of the great masters speak to a part of the psyche deeper than thought, and these were no reproductions. Each canvas glowed with immanent passion; Ilse's eyes danced from painting to painting in wonder.

"My God," she murmured. "Where *are* we?"

Linah caught hold of Ilse's arm and tugged her along like an awestruck child. Even the marble floors bore their share of the treasure. Classical sculptures, some over twelve feet high, rose like marble ghosts from pedestals in the center of each room. Ilse noticed that no work in any of the rooms seemed modern. Nothing had the asymmetrical distortions of Picasso, the geometric puzzles of Mondrian, or the radically commonplace ugliness of the "sculpture" so common in Berlin office parks. Everything was soft, romantic, inward-pulling. Had she not been so stunned, she might have noticed that all the objets d'art—Egyptian and Greek sculpture, paintings from Holland, Belgium, and France—had come from countries plundered behind the merciless boot of the *Wehrmacht* during the 'thirties and 'forties. But she didn't notice. She simply stared until the dazzling exhibition ended and she found herself in the dark, wood-paneled billiards room where Pieter Smuts and the young Englishman had finished their second game.

"Well, take your bloody winnings!" Lord Grenville snapped.

"Don't mind if I do," Smuts retorted, grinning. He pocketed the crisp fifty-pound note that the Englishman handed over as casually as a wrinkled fiver.

"Herr Smuts?" Ilse said. "Herr Horn wishes you to join him."

The Afrikaner's smile faded as he hurried into the hallway.

"Up for a game, Fräulein?" the Englishman asked, tilting his cue toward Ilse.

"It's *Frau*," Ilse corrected coldly. "And I'd prefer to return to my room."

As Linah turned to lead her out, Ilse got the impression that the Bantu woman approved of her decision not to remain. But as she followed the housekeeper out, she felt a light touch on her arm.

"Why not stay a moment?" whispered the Englishman. "It might do wonders for your husband's health."

Ilse froze. Without even thinking, she told Linah that she'd changed her mind. She would play one game before she retired.

The tall Bantu eyed the Englishman warily through the door. "I watch for Madam in the hall," she said. "You come soon."

"Soon," Ilse promised, closing the door.

"What do you know about my husband?" she asked pointedly.

"Not so fast, *Fräulein*." The Englishman racked the balls for another game. "Why don't you try being friendly? Since we're the only two civilized people in this godforsaken place."

"What do you mean?"

"What do you think I mean? Couldn't you tell at dinner? They're mad as hatters, both of them! I'm almost mad myself from listening to them. I'm also the only chance you have of getting yourself and your husband out of here alive. Break."

Ilse took a cue from the wall, walked to the table and opened the game by sinking the one and the five. She didn't know what to make of the arrogant Englishman. She suspected this was a trick to extract information from her, yet a voice deep inside her said to try to use this man—to try anything that might help her escape.

"How did you come to be here?" she asked. "I assume you weren't kidnapped, like me?"

The Englishman chuckled. "Not exactly. But I wouldn't be averse to leaving, I can tell you that. For some years now Herr Horn and I have been involved in a very profitable business arrangement. Until recently it's been mostly from a distance. Alfred knew my grandfather—William Stanton, Lord Grenville—before the war. I'm afraid my character runs a bit differently than my grandfather's, though. My primary interest is making money. Along with certain other distractions."

"Herr Horn is not interested in money?"

"Not for its own sake, no. He's very political. Fancies himself a bloody Messiah, if you want to know. He and my grandfather did something big in England during the war, though neither of them ever told me what. Alfred has some kind of political agenda that dictates every move he makes. All very hush-hush. And very silly, if you ask me."

"Does he ask you?"

The Englishman tried an extravagant bank shot and muffed it. "No," he said, "he doesn't."

"Lord Grenville," Ilse mused. "Is that a real title?"

"Yes, actually. I really am a lord. My name is Robert Stanton, Lord Grenville. Call me Robert, if you like."

"What about the other man?"

"The Afrikaner? Smuts? He's a commoner. A real bastard." Stanton chuckled. "A real common bastard, that's him. He's Horn's chief of security. I don't like him, but I stay clear of him, you know? He'd like to cut my throat some dark night."

"Why doesn't he?"

"Alfred protects me. Or he has up till now, at any rate. But my protector's patience wears thin . . ."

Ilse pocketed the three, nine and fifteen before missing the seven in the side pocket.

"Very nice, *Fräulein.*" Stanton eyed Ilse's hips. "Yes, I'm getting the feeling that dear Alfred's use for me is rapidly coming to an end. And I don't fancy waiting for the axe to fall."

"Exactly what business are you and Herr Horn in?"

Stanton sank the twelve with a crack. "Import-export."

"Of what?"

"Drugs. And money, of course. Lots of pretty pounds."

"Pharmaceutical drugs?"

Stanton laughed. "The odd lot now and then. But we generally handle drugs in their more elementary state. Morphine base, poppies, ether, coca paste . . ."

"*Narcotics* are the basis of Herr Horn's empire?"

"No, no. He's ninety percent legitimate now. But our little joint venture provides him with quite a bit of untraceable cash. That's a valuable commodity in the business world, as you probably know, rarer and rarer these days."

"I see."

"Don't think 'legitimate' carries any great moral weight, though. Alfred brokers chemicals to Iraq for weapons, conventional arms to the third world, nuclear and computer technology to half a dozen maniac governments—it makes the narcotics business look like a bloody jumble sale."

"So what exactly do you want from me?" Ilse asked warily.

Stanton stepped close to her. "I want to know what the old man's planning," he whispered. "Something big is in the works, and I think he's going to let you in on it. The old bird's got the idea you're some kind of avatar of Teutonic womanhood. He's mad about you."

"No," Ilse said quickly, fighting a strong feeling that Stanton's words were true. "You're wrong."

"Spare me, *Fräulein*. I can see it."

Ilse moved to leave, but Stanton barred the door. "If you find out anything," he said, "you come see me. I can help you."

Ilse tried to pass, but Stanton remained in front of her. "If you don't," he warned, "neither you nor your husband will get out of this house alive, I guarantee it."

Ilse stopped trying to pass and looked into Stanton's eyes. "What do you mean?"

"Nothing at all, love. But you think about it. Do you really believe that one-eyed madman brought you all the way here just to send you smiling back to Germany? Five thousand bloody miles?"

Ilse shook her head in denial.

"Come on, *Fräulein*, you're no fool." Stanton caught Ilse's shoulders and drew her tight against him. "I'll tell you something else for free," he said heavily. "Alfred's got the right idea, but he's much too old for you."

He pressed his mouth hard against hers. Ilse twisted her head away roughly. "Let go of me! Let me *go!*"

Stanton groped for her breasts. Truly frightened now, Ilse caught his arms and tried to push him away. Just as he got one hand free and raised it to strike, someone flung open the door.

Tall and menacing, the Bantu housekeeper fixed her imperious gaze on the Englishman. "Time for bed, Madam," she said in a dangerous voice.

"Yes—yes, thank you, Linah," Ilse stammered.

"Bloody *wog*," said Stanton. "You ought to keep out of where you're not wanted. I'm going to talk to Master about you."

Her face unchanging, Linah pulled the door shut and led Ilse to her bedroom.

"Thank you," Ilse said again.

Linah looked deep into her eyes. "Careful with the English, Madam," she said in her deep voice. "He is spoilt, and does not understand 'no.' "

Ilse listened hopefully as Linah shut the door, but the lock clicked fast.

Back in the dining room, Alfred Horn addressed Smuts liked a general briefing his adjutant before a battle.

"The airstrip extension?"

"One hundred feet to go, sir. They finished the southeast end at dusk. It should set up fine by tomorrow night."

"Is the basement secure?"

"Tight as a Zulu drum."

"What about the conference room video cameras? We *must* have a record of this meeting. Our fallback plan depends on it."

"All four cameras loaded and in position, sir."

"Any questions for me, Pieter?"

"What about the policeman in the basement? Lieutenant Luhr."

Horn's face hardened. "He's fine where he is until after the meeting."

"And the girl?"

"I'm quite taken with her, Pieter. I've asked her to sit in tomorrow night as my secretary."

"*What!*"

"No arguments," Horn said. "I've decided."

"But the Arabs won't stand for a woman there!"

Horn smiled. "What can they say? I am the only man who possesses the commodity they want. They certainly can't afford to make trouble about a secretary."

Smuts shook his head. "What about Stanton? He's getting insufferable."

"I agree," said Horn. "But you should have known his grandfather, Pieter, a visionary. It's a good thing he's not around to see his heir."

Smuts grunted in agreement.

"Let Robert take this last delivery, Pieter. Two million rand in gold bullion is worth waiting for, I think. Then he's yours."

Smuts grinned a death's-head.

"Less than twenty-four hours now," Horn intoned. "The wheels are in motion." He looked up. "Take me to the study, Pieter. I want to sit by the fire."

"Should I get the chair?"

"No. I feel strong. Tonight I walk like a man."

"A man among men, sir," Smuts said reverently.

"Thank you, Pieter. The last of a breed, it's true."

Together the two men—one ancient, the other in his midforties—set out upon the long journey to the study, where the old one would await the dawn with bright, unsleeping eyes.

CHAPTER TWENTY-FIVE

9:30 A.M. *Horn House: The Northern Transvaal*

Ilse had no warning of the horror to come. She had awakened several times during the night, but the periods of sleep had been mercifully dreamless. When her door opened, she expected to find the tall Bantu housekeeper waiting behind it. Instead she saw Pieter Smuts, Horn's Afrikaner security chief. Smuts's smile did not quite reach his eyes.

"I'm here to give you the threepenny tour," he announced.

"That's not really necessary," Ilse said uneasily. "I'm sure I can find my way around."

Smuts sighed with enough resignation to indicate he would remain in the doorway as long as he had to. After closing the door and dressing, Ilse allowed herself to be led out of the room and down the long corridor. The lanky Afrikaner towered above her. Again she felt like a child being led through a museum. Smuts delivered his information in a monotone.

"Horn House," he said, "stands in one of the most isolated regions of South Africa—the northeast corner of the northern Transvaal. Boer country. The nearest town is Giyani to the west, and the nearest landmark to the east is the Kruger National Park. Not many roads up here to speak of."

Point taken, Ilse thought bitterly.

"The estate itself is one of a kind, as you'll see when you get outside. The residential compound encompasses twelve thousand square feet of living space. We've got an indoor swimming pool, a gymnasium, an art gallery, an astronomical observatory, and something quite unusual for a private dwelling—a hospital. Because of Herr Horn's advanced age, he suffers from a number of chronic conditions, but here he is able to obtain optimum health care at all times. The medical complex is at the end of this hall. We have a resident cardiologist on duty at all times."

"My God," Ilse said, genuinely shocked.

"The cost of maintaining this unit out on the veld like this would bankrupt a small town," Smuts boasted, "but for Herr Horn . . . ah, here we are."

They had come to a door with no knob; brass letters on its face read KRANKENHAUS. Smuts pushed open the door. "After you," he said.

The astringent smell of alcohol and disinfectant wrinkled Ilse's nose. She found herself in a large examining room replete with all the paraphernalia of modern medicine. Blood chemistry machines, centrifuges, autoclaves, and various instruments lined the shining countertops. Two doors were set in the opposite wall. Smuts led her to the one marked ICU. Behind it was a fully equipped intensive care facility. Cardiac monitor screens, a defibrillator cart, a ventilator, and two cylinders of oxygen waited beside an electric hospital bed. Ilse wondered if Horn was in poorer health than he appeared. "Very impressive," she said, not knowing what else to say.

Smuts nodded curtly and led her out, closing the door softly behind them. The other door was marked only with a warning symbol—three inverted yellow triangles inside a circle of black. Smuts opened the door and stepped inside, motioning for Ilse to follow.

"This is our X-ray unit," he said. "It's state of the art, but I'm afraid our cardiologist has to do double duty as a radiographer. He's not too happy about that, as you might—"

The moment Ilse stepped across the threshold, someone seized her violently from behind, pinning her arms to her sides. Before she could scream, Smuts stuffed a handkerchief into her mouth. The unseen attacker lifted her off her feet, then heaved her high and dropped her heavily onto a hard surface. An ugly, sweating black face appeared above her; powerful hands crushed her flailing arms against the cold Formica while Smuts worked at something she could not see. Primal terror gripped her. Even without seeing the thick leather belts that now bound her to the table, Ilse registered and identified the sensation. *Restraining straps,* she thought wildly. White light speared into her brain from above.

"Be still!" Smuts shouted. "Be *still!*"

Ilse drew in all the breath she could and tried to scream, but the bunched handkerchief in her mouth choked her effort to an anguished groan. Her throat felt near to bursting. The man panting above her was so black he looked blue. He buckled a thick strap across Ilse's chest, then forced her right cheek flat against the table and fastened another strap across her head. All she could see now was a huge lead shield. Pieter Smuts's hard, angular face floated inside a thick bubble window set in its middle.

Ilse struggled to rise, but the heavy-buckled straps held her motionless. When she tried to shift even slightly, the straps scoured her flesh like sandpaper. As she lay there, chest heaving, Smuts stepped around the lead shield. From his right hand a long cable dropped to the floor and snaked around the shield to the X-ray machine. With his left hand Smuts reached up and took hold of a hammerhead-shaped mechanism suspended above Ilse's head. The X-ray tube. Painted a metallic orange, it hovered above Ilse like an alien being, a deadly thing that moved silently on tracks and cables. Smuts raised the housing to its highest position; then he returned to safety behind the lead shield.

Two seconds later every muscle in Ilse's body constricted in terror. A deep electrical surge, a subsonic roar shuddered through the table, lasting three full seconds before it ceased with a sharp clang. Ilse's mouth went dry. Her forehead beaded with sweat. Just as she realized what the sound signaled, it came again, the heart-stopping buzz of electricity converted into a barrage of irradiated particles and fired through her body like invisible bullets. Her teeth ground furiously as she fought the leather straps. The hide scraped her flesh raw. Again the awful sound came. Ilse heard herself screaming, the voice tiny and shrill and meaningless inside her head. *What have I done? What do you want!* Without a single word from Smuts, she had made the mental leap from resistance to abject servitude. She sought only to know what was required of her, and she would comply. Yet still the machine fired. Deeper than sound, she sensed a vibration barely within the realm of human perception, the vibration of accelerated electrons focused into a beam that, even when guided by healing hands, poured deadly poison into living cells. The sound came again and again, until finally, in a silence made deeper by Ilse's utter despair, Smuts stepped around the shield, the cable trigger in his hand, and began to speak.

"Frau Apfel," he said. "I don't believe in messing about— not where my job is concerned. You have certain information I need, and you are going to provide it."

Ilse tried to nod beneath the head strap.

"During the past several minutes, I have exposed you to the maximum allowable three-year dosage of radiation for a nuclear plant worker. In an hour or so, you will probably experience some nausea and vomiting, but let us hope that is all you must endure. Far worse outcomes are still possible. Blindness, burns . . . other things." Smuts held a finger in Ilse's face. "What happens next, Frau Apfel, is up to you."

While Ilse stared with wild eyes, the Afrikaner crouched and laid the cable trigger on the floor. Then he stood, loosened a bolt on the housing above Ilse, and lowered the hammerhead barrel to a position six inches above her abdomen. He tightened the bolt again, locking it in place.

"Frau Apfel, I am going to remove the gag now, and you will cooperate fully. I have focused the X-ray beam on the approximate area of your ovaries. Radiation has an enhanced effect on such cells—cells that are still dividing, as it were. Exposure in this region could seriously jeopardize your chances of ever having children." Smuts grinned. "Are you ready to talk?"

Ilse's eyes widened in horror. Her *baby!* She began to shiver uncontrollably. Her urinary sphincter let go, flooding both her dress and the table. Smuts drew back from the pungent smell. As he reached for the handkerchief gag, tears welled up in Ilse's eyes and streamed down onto the table.

"Listen," said the Afrikaner, his voice slightly softer. "As of this moment you are still all right. Only if you refuse to answer will you be injured. The dosage you have received so far would only be excessive for a woman already pregnant."

Ilse's body convulsed against the straps. She fought like an animal, expending every ounce of her remaining strength. Smuts—who had used this interrogation technique on many previous occasions—could not recall anyone resisting so fiercely once the prospect of escape had been offered. One never knew who the tough ones would be, he reflected. When Ilse finally went limp, he loosened the strap at her head and carefully removed the gag.

"Now," he said. "I need to know some things about your husband. Can you hear me?"

Ilse's eyes opened. Slowly she focused on Smuts's face.

"Good. Your husband did not take the plane he was instructed to take to Johannesburg. Nor has he checked into the hotel he was ordered to stay in. By the terms of the agreement, he has already forfeited your life. Why would he do that? Doesn't he want to save you?"

Ilse closed her eyes. More tears dribbled out. When she opened her eyes again, Smuts was shaking the cable trigger in her face. "Does your husband have any Jewish blood in his family?"

Ilse shook her head, her eyes blank in despair. Smuts stepped momentarily out of her field of vision, then reappeared with a damp rag. He squeezed a few drops of water into her mouth.

"Now," he said. "No Jewish blood?"

"No," Ilse coughed.

"What about friends? Does he have any Jewish friends? Has Hans ever been to Israel?"

Ilse shook her head.

"You're sure? What about England? Or anywhere else in Britain?"

"No."

"What is your husband's connection with Captain Dieter Hauer?"

Ilse hesitated. "Fr—friend," she rasped. It was difficult to concentrate hard enough to lie, but she sensed that to reveal Hans's blood relationship to Hauer might somehow be dangerous.

"Are you aware that Captain Hauer works with the German counterterror unit GSG-9?"

Ilse silently mouthed the word no.

"Undoubtedly your husband is." Smuts clucked his tongue thoughtfully. "I want you to tell me about the Spandau papers. Did your husband show them to anyone before you gave them to your grandfather?"

Ilse shook her head again.

"Do you understand these questions?"

She nodded.

"Think carefully, Frau Apfel. Think about the names you saw in the Spandau papers. Did you see the name Alfred Horn?"

"No."

"You didn't recognize the name when Herr Horn introduced himself last night?"

"No."

"You were staring at his eye—his artificial eye. Why were you so interested in that? Did you come here expecting to find a man with one eye?"

"I couldn't help staring."

"What names *were* in the Spandau papers?"

Ilse's voice cracked as she spoke. "Hess, of course. Hitler. Hermann Göring. Reinhard Heydrich, I think."

Smuts nodded. "Did you see the name Zinoviev?" he asked softly. "It's a Russian name."

Ilse thought a moment, shook her head.

"Helmut? Did you see that name?" Smuts shook the trigger in her face. *"Did you?"*

"No!"

"Frau Apfel," he said coldly, "if you're thinking of informing Herr Horn of what happened here this morning, I tell you now to abandon the idea. Whatever his reaction might be, I assure you that it is within my power to have you back on this table before anything could be done to me. Do you understand?"

"Oh God!" Ilse wailed, her voice choking into a sob. "You *bastard*! You've hurt my baby! You've killed my *baby*!"

Smuts's eyes widened. "You are pregnant now?"

"You know that! I said so on the tape!" Ilse squeezed her swollen eyes shut in anguish. She did not feel Smuts unbuckling the leather straps; only when she felt herself lifted from the table did she look again. The Afrikaner carried her over to the lead shield, then behind it to where the tall, rectangular X-ray machine stood with its glowing dials and meters.

"Look!" he said angrily. "Look here!" His tanned hand pointed to a scalloped black knob. "This displays MA—milliamperes. It's the measure of radiation." He moved his hand to another dial. "This is KV—kilovolts. It's the measure of power driving the tube. *Look, woman!*"

Ilse looked. Both dials were set at zero. She coughed and rubbed her eyes, fighting down waves of nausea.

"Do you *understand*?" Smuts asked. "I never heard the

tape you made, but it doesn't matter. You have received no radiation! You are *all right*. Your child is unhurt!"

Ilse looked into the Afrikaner's eyes for deception, but saw none. "Wh—why?" she stammered.

"I protect Herr Horn, Frau Apfel. At any cost. I had to know that you would tell the truth. And you did, didn't you?"

Ilse nodded, wiping her face on her blouse.

"Good. Now get back to your room and clean yourself up. Herr Horn is not to see you like this." His eyes fixed Ilse with frightening intensity. "But you remember what that table felt like. When Herr Horn asks you to do something, you do it, no matter how crazy it might sound. *Especially* at tonight's meeting. Remember your child, Frau Apfel. I can have you back on that table any time I decide. *Any* time!"

Unable to restrain herself any longer, Ilse clenched her stomach with both hands, doubled over, and vomited on the Afrikaner's boots.

Shaking with rage, Smuts stormed out and went in search of his Zulu driver, leaving Ilse coughing on the floor. He could not believe he had to put up with such outrages. Perhaps after tonight's business had been concluded, Horn would see that the best policy was to kill the girl and be done with it. The husband could be killed as soon as he turned over the Spandau papers, and the Berlin police could take care of the girl's grandfather at their leisure. Things were so simple, if people would only focus on the facts. As Smuts passed through the spectacular gallery rooms, he tried in vain to ignore the stench rising from his boots.

9:58 A.M. *Tempelhof Airport: American Sector, West Berlin, FRG*

Detective Julius Schneider climbed out of the Iroquois helicopter gunship and shook his head in wonder. Colonel Rose, bundled to the eyeballs in a goosedown parka, stood on the tarmac beside a drab Army Ford. Sergeant Clary waited faithfully at the wheel. Rose's face was clean shaven, but his eyes were red and swollen. He waved Schneider into the Ford. Pressing his hat to his head to keep the icy wind from blowing it off, the big German ran to the car and climbed in.

Rose skipped the formalities. "The shit has hit the fan,

Schneider. Remember my FBI guy? The one who was going to get that Zinoviev file for us?"

Schneider nodded.

"Well, he got it. He Fed-Exed a copy to me at nine-thirty this morning." Rose shook his head. "Ten minutes later he was arrested on charges of espionage. His computer query on Zinoviev apparently rang some kind of warning bell at Langley, and that set the dogs on him. I guess the FBI computers aren't as secure as the Bureau likes to think they are."

"What was in this Zinoviev file?" Schneider asked.

"We won't know till tomorrow when I get the file. *If* I get the file. If the FBI knows he shipped it, they can probably stop it before it gets here. If it *does* get here, I've got Ivan Kosov waiting to double-check what he can in the KGB files."

Schneider scowled. "Why do you need Kosov?"

"When my buddy called, he told me a little about the Zinoviev file, Schneider. He said the file claims that the United States, Britain, and the Russians have all known for years that Prisoner Number Seven was not Rudolf Hess."

Schneider's eyes narrowed.

"I asked him why, if that was true, the Russians had kept quiet about it all these years. You know what he told me? He said it didn't matter *what* the Russians knew about Hess, because in 1943 Winston Churchill *blackmailed* Stalin into silence."

Schneider looked bewildered. "What do you mean? Blackmailed him with what?"

Rose shrugged. "My guy said it had to do with Zinoviev's part in Hess's mission, but that it was too complicated to explain on the phone. He said I wouldn't believe it when I saw it, but that the Russians were the good guys in this mess. I told him I *would* believe it, and that I thought the Brits were still neck-deep in some kind of stinking coverup." Rose's eyes flickered. "He told me I might be right, Schneider. But I guess we'll have to wait for our copy of the Zinoviev file to find out."

"Where is your new partner now?" Schneider asked.

Rose hooked his thumb toward Tempelhof's observation deck, eighty meters away. Above the rail Schneider saw a solitary figure wearing a hat and a raincoat, the only person braving the cold of the deck.

"There he is," Rose said. "A week ago I'd have considered it sacrilege to bring that bastard to the home of the Berlin Airlift. Today I trust him more than some of my own people."

Schneider looked skeptical. "Why are you here now?"

"To give you a little tactical update, my friend. One hour ago Prefect Funk arrested one of your brother officers on espionage charges. Seems this guy was passing secret information to the British government."

"Scheisse!"

Rose nodded in disgust. "You should regard everything we knew as of this morning—including the names on Hauer and Apfel's false passports—as blown to the Brits. If you get anywhere near those cops, Schneider, you keep your eyes peeled for British spooks."

Rose looked out the window at an F-16 fighter parked in a concrete revetment twenty meters away. "One more thing," he said. "Kosov told me to tell you to watch your back. He wouldn't tell me why. I think he's in the same spot I am, Schneider. He doesn't know who to trust. He wants to help me, but he's being muzzled from above. I think he's waiting for some kind of clearance to come clean with me."

Schneider grunted. It wasn't easy for a German to see any Russian in a positive light. "Don't trust him too much, Colonel," he said. "Kosov would sacrifice you without a thought."

"You worry about your own ass," Rose advised. "Kosov's got enough to do without yanking my chain. Moscow went nuts when they found out about Axel Goltz's mutiny. The KGB is interrogating every Stasi agent in Berlin, trying to figure out what's going on. If they crack this Phoenix thing, they'll be lining those tattooed bastards up against the Wall by the dozen and passing out blindfolds and cigarettes." Rose punched a stiff forefinger into Schneider's barrel chest. "If you find Hauer and Apfel, you bring 'em back here with the papers. Hauer's probably the only guy who can straighten this mess out now. And those Spandau papers are the only thing that could buy my ass out of the sling. Oh yeah, one more thing. If you happen to find the guy who killed Harry Richardson"—Rose smacked the car window with the meaty end of his fist—"you have my permission to gut and skin the son of a bitch. Briefing concluded, Detective."

Schneider smiled coldly. *"Auf Wiedersehen, Herr Oberst."*

He climbed out of the Ford and clambered into the waiting gunship. He was still 150 miles from Frankfurt Airport, and thirteen air-hours away from South Africa. Plenty of time left to figure out how he was going to find Hauer, and plenty of time to figure out what he was going to say when he did. The questions he could not get out of his mind were the ones Rose had barely touched on. What was Phoenix, really? Was it a secret subsect of *Der Bruderschaft*? If so, if it was a neo-fascist group that had penetrated both the police and political hierarchies, Schneider feared not only for his police department, but for Germany itself. The primary goal of all neo-Nazis was German reunification. It was easy enough to see that a premature grab for that goal could result in catastrophe for the country. Russia might be flirting with *glasnost* and *perestroika*, but faced with the specter of two fascist-led Germanys pressing for reunification, the nation that had lost twenty million citizens to Hitler's armies might respond with unimaginable force and fury.

Kosov's warning to Colonel Rose about "watching his back" brought Schneider back to more immediate concerns. Who besides Kosov even knew that he was involved in the Phoenix case? Schneider remembered Harry Richardson's mutilated corpse baking in the overheated apartment. Did Kosov know the animal who had killed him? Schneider thought of the mysterious *B* written in Richardson's blood. Had Kosov been able to read its significance? If so, why couldn't he give Rose a name to go with his warning? Could Harry Richardson have been killed by a *Russian* only an hour after Kosov released him at the Wall? Schneider knew Colonel Rose saw the British as the villains in this case, but he suspected it was somehow more complicated than that. As a homicide detective, he had found that 99 percent of all "mysteries" could be solved by reasoning out the simplest explanation for any event. But this mystery—he had felt from the beginning—fell into the 1 percent category.

10:20 A.M. Frankfurt-Main International Airport

Twelfth Department agent Yuri Borodin sat eating a Wienerschnitzel in the large restaurant overlooking the main runway of *Flughafen* Frankfurt. Every two minutes a huge jet would swoop down from left to right across the giant picture window and settle silently onto the tarmac. Borodin had seen everything from Japan Airlines 747s to Aeroflot airliners to U.S. Air Force C-130s. To the right of Borodin's Wienerschnitzel lay a red file a half inch thick. It contained a concise summation of the KGB file on Rudolf Hess, a multivolume collection of data amassed over fifty years. A courier from Moscow had delivered the file to Borodin at the Frankfurt Airport Sheraton thirty minutes ago.

Borodin had scanned its contents with only desultory interest. The file described a convoluted plot to kill the British heads of state during World War Two, a plot involving high-ranking British Nazi sympathizers, the British royal family, and a British communist cadre manipulated by a tsarist Russian named Zinoviev and a young German agent named Helmut Steuer. It told of the KGB's certainty that Spandau's Prisoner Number Seven was not Rudolf Hess but his wartime double, and of that double's murder just five weeks ago. KGB Chairman Zemenek stated his belief that the killing had been done by an assassin paid by Sir Neville Shaw of Britain's MI-5. Borodin admired the nerve and resourcefulness shown by Vasili Zinoviev and Helmut Steuer, but the rest of the story essentially bored him.

Except for the part about the blackmail. When Borodin saw how Churchill had forced Joseph Stalin to keep silent about the Hess affair, he had come instantly alert. Because he saw then how important the recently discovered Spandau papers could be to KGB Chairman Zemenek. The Spandau papers could conceivably clear the way for the Kremlin to tell the world what it knew about British collaboration with the Nazis during the war, and thus force them to share responsibility for the Holocaust. Borodin also saw that if he were the man who recovered those papers, his already advanced career would take a critical leap forward.

He had only one problem. At the end of the Hess file he had found a message inserted by the chairman of the KGB. It said:

Borodin: General Secretary Gorbachev currently exploring possibility of collaborating with U.S. State Department regarding joint disclosure of the truth about Hess's mission. Do nothing to antagonize any U.S. operatives you may encounter in pursuit of the Spandau papers. British operatives fair game.

Zemenek

Yuri Borodin wiped his mouth with his napkin, shoved his empty plate aside, and pulled the file to him. He reread Chairman Zemenek's note. At this point, he reflected, another agent in his position might have trouble digesting the meal, since less than eighteen hours ago he had tortured and executed an American Army Intelligence major. But Borodin wasn't worried. The Hess file had told him one thing: if he returned to Moscow with the Spandau papers, no one would ask whom he had killed to get them.

He glanced at his watch. The next flight to South Africa took off in just under four hours. Borodin chuckled. The big German Kripo detective had not arrived from Berlin yet, but he would, with predictable German punctuality. And then he would lead Yuri Borodin to the Spandau papers like an elephant leading a lion to water.

CHAPTER TWENTY-SIX

11:35 A.M. El Al Flight 331: Zairean Airspace

The deadliest woman in the world stepped out of the forward lavatory of the 747 looking like a grandmother on holiday, a role she assumed with ease. Swallow's stylish outfit reflected modest wealth; her hair shone with the almost-blue tint unique to elderly ladies still courting their vanity; and she smelled of body powder and a very expensive vintage perfume—an alluring concoction called *Claire de Lune*. She carefully made her way up the first-class aisle, then, just as she passed Jonas Stern, she stumbled. She cried out in Yiddish—a nice touch—and landed directly beside Stern's seat. Gadi Abrams, who'd been sitting in the seat across the aisle, leaped up and helped her to her feet.

"Thank you, young man," she said weakly, her face flushed with embarrassment. "I'm afraid I'm not used to airplanes."

Stern glanced up. Had he met the woman's eyes, he might have seen the danger; he might even have recognized her by the dark fire that burned there. But he might not have. The road that had led Swallow to this airplane was a long and tortuous one. In any case, he did not meet her eyes. He glanced over at Professor Natterman, who slept noisily beside him, then went back to reading his *El Al* magazine.

"This flight seems as though it will never end," Swallow complained.

"It's a long one," Gadi agreed.

"How much longer, do you think?"

"About five hours."

Swallow sighed. "It's worth it in spite of everything. My

granddaughter just turned eighteen months old, and I've yet to see her."

"She lives in Johannesburg?" Gadi inquired politely.

"No, Pietersburg. It's far to the north, I think."

Gadi nodded. "Are you all right now?"

"Yes, but I'd better sit down. Thank you again."

Swallow slowly made her way to her seat, one of three near the spiral staircase leading up to the 747's cocktail lounge. After situating a small pillow behind her head, she pulled a romance novel from her handbag. Glancing up for a moment, she caught Gadi staring. The Israelis were professionals—she had to admit that. Though Jonas Stern sat only four rows behind her, his three young escorts had surrounded him in a protective triangle. And with Stern in an aisle seat, no one meaning harm to his slumbering companion could get to him without going through all four Israelis first—an impossible task. Stern himself, however, was a different matter. Swallow could have taken him as she passed only moments ago.

In a way she had. While Gadi helped her up, she had pressed an adhesive-backed microtransmitter against the underside of Stern's seat. Everything the Israelis said during the remainder of the flight would be picked up by a tiny receiver in the flesh-toned hearing aid she wore in her right ear. The unit whistled for a few seconds as she dialed in the frequency, but she could clearly hear Professor Natterman snoring in his seat by the window.

"This is Captain Lev Ronen," announced a disembodied voice with the accent of a Sabra, or native-born Israeli. "As a point of interest, we are now crossing the equator. And about four hundred miles to our left is Lake Victoria, Africa's largest lake and the source of the Nile. I'm sure our first-time travelers will be glad to know that as we cross into the southern hemisphere, the seasons are reversed. That means we're flying into summer. We should arrive in Johannesburg on schedule at 5:40 P.M. South African time, and we hope everyone is having a pleasant flight."

Gadi Abrams leaned across the aisle toward Stern. "Also about four hundred miles to our left," he said, mocking the captain's officious tone, "is Entebbe, site of the July fourth, 1976, rescue of over a hundred Israelis from the hands of international terrorists." His tone changed to indignation.

"You'd think they'd mention it, at least. We are on El Al, for God's sake."

Stern gave a dismissive wave of his hand. "Old news, Gadi. Besides, you never know who's flying El Al. We don't want to offend the paying customers."

Four rows ahead, Swallow smiled with satisfaction. The conversation had come in loud and clear over her receiver.

"I'm surprised at the number of passengers," Gadi remarked. "Since you arranged the flight privately, I didn't expect any."

Stern chuckled softly. "I arranged this flight thirty hours ago. General Avigur said he would get me to South Africa. He didn't say he wouldn't try to defray the cost any way he could."

"I don't like it."

"Two passengers are always air marshals," Stern reminded him. "Leave the security to them for once and go to sleep. It might be your only chance for a while."

"You're not sleeping."

Stern reclined his plush seat and closed his eyes. "Good night."

Gadi pulled a wry face and glanced around the First Class cabin. The blue-haired grandmother was the only other passenger up here. That meant the air marshals had to be in Tourist. He considered walking the length of the plane once more to try to pick them out, but decided against it. Stern was right: he needed rest. The old woman was certainly no threat. Reclining his seat, Gadi closed his eyes and, like professional soldiers everywhere, dropped off to sleep only moments after making the decision to do so. His last mental picture was of himself helping the old grandmother to her feet, his good deed for the day.

As the "grandmother" pretended to concentrate on the novel in her lap, a new voice mumbled in her receiver. Professor Natterman had awakened.

"What time is it?" he asked groggily.

"Almost lunchtime," Stern answered, half-asleep already. "How do you feel?"

"I feel like getting some answers is how I feel," Natterman grumbled. "I think it's time you told me your half of the story."

Stern opened his eyes and turned irritably toward the professor, but the large white bandage over Natterman's lacerated nose kept him civil. He jerked his head toward Gadi, reminding the professor of their agreement not to discuss anything about Rudolf Hess. "What do you want to know, Professor?"

"Everything. What about this Phoenix AG? Why did you come to Berlin in the first place? I want to know why Ilse was taken to South Africa. What's the significance of that?"

Stern looked over at Gadi. "I've thought a lot about that," he murmured. "And I'm sorry to disappoint you, but your Nazi angle doesn't fit here. At least not in the way you think. The Afrikaners are white supremacists, of course, but that's no secret. They fought *against* Hitler during the war, and damned valiantly. And in spite of their prejudice against blacks, they've got a pretty good record on Jews. They allowed a great deal of Jewish immigration during the war, which is more than a lot of countries did."

"What about the present day? What are their ties with Germany?"

Stern shook his head. "Limited. During the past several years, South Africa has quietly developed extremely close relations with another country in a very similar geopolitical situation. That country is not West Germany, however, but Israel. It doesn't sound like we're flying into a nest of neo-Nazis, does it?"

"No," Natterman agreed. "But you obviously have some suspicions about South Africa and Germany. Where is the fox in the henhouse?"

"South Africa's nuclear program. The darkest corner of this dark country."

"Does South Africa actually possess nuclear weapons? I've heard it speculated in the news, but never confirmed."

Stern smiled wryly. "Oh, I can confirm it for you. In 1979, an American VELA satellite detected a distinctive double flash off the South African coast, in the South Atlantic. That flash was the result of a joint nuclear test carried out by South Africa and Israel."

"How do you know that?"

"Because for all practical purposes, Professor, Israel gave South Africa the bomb. Nuclear weapons are one of the main pillars of the Israeli/South Africa relationship."

"*What?*"

"It was an inevitable partnership. Israel developed its first bomb in 1968, but we had several limitations. We couldn't test our weapons without being detected; South Africa had vast deserts and two oceans. We needed raw uranium and other strategic minerals; South Africa had extensive reserves. South Africa also had a great deal of ready cash. But the main tie was psychological, emotional. As the world closed ranks against apartheid, South Africa grew ever more isolated. Before long it was an international pariah surrounded by hostile enemies. The siege mentality was a natural reaction, and we in Israel are the masters of that particular neurosis."

"But how do you know all this, Stern?"

The Israeli looked at Natterman for a long time. "You asked me before if I worked for the Mossad, Professor. Right now I am exactly what I told you in the beginning, a retiree. But I have done a bit of work for several government agencies. Shin Beth and the Mossad, yes, but my longest service was with an agency called LAKAM. Have you heard of it?"

Natterman shook his head.

"LAKAM is Israel's nuclear security force. Not in the sense of *operating* the weapons, but in protecting them. LAKAM safeguarded Israel's nuclear program from inception to completion. That's why I know so much about the South African program."

"And is this LAKAM work what led you to Berlin? To Spandau?"

"Not exactly. What led me to Spandau was a chain of facts. A very fragile chain with four links that spans three decades. The first link was a warning note—an anonymous, cryptic note written in Cyrillic handwriting and delivered to Israel in 1967. It warned of terrible danger to Israel and spoke of 'the fire of Armageddon.' This note claimed that the secret of this danger could be found in Spandau. That, of course, was a very broad hint. Did the writer mean Spandau the city? Spandau the prison? What? Two days later, the Six-Day War broke out and the note was dismissed as a warning of the Egyptian attack, probably written by a Russian with a conscience." Stern rubbed his temples. "Now, jump ahead to the early 1970s. I was working for LAKAM by then, and we in the agency became aware that certain German scientists—former Third Reich physicists—were working in the rocketry section of South Africa's nuclear program. This by itself was not unusual. After all, it was German scientists who

built the bombs for America and Russia. But when you consider that the prime minister of South Africa in 1979—the
year of the secret Israeli/South African nuclear test—was
John Vorster, a man who had supported the Nazis during
World War Two, it takes on a rather different significance.

"Now, let's jump ahead again, to the 1980s. It was then,
through contacts in the Mossad, that I became aware of a
neo-fascist police organization called *Bruderschaft der
Phoenix*, headquartered in West Berlin—"

"Phoenix!" Natterman exclaimed. "Hurry, Stern, tell me!"

"Again, this by itself was not of great import. It took the
fourth and final link to join the others in my mind. Just three
weeks ago, the Israeli Foreign Ministry received a typed
warning from an anonymous source. The writer obviously
knew of the secret Israeli/South African nuclear partnership,
and stated that he had personal knowledge that there were
some in the South African defense establishment who had
anything *but* Israel's best interests at heart. The writer
claimed he believed that Israel might actually be in danger
of a nuclear attack, and that the best line of inquiry for us to
pursue was with a South African defense contractor called
Phoenix AG."

Natterman caught his breath. After several moments, he
said, "Forgive me, Stern, but there's something I don't understand here. You told me you were retired. This situation
seems serious enough that Israel would be making a significant effort to investigate it." .

Stern's smile carried the bitterness of a lifetime's disillu-
sionment. "You would think that, wouldn't you? But some
people don't see it that way, Professor. South Africa is Israel's nuclear partner, remember? No one in Jerusalem wants
to upset that status quo. The Israeli/South African 'special
relationship' is so close that, as we speak, a secret contingency plan exists to remove South Africa's entire stockpile
of nuclear weapons to Israel in the event that the blacks
appear likely to overthrow the government."

Natterman's eyes grew wide. "My God. This is all so unbelievable. Why would Israel support a repressive, even
genocidal state like South Africa?"

"The Israeli *people* probably wouldn't, Professor. But decisions guiding Israel's nuclear program were never voted on
in the Knesset. Israel's nuclear policy is formed by a very
few men who happen to hold the key positions in the gov-

ernment." Stern sighed. "And some men will do anything in the name of survival. For some Jews, the Holocaust justifies any act to prevent a repetition of history, even a preemptive Holocaust perpetrated *by* Jews." Stern reached beneath his seat, withdrew an orange from his leather bag, and slowly began to peel it. "Professor, how much do you know about Israel's resistance to the British during the Mandate and World War Two?"

Natterman shrugged. "I know about the Haganah."

"What about the Zionist terrorist groups?"

"The Stern Gang and the Irgun?"

"Yes."

"Some. Which did you fight with?"

"That is unimportant now. What matters is that prior to World War Two, both groups violently resisted the British occupation of Palestine. But when the war broke out, the two groups split. The Irgun supported the British, rightly believing that Israel could never be born in a world under Hitler. But the Stern Gang believed that driving out the British was more important than defeating the Nazis."

Natterman's eyes widened in disbelief.

"The Stern Gang actually sent delegations to meet with representatives of Hitler's Reich and Mussolini's Italy. They actually promised to fight for the influence of Germany and Italy in the Middle East, if Hitler and Mussolini would agree to allow Jews to leave their countries and also guarantee the safety of Israel after the war."

"Madness," Natterman breathed. "What fools could have believed that a guarantee from Adolf Hitler was worth anything?"

Stern shook his head in disgust. "One of those fools was Yitzhak Shamir, the prime minister of Israel."

Natterman sat in stunned silence. "Shamir *was* a Zionist terrorist, wasn't he? The Stern Gang . . . my God."

"And that," said Stern, "brings us to the present, to the new LAKAM. I left the agency seven years ago. At that time it was a model intelligence organization. But under Shamir, LAKAM has grown completely out of control. Up until two years ago, they actually ran a spy *against* the United States. Jonathan Pollard gave LAKAM information on U.S. weapons systems, satellite capabilities, even nuclear targeting data—the most sensitive intelligence in America. And do you know what Shamir did with this booty stolen from Israel's greatest ally?" Stern's tanned face paled with fury. "He sent it to *Moscow*. That bastard risked the life-giving support of America to prove that Israel could not be told what to do by anyone, even the United States!"

"Does LAKAM know about the Phoenix AG warning?"

Stern answered with bitter sarcasm. "The current chief of LAKAM feels that the Phoenix warning was fabricated by someone who wants to start us on a destructive mole hunt. LAKAM is pursuing the warning, but very slowly, like a man walking on ice. There are 'constructive discussions' going on between Jerusalem and Pretoria. The only reason I found out about the Phoenix warning at all was that an old friend at LAKAM felt that the warning was not being taken seriously enough."

Stern smiled mischievously. "*That* is the main reason I went first to West Berlin rather than South Africa—to stay out of LAKAM's way. But there were other reasons. The name of the company—Phoenix AG—reminded me of *Bruderschaft der Phoenix* in Berlin. And when an old friend happened to mention that Spandau Prison was being torn down only two weeks after the warning arrived, the timing seemed impossibly coincidental. All I could think of was the 'fire of Armageddon' note that had mentioned Spandau. Spandau as a city had always been too large to investigate, of course. And while Hess—excuse me, Hess's double—was being held in Spandau Prison, it was one of the most closely guarded buildings in the world. But when I heard it was to be knocked into pieces, well . . . it was enough to get me on a plane to Berlin."

"But how are all these things connected?" Natterman asked. "Where is the direct link between South Africa and Germany?"

Stern pursed his lips. "I don't think there is one, Professor. I think the link runs through England. The British governed South Africa until 1961, remember. They're a minority now, but a powerful one. Take Phoenix AG: it's a defense contractor based in South Africa, but the majority stockholder is a young Englishman named Robert Stanton, Lord Grenville. His father and grandfather owned the company before him."

"Grenville!" Professor Natterman shook his forefinger excitedly. "*That's* why you brought me with you. You think this nuclear danger to Israel could somehow be connected to the Hess case. To the English conspirators!"

"Keep your voice down!" Stern glanced across the aisle to make sure Gadi was still asleep. "LAKAM traced the paper used for the Phoenix AG warning to an English mill. Lord Grenville's family has owned and operated the corporation since 1947. But it still doesn't add up. Britain has always been anti-Semitic, but what motive could Englishmen have to support fascist groups now? Captain Hauer mentioned German reunification to you. Could these Englishmen stand to make great profits if Germany reunifies? Or could they have been blackmailed all these years by Germans who knew their dark secret? Germans who had secret ends of their own?"

Natterman was shaking his head. "I keep coming back to the past, Stern. Consider our highly placed clique of Nazi sympathizers in the wartime Parliament. I would imagine they had quite a bit of 'old boy' control over British policy vis-à-vis Palestine, wouldn't you? Think about it. In 1917 Britain promised the Jews a national home in Palestine. Yet while England drifted into war with Hitler—the man who had vowed to *exterminate* world Jewry—the British government used military force to prevent every European Jew it could from reaching safety in Palestine—the country Britain had *already promised them*. Was that rational policy? Who really made those decisions? Could those anti-Semitic feelings still be thriving in some families in Britain?"

Stern's face burned red with anger. "Professor, I can't even think about those days without feeling rage toward the British."

Natterman was staring at Stern with strange intensity. "Tell me," he said softly. "Were you part of the Stern Gang? Is that how you know all this? Or were you Irgun?"

Stern's eyes bored in on Natterman. "Neither, Professor. A very long time ago—before LAKAM—I helped found the Haganah." Stern glanced past Natterman, to the small window-square of cerulean sky. "In the winter of 1935, I emigrated with my mother to Palestine. My father refused to leave our homeland, which happened to be Germany. Despite my youth, I did a bit of everything for the Haganah: fought Arabs, procured illegal arms, set up radio links across the Arabian peninsula, smuggled in Jews from Europe—but mostly I fought the British." The Israeli's face hardened.

"But I was no terrorist. Haganah was a moral army, Professor. The moment Israel declared nationhood, we emerged as her legitimate defense forces. I've never believed in senseless violence to achieve political ends. I saw too many men start out as patriots and end up as criminals." Stern's eyes misted with some half-forgotten emotion. "Terror is a tempting tool in war, Professor. The easiest short-term solution is always to lash out—to murder. I know. I tried it once." He sighed deeply. "But 'an eye for an eye' is no road map to a better world."

In her seat near the staircase, Swallow clenched her trembling hands. Jonas Stern's voice—his hypocritical, Zionist voice—had hurled her back into the past, back to Palestine. Swallow knew all about Jonas Stern's flirtation with revenge, and she had a very different opinion about the merits of the concept. She could no longer even think coherently about her pain. Her clearest memory was of her time as a mathematics prodigy studying at Cambridge, her time as Ann Gordon. She still remembered the stunned expressions of the dons as she soared through the nether reaches of theoretical calculus at age sixteen. When the war broke out, British Intelligence had snatched her up with the rest of the savants and whisked her into cryptography. Her parents lived in London, but her two brothers were stationed abroad: the elder an RAF bombardier on Malta, the younger—Ann's fraternal twin—a military policeman in Palestine. Ann and her twin brother, Andrew, had been inseparable as children, and they had danced with joy when fate landed them both in the same theater of the war.

The family had a splendid war—right up until the end. In 1944 both of Ann's parents were killed by one of the last V-rockets to fall on London. Then her elder brother was shot down over Germany and lynched by civilians while the *Waffen*-SS looked on. That left only Ann, decoding German signals in a stifling shed in Tel Aviv, and Andrew, caught in the escalating violence between Jews, Arabs, and the British in Palestine. With the rest of the family dead, the twins had grown closer than ever. They even shared a small apartment in the poor quarter of Tel Aviv—until the night Andrew was blown into small pieces as he sat on a toilet in the British police barracks. His brutal death finally shattered Ann's English stoicism. During the long, desolate months of anguish, her grief slowly metamorphosed into a dark, implacable fury. The war with Germany ended, but she had found a new war to fight.

With methodical fanaticism she set to work finding out who had killed her twin brother. It didn't take long. The bomb that killed Andrew had been a Zionist reprisal attack, revenge for some filthy Jews who had died in a British deportation camp. And the name of the young firebrand who had planned and carried out that reprisal? Jonas Stern. It had taken Ann just two hours to learn everything the local authorities knew about Stern. He had apparently helped the British quite a bit during the war, but before and since, the young Zionist had killed enough Englishmen to earn an unofficial bounty of a thousand pounds on his head. Ann Gordon didn't give a damn about the bounty. All she cared about was avenging her dead brother.

The next day she volunteered for the operations side of British Intelligence, and they accepted her. She was brilliant, tough, and best of all an orphan. After rigorous training in England, they christened her Swallow and put her to work. As an assassin. The trouble was, she had no say in her choice of assignments. She spent year after year luring IRA gunmen, Arab terrorists, African communists, anti-British mercenaries and other hard cases to their doom, instead of hunting down the Zionist demon from her past. In all the years Swallow worked for British Intelligence, not once did she manage to get within striking range of Jonas Stern. To her everlasting fury, the young Zionist fanatic had evolved into a singularly gifted field agent. And long before Swallow was pensioned off, Stern himself had retired to a fortified haven in the Negev desert, apparently never to emerge.

Twice since then Swallow had attempted to breach the defenses of Stern's desert refuge. She had drawn Jewish blood on both occasions, but she had failed to reach her hated target. After that, the Mossad had learned her identity and warned her off. For Swallow, crossing into the Holy Land meant certain death. And so she had returned to England. And waited. Until yesterday. Yesterday, like a call from Olympus, Sir Neville Shaw's summons had come. *Something* had drawn Jonas Stern out of Israel at last. Out of his sanctuary . . .

Swallow's eyes popped open as Professor Natterman's voice crackled in her ear receiver, breaking her reverie.

"Can't you see it, Stern?" he said forcefully. "Somehow,

for some unknown reason, the past and present are converging toward some mysterious meeting point . . . a kind of *completion.* It's like the Bible. The sins of the fathers, yes? Or as the Buddhists teach, *karma.*" The old professor raised a crooked finger and shook it slowly. "You still think my suspicions about Rudolf Hess are unfounded? If ghosts like Yitzhak Shamir can survive to haunt the present, so can Hess. I tell you, Stern, the man is *alive.*"

Stern closed a strong hand over Natterman's upraised finger, hard enough to cause pain. It infuriated the professor, but it shut him up. Stern leaned back in his seat and sighed. "I do wonder sometimes who is pulling the strings of this invisible cabal. Is it Lord Grenville, the young Englishman? Is it some madman? Some would-be Aryan Messiah? *Is* it another ghost from the past? Your Helmut, perhaps?"

Natterman fixed the Israeli with a penetrating gaze. "Jonas," he said gravely, using Stern's first name for the first time. "What will you do if . . . if we find that I am right? If we find living men who bear direct responsibility for the Holocaust? Will you kill them?"

Stern ran a hand through his thinning hair. "*If* we were to find such men alive," he said quietly, "I would take them back to Israel. Take them to Israel for a public trial. That is the only end from which justice can come."

Natterman scratched at his gray wisp of beard. "You're a strong man, Jonas. It takes great strength to show restraint."

"I'm not that strong," Stern murmured. "If I couldn't get them back to Israel, I would kill them without hesitation."

Glancing across the aisle for the first time in several minutes, Stern saw that his three young companions had awakened. They were listening wide-eyed, like children around a campfire. The Haganah years Stern had spoken of resonated like myths in the hearts of the young sabras, and they stared at him like a hero of another age. Beyond that, they now knew something about their mission. They were to be given the chance of a lifetime—the chance to strike back through the pages of history—to punish men who had never been justly punished—men who had tried to make the State of Israel a stillborn nation! Stern's commandos were lean and hard in body and spirit, and from that moment on they were as soldiers in a holy war.

Four rows ahead of them, another soldier also awaited her chance to strike. As the El Al jetliner soared southward through the glorious vault of sky, the woman code-named Swallow reveled in the knowledge that she could destroy Jonas Stern right now. Stern had at least part of the Spandau diary, but what did she care for papers? If she killed Stern here, of course, she would die. She thought of Sir Neville Shaw, the nerveless director general of MI-5. She certainly felt no loyalty to that old serpent. Shaw and men like him had used her ruthlessly throughout her career, wielding her like a razor-sharp sword, all the while ignoring her quest for private justice. But what of England, that hazy, increasingly obsolete concept? In spite of her coldness, Swallow had always possessed a strong, rather maudlin streak of patriotism. Was preserving British honor worth deferring her sweet revenge for one more day? Professor Natterman had spoken of ghosts from the past. Swallow knew that once she unmasked herself—today, tomorrow, whenever—she would be one ghost that Jonas Stern would be very surprised to see.

CHAPTER TWENTY-SEVEN

11:40 A.M. *Pretoria*

More than fifty knives of all types gleamed inside the brightly lit display case. Hauer leaned over until his nose touched the glass. This immediately drew the attention of a nearby salesman, a freckled, red-haired man of about thirty.

"Any particular style you're looking for, sir?" he asked in a British accent. "Are you looking for a souvenir, or might you be doing some hunting with it?"

"Good point," Hauer said in English. "Could be doing some hunting. Still, we don't want anything too big. Quality, that's the thing."

"Of course, sir. I believe I've got just what you need."

When the young man moved down the row of display cases, Hans leaned close to Hauer. "What about a gun?" he whispered.

Hauer didn't reply. This was their fifth stop of the day, and he was beginning to feel overexposed. After checking into the Burgerspark Hotel and changing their Deutschemarks for rand, they had slipped out the rear entrance of the hotel and into their taxi. They clung to the armrests of the Ford while Salil made short work of their British tail car. The loquacious Indian had shepherded them around the city while they purchased several changes of clothes and enough food to last two days without leaving whatever hotel room they finally settled into. Salil had also recommended the large sporting goods store.

"Here you are, sir," the salesman said, proudly holding out a sleek six-inch knife for Hauer's inspection.

Hauer took the weapon and turned it in the light. He hefted it in his palm, feeling the balance. The knife had a plain varnished handle—not nearly so ornate as the engraved showpieces glinting in the display case—but Hauer's approval was evident.

"I see you know your knives, sir," said the salesman. "Made in West Germany that was. Solingen steel, finest in the world."

Hauer flicked the knife back and forth with practiced ease. "We'll take two."

The salesman's smile broadened. Already these two tourists had purchased an expensive hunting rifle, scope, and a Nikon camera with mini-tripod and hand-held light meter. "I notice your accent, sir," he said with a sidelong glance at Hans. "German, are you?"

"Swiss," Hauer said quickly.

"Ah." The salesman realized he had asked the wrong question. "I'll just wrap these for you." After another long look at Hans, he disappeared through a narrow doorway behind the counter.

"Why does he keep staring at you?" Hauer muttered. "Is he queer?"

"He thinks I'm a goddamn tennis star."

After a moment, Hauer nodded with relief.

"What about *guns*?" Hans asked again. "The rendezvous is tonight. Eight o'clock."

"Hans, if the kidnappers are smart—and so far they have been—they'll just sniff you out tonight. You didn't take the plane they told you to. That will put them off balance. For all they know, a hundred Interpol agents are going to descend on the Burgerspark Hotel tonight. No, they'll either send a drone or telephone you with further instructions. My guess is they'll call."

Hans looked far from satisfied. "I'd feel a lot better if I had a pistol, and there are dozens right in that case."

"True," Hauer acknowledged. "But I don't see any silencers, do you? We can't go around Pretoria firing off pistols. Our badges are worthless here. Plus, I don't want to subject our papers to even a cursory background check."

While Hans sulked, Hauer glanced around the store. "All right," he said resignedly. "You see that rack over there?" He pointed across the store to a large display of hunting bows.

Hans nodded.

"Go over and tell that salesman you want the smallest

crossbow he has with a seventy-pound draw, and six of the sharpest bolts he has." Hauer pulled a wad of bills from his trousers pocket and peeled off four hundred rand.

Still looking longingly at the gun case, Hans took the money.

"Here you are, gentlemen." The salesman had reappeared in the doorway with a small brown-wrapped parcel. "That comes to, ah . . ." He trailed off, looking past Hauer.

Hauer turned and followed his gaze. The salesman was staring at Hans, who now stood with his hands on his hips, scrutinizing a rack of expensive tennis racquets with an expert's disdainful eye.

The salesman cleared his throat. "Could I show you something else, er . . . sir?"

Hans continued to stare silently at the racquets.

The salesman reached out timidly and touched Hauer's sleeve. "Pardon me, sir, but isn't he . . . ?"

Slowly Hans turned to the salesman and smiled the confiding, slightly embarrassed smile celebrities use when they would prefer that no one make a fuss over them. "Could I possibly see a few racquets?" he asked. "Estusas? Preferably the N1000."

The salesman almost tripped over his feet in his haste to get around the counter. "Why *certainly,* sir. I am at your complete disposal." He blushed. "I'm a terrific fan, you know. We have just the racquet you want, and I'm *positive* that a very agreeable discount could be arranged . . ."

As the gushing salesman led his prize across the store, Hans looked back over his shoulder and glared pointedly at Hauer, then at the gun case, talking all the way. "Normally my racquets are supplied directly from the factory," he explained, "but the stupid airline put my bag aboard the wrong plane . . ."

Stunned by Hans's boldness, Hauer took one look around the store for surveillance cameras, slipped quickly behind the gun case, dropped to his knees and went to work on the lock.

When Hans stepped out of the store twenty minutes later, he saw Hauer waiting for him at the end of the block, surrounded by shopping bags. Stuffing a large, oblong parcel under his arm, he jogged awkwardly up the street.

"Don't tell me," said Hauer. "You bought the tennis racquet."

"The crossbow," Hans muttered. "I wasn't sure you could break into the gun case."

Hauer opened his jacket slightly. The handgrips of two gleaming black pistols jutted from his waistband. "Walthers. Matched pair. A child could have sprung the lock on that case." He closed his jacket and laughed softly. "That was pretty good acting in there, Boris. You almost had me convinced."

"Let's just get the hell out of here," Hans snapped. "I had to sign six autographs before they let me out of the store."

At that moment Salil pulled his taxi smoothly up to the curb. "Your carriage awaits," said Hauer. He reached down and picked up the boxed rifle, scope, and camera, and loaded them into the trunk of the Indian's Ford. "Let's go shoot some pictures."

11:44 A.M. MI-5 Headquarters, Charles Street, London, England

Sir Neville Shaw had not slept in his office for quite some time—not since the Falklands War, his deputy had reminded him. But now he lay sound asleep on a squeaky cot he had ordered brought to his office early this morning. When Deputy Director Wilson came barging into the office without even a perfunctory knock, Shaw came up off the cot like he had as a child during the Blitz.

"What in God's name is it?" he bellowed. "World War Three?"

Wilson was breathless. "It's Swallow, sir. She's picked up Stern."

Shaw pounded his fist on his thigh. "By God, I knew that woman could do it!"

"She boarded his plane at Ben-Gurion. They're airborne now, and Stern is definitely headed for South Africa. Not only did Swallow overhear Stern say that he had part of the Spandau papers, but she also heard him discussing the involvement of the Duke of Windsor in the Hess affair."

"Good Christ! Discussing it with *whom*?"

"A German history professor. He's a relative of one of the Berlin policemen who found the Spandau papers. Swallow thinks Stern plans to use him to make contact with Hauer and Apfel. She called from the aircraft telephone. She used a verbal code from the nineteen *sixties,* sir. It took a crypto team two hours to dig the cipher key out of the basement."

Shaw left his cot and walked toward his desk. "With Swallow on his tail, Stern's as good as dead. We can count on getting whatever portion of the papers he's carrying."

Wilson looked uncomfortable. "If Swallow does kill Stern, sir, do you think the fact that she's retired is enough to shield us from an Israeli protest?"

"Protest! What do we care about one scruffy Yid? You can bet Stern asked for it somewhere up the line. The Zionist terrorists in Palestine were a damned sight more ruthless than your Palestinian today, Wilson. A damned sight!" Shaw rubbed his hands together anxiously. "South Africa," he murmured. "How in blazes did that old fox figure that out?"

Wilson looked puzzled. "I'm not sure what you mean, but Swallow overheard Stern discussing the wife of Sergeant Apfel. Frau Apfel seems to have been kidnapped by someone in South Africa who is demanding the Spandau papers as ransom."

For a moment Shaw seemed to have lost his breath. "Where's my bloody ship, Wilson?"

"Ship, sir?" Wilson reddened. "Oh, yes. *Lloyd's List* has the MV *Casilda* bound for Tanzania. However, I managed to get hold of some American satellite photos which show her anchored in the Mozambique Channel, off Madagascar. There are two helicopters lashed to her decks."

"Thank God," Shaw said under his breath.

"Sir Neville?" Wilson said softly. "Does that freighter have something to do with the Spandau affair?"

"Better if you don't know just yet, Wilson. If all this blows up in my face, you'll be able to swear you never knew a bloody thing."

Wilson looked distraught. "For God's sake, Neville, at least let me help you!"

Shaw pursed his lips thoughtfully. "All right, man. If you really want to help, I've got something that's just your line of country."

"Name it."

"There are some files I need. If this thing goes sour, we'll want them shredded and burned in a hurry." Shaw picked up a pen and scrawled three names on a sheet of notepaper.

"Might be a bit sticky, but you've done this kind of thing before." He handed over the paper.

Wilson read the names:

Hess, Rudolf
Steuer, Helmut
Zinoviev, V. V.

"And where are these files, sir?"

"The Public Records Office." Shaw watched Wilson closely. "Although technically they're Foreign Office files. There is also a Hess file in the War Office, but it's sealed until 2050. I don't think anyone could get at that."

Wilson swallowed hard. "You mean . . . you want me to steal files from the *Foreign Office?*"

"Be thankful it's only paper, man. There are much dirtier jobs involved in this case."

Wilson met Shaw's steady gaze. "Won't the missing files be noticed?"

"Probably." Shaw reached into a drawer and withdrew a thick, dog-eared file. "That's why I'm giving you this." He handed the folder across to Wilson. "It's also a Hess file, but it's been . . . *amended.* The Zinoviev and Steuer files simply have to disappear, but you can fill the Hess gap with that. It was prepared in the early seventies, after we were forced by statute to reveal certain information on Hess. It was our insurance against the day some hothead like Neil Kinnock started pressing for radical disclosures. I think it will serve very well in this situation." Shaw sighed contentedly. "Now pour us a Glenfiddich, eh, Wilson? You look like you need one."

1:05 P.M. *Room 604, The Protea Hof Hotel: Pretoria*

Hauer looked forlornly around the hotel room. He had steeled himself for an explosion that never came. Perhaps Hans was simply too exhausted to get upset. And then perhaps it was something else. His reaction did not fit the stimulus, and that bothered Hauer. The fact that three pages of the Spandau diary were missing clearly reduced the chances of getting Ilse back alive; yet when Hauer had revealed that the pages were missing, Hans hadn't said a word. His eyes had widened in disbelief; he'd rubbed his temples, seemed to sag a little; but he had not shouted at Hauer for pilfering the papers on the plane, or blasted Professor Natterman for his cowardice, or tried to attack Hauer as he had done to the professor at the cabin. He'd simply stood up and walked into the bathroom. Hauer could hear water running in the sink now.

He unboxed the Nikon N/2000 camera with macro/micro lens that he had bought at the sporting goods store. Then he set up the special tripod he had bought to facilitate the time exposures. Less than a foot high, the squat instrument had short, splayed legs and fully pivoting head. It reminded him of a robot from a 1950s science fiction movie. He set it up on the table near the window and opened the drapes; then he mounted the Nikon.

"Hans!" he called to the bathroom. "I need the papers!"

Thirty seconds later Hans emerged from the bathroom with the crinkled foil packet containing the Spandau papers. He handed it to Hauer without a word.

"Cover the door," Hauer said. "If anyone knows where we are, now is the time they'll hit us."

Instead of drawing the Walther from his waistband, Hans leaned over and picked up the crossbow he'd bought.

Hauer gingerly unwrapped the foil while Hans loaded a stubby, razor-sharp bolt. "I'm going to bracket the *f*-stops," he said. "I'll shoot at the widest aperture—*f*1.8—at one-thirtieth of a second. Then progressively longer exposures until we reach two full seconds, just to make sure."

Hans said nothing.

"I know you're still worried about the pictures, but Ilse said the kidnappers could detect whether photocopies of the papers had been made. This is no different than *looking* at the papers. We've got no choice, Hans. We're going to have to trade the original Spandau papers for Ilse. This is our fallback. Besides, to crack Phoenix in Berlin, we're going to need a copy of the papers, plus the evidence in the fire safe at Steuben's house."

Hauer worked his way through the exposures for the first page—seven shots altogether—then carefully set it aside. Hans handed over the second page; Hauer repeated the procedure. The first roll of film ran out halfway through page four. While Hauer reloaded the Nikon, he heard Hans whisper: "*Damn* that old man."

Hauer kept working while he talked. "It isn't the professor's fault, Hans. That blond Afrikaner got them, and whoever killed him got the papers. The professor should have told us about the missing pages, but you know why he didn't. He couldn't bring himself to admit he'd lost them. He knew you'd go crazy, and to no avail. We couldn't have done anything about it anyway."

Hans sat silently.

"Listen," said Hauer. "Natterman was stupid to put these blank sheets in with the papers. It made the missing pages twice as obvious. When we make the exchange, we'll use only the six matching pages. The kidnappers won't know the difference."

Hans's opinion of this theory was painfully clear on his face. "You know better than that," he said softly. "They have Ilse, and she knows exactly what I found. She can describe it down to the—" Hans's mouth stopped moving. "Phoenix would *torture* her to find those things out!"

"Stop talking like that!" Hauer snapped. "Ilse's smart. She'll tell them what they want without a fight. Look, Hans, all we need is Ilse in the open and ten seconds to get her clear. The kidnappers won't have more than ten seconds to examine the papers. That's the situation I intend to arrange. Anything else is unacceptable."

"Ten seconds is enough time to count pages," Hans observed.

Hauer sighed heavily. "At the cabin you said you trusted me, Hans. Now you've got to prove it. *We've* got the leverage here, not them. They know they'll never get the papers back if they kill Ilse. The moment they make contact, we set out *our* terms for the exchange. They have to accept them. And once they accept our terms, we've got them."

Hans met Hauer's eyes. "But do we have Ilse?"

Hauer picked the last diary page up off the bed, shot his last seven exposures, then removed the film from the camera. He folded the Spandau papers into quarters, then eighths, then he wrapped the aluminum foil tightly about them again.

"I'm going to find a lab that can process the film in an hour or two," he said, slipping the cartridges into his pocket. "I want you to sleep while I'm gone. You've been up for thirty-six hours, and I've been up longer than that. Airplane sleep doesn't count. The Burgerspark rendezvous is at eight tonight. Call the desk and set a wake-up call for seven-thirty."

Hans looked up stonily. "You expect me to sleep now?"

"Just shut off the light and breathe deeply. You won't last five minutes. You should see your eyes right now. They look like they're bleeding."

Working his jaw muscles steadily, Hans finally said, "Shouldn't I keep the papers here?"

Hauer considered this. Hans had held the papers until now ... "They're safer on the move," he said suddenly. He slipped the packet into his trouser pocket and headed for the door. "Get some sleep. I'll see you when we wake up."

Outside the hotel the sun burned down without mercy. Hauer wished he'd thought to bring a hat. Moving watchfully through the tree-lined streets, he tried to gauge their chances of success. Tonight would be their first and possibly only chance to turn the tables on the men who held Ilse, the men behind Phoenix. And with no backup to rely on, every move could be their last. Hauer needed time to think. And most critical now, he needed sleep. Maybe worse than he ever had in his life. He could feel the sun sapping his energy by the minute.

He paused in the shade of a purple-blossomed jacaranda tree. He leaned against its trunk, folded his arms, and waited for a taxi. None passed. He did not know that in South Africa taxis may not legally cruise for business, but must wait in ranks at designated locations. Struggling to keep his eyes open, he wondered if Hans might be right. Would the kidnappers make their main move at the Burgerspark tonight? Would they risk showing themselves this early in the game? He didn't think so, but this wasn't Berlin. Maybe on their own territory the bastards would act with impunity. Maybe he should find a place to hide the papers before the rendezvous. Maybe—

"*Taxi!*"

A red Madza driven by an enterprising soul made an illegal U-turn and screeched up to Hauer's shade tree. For a moment Hauer thought the driver was Salil, the talkative Indian, but it was only his exhausted mind playing tricks on him. A tanned Afrikaner leaned out of the window.

"Where to, mate?" he asked in English.

"I need some film developed," Hauer replied. "Fast."

"How fast?"

"Yesterday."

"Got money?"

"All I need."

"Right," said the driver. "Get in, then."

CHAPTER TWENTY-EIGHT

1:30 P.M. Horn House, Northern Transvaal, RSA

Seated in his motorized wheelchair on the north lawn, Alfred Horn chewed an Upmann cigar while Robert Stanton, Lord Grenville, paced nervously around him, gulping from an enormous Bloody Mary. For an hour the young Englishman had been ranting about "corporate expansion." The corporation he referred to was the illegal and wholly invisible one which carried on the lucrative drug- and currency-smuggling operations he had administered for Alfred Horn for the past eight years. The old man had sat silent during most of the tirade. He was curious, but not about increasing his illegal profits. He was curious about Stanton himself. Today the young nobleman's voice had the semblance of its usual brashness, but something in it did not quite ring true. He was drunk, and Horn intended to give him as much rope as he would take.

"I don't even know why I'm trying," he lamented. "Do you realize how much money we have lost in the past three days, Alfred? Over two million pounds! Two *million*. And I have no idea why. You shut down our entire European operation without a word of explanation."

"To whom do I owe explanations?" Horn rasped.

"Well . . . to no one, of course. But Alfred, certain people might get angry if we don't resume operations very soon. We have *commitments*."

A faint smile touched Horn's lips. "Yes," he said softly. "I'm curious, Robert, this gold that is scheduled to arrive day after tomorrow. Why is it coming by ship? Normally those deliveries are made by air."

This question surprised Stanton, but he recovered quickly.

"The final leg will still be made by air," he said. "By helicopter. I don't know *why*, Alfred. Perhaps the currency export restrictions were tightened at Colombia's airports. Perhaps it was easier to take the gold out by ship. Who knows?"

"Indeed." Horn glanced at the thin face of Pieter Smuts. "Tell me, Robert, do you miss England? You've been with us a month now."

Stanton took a huge swallow of his Bloody Mary. "Glad to be away from the bloody place. It's winter there, isn't it? Though I must admit I'd like to get down to Jo'burg for a weekend. Not much female companionship to choose from here. I don't have the fancy for dark meat Smuts has. I suppose it's an acquired taste." Stanton grinned. "There's always the pretty new *Fräulein*, of course, our own Aryan princess."

Horn's solitary eye burned into Stanton's face. "You will keep your distance from Frau Apfel, Robert," he said sharply. "Is that absolutely clear?"

"Wouldn't dream of it, old boy. Not my type at all." The young Englishman tried to look nonchalant, but he could not remain cool under the smoking gaze of Horn's security chief. "Would you mind terribly not doing that, Smuts?" he said irritably. "Gives me the galloping creeps."

Smuts continued to stare like a wolf at the edge of a dying fire. After several moments, Horn said, "It won't be long now, Robert, and everything will be back to normal. I have some business to take care of first, that is all. It's a matter of security."

Security, Stanton thought contemptuously. *In two days you're going to find out about bloody security.* He slipped on a pair of Wayfarer sunglasses to hide his eyes while he considered his remarkable position. Three months ago, two very powerful people had decided they wanted Alfred Horn dead. One was a ruthless Colombian drug baron who wanted access to Phoenix's European drug markets. His motive—greed—Stanton clearly understood. The other was a rather terrifying gentleman from London named Sir Neville Shaw. Stanton knew nothing about his motive. All he knew was that both Shaw and the Colombian had asked him to assassinate Alfred Horn. With his own hands! Stanton had refused, of course. He didn't want to murder the old man. Horn had made him rich—something his worthless title had never done. But the terrible pressure to kill the old man had not relented. The Colombian had threatened Stanton's life, a threat Stanton could afford to ignore as long as he lived under Horn's protection. Sir Neville Shaw had also begun with threats. *I'll bury your title under a mountain of dirt and blood,* he'd said. Stanton had laughed. He didn't give two shits about his title. Even as a child he had sensed that the name Grenville was held in quiet, profound contempt among most of the British peerage. That was one reason he'd turned to the life he had, and also why, upon his father's death, he had accepted the aid and protection of Alfred Horn.

But then Shaw had changed tactics. Kill Horn, he'd said, and the Crown will allow you to keep the companies you own and operate under Horn's supervision. Stanton had paused at that. Because the time was long past for Alfred Horn to pass on his empire to a younger man. For five years Stanton had been the majority stockholder of Phoenix AG, yet not one decision regarding the administration of the giant conglomerate had been made by him. His father had played a similar role before him, but his father had been allowed to make decisions—his father had been trusted. Robert was a mere figurehead, almost a joke. Yes, the time for change had come. Yet Stanton could not do the dirty work himself; even if he succeeded in killing Horn, Pieter Smuts would tear him limb from bloody limb. No, the old man would have to be killed in such a way that Smuts and his security force died with him. Stanton had pondered this problem for a week, after which time he had hit upon a rather brilliant plan. He would simply bring together the two parties who shared a common goal. On a day trip to London he had communicated his plan to Shaw, then left the devious MI-5 chief to work out the details. Thus the present plan; thus the ship. All that remained now was the *execution.*

"Drunk already, are you?" Smuts goaded in his flat voice.

For once Stanton looked the Afrikaner dead in the eye. "Just thinking," he said. "You should try it sometime, old sport."

Ilse Apfel stood on a gentle swell of grass and stared across the vast high-veld. She had fled Horn House after the nightmare in the X-ray room, running as far and as fast as she could. No one had stopped her, but Linah had followed at a respectful distance, pausing whenever Ilse did, keeping pace like a distant shadow. After Ilse's panic had carried her nearly two miles from the house, she'd calmed a little and smoothed out a place in the rough grass to rest.

Alfred Horn had spoken the truth at dinner, she realized. On this empty plateau there was simply nowhere to escape *to*. Not without a map, a gun, and a good supply of water. Far to her left, scrawny, humped cattle grazed. Beyond them a pair of reddish horses pranced in the sun. A black haze hung low in the distance, touching the brown horizon. Though Ilse did not know it, the black smoke rose from the coal-fueled cookstoves of a small native *kraal,* or village. Such smoke marked most native dwellings from Capetown to the Bantustan of Venda. In winter it was worse. Then the dark palls hung perpetually over the settlements, blocking out the sun. In South Africa electricity is a selectively provided commodity.

Ilse looked down at the sun-baked earth. What hope had she here, so far from Germany? What chance did her child have? Hans was on his way here now, if Horn could be believed. And from Smuts's questions in the X-ray session, she thought there was a chance Hans's father might be coming too. She hoped so. Even from Hans's rare and bitter comments about Dieter Hauer, Ilse had gleaned that he was a highly respected, even feared, police officer. But what could he do against men like Pieter Smuts? Against men like Jürgen Luhr, who had slashed a helpless policeman's throat before her eyes?

She thought of Alfred Horn. Lord Grenville had been right about one thing—the old man had taken a strong fancy to her. Ilse had enough experience with men to recognize infatuation, and Horn had definitely fallen for her. And out here, she realized, his infatuation might be the key to her very survival. And to her *child's* survival. She wondered what madness the old man had planned for tonight. From what Stanton had told her of Horn's business dealings, the meetings could augur no good for anyone. Still, she could not very well refuse to attend—not if she wanted to ingratiate herself further with Horn. And she might learn something that could help her escape.

Pulling a long blade of grass from the ground, she rose and started back toward the house. She had wandered further afield than she'd thought. Linah was no longer in sight, and before Ilse had covered fifty meters, she confronted something she had not seen on her way out: a shimmering stretch of hot asphalt running off through the grass and scrub. *A road?* Her heart quickened with hope. Then she saw the plane. Three hundred meters to her right, on a round asphalt apron, sat Horn's sleek Lear-31A. Ilse sighed hopelessly, crossed the runway, and continued west.

Topping a long rise, she caught sight of Horn House about a kilometer away. She gasped. Fleeing the house earlier, she had not looked back. But now she saw the whole estate laid out before her like a postcard photograph, stark and stunning in its originality. She had never seen anything like it, not in magazines, not even on television. Horn House—a building that from inside gave the impression of a classical manor filled with ornate rooms and endless hallways—was actually an equilateral triangle. A triad of vast legs surrounded a central tower that rose like a castle keep above the three outer wings. Crowning this tower was a glittering copper-plated dome. *The observatory,* Ilse remembered. Hexagonal turrets spiked each vertex of the great triangle. She half expected to see archers rise up from behind the tessellated parapets. With a sudden shiver, she realized that Horn House was exactly what it appeared to be—a fortress. On the seemingly featureless plain, the massive citadel stood on a hill set in the center of a shallow, circular bowl created by gradually rising slopes on all its sides. Anyone approaching it would have to cross this naked expanse of ground beneath the gaze of the central tower.

Ilse pressed down her apprehension and set off across the grass, using the observatory dome as her homeward beacon. She was quickly brought up short by a deep, dry gully. She remembered crossing a shallow defile earlier, but nothing like this. She must have crossed it at another point on her way out from the house. Easing herself down over the rim, she slipped carefully into the dusty ravine.

Pieter Smuts had christened this dry creek bed "the Wash," and it served as the first barrier in an impregnable security screen which the Afrikaner had constructed around his master's isolated redoubt. If Ilse had known what lay between her and Horn House, she would have hunkered down in the Wash and refused to take another step. The Afrikaner had used all his experience to turn the grassy bowl between the Wash and his master's fortress into a killing zone from which no intruder could escape alive. Every square meter of the circular depression was protected by Claymore mines, explosive devices containing hundreds of steel balls that, when remotely detonated, blasted outward at an angle and cut any living creature to pieces in a millisecond. Concrete bunkers, each armed with an M-60 machine gun, studded the inner lip of the huge bowl. Each was connected to the central tower by a network of underground tunnels, providing a secure means of directing fire and reinforcing the bunkers in the event of casualties. But the linchpin of Horn House's defenses was the "observatory." The nerve center of the entire security complex, the great copper dome housed closed-circuit television monitors, radar screens, satellite communications gear, and the pride of Smuts's arsenal—a painstakingly machined copy of the American Vulcan mini-gun, a rotary cannon capable of pouring 6,600 armor-piercing rounds per minute down onto the open ground surrounding Horn House.

None of these precautions was visible, of course; Pieter Smuts knew his job. The Claymore mines—designed to be spiked onto the ground surface—had been waterproofed and hidden beneath small mounds of earth. The bunkers had sheets of sun-scorched sod laid over their outward faces. Even the Vulcan gun slept silently behind the retractable "telescope cover" of the "observatory," waiting to be aimed not at the heavens, but at the earth.

Oblivious to the matrix of death that surrounded her, Ilse fought her way up and over the far rim of the Wash, brushed herself off, and continued toward the still distant house.

With a soft buzz Alfred Horn turned his wheelchair away from his security chief and gazed across the veld. Ilse had just topped the rim of the bowl to the northeast. With her blond hair dancing in the sun, she looked as carefree as a *Jungfrau* picnicking in the Grunewald. Without taking his eyes from her, Horn asked, "Is the helicopter available, Pieter?"

"Yes, sir."

Horn watched Ilse make her way across the long, shallow depression and climb the hill to the house. It took several minutes. When Ilse spied the Afrikaner, she started to avoid the table, but Horn motioned her over. She stepped tentatively up to his wheelchair.

"Is there any news of my husband?" she asked diffidently.

"Not yet, my dear. But there soon will be, I'm sure." Horn turned to Smuts. "Pieter, have one of the office girls order some clothes for Frau Apfel. They can fly them out in the helicopter. And make sure there's something conservative." He cast a surreptitious glance at Lord Grenville. "For tonight."

The young Englishman stared into his drink.

"Take Frau Apfel with you, Pieter," Horn suggested. "She can provide her sizes." He turned to Ilse with a smile. "Would you, my dear?"

Ilse hesitated a moment, then she silently followed Smuts. She didn't know what to make of Alfred Horn's eccentricities, but she remembered the Afrikaner's warning against disobeying him. She would do anything to keep her unborn child off the torture table that waited in the X-ray room.

Horn watched her walk into the house, a look of rapture on his face. Stanton observed him with growing disgust. *The old fool's past it,* he thought. *There's no stopping things now. You never learned the natural law, Alfred. You pass the torch to the young or you die.* As Stanton drained the dregs of his Bloody Mary, he made a silent toast to Sir Neville Shaw.

3:30 P.M. *Mozambique Channel, Indian Ocean*

Sixty-five miles off the wooded coastline of southern Mozambique, the MV *Casilda* hove to in the 370-mile-wide stretch of water that separates the old Portuguese colony from the island of Madagascar. A medium-sized freighter of Panamanian registry, her holds were full of denim fabric bound for Dar es Salaam on the Tanzanian coast to the north. After unloading this cargo *Casilda* would sail to Beira, the great railhead and port on the Mozambique coast, where she would take on a consignment of asbestos bound for Uruguay. But just now she had other business.

Strapped to the aft deck of the freighter like giant insects pinned to a display board were two Bell JetRanger III helicopters scheduled for delivery to RENAMO, the anti-Marxist guerrillas in Mozambique. Although the choppers would eventually be delivered to their official buyers, they had a job to do first—a slight detour to take. Supplied by a very wealthy gentleman in South America, the JetRangers were configured as commercial aircraft—with the papers required for legal transfer all in order—but a military man might be quick to notice that they could be easily modified for combat duty in a pinch.

The sun-blistered man who surveyed the two helos from the shadow of the wheelhouse awning was just such a man. An Englishman, and the only white man on the entire ship, his name was Alan Burton. During the entire five-week voyage, Burton had watched over the helicopters as if they were his own. In the next two days he would have to entrust his life to them, and as he did not particularly trust any of the men he would be working with, he felt that the most he could do was be sure of the choppers. They were his lifeline. His way in—his way out.

Casilda had been lucky so far. At no port of call had any customs officials conducted more than a cursory search of her holds. If they had, they would almost certainly have discovered the two large crates secreted in the stacks of bolted denim, which contained a rather amateurish assortment of assault rifles, ammunition, and grenades. They might even have discovered the special cargo hidden in Alan Burton's cabin, but the Englishman doubted it. He had hidden the mortar tube well.

In spite of this luck, Burton was angry. The man who had contracted for his services had led him to believe that his companions on this mission would know what they were about. They did not. Burton was the only man in the entire unit who knew this part of Africa, and, excepting the pilots, he was the only professional of the lot. The Cubans were all right, but there were only two of them—the pilots. The sloppiness of the Colombians was appalling. Burton considered them a rabble—no better than armed bandits. From his first contact with them, serious doubts about the mission had begun to eat at his confidence.

He lit a Gauloise and cursed the luck that had forced him to work under these circumstances. The company stank, but what could he do? He wasn't complaining about the money—the Colombian paid cash on the barrel head and lots of it. The Cuban pilots were getting six thousand in flight pay, plus salary, and Burton's bonus was twice that. But he had not taken this assignment for the money. He had taken it for The Deal. The Deal was a mysterious and wondrous arrangement of a kind he had never before heard—a solemn pact between a government and an exiled mercenary.

The price to be paid was not money, but a treasure that only one government in the world could pay. Burton didn't like to think about The Deal too much, for fear it would evaporate like every other precious hope in his life. Only in a few unguarded moments, on the foredeck at dawn watching the sea, had he caught himself thinking of green hills, of an old stone cottage, the smell of hothouse orchids, and sharing a pint with a man much like himself. At those times he would angrily push the visions from his mind.

He had enough to worry about. He worried what would happen if the Cubans discovered what lay inside one of the elongated boxes labelled RPG. Two million rand in gold was enough money to tempt even a man of Burton's high professional standards, and he doubted the Cuban pilots had any such pretensions. Strangely, the Colombians didn't worry him on that score. They would know enough about the price of betraying their master to keep clear of such temptations. But their lack of combat experience *did* worry him. He'd heard them boasting about violent shootouts in and around Medellín, but such hooliganism hardly qualified them to face the kind of opposition they were likely to meet in Africa.

They'll find out soon enough, he thought bitterly.

Burton expected a message today, relaying the latest situation from the target. There was supposedly an informer *inside* the target—an Englishman, no less—which Burton found very interesting. *At least he isn't a bloody Colombian,* he thought. Burton hoped the strike order would come today. He was ready to get off the goddamn ship.

As he smoked beneath the blue wheelhouse awning, a thin, deeply tanned man emerged from a hatch in the afterdeck and walked over to the helicopters. It was one of the Cuban pilots—a bright-eyed youngster named Diaz—checking the moorings of the choppers. Spying Burton, he made an O.K. signal with his thumb and forefinger, then disappeared back down the hatch.

Burton flipped his Gauloise over the side rail and walked out to the helicopters. *Maybe a few of them know what they're about after all,* he thought. *Maybe.*

CHAPTER TWENTY-NINE

6:55 P.M. Horn House: The Northern Transvaal

The Learjet appeared low in the east, a fiery arrow hurtling down the vast African sky. The dying sun glittered on the metal-skinned apparition as it settled onto the freshly laid asphalt runway. It taxied to the short apron, then turned slowly until it faced back up the strip, shimmering like a bird of prey next to Horn's helicopter.

A khaki-colored Range Rover trundled out to meet the plane. Pieter Smuts, dressed impeccably as a major of the South African Reserve, stepped from the driver's seat. He stood at attention, waiting for the Lear's short staircase to drop to the tarmac. He noticed that the aircraft bore no corporate or national insignia, only numbers painted across the gracefully swept tail fin.

When the jet's door finally opened, two dark-skinned Arabs stepped out. Each carried an automatic weapon that, from where Smuts stood, appeared to be the Israeli Uzi. *Hats off to the competition,* he thought dryly. The bodyguards made a great show of checking the area for potential threats. Then one of them barked some Arabic through the open hatchway. Smuts marched smartly toward the bottom of the staircase.

Four Arabs filed out of the aircraft and down the steps. Two wore flowing robes and sandals, two wore Western business suits. Smuts greeted the shorter of the two robed Arabs.

"Mr. Prime Minister?"

"Yes. Greetings, Mr.—?"

"Smuts, sir. Pieter Smuts, at your service. If you gentlemen will follow me into the vehicle, please."

The taller of the two robed Arabs—a man with piercing black eyes and a desert chieftain's mustache—surveyed the vast expanse of grass and scrub around them, then smiled. "This is not so different from our own country," he said.

The other Arabs laughed and nodded.

"Now," he said, "let us go to meet the man we have come to see."

Smuts led them to the Rover.

When they reached the main entrance of Horn House, all the servants—medical staff excluded—stood outside awaiting their arrival. This favorably impressed the Arabs, who walked disdainfully past the white-clad line and into the great marble reception hall. Almost immediately a low whirring sound drew their attention to the far side of the high-ceilinged room. A section of the wall slid swiftly back, revealing Alfred Horn sitting in his wheelchair inside a two-meter wide cubicle. On his gaunt body, the black suit and tie he wore gave him a rather funereal air. But something else about him had changed. The artificial eye was gone. Tonight Horn wore a black eyepatch in its place. Combined with the wheelchair, the eyepatch gave the wizened old man the quiet dignity of a battle-scarred war veteran.

"*Guten Abend,* gentlemen," he rasped. "Would you join me in the elevator, please?"

The elevator Horn occupied led down to a basement complex one hundred meters below the house. Only from this basement could one reach a second elevator that led up into the observatory tower of Horn House. When it became obvious that only four could fit comfortably into the elevator with the wheelchair, he ordered Smuts to wait with the Arab bodyguards.

"We'll see you in a few minutes, sir," Smuts said.

By the time the Afrikaner's party arrived at the second-floor conference room, Horn and his Arab guests were already seated around a great round table of polished Rhodesian teak. A large aluminum briefcase lay closed on the table before one of the business-suited Arabs. Linah had brought up chilled Perrier. Prime Minister Jalloud turned to the door and softly addressed one of the bodyguards.

"Malahim, we feel quite secure in Herr Horn's care. We wish you to wait downstairs for us. The housekeeper will give you refreshments."

The bodyguard melted away from the door. Smuts closed the door, locked it, then stood at attention beside it.

"Herr Horn," Prime Minister Jalloud said uncomfortably, "Our Esteemed Leader has asked us to obtain your permission to make a video recording of this negotiation, so that he may witness what transpires here tonight. He understands if you prefer not to have your face recorded, but in that case he asks if we might make an audio recording instead."

The room hung in tense silence. Alfred Horn laughed silently. He had four video cameras recording the meeting already. "You have video equipment in that case?" he asked.

"Yes," Jalloud replied, worried that he might already have overstepped the bounds of propriety.

"Set it up then. By all means. In negotiations of this magnitude, it is necessary to have an accurate record."

An audible sigh of relief went up in the conference room. At the snap of Jalloud's fingers an Arab opened the aluminum case and busied himself with a camcorder and tripod.

"I have a request of my own, gentlemen," Horn said. "I too keep records of meetings, but I'm old-fashioned. Do you mind if my personal secretary takes notes?"

"Certainly not," Jalloud replied courteously.

Horn pressed a button. In a few seconds the door opened to reveal a striking young blonde wearing a severely cut blue skirt and blouse. Ironically, the two Arabs who affected Western dress seemed most shocked by Ilse's sudden appearance.

"As you can see, gentlemen," said Horn, "my secretary is a woman. Is that a problem?"

There were some uncomfortable glances, but Jalloud ended any discussion before it could begin. "If you wish it, Herr Horn, it is so. Let us begin."

Ilse took a seat behind Horn, crossed her legs, and held a notepad ready to take down anything Horn might instruct her to. She ignored the Arabs completely, her attention on Horn's eyepatch.

Jalloud said, "Herr Horn, allow me to introduce my companions. To my right is Major Ilyas Karami, senior military adviser to Our Esteemed Leader. He is understandably out of uniform."

The tall, mustached Arab wearing robes stood and nodded solemnly.

"To my left," Jalloud continued, "is Dr. Hamid Sabri, our

nuclear physicist. Do not let his youth mislead you. In our country he is the preeminent expert in his field."

A bookish young man wearing a business suit stood and bowed his head.

"And finally," Jalloud concluded, "Ali Jumah, my personal interpreter. He speaks excellent German and humbly waits to serve you."

"Excellent," Horn said in German. Until now they had all spoken a very uncomfortable English.

"And I," the robed Arab said proudly, "am Abdul Salam Jalloud, prime minister of my country."

"Of course," Horn said. "Do you mind if I smoke?"

Instantly the Arabs brought out packs of American cigarettes and lit up. Horn accepted an Upmann cigar from Smuts's pocket supply. As Smuts lit the cigar, Horn noticed a rectangular swatch of color emblazoned on Major Karami's gold lighter. A solid field of blue-green—the flag of Libya. *A military man to his bones,* Horn thought. *The homeland is never far from his mind.* A quick glance at Smuts told Horn that his security chief had also noticed the lighter.

"Perhaps you gentlemen should begin by stating your requirements," Horn suggested. "That should give us a clear idea of where we stand."

Jalloud yielded the floor to Dr. Sabri, the physicist. The bespectacled young Libyan spoke soft, precise Arabic. Jumah the interpreter translated whenever he paused for breath.

"What we need," Dr. Sabri began, "is fissile material. Either highly enriched uranium (U-235) or plutonium (Pu-239). We need as much of either isotope as you can supply, both if possible. At the very least, we need fifteen kilograms of uranium or five kilograms of plutonium. By 'highly enriched' I mean uranium enriched to at *least* eighty percent purity. Anything less is useless to us. We also need triggers—either lens or krytron types—and sculpted steel support tubes." He paused nervously. "These are our requirements," he concluded, and resumed his seat.

When the interpreter's voice faded, there was silence in the room. The Libyans, watching Horn closely, failed to notice the shock whiten Ilse's face as she realized the implications of the young scientist's words. She had not seen the Libyan flag emblazoned on Major Karami's lighter, and even if she had, she wouldn't have recognized it. But she knew enough science to understand that these men were discussing atomic weapons. It took all of her willpower to remain seated and silent. She watched the remainder of the meeting through a gauzy haze of unreality, like someone who has stumbled onto the scene of a bloody traffic accident. Alfred Horn, however, watched the Libyans as affably as if he were negotiating the price of Arabian horses.

Prime Minister Jalloud finally broke the silence. "We are prepared to pay any reasonable price for these items, Herr Horn. In the currency of your choice, of course. Dinars, dollars, pounds, marks, ECUs, rand ... even gold bullion. The question is, are these items available at *any* price? Do you actually have access to them?"

Alfred Horn smiled. This was the moment he had been waiting for—not for weeks or months or years, but for decades. For a *lifetime*. He could barely suppress the excitement he felt on the threshold of realizing his life's work. "Gentlemen," he said softly. "Allow me to be frank."

The Libyans nodded and leaned forward. Ilse held her breath, praying she would awaken from the nightmare. Pieter Smuts remained impassive as ever, his gray eyes glued to his master's face.

"For over a decade," said Horn, "your leader has sought to obtain nuclear weapons. He has attempted to develop a manufacturing capability in your home country, and also to purchase weapons ready-made from other nations. The first avenue proved impossible; students from your country aren't even allowed to study nuclear physics in the great universities of the world. And the second option, while theoretically possible, has proved to be an embarrassing circus of bribery, scandal, and hoaxes. The Chinese sent you packing in 'seventy-nine. India backed out of a proposed deal and refused to fulfill her obligations to you, even after you cut oil shipments to New Delhi by one million tons. Belgium yielded to U.S. pressure, and Brazil has refused to give any valuable assistance, in spite of the fact that you sold them massive amounts of arms in 'eighty-two ..."

The Arabs tensed in fury, but Horn continued reeling off his grocer's list of Libyan misadventures in a voice that was its own arbiter of truth. Finally Prime Minister Jalloud, white with indignation, rose from his chair.

"We did not come here to be insulted, sir! If you have nothing but words for us, there are other suppliers!"

"Like Edwin Wilson?" Horn countered. "And his grubby Belgian compatriot Armand Donnay? The uranium they offered you might—I say *might*—have been worth using as nose-weights for jets, but I doubt it. You're lucky you had young Sabri to recognize Wilson's proposition as garbage."

The young physicist nodded modestly, but Major Karami said, "Perhaps we planned to irradiate their uranium at our Tajoura reactor, to produce plutonium for a weapon of our own."

Dr. Sabri's sarcastic expression instantly undercut this feeble attempt to save face.

"Gentlemen," Horn said soothingly, "I did not bring you here to insult you. I merely state these facts so that the true basis of our negotiations will be plain, and so that you will understand the necessity of paying the price I ask."

The mention of money placated the Arabs somewhat. It suggested that the man in the wheelchair—whatever his opinion of them—might actually have access to the materials they had come to purchase. And that was all that mattered.

"Go on," said Jalloud, taking his seat again.

"Here is the situation as I see it," said Horn. "As we speak, the world does not even perceive Libya as a nuclear threshold country. Your requirements, however, paint a significantly different picture. The need for highly enriched uranium, triggers, and sculpted tubes tells me that you are building your own weapon, and that you have probably already obtained all the necessary components other than those you seek from me. Your request for an absolute minimum of fifteen kilograms of U-235 or five kilograms of plutonium suggests that you have procured tamper/reflector technology and are trying to build the smallest bomb you can—possibly even a portable weapon. Am I correct?"

No one disputed him.

Horn turned directly into the lens of the softly humming video camera that had been forgotten by everyone in the room but him. "I propose something quite different," he said solemnly. "I am offering you an aircraft-deliverable nuclear weapon with a forty-kiloton yield, completely assembled *with* fissionable core, ready for detonation."

In that moment the air in the conference room seemed to

turn to water. Although the Arabs knew their leader would not view the videotape for many hours yet, they also knew that the words spoken by the old man in the wheelchair were for him alone. Their presence had become irrelevant.

Horn spoke softly to the humming camera. "I can offer you a weapon of the implosion or the gun-assembly type, and, subject to certain conditions, I can continue to provide these weapons at the rate of one every forty days."

Major Karami's black eyes glittered as he fumbled for another cigarette. At length Jalloud asked softly, "Are you serious, sir?"

Horn's single burning eye was answer enough.

Major Karami regained his composure first. "And what is the price of this great gift?" he asked warily. "There are only so many billions of dinars in our treasury."

"Not a single piece of gold do I desire," Horn rasped.

"What then?" Jalloud asked, puzzled. "Oil?"

"My price, Herr Prime Minister, is *control*. I will provide you with a *single* weapon. You will not stockpile it and wait for more weapons. You will use it—and against a target *specified by me*." Horn raised a spindly finger. "Only then will more weapons be provided."

"That's ridiculous!" Major Karami exploded. "Why not use it yourself? We have our own targets and we'll use our weapons as we see fit! Your price is too high!"

"One moment, Ilyas," Jalloud cautioned. "What is your target of preference, Herr Horn?"

"Thank you for asking," Horn said softly. "It so happens that the target I want destroyed coincides with the one your leader has unsuccessfully tried for years to destroy—the State of Israel. To be exact, Tel Aviv."

Ilse let out a short gasp from her chair behind Horn.

"Tel Aviv!" Karami exclaimed, unbelieving. He turned to Jalloud. "Does he speak the truth?"

"Do you?" the prime minister asked.

"Tel Aviv," Horn murmured. "I want the Jews wiped from the face of the earth."

"As do we!" Jalloud retorted. "But what good is one weapon to us? If we have to wait forty days for another, we will be annihilated. The Zionists have two *hundred* nuclear bombs."

Horn smiled. "Yes, they do. But think for a moment. I assume you do not want Palestine rendered permanently uninhabitable. You merely wish the Jews pushed into the sea, yes? Tel Aviv is the first step on the road to reclaiming Jerusalem. If skillfully managed, your attack could even be made to appear as an Israeli nuclear accident."

Major Karami seemed to be debating with himself. "Herr Horn," he said hesitantly, "Israel's air defenses are the toughest in the world. Even with the best of luck, it would be difficult to guarantee that a single plane carrying this warhead could get through to Tel Aviv. And even if it did, we would have no chance to mask our responsibility for the attack."

Horn saw that admitting this weakness had cost the Libyan major dearly. "I appreciate your frankness," he said. "If you would prefer, I could arrange to deliver a slightly smaller warhead—a thirty-kiloton yield—that could be fitted with a timer and concealed inside a large crate. It would not be nearly as compact as the American SADM—the famous "suitcase bomb"—but it could fit easily inside a small truck."

Prime Minister Jalloud started to speak, but Major Karami restrained him. "I believe we can do business," he said hoarsely, trying to maintain some semblance of composure. "Are there any other restrictions?"

"Time," Horn replied. "I want Tel Aviv destroyed within ten days."

Stunned, Major Karami sat back in his chair. Horn's words coursed through his veins like a powerful narcotic. After endless years of cowering beneath the Zionist nuclear threat, Libya would finally possess the means to strike back! Karami clenched and unclenched his fists in anticipation of wielding the deadliest sword ever to fall into Muslim hands. Then he went still.

"How do we know that you actually have access to such weapons?" he asked. He was almost afraid to hear the answer—afraid that his heady dreams of conquest would disappear like smoke from a tent fire.

Horn smiled. "Because I have one in the basement complex of this house, ready for Dr. Sabri's inspection. If you gentlemen will follow me . . ."

Gasps went up around the table. The Arabs began shaking each other's hands and talking rapidly among themselves. The interpreter did not even attempt to translate the effusive congratulations that filled the room.

In the corner behind Horn, Ilse's face had gone slack. After Luhr's drugs and the horror in the X-ray room, witnessing this nightmarish conclave had pushed her over the edge of endurance. As the Libyans filed out of the room behind Horn's motorized chair, she slid awkwardly to the floor, tiny beads of cold sweat sparkling on her bloodless forehead.

7:30 P.M. Burgerspark Hotel, Pretoria

In a small room on the fourth floor of the Burgerspark Hotel, Jonas Stern reviewed his interception plan with his men. Gadi Abrams lounged on one of the hotel beds. Professor Natterman sat in a chair by the window, wearing a bulky bulletproof vest beneath his tweed jacket. Stern himself sat on the bed opposite Gadi. Yosef Shamir stood in the lobby four floors below, listening through a hand-held radio.

"Thirty minutes until the rendezvous," Stern said. "Where's Aaron?"

Just then they heard a key in the door. The young commando stepped in. "The elevator control box is in the basement," he said. "I can stop the elevator wherever you want it."

Stern nodded. "What about the radio?"

Aaron frowned and pulled a small walkie-talkie from his pocket. "I could hear you, but there's static. And you were only on the fourth floor. With eight floors between us, I'm not so sure."

"We'll check it when we get up there." Stern consulted a drawing he had made on a piece of hotel stationery. "All right, here it is. I've taken a second room on the eighth floor of this hotel. The closest I could get to suite 811—the room where Sergeant Apfel is registered—was 820. It's down the hall, past the elevators, and around the corner. Gadi and I will be in that room. Yosef will be watching the lobby. Aaron will be in the basement. Professor Natterman will wait here." Stern tugged at the flesh beneath his chin. "Before we intercept Hauer and Apfel, I intend to let the kidnappers make contact in whatever way they choose. I suspect that they will call suite 811 and instruct our German friends to meet them at a different place. If they attempt to seize or kill the Germans, however, we will intervene."

Stern looked over into the corner. There, in a large open suitcase, lay the fruits of one of the telephone calls he had made from Natterman's Wolfsburg cabin. A Jewish arms dealer of Stern's long acquaintance had had the suitcase ready when Stern arrived at his Johannesburg home this afternoon. In the suitcase lay five short-barrelled Uzi submachine guns, four silenced .22 caliber pistols, two of five walkie-talkies, silencers for the Uzis, and a small hoard of ammunition.

"Obviously," said Stern, "Professor Natterman must make our initial contact with the Germans. Of the five of us, Captain Hauer knows only him. Hauer is likely to shoot anyone else who exposes himself too soon. Ideally, the professor will make the contact by telephone. When Yosef sees the Germans enter the lobby, he will radio Gadi and me in room 820. Gadi has already bugged suite 811, so we will be monitoring what transpires after Hauer and Apfel get inside. After the kidnappers have made their contact, we will call Professor Natterman here. Professor, you will immediately call suite 811. If you reach Hauer or Apfel, you will give the little speech we went over together."

Natterman nodded attentively.

"If you cannot reach them—because of a busy signal or anything else—we will go to the backup plan. Gadi and I will observe the Germans as they leave suite 811. If they take the stairs down, we will radio you here, whereupon you will walk immediately to the stairwell and wait for them." Stern smiled encouragingly. "You don't need to run, Professor. The stairwell is less than twenty meters from this room. Hauer and Apfel must cover four floors before they reach you."

Natterman nodded again.

"If they take the elevator down, however, it gets a bit more complicated. In that case Gadi will radio Aaron in the basement, and Aaron will stop the elevator between floors— hopefully between the fourth and third. I will radio you"— Stern pointed his finger at Natterman—"and tell you to go to the elevator shaft. Yosef will be here with you. He will have come up from the lobby, after making certain that Hauer and Apfel are not being followed. He will pry open the elevator doors for you, and you will speak to Hauer while he is trapped below you. He'll probably be trying to get out through the roof anyway."

Natterman looked anxious. "The elevator scenario seems rather complicated."

"It's the only way we can insure contact without frightening Hauer away or getting killed ourselves."

"Why can't I just wait in the lobby for them?"

Stern sighed heavily. "Because we would then risk frightening the kidnappers away. And the kidnappers, Professor, are the men I came to South Africa to get."

Natterman looked glum. "Can your men do all they're supposed to? The timing seems close."

Gadi Abrams grinned. "We are *sayaret matkal,* Professor," he said proudly. "This is child's play for us."

Stern shot him a dark look. "Hauer will not be child's play, Gadi. You boys have trained with GSG-9, so I shouldn't have to amplify that. Captain Hauer is an *extremely* dangerous man. Don't underestimate Sergeant Apfel either. He is under unimaginable pressure, and a man like that is capable of anything."

Gadi nodded. "Yes, Uncle."

Stern glanced at his watch, "Let's move. Twenty minutes to the rendezvous, and we still need to test the radio reception from the basement."

As one, Stern, Gadi, and Aaron collected their weapons from the suitcase and moved toward the door. "Good luck, Professor," Stern said, then they went out.

As Stern moved toward the elevators, Gadi fell back beside him and whispered, "I didn't want to alarm anybody, Uncle, but what happened to our body armor?"

Stern grimaced. "Another buyer came along and offered more money."

"But why give the Professor the one vest we have? You should be wearing it."

Stern shook his head. "Natterman may have to stand in the stairwell and wait for Hauer and Apfel to come running down. There's a strong chance Hauer will fire a reflex shot before he even recognizes the professor. *That's* why he gets the vest."

In room 401, Professor Natterman sat with the walkie-talkie clenched in his hand. It was sticky hot inside the armored vest. He wanted to take it off, but he reasoned that if Stern had given him the only vest they had, he probably needed it. Setting the walkie-talkie on the table, he stood and stretched. His joints ached terribly from all the unaccustomed exercise. He had been on his feet for less than a minute when the door slid open.

Facing the professor stood a woman wearing an expensively cut red skirt, a white blouse, and a red hat. She carried a Vuitton handbag in her left hand. It took Natterman several moments to realize that she also held a gun.

Swallow stepped inside the room and closed the door. "I've come for the Spandau papers, Herr Professor," she said in a crisp, low voice, her British accent unmistakable. "Would you be so kind as to get them for me?"

"I . . . I don't have them," Natterman stammered.

"Stern has them?" Swallow asked sharply.

Stunned by her knowledge, Natterman said, "Who are you?"

Swallow's lips drew back, exposing her small teeth in a fierce animal glare. *"Does Jonas Stern have the papers?"*

With a fool's courage Professor Natterman grabbed for the walkie-talkie on the table. Swallow destroyed it with a three-shot burst from her silenced Ingram machine pistol.

"Take off your clothes," she ordered. "Every stitch." When Natterman hesitated, Swallow jerked the Ingram in his direction. *"Do it!"*

While Natterman, pale and shaking, removed his clothes, Swallow began searching the hotel room.

CHAPTER THIRTY

7:40 P.M. *Horn House: The Northern Transvaal*

Deep in the basement complex of Horn House, Alfred Horn shepherded his Libyan guests through a maze of stainless steel and glass and stone. Huge ventilator fans thrummed constantly, forcing filtered air down from the surface one hundred meters above. An intricate network of cooling ducts maintained the silicon-friendly environment required by the formidable array of computers purring against the walls; the brittle air also extended the life of the manifold chemicals and weapons stored here. The Libyans surveyed the labyrinth of tubing, hoods, and pipes in reverent silence. Only young Dr. Sabri, the Soviet-educated physicist, found it hard to suppress his enthusiasm as he toured the lab. Most of the visible hardware had been produced by one or another of the various high-tech subsidiaries of Phoenix AG, but the man who controlled them all was about to reveal a product of very different pedigree. Horn gradually led the Libyans toward the rear of the basement, where something resembling a giant industrial refrigerator stood gleaming in the fluorescent light. Stretching from floor to ceiling and wall to wall, the aluminum-coated lead chamber awaited the men like a futuristic crypt. Three great doors without handles were set in its face.

"Pieter," Horn said softly.

The tall Afrikaner stepped over to an electronic console and flipped a switch. An alarm buzzer sounded briefly; then, with a sucking sound, the center door opened a fraction of an inch. A sickly orange-yellow light dribbled out of the crack. Smuts slipped a hand inside and pulled. When the door opened completely, the Libyan physicist gasped.

"Go ahead, Doctor," said Horn, "have a look."

Sabri looked shaken. "You don't store the weapon in halves?"

"It's quite safe," Horn assured him. "The core has been temporarily removed. The weapon can be disassembled with the tools beside it. You may verify the soundness of the design at your leisure."

Dr. Sabri stepped gingerly into the storage chamber and tiptoed around the weapon. The blunt-nosed cylinder stood menacingly on its tail fins like a blasphemous icon. Painted a gleaming black, the bomb bore a single marking, emblazoned on one of its fins: a rising Phoenix. The bird's head was turned in profile, its sharp break screeching, its single fierce eye wide, its talons engulfed by red flames. Sabri's left hand caressed the cool metal of the bomb chassis like a woman's thigh. Horn watched the Libyans with thinly veiled curiosity. Prime Minister Jalloud stood well back from the vault, his eyes on the physicist. His interpreter did the same. Major Karami stood rigid, his black eyes fixed unwaveringly on the upended weapon. "Where is the core?" he asked hoarsely.

"The fissile material," Horn replied, "in this case plutonium 239—lies in a lead vault below our feet."

"We must see it."

"I'm afraid you can't actually *see* it, Major, not without more safeguards than are available in this room. But you can see its effects." Horn waved his right hand.

Smuts pressed another button on the console. Instantly a section of the metal floor to the left of the storage chamber whirred out of sight. Beneath it lay a lead-lined vault containing a wooden pallet stacked with orange fifty-five-gallon drums.

"The plutonium is in those drums?" Jalloud asked, instinctively stepping back from the gaping vault.

"They're lined with concrete," Horn explained. "We're perfectly safe. For a short time, anyway. Look while you can. Those drums contain enough plutonium to turn the State of Israel into a smoking cinder."

While the Arabs made approving noises, Smuts took a small metal box from a nearby shelf. The box had a long cable dangling from it with some type of sensor on the end. When Horn explained that the machine was a portable radiation detector, Dr. Sabri came out of the chamber and followed Smuts to the edge of the vault. He watched the Afrikaner lower the sensor until it hung just above the row of drums. Most modern radiation detectors emit no sound, but Smuts's "Geiger counter" began to crackle like an untuned radio dial. All of the Libyans but Sabri drew back in terror. While the interpreter held both hands protectively over his genitals, the physicist leaned over to read the instrument.

Major Karami asked, "How can we be sure the drums contain plutonium?"

Horn shrugged. "I have no motive to deceive you. Have I asked you for any money?"

"You are a rich man," Karami pointed out. "Perhaps your only goal is to make our country look foolish in the eyes of the world. In the eyes of the Zionists."

"Silence, Ilyas!" Prime Minister Jalloud commanded.

Horn smiled knowingly. "My intentions regarding the Jews are identical to your own, Major. You can be sure of that."

Karami looked skeptical. He turned to Dr. Sabri and spoke rapidly in Arabic. "Could not spent reactor fuel produce this reaction? Couldn't the instrument be tampered with to produce any desired reading?"

Already protective of his new toy, Sabri spoke defensively. "Spent fuel alone would not produce the reaction you see, Major. The drums contain plutonium."

"You sound very sure of yourself for an inexperienced young man."

"I am the most experienced man you will find in our country!"

"Yes, yes, we know that," Prime Minister Jalloud said, switching back to English. "Why don't we close the vault now?"

Horn nodded. Smuts pressed the button that hydraulically moved the lead-lined cover back into place. Angered by Major Karami's skepticism, Dr. Sabri returned to the bomb chamber. In a few seconds he had the weapon open for inspection. His eyes glinted like those of a boy over his first electric train. Major Karami, however, looked far from satisfied.

"I understand your skepticism, Major," Alfred Horn said. "And under the circumstances, perhaps you deserve more assurance of my motives than my word alone." Pieter Smuts shifted uneasily. "If you gentlemen will join Dr. Sabri," Horn went on, "I believe I can satisfy all doubts as to my motives regarding the Jews."

Major Karami stepped quickly into the yellow-lit chamber. Jalloud and his interpreter reluctantly followed him inside, where they formed a respectful half-circle around the bomb.

Smuts leaned down and whispered into Horn's ear, "I don't think this is a good idea."

"Nonsense," Horn said. He buzzed his wheelchair up to the door of the chamber. "The time for secrecy is past. Remove the decal, Pieter."

With a sigh of frustration the Afrikaner flipped a wall switch, flooding the storage chamber with fluorescent white light. Then he shouldered past the Libyans and knelt beside the upended weapon. Taking a penknife from his pocket, he unfolded a short blade and began to scrape lightly beneath the flames of the painted Phoenix. Soon he had pried up a triangle of black polyurethane. He put the knife back into his pocket, then took the curled edge between his thumb and forefinger and pulled with a gentle, steady pressure. There was a soft, adhesive ripping sound as the black decal tore away from the metal fin.

Prime Minister Jalloud gasped.

"Allah protect us," whispered the interpreter.

Dr. Sabri stared in mute wonder.

But Major Karami smiled with wolfish glee. For hidden beneath the black polyurethane decal was Alfred Horn's true Phoenix design—a blood red planet Earth clutched in the flaming talons of the Phoenix. And spanning the red globe—a curved black swastika. Karami's sigh of satisfaction told Horn that his revelation had produced its desired effect.

Horn smiled. "It will take the doctor a half hour at least to complete his inspection. Why don't we go upstairs and wait in more comfortable surroundings? Smuts will stay until he has finished."

"An ... an excellent idea," Jalloud stammered.

Jumah the interpreter stumbled out of the chamber, his face ashen. He and Prime Minister Jalloud followed Horn's wheelchair to the elevator at the far end of the basement lab. But Major Karami lingered behind. At the elevator Jalloud turned and watched him. Still only halfway to the elevator, the stubborn major stood staring back down the length of the lab to the vault where Sabri—under the watchful gaze of Pieter Smuts—toiled over his deadly prize.

Horn called, "More questions, Major?"

Karami turned and walked toward the elevator. "What is behind the other two doors? More bombs?"

Horn's smile faded. "No. I keep only one weapon here. They're too dangerous."

"More dangerous than raw plutonium?" Karami stepped into the elevator.

Horn smiled thinly. "Far more dangerous. There is always the chance that some unscrupulous individual or nation might attempt to steal them."

The elevator closed with a hydraulic hiss.

"I'm sure this house is well protected," Karami baited.

"Did you see any security on your way in?" Horn asked gamely.

Karami's eardrums registered a painful relief of pressure as the elevator rocketed toward the surface. He had already noted the lack of security with great satisfaction. "No, I didn't."

"It's there, Major. Smuts is the best in his field."

"And what is his field, Herr Horn? Personal security?"

The old man smiled. "I believe the English term is 'asset protection.' "

"Translate," Karami commanded. When the prime minister's interpreter obliged, Karami said, "Ah. Was he a soldier, then, this Smuts? Where did he train?"

Horn folded his spotted hands in his lap. "He served in the South African army as a young man. But he has a varied background. By the time I found him, he'd fought all over Africa."

The elevator opened on the ground floor.

"And who trained him in this 'as-set protection,' as you call it?" Karami asked. "The South African Army?"

"I did," Horn said tersely, rolling into the spacious reception hall.

"With all due respect," Karami called, "who trained *you*?"

Horn stopped his wheelchair and whirled to face the Libyan. "The German Army," he said quietly.

The Arab's eyelids fell, hooding the yellow sclera of his eyes.

"More questions?" Horn challenged.

Fearing a deal-breaking dispute, Prime Minister Jalloud stepped between the two men. "The major has a great curiosity, Herr Horn. He's known as a zealous military historian in our country."

Karami ignored him. "You must have fought in the Second World War, Herr Horn. Were you SS?"

Horn spat contemptuously on the marble floor. "I said the army, Major, not Himmler's lapdogs. The *Wehrmacht* was my home!" Horn had taken all he intended to from this arrogant Bedouin. "Listen to me, Arab. In 1941 the mufti of Jerusalem went to Berlin to *beg* the Führer's help in destroying the Jews of Palestine. The Führer generously armed the Arabs"—Horn stabbed a finger at Karami—"yet *still* your fathers could not push the Jews into the sea! I hope you do better this time!"

Major Karami shook with rage, but Horn simply turned his wheelchair away and whirred off down a long corridor.

Jalloud shot Karami an angry glance. "Fool! What are you trying to do?"

"Just testing the old lion's claws, Jalloud. Calm yourself."

"Calm myself?" The prime minister caught hold of Karami's robe. "If you wreck this negotiation, Qaddafi will have your head on a spike! And mine with it!"

Karami easily pulled his arm free. "If you had half the cunning of a rug peddler, Jalloud, you'd see that this old Nazi needs us as much as we need him. Probably more." Karami reached out and laid his forefinger lightly on Jalloud's cheek. "When our business is done," he vowed, "I will gut that old man for his insult."

Jalloud stared at Karami with horror, but the major only smiled.

"Hurry!" the interpreter whispered. "He's already around the corner!"

"Let us go, my friend," Karami said pleasantly. "We'll see what else our host has to offer us." He started down the hall.

Jalloud followed slowly. He didn't know exactly what the second-in-command of the Libyan People's Army had in mind, but he knew already that he didn't like it. He also knew that the fanatical, impulsive dictator who still held the reins of power in Tripoli would probably love it. "Allah protect us," he murmured, hurrying after the receding figure of Karami. "From ourselves, if no one else."

* * *

Ilse Apfel opened her eyes and stared at the ceiling of her bedroom prison cell. *How did I get here?* she wondered. As she lay there, trying to gather her thoughts, a key scratched in the door. Ilse sat up slowly, her eyes on the knob. It turned slowly; then the door burst open. Robert Stanton stood there wobbling, with two crystal goblets in one hand and a bottle of cognac in the other. The Englishman smiled crookedly.

"Guten Abend, Fräulein!" he bellowed.

While Ilse stared, he stepped in, closed the door, and propped himself haughtily against it.

"Get out of my room," she said forcefully.

"Now, now, *Fräulein,* let's just relax and have a sip of something nice, shall we?"

"I'll scream," Ilse threatened, though she knew it sounded ridiculous.

"Wonderfully solid house, this," Stanton said, grinning. "Damned near soundproof, I should think."

Ilse summoned her coldest voice. "If you touch me, Herr Horn will make you pay."

Stanton raised an eyebrow. "The old goat's taken quite a fancy to you, it's true. But he's terribly busy just now, hob-nobbing with the Great Unwashed. He doesn't have time for domestic squabbles. So, it's up to us to have a good time while the business gets done." Stanton poured two brimming glasses of Rémy Martin V.S.O.P., spilling as much again on the floor.

The mention of the Arabs brought the earlier meeting back in a rush. "Business?" Ilse echoed. "You're aware of what he's doing, and you call it *business*? Aren't you an Englishman, for God's sake?"

"The genuine article," Stanton said with a mock bow. "I told you, my blood's nearly as blue as the queen's."

"Then why don't you try to stop him?"

Stanton shrugged. "What's the point? Alfred stopped listening to me long ago. Although what he thinks he can get from those flea-ridden Arabs, I haven't the slightest idea. Poppies, I suppose. Very old hat. He certainly can't *sell* them anything—they've got their own sources of supply in the trade, haven't they? Rather like trying to sell them oil, what? Now, come here and give us a kiss."

"My God," Ilse whispered. "You don't even know what he's doing! What he's selling!"

Stanton lurched forward, sloshing cognac onto her blouse. "I don't care if he's selling the bloody crown jewels, love. I'm well out of it now and . . . darling, you make quite a dish in those natty secretary's clothes. Makes one quite anxious to see what you look like out of them."

Leering through a haze of alcohol, Stanton set the bottle on the bedside table, drained his glass and smashed it against the door with a flourish.

Ilse struggled to stay calm. "Lord Grenville," she said evenly, "you're drunk. You don't know what you're doing. Herr Horn will have you killed if you do this. Don't you know that?"

Stanton laughed raucously, then his face grew deadly serious. "I advise you to choose your allies with care," he said, wagging a finger in her face. "Very soon dear Alfred may no longer be in a position to have *anyone* killed."

Ilse thought swiftly. She was afraid, but not in the way she had been on the X-ray table. This babbling Englishman was no Pieter Smuts.

"All right, then," she said. "I suppose there's nothing I can do." As Stanton watched fascinated, Ilse lifted the bottle of Rémy Martin and swigged from the mouth of the bottle. She let some of the brandy dribble down her chin, her eyes fixed on Stanton's. "Lock the door," she said. "I don't want to be interrupted."

With an astonished gape Stanton turned around and lurched toward the door. The half-full bottle of Rémy Martin crashed against the base of his skull like a glass avalanche. He staggered and fell to the floor. Ilse rifled his pockets and found the key he'd used to enter her room. Praying he didn't have access to any others, she flung the bedroom door wide, dragged his unconscious body into the hall, then jumped back into her room and slammed the door. She tried to lock it with the key, but it didn't seem to fit. She cursed as the useless metal bent in the lock. Either she'd taken the wrong key from Stanton, or the proper key only worked from the outside. She thought of opening the door and searching him again, but she had lost her nerve. Her entire body was shaking. Ilse lurched into the bathroom and locked it with the flimsy door latch.

"Please hurry, Hans," she murmured. "God, please hurry."

7:55 P.M. Burgerspark Hotel, Pretoria

When Hans Apfel walked into the lobby of the Burgerspark, Yosef Shamir felt his heart thump with excitement. Hans looked neither left nor right as he walked, but marched straight across to the elevators set in the far wall. Yosef lifted the walkie-talkie that connected him to Stern's room on the eighth floor.

"Apfel has arrived," he said. "He's going for the elevators."

"Any sign of Hauer?" asked Gadi Abrams.

"No. Should I wait?"

A pause. "No. Get up to Natterman's room."

Yosef scurried to a second elevator. Just as he stepped inside, he glimpsed the broad back of a man wearing a dark business suit disappear through the fire stairs door. "I think Hauer's here," he said as the elevator doors closed. "He's coming up the stairs."

"Acknowledged," Gadi replied. "Get the professor ready to move."

Dieter Hauer crashed through the third floor fire door and hit the UP elevator button. The stairs were taking too long, and if anything rough was going to happen in suite 811, he didn't want to be too late or too exhausted to participate. After a brief wait, he darted into an empty elevator and punched 8. The car whooshed up the remaining floors in seconds. It took Hauer a moment to get his bearings, but within fifteen seconds he was knocking on the door of suite 811.

Hans opened the door after scrutinizing him through the fisheye peephole. "See anyone?"

Hauer stepped into the suite. "No, but I went through the lobby pretty fast."

"The room's empty," Hans informed him. "Do you think they'll call, or send somebody up?"

"I think they'll call." Hauer glanced at his watch. "In one minute we'll know for sure."

Gadi Abrams adjusted the headphones he was wearing and looked up at Jonas Stern. "Hauer's inside," he said.

Stern nodded. "Let's see if anyone shows up."

The unexpected ring of the telephone in the Israelis' room

startled both Gadi and Stern. Gadi asked sharply, "Who besides our own men knows we're here?"

Stern tightened his lips. "No one. Except maybe the kidnappers." He lifted the receiver. "Yes?"

"Someone's trying to hit us!" shouted a voice in Hebrew. *"The professor's stark naked!"*

"Yosef?" Stern said. "Yosef, what's happened? Where are you?"

"In the professor's room! Just after we left Natterman, someone came in here looking for the papers. A *woman*. I used the phone because she blew the professor's radio to pieces. He's hysterical!"

Stern touched the bulge in his pocket where the three Spandau pages lay. "Yosef, stay where you are. Stay on the line—"

"Telephone ringing in Apfel's room," Gadi said, pressing the headphones to his ears.

"Yosef," Stern instructed, "wait five seconds, then start calling suite 811. Make certain the professor is ready, and keep trying until you get through."

Yosef rang off.

Hans jumped a foot off the bed when the ringing telephone fulfilled Hauer's prediction. Hauer glanced at his watch: eight P.M. exactly. Hans darted between the beds and snatched up the receiver.

"Hello?"

"Sergeant Apfel?" said a male voice.

"Yes!"

"You know the Voortrekker Monument?"

"What? Wait ... yes, the big brown thing. I saw it as I drove into town."

"Be there tomorrow at ten A.M. Come alone. Ten A.M. Do you have that? The Voortrekker Monument. Ten in the morning. Alone."

"What about my wife? Will Ilse be there?"

"*You* be there. If you're not alone, she dies."

The caller broke the connection.

Hans dropped the receiver onto the floor, his face slack. "Well?" said Hauer. "What did they say?"

Hans stood silent for several seconds. "They want me to meet them tomorrow," he said finally. "At the Voortrekker Monument."

Hauer nodded excitedly. "That's a good place for us. Very public. That's where I'll lay out our terms for the exchange. What time is the rendezvous?"

A strange calm seemed to settle over Hans. His eyes seemed unfocused. He sat down hard on the bed.

"What *time,* Hans?" Hauer repeated softly, his eyes straying to the door. "What time is the rendezvous?"

Hans looked up, straight into his father's eyes. "Six," he said in a robotic voice. "Six P.M. at the Voortrekker Monument."

Down the hall and around the corner, Gadi Abrams shook his fist in triumph. "The rendezvous is at six," he murmured, "at the Voortrekker Monument. Apfel's off the line, but I didn't hear him hang up." Gadi pressed the headphones to his dark head. "No phone ringing. Come on, Professor . . ." Suddenly Gadi jumped up and pulled off the headphones. "The professor can't get through! Apfel didn't hang up the phone!"

Stern forced himself to think clearly. His well-planned operation was unraveling around him. Snatching up the phone, he tried to call Yosef and the professor. "Busy," he said. "They're still trying to reach Hauer. That means the stairs won't be covered."

"Aaron has to stay at the elevator box," Gadi said quickly. "You've got to keep trying to reach the professor. That leaves me to cover the stairs." The young commando picked up his Uzi and started for the door. He had not heard it open.

With the mute surprise of a man watching the earth split open at his feet, Gadi watched a small round fragmentation grenade rolling toward him through the foyer. The door slammed shut.

"Grenade!" he shouted.

While Stern—a veteran of three desert wars and countless guerilla actions—dove behind the far bed, Gadi Abrams proved the boast he had made minutes before about the *sayaret matkal* commandos. With the reflexes of a gifted soccer player, he stopped the grenade's forward motion with his right foot, then kicked it sideways into the bathroom. Then he hurled himself backward into the space between the two double beds.

Hauer was leaning out of the door down the hall, straining his ears for the slightest sound, when Swallow's grenade exploded in the bathroom of room 820.

"Donnerwetter!" he roared. "What the hell was that?"

Reaching back blindly, Hauer wrenched Hans through the door. "Stay with me!" he commanded. "And don't use your gun unless you absolutely have to!"

Hauer dragged Hans toward the fire stairs, away from the explosion. They crashed through the metal door at speed, careening headlong down concrete steps like teenaged hoodlums. As they passed a large, red-painted 5, Hauer caught hold of Hans's jacket and pulled him against the wall. He clapped a hand over Hans's mouth and listened for any sound of pursuit. At first he heard only their own ragged gasps. Then a slow creak, as of someone attempting to silently open a disused fire door, echoed through the stairwell. When the crash came, Hauer knew that their pursuer had given up all hope of stealth. He shoved Hans downward and charged after him.

They took each flight in two leaps, only lightly touching the rails as a guide. On the third-floor landing Hauer grabbed Hans and growled a dozen words into his ear, then slipped through the fire door while Hans continued downward. Hauer drew his stolen Walther—then he recalled his warning to Hans. The explosion upstairs would draw all attention to the eighth floor. If he fired the unsilenced Walther here, he would certainly draw some attention to himself. With a curse of frustration he slipped the Walther back into his pocket and waited.

Four floors above him, Yosef Shamir flung himself down the stairs like a man possessed. From the moment he'd gotten off the telephone with Stern, the young commando had been battling his instincts. Stern had ordered him to stay put, but from what Natterman had told him, Yosef feared that the woman with the machine pistol was now on her way up to find Stern. Leaving Natterman to complete the call to the Germans on his own, Yosef had raced upstairs to help Gadi and Stern. He had reached the seventh floor when he heard the door just above him crash open. He slipped quietly through the seventh floor door just in time to see Hauer and Hans rush past him down the stairs. With a sudden sick feeling, Yosef realized he was probably the sole remaining link to Stern's quarry. The young Israeli bounded down the fire stairs with no regard for safety, his mind only on regaining contact with the Germans.

When the steel edge of the fire door materialized in front

of him like a phantom, time slowed down. Yosef twisted his body to avoid the deadly obstacle, but he simply couldn't move fast enough. The door caught the side of his forehead, opening a three-inch gash and dropping him like a stone on the landing.

Hauer threw his weight against the third-floor fire door and forced Yosef's unconscious body out of the way, then knelt to examine him. He didn't recognize the face, but he hadn't expected to. Yosef's pockets were empty. No wallet, no coins, no clue to his name or nationality. Even his clothes had no labels. On impulse Hauer took hold of Yosef's head and lifted it to search for the tattooed eye ...

A scream of agony rebounded up through the stairwell. A man's scream. Then a pistol shot exploded.

"Jesus!" Hauer cried. He dropped Yosef's head on the concrete and raced down the steps after Hans.

As Gadi Abrams came to his knees and leveled his Uzi at the smoke-filled foyer, the first spray of bullets from Swallow's Ingram tore into room 820. Gadi hit the floor and cursed in fury. Either the gunman was using a silencer, or the grenade had blown out his eardrums. Beneath the far bed he saw Stern speaking into his walkie-talkie.

"Aaron, this is Jonas. We are pinned down here. Please respond." Stern waited while Gadi rose up and peppered the door with a burst from his silenced Uzi. "Aaron!" Stern tried again. "Please respond!"

"He can't hear you!" Gadi shouted. "Too much concrete between him and us! We've got to storm our way out, Uncle! We're going to lose the Germans otherwise. It's the only way!" The young commando leapt to his feet.

Feeling a surge of adrenaline unlike any since the '73 war in Sinai, Jonas Stern clutched his own Uzi, rose up, and followed his shouting, blasting nephew into the smoke of battle.

Hauer found Hans on the garage landing, standing silently over a corpse. The body was blond and fair-skinned and looked about thirty-five. Its right hand gripped a pistol.

"I told you not to use your gun!"

"I didn't!" Hans shot back.

Then Hauer saw the knife. The German knife from the

sporting goods store. It was buried to the hilt in the dead man's left side. "I'll be damned," he said.

He fell to his knees and searched the dead man's clothes. He immediately found a British passport—which he placed in his own pocket—and a wallet, from which he removed the money. Robbery was the most plausible option under the circumstances. He glanced quickly behind the dead man's ears for the Phoenix tattoo, but saw no mark. It took a considerable effort to dislodge Hans's knife. Hauer wiped it clean on the corpse's jacket, then slipped the knife into his belt.

"Who is he?" Hans murmured.

"Worry about it later. Let's go."

As Hauer turned and grabbed the door handle, he felt motion behind him. He turned again, then froze. Hans had snatched up the corpse by the collar and he was screaming, screaming in German at the top of his lungs: *"Where is she, goddamn you? Where is my wife?"*

Gadi and Stern burst out of room 820 to find an empty hallway. A strange, cloying scent lingered in the air. Perfume.

"Who the hell was that?" Gadi shouted. "The Germans? They must be in one of these rooms."

"They're gone!" Stern called from the door of suite 811. "Come on!"

Together they raced to the elevator. As the doors slid shut, Stern tried again to reach Aaron at the elevator-control box. "Aaron!" he cried. "Forget the elevator! Try to stop the Germans! Aaron!"

In the concrete basement of the hotel, Aaron Haber heard Stern's crackling commands as: "Aaron! ... elevator! ... stop the Germans!" Dutifully, the young Israeli threw the switch that stopped the elevator between the fourth and third floors.

When the car jolted to a stop, Stern and Gadi stared at each other with ashen faces. Gadi punched the button to open the door, but got no response. He tried to pry the doors open with his Uzi, but they wouldn't budge. Whirling around in fury, he saw no one. Stern had sat down on the floor of the elevator and leaned against the veneer wall, his eyes closed.

"Child's play," he said softly. "Isn't that what you said?"

* * *

Hauer wrenched the rented Toyota over to the curb in front of a government sandstone office building. He leapt out of the car, ran to the left front wheel well, and crouched down. Eight seconds later he was back beside Hans, holding a heavy paper packet covered with duct tape. The packet held the Spandau papers and the photos Hauer had shot during the afternoon.

"So much for the Burgerspark," Hauer said. "We're not going back to the Protea Hof, either. Our passports are obviously blown."

Hans rocked back and forth in the passenger seat.

"That explosion sounded like a grenade," said Hauer. "Who in hell could have thrown it? The kidnappers?"

"We got out," Hans muttered. "That's all that matters. We just have to stay alive until the rendezvous tomorrow."

"We need cover," said Hauer. "This time we ignore our friendly cabbie's advice, though. This time we're going to a real fleabag. Somewhere we won't need any identification at all."

Hans nodded. "How do we find that?"

"Just like we would in Berlin."

Hauer let in the clutch and pulled onto Prince's Park Straat, then turned southwest onto R-27. He slowed at each intersection and peered down the side streets. He knew what he wanted: garish neon, street people, liquor advertisements, the howl of bar music. The universal siren song that draws the lonely and the bored and the hunted to the dark marrow of every city in the world. From what Hauer had learned already, he suspected it would be easier to find such a place in Johannesburg than in Pretoria. But he knew that anonymity could be had anywhere for a price.

With Hans watching the streets fanning north, he drove on.

8:26 P.M. Horn House: The Northern Transvaal

Alfred Horn sat beneath the greenish glow of a banker's lamp in his dark study. Opposite him, immersed in shadow, Pieter Smuts awaited his questions.

"They're gone?" Horn said quietly.

"They're gone."

"Comments?"

Smuts glowered from the shadows. "I don't like Major Karami. I don't trust him. I think it was a mistake to show him the plutonium. It was a mistake to show him the Phoenix mark."

Horn laughed softly. "Is there anyone you do trust, Pieter?"

"Myself. You. No one else."

"You must have a little faith in human greed, Pieter. The Arabs want the weapon too desperately to risk losing it through treachery. Now, what of the cobalt case?"

"Can't be done, sir. Not in ten days."

Horn let out a sigh of exasperation. "What about using a standard cobalt jacket?"

Smuts shrugged. "It would work, but the Libyans would realize what they were dealing with. They'd probably remove the jacket before the strike. The only way we can fool them is by having the bomb case itself seeded with cobalt. And our metallurgists are having serious problems. We had delays getting the cobalt itself, and the casting is far from simple. It's the rush, sir. If we could slow down a bit, go back to the original plan—"

"Out of the question!" Horn snapped. "I may be dead in twenty days. The British are coming for me, I'm certain of it. What will the bomb do without the cobalt?"

"To be honest, sir, the short-term damage will be just as severe without it. And with the prevailing winds in Israel at this time of year, a direct forty-kiloton strike on Tel Aviv may well take out most of the population of Jerusalem with radiation alone."

Horn nodded slowly.

Smuts reached out of the shadows and laid four videocassettes in the pool of light on Horn's desk. "There," he said forcefully, "is the proof of Libyan involvement with the bomb. I must ask again, sir. Why trust the Arabs at all? My men and I can place the weapon in Tel Aviv ourselves, and we can use a standard cobalt jacket. Your original goal will be accomplished with half the risk and twice the likelihood of success."

Horn shook his head. "Not half the risk, Pieter. *You* would be at risk. I cannot allow that. Besides, Israeli Intelligence is very good. This must be a genuine Arab attack. Only that will bring about the outcome I want. If the Libyans fail, you will get your chance. But we'll speak of that no more for now. Tell me, what of our German policeman?"

"I made the call myself. Sergeant Apfel took it. I think Hauer might be with him, but it doesn't matter. One of my men is meeting Apfel tomorrow morning at the Voortrekker Monument. We'll kill Hauer there if he shows up, and we'll have both Apfel and the papers here by tomorrow afternoon."

Horn toyed with his eyepatch. "And what has dear Lord Grenville been up to?"

Smuts wrinkled his nose in disgust. "He's spoken to no one outside the house. I'm monitoring all the phones to make sure. He's got his eye on Sergeant Apfel's wife, though, I can tell you that."

Horn's face hardened. "See that he makes no trouble for her."

"I'll see he makes no trouble for anyone ever again."

"Not yet, Pieter," Horn said gently. "We're not sure of anything yet."

"He asked me again if he could go up in the tower."

Horn smiled wryly. "Robert is a good boy, Pieter, but he's mixed up. We don't want him to know all our secrets, do we?"

Smuts snorted. "Have you seen that runny nose of his? I think he's using what he's selling." The Afrikaner drew a short, double-edged dagger from his belt and held it in the light. "I tell you, one false step and I'll cut that bastard's balls off and feed them to him with parsley."

Horn cackled softly. "*Gute Nacht,* Pieter."

Smuts stood and sheathed his knife. "Good night, sir."

As the Afrikaner passed Ilse's bedroom, he listened at the door. He heard nothing. Had the hall light been on, he might have noticed the dark bloodstains on the carpet. But it wasn't, and he didn't. He moved on. He had a treat waiting in his room. A village girl from Giyani—a virgin, if the headman could be believed—no more than thirteen, and black as coal dust. Alfred Horn's Aryan princess could sleep the night in peace; Smuts knew what he liked: a sweating *kaffir* girl with the smell of coal smoke still on her. When he first came into the bedroom, he liked to ask the girls if they'd brought their passes with them. Sometimes the young ones were so scared they broke down and cried. It was a good way to set the tone for the evening.

CHAPTER THIRTY-ONE

The South African Airways 747 landed with the dawn.

As the jet taxied up to the terminal, Kripo detective Julius Schneider collected his flight bag from the overhead compartment and prepared to deplane as quickly as possible. Twelve hours was too long to sit in a seat booked for a dead man. Schneider edged his bulk into the crush of honeymooners, big-game hunters, and businessmen jamming the aisle, all the while wishing that Colonel Rose could have managed to get him a military flight. He took a deep breath when he finally made it out of the aircraft. The anxious passengers and the South African summer heat had combined to produce a singularly unpleasant closeness, even at dawn.

"What a change," he muttered, thinking of the snowdrifts he'd left behind at Frankfurt. He slung his flight bag over his shoulder and headed for Customs.

Standing in the long queue, Schneider looked impatiently at his watch. He wanted to get to a telephone as soon as he could. If he was lucky, he thought, he might trace Hauer's and Apfel's false passports to a hotel before they got moving for the day. He wondered what Hauer was doing now. Schneider did not know Hauer personally, but he knew his reputation. He figured a lone wolf like Hauer would keep an open mind long enough to listen to his arguments about Phoenix. Schneider didn't give a damn about the Spandau papers; all of Rose's ranting about them meant little. What Schneider wanted was to sever all contact between Wilhelm Funk's neo-Nazi fanatics in West Berlin and their Stasi counterparts in the East, and then to drive both Phoenix groups back into the dark hole from which they had sprung.

His instincts told him Dieter Hauer was the man to help him do that.

Before he contacted Hauer, however, he intended to check out the local Russian situation. Because no matter what Kosov was telling Colonel Rose, the KGB *would* have people here in South Africa—probably at the head of the pack chasing the Spandau papers. Schneider wondered where they would be based. The South African government allowed no Soviet embassies on its soil; he had checked. Thus the KGB had no legal residency from which to conduct operations. That complicated things. In fact it made him downright nervous. And the more he thought about it, the surer he became that he would be making a mistake if he talked to Hauer before he knew *exactly* where the Russians were.

He would not have to look far. Yuri Borodin stood just four places behind Schneider in the sweltering line. The Twelfth Department agent had easily stayed clear of the big German during the flight from Frankfurt. Borodin always traveled First Class, and he had spent the entire journey in the second-story lounge of the 747. He laughed aloud as Detective Schneider lumbered through the Customs gate. Comparing his own spare frame to the German's, the Russian saw a mental image of a sleek Jaguar following a double-decker bus. It did not occur to him what was likely to happen if the Jaguar hit the bus head-on.

9:10 A.M. Bronberrick Motel: South of Pretoria

Hauer closed the door to the dank-smelling motel room and leaned against a battered veneer desk. After much searching last night, he and Hans had finally taken this rathole just off the N-1 motorway, ten miles south of the capital. Hans sat sullenly on a twin bed, fanning himself with a magazine he'd found in the mildewed bathroom. His knife was jammed into his belt; his Walther lay a few inches from his right hand.

"I found another car," said Hauer, his face slick with sweat. "A Ford. From a small firm, just what we wanted. I dumped the Toyota in an underground garage."

"Good," Hans replied without looking up.

"I really think it would be safer if you came along," Hauer pressed.

"You don't need me to help you calibrate the scope. And I'm not taking any chances on missing the rendezvous."

"But you're not going to the rendezvous," Hauer said, pocketing the keys. "Didn't you realize that? This rendezvous is where I use our leverage to turn the tables on the kidnappers. If you show up, Phoenix will assume you have the papers with you. They'll simply kidnap you, then kill you. I'm going to the Voortrekker alone. You'll keep the papers safe here."

Hans nodded slowly. "I see. But I'm still not going with you now. Anything could happen out there. You could kill us both just by forgetting to drive on the left side of the road. Where would we be then?"

Hauer nodded pensively. "All right. But don't leave this room for anything, understand? I'll be back in three or four hours. After I zero-in the scope, I'm going to scout for an exchange location. I saw a stadium on the map that looks good. I'll be back long before six."

Hans forced a smile. "I'll be waiting."

"Fasten the chain behind me."

Hans stood to see him out.

"And for God's sake get some sleep, would you?" Hauer said. "Ilse wouldn't even recognize you like this."

As soon as he heard Hauer's car pull away, Hans picked up the telephone. "This is room sixteen," he told the desk clerk, his voice edgy. "Call me a taxi. *Bitte?* Of course I can pay for it!"

He slammed down the phone and trudged over to the lavatory. The mirror was cracked in a starburst pattern, causing his reflection to stare back at him like jumbled pieces of a puzzle. Hauer was right. He looked as bad as he felt. Bloodshot eyes, sallow cheeks, dirty blond hair sticking out in all directions. If he didn't sleep soon, he would collapse where he stood. All night he had lain awake in the stifling heat, listening to Hauer's steady snoring, fighting the solitary horrors of his imagination. From the moment he had learned the Spandau diary was incomplete, his fears had been working on him, tapping in the back of his brain like a dull pick hammer.

Hans turned the cold tap, wet a washrag, and brought it to his stubbled face. The water felt good, but it didn't improve his appearance. He stuck his head under the tap and soaked his hair, then smoothed it as best he could with his fingers. He hadn't *planned* to lie to Hauer about the rendezvous time. But when he heard the cold voice on the telephone last night in the Burgerspark suite, some deep part of him had simply overridden his conscious will. He believed in Hauer's abilities. If anyone could save Ilse by using force, his father could. But what if *no one* could? Hans had seen miraculous rescues during his short tenure with the police department. But he had seen other cases, too. And the harder he tried to shut those cases out, the clearer they became in his mind.

Throughout the night vague images had turned to searing nightmares. The dead blond girl from the Havel, fished out of the muck by a grappling hook two days after the "failsafe" police rescue operation. Anonymous Berliners who had died by gunfire, by stab wounds, other ways. Erhard Weiss's gouged and bloody chest. He thought of the girl from the Havel. The police had used the ransom as bait, as they always did. A half-million Deutschemarks in cash. But the kidnappers had managed to withhold the girl just long enough to escape. For Hans the lesson was clear. No plan was fail-safe. And no matter how deeply he believed in Hauer's commitment, he could not risk seeing Ilse pulled from that river, or one like it. Who could predict how the kidnappers would react when Hauer tried to turn their operation back against them? Rational men would probably make a deal. But rational men did not tattoo eyes on their scalps or gouge religious symbols into the chests of Jews.

At the veneer desk, Hans scribbled a note to Hauer on the back of a promotional flyer. Then he picked up his Walther from the bed and laid it on top of the note.

The ring of the telephone startled him. "Taxi's here," growled the desk clerk.

Hans took a long last look at his pistol, but he knew he could not take it where he was going. He reached beneath the mildewed mattress and withdrew the Spandau papers, which he had stolen while Hauer showered. He slipped them into his shirt (beside the knife he had taped to his ribs); then he stepped out into the glaring sun. A blue Mazda 323 sat idling in the parking lot. He walked over to the driver's window.

"You know the Voortrekker Monument?" he asked in English.

The driver rolled his eyes and jerked his thumb toward the backseat. Hans climbed in and the cab screeched away.

The Voortrekker Monument sits atop a hill three miles south of central Pretoria. Visible from most parts of the city, this dun-colored building is the spiritual symbol of the Afrikaner nation. Its domed Hall of Heroes holds a huge frieze commemorating the Great Trek of the Boer pioneers, who fled northward from British colonial rule in 1838. Hans caught a glimpse of the massive dome as his driver exited the N-1 freeway, then swung back under and headed west. Climbing the monument hill, he realized he would be ten minutes early for his rendezvous.

He paid off the cab, then moved as instructed to a spot directly beneath the frieze in the Hall of Heroes and studied it like a Muslim who has finally reached Mecca. The tourists shuffling around him were mostly Afrikaners. With his classic German looks, Hans thought he probably looked as Afrikaner as the rest. He was wrong. Feeling a tap on his shoulder, he whirled to see a Bantu man of medium height—a Zulu, actually, but Hans knew nothing of such distinctions—with a large camera bag slung over his shoulder. Hans failed to notice the irony of a black man visiting the monument that memorialized the conquest of his native country. The Zulu never once glanced up at the frieze. He hurried out of the building and down the slope, Hans scrambling after him. A shining blue Range Rover waited at the base of the hill. The Zulu indicated that Hans should get into the rear seat. Hans climbed in.

"You have the papers?" asked the Zulu in broken German. Hans nodded. "Are you taking me to my wife?"

Without a word the Zulu started the engine and drove down the hill, then swung the Range Rover onto R-28 and headed into central Pretoria. He drove until they intersected the N-1 freeway, then climbed into the northbound traffic. Hans looked blankly out the window as the suburbs gave way to gaudy storefronts, liquor stores, and finally the government matchboxes of black settlements outside the city.

Hans fingered the knife beneath his shirt. The thought of what the kidnappers might do if they realized the diary was incomplete made his bowels squirm, but what choice did he have? At least by acceding to their demands he had gained a chance to try to explain the missing pages. In the middle of some football stadium, with a dozen guns sighted on Ilse and himself, anything could happen.

Suddenly Hans felt his throat tighten. Though he had been staring straight at the back of the Zulu's head, his conscious mind had only now registered what his eyes were seeing. Behind the Zulu's right ear—in plain sight—was the ominous design sketched in the Spandau papers: the eye—the mark of Phoenix! Yet unlike Funk's men, this tribesman wore no tattoo. The eye had been *branded* onto his scalp with a red-hot iron! The ugly, whitish-pink keloid scar chilled Hans's blood. He stared, hypnotized by the mark. What did it really symbolize? *Follow the Eye,* the Spandau papers had charged. Yet it seemed to Hans that the eye was following him!

"How . . . how far do we have to go?" he stammered, trying to keep his anxiety in check.

The Zulu said nothing.

Hans touched the haft of the knife in his shirt. Obviously the black man didn't intend to reveal anything about the upcoming rendezvous. Hans forced his eyes away from the scar and concentrated on the road. The shimmering highway stretched in a seemingly endless line across the veld, toward a destination Hans could only pray would reunite him with Ilse. If the kidnappers were as hard as the land they now passed over, he thought, their chances of getting out alive were small. He caught himself wondering if he should have told Hauer the truth about the rendezvous after all. Maybe Hauer *could* have pulled off the exchange. Maybe . . .

"Too late now," he muttered.

"*Bitte?*" the Zulu said sharply.

"*Nichts!*" Hans snapped. He tried not to stare at the branded eye as the Range Rover droned on.

10:45 A.M. Horn House: The Northern Transvaal

Linah had set out a fine brunch in the enclosed garden near the southwest turret of the estate. Subtropical fruit trees splashed blossoms of color against the high stone walls. Alfred Horn and his security chief sat together drinking coffee and speaking quietly.

"And what of Captain Hauer?" the old man asked.

Smuts shrugged. "I had four men at the Voortrekker ready to kill him, but he never showed up."

"Could he be following Sergeant Apfel?"

Smuts shook his head. "He might try, but my driver will know if he does. We'll have no problems from Hauer."

Horn nodded.

"How long do you expect it will be before we hear something from the Arabs? Three days? A week?"

"I've already heard," Horn said casually, and took a sip of his coffee. "Qaddafi himself called me an hour ago. He has accepted our terms. What did I tell you, Pieter? If you want a job done quickly, hire a hungry man. Prime Minister Jalloud will return tomorrow night with men to transport the weapon."

"Tomorrow night!" Smuts exclaimed. "I had no idea it would be that soon. Two hours ago I sent half my men back to the mine."

Horn smiled. "That was a little premature, Pieter. But I shouldn't worry. There will be no problems with the Libyans. And if there were, I am confident that you could protect us from that. You have had years to prepare your defenses."

Smuts looked uncertain. "Did Qaddafi mention Major Karami?"

"No."

Smuts nodded suspiciously. "Karami is planning some kind of double-cross. I'm certain of it. I'd better make additional security arrangements."

Horn smiled cagily. "You might want to make some arrangements before tonight, Pieter. I have the feeling we may need a few extra men."

Smuts squinted curiously at his master. But before he could ask for clarification, Lieutenant Jürgen Luhr opened a sliding glass door and marched toward the table. Horn eyed the tall German suspiciously, but Smuts waved a greeting.

"*Guten Morgen,* Herr Oberleutnant."

"*Guten Morgen!*" Luhr replied, clicking his heels together smartly. He inclined his head first to Horn, then Smuts.

"Sit," Smuts commanded.

"Just a moment," Horn interjected. "Show me your mark, Herr Oberleutnant."

Instantly Luhr moved to the old man's wheelchair and leaned down so that Horn could inspect the tiny tattoo behind his ear. Horn actually licked his finger and rubbed the mark to make sure it was indelible. When he was satisfied, he gave Luhr permission to sit down.

"*Danke,*" said Luhr, taking a chair and sitting ramrod straight.

Horn stared at Luhr some time before speaking. His one flickering eye lingered on the blond hair, the hard blue eyes, the trim figure and classical features. He nodded slowly. The young policeman had sparked something in his memory.

"Has your stay in our cell taught you some respect for orders?"

Luhr had prepared for this. "Sir, I drugged Frau Apfel only for her welfare, I assure you. She struggled so hard against her bonds that I feared she might injure herself."

Horn's single eye glazed like a chip of ice. "There is no excuse for insubordination! A man who disobeys orders is a threat to everyone around him!"

Luhr wiped a sheen of perspiration from his forehead.

"But," Horn went on in a softer tone, "my security chief seems to think I should give you a second chance. He speaks highly of your work in Berlin."

Luhr raised his chin proudly.

"Frau Apfel will be joining us soon, Herr Oberleutnant. When she arrives at table, you will issue an immediate apology. Then the matter will be closed. Clear?"

"Absolutely," Luhr said solemnly. He had never balked at licking the proper pair of boots.

While Linah poured coffee for Luhr, the sound of someone talking softly drifted around the corner of the house. Shortly Lord Grenville appeared, wearing dark sunglasses and muttering to himself. A huge white square of gauze was taped high on the left side of his head, but it did little to conceal the massive purple bruise that extended from behind his ear to his left eye.

"My God!" Smuts exclaimed, as the Englishman wobbled to the table.

"What have you done now, Robert?" Horn asked wearily.

"Got pissed again. Literally. Took a fall in the loo last night that would have killed a bloody wildebeest. Didn't break the skin, though, thank God. I'd have bled to death on the spot." He pulled a silver flask from his pocket and poured two jiggers of brandy into his coffee. "King and country," he toasted, and drained the mixture.

Smuts glared. Such conduct by anyone else in the old

man's presence would be unthinkable, yet Stanton made it a rule.

"Robert," Horn said, "when will our next payment from the Colombians arrive?"

Stanton tried in vain to mask his surprise at this question "What? Oh. It's coming in by ship next week, remember? Brazilian gold this time. Supposedly it's never even seen the inside of a bank."

Horn leaned his head back and smiled. His good eye looked past Stanton and settled on a fragrant eucalyptus tree. "And how will our gold get from this mysterious ship to here?"

"By helicopter," the Englishman said, frowning now. "I told you that yesterday."

Pieter Smuts looked quizzically at his master.

"Yes," Horn said, "yes that's right. You did."

Everyone looked up at the sound of the garden gate. Ilse stood there, her blond hair uncombed, her eyes swollen from lack of sleep.

"Guten Morgen," Horn called. "Please join us."

Ilse edged toward the table, her wary eyes on Stanton.

With an effort that stunned all present, Alfred Horn struggled from his wheelchair and stood until Ilse had seated herself in the wrought-iron chair Smuts offered her. Jürgen Luhr rose immediately to deliver the apology demanded by Horn, but before he could speak, Lord Grenville slid his chair away from the table.

"If the company will excuse me," he mumbled. "My apologies."

While everyone stared, Stanton rose and left the garden by way of a glass door leading into the main house.

Inside Horn House, Stanton hurried to Alfred Horn's study and locked the door. He felt surprisingly calm, considering what he was about to do. He lifted the telephone receiver and dialed a London number that he had committed to memory.

"Shaw," growled a tired voice.

"This is Grenville."

"Where are you?" Sir Neville Shaw asked sharply.

"Where do you think?"

"Good Christ, are you mad?"

"Shut up and listen," Stanton snapped, feeling his pulse

start to race. "I had to call from here. They won't let me go anywhere else. Look, you've got to call it off."

"*What?*"

"He knows, I'm telling you. Horn knows about *Casilda*. I don't know how, but he does."

"He can't know."

"He does!"

There was a long pause. "There's no stopping it now," Shaw said finally. "And your information on Horn's defenses had better turn out to be good, Grenville, or you'll answer to me. Don't call again."

The line went dead. Stanton felt sweat running down the small of his back. The die was cast. Somewhere off the coast of Mozambique, a man named Burton waited to change his life forever. *Perhaps Alfred was merely toying with me,* Stanton thought hopefully. Smuts had evinced no more suspicion than was usual. Yet Stanton had but one choice in any case—hold firm. If he could do that for eight hours, Horn's days of power would end, and he would be free. London would be satisfied, and one of the largest conglomerates in the world would become the property of Robert Stanton, Lord Grenville in fact, as well as in name.

For a brief moment, Stanton worried that Ilse might betray his advances of last night, but he dismissed the thought. If she had intended to do that, she would have done it already. Unlocking the study door, he set out for the garden in better spirits than he had been in for some time. All he had to do now was find a way into the basement complex before the attack came. He had never entered it before, but he would today.

He could hardly wait.

11:00 A.M. MV Casilda: *Madagascar Channel, Off Mozambique*

The laden helicopters lifted off the deck of the ship like pregnant birds, but they lifted. Juan Diaz, the pilot of the lead chopper, looked over to see that his *compadre* flying the second ship had taken off safely. He had. Diaz turned to the tanned Englishman sitting in the seat beside him.

"They're up, English. Where we going?"

Alan Burton tossed a folded sheet of paper into the Cuban's lap. A mineral survey map of Southern Africa. "First stop, Mozambique," he said. "Just follow the lines on the map, sport."

Burton turned and looked back at the two rows of Colombians who sat shoulder-to-shoulder against the cabin walls of the JetRanger. With their dark faces, scruffy beards, and bandolier ammunition belts, they looked like armed migrant workers. Sick ones, at that. The greenish cast of their skin suggested that by leaving the ship, they would merely exchange their seasickness for airsickness. Burton didn't care what they looked like, as long as they could cause some commotion. He could do the job alone if someone provided a sufficient diversion.

He was glad the end of the mission had finally arrived, not least because they were finally leaving the *Casilda*. He didn't care if he never saw another ship in his life.

"I'm supposed to fly by these goddamn chicken scratches?" Juan Diaz complained, shaking the map in the Englishman's face.

Burton gave the Cuban a black look. "That's what you're being paid for, sport. Now let's move."

"What about a flight plan?" Diaz asked. The two choppers still hovered over the old freighter.

"You're holding it," said Burton. "I can show you the landmarks. Just watch for enemy aircraft."

The Cuban narrowed his eyes. "How do I know who is the enemy?"

Burton grinned. "It's everybody, sport. Simple enough?"

After a grim moment of reflection, Diaz nudged the stick, and as one the two JetRangers moved out over the ocean, toward the coastline, toward Africa.

11:25 A.M. *Room 520, The Stanley House, Pretoria*

Gadi Abrams let the drapes fall closed and turned back to Stern. "Still no sign of them, Uncle. No Hauer, no Apfel."

Stern got up from one of the beds and rolled his shoulders. He had said little since last night's fiasco at the Burgerspark Hotel. "They're probably holed up in some cheap hotel, waiting for the rendezvous at the Voortrekker Monument."

Professor Natterman was pacing out the far end of the

room. "So why are we watching the Protea Hof?" he snapped.

"We can always intercept them at six at the Voortrekker Monument," Stern replied. "But I think Hauer might return to the Protea Hof before then."

Natterman snorted with contempt. "What about that woman?" he asked. "Are you sure it was the same woman from the plane?"

"Absolutely," Gadi said. "From the description you gave and the perfume I smelled in the hall, I have no doubt at all."

"Who is she, then?" Natterman asked. "What does she want?"

"She wants me," said Stern.

"What makes you say that?" Gadi broke in. "Nobody knows where you are."

Stern half-smiled.

"Who wants you dead?" Professor Natterman asked.

"Who doesn't?" said Gadi. "The Syrians want him, the Libyans, the Palestinians ... you name it. That's why he has to live where he does."

Stern shot his nephew a warning glance; then his face softened. "I suppose it doesn't matter," he said. "Remember the kibbutz I described to you, Professor? My retirement home? Well, it's no ordinary kibbutz."

"How do you mean?"

"It's a special settlement for men like me. Retired fieldmen. Men who have prices on their heads."

Gadi grinned. "Uncle Jonas's head carries the highest price in town."

Stern frowned.

"But Gadi said the woman on the plane was European," said Natterman. "Not Arabic."

"Precisely," said Stern. "And of the European countries, only one has agents who might want me dead."

"*England?*" Natterman asked, his eyes alight.

Stern ran his hand across his chin. "I know who the Englishwoman is. Her name is Swallow. Or it was, many years ago. But right now she concerns me much less than the big fellow who checked in here this morning."

"I say he's a friend of Hauer's," Gadi declared. "Backup from Berlin. He's obviously doing the same thing we are—

watching Hauer's room. He's right beneath us, by the way, though I don't think he knows it."

"Why do you insist he's German?" Stern challenged.

"Don't give me that, Uncle. A Jew can smell a German, can't he? No offense, Professor."

"None taken. A German can smell a Jew just as well."

Gadi glared at Natterman. "His name's Schneider, which is German enough. We'll know what he is for sure in an hour, in any case. Tel Aviv is checking him out. By the way, they told me Hauer *was* one of the sharpshooters at the Munich Olympics. How did you know that?"

Stern half-smiled. "I had one of my notorious intuitions when I read his police file. We might be able to use that somehow."

"Could this Schneider be part of Phoenix?" asked Yosef Shamir. The young commando wore a large white bandage around his forehead. "Maybe he threw the grenade last night. Maybe he was the one who hit me with the door."

"That was Hauer," Stern said firmly.

"Who fired the gunshot?" asked Yosef. "I was only semi-conscious in that stairwell, but I'm certain I heard a shot."

"Nothing about it in this morning's newspapers," Gadi said. "There was no body in the stairwell. If our German cops shot at someone, they must have missed."

Stern smiled. "I think it went this way: Swallow's grenade panicked the Germans. They fled down the stairs, Apfel in front. They ran into trouble, Apfel panicked and fired his gun. I read Hauer's police file. If he'd fired his gun, he wouldn't have missed."

"I'll keep that in mind when we meet him," Gadi said soberly.

"You're not *going* to meet him!" Natterman flared. "He's given you all the slip!"

Stern padded slowly over to the hotel window. "Hauer is coming back to the Protea Hof," he declared, parting the drapes and staring across at the seven-story hotel. "I don't know how I know it, but I do."

One floor below the Israelis, Kripo detective Julius Schneider held the telephone against his sweating cheek as he sat on the edge of the bed. Beside him lay his hat, half a sandwich, and two empty bottles of beer. Into his ear came the angry drawl of Colonel Godfrey Rose.

"You too proud to take a tip from a Russian, Schneider?"

"No, Colonel."

"Kosov gave me the name of the son of a bitch who mutilated Harry. I think he suspected it all along. He's a Russian too, you believe that? Name's Borodin, Yuri Borodin. Twelfth Department, KGB. According to Kosov, he's a real hotshot. Renegade out for glory, that type. I guess that's what Kosov meant about you watching your back."

Schneider made a sound in his throat that was halfway between a growl and a sigh. "So Borodin could have seen me leaving Major Richardson's apartment. He could be following me now."

"Could be, Schneider. Have you located Hauer and Apfel yet?"

"I'm watching their hotel room now. They aren't in it, though."

"Hmm. You decided how you're gonna handle Hauer? You gonna try to take the papers?"

"I don't know yet. Hauer may have better ideas than I do about crushing Phoenix."

Rose was silent for a moment. "Yeah, well, the Russians are getting pretty itchy about Phoenix themselves. Kosov heard that a low-ranking Stasi agent cracked under torture this morning. Seems he's a member of something called *Bruderschaft der Phoenix.* The Russians are already talking to the State Department about setting up a special inter-Allied commission to deal with the Rudolf Hess case, Phoenix, and all related affairs. Sort of an international Warren Commission."

"A what, Colonel?"

"Never mind, Schneider." There was a sibilant rustle of paper in the background. "You want a quick rundown on Yuri Borodin's file? Reads like the friggin' Count of Monte Cristo."

"Please."

"Got a pencil?"

The German heaved his bulk back on the bed and closed his eyes. "I'm ready."

2:02 P.M. Bronberrick Motel: South of Pretoria

The moment Hauer saw the note, he knew that Hans had tricked him. He knocked Hans's abandoned Walther aside and read swiftly:

> *I'm sorry, Captain. I've thought it through, and I feel the risks of an armed exchange are just too great. I couldn't tell you before, but Ilse is carrying a child. I didn't want to lie about the time of the rendezvous, but I knew you'd never let me try it this way. Please don't follow me. I'll meet you back here when I've got Ilse.* [Here the name "Hans" had been signed, then scratched through.] *If it goes bad, I want you to know I don't blame you for anything in the past. We found each other in time. Your son, Hans.*

Hauer stood rock still as waves of anger and panic swept over him. He dug the foil packet from his pocket and ripped it open. The negatives he had taken at the Protea Hof were there, but the Spandau papers were gone. In their place lay five sheets of crumpled motel stationery. Hauer tried to breathe calmly. Hans had struck out on his own to meet the kidnappers. He had to accept that. It wasn't hard to understand. Not if the hostage was *your* wife, and she was carrying *your* child. Yet Hans was *his* son. Ilse was his daughter-in-law. And the child she was carrying—Hauer felt a thick lump in his throat—that child was *his* grandchild— his blood heir. Hauer sat down hard on the bed. For the last twenty years he had lived alone, resigned to a solitary life. Yet in the past forty-eight hours he had been given not only a son, but a family. And now he had lost that family. He read the note again. *Your son, Hans.*

"Fool," he muttered.

It took him twenty minutes to reach the Voortrekker Monument. All the way he cursed himself for leaving Hans alone. He had known something like this might happen, that Hans had been walking an emotional razor edge. This morning, while zeroing-in his rifle scope, he had almost packed up the gun and driven straight back to the motel. But he hadn't. He had finished with the rifle, then gone ahead and scouted for an exchange location. And he'd found one, an empty soccer stadium. Perfect. *Damn!*

Hauer saw no sign of Hans at the Voortrekker Monument. For an hour he circled the base of the dun-colored building on foot, but he knew it was hopeless. Hans was gone— maybe dead already. Faced with this heart-numbing reality, Hauer realized he had but one slim chance to save his son's life. When the kidnappers realized that the Spandau papers were incomplete, they would demand answers. And when they got them, they might—just might—come looking for Captain Dieter Hauer. He would make it very easy for them to find him.

In the Ford again, he checked his map. Then he swung east and headed back toward the Protea Hof Hotel. He pulled straight up to the main entrance, removed a long leather case from the Ford's trunk, and tipped the doorman to park the car. The hunting rifle felt heavy but reassuring against his leg as he strode toward the elevators. In a European city the oddly shaped case might have attracted unwelcome attention, but in South Africa rifles are as common as golf clubs.

Their room looked just as they'd left it yesterday. In a shaft of light leaking through the drawn drapes, Hauer saw the clothes and food they had bought still lying in crumpled shopping bags on the beds. Hans's loaded crossbow leaned in the corner space between the near bed and the bathroom wall. Hauer laid his rifle on the bed. Then he felt the hairs on his neck stiffen.

There was someone else in the room. He turned very naturally, as if unaware of any danger. *There.* Sitting in the chair by the window. A thin shadow silhouetted against the dark drapes. Hauer jerked his Walther from his waistband and dived behind the bed, pulling back the slide as he hit the carpet.

"Don't be alarmed, Captain," said a deep, familiar voice. "It's only me. I managed to get here in spite of you."

Hauer thrust his pistol over the top of the mattress, put two pounds of pressure on the trigger, then slowly lifted his eyes above the edge of the bed. Sitting in a narrow shaft of light coming through the drapes was Professor Georg Natterman.

CHAPTER THIRTY-TWO

2:25 P.M. The Northern Transvaal

One mile northeast of the village of Giyani, the Zulu pulled the Range Rover onto the gravel shoulder and climbed out. Hans stayed put. The Zulu shielded his eyes and stared back down the long highway. Lean as an impala, he looked as if he were scanning the veld for game herds. Whenever a car or truck whizzed past, he stared into the vehicle as if searching for someone he knew.

Hans was getting angry. They had been on the road for hours, and they had stopped like this twice before. After a quick glance at the Zulu, Hans climbed out of the Rover on the shoulder side and looked around. Back toward Pretoria, the sun burned down relentlessly, shimmering like a layer of oil just above the road. To the north, however, Hans saw a vast wall of slate gray clouds. Beneath the leaden ceiling, sheets of rain rolled south toward the Rover, seeming to carry the night behind.

"In," the Zulu commanded, scampering back into the driver's seat.

When Hans climbed into the backseat, he found a thin black arm dangling a long black cloth before his eyes. "No," he said.

The Zulu dropped the blindfold in Hans's lap and turned back to the windshield. His posture told Hans that unless he obeyed, the vehicle would not move one inch further toward his wife.

Hans cursed and tied the scarf around his eyes. "Now," he muttered, "move your ass."

The next thirty minutes felt like a G-force test. The Zulu swung off of the road immediately, and the bone-crushing ride that followed would have totaled a vehicle less sturdy than the Range Rover. Hans peeked around the blindfold when he could, trying to maintain some rough idea of their progress, but taking accurate directional bearings was impossible. By the time they finally leveled out, his head had taken several vicious knocks and the Zulu's goal of disorienting him had been well and truly achieved.

The road surface felt like rock scrabble now, but that didn't help Hans. All he could do was press himself into the rear seat and wait for journey's end. Thirty minutes later the Rover stopped and the Zulu ordered him out. When Hans's feet hit the ground, the Zulu pushed him against the side of the vehicle and searched him. He immediately discovered the knife taped to Hans's ribs, and ripped it away from the skin. He told Hans to wait.

When Hans heard receding footsteps, he pulled off the blindfold. He stood before an enormous building unlike any he had ever seen. Before he could examine it in any detail, however, a great teak door opened and a tall blond man stepped out, his well-tanned arm extended in greeting.

"Sergeant Apfel?" he said. "I'm Pieter Smuts. I hope the ride wasn't too rough. Come inside and we'll see about getting you more comfortable."

"My wife," Hans said awkwardly, holding his ground. "I've come for my wife."

"Of course. But inside, please. Everything in good time."

Hans followed the Afrikaner into a majestic reception hall and down a long corridor. In a cul-de-sac full of shadows, they stopped beside two doors. Smuts turned to him.

"The Spandau papers," he said softly.

"Not until I see my wife," Hans retorted, raising himself to his full height—which was about eye level with the Afrikaner.

"First things first, Sergeant. That was our agreement. When we are satisfied that no copies exist, you will be reunited with your wife."

Hans made no move to comply.

A brittle edge crept into the Afrikaner's voice. "Do you intend to break our agreement?"

Hans held his breath, struggling to cling to the illusion that he had entered Horn House with bargaining power. It was now painfully clear that he had not. He had probably made the worst mistake of his life by coming here. He had gone against the advice of the one man who might have been able to help him, and now Ilse would pay the price for his stupidity.

Smuts saw Hans's pain as clearly as if he had burst into tears. He opened a door and motioned for Hans to enter the small bedroom beyond. "The papers," he repeated.

Like a zombie Hans withdrew the tightly folded pages. Smuts did not even look at them. He slipped the wad into his pants like pocket change, then nodded curtly. "I'll be back soon," he said. "Get some rest."

"But my wife!" Hans cried. "You've got to take me to her! I've done everything you asked!"

"Not quite everything," Smuts admonished. "But enough, I think." He closed the door solicitously, like a well-tipped bellman.

"Wait!" Hans shouted, but the Afrikaner's footsteps faded into silence. Hans tried the door, but it was locked. *It's out of my hands now,* he thought hopelessly. *Is that what I wanted all along?* He wondered how long the procedure to detect photocopying would take. He was still wondering that when the countless hours without sleep finally overpowered him. He collapsed onto the small bed, his mouth moving silently as exhaustion shut down his frazzled brain. For the first time since childhood, Hans Apfel fell asleep with a prayer on his lips.

When the Afrikaner jerked him awake ten minutes later, Hans knew that his desperate gamble had failed. Smuts's eyes burned with feral fire, and though he spoke even more quietly than before, violence crackled through his every syllable like static electricity.

"You have made a grave mistake, Sergeant. I will ask you only once. Your wife's life depends upon your answer. *Where* are the three missing pages?"

Hans felt as if he had suddenly been sucked high into the stratosphere. His ears seemed to stop up. He couldn't breathe. "I—I don't understand," he said stupidly.

Smuts turned and reached for the doorknob.

"Wait!" Hans cried. "It's not my fault! I don't *have* the other pages!"

"Dieter Hauer has them," Smuts said in a flat voice. "Doesn't he?"

Hans gulped in surprise. "Who?" he asked lamely.

"Polizei Captain Dieter Hauer!" Smuts roared. "The man who helped you escape from Berlin! What kind of game is the fool trying to play? Where is he now?"

Hans felt suddenly faint. Phoenix knew everything. They had known from the beginning. "Hauer doesn't have the pages," he said. "I swear it. The pages were stolen in Germany."

Smuts grabbed him by the sleeve and jerked him across the room toward the window. Hans was amazed by the strength in the wiry arm. Pulling back the curtains, Smuts waved his arm back and forth across the pane. Satisfied with what he saw, he motioned for Hans to step forward.

Puzzled, Hans put his face to the glass. When he saw what waited beyond, every muscle in his exhausted body went rigid. Thirty meters from the window, Ilse Apfel stood facing the house. Her hands were bound with wire. Affixed to the wire was a long chain, held at the other end by Hans's Zulu driver. At the Zulu's feet lay an old black tire; beside him stood Lieutenant Jürgen Luhr of the West Berlin police. Luhr wore civilian clothes, but his tall black boots gleamed in the sun. Seeing Hans in the window, Luhr smiled and pressed a Walther P1 against Ilse's left temple. Smuts caught Hans in a bear hug and held him still.

"*Ilse!*" Hans shouted.

Ilse moved her head slightly, as if she had sensed the sound but could not locate its source. When Luhr jabbed the pistol barrel into her ear, Hans jumped as if the gun had struck his own head. He sucked in a rush of air to shout again, but Smuts cut him off.

"Scream again, Sergeant, and she dies. I presume you know that man out there?"

Hans had only spoken to Jürgen Luhr in person once, but he would never forget it. Luhr had called him in for the polygraph session at Abschnitt 53, the call that had started all the madness. Luhr was the man who had gouged the Star of David into Erhard Weiss's chest. His presence here, five thousand miles from Germany, compounded Hans's sense of dislocation.

Smuts released Hans. "Step back from the window," he commanded.

Hans didn't move.

"*Step back!*"

When Hans refused, Smuts gave another hand signal. The

Zulu handed the leash chain to Luhr, then reached down and lifted the tire high into the air. As it hung suspended like a black halo over Ilse's head, amber liquid sloshed out of it onto her hair. With a sadistic grin the Zulu jerked the tire savagely down around Ilse's torso, pinning her arms to her sides.

Smuts spoke from behind Hans. "Are you familiar with the 'necklace,' Sergeant? It's a local native specialty. They fill an old tire with gasoline, pin the victim's arms to his sides with the tire—thus the term 'necklace'—then they set the gasoline afire. The results are quite ghastly, even to a man of my wide experience. A human torch running about like a dying chicken—"

Blind with rage, Hans hurled himself backward and hammered his elbow into Smuts's chest. Then he whirled, lowered his head like a bull, and drove the Afrikaner back toward the heavy door. The sudden attack startled Smuts, but as the Afrikaner backpedaled toward the wood, he bucked his knee into Hans's ribs—an upward blow so sharp and quick that Hans did not even realize what had hit him. He went down gasping. When he looked up, Smuts was standing across the room, arms folded, glaring at him.

"Let her go!" Hans begged. "What has she done to you?"

"Where is Captain Hauer, Sergeant?"

Hans staggered to his feet and went to the window. Ilse's face had taken on an ashen pallor. She had recognized the smell of gasoline, and with it the terrible danger. She swayed slightly on her feet. Luhr jabbed his pistol at her. Behind Hans, Smuts lifted his hand yet again. Grinning, Luhr reached into his pocket, withdrew a cigarette lighter, and flicked it alight. He held the flame less than a meter from Ilse, his arm stretched to its limit in case the gasoline vapor should accidentally ignite.

"Don't make me do it, Sergeant," Smuts said into Hans's ear. "Why give Lieutenant Luhr the enjoyment at your expense?"

"You fucking animal! Hauer's at the hotel!"

"Which hotel?"

"The Bronberrick Motel! Now let her go!"

Smuts raised his hand once more, and Luhr, his face red with anger and disappointment, snapped his cigarette lighter shut. The Zulu shoved roughly down on the tire until it dropped at Ilse's feet, then he led her away.

"Let's go, Sergeant," said Smuts, pulling Hans toward the door. "You've got a telephone call to make."

3:26 P.M. Room 604: The Protea Hof Hotel

"I ought to shoot you!" Hauer growled. "You senile idiot!"

"Steady, Captain," Professor Natterman urged. "I told you I meant to get here one way or another."

Hauer's mind reeled. How could he have been so stupid as to leave Natterman holding a shotgun on the forger in Wolfsburg? The professor had probably gotten the false passport names before he and Hans had driven a mile from the cabin!

"Are you alone?" Hauer asked sharply.

Natterman's eyes flicked to the door. "Please don't over-react, Captain. I was in no position to get here on my own."

"Who is with you?"

"Another old man like me. He's a Jew."

Hauer whirled around toward the foyer and covered the door with his pistol. "Where is he?"

"Is Hans with you?" Natterman asked.

"Where is this Jew?"

Hauer's question was answered by a deep, unfamiliar voice. "I am standing alone in the washroom," it said.

Hauer dived into the space between the bed and the bathroom wall, clutching his Walther to his chest.

"I'm unarmed, Captain," said the voice.

"Shut up! Stay where you are!" Hauer jabbed his pistol at the professor. "You too, damn you. Don't move."

Natterman snorted. "You're being ridiculous, Captain. Herr Stern is harmless."

"You couldn't stay away, could you?" Hauer thought furiously for several seconds. "All right!" he called finally. "You in the toilet—walk out slowly with your hands over your head! I won't hesitate to shoot!"

"Can I put on the light?"

"No!" Hauer lay prone in the space between the beds with only his head and his gun hand exposed. When the tall silhouette appeared in the dim foyer, Hauer trained his Walther on the man's head. "Start talking," he growled. "And keep your hands up."

"My name is Jonas Stern," said the tall shadow. "I assure

you that I mean you no harm, Captain. I suspect that my interest in this case is similar to your own, and I would like to discuss it with you."

"Who do you work for?"

"For myself. But to give you a frame of reference, my native country is Israel." Stern paused. "May I switch on the light now?"

"The bathroom light. That's enough to talk by."

Fluorescent light flickered from the small cubicle. The fixture buzzed softly. Stern stood squarely in the pool of light so that Hauer would feel at ease, but Hauer kept his Walther trained on him anyway. As the silhouette took on human features, Hauer noted the tanned, angular face with its quick, piercing eyes.

"Captain Hauer," said Stern, "would you mind telling me where Sergeant Apfel is now?"

"I'd rather find out how you arrived on my doorstep."

Stern's eyes met Hauer's with steady assurance. "Frankly, that would be a waste of time. Suffice to say that I have been involved in this situation since the first night at Spandau. I'm sure the most important detail from your perspective is that I have the three missing Spandau pages in my possession."

Hauer felt his heart stutter. *So you're the one. You slashed that Afrikaner's throat like a suckling pig.* "You still haven't explained your interest in this matter."

Stern sighed. "We're all concerned for the girl, Captain, let's have that said. But I suspect that your interest, like mine, runs a bit deeper than simple kidnapping. To the safety and future of Germany, perhaps?"

Hauer waited.

"I am a Jew, Captain. An Israeli. I believe that the men who want these Spandau papers pose a very serious threat to my country. They may pose a different but equally perilous danger to democratic Germany. I have come to root these men out."

"How do you propose to find them?"

"With your help."

Hauer shook his head in amazement. "You expect me to drag the two of you along with me? Is that what you think?"

Stern smiled. "I do bring certain assets to the game."

Hauer raised a skeptical eyebrow. "Such as?"

"Superior intelligence experience. The professor tells me

that you have counterterror training, Captain. That is of limited value under the circumstances. We're not dealing with the Red Army Faction here. This is the 'big league,' as the Americans say. I've fought in the secret world for many years. I can keep you from making some very serious mistakes."

Hauer shook his head. "I don't think your experience offsets your age. This is a hostage situation. Speed and reflexes will be critical."

Stern suppressed his anger. "If you see this as merely a hostage situation, you are fatally mistaken. We are at the edge of a web of intrigue spun fifty years ago, a web that has grown more complex with each passing year. Ilse Apfel is but a speck of dust trapped inside it." Stern raised his hand and plucked an imaginary mote from the air. "Every time you take a step toward her, Captain, the entire web shakes. The spider knows where you are at every moment, and when you finally make your move, you will find that it is *you* who are trapped."

"Interesting metaphor," said Hauer. "What lesson should I draw from it?"

Stern smiled patiently. "Your attention should be fixed upon the spider from the start, not the speck of dust. Eliminate the spider, you can plunder the web at your leisure."

Hauer said nothing for a while. "I'll take my chances alone," he answered finally. "I've handled a few spiders in my time."

Stern's jaw muscles tightened. "You'd stand a much better chance with my help."

Hauer raised his Walther. "If information is all you have, Stern, you can give that to me right now."

In the instant Hauer's finger hesitated on the trigger, Stern slipped out of the door. He reappeared moments later. Behind him stood three very fit young men. Their hard faces and burning eyes told Hauer everything he needed to know about their probable areas of expertise.

"These are my other assets, Captain," Stern said. *"Sayaret matkal*—Israeli commandos. You may have heard of them. If you're any judge of men, you will recognize their value vis-à-vis our particular situation."

Hauer instantly revised his estimate of Stern's possible contribution. Even the elite officers of Germany's GSG-9 spoke of the *sayaret matkal* with respect.

"You!" he cried suddenly, recognizing the bandaged Yosef Shamir from the stairwell of the Burgerspark Hotel. "You were following me last night!"

Stern quickly interposed himself between Hauer and the young Israeli. "Yosef was there at my request," he explained. "I had hoped to meet you at the Burgerspark myself, Captain, but unexpected trouble prevented me. I'm only thankful you decided to return here this evening. I assume you found another hotel last night after your brush with Yosef?"

Hauer nodded reluctantly.

"And you returned here because . . . ?"

"Because our distraught young husband decided to lie to me. He made contact with the kidnappers on his own."

Stern closed his eyes.

"Oh, no," Natterman groaned. *"Why?"*

"Because he realized that any attempt to free Ilse by force might well bring about her death. I believe that was the same position you took back in Germany, wasn't it, Professor? Also because Ilse is pregnant."

Natterman's eyes widened.

"Is the boy mad?" Stern asked. "Doesn't he know the kidnappers will kill both him and his wife no matter what he does?"

"No. I don't believe he does. He thinks with his heart, not his head."

"An often fatal mistake," Stern said dryly.

"Ilse is pregnant?" Natterman murmured.

Hauer walked to the window and opened the drapes. Van Der Walt Street looked as calm as the Kurfürstendamm on an early Sunday morning. In the corner of the room, Aaron Haber picked up Hans's loaded crossbow and showed it to his fellow commandos, an amused smile on his face. Stern motioned for him to put it down.

"What had you planned to do before we arrived, Captain?" Stern asked. "Play bait? Tell the kidnappers you had the missing pages of the Spandau diary and try to turn their trap inside out?"

Hauer grunted. "That's about it."

"A dangerous game."

"The only one left."

"Not quite," said Stern. "You're forgetting something."

"I am?"

"I really have the missing pages. I would think they rate us an invitation to the Kidnapper's Ball, wouldn't you?"

Hauer's lips slowly spread into a smile.

Everyone froze as the telephone rang, faded.

"You answer it," Stern advised.

Hauer darted between the beds and picked up the receiver. "Yes?"

"Captain!"

Hauer kept his eyes on Stern. "Where are you?" he asked through gritted teeth.

"I can't say," Hans replied. "I'm not sure, anyway. Captain, I've got to have those missing diary pages. I made a mistake in leaving you, I'm sorry. But these men really will kill Ilse unless they get all the pages. They're insane!"

Hauer thought silently. "But I don't have the pages," he said at length, still watching Stern.

"I know," Hans said quickly. "But you can *find* them. You've got to! Go back to Germany! To the cabin! You can find them, Captain, you *must*. It's simple police work!"

"Not so simple," Hauer stalled. "Not when I'm wanted for murder in Germany."

"They can fix that!"

Hauer sealed the mouthpiece with his palm and whispered to Stern. "Phoenix wants the rest of the diary. Do I tell them I have it?"

Stern shook his head vehemently. "They won't believe that. If you'd really had the other pages, Hans would have found a way to steal them before he went to the rendezvous."

"Hurry!" said Hauer, wondering why he was asking this strange old Israeli for answers anyway.

Stern jabbed his finger at Professor Natterman. *"He's* got them. Tell them the professor followed you and Hans to South Africa, and that he brought the missing pages with him."

Hauer shook his head angrily, but he could think of nothing else to say. "Hans?"

"I'm here!"

"Can the kidnappers hear me?"

"Yes!"

"Don't hurt the girl," Hauer said slowly. "Do you hear me? *Do not hurt the girl.* Her grandfather is here with me, and he has what you want."

Hans gasped.

A new voice came on the line. "Listen well, Captain Hauer," said Smuts. "You will send the old man to the same place as before, the Voortrekker Monument. He must be there thirty minutes from now, alone, *with* the missing pages. After we are satisfied that no copies exist, we will release our prisoners. If you attempt to follow the vehicle that picks up the professor, the driver will shoot him on the spot." Smuts's voice went cold. "And *you* will never leave this country alive. Do you understand?"

"*Ja,*" Hauer growled.

The phone went dead.

Hauer whirled on Stern. "Well, Herr Master-Spy, you've painted us into some damned corner. They want the professor to deliver our last bargaining chip to them, and if we try to follow, they'll kill him. Now three hostages will die instead of two."

Stern smiled enigmatically. "Captain, where is your imagination?"

Hauer flushed with anger. "I try to be practical when lives are at stake."

"As do I," Stern said calmly. "But pragmatism alone is never enough. You should know that, Captain. It is imagination that wins the day."

"And what miracle does your imagination suggest for this problem?"

"A simple one." Stern's eyes had settled on a bedfuddled Professor Natterman. "Does your granddaughter carry any pictures of you in her handbag, Professor?"

Natterman looked mystified. "I . . . I don't believe so."

"Well," Stern said brightly, "there it is."

Hauer's eyes widened in comprehension.

Stern smiled. "It's the perfect solution, Captain. I become the professor."

Hauer was shaking his head, but he knew that he had been trapped by a master. Stern was already disrobing. "It's too risky," he objected.

"Let's have that jacket, Professor," said Stern. "I must wear something Ilse can recognize immediately."

Hauer wanted to argue, but he could think of no better plan. He watched enviously as the Israeli prepared to slip into the very center of his metaphorical spider's web.

As Stern stripped, Professor Natterman leaned over and

whispered in his ear. "Remember what we talked about on the plane, Jonas? About the man with one eye? About Hess—"

Stern gently but firmly shoved Natterman away. Naked to the waist, he handed his pistol to Gadi, then turned to Hauer and smiled.

"Sorry, Captain," he said. "You're just too young for the job."

CHAPTER THIRTY-THREE

3:37 P.M. *Van der Walt Straat, Pretoria*

Yuri Borodin wiped his neck and forehead with a silk handkerchief. It was beastly hot in the van, with the oppressive closeness of impending rain, and it stank. The van's engine was not running, so there was no air conditioning. Borodin looked up. Five fleshy faces stared dumbly back at him. Gorillas. That's what Borodin called them. Embassy gorillas. They were the KGB muscle available at every Russian embassy in the world, and everywhere in the world they looked the same. Off-the-rack suits, pomaded hair, big faces, big fists, and most of them smelled. Of course there were no Russian embassies in South Africa, but there was an illegal residency in Johannesburg. And the gorillas from the residency had the same aroma, a cloying mix of body odor and aftershave.

"Crack a window," said Borodin.

The driver did.

"Gentlemen, Captain Dieter Hauer is in the hotel on my right, the Protea Hof. With him are some scruffy fellows who look suspiciously like Jews." Borodin clucked his tongue. "Germans and Jews . . . an often explosive combination."

One of the gorillas chuckled appreciatively. *Ah,* Borodin thought, *a rudimentary sense of humor.* "Across the street in the Stanley House," he went on, "we have our restless German Kripo detective. He's big, but he shouldn't be much trouble. Two of you should be enough for him. When he's dead, leave his ID but take his money." Borodin took a Heckler and Koch MP-5 submachine gun from a leather attaché case. "The rest of us will take room 604." He singled out the leanest of the gorillas. "You know the window?"

The lean man lifted a Dragunov sniper rifle from his lap and zipped it into a soft case. "Sixth floor," he said, "third window from the left."

Borodin screwed a long silencer onto the muzzle of his MP-5. "Let's go."

3:42 P.M. Room 604: The Protea Hof Hotel, Pretoria

Jonas Stern would have verbally crucified Gadi and his men for their laxness, but had they not been so attuned to Stern's absence, they might have defended themselves better. When the telephone rang, everyone turned toward it thinking it was Stern. Hauer turned from the window, Natterman from one of the beds, Yosef from the space between the other bed and the bathroom wall, and most importantly, Aaron from the foyer. No one heard the key turning softly in the door.

Closest to the phone, Gadi Abrams snatched it up and said, "Hello? Hello? Uncle Jonas?"

In that instant of shared bewilderment, a rifle slug shattered the hotel room window, missing Hauer by a centimeter. Everyone whirled toward the crashing sound. A half second later one of Borodin's gorillas charged through the foyer and bowled Aaron Haber over like a child. Hauer looked around wildly. His Walther lay on the bed six feet away. He started to dive for it; then the second gorilla came through the door with his pistol aimed at Hauer's chest. Standing open-mouthed with the telephone to his ear, Gadi Abrams was also trapped in the newcomer's line of fire.

Only Yosef Shamir moved to counterattack, and it was Yosef who died. He had been toying with Hans's crossbow in the narrow slot between the bed and the bathroom wall when the Russians burst in. With lightning reflexes he dropped the bow, drew his silenced .22 and fired three shots in rapid succession as the second gorilla emerged from the foyer and barreled past him.

All three bullets embedded themselves high in the Russian's broad back. He went down on top of his compatriot, who was wrestling with Aaron on the floor. The small-caliber slugs only slowed the Russian giant, but that slowness saved his life. As Yosef stepped forward to finish him off, Yuri Borodin somersaulted through the foyer and shot the young Israeli through the throat.

By the time Gadi got his hand on Hauer's Walther, Borodin was covering the entire room. Faced with the deadly MP-5 submachine gun, Hauer, Gadi, and Aaron realized the futility of further resistance. They slowly raised their hands, their eyes locked on Yosef's convulsing body.

It took the young commando forty seconds to die, and no one spoke while he did it. They had all seen death before, and knowing that no help would be called imposed a solemn silence on both attackers and hostages. Professor Natterman was the first to make a sound, chattering *"Why? Why?"* to everyone and no one at the same time.

"You," said Borodin, pointing his weapon at Hauer. "Close the drapes."

Hauer didn't move.

Borodin checked his watch. "Close the drapes within twelve seconds or you will be shot by my sniper. Everyone else against the window."

Hauer obeyed. Gadi and Aaron backed against the closed drapes and stood beside Hauer. The gorilla that Yosef had shot was straining without success to reach the wounds on his back, and moaning like a dying ox. Borodin ordered the other gorilla to take him into the bathroom and see to the wounds; then he casually seated himself on the bed nearest the door. Natterman sat gibbering on the bed opposite Borodin, but the immaculately dressed Russian took no notice. He took out a cigarette and lit it with great deliberation.

"Gentlemen," he said in English, "I have come for the papers unearthed at Spandau Prison. Which one of you has them?"

"None of us," Hauer replied in the same language.

Borodin took a drag from his cigarette. He had noticed the German accent. "You are Captain Hauer, I take it?"

Hauer nodded. "Who are you?"

Borodin smiled, revealing a dazzling set of Swiss dental crowns. "Once again, Captain, which of you has the papers?"

"How did you find us?" Gadi asked, stalling.

Borodin laughed softly. "A fat Kripo detective named Schneider led me right to you. I assume he's a friend of Hauer's."

Hauer's eyes darkened in confusion.

Borodin smiled. "Of course the detective is dead now, Captain. As you will be if you don't give up the papers."

"I told you before, we don't have them."

Borodin's smile stretched to a grimace. He called one of the gorillas back from the bathroom and barked several phrases at him in rapid Russian. Of the captives, only Aaron Haber—the son of a Lithuanian Jew—understood the exchange, but the color draining from his face told the others all they needed to know. The big Russian jerked Aaron away from the curtained window and kicked his legs out from under him. When the young Israeli tried to rise, the Russian locked a thick forearm around his neck and pressed the barrel of a silenced Browning 9mm pistol into his ear.

"The foreplay is over, gentlemen," Borodin said. His voice had not risen a single decibel, yet it had lost all trace of humanity. Everyone in the room knew that the Russian would not hesitate to order Aaron's execution. Yet the young commando made no sound. He left his fate entirely in the hands of Gadi Abrams, who had been designated senior officer by Stern just before he left to rendezvous with the kidnappers.

"At the risk of sounding melodramatic," Borodin went on, "I'm going to count to five. If I do not have the Spandau papers when I reach that number, my loyal assistant will transform this young man's brain into kosher caviar."

"We don't have them," Hauer said again.

Borodin counted quickly. "One, two, three, four—"

"Stop!" Professor Natterman cried, surprising everyone. "In God's name stop! Listen to me, you barbarian! Hauer is telling the truth. Hans Apfel has the original diary. Most of it, anyway. The Jew who left here a few minutes ago has the rest. My granddaughter has been kidnapped. We've come to exchange the papers for her life. Surely even you can understand that?"

Borodin stared at the historian. "How does that help me, old man? I need results, not excuses."

"There is a *copy,*" Natterman explained. "A copy of the papers. *Photographs.* You're Russian, correct? If you want to expose the truth about Rudolf Hess, that's all you need." Natterman pointed across the room at Hauer. "He has them. I'm sorry, Captain, those papers mean far more to me than to you, but they're simply not worth this boy's life."

Hauer stared at the old man with incredulity. This did not

sound at all like the fame-obsessed professor he had come to know.

Borodin raised the MP-5 to Hauer's face. "The photographs, Captain."

Hauer didn't move.

"Kill the Jew," Borodin said calmly.

"Bastard," Hauer muttered. He jerked the envelope from his hip pocket and tossed it onto the bed.

Borodin held the negatives up to the overhead light, examined them briefly, then slipped them into his inside coat pocket. "I assume that none of you know the location of the people to whom your friend is trading the original papers?"

"That's right," Natterman said.

Borodin chuckled. "I thought not. If you did, this wonderful little commando unit wouldn't be sitting on its collective ass in a hotel room."

In spite of the gun at his temple, Aaron cursed and tried to lash out at the Soviet agent. Borodin stepped aside and called to one of the residency men, "Dmitri! Leave their weapons, but take their ammunition!"

Two minutes later Borodin stood smirking in the foyer, flanked by his gorillas. The Russian who had not been wounded held a pillowcase weighted with Uzi ammunition clips, boxes of shells, and loose .22 rounds.

"This soirée is over, gentlemen," Borodin said. "I'll take my leave now." He accented his farewells with a broad flourish of his hand. *"Do svidaniya! Shalom! Auf Wiedersehen!"* Borodin burst into laughter, then motioned for one of the gorillas to open the door.

The moment the Russian holding the pillowcase turned the doorknob, the door burst open and knocked him backward against his wounded comrade. From the window, Hauer gaped as the back of the wounded man's head exploded.

The second Russian groped at his belt for his pistol, but two bullets hit him low in the stomach and severed his spine.

Yuri Borodin backpedaled out of the foyer and spun toward the window. Hauer and the Israelis dropped to the carpet as slugs from his MP-5 peppered the bed and the wall and the ceiling. Hauer looked up just as two bright red flowers blossomed on Borodin's shoulders.

Hauer and Gadi were on their feet by the time Borodin's

body hit the floor. Standing in the doorway, his shoulders stretching from post to post, was a very large man holding a Walther pistol in his hand. A gray hat was pressed down over his bloody head, and a brass gorget plate hung from his neck. On it was a capital *K,* the emblem of the Berlin *Kriminalpolizei.*

"Captain Hauer?" Schneider said.

Hauer stepped forward and nodded.

Schneider put his gun in his pocket. "I need to talk to you."

Gadi Abrams crouched over Borodin, who lay pale and shaking on the carpet. He rifled Borodin's pocket for Hauer's envelope, found it, and tossed the negatives to Hauer. Then he leaned down over Borodin's face. "Where is your sniper?" he shouted. "Where!"

Borodin smiled. "Fuck you, Jew."

Gadi snatched up a pillow, crushed it over Borodin's face and punched him hard on his wounded shoulder. The muffled howl that followed did not sound human. Gadi pulled the pillow away.

"Across . . . across the street," Borodin croaked. "Room 528 . . . the Stanley . . . House."

Gadi closed his brown hands around Borodin's throat and began to squeeze. "For Yosef," he said softly.

Detective Schneider crossed the room and shouldered Gadi off of the Russian. He crouched down beside him. "Are you Yuri Borodin?" he asked tersely. "Are you the man who killed Major Harry Richardson?"

Borodin stared up with glassy eyes. He saw little chance of leaving this room alive. His pale face wrinkled into a sneer. "The Swastika was a nice touch . . . don't you think?"

Schneider sighed heavily. In his mind he saw the dim, overheated bedroom where he and Colonel Rose had examined Harry's mutilated corpse. In the close South African heat, it wasn't hard to recall. "I should let you bleed to death," he growled.

"Fuck you too, you stinking German."

While Hauer and the Israelis watched in disbelief, Schneider closed one huge hand around Borodin's throat and squeezed with the remorseless force of a root cracking concrete. Schneider did not see Hauer signal to Gadi, or the two Israelis approach him from behind. The moment Borodin's legs stopped thrashing, the Israeli commandos seized him.

Schneider did not struggle, not even when Gadi took the pistol from his pocket.

Hauer stepped forward and checked the scalp behind both of Schneider's ears. Satisfied, he stepped back and motioned for the Israelis to release him.

"I don't have the damned tattoo," Schneider muttered.

In the awkward silence that followed, Hauer finally noticed the weak moaning coming from somewhere inside the room. He walked around and looked on the floor between the beds. Professor Natterman lay there, deathly white, both hands clutching his side. "Captain . . . ?" he whispered uncertainly.

Hauer knelt and examined the old man. The professor had been lying on the bed when Schneider burst in, and he had been too slow to seek cover. Two bullets from Borodin's final spray had struck him. One had nicked the flesh above his left hip, the other grazed his left thigh. Hauer could see that the wounds were superficial, but the professor obviously believed he was in danger of dying. He raised his quivering arms to Hauer's collar and pulled him down to his face.

"There really is . . . a copy, Captain," he rasped. "A copy of the Spandau papers."

Hauer pulled himself free of the old man's grasp. "What did you say?"

"Tell Stern to remember the copy I made in Berlin!"

"What?"

Natterman nodded weakly. "Stern . . . was following me. He saw me do it. I made a copy of the Spandau papers before I ever left Berlin for the cabin. I mailed it to one of my old teaching assistants for safekeeping. Kurt Rossman. If . . . if you get to Ilse, don't worry about the papers. Just get Ilse out. Tell Stern to get Ilse out!"

Hauer sat stunned. He couldn't believe that through all the warnings against photocopying the Spandau papers, Natterman had risked Ilse's life by not admitting that he had already done so. As he opened his mouth to rebuke the old man, Aaron Haber appeared at his side with a canvas overnight bag. The young commando withdrew a kit containing Betadyne, Xylocaine, sutures, syringes, gauze bandages, a blood-pressure indicator, morphine, and a cornucopia of emergency drugs. "We came prepared for casualties," he said. He propped Natterman's legs on some pillows to maximize the flow of blood to his brain.

Hauer stood up and gave his full attention to Schneider. "What's your story, Detective?"

Schneider produced a handkerchief and wiped some blood from his face. "I've come here to help you, Captain. You are in a great deal of trouble in Berlin. Both you and Sergeant Apfel are wanted for murder there."

"I'm no murderer," Hauer said gruffly.

"I didn't say you were. I know all about the Spandau papers, Captain. I know about Phoenix. I'm working with the Americans, with Colonel Rose of the U.S. Army. That's how I traced you."

"I suppose you want the Spandau papers?"

Schneider shrugged. "Only if they can help to crush Phoenix."

Hauer digested this slowly. "Why did you kill that Russian?"

"He killed an American intelligence officer named Richardson. Richardson was the man who discovered that Phoenix extends into East Germany as well as West Berlin."

"I've known that for months."

"Then why didn't you report it?"

Hauer snorted. "Report it? Phoenix has men in the police department, the BND, the West Berlin Senate, the federal government in Bonn, and all the states. If I'd reported what I knew to the wrong person, you and your Kripo friends would have been visiting me at the morgue twelve hours later."

Schneider nodded slowly. "The Americans can help you, Captain. Colonel Rose will help."

"You said this Russian here already killed one American officer. That kind of help I don't need." Hauer studied the big German. "Why do you think I should trust you?"

"Because I saved your life."

Hauer shrugged. "Anyone from Phoenix would have killed those Russians just as quickly as you did. They can't afford to let the Russians know what Phoenix truly exists for. Not yet."

Schneider met Hauer's eyes. "Come back with me to Berlin, Captain. Help us root out Funk and his men. Colonel Rose would like nothing better than to order an assault on Abschnitt 53. But his hands are tied. His superiors are holding him back because of the Hess business, and he doesn't have nearly enough evidence against Prefect Funk. You could provide that evidence, Captain. You *must* trust me. I want the same thing you do—to clean those scum out of Berlin." Schneider turned his broad hands upward. "I know you don't know me, but you must have known my father. Max Schneider. He was a Kripo investigator too. Big like me."

Hauer searched Schneider's face for a full minute. Two rivulets of blood trickled down from the sweatband of Schneider's hat. Behind Schneider, Gadi was moving the dead Russians into the bathroom, while Aaron worked on the professor. The professor's revelation that he had made a copy of the Spandau papers pulsed in the back of Hauer's brain like a second heartbeat. The situation had changed. Profoundly. A copy of the Spandau papers, combined with the evidence he and Steuben had already compiled, meant that direct action in Berlin might now be possible. Things were moving too quickly here in South Africa. Hans's betrayal, Stern's sudden appearance, the Russian assault, Schneider's unexpected rescue. Schneider . . .

"Your father wore a hat like yours," Hauer said absently.

"You did know him," said Schneider.

Hauer turned and stared pensively out the window. "You say you're working with the Americans?"

"Yes. Colonel Godfrey Rose, of Military Intelligence."

"Can you get him on the phone?"

"Yes."

"Do it."

4:00 P.M. *The Voortrekker Monument, Pretoria*

After forty-five minutes of lying blindfolded in the backseat of the speeding Range Rover, Jonas Stern had lost all sense of direction. The Zulu driver who had met him at the Voortrekker Monument drove with the windows down, and Stern could smell rain on the wind. He had peeked around his blindfold once, and it seemed to him that night had fallen early. In fact the darkness was caused by the thick ceiling of storm clouds Hans had earlier seen rolling in from the north. It was part of a front that had blown in from the Indian Ocean; it stretched southward from the Mozambique border almost to Pretoria.

Stern tensed as the Range Rover swerved onto a rocky

shoulder and shuddered to a stop. He heard the driver's door open and close. Stern pulled off the blindfold and looked around. Down the highway, he saw a small speck of light. It shone from the direction they had come. Yet as he tried to focus on the yellow glimmer, it winked out. The Zulu driver turned to Stern, the whites of his eyes flashing angrily. He jabbed a finger toward the blindfold. Pulling the black scarf back around his eyes, Stern heard—or thought he heard—the sound of an automobile engine in the distance.

The Zulu clambered back into the Range Rover and screeched onto the highway, accelerating to a ridiculous speed. He raced on that way for three or four minutes; then he geared down and turned off the highway again. When the Rover finally stopped, he leaped out and ran away.

Stern moved the blindfold enough to see his surroundings. The Rover had stopped at some type of roadside park. A knot of brightly dressed Africans lounged around the single building. Several held liquor bottles in their hands. Their focus seemed to be a public telephone mounted on a wall. One of their number was talking into it. Stern watched as his Zulu driver approached the men. Rather than slow down, the Zulu swiped the air with a broad sweep of his arm. The tribesmen scattered like frightened children. They knew the Zulu, Stern thought.

The Zulu shouted into the telephone for a minute or so, bobbing his head up and down like a bird. Abruptly he ceased this motion and looked back down the highway. Stern followed his gaze. The light was there again, but larger now—and it was no longer one light, but two.

Hauer, Stern thought suddenly. *Damn him!*

As the Zulu came running back to the Rover, Stern stiffened, fearing the bullet that had been promised if anyone followed the pickup vehicle. None came. The driver's door slammed shut; then the Rover roared out of the park and accelerated to 150 kilometers per hour. Over the edge of his blindfold Stern saw the Zulu checking his rearview mirror every few seconds. *So Hauer's still there,* he thought. *How the hell did he get past Gadi?*

The engine screamed as the Zulu pushed the Rover to a frightening speed. Stern wondered if the driver really expected to shake Hauer by this simple tactic. On a paved highway Hauer's rented Ford could overtake the Range Rover without much trouble.

Suddenly the Zulu savagely twisted the wheel, throwing the Rover into a two-wheeled skid that hurled it down a shallow slope onto the hard, rolling veld. The vehicle decelerated rapidly, but the torturous terrain more than made up for the reduction in speed. No conventional automobile could catch them now. Stern tried to keep his head from slamming into the roof as the Rover vaulted humps, leaped ditches. When the Rover finally shuddered to a halt, Stern collapsed against the door and tried to catch his breath.

The Zulu wrenched the door open, jerked Stern out and ripped off the blindfold. On all sides Stern saw the seemingly limitless veld, lit by an eerie blue light filtering through the storm clouds above. The first heavy drops of African rain smacked against the roof of the Rover. Then the clouds opened with a crash. Following the Zulu's line of sight, Stern spotted the fast-approaching headlights, now jinking wildly up and down as if manipulated by some mad puppeteer. The African raised his face to the dark clouds as if beseeching some native god to lift him up and away from his pursuer. While Stern stared through the rain, hypnotized by the dancing headlights, a new sound rumbled into his ears. At first he thought it was rolling thunder. Then the engine of the pursuing car. But the sound grew nearer much faster than the headlights. Soon it was a buffeting roar, terrifying in intensity. When Stern finally looked up, he saw that the roar had blotted out the sky. He crouched beneath the blast of the rotors and shielded his eyes against the whipping rain, but the Zulu jerked him up and into the gaping maw of the helicopter as it hovered briefly near the earth.

As they lifted away from the hurricane below, Stern heard another sound cutting through the din of the rotors—a higher sound, like the rim of a crystal goblet singing. Then it came to him—the brief whine punctuated by the dull thwack— *bullets!* Two more slugs punctured the thin aluminum skin of the chopper but miraculously missed the vitals of the machine—the cabling, hydraulics, and precious rotors.

The helicopter yawed at a sickening angle as it climbed, but the Zulu held Stern fast. Far below, Stern saw the pursuer's headlights, spinning and shrinking to unreality. The chase car had stopped now. It merged with the Rover, a tiny bright speck against the rain-swept veld. Stern thought of Hauer, of how angry he must be at this unexpected tactic. He pictured the furious German kicking the Rover or even firing a few slugs into it for good measure. He couldn't help but smile.

But the man below was not kicking the Range Rover, or stupidly firing his pistol into the lifeless steel hulk. For the man below was not a man at all, but a woman. An English-woman smelling of powder and expensive perfume. *Claire de Lune.* And if Jonas Stern had known that, he would not have been smiling.

4:10 P.M. Room 604: The Protea Hof Hotel, Pretoria

Hauer and Schneider sat facing each other across the narrow space between the two double beds. Hauer held his Walther loosely in his hand; Schneider's hands were empty. Gadi sat by the window, hands clenched around his Uzi. After piling the dead Russians in the bathroom, he had gone over to the Stanley House to try to capture Borodin's sniper, but the sniper had disappeared. Professor Natterman lay asleep on the bed, his thigh and his side wrapped in gauze. Aaron Haber guarded the door. There would be no more surprise entries.

"Do you believe me now?" Schneider asked.

Hauer had spent five minutes on the phone with Colonel Rose. "I believe you," he said. "But not because of what the American said."

"Why, then?"

"Your father. He was an investigator during the student riots in the sixties. Back then a lot of police officers would just as soon have shot a student as talked to one. Your father was different."

Schneider nodded.

"Unless the acorn fell a long way from the tree, you're not part of Phoenix. Besides, why would Funk need to send you? Phoenix must have an army here in South Africa."

"Will you come back to Berlin with me?"

Hauer shook his head. "Right now I care about only one thing—saving my son's life. After that's done, I'll remember that I need to care about cleaning Funk and his stormtroopers out of Berlin. But by then it may be too late." Hauer stood. "I've got a feeling I may not be coming back from this trip, Detective. So I'm going to trust you to handle Berlin. I have to trust you."

Hauer felt every eye in the room upon him.

"Here is the situation as I see it: The British want to suppress the Spandau diary, and the Hess story with it. The Americans—at least in the past—have been willing to go along with the British. The Russians want to expose the papers and force the British to accept partial blame for what the Nazis did in the war. It's political one-upmanship." Hauer turned his head. "Have I got that right, Professor?"

"Succinctly put, Captain."

"From the Russian point of view, one would think the Spandau papers are a minor consideration compared to the very real danger of Phoenix. If the Russians learn that a secret, extremely nationalistic group exists within the police and political hierarchies in both East and West Germany, a group bent on breaking the DDR away from Russia and uniting with West Germany, a group that has infiltrated the Stasi, there is really no telling what they might do."

"What are you saying, Captain?"

"I'm saying that the Russians *need* to learn about Phoenix. In the right way, of course. I didn't tell Colonel Rose any of this, so it will all be up to you. You heard Professor Natterman. In Berlin there is a photocopy of the Spandau papers. Also in Berlin—in the house of a dead policeman named Josef Steuben—there is a fireproof safe. In that safe is a year's accumulation of evidence of drug crimes against Funk and his men. But more importantly"—Hauer paused, reluctant to reveal something that a friend had died to protect—"there is a list of every member of *Bruderschaft der Phoenix* whose name I could learn. The list names members on both sides of the Wall. Once the Russians know what Phoenix is, Schneider, they will give anything for that list."

The light of admiration dawned in Schneider's eyes.

"We want Phoenix crushed, yet we can't trust our own countrymen to do the job. So, as painful as it may be, we must turn to the Allies. That means the Americans. When you get to Berlin, retrieve the photocopy and the list, then hide them. Then tell Colonel Rose what you have, and what you want. What you want is clandestine American supervision of a German purge of Phoenix. When the Americans agree to that, let them present the Russians with their own offer. I suspect it will run something like this: In exchange for continued silence about the Hess affair—which is what the British and Americans want—the Russians will be given the names of Phoenix members in the East. They can purge the Stasi at their leisure, and get the higher-ups by interrogating the Stasi members." Hauer cracked his knuckles. "As far as I can see, everybody should be happy with that arrangement."

A strange smile flickered across Schneider's face. "I think you're in the wrong line of work, Captain. You should have been a negotiator."

"I am," Hauer told him. "A hostage negotiator."

"I thought you were a sharpshooter."

Hauer sighed. "Sometimes negotiations fail."

Schneider stood. "I'd better go. Colonel Rose said there's a plane leaving for Cairo in forty minutes, and there'll be an Army jet waiting for me there."

Hauer offered his hand. "Good luck, Detective."

Schneider's grip was like a bear's. "You come back to Berlin, Captain. And bring your son. We need more men like you."

At the door Hauer spoke softly. "It's funny, Schneider. I want the same thing Phoenix wants, a united Germany, but—"

"We all want that," Schneider cut in. "But we don't want men like Funk running it. There is a better Germany than that."

Hauer met Schneider's eyes. "We'll never get them all, you know. Not the ones at the top. Those bastards never pay."

Schneider laid a hand on the Walther in his belt. "If the courts don't get them, Captain, there are other ways. And don't take too long here. The local police are going to start discovering corpses soon."

With that, Schneider turned and walked away, a hatted man whose shoulders stretched half the breadth of the hallway.

When Hauer walked back through the foyer, Gadi said, "Isn't there something else we can do while we wait?"

Hauer shook his head. "Stern is our only chance. We've got to wait until he calls us."

"I've got a bad feeling about this," Gadi confided. "What if Uncle Jonas can't find a way to call?"

Hauer shrugged. "Then he dies. Just like Hans and Ilse." Perhaps inspired by Schneider, he touched the grip of his own pistol. "Then we hunt the bastards down and kill them. Every one of them."

Gadi exhaled in frustration. "So we just sit here?"

"We sit here."

"How long?"

"As long as it takes."

"I don't like it, Captain. And I don't trust that detective, either."

Hauer lay back on the bed and closed his eyes. "Who cares."

CHAPTER THIRTY-FOUR

4:55 P.M. MI-5 Headquarters, Charles Street, London

Sir Neville Shaw sat alone in his darkened office, clutching the telephone receiver to his ear.

"What do you mean, you *lost* him?" he asked.

Swallow's low voice quavered with barely controlled hysteria. "Someone picked him off a motorway with a helicopter. I was too far back to stop it."

Shaw rubbed his forehead. This was bad news indeed. "Thank you for informing me," he said at length. "Your services have been appreciated, but they will no longer be needed."

"*What?*"

"There will be no further contact between you and this office."

"Don't give me that, you bastard!" Swallow shrieked. "I want to know where Stern went! I know you know, and you had better tell me!"

Shaw straightened up at his desk. "Listen to me very carefully. Your orders are to stand down. Stand down *as of this moment.* Any further action on your part may disrupt a parallel operation, and will thus be considered not insubordination, but treason to the Crown. Is that clear?"

Swallow's laugh was like the cackling of a witch. "The Crown," she scoffed. "Listen to me, little man. I know what kind of operation this is. I know you ordered the murder of Rudolf Hess in Spandau. And if you don't tell me where Stern is now, I'll blow this story wide open. I'll kill Stern one way or the other, and when I've done with him, I'll come for *you.* Now—"

Shaw broke the connection. The light on his phone went

dark. Seconds later Deputy Director Wilson appeared in his doorway, a darker shadow in the dim office.

"What did she want, Sir Neville?"

Shaw stared at Wilson's anxious face for a long time. "Nothing," he said finally. "Stern's mucking about Pretoria, Swallow's on his tail. Why don't you send out for some food, old man? Get enough for yourself. It's going to be a long night, and I want you with me."

Wilson nodded crisply. "Certainly, Sir Neville."

When Wilson had gone, Shaw consulted his map of southern Africa. He checked the scale against a line he had drawn from the Mozambique Channel to a sand-colored blank spot near the Kruger Park. As if in a dream, he saw two tiny helicopters flying slowly across the map, somewhere along that line. *Parallel operation,* he thought, remembering his words to Swallow. He hoped Alan Burton had better luck than Swallow did. Burton was the last chance for the secret to stay hidden. Shaw took his favorite pipe from the stand on his desk and began rummaging for his tobacco. *Jonas Stern must be good indeed to have eluded that she-devil,* he thought. He wondered about Swallow's death threat as he sucked on the cold pipe stem, but he soon put it out of his mind. At this point in time, a deranged assassin was the least of his worries.

5:00 P.M. Mozambique/South Africa Border

The two helicopters flew in tandem, noses dipped for speed as they swept across the coastal plain north of Maputo. In the seat next to Alan Burton, Juan Diaz cursed under his breath. They had spent half the day in a guerilla camp that looked like an outpost from hell. Ragged tents pitched in the middle of a desert, cannibalized army trucks, emaciated black men carrying rusty AK-47s, girls of twelve or thirteen stolen from nearby villages and forced into whoredom by the soldiers: the dogs had looked healthier than the people.

"Who were those bastards?" asked Diaz, who had a fair grasp of English.

"The MNR, sport," Burton replied. "Bloody wogs. Fascists, to boot. You're lucky they didn't know you were a communist."

Diaz spat and muttered something in Spanish.

"I didn't like it any more than you, Juan boy. But we had to stop to pay them. Those fuzzy-wuzzies are providing our diversion this evening. Plus, it was a good place to lie up. That freighter was too exposed."

Diaz leaned out to make sure his sister ship was close behind. "Who are they trying to *di-vert* for us, English?"

"Government air forces. There's a Mozambican base about a hundred miles south of here, and a South African one further south."

"Ay-ay-*ay*," Diaz groaned. "What's based there?"

"In Mozambique? The usual African complement. Transport craft, helos, a few outdated fighters. But the South Africans have it all."

The Cuban crossed himself and dropped the chopper even closer to the plain.

"You didn't think an incursion into South Africa would be a stroll on the beach, did you?"

Suddenly a torrent of what sounded like gibberish to Diaz burst out of the African ether and filled the cabin. Burton leaned forward and began transmitting in a slower, broken version of the same language. When he finished, he replaced the transmitter and settled back into his seat with a trace of a smile on his lips.

"Takes me back, that does."

"What was that shit?"

"Portuguese, sport. Language of a lost empire."

"Everything still okay?" the pilot asked nervously.

"Bloody marvelous, I'd say."

Burton felt like a different man after the confinement of the ocean voyage. He was glad to be back in Africa. The only complication so far had been the "observer" that the MNR guerilla chief had foisted on him. The observer was a giant black named Alberto who carried a frightening arsenal of grenades, knives, and pistols. But when Burton thought of The Deal, he refused to let Alberto worry him. The guerilla looked like more of a soldier than any of the Colombians, and if he got in the way, Burton could always kill him. The Englishman reckoned there might be a good deal of killing before this mission was done. But that was all right. England had never seemed closer than it did just now.

6:07 P.M. Horn House, The Northern Transvaal

Jonas Stern waited alone in the vast reception hall of Horn House, praying that Ilse Apfel possessed more nerve and presence of mind than her overwrought husband. By all rights she should be in worse shape, emotionally speaking. But something about the way Natterman had talked about the girl gave Stern hope. Maybe she had the sand to do it. Maybe—

"Herr Professor?"

The voice emanated from a dark hallway to Stern's left. He turned to see Pieter Smuts emerge from the shadows.

"That's right," said Stern, putting his full concentration into each syllable of German. "Professor Emeritus Georg Natterman, of the Free University of Berlin. Who are you?"

Smuts smiled bleakly. "I believe you have something for me, Professor?"

Stern regarded the Afrikaner with imperious detachment. "Where is my granddaughter?"

"First the papers."

Playing the role of arrogant academic to the hilt, Stern raised his chin and looked down his nose at Smuts. "I'll not give the Spandau papers to anyone but the man who can prove they are his rightful property. Frankly, I doubt anyone here can do that."

The Afrikaner grimaced. "Herr Professor, it is only my employer's extreme patience which has kept me from—"

An invisible bell cut Smuts off in midsentence. "One moment," he said, and disappeared down the hall from which he had come.

Glancing around the grand reception hall, Stern wondered what madman had constructed this surreal *schloss* on the highveld. He took a couple of tentative steps down the opposite corridor, but Smuts's returning footsteps brought him back almost immediately.

"Follow me, Herr Professor," the Afrikaner said stiffly.

In the dimly lit library, Alfred Horn sat motionless behind an enormous desk, his one good eye focused on the man he believed to be Professor Georg Natterman.

Stern hesitated at the door. He had expected to be brought before a young English nobleman named Grenville, not a man twenty years his senior.

"Come closer, Herr Professor," Horn said. "Take a seat."

"I'll stand, thank you," Stern said uncertainly. He saw little more than a shadow at the desk. He tried to determine the shadow's nationality by its voice, but found it difficult. The man spoke German like a native, but there were other inflections too.

"As you wish," Horn said. "You wanted to see me?"

Stern squinted into the gloom. Slowly, the amorphous features of the shadow coalesced into the face of an old man. A very old man. Stern cleared his throat. "You are the man responsible for my granddaughter's abduction?"

"I'm afraid so, Professor. My name is Thomas Horn. I'm a well-known businessman in this country. Such tactics are not my usual style, but this is a special case. A member of your family stole something that belongs to some associates of mine . . ."

Horn sat so still that his mouth barely moved when he spoke. Stern tried to concentrate on the old man's words, but somehow his attention was continually drawn to the face—or what little he could see of it. A low buzz of alarm began to insinuate itself into his brain. With a combat veteran's sensitivity to physical wounds, Stern quickly noticed that the old man had but one eye. Watery and blue, it flicked restlessly back and forth while the other stared ever forward, seeing nothing. *My God!* Stern thought. *Here is Professor Natterman's one-eyed man!*

". . . but I am a pragmatist," Horn was saying. "I always take the shortest route between two points. In this case that route happened to run through your family. You have a fine granddaughter, a true daughter of *Deutschland*. But in matters such as this—matters with *political* implications—even family must take second place."

Stern felt sweat beading on his neck. Who in God's name was this man? He tried to recall what Natterman had said about the one-eyed man. *Helmut* . . . That was the name the professor had mentioned. But of course Natterman had thought "Helmut" was a code name for the real Rudolf Hess. Stern felt his heart thud in his chest. *It can't be,* he thought quickly. *It simply cannot be.*

"And so you see how simple it is, Professor," Horn concluded. "For the Spandau papers, I give you back your family."

Stern tried to speak, but his mind no longer controlled his

vocal cords. The man murmuring to him from the shadows was at least twenty years older than himself. The face and voice had been ravaged by time, but as Stern stared, he began to discern the telltale marks of authority, the indelible lines etched into the face of a man who had held great power. *Could it be?* asked a voice in Stern's brain. *Of course it could,* answered another. *Hess's double died only weeks ago, and he had endured the soul-killing loneliness of Spandau Prison for almost fifty years . . . This man has lived the life of a millionaire, with access to the best medical care in the world—*

"I've read your book, Professor," Horn said smoothly. *"Germany: From Bismarck to the Bunker.* A penetrating study, though flawed in its conclusions. I would be very interested to hear your opinion of the Spandau papers."

Stern swallowed. "I—I haven't really had that much time to study them. They deal mainly with the prisoners at Spandau."

"Prisoners, Professor? Not one prisoner in particular?"

Stern blinked.

"Not Prisoner Number *Seven?"* Horn smiled cagily. "Have no fear, Professor, my interest is purely academic. I'd simply like to know if the papers shed any light on the events of May tenth, 1941—on the flight of Rudolf Hess. The solution to that mystery has always eluded me"—he smiled again—"as it has the rest of the world."

Stern fought the urge to step backward. What kind of game was this? "There is mention of the Hess flight," he whispered.

"And are you familiar with the case, Professor?"

"Conversant."

"Excellent. I happen to have a unique volume related to it here in my library. The only one of its kind." Horn tilted his head slightly. "Pieter?"

Smuts crossed to some tall shelves at the dark edge of the library and pulled down a thin black volume. He hesitated a moment, but Horn inclined his head sharply and Smuts obeyed.

Stern accepted the thin volume without looking at it.

"You hold a piece of living history in your hand, Professor," Horn said solemnly. "A piece no historian has ever seen before. May of 1941 was a critical juncture in the march of Western civilization. A time of great opportunities." He sighed. "Missed opportunities. I'd like you to read that while we verify the Spandau papers. Perhaps it will help you to do what no one else has yet been able to do—solve the Hess mystery."

Stern looked down at the book in his hands. It was a notebook, he saw, bound in black leather with a name stamped in gold on its cover: *V. V. Zinoviev.* The name meant nothing to Stern. What was he holding in his hands? Had this man Horn threatened to kill Ilse Apfel in order to suppress one clue to the Hess enigma, only to give the man he thought to be her grandfather another? Was he a fool? Of course not. He was a snake allowing the sparrow one last song before it felt the fangs strike. Any knowledge that "Professor Natterman" gained from the Zinoviev notebook in the next few hours would perish with him.

"Come closer, Professor," Horn said, raising his chin like a connoisseur examining an antique for authenticity. "Do you have Jewish blood in your family?"

The flickering blue eye fixed on Stern and bored in, searching for the slightest hint of deception. Stern struggled to maintain his calm. During the helicopter flight he had worried that his rusty German would give him away, yet no one seemed to have noticed it. Would it be his Semitic nose that betrayed him? That put the final bullet through his heart?

"Nein," he said, forcing a smile. "This nose has been the bane of my life, Herr Horn. There's some Arab blood far back down the line, I think. It almost cost me my life several times during the thirties."

"I can imagine," Horn said thoughtfully. "So. The Spandau papers. You have brought them to me?"

Horn's cadaverous face seemed to waver ghostlike in the shadows. As if by its own volition, Stern's right hand burrowed into his trouser pocket and brought out the missing pages. Before he even realized what he meant to do, he had lurched forward and laid the three sheets on Horn's desk.

"You have it all now," he blurted. "Make what you wish of it. Just give me back my granddaughter."

He turned and moved zombie-like toward the door. His eyes focused on the handle as he neared it.

"Herr Professor?"

Stern froze.

Horn's warbling voice floated through the darkness like a

phantom, ancient and unreal. "I called the Document Centre in Berlin. They informed me that you were at the Siege of Leningrad. This shouldn't be too great an ordeal for an old *Wehrmacht* soldier. Have a rest, see your granddaughter. All will soon be back to normal, and you and I will exchange old war stories. And don't forget to read the Zinoviev book."

Stern peered through the shadows. The conversation seemed to have tired the old man. The face which had looked so alive at the beginning of the meeting now sagged as if drained by chronic pain. Stern groped behind him for the door. Pieter Smuts turned the knob and slipped into the hall ahead of him. Stern saw Horn raise a skeletal arm in farewell, and then Smuts pulled the door shut.

Dazed, Stern followed the tall Afrikaner down the long corridor toward the reception hall. They crossed it, then walked the length of several dim passages. Stern felt like Alice being led through the warrens of the looking-glass world. Finally, Smuts stopped before a door and opened it.

Stern saw a striking young blond woman dressed in a smart navy skirt and white blouse. From Natterman's description, he recognized Ilse Apfel immediately, but he was still so deep in frenzied speculation about the old man that he failed to notice the shock on her face. Ilse looked from Smuts to Stern, then back to Smuts. She started to speak, then held her tongue, waiting for the Afrikaner to explain the intrusion. Smuts said nothing. Ilse's eyes moved up and down Stern's lean frame, lingering on his unfamiliar face, finally settling on Professor Natterman's patched tweed jacket. Smuts—who was normally quite sensitive to subtleties of human behavior—put Ilse's awkwardness down to surprise.

"I hope you both appreciate Herr Horn's generosity," he said.

The words woke Stern from his trance. Instantly he registered the dangerous bafflement on Ilse's face. *Steady, girl,* he thought. *Steady* . . . "Ilse!" he cried. "My little *Enkelkinder!* Come to me!" He took a step forward and held out his arms. *Come on girl, get it.*

Without quite understanding why, Ilse moved forward. First hesitantly, then in apparent jubilation, she rushed to the stranger and pressed her head against his jacket, clinging to him like a child. She would never know why she did it. It was an impulse, a tingling flash of inexplicable certainty like those that sometimes hit her as she watched the stock quotes flickering across the toteboard at work. She didn't question it, she simply obeyed.

"My little darling," Stern said soothingly, stroking Ilse's cheek. "Are you all right?"

"Yes, *Opa,* yes," Ilse murmured. "Can we go home now?"

"Not yet, little one. Not quite yet. But soon."

Stern glared at Smuts over Ilse's blond hair. "Could we have some privacy?" he asked icily.

A tight grimace plucked at the corner of the Afrikaner's mouth, but he left them.

Ilse immediately pulled away from Stern and opened her mouth to speak. Stern stifled her with an upturned palm, then pointed to the door.

Who are you? Ilse mouthed silently.

Stern leaned over until his lips touched the shell of Ilse's ear. "A friend," he whispered. "Thank God you managed to suppress your shock. I believe you just saved my life."

"It was the jacket," Ilse whispered excitedly. "You're wearing *Opa*'s jacket. At first I thought it was some kind of crazy trick, but—"

"No trick."

"Where is *Opa?*"

"He is safe. He's with Captain Hauer."

"And Hans? Is Hans safe?"

Stern nodded impatiently, as if Hans were merely a secondary problem to be dealt with when and if possible. "Hans is here now. He tried to trade the Spandau papers for your life, but failed."

Ilse's eyes widened. "Hans is *here?*"

"Yes, but we can't worry about that now. If we don't figure out exactly where we are and get me to a telephone, we'll probably be dead within an hour."

Ilse shook her head. "You'll need an airplane to get out of here."

"You know where we are?"

"Not exactly, but I've been outside. We're far out in the wilderness. Near something called the Kruger Park, I think."

"The Kruger National Park?" Stern looked at his watch, estimating the distance he had traveled by road and by helicopter. "Yes, that would be about right." His voice grew urgent. "Ilse, I don't know how much you know about the situation you are in. You may, like your grandfather, see it as merely a squabble over the Rudolf Hess case, but it is much more than that. I believe that somewhere in this country there are men who mean to cause great harm to my country—Israel. Damn it!" Stern cried suddenly. "What is hiding here? That bastard asked me if I had any Jewish blood in my veins, and I—*an Israeli*—denied that I did!"

He threw the Zinoviev notebook onto the bed and tried the doorknob again, shaking it furiously. Ilse reached out and clutched the sleeve of her grandfather's jacket.

"You're right," she whispered. "About Israel."

"What?" Stern turned to face her. "What do you mean?"

"I mean that Horn wants to destroy Israel."

Stern clutched her arms. "How do you know that? Out with it, girl! Speak!"

"You're hurting me!"

Stern released her. "What are you talking about?"

Ilse brushed a strand of hair out of her eyes. "Last night, Herr Horn met with some Arabs up in the central tower of the estate. For some reason he wanted me there, I don't know why. He offered to provide these Arabs with a nuclear weapon—one or more than one, I'm not sure. He said he would provide it free of charge if the Arabs would use it as he wished. He said there was a nuclear weapon somewhere beneath this house."

Stern swallowed hard, his eyes burning into Ilse's. "Did you believe him?"

She hesitated a moment; then she nodded very slowly.

"How did he say he wanted the weapon used?"

"He said he wanted it exploded in Tel Aviv."

Stern felt his bowels roll. "When?"

"Within ten days, he said."

Stern crossed to the bed and picked up the thin black notebook Horn had given him. Again he read the gold letters stamped on the cover: *V. V. Zinoviev.* Still the name meant nothing. He slipped the notebook inside his shirt, backed against the far wall, and without a sound threw himself across the room and against the heavy wooden door.

Ilse screamed.

The door didn't budge. Stern gasped for breath, backed up, charged again. His wiry frame smashed into the wood with a sound like a child falling down stairs. Ilse cringed. Twice more the old Israeli flung himself at the door, but it refused to give. Bruised and winded, Stern raised his right leg and kicked at the knob with all his strength.

"It's no good!" Ilse cried. "Please stop! You're hurting yourself!"

Stern did not even look at her. With a howl of rage he kicked at the knob again. When it refused to yield, he backed up and launched his body at the door yet again. This time the impact knocked him to his knees. He got unsteadily to his feet and prepared to try again. Ilse caught his arm, meaning to restrain him, but when Stern whirled, something in his eyes moved her into some region beyond logic, beyond reason. She counted to three, and together they flung themselves against the wood.

CHAPTER THIRTY-FIVE

7:05 P.M. *Mozambique/South Africa Border*

The helicopters stormed northward on the Mozambique side of the border, hugging the plain between the Lebombo Mountains and the Limpopo River. Occasionally they jinked westward long enough for Burton to take bearings. The Englishman knew this part of Africa well, and the Kruger Park had enough landmarks to keep him oriented.

The border itself, a garish scar of bare earth bisected by a huge electric fence, divided two countries that might have been different continents. On the Mozambique side, a desolate war-ravaged plain stretched toward the sea. On the South African side, the lushness of the Kruger Park began immediately. Wide green troughs of riverine vegetation snaked westward out of sight. Forests of mopane, Sycamore fig, and Natal mahogany sheltered herds of elephant and zebra, white rhino and lion.

"Take her back up!" Alan Burton ordered.

Juan Diaz breathed a sigh of relief. The Cuban pilot prided himself on his flying skill, but this crazy English *gringo* had badgered him about the altitude until he wondered if the man had a secret death wish. Burton pointed to the north and shouted above the rotor noise.

"We want to keep on this heading until we see the Olifants River! Then we'll veer west and cross the park at treetop level!" He showed Diaz the map. "The house we want lies about halfway between the western edge of the park and this little town here." Burton pointed to Giyani, then indicated an X marked about fifteen kilometers from the western edge of the Kruger Park.

Diaz nodded, then returned his gaze to the plain below.

"The Kruger Park's about the size of Wales," Burton told him. "But it's thin—runs north to south."

Diaz ignored him.

"Probably never heard of Wales, eh?" Burton laughed. "The Prince of Wales?"

Diaz shook his head. Either the Cuban hadn't understood or he simply did not want to be bothered. Burton switched to a more relevant subject. "That fence down there," he yelled, pointing westward, "11,500 volts! They fry a whole gang of Mozambican refugees on that thing every year. Bloody awful."

The Cuban grimaced. He knew about dead refugees.

Glancing back into the cabin of the JetRanger, Burton looked the Colombian soldiers over again. The presence of Alberto, the big MNR observer, made them look even more unprofessional. "What do you think of our South American friends, Diaz?" he yelled.

The Cuban pilot did not share Burton's confidence in the deafness of the Colombians. He pulled the Englishman's head down near his own. *"Banditos,"* he muttered. "No soldiers." He cut his eyes back toward the cabin, then crossed himself so that only Burton could see.

"Bloody hell." Burton had hoped Diaz might know something encouraging about the Colombians that he didn't. Suddenly the Englishman sighted a silver serpentine glittering beneath the dark clouds to the north. "There's the river!" he shouted.

Diaz nodded, then banked westward and dove for the plain. Their sister ship followed closely, behind and to the right. The green sea of the Kruger Park rushed toward them. The JetRangers skimmed over the border fence and swept westward over the verdant foliage below. Burton saw a herd of antelope raising a huge cloud of dust as they fled the noise of the approaching choppers. Diaz pointed to the dark cloud ceiling above them.

"Much rain when it comes?"

"Buckets this time of year!"

Diaz frowned, but Burton smiled wryly. The weather didn't worry him; that was the pilots' problem. But the accuracy of his intelligence reports did. Who in hell was the English informer who supposedly waited inside the target house? Probably anything *but* a soldier, Burton thought ruefully. The informer had reported that Alfred Horn relied primarily upon isolation for security—isolation and a neo-Nazi security chief. Burton wondered if the informer would even recognize defensive measures if he saw them. Swallowing his anxiety, he slapped Diaz on the back and grinned.

"Rain's good for us!" he yelled. "Better cover!"

Diaz glanced doubtfully back into the cabin where the bearded Colombians crouched. He dropped a little closer to the trees.

Horn House: The Northern Transvaal

Ilse sat opposite Alfred Horn at the long mahogany dining table and stared sullenly at her plate. All the other chairs were empty. In spite of their furious efforts, she and Stern had been unable to break out of the bedroom before Linah arrived to take them to dinner. Stern had pleaded an unsettled stomach, so Ilse had come alone. She wondered if the old Israeli was still trying. As Linah leaned over her left shoulder to pour white wine, she looked up at Horn.

"Where is everyone?" she asked, trying to hold her voice steady.

"Pieter has work to do," Horn replied. "And of course your grandfather remains in your bedroom." He smiled. "I believe he would rather finish reading that notebook I gave him than eat."

Ilse lifted her fork and tried to make a show of eating. Stern had advised her to carry on as she had been, but now that she knew Hans was almost surely somewhere inside the house, she couldn't contain herself. "Where is my husband?" she cried suddenly.

Horn looked up slowly from his plate. "He has not yet arrived, my dear."

"*Liar!* He's here!"

Horn swallowed some wine, then set his crystal goblet on the table. "Who told you that?" he asked quietly. "Your grandfather?"

"No one. I . . . I just feel it."

"Ah, woman's intuition. An overrated faculty, I've found. Do not worry, your Hans will arrive soon."

Ilse quivered with anger. "You're lying," she said stubbornly. "Hans is here."

Horn slammed his frail hand against the table, rattling the

silver. "*I will not tolerate this at my table!* You will behave as a German woman should or—"

At that moment Pieter Smuts marched into the dining room with Jürgen Luhr on his heels. "Aircraft approaching the house, sir," he announced. "Two blips, so far. They're at the edge of the Kruger Park now."

"What type of aircraft, Pieter?"

Smuts smiled coldly. "No radio contact, no IFF, but from their speed I would guess helicopters."

Horn sighed deeply. "Are the bunkers manned?"

"Yes, sir." Smuts's face was taut. "Everyone's in place."

"And Lord Grenville?"

The Afrikaner shook his head. "I'm not sure where he is."

While the men spoke, Ilse slid her right arm off of the table, taking her silver dinner fork and salad fork with it.

"Take Frau Apfel to her room," said Horn. "Then get to the tower. I'll be in my study."

"But, sir, with Grenville loose—"

Horn silenced the Afrikaner by ringing a hand bell that summoned Linah. "To the tower, Pieter," he commanded. "I am in no danger."

"Bring the girl," Smuts told Luhr, and hurried out.

"Frau Apfel?" Luhr motioned for Ilse to stand. He forced himself to smile. As soon as Linah had wheeled Horn out of the dining room, however, he snatched Ilse up by the arm and dragged her into the hall.

"Lock her in!" Smuts called from up the corridor. "Then meet me at the reception hall elevator!"

When Ilse and Luhr reached the bedroom door, she reached into her pocket and closed her hand around one of the forks. She thought of driving it into Luhr's neck, but she did not. Better to let Stern make a move if he thought the time was right.

Stern didn't get the chance. Luhr turned the knob quickly and kicked open the door, knocking the Israeli backward onto the floor. He laughed, then shoved Ilse inside and jerked the door shut.

Ilse pulled the silver forks from her pocket and tossed them to Stern. "Get us out of here!" she snapped. *"Now!"*

When the elevator door opened in the domed observatory tower, Jürgen Luhr stepped into a room unlike any he had ever seen. He had once been admitted to the control tower of Frankfurt International Airport, but even that seemed primitive compared to this futuristic command post. Computer screens, satellite receivers, amplifiers, massive banks of switches, closed-circuit television monitors, and countless other pieces of high-tech equipment hung from the ceiling and rose from the carpeted floor. An eerie green glow bathed the circular room, silhouetting three men dressed in khaki who ceaselessly monitored the various surveillance consoles. One man made way for Smuts, who took a seat before a phosphorescent radar screen.

"Who is in the helicopters?" Luhr asked.

Smuts smiled thinly. "I'm not sure, but you can bet they're friends of Lord Grenville, our pet English nobleman. You see those switches there? The red ones?"

"Here?" asked Luhr, reaching.

"Don't touch them! Christ! Look at the markings. North, East, South, West. When I call a direction, pull the first switch for that heading. When I call it again, pull the second. Got it?"

Luhr nodded. "What do they do?"

"You'll find out soon enough."

Taking a last look at the radar screen, Smuts moved to the center of the room, ascended a short ladder, and climbed into the strangest contraption Luhr had ever seen. A monstrosity of steel tubing, pedals, gears, and hydraulic lines, it looked like something stripped from the belly of a World War Two vintage bomber. Protruding from this strange machine were six long narrow metal tubes joined at the center and extending to within an inch of the dome's wall. Suddenly, Luhr realized what he was looking at: a Vulcan 20mm rotary cannon. He had seen them many times in Germany, jutting from the stubby snouts of American A-10 tank-killing warplanes.

"Hit the blue switch," Smuts ordered.

Luhr obeyed, and watched in wonder as a narrow oblong section of the domed ceiling receded into a hidden slot in the wall. Smuts touched a button; the barrels of the Vulcan gun moved forward through the opening like the barrel of a telescope. Now the gun could be traversed on a vertical axis.

"Hit the next switch down."

Luhr gasped as the middle four feet of the circular wall sank into the floor with a deep hum. Through the bullet-resistant polycarbonate glass that now served as the wall, Luhr could see a 360-degree panorama of the grounds surrounding Horn House. The sky was heavy and nearly black with impending rain. Four hundred meters to the north, Horn's Learjet and helicopter sat like toys in the fast-fading light.

"Next," said Smuts.

Luhr hit the final blue switch, immersing the room in near-total darkness. Only the luminous green radar screens competed with the gray light outside the turret. Smuts pulled down a leather harness and buckled it across his chest. Then he grasped two elongated tubes and positioned them directly over his eyes. Luhr realized they were laser targeting goggles.

"Sit down and strap yourself in," Smuts ordered.

"Why?"

Scowling, Smuts jabbed a foot pedal. Instantly the turret began to rotate, throwing Luhr to the floor.

"Don't ever question my orders, Lieutenant."

Luhr scrambled to his feet and buckled himself into the chair. On the radar screen to his left, two tiny blips crossed the line indicating the western edge of the Kruger National Park, then turned southwest toward an *H* marked on the screen in grease pencil.

"Fifteen kilometers and closing," announced a khaki-clad technician. "Approach speed 110 knots."

Luhr watched the fuzzy green specks pass slightly to the north of the *H*, then veer left and bore straight in. "Who *are* they?" he asked, unable to suppress his apprehension.

"Dead men," Smuts replied from the gun cage.

Hans Apfel could not move. He lay in the absolute darkness of a cell one hundred meters below the earth. This was the same cell in which Jürgen Luhr had spent his first night in South Africa. Hans was bound to a heavy cot with rope and gagged with a thick strip of cloth. He could only breathe through his nose. No sound had reached his ears for hours, save the occasional sibilant hiss of a ventilator blowing air into his cell.

Suddenly, a deep, buzzing alarm blasted through the basement complex. Every muscle in Hans's body contracted in shock. What was happening? A fire? For the hundredth time he expelled every ounce of air from his lungs and tried to shift his body on the cot. It was no use. He had never felt so helpless in his life. Yet despite his fear for Ilse, one desperate hope flickered in his brain: *Is it my father?*

"I've almost got it," Stern grunted, working feverishly at the lock on the bedroom door. By intertwining the tines of Ilse's stolen forks and snapping off several, he'd managed to fashion the dinner fork into a serviceable lock pick.

"Hurry!" Ilse urged. "I don't think we have much time."

"Did Horn seem upset?" Stern asked, still working. "Surprised? Frightened?"

"Not really. Please, *hurry.* We must find Hans!"

At that moment the clouds opened. The rain lashed the roof of Horn House in great sheets, then settled into a steady torrent that would soon turn the surrounding gullies into raging rivers.

"Got it!" Stern cried. He cracked the door slightly, then flung it wide.

Ilse darted into the hall. "Where should we start?"

"Beat on every locked door you can find. If Hans is here, he'll be behind one."

"Aren't you coming?"

"You don't need me to find your husband. I've got something else to do."

"What?"

"After what you told me, you ask me that? *Move* girl!"

Stern spun Ilse around, put a hand between her shoulder blades and shoved her down the hall. She hesitated a moment; then, seeing that the Israeli meant what he said, she started slowly up the corridor. Stern clenched the broken fork tightly in his fist and set out in the opposite direction.

The JetRanger helicopters skimmed across the veld like great steel dragonflies. In the distance Burton could just make out the copper dome of Horn's "observatory" glinting through the heavy rain. He flattened his palm and dropped it close to his thigh, indicating that Diaz should fly still closer to the earth. The Cuban muttered something in Spanish, but the scrub brush rose up into the Plexiglas windshield until Burton felt he was tearing across the veld on a horse gone mad. Even the few stunted trees they passed rose higher than the chopper's rotors.

"See it?" Burton yelled, pointing.

The Cuban nodded.

"We should see an airstrip soon. That's your objective. Set right down on it!"

Burton poked his head back into the crowded cabin and gave the Colombians a thumbs-up signal. Most of them looked airsick, but Alberto—the guerilla observer—grinned back, his square white teeth flashing in the shadows.

Forty seconds later, Diaz wheeled the JetRanger in a wide circle and settled onto the freshly laid asphalt fifty meters from Horn's Learjet. Burton punched open the Plexiglas door and jumped to the ground. Just as they had practiced a dozen times on the *Casilda*'s afterdeck, the Colombians poured out of the chopper one after another, looking, for all their amateurishness, like a squad of marines securing a hot LZ. A quick glance across the tarmac told Burton that the men on the other chopper were doing the same. "See you after the party!" he shouted to Diaz.

The Cuban shook his head. *"English loco,"* he muttered, twirling his forefinger beside his temple.

The Colombians crouched at the edge of the rotor blast, waiting for Burton to take the lead. The mercenary jumped to the ground and immediately started toward the distant dome at an easy trot. The Colombians, twenty-two in all, followed closely.

Thirty seconds' running brought them up short at the rim of the Wash. Burton stared angrily into the ravine. He'd been told to expect a shallow trench, no more than a thirty-second delay. But the summer cloudburst had turned this steep-sided gully into a treacherous river that would take minutes, not seconds, to cross. Three feet of muddy runoff churned through the undergrowth near the bottom, and the water was rising fast.

"Move!" Burton shouted, and leaped over the lip of the ravine. He half-fell, half-slid toward the torrent below. Looking back, he saw the Colombians skidding down behind him. Two minutes later they all stood on the opposite rim of the Wash, huddling against the rain. Burton started slogging westward again without a word. For a few minutes he saw nothing ahead but rain. Then, like a mirage, the whole stunning specter of Horn house appeared out of the downpour. Burton's blood ran cold. One glance told him that his "inside" informer didn't know his ass from his elbow. The "soft" objective he had been briefed to expect stood like a medieval fortress on a hill at the center of a huge expanse of

open ground. Ten men armed with medium machine guns could defend that house indefinitely against a force the size he had brought. His ragtag outfit had only one hope—surprise.

The Colombians had not yet picked up on the alarming deterioration of their situation, and Burton didn't intend for them to. "All right, lads!" he barked. "Change of plan! I'd intended to use the mortar to soften the target for you"—Burton paused while a bilingual Colombian interpreted—"but this open ground changes everything. If I open up before you go in, the target will be warned. Many of you could die in the charge." Burton saw several faces nod warily as the interpreter conveyed his words. "My suggestion is that you all go in at the double—a quick, silent run. You go in very fast and close to the ground. The Israelis favor this tactic, and they've surprised a lot of Arabs with it, I can tell you." He summoned a bluff grin. "Ready, lads?"

Two or three Colombians nodded, but most looked a shade paler than they had when they thought Burton's mortar barrage would precede their attack. The Englishman took a final look at his unit. They were a ragged lot by any standard, standing there in the rain, weighted down by bandolero ammo belts, grenades, and LAW rockets. They would have been comic but for the near certainty of their impending deaths. Looking past them to the distant house, Burton felt a sudden, almost irresistible urge to order them back to the choppers, to save their miserable lives before they charged the fortress that waited beyond the gray wall of rain. But then he remembered The Deal.

"Move out!" he shouted angrily. "Goddamn it, *charge!*"

The Colombians stared dumbly for a moment; then they turned and trotted down the slope into the shallow bowl. One hung back—a teenager named Ruiz, whom Burton had tried to instruct in the finer points of mortar operation—waiting to see if he was needed. Burton started to nod, then he sensed someone behind him. He turned to see Alberto, the huge MNR guerilla observer. Burton pointed to the mortar tube he had dropped onto the grass and eyed the guerilla questioningly. When Alberto nodded with confidence, Burton decided he would prefer skill to good company today. He motioned for Ruiz to follow the charge.

Alberto immediately began setting up the mortar, but Burton, impelled by some morbid instinct, crouched on the rim of the grassy bowl and watched the Colombians go in. As his eyes followed the camouflaged figures—running now—he suddenly noticed something odd about the floor of the bowl. Subdividing the approaches to Horn House into measured sections were dozens of small, grass-covered mounds. At first glance they seemed only natural irregularities in the ground—animal spoor, perhaps—but Burton soon realized that the humps were anything but natural. His mind faltered for a moment, not wanting to accept it; then his gut instinct grasped the whole ghastly scene. *A killing ground.* Those innocent-looking mounds concealed land mines. Burton shouted a warning, but the Colombians had already passed out of earshot. Alberto raised his head at Burton's shout—

Then it started.

Sixteen Claymore mines exploded simultaneously, sending thousands of steel balls scything through the air at twice the speed of sound. Half the Colombians were shredded into bloody pulp before they could scream. The sound came in waves, deep, shuddering concussions muted by the rain. Most survivors of the first blast staggered to the ground, mortally wounded. Shrapnel detonated some of the Colombian ordnance. Grenades flashed in the dusk; one of the LAW rockets exploded in a blinding fireball, consuming the man who carried it.

Burton lay stomach-down, shielding his eyes against the flashes. Alberto tugged at Burton's pack, groping for mortar rounds so that he could return fire. Burton slapped the big guerilla's hand away. "Bloody *hell!* All you'd do now is pinpoint our position!" He punched his fist into the soggy veld. "Poor bastards."

In spite of the Englishman's pessimism, Alberto grinned and pointed down the slope to where, unbelievably, a half-dozen Colombians still crawled doggedly toward Horn House. Having gone too far to retreat with any hope of survival, they went blindly on. Forty meters from the great triangular structure, one of them rose to one knee and let off a LAW rocket. The smoke trail arrowed across the grass, and the exploding warhead tore a jagged hole in the wall above a shuttered window. Emboldened by their comrade's success, three wounded Colombians got up and cheered, then charged the main entrance with their AK-47s on full automatic.

At that moment—with a sound like a bandsaw ripping tin—Smuts's Vulcan gun opened up from the observatory.

From the tower, Jürgen Luhr watched the carnage with morbid fascination. He could not quite comprehend the fact that he had obliterated a dozen human beings with the flick of a switch. The land around Horn House looked as if a hundred plows had passed over it, sowing blood and fire. The remotely detonated Claymores had churned the earth into a smoking graveyard. When the Vulcan gun began to fire, Luhr thought he had gone deaf. White flame spat out of the six spinning barrels; the unbelievable rate of fire made the scarlet tracers look like laser beams arcing across the slope below. Anywhere the gun lingered for a full second, more than a hundred depleted-uranium-tipped slugs impacted in a steady stream of death. The rain and darkness obscured the remaining attackers, but Smuts seemed to have no trouble finding them. Wearing ear protectors now, he worked the pedals with practiced skill, traversing the gun with remorseless accuracy. Watching Smuts's slit-eyed face behind the Vulcan, Luhr actually pitied the men who remained alive.

Four floors below the observatory, Robert Stanton, Lord Grenville, watched the weapons he had known nothing about blast his dreams of power into oblivion. *If Alfred survives this night,* he thought desolately, *what will Shaw give me? Not a fucking thing, that's what!* He shook his head in wonder. Not one member of the assault team remained standing! Unbelieving, Stanton pressed his palm against the windowpane, watching in horror as the Vulcan's terrible tracer beam climbed the slope, then disappeared over the ridge. Seconds later a fireball mushroomed into the sky. *Probably a helicopter,* he realized. Stanton could bear no more. He knew he had but one chance now: to find Horn and allay any suspicion that he was connected with the attack. *If Burton is killed,* he thought hopefully, *I might just bring it off.* He dashed into the dark hallway and made for the study, almost sure that Horn would be closeted there.

Scurrying through the vast reception hall, he saw Ilse jerk back into one of the corridors, but she meant nothing to him now. In seconds he would be fighting for his life. A quick sprint brought him to the study door, which he found unlocked. He burst through it like a man in blind panic. A green-shaded lamp burned at Horn's desk, but the old man was not there. Then, slowly, Stanton made out the wheelchair, silhouetted against the rain-spattered picture window. Scarlet tracers sliced through the darkness outside, giving the room a surrealistic sense of drama, like the bridge of a ship during battle.

"Alfred!" Stanton cried with exaggerated relief. "Thank God you're safe!"

Slowly Horn rotated his wheelchair until he faced the young Englishman. His face was haggard, but his solitary eye burned with black contempt. "So, Robert," he rasped, "you would be my Judas."

Ilse tore through the halls like a madwoman. She had searched every unlocked room and pounded on every locked door in the house, but she'd found no sign of Hans. Nor had she seen Stern since they parted at the bedroom door. She had found one useful thing. In a spartan bedroom decorated only by an eight-by-ten photograph of a younger, uniformed Pieter Smuts, she'd found a Beretta 9mm semi-automatic pistol in a holster hanging from the bedpost. She wasn't sure she could use it, but she had no doubt that Stern could. Or Hans, if she could find him.

Approaching the reception hall at a full run, she saw Lord Grenville sprint across it in another direction. She skidded and tried to backpedal into the narrow corridor, but she was too late—Stanton had seen her. Yet just as she turned to flee, she heard the Englishman's footsteps echoing down one of the main passageways—*away* from her. Carefully she crossed the reception hall and peered down the corridor into which Stanton had vanished. *What's he after?* she wondered. *What is so important that he would ignore me running loose? Another prisoner, perhaps? Hans?*

Ilse darted down the hallway after Stanton. Toward the far end of the dark corridor she saw a vertical crack of light. As she neared it, she heard voices. One was unmistakably Stanton's, the other . . . she couldn't be sure. Pulling off her shoes, she slipped quietly through the door.

She pressed herself flat against the paneled wall of the study. Alfred Horn sat hunched in his wheelchair before a large picture window, barely discernible in the shadows. Beside an ornate desk four meters away stood Lord Grenville. He was gesticulating wildly with his hands.

"I told you, Alfred!" he shouted. "Smuts is insane! He knows nothing of my loyalty! I'm your *partner*, for God's sake!"

"You are a liar and a coward," Horn said evenly. "And you care for nothing but money." He swept a hand toward the window, where sporadic tracer fire still illuminated the grounds in short bursts. "You see how your greed ends, Robert?"

Stanton raised his arms in supplication. "But I know nothing of that! It's another of Smuts's schemes to discredit me! He's always been jealous of me, you know that!"

Horn shook his head sadly. "Dear Robert. How is it that great men produce heirs such as you? It is the bane of the world."

"Please!" Stanton begged. "What proof is there against me?"

Horn rubbed his wizened forehead. "Reach beneath the desktop, Robert."

Stanton did. His fingers touched a toggle switch. He flipped it reflexively. A male voice boomed from speakers on the bookshelf: *"Good Christ, are you mad?"*

Stanton felt faint. "Shut up and listen!" snapped a voice he recognized as his own. "I had to call from here. They won't let me go anywhere else. Look, you've got to call it off."

"What?" asked the incredulous voice, the British accent unmistakable.

"He knows, I'm telling you. Horn knows about *Casilda*. I don't know how, but he does."

"He can't know."

"He does!"

"There's no stopping it now," said Sir Neville Shaw. "And your information on Horn's defenses had better turn out to be good, Grenville, or—"

Alfred Horn's bitter voice rose above the recording. "You don't even make a good Judas, Robert! You're pathetic!"

"But ... but it's not what you think!" Stanton wailed. "That call was about the gold we're expecting!"

"Liar! You've betrayed me! I will coddle you no more!"

With a sudden straightening of his body, Stanton pulled a .45 caliber pistol from his belt. *"You're* the fool!" he cried, his eyes burning with maniacal hatred. "Doddering around this carnival house, clinging to your rotting fortune like a sick lion. Blubbering your idiotic racial philosophies through these empty halls. You're daft! Your day is *past,* old man! It's my turn now!" Stanton aimed the pistol at Horn's head.

"Put down the gun, Robert," Horn said quietly. "I will forgive you. Please, for your grandfather's sake."

"Shut up! You'd never let me live now!"

"I will forgive you, Robert. But first you must tell me all about your friends from London."

Stanton shook his head like a terrified child. "I can't! I tried to protect you, you know. They wanted me to kill you myself, but I refused. They offered me the bloody moon! They threatened to blackmail me, to expose some horrible secret about my grandfather"—Stanton grinned wildly—"but then I realized they were more afraid of the secret than I was!" The petulant scowl returned. "But they mean to kill you, Alfred. One way or the other. Don't you see? I had no choice. London will only send someone else for you."

"Perhaps," Horn said wearily. "Perhaps I made a mistake, Robert. Because you are . . . like you are, I never revealed to you my true identity. My true mission. Even your father kept it from you—wisely, I thought. But the time has come for you to know. I *will* forgive your treachery, but first you must put down the gun. Put it down, and learn the true story of your noble heritage."

"You bastard!" Stanton screamed. He charged forward and kicked Horn's wheelchair over, spilling him onto the parquet floor.

Drawn inexorably forward by the madness of the scene, Ilse edged along the wall until she could see Horn lying on his back. Erratic flashes through the picture window fell on his gaunt face, contorted with pain and confusion. Above him, Stanton, his eyes alight with maniacal fury, held the gun in his quivering right hand. "You talk of forgiveness!" he shouted. *"Who are you to forgive?"* He jerked back the slide of the .45 and aimed at Horn's glass eye. "What did you make my grandfather do?"

"Nothing!" Horn said pleadingly. "You have it all backward! Please, Robert! I do not fear death, but I fear for my mission. For your grandfather's mission. For mankind!" Horn's voice rose in desperation. *"Do not end the work of half a century!"*

Stanton laughed wildly, then he tightened his mouth into

a grimace and steadied the gun with both hands. "Death at last, Alfred!" he cried. "It's long overdue!"

As if in a dream, Ilse raised Smuts's Beretta and pulled back the slide, just as she had seen Hans do a hundred times in their apartment. Stanton heard the metallic click. He whirled, trying to pinpoint the source of the sound ...

Ilse fired.

CHAPTER THIRTY-SIX

Stern ran silently, swiftly through the house. Ilse had described the triangular layout of Horn House to him, but from inside, the myriad halls and passages seemed only to lead back upon themselves. He had tried to always turn inward, toward the central tower that Ilse had told him would lead to the basement, but each time he was eventually stopped by the same obstacle—an impenetrable sheet of black anodized metal. The heavy shields blocked every inward-facing door and window he could find. The central tower and basement complex had obviously been sealed for battle.

Stern paused for breath beside a wide metal door marked KRANKENHAUS. He had yet to find a telephone, and even if he found one, he could only give Hauer the most general idea of where he was being held. He needed a map. *Who is attacking this house?* he thought angrily. *The Arabs come for their damned bomb, if it even exists?* In any other country, the idea that a private citizen had gained possession of a nuclear weapon would be ludicrous. But Stern knew that in South Africa no normal rules applied. In a nuclear-capable state that had developed beyond the scrutiny of any regulatory entity, anything was possible. A man of Horn's wealth might well have been instrumental in South Africa's nuclear weapons program, and God alone knew what price he would have exacted for his aid. *And if he does have the bomb?* Stern asked himself. *What then?* Visions of Israeli commandos parachuting into the courtyards of Horn House made his pulse race, but he knew that such a raid would not happen here. When he finally found a telephone, he would not have time to make the six or eight calls it would take to reach the proper members of the Israeli General Staff—*if* they weren't out playing golf somewhere. And even if he did reach them, what action could they take? South Africa wasn't Lebanon or Iraq. Violating South African airspace would be a dangerous act of war. The unofficial motto of the South African Army was "Thirty days to Cairo"—meaning that the South African Defense Forces could fight their way up the entire length of Africa in a month. Few experts argued the point. No, Stern realized, Hauer was his only chance. Hauer was in South Africa, he was one phone call away, and he was ready to act. Stern wondered what the mandarins in Jerusalem would say if they knew the future of Israel might depend on a single German.

Stern pushed open the infirmary door and looked for a telephone. He saw an EKG machine, an IV stand, several laboratory instruments—but no telephone. There were two doors set in the far wall. One was marked INTENSIVE CARE, the other bore the international warning symbol for radiation. Behind the first Stern found a plethora of life-support equipment, but no telephone. Behind the second he found an X-ray machine and table, a paneled door marked DARKROOM, fluorescent screens for examining printed X-ray films, and shelves of manila folders for storing them. No telephone.

Stern hurried back into the hallway. After trying another half-dozen rooms, he found himself standing in the library where he had initially confronted Horn. Though empty now and shrouded in darkness, the room seemed to retain some residue of human presence. Stern saw no one, yet he *felt* something, a strange aura of awareness. Was someone watching him from a corner? Uneasy, he moved toward the desk from which Horn had interrogated him. His common sense told him to get out of the library fast, yet his intuition told him he was close to something important.

He switched on the green-shaded desk lamp and stared at the books lining the library walls. They were standard volumes, the generic fare that adorns the shelves of gentlemen of great wealth but little culture. Driven by a vague premonition, he stepped closer to the shelves. He touched the books first, then the wood between them, working his way to the corner of the library, probing with his long fingers. As he neared the corner he felt cool metal graze his fingertips. He peered between the shelves. Just where the wood met the wall was a tiny brass knob.

He closed his thumb and forefinger over it, then gently pulled. The resulting snick made him jump, but instantly a thin crack appeared around a three-by-six-foot section of shelving. He pushed forward slowly, slipped his arm into the dark cavity, and felt for a switchplate. *There.* After ten silent seconds, he flipped the switch and lunged through the secret door.

Stern recoiled in dread as bloodred and black assaulted his senses. The room beyond the door was small but high-ceilinged, like an upended coffin. Great scarlet drapes fell from the vaulted ceiling, to be gathered chest-high by black silk sashes. He felt an involuntary shudder pass through his body. Sewn into the center of each black sash was a glittering white medallion, and crowning the center of each medallion—a black-painted swastika! From the wall opposite Stern, a grouping of black-and-white photographs leaped out like phantoms from a mass grave. Thousands of gray uniforms stood in endless rigid ranks; hundreds of jackboots goose-stepped down a depopulated Paris boulevard; dozens of young lips smiled beneath eyes that had witnessed the unspeakable. As Stern stared, individual faces emerged from the collage of depravity. Göring and Himmler . . . Heydrich . . . Streicher . . . Hess and Bormann . . . Goebbels . . . they were all here. Fighting a growing sense of dislocation, Stern turned, only to confront still another demon from his past.

Rearing high above him, its enormous bronze wings stretching from one corner of the red-draped wall to the other, was an imperial Nazi eagle. *Speer's eagle,* he thought with a chill, *risen again.* Yet the great bird was not an eagle. For its legs were engulfed in bronze flames, and clutched in its talons like a world snatched from the primordial fire was a bloodred globe emblazoned with a swastika. *The Phoenix!* exulted a voice in Stern's brain. Professor Natterman's voice. Stern stared in wonder. The head of the mythical bird was turned in profile. Its sharp beak was stretched wide in a defiant scream, its solitary eye blazed with fury. Stern felt his knees tremble. *Here is your Egyptian eye, Professor. The exact design! The tattoo used by the murderers of Phoenix . . . the mark sketched on the last page of the Spandau papers.* With dreamlike clarity Stern remembered Natterman's explanation of Rudolf Hess's Egyptian connection. This Phoenix looked almost identical to the old Nazi eagle, but the Egyptian character of its eye could not be denied. The eye did not match the rest of the sculpture at all. Neither did the flames at the bird's feet. They looked grafted on somehow, as if they had been added long after the original sculpture was cast. *But by whom?* Stern wondered. *By a man who spent the first fourteen years of his life in Egypt? By a man who lost one eye sometime after 1941? By Rudolf Hess?*

Under other circumstances, Stern reflected, this strange sanctum might pass for a private trophy room—a perverted version of the narcissistic shrines one often found in the homes of vain old generals. But *here*—hidden in a fortress at the end of a twisted trail that began at Spandau Prison— these relics suggested something else altogether. This room was no museum, no maudlin monument to the past. It was a time warp, a place where the past had not been merely preserved, but *reanimated* by a personality bent on resurrecting it. Stern felt a wild urge to leap up and tear the effigy down, like Marshal Zhukov's Russians atop the Reichstag. He stretched up on tiptoe, then froze.

Mounted on the wall beneath the huge Phoenix he saw what he had come looking for: *maps*. And not only maps, but a telephone! The map on the left—a projection of the African continent—Stern ignored. But the other—a topographic survey of the northern Transvaal—was just what he'd wanted. Quickly orienting himself to Pretoria, he slid his finger northeast toward the splash of green that represented the Kruger National Park. His fingernail stopped an inch short of the park border. "There you are," he said aloud. Just as on the radar screen in the turret high above, the location of Horn House had been clearly marked with a large red H. Stern figured the distance from the H to Pretoria at just under three hundred kilometers. Roughly three and a half hours overland, making allowances for what appeared to be trackless wilderness surrounding Horn House itself. He snatched up the telephone from the desk, his heart pounding. Then—as he punched in the number of the Protea Hof Hotel—he heard muted voices. He dropped into a crouch behind the desk, taking the phone with him.

The voices were not coming from the telephone. Nor were they getting any closer. Stern got cautiously to his feet. By moving to different parts of the room, he soon located the source of the sound. The voices were coming from behind the wall of photographs. He flattened his ear to the wood. Both voices were male, one much stronger than the other. The stronger voice spoke with a British accent.

Feeling his way across the wall to get closer to the voices,

Stern touched cold metal with his right hand. *Another knob.* Now he understood. This unholy shrine adjoined the library and study by means of *two* hidden doors. Horn had made sure that his secret sanctuary had two routes of egress. Taking a deep breath, Stern turned the knob. He heard the familiar snick of metal, but the voices went on talking. He pushed open the door.

The study beyond was dim but not lightless. Flashes from the picture window intermittently lit the room. Stern could hear the rattle of small arms fire outside, punctuated by the occasional burp of some heavier weapon. He edged into the room and pressed himself against the paneled wall. By the greenish light of a desk lamp he picked out the man with the British accent. He was pointing a large pistol across the desk at a shadow seated before the window.

Stern jumped when he heard the voice of the man in the chair, a gravelly rasp, full of contempt. It was Horn. He couldn't make out all the words, but the old man—despite his vulnerable position—seemed to be offering the Englishman mercy. This only infuriated the younger man. With a cry of rage he charged the wheelchair, kicked Horn over, then raised his pistol and jerked back the slide. *By God, he means to kill him,* Stern realized. He started forward instinctively, then he stopped. A broken fork was not much good against a semi-automatic pistol. Yet beyond that, something deep in Stern's soul, something angry and crusted black, told him to do absolutely nothing. If the old man lying helpless on the floor actually *had* gained possession of a nuclear weapon, Stern could neutralize him now by simply allowing the enraged Englishman to blow his brains out. Perhaps that was best . . .

The next moments passed like chain lightning. Stern heard Horn mutter something from behind the sofa. The young Englishman, driven beyond his limit of endurance, steadied his gun with both hands and prepared to fire.

"Death at last, Alfred!" he cried. "It's long overdue!"

Stern stopped in his tracks. *Alfred?* He felt a jolt of disorientation. *Alfred Horn?* But the old man had introduced himself as *Thomas* Horn—

A sharp metallic click froze everyone in the room. The sound was unmistakable—an automatic pistol being cocked. As if controlled by the same brain, Jonas Stern and Robert Stanton whirled toward the sound. Stern glimpsed a swatch of blond hair in the shadows; then the muzzle flashes blinded him. Five in a row, very fast. The first shots went wild, but the last two snatched the Englishman off his feet and drove him through the picture window, shattering the panes into a thousand glittering razors.

Stern dropped to the floor. The blond hair he had seen told him one thing: Peter Smuts had arrived to save his master. As Stern peered through the darkness, trying to pick out the Afrikaner, the study door burst open and the overhead lights flashed on. What Stern saw next stopped the breath in his lungs. Ilse Apfel stood rigid at the center of the room, a smoking pistol clenched in both hands. *She* was the blond who had saved Horn from his would-be executioner! Pieter Smuts bounded across the room and tackled her, one hand immobilizing the pistol as he knocked her to the floor. She went down without a sound. The Afrikaner came to his feet almost instantly, scanning the room for his master.

"Pieter," cried a weak voice. "Behind the sofa."

Smuts darted to the old man and fell to his knees. "Are you hit?"

"What ... ? No. You saved me, Pieter."

"Linah!" Smuts shouted. "Get the doctor!"

Stern heard footsteps scurrying down the hall.

Only now did Smuts notice the broken window. Stanton's mangled corpse lay half in and half out of it, his lifeless eyes turned upward, open to the rain. The Afrikaner's mouth dropped open in wonder as he realized what must have happened.

"Thank God you arrived, Pieter," Horn mumbled. "The swine meant to kill me. I didn't think he had it in him."

Watching Ilse closely, Smuts righted the wheelchair, lifted the old man into it, then crossed the study and pulled Ilse to her feet. She looked no more alert than she had when Smuts bowled her to the floor. The Afrikaner led her gently over to Horn.

"Sir, when I got here I saw Frau Apfel standing over there with a pistol raised. It was she that saved you." Smuts made a sudden sound of astonishment. "It's my Beretta! By God, she shot Lord Grenville with my bloody Beretta!"

Ilse's face remained expressionless, but Horn's eyes began to shine. "I *knew* it, Pieter," he said triumphantly. "She couldn't stand by and watch me die. She is a true German!"

Horn rolled his chair forward and took Ilse's hand. "Did you kill Lord Grenville, my child?"

Ilse said nothing.

"She's in shock," Horn murmured, shaking his head. "It is a miracle, Pieter. Fate brought this woman here to me."

While appreciative of Ilse's actions, Smuts would not have carried the praise so far. "Sir," he said carefully, "it appears to me that Frau Apfel acted purely by reflex. She was trying to escape. She saw a murder about to be committed; she fired blindly to prevent it. I don't think we should attach more significance to it than that."

Ignoring Smuts, Horn squeezed Ilse's hand in his own. "My child," he said softly, "by your action tonight you not only saved my life, but your husband's also."

"But sir!" Smuts protested. "Think what you're saying."

"Silence, Pieter!" Horn exploded. "I want half a million rand transferred to the Deutsche Bank in Berlin, under Frau Apfel's name." He smiled at Ilse. "For the child," he said. "Pieter told me that you are pregnant, my dear."

Smuts stared incredulously at his master. This was insane. He had never seen the old man make decisions based on sentimentality. Somehow, the Apfel woman had acquired a dangerous amount of influence over Alfred Horn, and that influence was obviously growing. A tragic accident might soon be required.

A sudden roar from outside rattled the shattered window. From his position by the hidden door, Stern saw a line of tracers arc out toward the rim of the bowl.

"What of the attack?" Horn asked.

"The house is secure," Smuts said tersely.

"And Oberleutnant Luhr?"

"A good man. That's him firing the Vulcan."

Horn smiled. "I imagine your little toys came as something of a surprise to Robert's friends, eh?"

Smuts grinned nastily.

"Do you know who they are yet?"

"We'll round up the bodies tonight. Then we'll see."

Horn nodded, then turned to Ilse and spoke softly. "Pieter will take you to your husband now. A matter of minutes. Do you hear me, child?"

Motionless until now, Ilse suddenly began to shiver. A single tear streaked her face. She looked as if she might collapse.

"Take her now, Pieter," Horn commanded. *"Schnell!"*

"Sir!" The Afrikaner snapped into motion.

Realizing that he had only moments to reach safety, Stern ducked back into the shrine room and reached for the telephone. He was about to punch in the number of the Protea Hof when he heard a voice coming from the phone. His throat tightened in disbelief. Who could it be? One of Smuts's soldiers? Did it really matter? Closing his palm over the mouthpiece, Stern stuck his head back through the little door. He saw the Vulcan's bright red tracer beam climb the distant ridge, searching out more victims. Horn, too, had wheeled his chair around to watch. The tracer beam jinked back and forth beyond the dark horizon, steadied a moment, then lurched into the sky. For an instant the end of the deadly arc became visible—then it detonated in a huge fireball.

The shock wave blasted a sheet of rain and glass into the room. Several shards fell onto Horn's lap, but the old man didn't seem to notice. He reached for a button on the arm of his wheelchair, preparing to turn. Stern hunkered down, hoping to see the gray face once more in the light. He heard the hum of the wheelchair's electric motor, saw the face in profile—then his survival instinct overrode his curiosity. He scrambled back into the secret room and pulled the door shut behind him. When he put the phone to his ear, the voice was still talking. With a silent curse he slipped the receiver back into its cradle. There would be no call to Hauer. Stern estimated he had less than a minute to become Professor Natterman again.

Alan Burton lay belly-down in the mud, humping it with the infantryman's desperate love. Even before he heard the apocalyptic roar of the Vulcan gun, he had seen the deadly tracer beam reach out from the tower. Now the gunner was raking repeatedly over the corpses of the Colombians—for corpses they surely were. When a stream of armor-piercing slugs intersects a human body at the rate of sixty-six hundred rounds per minute, the result cannot be described. Burton had seen it before; he had no desire to again.

Apparently Alberto did. Four times already the big guerilla had lifted his head over the rim of the bowl to watch the slaughter. The last time he must have gotten his fill, because Burton could hear the giant African whimpering beside him in the mud. When one of their escape helicopters exploded behind them, Alberto began babbling to himself. The incoherent syllables sounded vaguely religious to Burton, and the Englishman decided that a bit of prayer might not be out of order, even for a confirmed old sinner like himself.

When the terrible roar of the Vulcan diminished to desultory bursts, Alberto tried to jump up and race back to the airstrip. Burton pressed him violently back into the mud. As far as Burton knew, they still had one operable helicopter and, hopefully, a pilot. But to run for it now would be suicide. Any idiot could see that the gunner in the turret was using night-vision equipment. Burton could picture the smug bastard, perched up there behind his monstrous weapon, waiting for one desperate survivor to jump up and bolt for the airstrip. Burton didn't intend to be the moron who tried that.

But Alberto did. After the Vulcan had lain silent for ninety seconds, the big African rose tentatively to his knees and beckoned Burton to follow. The Vulcan burped just once: the three-second burst flashed up the slope like a lightning bolt. Approximately ninety bullets tore into Alberto's body, eviscerating and then decapitating him. The mangled hulk that thudded into the mud next to Burton would be food for the jackals in an hour.

The Englishman decided not to wait around to see the feast. *The Deal be damned,* he thought bitterly. *Maybe Shaw will give me another chance. God knows I didn't have much of one today.* With movements so subtle only a serpent would perceive them, Burton slithered backward through the mud until he dropped below the Vulcan's angle of fire. Then he jumped to his feet and ran as he never had in his life, low to the ground, but fast. When he felt the ground rising beneath his feet, he knew he was nearing the airstrip.

The Wash brought him up short. Three feet of water raged through its bottom now, but Burton tobogganed down the steep slope as if the torrent represented safety rather than potential death. Hoisting his MP-5 submachine gun high above his head, he waded into the flood. It took superhuman strength to hold himself upright against the current, but he made it across. He scrambled up the far side of the ravine in twenty seconds flat and found himself staring into the face of Juan Diaz.

"Madre de Dios!" the Cuban cried.

"The helo?" Burton gasped, his chest heaving.

"They got ours, English. But Fidel—the other pilot—he's waiting for us. Come! Before they shoot the runway again!"

They ran. Burton could see the airstrip ahead, a glistening asphalt line. Horn's Learjet waited silently on the apron like a falcon sitting out a storm. The surviving helicopter stood about forty meters from the Lear, only twenty meters from the still-burning wreck of its sister ship. Burton heard its rotors whining as he neared the runway, running full out.

Then the whine was swallowed by the furious ripping sound of the Vulcan. Burton looked back. He saw the terrible tracer beam race across the bowl, leap over the Wash, and streak up behind them. *"Run!"* he screamed at Diaz.

The Cuban needed no prodding; he was ahead of Burton already. The tracer beam actually passed between the two men as it raced toward Fidel's chopper, churning the earth into a furrow of death.

Then it happened. Fidel lost his nerve. Seeing the tracers closing in on him, he simply could not control his panic. With the only survivors of his team less than thirty meters from his chopper, the terrified Cuban lifted off. Diaz screamed for his comrade to wait, but the terrified pilot ignored him.

Burton had seen this a hundred times before. Slowing his sprint, he unslung his MP-5 and dropped to his knees. The only way to stop a panicked man from bolting was to put an equal or greater threat in front of him. Burton sighted his submachine gun in on the windshield of Fidel's chopper and squeezed off a three-round burst.

"Are you *loco?*" Diaz screamed. "You'll crash him."

"Signal him to put down!"

Fidel's chopper bucked wildly, hovering ten meters off the ground. Unaccustomed to firing the Vulcan, Jürgen Luhr had missed the chopper on the first pass. Tracers danced wildly above the chopper's rotors.

Diaz signaled frantically for his *compadre* to put down, but Fidel still seemed uncertain of where the greater danger lay. Burton convinced him with a sustained burst that fragmented the chopper's windshield. The JetRanger dropped until it hovered a meter above the runway. Burton dashed for its side door, passing Diaz on the way. He leaped into the shuddering machine and trained his weapon on Fidel. "Don't take off till Diaz is in!"

The little Cuban was close, but not close enough. Without even meaning to, Fidel jinked his ship two meters higher.

"Down!" Burton roared.

The JetRanger settled, then jerked up again.

Luhr backed his tracers off about forty meters from his target and began vectoring in again. This time the deadly beam held steady as he walked it in on the struggling helicopter.

"Jump!" Burton yelled.

Diaz leaped for the chopper's right skid, caught it. Burton got one hand on the Cuban's collar, saw the fear and anger in his eyes—then he felt the wild impact. For the briefest instant the tracer beam had sliced up and nicked Diaz in the side. One bullet plucked him off the skid as deftly as the finger of God.

The chopper yawed wildly as Fidel sought to avoid the tracer beam.

"Set this whore down!" Burton cried. He fired a round through the Plexiglas two inches from Fidel's head. The panicked Cuban shrieked in terror. Leaning out of the side door, Burton saw Diaz lying in the mud below, one arm raised in supplication.

Without any warning the chopper tilted ninety degrees and, whether by Fidel's design or not, Burton tumbled out. He caught himself on the skid and hung on with claws of desperation. He felt the JetRanger start to rise. Fidel had made his decision: he was clearing out. In a split second Burton made his own. With a curse on his lips he let go of the skid and fell six meters to the ground.

He landed badly, but the muddy earth cushioned his fall. Above him, Fidel's chopper climbed rapidly, but not rapidly enough. Luhr had finally got the hang of the Vulcan. The fiery stream of slugs intersected the JetRanger amidships and nearly cut it in two before the fuel tanks blew. The chopper fireballed like its sister ship, blasting wreckage all over the runway.

Burton threw himself over Diaz as the shrapnel tore the asphalt all around them. Without waiting for any further fire from the Vulcan, he took hold of the Cuban, heaved him over his shoulder like a sack and started slogging toward the Wash. *If that gunner's still watching the fireball,* he thought, *we might just make it. But if he saw me jump, he's sighting in on us right now. Ten meters to the edge . . . seven . . .* Burton sped up, leaned forward . . .

He leaped.

The two men tumbled head over heels down the steep slope and skidded to a stop at the edge of a raging flood. Burton made sure Diaz wasn't about to be swept into the water, and then he glanced around for a hiding place. The Cuban caught his sleeve and pulled his face down close.

"Gracias," he coughed. *"Gracias,* English."

Burton looked down at the tough little Cuban. Diaz's camouflage shirt was soaked with dark blood, but his lips and eyes showed the trace of a smile. "Don't thank me yet, lad," the Englishman said quietly. "It's going to be a long bloody night."

With the stealth that had carried him safely through four wars and countless intelligence operations, Jonas Stern made his way back to the bedroom he had briefly shared with Ilse. His brain thrummed wildly. He *had* to get back to that telephone. He had scratched a mark deep in the library door with his broken fork so that he could quickly find the secret room again. But would he get another chance? Horn's security chief would surely check the bedroom soon. The Afrikaner would naturally assume that "Professor Natterman" had tried to escape with his granddaughter. And when he found Stern waiting here, what would he think? Would he believe that "Natterman" had sat like a rabbit in an open cage while his granddaughter risked her life to escape?

Stern had heard Horn's promise to spare Hans Apfel's life, but he doubted if the old man's clemency would extend to Ilse's "grandfather." To survive the next few minutes, Stern knew, he would have to find some plausible reason for having stayed behind while Ilse fled. Boot heels were already pounding up the hall when he remembered the Zinoviev notebook. Snatching it from inside his shirt, he darted to the little writing desk, mussed his hair, and opened the leather-bound volume at the middle.

The boots stopped outside his door.

CHAPTER THIRTY-SEVEN

Stern did not look up when Smuts opened the door. He pored over the thin black volume as if it were a lost book of the Bible. The Afrikaner stood silent for some time, watching him.

"What are you doing, Professor?" he said finally.

"Reading," Stern muttered.

"I can see that," snapped Smuts. "Where is your granddaughter?"

"I have no idea."

"How did she get out of this room?"

Stern looked up at last. "She picked the lock."

"With what?"

"A fork from your dinner table, I believe."

Smuts frowned. "Why didn't you go with her?"

Stern shrugged. "She is young, I am old. With me along she would have little chance of escape. Without me . . . who knows?"

"She did not escape," Smuts said, smirking.

Stern sighed and let a hand fall from the desk to his knee. "Will you bring her back to me, please?"

"Impossible. She must pay for her insolence."

Recalling Horn's promise of mercy to Ilse, Stern suppressed a smile as he brought a hand to his forehead. "She's only a young girl who wanted to find her husband. Where is the crime in that?"

"Herr Horn will decide," Smuts answered stiffly. "I think you're lying, Professor. You tried to escape and failed, didn't you? You ran into the shields."

"You underrate my devotion to history, young man." Stern laid a hand on the Zinoviev notebook. "This volume is a treasure—a lost fragment of history. Already I've learned things my colleagues would trade a limb for."

Smuts shook his head slowly. "You're past it, old man. You can't see anything, can you?"

"I see that this book is far more valuable than the rubbish Hans found at Spandau."

"I'll tell you what that book is, Professor," Smuts snarled. "It's your bloody death sentence. Only one man has read that book and remained alive, and you've already met him." Smuts reached for the doorknob. "Enjoy it while you can," he said, and went out.

Stern stared at the closed door. He knew he could pick the lock again, but the Afrikaner might be waiting for just such an attempt. He took a deep breath and rubbed his temples. He was sweating. Sixty seconds ago he had seen something so shocking it had wiped the ghastly Nazi shrine room from his mind.

It was the book. Zinoviev's notebook. The moment he had opened it, the moment before Pieter Smuts marched into his room, Stern had seen the strange black characters marching like foreign soldiers down the page. *Cyrillic* characters. Paragraph after paragraph of laboriously handwritten Russian covered the left-hand page. And on the right—neatly typewritten on an old German machine—Stern had seen what he prayed was a German translation of the Russian handwriting. But what had so shocked him—what had blown everything else out of his mind—was his near-certainty that the Cyrillic characters had been written by the same hand that wrote the "fire of Armageddon" note warning of danger to Israel in 1967. The same note which had said the secret of that danger could be found in Spandau.

Now he leafed quickly through the thin volume. The pages—twenty in all—were merely sheets of heavy typing paper glued amateurishly into a leather spine. The same strange configuration over and over: first Russian, then German. Stern could not verify his intuition about the author of the Spandau note. The note was in his leather bag, back in Hauer's room at the Protea Hof. But he did not need to verify anything. He *knew.* He closed the black notebook and re-read the name on the cover: *V. V. Zinoviev.* Who was this mysterious Russian? How was he tied to the Rudolf Hess case? If Zinoviev had warned Israel in 1967 of some apocalyptic danger, had he voluntarily given this book to Alfred

Horn? Stern shivered with a sudden rush of déjà vu. *Alfred Horn*. The name buzzed in his brain like a swarm of bottleflies. Where had he seen it before? In some intelligence report? On some tattered list of Nazi sympathizers crossing a desk in Tel Aviv?

He forced his mind away from the question. He forced himself to think of the telephone, the phone that waited in the bizarre Nazi shrine room. To think of Hauer and Gadi, waiting anxiously for his call. He had to make contact with them. Yet in spite of Ilse's warning about a nuclear weapon, in spite of his conviction that Israel actually *was* in danger, Stern felt oddly certain that the key to the whole insane business—both past and present—lay within the thin volume in his hand. If the papers Hans Apfel found in Spandau Prison proved that Prisoner Number Seven was not Rudolf Hess, what did this strange book reveal? Horn had said it related to May of 1941. Did this book, finally, reveal the secret of Rudolf Hess's real mission to England? Did it name Hess's British contacts? Did it reveal the full scope of the threat to Israel? Could it silence the maddening hum at the back of Stern's brain when he heard the name Alfred Horn? *This notebook*, he thought, *not the Spandau papers, is Professor Natterman's Rosetta stone of 1941. I only hope I live to tell the old fool about it.* Stern opened the black cover and began to read:

I, Valentin Vasilievich Zinoviev, here record for posterity the facts of my service to the German Reich, specifically my part in the special operation undertaken in Great Britain in May 1941 known as "Plan Mordred." I do so at the request of the surviving Reich authorities, to the best of my ability, adding or omitting nothing.

I was born in Moscow in 1895 to Vasili Zinoviev, a major in the army of Alexander II. At seventeen I became a soldier like my father, but after rising to the rank of sergeant I was recruited into the Okhrana, the Tsar's secret police. I was promoted rapidly there. Some of my colleagues criticized my methods as overly harsh, but no one denied the results I achieved. Looking back on the bloodbath of 1917, I believe many of those same colleagues would say that my methods were not harsh enough. But they are dead now, and that is another story.

When I received word in 1918 that Tsar Nicholas II and

his family had been executed by the Bolsheviks, I decided to make my way to Germany. Strange to choose the vanquished nation as my sanctuary, but I did. Of all the Western nations, I had admired Prussia's military most. The journey was a nightmare. Europe was a shambles, but by using Okhrana contacts I finally managed to pass through the frontier into Poland. From there I had little trouble.

Germany was in chaos. The people were starving. Armed gangs roamed the streets at will, preying on the unwary and stripping returning soldiers of their decorations. Chief among these gangs were the Spartacist Communists. I could scarcely believe I had fled Lenin's revolution only to find more of the same madness awaiting me. Quickly seeing how things stood, I offered my services to a band of Friekorps, one of the groups of German ex-officers and enlisted men who were trying to reestablish order in their country. The Friekorps leadership appreciated my special talents and put me to work immediately.

These were farsighted men. Even at that early stage they were planning for the next war. At their request I refrained from joining the Nazi Party throughout Adolf Hitler's rise to power. They preferred to use me as a "cat's paw" whenever actions were required where absolutely no risk of being traced back to the Party could be tolerated.

Because the chief enemy of the Nazis was the Communist Party, I proved invaluable, and soon came to the attention of Heinrich Himmler, Reichsführer of Hitler's newly created SS. Though I never developed more than the most superficial personal relationship with this strange character, I admired his efficiency. Himmler saw to it that some of my Okhrana methods were taught to members of his counterintelligence unit—the SD. It was through these endeavors that I came to know a promising young officer named Reinhard Heydrich.

Because of what happened later, I should mention my service in Spain. In 1936 I accompanied Germany's Condor Legion to Spain, to help Generalissimo Franco in his struggle against the Republican Forces—which were actually controlled by the Spanish communists and a few generals borrowed from Stalin. I served as an interrogator, my chief responsibility being interrogation of communist prisoners. It was this eighteen-month period that would later rise up to thwart my greatest mission, but who could foresee it then?

Back in Germany, I worked closely with Heydrich on a

special program which I had helped initiate after the 1919 communist uprisings in Germany. Because yet another world war seemed inevitable, certain Nazi leaders expressed a desire that we should infiltrate not only the German Communist Party, but the communist organizations in those countries likely to be enemies of Germany in the next war. By 1923 we had put a large number of agents in place, and by 1939 we had the most extensive anti-communist intelligence network in the world. There were losses and defections, of course, but the strategy remained sound.

Two years later (January 1941) Hitler informed Heydrich that a powerful, highly placed clique of Nazi sympathizers existed in England, men who wished to arrange a peace treaty with Germany. These Englishmen claimed to be in a position to seize their government, if only two obstacles could be got out of the way. The main obstacle was Winston Churchill, who considered Adolf Hitler his personal nemesis. The second was King George VI, who, unlike his dethroned older brother, was a fervent anti-Nazi. Hitler's English sympathizers saw this dethroned brother—then called the Duke of Windsor—as a malleable alternative British monarch. Hitler charged Heydrich with removing the human obstacles to this alliance, and Heydrich naturally turned to me. Because an Anglo-German alliance would virtually guarantee the destruction of Stalin's regime, I volunteered immediately.

Heydrich's plan, though complex in execution, was simple and ingenious in theory. We would assassinate both Churchill and the king, then lay the blame on our archenemies the communists—just as the Nazis had done with the Reichstag Fire! To accomplish this, Heydrich envisioned using one of the British communist cells infiltrated by our agents. He asked if I thought we might dupe one of these groups into carrying out the assassinations for us, and I must admit that I expressed pessimism. The revelation of the Hitler-Stalin pact of 1939 had disillusioned communists around the world; consequently, I considered the chance of finding western communists still fanatical enough to attempt a suicide mission very small.

But Heydrich was undaunted. On his orders I set to work bringing his plan to fruition. The communist cell I chose for the operation was based in London, and, from our point of view, was under the command of one Helmut Steuer—a former Wehrmacht sergeant. This Helmut deserves special

*mention, for he—like the unit he had created—was unique.
Helmut had been spying on communists since Munich, where
he was "sole survivor" of the massacre at the Hauptbanhof.
When he "fled" to Britain (on our orders) the British communists welcomed him as a hero. His bond with them was so
strong that when these communists went to Spain to fight in
the International Brigades in 1936, Helmut went with them.*

*Heydrich could not believe it. It was an insanely danger-
ous thing for Helmut to do, but I understood. He was a
young man then, a man of action, and he craved danger. In
Spain he fought heroically for the Republicans, all the while
feeding to the Fascists information on the movements of the
very armies he was fighting in! Helmut lost an eye at
Guernica, and probably because of the accuracy of his own
reports! It was truly a miracle that he survived at all, yet his
service in Spain made him irreproachable in the eyes of his
English comrades. After returning to England—*

Stern stopped reading. His heart was pounding. He put his
finger to the paper, traced the sentences backward and read
again: *Helmut lost an eye at Guernica* ... "My God," he
muttered. "I've found you out at last. Alfred Horn ...
You're not Rudolf Hess, and you're not Zinoviev either."
Stern's mind raced as he tried to assimilate this new information. There actually *was* a Helmut involved in the Hess
affair—just as the Oxford draft research had claimed. Professor Natterman would be extremely disappointed to hear
it! Stern heard himself laughing. *It all fits,* he thought with
satisfaction. *I simply couldn't accept the idea that Rudolf
Hess had survived the war, that he had wormed his way into
South Africa's power elite, and I was right!*

"Well," he murmured, "let's find out exactly what Helmut
the great German spy did during the war." Stern picked up
reading Zinoviev's narrative where he had left off:

*After returning to England, Helmut—on our orders—
organized his own communist cell. It was small (six men, not
counting Helmut) and every man had been seriously
wounded either in the Great War or in Spain. In his commu-
niques Helmut called them his <u>Verwunden</u> Brigade—the
"Wounded Brigade." These men had come from the British
working class, and no men ever felt more betrayed by their
government than they. The flower of their generation had*

been slaughtered in the Great War, yet they had survived. And when a neighboring republic was threatened by a newly risen German monster, their government had not only turned its back, but disparaged its sons who went to defend the democratic ideal that their friends and brothers had died for in the Great War.

There is no hatred like that of idealistic men who have been betrayed. Even the Hitler-Stalin pact had not disillusioned these men. They saw it merely as an adroit political move by Stalin—a temporary alliance that would be rescinded as soon as Russia could defend herself against Germany. If any Englishmen could be made to take up arms against Churchill and their king, I knew, it was Helmut's Verwunden *Brigade.*

I arrived in London in April of 1941, armed with secret documents bearing the signatures of the highest officials of the Soviet Communist Party—all excellent forgeries, of course. This deception was risky but necessary. No communist cell, however fanatic, would undertake an operation of the magnitude we planned without the full weight of the Party International behind them. My mission was to symbolize this authority. I was the holy messenger sent from Moscow, the sacred city, and the documents I carried sanctified my crusade. They made the planned assassinations sound like the first shot of a worldwide communist revolution. One document even bore Stalin's signature! The SD forgers had done their jobs so well that I myself was tempted to believe in my newfound power.

Of the operation itself there is much to tell, and yet little. The mechanics were relatively simple. From English collaborators and German agents-in-place we received regular reports on our targets' daily movements, along with predictions of their future agendas. That part was easy. Churchill tramped all over the country with his fat cigar, inspecting troops or viewing air-raid damage. With an assassin willing to die in the deed, the prime minister was as good as dead. King George presented a more difficult problem, but not insurmountable. Though better protected than Churchill, he occasionally left Buckingham Palace to put on a show of solidarity with the common people.

What made the mission impossibly difficult was Hitler's commandment that the operation be carried out on the tenth of May. Limiting the mission to a single day meant that our

*assassins would have to strike regardless of circumstances.
I wasn't concerned about their chances of survival; on the
contrary, we wanted to insure that the assassins would be
killed in the accomplishment of their mission. But I also had
to be reasonably sure that the targets would be sufficiently
exposed for our men to reach them. When I expressed my
apprehension to Heydrich, however, he assured me that Hitler had devised a diversionary ploy that would bring our
targets into the open on the given day. At the time he would
tell me no more than that.*

*With Helmut's help I set to work selecting our assassins.
We had decided to choose three men—one man for each target, with one backup man in case of unforeseen circumstances. The men we ultimately chose were named William
Banks and William Fox. I shall never forget them. The confusion caused by the similarity of their names was circum-
vented by their nicknames. Banks, a red-haired giant, was
known as "Big Bill," and the more diminutive Fox as "Little
Bill." The backup man—selected by Helmut—was a distasteful little fanatic named Sherwood.*

*This Sherwood almost wrecked the operation on the first
day. During the Spanish war he'd been captured at Jarama,
and the first time he saw me he turned pale as a fish. When
Helmut asked him what was wrong (I spoke little English)
Sherwood asked if I had ever been in Spain. Naturally I said
I hadn't, whereupon the little man told his comrades that I
could have been the twin brother of a certain El Muerte—a
sadistic Russian interrogator who worked for the Germans
in Spain. Helmut laughed outright, and the rest of us joined
in. All but Sherwood. The memory had shaken him badly. It
had shaken me too. In Spain—where I had used my Okhrana
methods ruthlessly—the communists had christened me El
Muerte.*

*My job was to motivate Banks and Fox to carry out their
suicidal attacks. Helmut had prepared them well, and this
made my role much easier. From the day he founded his tiny
cell, Helmut had promised his disenchanted men that when
the revolution came, they would be called on by Moscow to
carry out the first strikes against the imperialist oppressors.
My years in the Okhrana had given me an encyclopedic
knowledge of communist methods and terminology, and I
used it to the full in dealing with these Englishmen.*

I told them solemnly that Hitler intended to break his pact with Stalin and attack Russia within thirty days. To this ter-rifying news I added the usual Stalinist drivel, i.e., that while the industrialized nations would eventually fall like rotten apples from the tree, the war had presented an oppor-tunity we could not afford to let pass. Now was the time for revolution, I cried with passion, and the names of the mar-tyrs who struck down the imperialist leaders would be en-graved forever in the histories of the new world.

Stalin, I told them, had decided to save Russia and ignite the worldwide revolution in one daring stroke. Not only were Churchill and George VI to die, but the leaders of imperial-ist France and the fascist leaders of Italy and Germany. The forged documents I carried added the weight of holy writ to my tale, and these two Englishmen accepted it all with grave pride. It was a sobering thing to see—two men who had fought so bravely for their homeland agreeing to bring it to its knees. Of course, in their minds they were liberators—downtrodden proletarians who would free their fellow-countrymen from the clutches of warmongers like Churchill.

One week before the target date we received reports that Churchill would be spending the weekend of May 10th at Ditchley Park, a private country house owned by a friend. The king, of course, would be at Buckingham Palace. Soon after, I received a coded message from Heydrich, outlining the "diversion" that Hitler would provide. The Führer had ordered an air raid on London for the night of May 10th—to occur simultaneously with our mission. And not just any air raid, Heydrich said, but the largest bomber strike yet visited on the city. Hitler believed that such a raid would not only provide us with a perfect diversion, but would also demon-strate to the English the futility of continued struggle against Germany.

The moment I read this message I decided to change the strike date to May 11th, regardless of Hitler's orders. I knew that our targets would not leave their protected shelters dur-ing the air raid; and if our assassins attempted to break into Ditchley Park or Buckingham Palace, they would be shot dead long before they reached their targets. But on May 11th—when both Churchill and the king would emerge to view the unprecedented bomb damage of Hitler's raid—the chances of success would be highest.

The weapon we chose for the attacks was the British Sten gun. Although prone to jamming, the Sten was easily con-

cealable and insured that a high number of bullets would penetrate the targets. Each man was to carry a revolver as a backup in the event of a jam.

Five days before the strike date, I suggested to Helmut that we dismiss the alternate—Sherwood—from training. Helmut agreed and informed Sherwood of the change. From this moment on, things began to go wrong. First "Big Bill" Banks, the man assigned to kill Churchill, refused to remain in the safehouse during the final days before the strike date. His parents lived in London, and he wanted to spend his last days with them. Helmut's best efforts could not change the man's mind. "Little Bill" Fox—the man assigned to King George—had no family, and agreed to stay in the safehouse with us. Together we passed the days playing cards and listening to the radio. At night around ten-thirty "Big Bill" would show up to make sure the plan had not changed.

Twice during this period Sherwood found an excuse to break orders and come to the safehouse. I should have found some way to kill the Bolshevik rat, but since "Little Bill" was with us all the time, I couldn't risk doing it in the house. I thought of ordering Helmut to slip out and kill Sherwood, but I must confess I had some doubt as to whether he would do it. Helmut had lived with—and fought by—these Englishmen for years, and I could see that the inevitability of their deaths was beginning to weigh upon him. Helmut wasn't disloyal, but the strain of living a perpetual lie had started to build up in him to a significant degree. Because of this, I let the Sherwood matter go unresolved.

On May 10th—the final night before the strike—the atmosphere in the house was electric. We had a car parked behind the house, filled with black-market petrol. Every minute it sat unattended was another minute of increased risk. Around ten p.m. we heard the first Luftwaffe bombs falling outside. They were far away from us—Heydrich had seen to that—but the noise was still frightening. I began to worry. By eleven p.m. "Big Bill" had still not arrived. I began to wonder if he had lost his nerve, or even—God forbid—if he might have been killed in the air raid. His lateness did not help Fox's resolve, either. The little man paced the room like a prisoner in solitary confinement.

At eleven-fifteen, disaster struck. The door burst open and "Big Bill" stormed into the room, his eyes blazing. "They're dead!" he shouted like a madman. "Dead dead dead!" I will *never forget his huge red face, shaking in anguish. I couldn't imagine what he was screaming about, but he soon told us. Both his parents had been killed in the air-raid, he wailed, burnt blacker than coal. He wanted revenge: revenge on Göring, on the Luftwaffe, and most of all on Hitler. I tried to turn this catastrophe to our advantage. Banks would have his revenge, I said. Tomorrow Hitler would be killed—just as Churchill would—by a communist martyr just like Banks. What better revenge could his parents have?*

When I mentioned Churchill, however, a strange look crossed Banks's face. Then an odd calm settled on him. "I won't do it," he said simply. I almost collapsed. "What?" I cried. Speaking in a voice almost too low to hear, Banks said that all along Churchill had been the man who had stood up to Hitler. That no matter what extremes of capitalist greed Churchill stood for, Churchill wanted Hitler dead. It seemed that this alone was now enough for "Big Bill" Banks. The man's fanatical communist zeal had disappeared in the blink of an eye.

I wanted to shoot him on the spot. I could see that his uncertainty was having a similar effect on Fox. Immediately I redoubled my efforts to convince Banks to push on. Helmut did his best to help me, and after several minutes of emotional appeals Banks started to come around. Somehow Helmut had redirected Banks's anger onto Churchill. It was Churchill who'd brought the air raids down on England, he said, Churchill who'd actually killed Banks's parents. "Big Bill" took hold of his Sten and began marching around the room, a snarl on his lips and tears in his eyes. His rededication steeled Fox for his task, and I believed that our mission might yet succeed.

But disaster struck again, this time in the form of Sherwood. We heard the group's secret knock at the door. Helmut answered it, ready to brain whatever fool had broken his order not to come around. The moment he unlatched the door, Sherwood burst in with a revolver and ordered me against the wall. Jabbing the gun at me, he told the others that I really was <u>El Muerte</u>, the Russian torturer from Spain. I calmly called the man a lunatic and told him he was about to wreck the greatest strike for world communism since 1917. Sherwood laughed wildly. Both Helmut and "Little Bill" Fox urged him to put the pistol down, but the fanatic showed no reluctance to point the gun at his own country-men if they interfered.

Sherwood stepped up to me and laid the barrel of the pis-tol between my eyes. "Tell them," he said. "Tell them who you really are." I could almost see Helmut's brain spinning. No one suspected him yet, but he had to be careful. "Com-rade Zinoviev comes from Moscow!" he told them. "From Stalin himself! Don't bring Stalin's wrath down upon us." But Helmut's words had no effect on Sherwood. "He thinks we're fools, Bill!" Sherwood shouted to Banks. "Wants us to kill our own King, he does! Wants us to kill Churchill and help Hitler!" Banks looked confused. "Why would a Russian want that?" he asked Sherwood. Sherwood scowled. "Aye, he's a Russian, Bill, but he's no Communist. He's a Tsarist killer and a bloody Nazi-lover too! Aren't you?" he said, jabbing me with the revolver.

I told Sherwood he was mad, all the while praying that Helmut had a pistol on him. This couldn't go on much longer, I knew, and it didn't. Sherwood suddenly called out a name, and a ragged old man shambled through the door. My blood ran cold. Before me stood the interrogator's nightmare—one of my former victims, a man whose arm I had ordered broken in several places. I could not conceal my shock. The man had only one arm now, but I remembered his face from Spain. While Sherwood pointed his pistol at me, the old man raised his one arm and slapped me in the face. "Bastard," he said. Then he turned to the others and said, "This is El Muerte."

Sherwood's eyes sparkled with glee. "Little Bill" Fox stood shaking his head in disbelief. Sherwood took two steps back and steadied his aim; he meant to kill me on the spot. In that moment Helmut saved my life. He jerked a knife from his pocket and buried it in Sherwood's heart. The stunned Englishman staggered back, gurgled once, fired the pistol and fell dead.

Everyone in the room stood still, not quite sure what had happened. I had the insane notion that we might yet salvage the mission. Then—in a flash of insight—"Big Bill" Banks understood it all. "You're a Nazi," he said to Helmut, his face slack with astonishment. "You—you always have been." He looked like a shell-shocked recruit. "But you fought with us at Jarama," he mumbled. "And Madrid."

Helmut tried to deny it, but Banks heard nothing. His eyes

narrowed and his lips grew white and thin. It was the killing look—I'd seen it a hundred times before.

Had Banks simply shot Helmut, I would not be here today—but Banks was a huge man, and his instinct was to smash what he hated with his hands. Clutching the Sten gun like a bat, he smacked its stock across Helmut's face. I felt Helmut's blood hit me as it sprayed across the room. He staggered, but held his feet. Dazed, he tried to reason with Banks, but the Englishman raised the Sten above his head and brought it down on Helmut's skull. Helmut crumpled to the floor. Banks's fury at the loss of his parents had been unleashed, and nothing short of death could stop it.

Fox and the old man who had pointed me out backed against a wall, cowed by the violence of their comrade. As Banks raised the Sten once more, I snatched up Fox's Sten from the table, pulled back the bolt, and pointed the gun at Banks. The man did not even notice me. I could have cut him down at that instant, but I hesitated. By killing him, I would be admitting that my mission had failed. Of course it already had, but I could not yet accept that. My finger quivered on the trigger. How could this specter from my past have traveled to this very room after so long? And the bombs—how could they have fallen right on Banks's house! How could it possibly have happened!

I saw Banks bring the Sten down once more onto—or rather into—Helmut's skull, and I pulled the trigger. Whirling around the room in fury, I cut them all down in seconds, then bolted for the car. I had just got it started when I remembered my forged papers—my "orders from Moscow." Dashing back inside, I searched for my suitcase, but couldn't find it in the main room. I checked the kitchen, found nothing, then returned to the room where the bodies lay. I caught sight of my case in a dark corner. I started toward it, then froze. A pair of tall workboots stood beside it. And standing in the boots was a thick pair of legs. "Big Bill" Banks, the red-haired giant, had somehow gotten to his feet, and he still held his Sten.

He wobbled, then fired. He hit me twice—once in the right arm, once in the right shoulder. I had no choice but to run. At worst, I thought, the forged papers implicated Stalin—not Hitler—so I ran. I cranked the old car, and in the confusion of the air raid I managed to escape to the countryside east of London. I used my escape plan just as if the mission had *been accomplished. I lay low for a few days on the British coast, with a German agent who maintained a radio link with Occupied France—then crossed the Channel to safety. I served out the remainder of the war in Heydrich's SD, and near the end fled with some others to South America.*

My dream of returning to my native Russia was crushed forever in 1944. I must live with the knowledge that the terrible shadow my Motherland lives under is in no small part due to my failure in England in the spring of 1941. Surely that knowledge is punishment enough for my failure.

> *Signed,*
> *V. V. Zinoviev, Paraguay, 1951*
> *Witnessed,*
> *Rudolf Hess, Paraguay, 1951*

Stern's stomach rolled. *Rudolf Hess? 1951?* Good God! What did it mean? Had Hess survived the war after all? Had he fled to Paraguay with Zinoviev after his failed mission? But what of Helmut, the daring German spy with the eyepatch? Had he really died from his terrible beating? Or had he somehow managed to escape and eventually make his way here, to South Africa? Stern felt more confused than he ever had in his life. *How are Hess and Zinoviev connected?* he wondered. *Where did their lives intersect?* Nowhere in Zinoviev's account was Hess mentioned, yet the date of the planned assassinations simply *couldn't* be coincidence. Hess had flown to Britain on May 10—the exact date that Zinoviev had been ordered to kill Churchill and the king. So why had Hess been ordered there at all?

Abruptly Stern stood and closed the notebook. *Of course!* Zinoviev's failed mission—the double assassination—as important as it was, was merely *preparatory*. The real objective was the replacement of Churchill's government—a *coup d'etat*. *That* was Hess's part of the mission, the *political* side. But what had gone wrong? The bombs had fallen as Hitler ordered, but Churchill and the king had not. As far as Stern knew, no assassin ever got close to either leader on May 10, 1941. So where did that leave the British conspirators who had planned to replace them? Where did that leave the real Rudolf Hess? Whatever Hess's mission had been, Zinoviev's failure had blown it. So where had Hess gone? When his mission failed, why didn't he go straight back to Germany? Why run to Paraguay, where he had apparently witnessed Zinoviev's document? Many Nazis fled to South America after the war. Had Hess been one of the first to go? And had he gone alone? No. Somehow, Stern realized, somewhere, Hess had met Zinoviev before Paraguay. Had it been in Germany? Or was it in England, on the run after the failed mission? *I'll bet dear Helmut of the one eye could answer that question,* Stern thought wryly. *And I've got the oddest feeling that he's sleeping in this very house!*

Stern hurriedly reconstructed Hess's flight in his mind. If what the Spandau papers said was true, the real Hess had taken off from Germany, picked up his double in Denmark, then flown across the Channel and reached the Scottish Coast around ten P.M. The real Hess had bailed out over Holy Island; then the double flew on, directly over Dungavel Castle—his supposed target—all the way to the western coast of Scotland. There he had turned, paralleled the coast for a while, then flown *back* toward Dungavel and parachuted into a farmer's field a few miles away. Why was the double needed at all? Stern asked himself. As a diversion? He pictured the lonely, frightened German falling from the Scottish sky—an image that had captivated the entire world. What had been in the double's mind at that moment? In the Spandau papers he had frankly admitted ignorance of the real Hess's mission. All the double knew was that the scheduled radio signal from Hess had not come, and rather than kill himself as ordered, he had bailed out of the Messerschmitt, broken his ankle, and then, when a shocked and sleepy Scottish farmer approached him, he had claimed to be Rudolf Hess—just as he'd been ordered to do had the proper signal come.

Stern felt the breath leave his lungs in a rush. *My God!* he thought. The double had *not* claimed to be Rudolf Hess! Not at first, anyway. He had not given the farmer Hess's name, but *another* name—a name always thought to have been a cover. But that was ridiculous, Stern realized, because *Rudolf Hess* was the double's cover name! After his failure to swallow the cyanide pill, after his bloodcurdling first-time parachute jump, the confused pilot had given the farmer his *real name.* And his real name was *Alfred Horn!*

Stuffing the Zinoviev book under his shirt, Stern snatched the broken dinner fork from beneath his mattress and went to work on the door lock. Thirty seconds later, he switched off the light and peeked outside. Two soldiers wearing khaki uniforms and carrying South African R-5 assault rifles guarded both ends of the dark corridor. Apparently the abortive attack had prompted Pieter Smuts to post sentries against anyone who might have leaked through his defenses. *Or perhaps,* Stern thought desperately, *perhaps Horn's Arab friends are scheduled to return sooner than I thought.* With his chest pounding, he eased the door shut and slumped against it. He *had* to find a way out! He knew exactly where he wanted to go, and it wasn't to the basement in search of Frau Apfel's alleged nuclear weapon. Nor was it to the shrine room telephone to call Hauer. All he could think about was something Professor Natterman had reminded him of during the flight from Israel. Something he had known for so long that he had forgotten it . . .

Something about Rudolf Hess.

CHAPTER THIRTY-EIGHT

11:40 p.m. Horn House

Hans and Ilse lay in darkness in the opulent main guest room of Horn House. They left the light off, for they knew each other better without it. Ilse's face, wet with tears, nuzzled in the hollow of Hans's neck, Piled upon the tortures she had already endured, killing Lord Grenville had caused Ilse's brain to spin a protective cocoon around itself. After a time, though, the barrier began to thin and stretch. When it finally broke, the tears had come, and she began to answer Hans's questions. His first was about the baby, and Ilse's confirmation of what he had been too frightened to believe engendered a deep and dangerous tension within him. His left hand stroked Ilse's cheek, but his right fist clenched and unclenched at his side.

"Don't worry," she whispered from the darkness. "Herr Stern is going to help us."

Hans went still. "Who?"

"Herr Stern. I thought you knew about him. He came here impersonating *Opa*. He's come to help us."

"What?" Hans rolled out of the bed, stumbled over to the wall and found the light. "Ilse, what have you done?"

She sat up. "Nothing. Hans, my grandfather is here in South Africa. He's with your father in Pretoria. Herr Stern is working with your father."

Hans's eyes grew wide. "Ilse, this must have been some kind of trick to get you to talk! What did you tell them?"

"Nothing, Hans. I don't understand it all, but Herr Stern came here wearing *Opa*'s jacket, and the kidnappers plainly believe that he is my grandfather."

"My God. Where is my father now? Did this man Stern say?"

"He told me that he left your father, *Opa,* and three Israeli commandos at a hotel in Pretoria. They're waiting for instructions from Stern right now."

"Israeli commandos?" Hans felt as if he had stumbled into a madhouse. "Where is Stern now?"

"I don't know. They were holding us together, but we split up when we escaped."

"Who *is* this Stern?" Hans asked irritably. "How did he even become involved?"

"He's an Israeli. He met *Opa* at the cabin in Wolfsburg. He is a good man, Hans, I could feel it."

"He told you he had *commandos* with him? How old a man is he?"

Ilse shrugged. "Somewhere around *Opa*'s age, I guess."

"And this is the man who's going to get us out?"

"He's done more than anyone else."

That stung Hans's pride, but he tried not to show it. If Ilse could cling to her optimism, all the better. But might they really have a chance? Had his father somehow managed to organize some kind of rescue? "Ilse," he said softly. "*How* can this man Stern help us?"

"I don't know," she said thoughtfully. "But I think he will."

Jonas Stern closed the infirmary door and flattened himself against the wall. His heart beat like mad as he waited for his eyes to adjust to the darkness. The astringent tang of isopropyl alcohol and disinfectant wrinkled his nose. He had been forced to wait almost seven hours before the guards outside his room finally left their posts. He had no idea if more would be sent to take their place, but he hadn't waited to find out. Even in the dark he could make out the high-tech gleam of stainless steel and glass. He eased forward. After eight short steps, he felt for the interior doors he remembered. Finding one cool metal knob, he turned it and hit the wall switch. He saw an empty hospital bed, oxygen bottles, telemetry wires, a dozen other gadgets. *Wrong room.* He killed the light and closed the door. Sliding his hands up the facing of the second door, he found the warning sign he remembered: three inverted triangles, yellow over black. *Radi-*

ation. Stern's pulse quickened as he opened the door and slipped inside.

There was light here, the dim red glow of a darkroom safelight. He moved quickly around the X-ray table to the file shelves. One way or the other, he thought, here would be the proof. He reached into the first compartment and pulled out a six-inch stack of fourteen-by-seventeen manila folders. Then he crossed to the viewing screens and hit the switches. Harsh fluorescent light flooded the room. While the viewers buzzed like locusts, he pulled an exposed X-ray film from the top file folder and clipped it against the screen.

Chest X-ray. It took him a few moments to orient himself. The spinal column and ribs showed clearly as strong, graceful white lines against the gray soft tissues and the almost burnt-black spaces of the body cavities. After that it got tougher. A dozen shades of gray overlapped one another in seeming chaos. Despite his initial confusion, Stern believed that what he sought should be reasonably apparent even to a layman. He tried to discern the subtle differences between the anatomical parts, then groaned as the outlines of two pendulous breasts emerged from the shadow of the internal organs.

"It's a bloody woman!" he muttered.

Then he noticed the small radiopaque ID-plate image on the top left corner of the film. It read: *Linah #004, 4-08-86.* Stern unclipped the film, thrust it back into the folder and dropped it on the floor. The outside of the next folder read: *Stanton, Robert B. #005.* He dropped it. *Smuts, Pieter #002.* The next file also belonged to Smuts. After three more names he did not recognize, he returned to the storage shelves.

The first folder he pulled out measured an inch thick by itself. The top-left corner read: *Horn, Thomas Alfred #001.* With shaking hands Stern removed the top film from the file and clipped it to the viewing screen. It showed two views of a hand positioned to reveal a hairline fracture that Stern couldn't see and cared nothing about. He jerked the film from the screen and let it fall to the floor. The next three films showed a series of intestinal views enhanced by the ingestion of barium sulfate. These, too, Stern let fall. A comprehensive X-ray anthology followed: grossly arthritic knees, lumbar spine, cervical spine—Stern tossed them all onto the growing pile at his feet. Finally he found what he wanted—an X-ray of Alfred Horn's chest. With mounting anticipation, he clipped the top edge of the film into the clamp and stepped back.

No breasts on this film. Stern began with what he clearly recognized—the spine. The ribs climbed both sides of the spine like curved white ladders. The lungs were the dark ovals behind them. A triangular white blob overlaid the spine. *The heart,* thought Stern. He knew the heart to be situated slightly left of center in the body—a fact he had learned during a silent killing course as a young man in Palestine. *So the left lung should be . . . here.* He touched the film with his right forefinger. *Now . . . compare. Check each lung against the other until I find a discrepancy.*

He immediately found several. Opaque disks the size of small coins seemed to float like celestial bodies in the dark lung spaces. These disks were small scars left by a mild case of tuberculosis. Stern did not know this, but he soon dismissed the disks as unrelated to what he sought. The first suspicious thing he saw was a kind of widening of two rib bones at one spot in the left lung. They seemed thicker than the other ribs, more *built up* somehow, not quite as smooth.

Stern had an idea. Pulling another stack of films from Horn's folder, he rifled through them until he found what he wanted—an oblique X-ray of Horn's chest—a picture shot from the side with both arms held above the head. When he pinned this film to the screen, the mark he sought jumped out at him like a contrail against the sky. He swallowed hard, raised a quivering finger to the film. Crossing the dark left lung in a hazy, transverse line was the scar of a rifle bullet. A rifle bullet fired seventy-one years ago. The opaque track diffused rapidly into the surrounding shadows, but the path of the old bullet fragments was plainly visible. With his heart pounding, Stern counted downward from the collarbone to the scarred area—one rib at a time.

". . . four . . . five . . . six . . . *seven.*"

He switched back to the first X-ray—the posterior/anterior view—and carefully counted down again, this time searching for the ribs with the strange built-up areas.

". . . three . . . four . . . five . . . six"—Stern felt sweat dropping into his eyes—"*seven.*"

"My God," he murmured, feeling a catch in his throat. "Hess is alive." Simultaneously a voice reverberated in his brain: *The bomb for Tel Aviv is real!*

Folding the two stiff chest X-rays in half, Stern thrust them inside his shirt between Zinoviev's notebook and his pounding heart. He quickly gathered up the discarded films and folders from the floor, shoved them back into the shelves, then slipped quietly out of the X-ray room and into the dark hallway.

He sprinted to the library. In the musty darkness he tripped, picked himself up, then moved carefully on toward the tall bookshelves. Feeling his way across them to the corner, he found the tiny brass knob. He turned it. He had already resolved that if he found anyone other than Hess himself inside the secret shrine room, he would kill him.

The room was empty. Stern sat down behind the mahogany desk and breathed deeply. He wanted to slow his racing heart. Above him the bronze Phoenix screamed silently. From the wall to his left a hundred Nazis gazed at him. As Stern reached for the phone to call Hauer at the Protea Hof, he froze. Someone had been in the room since his visit. Across from the desk—where there had been only red drapes before—hung a gigantic oil painting—twice life-size—of Adolf Hitler. Rendered in muted greens and browns, the dictator gazed down with sullen intensity at the Jewish intruder. Someone had pulled back the drapes to admire the Führer. Gooseflesh rose on Stern's neck. His left cheek began to twitch. After working his dry mouth furiously, the old Israeli spat a wad of mucus across the desk onto the canvas. It struck Hitler just above his groin. Stern raised his left arm, made a fist, and shook it at the portrait.

"Never again!" he vowed. He lifted the phone.

4:55 A.M. *Protea Hof Hotel, Pretoria*

Hauer came off the bed like a fighter pilot hearing a scramble alarm. Gadi and Aaron sat half-conscious against the foyer walls; Professor Natterman lay on the opposite bed, his right thigh wrapped in gauze, his eyes half-closed from the effect of the morphine.

"Stern?" Hauer cried.

"Yes."

"It's him!"

The young commandos leapt to their feet. Natterman tried to sit up, then lay back groaning.

"Get a pen and paper," Stern ordered. "Write down everything I tell you."

Hauer looked at Gadi Abrams, who stood ready to copy down every syllable he repeated. "We're ready," he said. "Go ahead."

Stern spoke in a rapid whisper. "I'm being held at a private estate in the northern Transvaal. It's situated halfway between the Kruger National Park and a village called Giyani. Have you got that?"

"Got it."

"The house belongs to a man named Thomas Alfred Horn, H-O-R-N."

"H-O-R-N, Thomas Alfred Horn."

Behind Hauer, Professor Natterman gasped. His right arm shot out and caught Hauer's sleeve. *"Captain!"*

"Hold it, Stern. The professor—"

"What did you say?" Natterman croaked. "What name did you *just* say?"

Gadi read from his notes. "Horn, Thomas Alfred. H-O-R-N."

"Mother of God. It can't *be.*"

"Go on, Stern," Hauer said angrily. "I think the professor is hallucinating."

"No, he recognizes the name."

"He's alive!" Natterman cried. "I was right! Hess is alive!"

Hauer pulled away from Natterman's grasp. "Stern, the professor's yelling about Rudolf Hess."

"You can tell the old fool he was right. Rudolf Hess is alive and reasonably well. He is also quite mad."

Natterman clawed at Hauer. "Give me the phone, Captain!"

Hauer held the receiver away. "Stern said to tell you that you were right, Professor. That Rudolf Hess is alive. I think you're both mad."

Natterman shook his head. "Perfectly sane, Captain. I understand it *all* now, every wretched bit of it. Alfred Horn was the name Hess's double gave the farmer when he first parachuted into Scotland. My God, it's so obvious!"

"Hauer!" Stern snapped, his voice strained. "Forget about Hess. We've got a crisis here."

"I'm listening."

"Mounting a rescue along the lines we discussed is no

longer an option. Whatever security forces Hess has here, they were sufficient to repel a determined attack by a force larger than yours. The stakes have gone up, Hauer, up beyond belief. Yesterday you asked me what I was after. Well, I've found it. Last night Frau Apfel witnessed negotiations between Hess and a group of Arabs for a nuclear weapon."

Hauer's eyes met Gadi's. The young Israeli was watching him like a cat.

"I haven't seen the weapon myself," Stern continued, "but I have no doubt whatsoever that it exists."

"What about Hans?" Hauer asked. "And Ilse. Are they still alive?"

"They are. But if you want to see your son alive again, Captain, this is what you must do. Go to the Union Building—that's the huge government building on the hill in central Pretoria. It's floodlit every night. On the third floor you will find the office of General Jaap Steyn, chief of the National Intelligence Service. That's S-T-E-Y-N. Jaap Steyn is a friend to me and to Israel. Explain the situation in the way you think best, but you tell him he needs to mount an assault of sufficient strength to reduce a fortified position. You're at least four hours away from me now, so you'll need to move fast. And keep Hess's name out of this altogether. From this moment on we speak only of Alfred Horn."

"Just a damned minute," Hauer protested. "You think I can waltz into the offices of South African Intelligence and demand a paramilitary operation on the basis of wild accusations? They'll laugh me out of the building. *If* they don't clap me in irons first."

"They'll have no choice but to cooperate," Stern said evenly. "My name should be sufficient to get Jaap Steyn moving, but in case it's not, I'm going to give you some information that will ensure his cooperation. Write down every single word of this."

Hauer signaled Gadi to hand over the pen and paper.

Stern spoke slowly. "There now exists between the Republic of South Africa and the State of Israel a secret military contingency plan called *Aliyah Beth*—Gadi can spell it for you later. In Hebrew, *Aliyah Beth* means 'going up to Zion.' This plan mandates the clandestine removal of . . ."

Hauer's throat went dry as Stern proceeded to describe in detail the most sensitive protocol of the secret nuclear agreements between the Republic of South Africa and the State of Israel. "Is that true?" he asked, when Stern had finished.

"Captain, with that information you will be able to blackmail General Steyn into giving you anything you want."

"Or force him to shoot me."

"No. To avoid that, leave Yosef behind at the hotel. Tell General Steyn that if you don't check in with Yosef by telephone at prearranged times, he will forward the details of Plan *Aliyah Beth* to the Western press."

Hauer sighed heavily. "I'm sorry, Stern. Yosef is dead. And Professor Natterman is wounded. Some Russians found us. We've got corpses piled in the bathroom like firewood."

"Leave Aaron at the hotel instead," Stern said tersely.

"The Russians also got hold of our photos of the Spandau papers," Hauer confessed.

"You thick-headed Kraut!" Stern exploded. "Those rags mean nothing now! You just get those troops out here!"

Hauer forced down his anger. "Listen, Stern, South African Intelligence isn't going to give in to blackmail no matter what I threaten them with. German Intelligence wouldn't."

"You must *force* them to. I've given you the leverage. But be careful. Horn didn't gain access to a nuclear weapon by playing recluse up in the Transvaal. He's probably a key figure in their defense industries. Trust only General Steyn. His loyalty to Israel is beyond dispute. Anyone else, God only knows."

"Great."

"Oh, a tactical tip for you, Captain. There's some type of rotary cannon on the roof here, and there could be any number of other surprises as well. Bring enough firepower to flatten this place if you have to. Now, could I speak to Gadi for a moment?"

Hauer handed over the receiver.

"Yes, Uncle?"

"Listen to me, Gadi. Captain Hauer is going to give you my instructions. I want you to listen to him as if he were me. Do you understand? On this mission Hauer will be in command."

Gadi clenched the phone tighter.

"I know it won't be easy taking orders from a German, but I believe Hauer is the man to carry this through."

Gadi ground his teeth. "I understand, Uncle."

"Good. Because we are dealing with a nuclear weapon

here, Gadi, possibly more than one. And it is targeted at Israel. At Tel Aviv, maybe Jerusalem."

Gadi felt his face grow hot.

"The other crazy thing you heard is also true. Rudolf Hess is alive. If there is any way possible, I mean to get him away from here and take him back to Israel for trial. But if I *can't*—or if for any reason you and Hauer cannot raise enough force to take this house—I will locate the weapon and try to detonate it."

Gadi felt his heart stop. "No, Uncle—"

"I'll have no choice, Gadi. Anything could happen before you get here. *If* you get here at all. It's like the Osiraq reactor in Iraq, only a hundred times worse. Do you understand?"

Gadi wiped the sweat from his forehead. "God in Heaven."

"Once you get within a few miles of here, you and every man with you will be within the blast radius."

"No one else will know," Gadi said in Hebrew.

"Good boy. There's one more thing. Once you learn the exact coordinates of Horn House, I want you to call Tel Aviv and ask for Major-General Gur. Explain the situation, give him the coordinates, then say *'Revelation.'* That's the IAF crisis code for imminent nuclear emergency. I doubt Jerusalem would give clearance for a raid here, but it's worth a try. If we fail, perhaps the air force will make an attempt. Now, Gadi, I must go. It's time to become the professor again. I hope to see you soon, my boy. *Shalom.*"

Gadi swallowed. "*Shalom,* Uncle."

Stern disconnected.

Hauer stared suspiciously at Gadi for a few moments, but he decided not to press. He shoved his Walther into his belt. "Let's go blackmail some spies," he said.

Separated from Jonas Stern by one thin wall, Lieutenant Jürgen Luhr held the silent telephone to his ear. Luhr had been unable to sleep after the exhilaration of the battle, and his wanderings through Horn House had eventually led him to Alfred Horn's study. He'd been standing by the shattered picture window through which Ilse had blasted Lord Grenville when he saw a yellow light flashing on Horn's desk. Hesitating but a moment, he had lifted the receiver and overheard the final few seconds of Stern's conversation with Gadi.

Now he stood still as stone, trying to comprehend what he had heard. It seemed impossible. Apparently Professor Natterman—or the *Jew* claiming to be Professor Natterman!—had made a call from somewhere inside this house. But to *whom?* From the little he'd heard, Luhr could not be sure. He would have suspected Dieter Hauer, but he'd heard the swine on the other end of the phone speak Hebrew, and Hauer wasn't a Jew. Luhr was sure of one thing. Alfred Horn and his Afrikaner security chief would be very grateful to the man who informed them not only that they had a Zionist spy in their midst, but that they might soon be the target of an Israeli air strike! With his pulse racing, Luhr dashed into the hall to rouse the house.

CHAPTER THIRTY-NINE

5:20 A.M. Horn House

They came for Jonas Stern as the Gestapo had come for his father in Germany. Four heavy-booted soldiers burst through the door with pistols drawn and snapped on the overhead light, shouting at the top of their lungs: *"Up Jüdin! Up! Schnell!"*

The sudden light blinded Stern, for he had been lying fully clothed in the darkness. He leaped from the bed with his broken fork raised, but the click of pistol slides made him freeze where he stood. There was only one explanation for this. The worst had happened. Somehow, on the same night he had discovered that Alfred Horn was not who he pretended to be, Alfred Horn had discovered the same thing about him.

Powerful hands seized Stern's arms and lifted him off his feet. The soldiers—their khaki uniforms now replaced by *Wehrmacht* gray—frog-marched him into the corridor and hustled him along at the double. When Stern glanced up, he saw the cold black eye of a pistol barrel. Above it hovered the face of Pieter Smuts.

"Where are you taking me?" asked Stern.

"Where do you think, Jew?" the Afrikaner jeered, walking backward. "To see the Führer!"

Stern stared across the mahogany desk with a lump in his throat. Ghostlike and gray, the old man who called himself Alfred Horn sat hunched in his wheelchair, an expression of bemusement on his deeply lined face. As Stern stared, he felt a sudden stab of doubt. Concealed in his shirt were the X-rays that he believed would prove beyond doubt that

Alfred Horn was Rudolf Hess. And yet . . . the old man sitting across from him no longer looked quite as he had before. Now, instead of a glass eye, Horn wore an eyepatch. All Stern could think of was Zinoviev's description of Helmut Steuer: *Helmut had worn an eyepatch.* Had Helmut Steuer survived his mission after all? Was Rudolf Hess really dead? Had Helmut somehow managed to hunt down Hess's X-rays to conceal the truth? Or had *both* men survived? Could it be that Hess had lived for a time as Alfred Horn, and then, after he died, Helmut had quite naturally taken over the false identity? Whatever his true identity, the old man across from Stern was not wearing the plain khaki uniform Rudolf Hess had worn as Deputy Führer of the Reich. He was wearing a gray suit jacket much like the one Adolf Hitler had worn as Supreme Commander of German Armed Forces. And suspended around his neck was the Grand Cross—Nazi Germany's highest military award. To Stern's knowledge, Rudolf Hess had never won that decoration.

Pieter Smuts stood rigid behind his master, eyes smoldering, mouth set in a grim line. Above him reared the bronze Phoenix; directly behind, the maps from which Stern had copied the coordinates he'd given Hauer. Stern sensed the soldiers standing behind him.

"We seem to have a problem of mistaken identity," Horn said. "Would you care to enlighten us, Herr *Professor*?"

Stern stood still as a pillar of salt.

Smuts nodded. One of the soldiers behind Stern smashed a savage fist into his right kidney. Stern crumpled, but managed to stay on his feet. As he straightened up, the two X-rays he had stolen from the medical unit made a crackling sound. Smuts came around the desk, ripped Stern's shirt open and jerked out the films. He handed them to Horn, who held them up to his desk lamp and clucked his tongue softly.

"You're a clever little rat, aren't you?" he growled. "Herr *Stern*?"

Stern struggled to hold his face immobile as his brain raced to adapt to the changing situation. If Horn knew his name, that meant that either Ilse had been made to talk, or Hauer and Gadi had been captured. Stern prayed it was the former. "I'd say we have two cases of mistaken identity," he said coolly.

Smuts signaled for another kidney blow, but Horn raised

a peremptory hand. "I think you know who I am," he said, his watery eye twinkling.

"Deputy Führer Rudolf Hess, I suppose?"

"That title is long out of date. After the Führer died, his responsibilities passed to me."

"You've pinched his uniform and decorations, at any rate," Stern needled. "I thought the dubious honor of the Nazi succession passed to Hermann Göring."

Hess colored. Another vicious blow hammered Stern's left kidney, driving him to his knees.

"The Reichsmarschall is also dead," Hess said testily. "And the Grand Cross was awarded to me by the Führer himself. Secretly, of course."

Stern looked up at the old man and stared into the single furtive eye. "If you are Hess," he said, "what happened to Helmut Steuer?"

"Helmut died a hero's death in 1941. He was a German patriot of the highest order, and I immortalized his efforts by awarding him the Knight's Cross."

"And the tattoo? The single eye?"

Hess shrugged. "I needed a symbol. I couldn't risk telling my associates my true identity. I wanted a mystical sign that would signify their bond to me and to each other. I remembered the All-Seeing Eye from my childhood in Egypt." Hess touched his eyepatch. "It certainly seemed appropriate. As did the Phoenix."

All just as Professor Natterman guessed. "How did you lose the eye?" Stern asked.

Hess grimaced. "A British bullet. I had no access to a doctor until it was too late." The old man jerked his finger away from his face. "This is ancient history! I want to know what you hoped to accomplish by your ridiculous deception, Jew. Other than suicide, of course."

Stern stared back with cold assurance. "I have come to take you back to Israel to stand trial for the crimes you escaped at Nuremberg—the crimes for which your double served a life sentence in Spandau Prison."

Hess's laugh was hoarse and hollow, but frightening all the same. "You should see a psychiatrist, Herr Stern. You suffer from serious delusions of the paranoid type. I will arrange for my personal physician to visit you."

Stern waved his arm, taking in the Nazi regalia that covered the walls. "You're the one who's mad. If you believe you're going to raise some kind of Fourth Reich in Germany, you're hopelessly senile."

Hess's eye brightened. "Is that what you think I want? A Fourth Reich in Germany? I'm afraid the only people with whom you share that fantasy are paranoid Russians and writers of pulp fiction." He glanced at Smuts. "Perhaps a few German policemen," he added.

"What is it then? I'm sure you have some master plan for German world domination."

Hess smiled. "Do you really think I need one? The postwar world has evolved along the very lines the Führer predicted. Germany—even when divided—is the most powerful nation in Europe. America has assumed Britain's imperial mantle and rules the seas in her stead. Japan rules the Pacific and a lot more besides. Which brings us to the Soviet Union. How far are we, really, from seeing Russia as an economic colony of Greater Germany? The Soviet economy is almost as weak now as it was just prior to the 1917 Revolution. How long before it explodes? When that explosion comes, it will be Germany who rebuilds the country. We'll trade cash for raw materials and gain access to the enormous markets that will be opened there. The final step toward economic hegemony over Europe. We already hold the purse strings to half the American national debt, and our power and influence grow stronger every day. Reunification is inevitable."

"Then why destroy Israel?"

Hess scratched beneath the black eyepatch. "For the most pragmatic of reasons, I assure you. In a way, I almost regret having to do it. Sometimes I think you Jews learned more from the Führer than anyone. Have you ever seen Israeli soldiers at the Wailing Wall, Herr Stern? Praying in formation? It is a sight worth seeing. The Israelis have become the new Germans! Isn't that a shock? Israel has become a supernationalist, expansionist, Blood-and-Sacred Soil state with the best-trained army in the world. It is surrounded on all sides by enemies, just as Prussia was. The Chosen People, yes? Just as we Germans were chosen to lead the Aryan race!"

Stern stared in wonder at the man before him. "If you strike Israel with nuclear weapons, you'll start a war that could wipe *every* country off the face of the earth. Israel has her own bombs, Hess, and she will use them."

The old man nodded excitedly. "I'm *counting* on Israel

using her bombs, Stern! I know exactly what the Zionists have in their arsenal, and more importantly, I know where their missiles and 'black' bomber squadrons are targeted. More than half of Israel's warheads are aimed not at the Arabs, but at the Soviet Union. Israel does this to prevent Soviet resupply of the Arabs in the next Mideast war." Hess's eye gleamed. "But times change, don't they, Stern? Old men know that best of all. Right now the Israeli warheads point at the Soviet Union. Ten years from now they will be aimed at Greater Germany!"

"My God," Stern breathed, "you're trying to provoke Israel into retaliating against Russia with nukes. When the Arabs wipe out Tel Aviv or Jerusalem with a sophisticated bomb, the Israeli government will have no choice but to respond in kind. And where will they respond? Where could Arabs have procured such a weapon? From the Russians, of course."

Hess smiled thinly. "I knew you'd appreciate the simplicity of it."

Stern's mouth went dry. "But you can't predict what will happen in a situation like that! You could ignite a full-scale thermonuclear war! There's no telling who might be drawn into it."

"It wasn't my original plan," Hess admitted. "But when the British started trying to kill me last month, I was forced to improvise."

"The British are trying to kill you? They know you're alive?"

"Oh, yes. Only tonight MI-5 sent men here to kill me—a force of filthy Colombians." Hess smiled. "But I'm afraid they are all dead now." He fiddled with a pen on his desk. "I suppose I owe the British a debt of thanks. By rushing me, they forced me to think creatively, and it was thus I came upon the Führer's old Palestine strategy. The very same year I flew to Britain, Hitler armed the Mufti of Jerusalem and bade him destroy the Jews of Palestine. Only it turned out that the Jews had been better armed by their Zionist relatives in America. I find that quite ironic, since it is ultimately for the Americans that I now arm the Arabs."

"*What?*" Stern's eyes widened in disbelief.

"Yes, Jew. The Americans are the inheritors of the Führer's work. Is that so hard to see?"

"You really are mad. America is the most liberal democracy in the world!"

Hess chuckled. "If all the Jewish tribe were so naive as you, my work would be greatly simplified. The Americans are a strange people, Stern. A violent people."

"They aren't Nazis."

Hess looked bemused. "The other day I was speaking with an American businessman on the telephone. Do you know what he said to me? He said, 'Hitler had the right idea, Alfred, he just had a poor marketing strategy.' "

"An off-color remark is a long way from a fascist revolution."

"Is it really? I suppose that depends on who's doing the talking. This man happened to be the president of a Fortune 500 company." Hess drew an imaginary line in the air. "A very thin line divides democracy and anarchy in America, Stern. It is concealed by vast material wealth, but *it is there*. And the Americans can be pushed over it. They have been before, and they will be again. Think about it. Whenever the Nordic American has felt the existence of his values and race imperiled, he has steeled himself and done whatever was necessary to insure his survival. Did Americans shrink from interning thousands of Japanese during World War Two? Did they shrink from ruthlessly hounding down thousands of communists in the fifties? In the sixties they even found a way to thin the ranks of the mongrel blacks, by sending them to die in Southeast Asia. Ingenious, and so subtle it would put Goebbels to shame! And what of their precious Constitution? To hell with it! In time of crisis, Jew, *expediency rules*!"

Stern was silent. He had seen that principle in operation many times in the political councils of Jerusalem.

"And what does he face today, the Nordic American? Abroad, violent terrorism. Arab jackals run mad with power, drunk on a great tide of oil which will run out in two or three decades, but not before the savages succeed in purchasing nuclear warheads *and* the delivery systems necessary to threaten the civilized nations! At home it's even worse! White Americans cannot even walk the streets of their cities at night. Robbery, murder, and rape are the rule, and all the work of the mongrel races! Armed gangs roam the streets, just as in Germany after the Great War. The defiled bloodlines drag America to her knees, while in the highest circles of power your Zionist Rasputins work their devious schemes."

Hess steepled his shriveled fingers. "But that is as it should be," he said softly. "As it *must* be. Fascism isn't gangs of ruffians scrawling swastikas on synagogues and tearing up Jewish cemeteries. It is the final distillate of human society, the purest system of government, born in the crucible of poverty, injustice, and war. *That* is why America is the last hope of the world, Stern. It is there that the final struggle will begin." Hess waved his hand in disgust. "Germany has become too fat, too rich. The Fatherland is governed by cowards who care only for money! Germany could have nuclear weapons of its own now, if Bonn had any nerve. Social Democrats!" Hess spat. *"The swine should be lined up in front of the Reichstag and shot!"*

Hess's solitary eye burned with evangelical fire. "But the change is coming, Jew. And Germany will be ready. Even now loyal Germans in both East and West work to push the communists out. When America calls, Germany will step forward. Already immigrants choke American employment lines; drugs poison the small towns; the people see that their government is powerless to stop the madness. In a few years the pressure will be so high that the smallest spark will set off the explosion. And when the spark comes—be it war or plague or economic catastrophe—when the price of petrol rockets to ninety dollars per barrel, when American cars sit empty on freeways while their owners freeze in their homes—*then* the great change will come. And it will come like a crash of lightning! A new leader will rise, Jew, and *it matters not who he is*! Like the Führer he will be a man of the people. He will be equal to the times, and when he steps forward *the people will recognize him*! They will follow him to glory! America will *finally* seize the reins of power she has shied away from for so long! *Then* countries like Germany can stand up and play their part!"

"My God," Stern murmured.

"The day of reckoning is nearly upon us, Jew. That is why your race must be purged. The incineration of Jerusalem will mark the birth of the new millennium. By the year 2000, the Nordic race will rule over three-quarters of the globe, and *the Jews will be no more*!"

Stern shook his head like a man faced with some human aberration of nature. "But this is so utterly insane," he said quietly. "Have you considered your family, Hess? Have you talked to your wife? To your son?"

Hess turned his face downward. "What could I expect from my son, Stern? A boy raised in a Germany poisoned by artificially imposed guilt . . . a Germany crippled by a psychological Versailles Treaty in which the people can never pay enough tears for dead Jews? My family has been the most painful burden of my life. To watch my son on television, fighting so valiantly to free the man he believed to be his father. And now that Horn has been murdered, to know that Wolf believes me dead. It tears my heart to pieces! So many times I have been tempted . . ." Hess wiped a tear from his eye and clenched his wrinkled hand into a fist. "My duty to the Fatherland and to history comes first. I alone have survived to carry on the Führer's work!"

Stern stared thoughtfully across the desk. "How have you managed to conceal your true identity when you so brazenly used the name your double gave when he landed in Scotland? Surely the name Alfred Horn is known to anyone familiar with the Hess case?"

Hess smiled cynically. "Why do you assume that I *have* evaded detection? Do you think your fellow countrymen are so constrained by moral absolutes that they would feel compelled to send an assassin to my door?"

"It's been known to happen," Stern said.

"Oh, yes," Hess agreed. "But my dear fellow, I was no Eichmann. The so-called 'atrocities' against Jews took place long after I left Germany. I signed a few pieces of legislation limiting Jewish social activities, but that was simply paperwork. Hardly a reason to execute a man who can be so helpful in vital areas of your country's national interest."

"I don't believe you had anything to do with Israel's nuclear weapons program," Stern said angrily. "No Jew would knowingly deal with you."

Hess leaned his head back with scorn. "Are you really so unworldly, Stern? You know the saying, 'Don't look a gift horse in the mouth'? I have found the Israelis to be great lovers of that proverb. No one can afford to quibble over moral distinctions when he's shopping for a nuclear bomb. Not even the Jews. It is poetic, is it not? In their lust for power, the Jews have sown the seeds of their own destruction. In its quest for nuclear weapons, Israel gave over its most precious secrets to South Africa. And I intend to give them back a thousandfold!"

"You won't succeed," Stern said.

Hess smirked. "I presume you're referring to the telephone call you made to your associates in Pretoria? Requesting the aid of the NIS? Of General Jaap Steyn, to be precise?"

Stern felt his heart stutter.

"In all fairness, I should tell you not to have any great hopes on that account. The NIS is thoroughly under the control of certain associates of mine. Respected members of the government." A cruel smile plucked at the corners of Hess's mouth. "So, perhaps I shall succeed, yes?"

Pieter Smuts chuckled softly. Stern tried to still his quivering hands, but the snuffing of his solitary hope for rescue drove him beyond reason. With a primal scream he flung himself across the desk, groping for Hess's throat. He felt his hands grasp the beribboned jacket, then the old man's spindly neck—

Smuts's Beretta crashed down on his skull and blotted out the light.

6:35 A.M. *The Union Building, Pretoria*

Hauer sat as still as possible and tried to control his frustration. He had been waiting this way for almost two hours. Across the desk from him sat a tall, sandy-haired young man of about thirty. His name was Captain Barnard, and he was one of General Jaap Steyn's two personal staff officers. Captain Barnard had been working a graveyard shift when Hauer and Gadi were ushered into his third-floor office by an armed duty officer. The young captain had listened patiently to Hauer's requests to speak to General Steyn, but he had acted on none of them. General Steyn, Captain Barnard explained, never woke before seven. And unless Hauer could be more specific about what he meant by "national crisis," he would have to wait until then, when Barnard would be happy to call the general at home. No, the captain had not heard of an Alfred Horn who had an estate in the northern Transvaal. At that point Hauer had resorted to blackmail. He mentioned plan *Aliyah Beth*, which Captain Barnard blandly explained was "Greek to me." In the face of this delay, Gadi Abrams stood and moved softly toward the door.

"Where are you going?" Captain Barnard asked sharply.

Gadi reached for the door handle and pulled. In the doorway stood the khaki-clad duty officer who had brought them upstairs. He leveled his pistol at Gadi's belly.

"I'd like to call my embassy," Gadi said evenly. He was gauging his chances of taking the sentry before the man could pull the trigger. The officer seemed to sense Gadi's intentions; he took a quick step backward.

"Which embassy would that be?" Captain Barnard asked.

"The Israeli embassy."

"You'd best not," said the Afrikaner. "Let's everyone just have a seat, shall we?"

Hauer sat still and tried to remain calm. To be forced to sit here while Hans and Ilse waited for a bullet, while Stern sweated out his deception, and while Schneider flew toward Berlin was maddening. Yet things could be worse. They had not yet contacted the right South African, but they had not run into the wrong one, either. Hauer studied the office. It was the twin of a hundred offices in Berlin. Outside, the Union Building was a massive colonnaded block built of ocher sandstone and crowned with twin domes. It sat high atop a ridge over the capital city, dominating the halogen-lit valley below. Yet inside, the building was as monotonously official as the Police Presidium in Berlin.

"I say there," Captain Barnard said suddenly. "You wouldn't be meaning *Thomas* Horn, would you? Thomas Horn the industrialist?"

"We might," Hauer said, cutting his eyes at Gadi.

"*Thomas* Horn has several houses throughout the country. I'm not sure about one near the Kruger Park, though." Barnard's face clouded. "Here now, is Thomas Horn in danger? He's a very important man in this country."

"He may be," Hauer said carefully.

Captain Barnard frowned. "Someone had better speak up about all this," he said. "And damned quickly."

"Captain Barnard," Hauer implored, "you *must* see how important this is. How often do foreign law enforcement officers come in here in the middle of the night and tell you that your country is in danger?"

"Not very often," Barnard admitted. "And I've half a

mind to let you and your rude companion wait for the general in a police holding cell."

"For God's sake!" Hauer pleaded, coming to his feet. "There's no time for that!"

Without warning, the door to Captain Barnard's office banged open and a short, heavy-set Afrikaner with carrot hair and lobster-red skin marched in. The sounds of early morning office traffic filtered through the doorway until the newcomer slammed it shut. He looked quizzically at Hauer, then at Gadi, and finally at Captain Barnard. Hauer was struck with a strange certainty that the red-haired man had been summoned by the duty officer, for the guard took up position in a corner with one hand on his holstered pistol.

"What's all this then, Barnard?" the red-haired man asked sharply.

Captain Barnard stood. "Major Graaff, this is Captain Dieter Hauer of the West Berlin police. Captain Hauer, this is Major Graaff, General Steyn's senior staff officer. Major, Captain Hauer claims to have very important information for General Steyn. He refused to discuss it with me, so I decided to wait until seven and call the general. As a matter of fact, I was just about to call—"

"Wake the general?" Graaff looked as if he were being asked to arrange a papal audience. "What the devil are you men doing here? Out with it!"

Hauer eyed Major Graaff uncomfortably. "Our message is for General Steyn," he said. "I'm sorry, Major, but that's the way it has to be."

Graaff's skin grew even redder. "You've got some bloody nerve, Jerry." He turned to Barnard. "I'm surprised you didn't throw these characters into a cell!"

"They mentioned Thomas Horn, sir," Captain Barnard said, surprised by Graaff's vehemence. "I think he may be in danger."

"Thomas Horn?" Graaff's eyes narrowed. "What's he got to do with this?"

"They won't say, sir."

"They won't. We'll see about that."

"They also mentioned what they said was a code, Major. What was it, Captain Hauer?"

Hauer didn't like the look of Major Graaff at all, but he'd already given the code to Captain Barnard. Maybe it would light a fire under Graaff. "The code is *Aliyah Beth*," he said.

Graaff's eyes narrowed. "Means nothing to me, Barnard."
Gadi flushed with anger.

"Why don't I call the general?" Captain Barnard suggested. "It's almost seven."

"Nonsense!" scoffed Major Graaff. "Not until we've found out what these characters are up to. Send them over to Visagie police station. Let the interrogators have a go at them. We'll soon get to the bottom of this. Call Visagie, Barnard. Have them send over a van." While Barnard made the call, Major Graaff glanced disapprovingly at Gadi. "Who's this dark one then? I don't like the look of him."

Captain Barnard tried once more. "You don't think perhaps I should call the general?"

"Don't be an idiot, Barnard. We'll know everything about this lot by lunchtime. I'll speak to the general then if it's worth bothering him about. They're probably journalists, trying to poke their noses where they don't belong."

Hauer considered telling Major Graaff about Aaron Haber—the "insurance" they had waiting at the Protea Hof—but something told him to keep silent, at least for the time being.

Major Graaff's police escort arrived in less than fifteen minutes. They brought handcuffs, but Graaff waved them aside. "These buggers won't be making any trouble." He laughed. "They're fellow police officers, after all. Where are their papers, Barnard?"

Captain Barnard looked sheepish.

Graaff shook his head. "Damn it, man, it's a wonder they didn't kill you and take the place over."

"It wouldn't have mattered," Hauer told him. "We're traveling under false papers."

"Are you, now?" Graaff said. "Well, let's just toddle down to the police station, shall we?" The major shoved his prisoners through the door.

Captain Barnard got up and closed the door. He was strangely irritated by Graaff's remarks. *Why didn't I ask to see their passports?* he wondered. But he knew why. Because the longer he had stared into the earnest eyes of the German policeman, the more convinced he'd become that the man was telling the truth. There *was* some kind of crisis going on. And what was the harm in calling the general, anyway? Jaap Steyn prided himself on keeping a hand in every case that directly affected his office. And if two foreigners asking to speak to the general on a matter of national security didn't directly affect his office, what did?

Barnard reached for the phone and dialed General Steyn's home number. He listened to it ring three times, then hung up with an oath. Graaff was probably right. Better to wait until they knew they had a problem before bothering the general. The Visagie interrogators would know everything about the strangers in a few hours, and South Africa's political battles kept General Steyn busy enough without jerking him away from his morning coffee to deal with a non-event. Captain Barnard took his car keys from his desk and wrote a note to his secretary. He'd been working all night. He was going home to shower, shave, and have a bite of breakfast. He would be back around ten A.M. *It will all be sorted out by then,* he thought as he slipped out of the office. But then he remembered the German policeman's sober gaze. And he wondered.

CHAPTER FORTY

Sir Neville Shaw looked up as Wilson rushed into his dim office. His deputy shook a thin piece of paper in his right hand.

"Cable, Sir Neville!"

"Well read it, man! What's the bloody rush?"

Wilson shoved the message across the desktop. "Personal for you, sir."

Shaw tore open the seal and read:

DIRECTOR GENERAL MI5:

THE MEN YOU SENT ARE DEAD STOP LORD
GRENVILLE IS DEAD STOP YOU BROKE
A SOLEMN AGREEMENT MADE MORE
THAN THIRTY YEARS AGO STOP I AM NO
LONGER BOUND BY TERMS OF THAT
AGREEMENT STOP I'VE NEVER KNOWN
AN ENGLISHMAN WHO KEPT HIS WORD
STOP SECRET NOW HELD AT MY DISCRETION
STOP BETTER LUCK NEXT TIME

HESS

Shaw felt his hands begin to shake. "Good God," he murmured. "Burton's dead." He looked up, his face red and blotchy. "Wilson! Do you have those files I told you to get?"

"In my office safe, sir. I don't believe the Foreign Office has noticed them missing yet."

"*Damn* the Foreign Office! Shred those files, then incinerate them in the basement! Do it yourself and do it now!"

Wilson moved toward the door, then paused and looked back at his superior.

"I was a bloody fool to order Swallow off the case," Shaw said hoarsely. "She could have killed Hess herself."

Wilson's eyes narrowed. "You mean Horn, sir?"

Shaw looked up with red eyes. "Horn is Hess, Wilson. Haven't you got that yet?"

Wilson took a step backward.

Shaw looked down at the wrinkled map on his desk. "Swallow could still be in South Africa," he muttered. "By God she might be able to save us yet. Wilson, put out a message to every resource we have in South Africa. Anyone who contacts agent Swallow should order her to call me here. And if she calls us *for any reason,* you put her through to me immediately. Do you understand?"

"Yes, sir!"

Shaw's eyes sparkled with excitement. "By God, I should have used that harpy in the first place! Murder has always been woman's work."

6:55 A.M. Protea Hof Hotel, Pretoria

Swallow had been waiting outside room 604 for twelve hours, and her patience had almost run out. In the half-dozen times she had approached the door, only once had she heard any conversation from the two men inside. For the hundredth time she glanced at her watch. Almost seven A.M. Maids would be coming on duty any moment. *To hell with it,* she thought, *I'm going in.* She already had a plan. Taking a last glance at the door, she headed downstairs to use the lobby telephone.

Inside room 604, Professor Natterman lay flat on the bed in a haze of morphine, fever, and pain. Thanks to Aaron's expert medical training, the gunshot wounds had at least stopped bleeding, if not hurting. The professor had spent the night wrestling with despair. Rudolf Hess was alive, as he had predicted, yet he would not be at Horn House to confront the old Nazi. And worse, Hauer had told Detective Schneider where to find his photocopy of the Spandau papers, wiping out any hope of his publishing an exclusive translation of the papers. All night Natterman had clutched his only consolation to his chest—the photographic negatives Hauer had made of six of the Spandau pages. When dawn began to creep around the edges of the drapes, Natterman wondered when or if Hauer would call back. Would the South Africans give Hauer the troops Stern had told him to ask for? And if so, could Ilse survive such an assault?

Natterman glanced over at the other bed. Aaron Haber lay there, watching a silent television. The young commando had lain that way most of the night, except when he took time out to check Natterman's bandages. He'd said he muted the sound so that he could hear anyone approaching the door. Natterman wiped a sheen of sweat from his brow. The hotel air-conditioning whooshed straight out of the window shattered by Borodin's sniper.

Natterman jumped as a sharp knock sounded at the door. Aaron came to his feet like a leopard startled from sleep, his Uzi cocked and pointed at the door. Natterman could just see the door from where he lay. As the Israeli tiptoed toward it, the knock sounded again. Aaron flattened himself against the foyer wall.

"Who's there?" he called.

"Messenger," said a male voice. "Telegram, sir."

Aaron's brow knit in furious thought. "Telegram from who?"

"From a *Meneer* Stern, sir."

The young commando's blood quickened. "Shove it under the door!"

There was a pause. "I'm sorry, sir. *Meneer* Stern's instructions say I must personally give this message to one of his boys."

Aaron nervously fingered his Uzi. "Which of his boys?"

"*Meneer* Stern does not say, sir."

Keeping his Uzi leveled, Aaron stepped warily up to the door and peered through the peephole. Through the blurred fisheye lens he saw a thin young black man wearing a blue messenger's uniform buttoned to the throat. "Hold up the telegram," he said.

The young Bantu held up a piece of yellow paper, too far back for Aaron to read. "I must hurry, sir," he said. "I have other stops to make."

Aaron muttered something in Hebrew, then reached for the door knob.

"Don't open it!" Natterman warned, but the young Israeli

signaled him to be quiet. Natterman heard the lock click; then the door opened and caught against the chain.

"Hand it through," Aaron said from behind the door. "I'm not letting you in."

After a moment's hesitation, a small black hand slipped the telegram through the crack in the door. Aaron reached out, then froze. A faint scent of body powder and perfume had wafted into the room. For an instant Aaron flashed back to last night. He heard Gadi's voice saying, ". . . and the perfume, I tell you, it was the same woman, the woman from the airplane." In a fraction of a second Aaron comprehended the danger, but he was too late.

Already a thin white hand had snapped through the four-inch space between the door and its frame. The hand held a silenced Ingram machine pistol. As Aaron looked down in astonishment, the Ingram spat three times, blowing him off his feet and dropping him less than a foot from the bloody stain where Yosef Shamir had died twelve hours ago.

Natterman tried to roll off the bed, but he was tangled beneath the covers. He heard two more spits, then a clinking rattle. Swallow had shot off the chain latch. He heard the door close, then a heavy thud. Somehow Natterman knew who the killer was before he saw her. He actually stopped breathing as the pale apparition glided swiftly to Aaron's body. With one chilling glance at Natterman, the thin woman bent down and tugged the Uzi from Aaron Haber's clenched hands. *Swallow,* Natterman thought, remembering Stern's words. *What's left of the girl whose brother Stern killed while he sat on a toilet in a British barracks a million years ago . . .*

Swallow glanced into the bathroom. She saw the Russians piled like cordwood in the bathtub, and Yosef Shamir propped against the white-tiled wall. Then she crossed immediately to Natterman, reached down, and jerked his gag aside. When he opened his mouth to gasp for breath, she jammed the barrel of the Ingram inside it.

"Hello again, Professor," she said in a low, flat voice. "Where is Stern?"

Natterman felt the gun barrel against the back of his throat, as cold and deadly as a snake's head. He desperately needed to gag, but he didn't dare. The woman leaning over him was like a creature from a nightmare, a ghastly grand-

mother with blue-rinse hair, yellowed pearls hanging round
her wrinkled throat—

"Jonas Stern!" Swallow snapped. *"Where is he?"*

Natterman nodded his head carefully. Swallow removed
the Ingram from his mouth. For a moment—thinking of
Stern and his mission—Natterman considered lying. He
changed his mind when Swallow jammed the gun barrel
down onto the bloody bandage that Aaron had wrapped
around Natterman's wounded thigh.

"Alfred Horn!" he gasped. "Stern went to see a man
named Alfred Horn!"

Swallow jabbed the Ingram deeper into Natterman's
wound. *"Where* to see Alfred Horn?"

Natterman felt his stomach heave. "Somewhere in the
northern Transvaal! That's all I know. It was a blind rendezvous. Stern didn't know where he was going himself!"

While Swallow considered this, Natterman looked past
her to the floor. He saw black skin and white eyes. The messenger. Now he understood the second thud. Swallow had
shot the Bantu boy in the throat. "Stern was wrong," he said,
thinking aloud. "He thinks you're after him. But you've
come to destroy the Spandau papers, haven't you?"

Swallow's nostrils flared. "I've come for Stern. If he has
the papers, that's a bonus."

Natterman glanced back at Aaron. The Israeli had fallen
with his back against the foyer wall. Except for the blood on
his chest, he looked like he was sleeping. Natterman remembered how innocent the young commando had looked watching the soundless television. "How do you do it?" he asked.
"That boy was hardly more than a child."

Swallow followed Natterman's gaze to Aaron's motionless body. She shrugged. "He was a soldier. Today was his
day."

Natterman shook his head. "Every bullet has its billet,
eh?"

"King William," Swallow murmured, recalling the quote
from her wartime service. "You're a philosopher?"

"I'm a fool. And you're a murderer, and a hypocrite as
well. That boy was probably someone's brother, too."

Swallow smacked Natterman on the mouth with the
Ingram, drawing blood. Her eyes, as cold and dark and
empty as deep space, settled on his face. Natterman had
never in his life felt such fear, not even as a young German

soldier patrolling alone in the shadow of Russian tanks outside Leningrad.

"You're going to kill me," he said *sotto voce*.

"Not quite yet." Swallow lifted the telephone receiver and dialed an international number. As she waited for an answer, she casually pulled off her blue-rinse hair. Natterman's eyes widened. Beneath the wig, Swallow's hair was iron gray and cropped to within an inch of her skull. She did not look like a grandmother anymore.

"Swallow," she said harshly.

In London, Sir Neville Shaw's heart leaped. "Good Christ! Where are you?"

Swallow's knuckles whitened on the telephone. "Listen to me, little man. I'm giving you one last chance to tell me where Stern is. He's gone to see a man named Alfred Horn. I want to know where—"

"I'll tell you exactly where to find him!"

Without wasting a second the MI-5 chief read out the overland directions to Horn House. Swallow repeated them as they came, her head bobbing with birdlike impatience, her eyes locked onto Natterman. When Shaw finished reading the directions, he said, "I'm modifying your assignment. You can still do what you like with Stern, but I need more than the Spandau papers now. I need Alfred Horn dead. You shouldn't have any trouble recognizing him. He's an old man, rides in a wheelchair most of the time. If you kill Alfred Horn, you can name your price."

Swallow laughed, a dry rattle. Her finger slipped inside the Ingram's trigger guard. As Natterman stared in horror, she reached out casually and laid the machine pistol against his cheek. Sir Neville Shaw's voice warbled from the telephone. Swallow drew back her lips, exposing her teeth like an animal preparing for a kill. Then her head snapped around toward the foyer. She dropped the telephone and raised the Ingram.

What is it? Natterman thought wildly. *Is someone at the door?* He couldn't hear anything but his hammering heart. Following Swallow's line of sight, he finally realized what she was looking at with such alarm. *Nothing!* Where less than a minute ago the bullet-riddled body of Aaron Haber had lain against the foyer wall, only bloodstained wallpaper remained.

Shrieking like a demon, Swallow fired a sustained burst

into the foyer, then adjusted her aim to the bathroom wall. The muted barks of the silenced weapon modulated quickly into loud bangs. Her silencer was burning out. Natterman threw off the sheets and rolled off the far edge of the bed. He had been on the floor for less than five seconds when the firing stopped. What the devil was happening? He raised his head above the line of the bed.

Swallow was crouched at the end of the bed nearest the foyer, trying frantically to clear the jammed receiver of her Ingram. Like a man rising from the grave, Aaron Haber lurched up from the narrow space between the bed and the bathroom wall. Natterman's heart leaped with joy and astonishment. Dark blood covered the young commando's neck and chest, but his eyes burned wildly. Swaying like a drunken madman, he steadied his .22 automatic and fired four shots in rapid succession.

Swallow was so desperate to reach the safety of the foyer that she actually leaped into Aaron's bullets. Two slugs slammed into her left shoulder, but the others went wild. She staggered into the foyer, spun around and collapsed. Hoping that the impact of the fall had cleared her weapon, she scrambled to her knees, thrust her Ingram around the corner and pulled the trigger.

Aaron fired the instant he saw the gun barrel appear. His bullet tore the gun from Swallow's hand. It spun through the air and landed against the wall, too far away for either of them to reach. All Aaron had to do was step around the corner to finish the woman off. He started forward, then wobbled to a standstill. Bright blood pumped through his shirt.

Why doesn't she just run? Natterman thought angrily. *She has the information she wanted!* And then he knew. Swallow meant to leave no witnesses behind.

A horrible coughing spasm racked Aaron Haber's body. He lunged forward, gurgled something in Hebrew, then dropped his pistol and collapsed at the mouth of the foyer. Natterman peered around the edge of the bed. The Israeli lay on his stomach with his head pointed toward the door. Swallow's Ingram lay at his feet. Natterman's heart sank. The gun might as well have been ten kilometers away. But as he jerked his head back behind the bed, he saw something that stopped the breath in his lungs—Hans's crossbow, loaded and lying beneath the bed. Yuri Borodin's gorillas had missed it during their sweep. Natterman lay flat and stretched his arm to its limit . . .

Swallow glided soundlessly out of the foyer and bobbed over the wounded Israeli. A knife flashed in the air. Swallow reached for Aaron's hair, meaning to jerk up his head and slash his throat, but at the last moment she leaned toward his feet and grabbed for the Ingram.

The decision cost her her life. The instant she moved, Aaron flipped over onto his back and grabbed her by the waist. Unable to reach the Ingram, Swallow twisted in his arms and brought the knife down into his chest. She raised it again for the deathblow, but Natterman struggled up over the bed, steadied the crossbow, and fired.

The razor-tipped bolt speared through Swallow's breastbone with a sickening crunch. Sucking for air she no longer needed, she pawed the air in maniacal fury. Her last cry carried all the atrophied rage and pain of her unfulfilled quest for vengeance: *"Sterrrn!"*

Swallow collapsed on top of Aaron, preceding the young commando into death by only seconds. Natterman stumbled over to the gasping Israeli and with painful effort shoved Swallow's corpse off his blood-soaked chest. Aaron strained to raise his head, then fell back and reached up to Natterman for succor. Natterman knelt over him. "Lie back," he said. "You're safe now."

A froth of blood bubbled from Aaron's mouth. "Did I stop her?" he asked softly. "She wanted . . . Stern."

Natterman looked over at Swallow. Lying dead with the arrow buried in her chest, she looked like a locust husk spiked to a display board. Natterman smiled at the young Israeli. "You stopped her."

"Tell . . . tell Gadi . . . did my duty." Aaron coughed once more; then he closed his eyes.

Natterman swallowed hard. This young soldier had given his life for Jonas Stern. Filled with a sudden rage, Natterman lurched to his feet and scrambled back to the telephone.

"Who is this?" he shouted. "Speak!"

"Who is *this?*" came the wary reply, the British accent clear.

Natterman felt his hands shaking. "Your assassin is dead!" he yelled. "Your secret will be secret no more!"

He threw down the telephone. Moaning in pain, he stripped off his shirt, picked up Aaron's first-aid bag, and began rummaging through the drug bottles. He wanted local anesthetic. He needed to dull the fire of his wounds, but he could not risk losing consciousness. He had to be able to board an airplane under his own power. He hated the idea of leaving Ilse and the others behind, but he suspected that if he did not get out of South Africa today, he might not get out at all.

7:01 A.M. MI-5 Headquarters: Charles Street, London

Sir Neville Shaw dropped the phone, his face ashen. Deputy Director Wilson faced him from the doorway.

"It's over," Shaw said quietly. "After all this time, it's over."

"What do you mean, sir?"

"Swallow's dead. There's no stopping the secret now. We've fired our last shell. From Churchill down to me, and all for nothing."

"Churchill, Sir Neville? I don't understand."

"Don't you? Haven't you got it yet, man? Horn is Hess, Hess is Horn. The great bloody secret. Ever since Churchill, it's been our sacred charge."

"Sacred charge?"

"This service, Wilson. My office, particularly. It was MI-5 who ran the original Hess double-cross in 1941. We intercepted the first letter from Hess to the Duke of Hamilton." Shaw lifted two sheets of paper from his desk. "Why don't you read this, old man? It's a memo to the prime minister. Typed it myself while you were getting tea."

Wilson stepped forward uncertainly and took the proffered pages. His eyes widened as they flew over phrases that made his blood run cold.

Dear Mrs. Prime Minister:

In May 1941, Rudolf Hess, Deputy Führer of the German Reich, flew to this country to assist in a coup d'état aimed at the government of Prime Minister Winston Churchill and King George VI. MI-5 was aware of this plot almost from its inception, and used it to buy time to forestall the German invasion of this country [Operation Sea Lion].

Regrettably, the success of the *coup* hinged on the participation of numerous ranking members of the wartime Parliament and the nobility, as well as a second accession of the Duke of Windsor to the throne. On 11 May 1941, Prime Minister Winston Churchill instructed this office [Secret Finding 573] to conceal all evidence of this Anglo-Nazi collusion, on the grounds that exposure of such high-ranking treason might bring down the government and possibly even prevent American entry into the war.

Events of the past five days have made the continued suppression of this information highly unlikely. I must inform you that Rudolf Hess is alive as of this writing, and is a citizen of the Republic of South Africa [living under the alias "Alfred Horn"]. Hess may soon reveal this fact himself, or certain papers unearthed at Spandau Prison may do so. My best efforts to silence Hess and to destroy the papers have failed. Hess's current activities fall into the realm of the criminal, and, if exposed, could put at risk a significant number of British nationals. The family of Lord Grenville, particularly, may soon be made public in this connection, as it has owned and operated Phoenix AG [a multinational defense contractor] at the bidding of "Alfred Horn" since 1947. Other families of the peerage [one of whom boasts a member of your cabinet] have lent their names to similar enterprises in exchange for large cash payments, and possibly for ideological reasons as well. I'm afraid issuing a D-notice at this time would be counterproductive, however, as it would tend to indicate prior knowledge by your office of these activities.

The suppression of the Hess information to date has only been possible thanks to the nerve and foresight of Prime Minister Churchill. In October 1944, Churchill flew to Moscow for a meeting with Joseph Stalin. With him he carried copies of assassination orders that were, to all appearances, signed by Stalin himself. These orders were actually forgeries fabricated by Reinhard Heydrich's SD.

They were brought into this country by a
German-trained White Russian agent named
Zinoviev, and recovered by MI-5 on 11 May
1941. In Moscow, Churchill warned Stalin that he
would inform the world press that Stalin had ordered
the murders of Churchill and King George VI,
if Stalin did not cease making accusations about
Anglo-Nazi collusion in the Hess affair.

Five weeks ago, on the strength of Secret Finding
573, I ordered the liquidation of Hess's double
[the real Alfred Horn] in Spandau Prison. On
my order the Foreign Office file on Hess has been
sanitized. I have placed in my personal safe papers
which washed ashore in Scotland on 11 May
1941, which were thought to have been ditched
from Hess's plane. These papers contain the names
of many of the British *coup* conspirators. The War
Office file on Hess contains damaging
information on the Duke of Windsor [which the
Royal Family is frightfully anxious to keep buried],
but that file is sealed until 2050. The F.O. file is
sealed until 2016.

We should meet as soon as possible.

Sir Neville Shaw
Director General, MI-5

P.S. This unfortunate situation has been
complicated by the arrest yesterday of an MI-6
intelligence analyst who for seven years made
available to agents of "Alfred Horn" some of our
most sensitive intelligence secrets, including
copies of American satellite photography. Three
weeks ago, this man inferred [from information which
had been requested by Phoenix AG] that some type
of attack [possibly nuclear] was imminent against
the State of Israel. In a belated fit of conscience,
he sent an anonymous warning to the Israeli Embassy
in London. We cannot discount the possibility that
my efforts to liquidate Hess prompted him to
attempt some desperate action against Israel, but
I consider this scenario unlikely. "Alfred Horn" does
have significant uranium holdings in South Africa,

but the possibility that he has acquired a nuclear device is infinitesimally small.

Deputy Director Wilson looked up at Shaw with horror on his face. "You don't really mean to send this?"

Shaw raised his eyebrows. "Of course I do. As far as I'm concerned, the Hess secret is blown. I'll be sacked tomorrow, so what do I care? I'm tired of protecting traitors, Wilson. It's time the world learned what a heroic mission this service performed in 1941. We saved Churchill and the King, man. We saved England! I should write it up for the bloody *Times!*"

The blood drained from Wilson's cheeks. "Surely you're joking, Sir Neville. You're overwrought."

"But I'm deadly serious."

The deputy director glanced behind him to the closed office door. "I'm sorry to hear that," he said softly. He pulled a revolver from his coat pocket.

Shaw studied the gun. "A bit noisy for murder, don't you think? Too many people around."

Wilson gave his superior a wintry smile. "Not murder, Sir Neville. Suicide."

Shaw smiled appreciatively. "Ah. I'm about to crack under the strain of a failed operation, eh? You'll 'discover' me with my head bleeding over the Hess file, the mandarins will cover it up 'for the good of the service,' and you'll take my chair as director general. Is that it?"

Wilson nodded. "I've been laying the groundwork ever since you locked yourself in here like a hermit. The secretaries are already whispering about you."

Shaw sighed. "You were Horn's man all along, weren't you? As long as my efforts went toward keeping the secret, you went right along. But you and your bloody uncle—Lord Amersham, isn't it?—you didn't know that some of the conspirator families had asked me to liquidate both Hess and Number Seven, did you? Gutless bastards. They claimed Horn had gone senile, that he had too much power. I saw the truth, though. *Glasnost* had those blue-blooded cowards pissing their beds at night. Gorbachev's whole program was openness, sweeping out the past. Couldn't have that, could we? Our brave peers were scared silly that the Russians might not veto Number Seven's release next time around." Shaw raised a forefinger. "And they were right, you know?

Two days ago I learned that Gorbachev had recently indicated to Hess's son that he was on the verge of releasing Prisoner Number Seven."

Wilson kept his pistol pointed at Shaw's chest. "How did you kill Number Seven without my knowledge?"

Shaw shrugged. "Easily. I used a retired SAS man. Michael Burton. The whole Hess business has always been run outside official channels. That's why you knew nothing about the *Casilda*. But you found out in time, didn't you? You warned Hess about the raid."

Wilson's face reddened. "I warned *Horn*."

"My God," muttered Shaw. "You didn't even know who you were working for, did you? Just like that idiot in MI-6. At least his mother was South African."

The revolver shook in Wilson's hand. "Why was Hess allowed to live? Why did we let him out of England at all?"

Shaw smiled humorlessly. "We never *had* Hess, Wilson. We only caught Horn—the double Heydrich sent to confuse us. We never found out how Hess escaped, *if* he came here at all. MI-6 finally located him in Paraguay in 1958. The Israelis and other Nazi-hunters never found him because they weren't looking. As far as they knew, Rudolf Hess was locked inside Spandau Prison."

"Why didn't you kill Hess in Paraguay?"

Shaw snorted. "You think your friends are afraid of the Spandau papers? Hess knew the name of every bloody British traitor involved in the *coup* attempt. He claimed he had taken steps that would make those names public in the event of his untimely death, and we believed him."

"But why kill Number Seven after all this time? He'd held his silence for decades. Why should he break it?"

"Because his wife and daughter were dead," Shaw explained. "Had been for years. We kept Number Seven quiet by threatening his family, just as Hess must have. If Number Seven had been released from Spandau, he might have discovered they were dead. And we would have lost our leverage. If the Russians hadn't vetoed his early release every year, we would have had to kill him years ago."

Sir Neville Shaw steepled his fingers. "Tell me one thing, Wilson. How much have you told Hess's people about Jonas Stern?"

"Nothing, until today. I assumed Swallow would kill Stern before he became a threat, and I didn't want to risk further direct contact. Stern must have blown his cover himself. Two hours ago Horn's security chief called me and asked if I knew anything about a Jew who had come after Horn."

Shaw nodded thoughtfully. "I suppose you intend to burn my memo?"

"Yes, actually."

Shaw reached out his hand. "Here. Let me shred it for you."

Puzzled, Wilson handed Shaw the letter, then watched incredulously as the MI-5 chief fed both pages into his high-speed shredder. "But . . . why? What are you doing?"

Shaw smiled. "Don't worry, there's a copy in my safe. But things haven't *quite* reached the stage where I feel compelled to send it." Shaw looked over Wilson's shoulder to a dark corner of the large office. "Sergeant," he said crisply, "please arrest Mr. Wilson. The charge is treason."

Like a thousand fools before him, Wilson whirled to face an imaginary threat. When he looked back at Shaw, there was a silenced Browning Hi-Power pistol in the old knight's hand.

"Sorry, old boy," Shaw said, but he had already pulled the trigger.

Wilson's astonished eyes went blank as the bullet tore through his heart. He dropped dead on the floor without a sound.

Shaw calmly lifted his telephone and punched in a number. The call was answered immediately.

"Rose here," said a gruff voice with a Texas twang.

"Good morning, Colonel," said Shaw. "I am authorized to agree to your terms—*if* you believe the Hess secret can still be kept."

"As if you had any choice," Rose growled.

"About Jonas Stern," Shaw said diffidently. "Her Majesty's government doesn't want the Israelis getting hold of this story."

"I figure Stern's dead by now," Rose said. "*Sir* Neville."

Shaw sighed with forbearance. "Is there any further word from South Africa?"

"Negative. Your precious secret's in Captain Hauer's hands now. Who knows what a friggin' Kraut'll do?" Rose laughed away from the phone. "Hey, Shaw, I've got a guy here, name of Schneider. He says Hauer'll kill Hess if he gets the chance. That make you feel any better?"

Shaw smiled with satisfaction. "Thank you, Colonel. I shall be in Berlin by noon."

CHAPTER FORTY-ONE

8:26 A.M. Angolan Airspace

At eighteen thousand feet the Lear 31-A turbojet knifed southward through the sky and down the length of Africa. In the sumptuously appointed passenger cabin, Prime Minister Abdul Bakr Jalloud sipped from a glass of sherry and contemplated the excited face of Dr. Hamid Sabri. The bespectacled young physicist could barely restrain his enthusiasm. In a matter of hours he would be shepherding back to Libya the first nuclear weapon ever to stock an Arab arsenal. Prime Minister Jalloud was more subdued. Despite Muammar Qaddafi's repeated assurances that all was well, Jalloud could not shake a vague suspicion that something was not as it should be.

"Are you all right, Excellency?" asked Dr. Sabri. "You look pale."

"It's the food," Jalloud muttered. "I shouldn't have eaten anything."

"I'm nervous myself," Sabri confessed. "I cannot wait to return home with the device."

"I can't wait to return home, period," Jalloud murmured.

This curious statement disconcerted the young scientist. He glanced through his window at the clouds below. "Excellency?" he said quietly. "I must admit I am glad Major Karami is not accompanying us on this trip. He makes me uncomfortable. I do not believe Mr. Horn liked him either."

"Major Karami makes a lot of people nervous," said Jalloud, glancing past Dr. Sabri. At the rear of the cabin, sitting on a pile of embroidered pillows, six very dangerous-looking soldiers quietly smoked cigarettes. Qaddafi had assured Jalloud that he'd ordered them along for extra security and to help with the loading of the weapon, but Jalloud doubted this. On the last trip two security guards had been considered adequate escort. Jalloud was almost certain that these men had been handpicked from Ilyas Karami's personal bodyguard.

"I'm not so sure we are free of Major Karami," he whispered, cutting his eyes toward the guards.

Dr. Sabri peered around the prime minister's *keffiyah* and looked at the sullen group. "Don't say that," he said quietly. "Allah protect us, don't even think it."

Twenty-eight miles behind the Lear, Major Ilyas Karami stepped onto the flight deck of a Soviet-built Yakovlev-42 airliner and leaned down into the pilot's ear. "Should I go over it for you again?" he asked.

"It's not necessary, Major," the pilot replied.

"Good." Karami laid a hand on the young man's shoulder. "Because what I told my commandos goes for you pilots too. Any man that makes a mistake on this mission will lose his head when we return to Tripoli."

The pilot strained to keep his hands steady on the controls. Ilyas Karami's threats were never empty.

"And his testicles will be in his mouth," Karami added.

The plane lurched violently, as if buffeted by turbulence. "I'm sorry, Major!" the pilot croaked.

"Low-pressure pocket," the copilot covered quickly.

Major Karami snorted and left the flight deck.

This Yakovlev aircraft—popularly known as the Yak-42 —had begun its life as an Aeroflot jetliner, then passed into Libyan commercial service. But for this mission Major Karami had ordered it configured as an Air Zimbabwe commercial airliner. Karami smiled with satisfaction as he walked through the stripped cabin of the plane. Lining both walls of the Yak-42 were fifty heavily-armed Libyan commandos; and filling the center section from front to rear were pallets stacked high with weapons, ammunition, a small truck, and at the rear of the cabin, lashed to the fuselage by chains, a 105-millimeter artillery piece.

Karami nodded to his company commanders as he made his way through the tangle of legs and equipment and stopped beside the small pickup truck. The bed of the Toyota had been padded with wrestling mats, and its sides fitted with cleats sized to take chains. Ostensibly the truck had been brought along to tow the 105mm howitzer into position. Only Major Karami knew what special cargo its bed and suspension had been modified to accept. When they got a little closer to their destination, however, Karami would let his men in on the secret. For what force could withstand the fury of Arabs come to claim the weapon that would finally wipe the Jews from the sands of Palestine?

8:40 A.M. *Northern Transvaal, Republic of South Africa*

Alan Burton scrambled over the lip of the Wash and down the slope to where Juan Diaz half-sat, half-lay in the slowly drying mud. He had bandaged the Cuban's wound as best he could; it was crusted with blood but not suppurating. Diaz opened his eyes when he heard Burton approach.

"Well, English?" he croaked.

"No chance," Burton said bitterly. "It's worse than it looked last night. Fidel's chopper blew itself all over the runway. It's a wonder we weren't cut to pieces. The tail of that Lear looks like scrap metal."

"The lateral fins?" Diaz asked hopefully. "Or the vertical?"

"Left lateral's completely gone. Vertical's got more holes than a Swiss cheese."

"Shit! What now, *amigo*?" Diaz tried to smile. "We're dead men, eh?"

"Not bloody likely," Burton said with an optimism he didn't feel. "That's an airstrip up there, isn't it? This place is too damned remote to service by road. It's bound to be just a matter of time before another plane lands."

Diaz squinted skeptically at the Englishman.

"And when it does, sport," said Burton, tapping his submachine gun against his chest, "I'm going to climb aboard and watch Captain Juan Diaz fly our wet *arses* right out of here."

The Cuban grinned, exposing dazzling white teeth. Burton pulled some more brambles around the little depression he had expanded into a hiding place during the night. A patrol from the house had come by just after last night's attack. It had missed them, but Burton wasn't sure the shelter would stand up to daylight scrutiny.

"I tell you, Juan boy," he said wistfully, "it's times like

this I wish I was back in England, fishing a stream in the Cotswolds."

"Why aren't you?"

Burton smiled sheepishly. "I'm *persona non grata* there, sport. Occupational hazard. Her Majesty takes a rather dim view of soldiering for pay. Not like your scruffy boss in Havana. The only thing waiting for me in England's a bloody jail cell."

Diaz tried to smile in sympathy.

"I had a chance to go back free and clear," Burton said quietly. "Last night. But we ballsed it up."

"What do you mean?"

"I mean while you were working for a Colombian drug baron, I was working for Her Majesty's Government. My pay was full reinstatement of British citizenship. I don't know why everyone wants the old man in that fortress dead. I don't care much, either. Maybe his drugs are ending up in London, and the bloody House of Lords wants him discreetly blotted from their universe." Burton grinned. "By God, if I thought I had half a chance, I'd give it another go on my own. I know, I know—English *loco,* right?"

Diaz nodded, then grimaced in pain.

Burton checked the barrel of his MP-5 for mud. "Who needs England, anyway?" he muttered. He fixed his gaze on the rim of the ravine. "You've got one job, Juan boy. Stay alive until I can commandeer some air transport. Then it's straight back to civilization. *Comprende?*"

Diaz coughed horribly.

Burton touched the Cuban's forehead. It felt cool and clammy. A fishy paleness had spread beneath his olive skin. "Can you do it, lad? Can you hold out?"

"Fucking-ay, English," Diaz grunted. "You get me a plane, and I'll fly the whore out."

"That's the ticket." Burton patted the Cuban on his good shoulder.

"But you better hurry, *amigo,*" Diaz coughed, gripping his torn side. "I can fly drunk, stoned, or bleeding, but I can't fly dead."

Burton nodded grimly.

1:40 P.M. The Union Building: Pretoria

Captain Barnard slammed down the phone and glared at his watch. He had been trying in vain to reach General Steyn since ten-thirty. When the general failed to show up for work this morning, Barnard had assumed he was simply late. But by ten A.M. Barnard knew something was wrong. No one answered at General Steyn's home, and none of the government ministries knew where he was. As Barnard continued his round of calls, a disturbing image kept coming back to him: the resolute eyes of the German police captain. Barnard was certain that Captain Hauer believed he possessed information vital to South Africa's security. Hauer might be insane, but he was *sincere*. The Afrikaner ground his teeth in frustration. Major Graaff had told him that the Visagie police interrogators would have the prisoners' story by lunchtime, yet Barnard had received no further word regarding them. Barnard had never liked Major Graaff, but in the NIS, like the army, you had to go along to get along. Especially with superiors. Barnard almost jumped out of his skin when the phone on his desk rang.

"General Steyn's office," he answered.

"Barnard?" boomed a husky voice.

"General Steyn! Where are you?"

"I'm out at the Pretoria office of Phoenix AG. The directors here seem to think that some type of shenanigans may be going on in their defense division. I felt I should handle it myself. Phoenix works on some very sensitive projects, you know . . ."

Captain Barnard felt sweat on the back of his neck. "Excuse me, General, but how did you learn about this problem?"

"Graaff called me at home this morning. He's right on top of this. Seems he's friendly with the people over here at Phoenix. He was the one who suggested I handle it personally, in fact."

"Where is Major Graaff now, General?"

"I haven't the foggiest, Barnard."

"General," Captain Barnard said hoarsely, "I think we've got a problem."

2:05 P.M. *Visagie Straat, Pretoria*

When General Jaap Steyn strode through the doors of the Visagie police station, the desk sergeant knew that his afternoon had just been shot to hell. The chief of South Africa's ruthlessly efficient intelligence service was a bluff, red-faced giant of a man. He stalked straight up to the high desk and planted himself like an admiral on the prow of a flagship.

"Sergeant!" he bellowed. "I want to see your foreign prisoners immediately. Where are they?"

"Um . . . yes, sir. Well, one is in the cellblock and the other . . . I believe Major Graaff is supervising his interrogation."

"Lead on, Sergeant!"

The desk sergeant wasn't sure if the NIS general had legal authority to give orders to a municipal police officer, but risking his career to find out didn't seem like the best of options. He jumped down from his stool and led General Steyn and Captain Barnard to a heavy steel door at the back of the station. He nodded once, then fled down the hall.

General Steyn grunted and pushed open the door. Inside he saw two bull-necked policemen holding a shirtless, gray-haired man against a cinder-block wall. The man's face was covered with sweat and blood. Major Graaff held a rubber truncheon high above his head, poised to strike.

"That will do, Major," General Steyn said icily.

Graaff whirled. When he saw his furious general filling the door, he froze, the truncheon still above his head. He looked back at his muscular accomplices, but after one look at General Steyn they released their bruised captive and came to stiff attention. Hauer slid slowly to his knees.

"Captain Barnard," General Steyn ordered, "place Major Graaff under arrest. You men clean the prisoner up and bring him and his companion to the visiting room." General Steyn stalked out.

Barnard drew a pistol and leveled it at Graaff. "Give me an excuse, you bloody bastard."

Hauer faced General Steyn across the long wooden table used to separate prisoners from their visitors. He had a bloody towel wrapped around his bared shoulders. Captain Barnard stood stiffly behind his superior. Gadi Abrams sat at

Hauer's left. Hauer had brushed aside their concern over his injuries and immediately gone over to the offensive.

"I simply don't have time to explain everything you want to know, General," he repeated. "Stern needs your help."

"I'm afraid that's just not good enough," General Steyn said. "Jonas Stern is a good friend of mine, a damn fine intelligence officer. He's a friend to this country. But I simply cannot agree to help without knowing more."

Hauer sighed. Stern had told him to call out the NIS in full strength—to request whatever was necessary to take Alfred Horn's isolated fortress by storm. But after what he had seen of Major Graaff, Hauer didn't share Stern's confidence in the South Africans who would be called upon to carry out that attack.

"General, did Captain Barnard inform you of the code word Stern told me to repeat to you?"

General Steyn's jaw muscles flexed. "He did."

"And still you won't agree to help me?"

"Captain Hauer, the South African government does not yield to blackmail. If by some remote misfortune Jonas Stern has seen fit to confide in you the true meaning of that code word—and if you have been trumpeting it about—I may decide that Major Graaff's tactics were *lenient*. Do you understand? Now, *do* you know the meaning of that code word?"

Hauer nodded slowly. "It's Hebrew. Literally, it means 'going up to Zion.' "

General Steyn's face flushed. "Leave us please, Captain Barnard."

Barnard reluctantly obeyed.

"General," Hauer said gravely, "*Aliyah Beth* is a secret contingency plan that mandates the evacuation by sea and air of South Africa's entire nuclear weapons arsenal and fuel stocks to Israel in the event of armed insurrection by the black population. This move will be considered a redeployment of weapons, as the warheads will remain under the control of the South African government—"

"*My God,*" General Steyn breathed. "Stern's gone mad."

"No!" Hauer argued. "General, Stern knew that the dimensions of this crisis are such that any other consideration pales beside it. I'm telling you that a nuclear threat exists *now*—*inside* this country!"

General Steyn slammed his fist down on the table. "Then

I'll have the bloody details now, Captain! Even if I have to torture you to get them!"

"You wouldn't get them in time, General. I'm sorry, but that's the way it is. Don't you understand? Your men can't be trusted. Major Graaff was on your personal staff, for God's sake! One phone call from an informant could bring about the very disaster that Stern is trying to avert. A nuclear weapon could be detonated before we leave this building!"

General Steyn came to his feet, knocking his chair to the floor. Startled, Captain Barnard rushed in with pistol drawn.

"It's all right, Barnard," the general said. The Afrikaner towered over Hauer. "Tell me something, Captain. What does Stern have to do with this? How is Israel involved?"

Hauer had been dreading this question. "General," he said slowly, "all I can tell you is that a madman possesses a nuclear weapon within the borders of your country. It could be detonated at any moment. In my opinion, any political considerations are secondary."

"Political considerations are never secondary, Captain. More's the pity. What about Thomas Horn? What's he got to do with all this?"

Hauer knew he had to tread carefully here. "General, how would you describe Herr Horn's ties to the South African government?"

"Well, he's what some would call a power broker, a behind-the-scenes type. Very reclusive. But I understand he's a force to be reckoned with in the ultraconservative enclaves. Very chummy with the old Afrikaner stock. It's the *military* Horn's tied to, you see. As you probably know, during the last few decades South Africa has been forced to become self-sufficient in many areas—especially defense. We build everything from bullets to heavy artillery and aircraft. We're damned proud of it, too. As you might imagine, anyone with Thomas Horn's industrial clout is courted constantly. His money and factories have produced untold amounts of ordnance for the army. He's involved in some very sensitive defense projects. I imagine—"

General Steyn's voice faltered. "My God. Horn is the *source* of this nuclear threat? But ... but he's one of the most patriotic men in the country!"

"Perhaps," Gadi said, speaking for the first time, "Mr. Horn isn't who he appears to be."

General Steyn eyed the Israeli suspiciously. "Just who the devil do you think he is, lad?"

When Gadi didn't reply, the general turned to Hauer. "What is it you want me to do, Captain? *Exactly?*"

Hauer looked straight into General Steyn's eyes. "I want you to place a small group of men under my command and give me until midnight before you call out the army."

The general gaped in astonishment. "You're mad! You're asking me to place South African officers under the command of a *foreign policeman?* So that he can carry out an unsanctioned and illegal operation within this republic? Is that what you're asking?"

"I'm not asking." Hauer's eyes were flat and steady. "I'm demanding it."

General Steyn reddened in outrage. "You're not in a position to demand a bloody toothpick!"

Hauer looked pointedly at his watch. "General, I have a man waiting in Pretoria for a telephone call. He has a full description of Plan *Aliyah Beth.* If he does not receive that call in the next twelve minutes, he will call the *New York Times*, the London *Daily Telegraph*, CNN, *Der Spiegel*—"

General Steyn raised his hand. "And if I don't consider that a strong enough threat?"

"You may be personally responsible for the deaths of millions of people."

Captain Bernard stood openmouthed in astonishment. He had never heard anyone speak to General Steyn like this, and the mention of hostile nuclear weapons on South African soil had all but pushed him over the brink. But General Steyn simply rubbed his right hand over his close-cropped scalp and said, "Excuse us for a moment, gentlemen. Barnard?"

When they had gone, Gadi leapt to his feet. "What the hell are you doing, Hauer? My uncle told you to get enough troops to flatten Horn's estate. You're asking for a small group of men! What are you up to?"

"I'm trying to save your damned country for you," Hauer snapped. "Since you don't have the presence of mind to do it yourself. Would you use your brain for one minute? Let's say I tell General Steyn everything. Where the bomb is, who really has it, everything. What will he do? His first impulse will be to do what Stern wants—take a battalion up there and flatten Horn's place. But guess what? While the good general is flying up to the Transvaal, he's going to realize something. He's going to realize that Alfred Horn's target is *not South Africa.* Eh? Because if it was, Horn could have sabotaged it a thousand ways before now. He'll realize that Horn's target must be *outside* South Africa, as *we* well know. And when General Steyn's political bosses find that out, they're going to realize that the smart thing to do— for South Africa—is to simply let the deal happen. Let whoever's buying that bomb land their plane, load it on board, and fly it right out of South Africa, thereby neutralizing the threat to their country."

The color drained from Gadi's face. "They wouldn't."

"They damn well would," Hauer asserted. "Even if they want to stop Horn, how can they? He's got the ultimate blackmail weapon. If they attack him, he can detonate the weapon right where he is—*inside* South Africa. And I imagine someone in the South African government knows he's crazy enough to do it."

"All right," Gadi said. "I see your point. But General Steyn isn't going to give you any men."

"He is," Hauer said calmly. "On one condition."

"What condition?"

Suddenly, the steel door clanged open. General Steyn marched in with Captain Barnard on his heels.

"Let's see," Hauer murmured to Gadi.

General Steyn stopped in front of Hauer. "Before I answer," he said, "I want to hear exactly what you want."

Hauer didn't hesitate. He'd made his shopping list while he waited in the cell. "I want an armored car. I want it mounted with a heavy machine gun, not a water cannon. I want five men from your elite counterterror unit. I don't want them to know where they're going or what the mission is, but I want them to bring along their whole bag of tricks: flash-bang grenades, body armor, flares, combat shotguns, the works."

"Mmm," the general murmured. "Is that all?"

"No. One more thing."

"Yes?"

"A Steyr-Mannlicher SSG.69."

General Steyn glanced at Captain Barnard.

"Our counterterror team uses a different sniper rifle," Barnard explained. "But I think we can get hold of a Steyr."

Hauer was still watching General Steyn. "Do I get my men, General?"

"On one condition," the Afrikaner said stiffly. "And it's nonnegotiable."

"I can't imagine what it is," Hauer said, almost smiling.

"I go with you."

Gadi's jaw dropped.

"But I'm in command," Hauer pressed.

General Steyn pursed his lips. "*Tactical* command," he allowed.

Hauer breathed a sigh of satisfaction. "Make your calls, General."

CHAPTER FORTY-TWO

5:51 P.M. *Horn House*

Jonas Stern's head, chest, and ankles had been scraped bloody by the leather restraining straps of the X-ray table. Blinding white light stabbed his eyes. He had counted forty blasts of the X-ray unit already, and in between he had heard the muffled voices of the men behind the heavy lead shield. His murderers. They had asked no questions, given no explanations, and Stern needed none. He was a Jew.

"That's 150 rads," said a voice Stern recognized as Pieter Smuts's.

"How much is that?" asked a second, eager voice. Jürgen Luhr. "How much can he take?"

"Oh, quite a bit more," Smuts replied. "And he will."

"Just a moment," said a hoarse, high-pitched voice.

Stern heard the hum of an electric wheelchair, and then Hess rounded the lead shield. Stern tried to move his head to look, but the straps held him fast. He saw only the brilliant white light overhead. Hess chuckled beside his ear.

"Pieter has devised a rather ingenious method of eliminating my Jewish problem, wouldn't you say, Herr Stern?"

Stern said nothing.

"I wanted you punished, you see," Hess explained, "but I also wanted you to live long enough to see your country destroyed."

"He may not actually *see* it, sir," Smuts interjected as he stepped around the shield. "In a few hours he will experience blindness similar to that caused by flashburns. He may or may not recover his sight."

Hess's face darkened. "But he will live long enough to know that Israel is no more?"

"If the Libyans stick to the schedule, yes. We could stretch this out for months, if you like."

Hess shook his head. "Just long enough for the Jew to see what happens to Israel. What will become of him after that?"

Smuts's voice took on a clinical detachment. "It varies. This dosage will cause severe nausea and vomiting for the next twenty-four hours. He'll have deep burns, bloody diarrhea, his hair will fall out, there'll be bone marrow destruction—"

Hess raised his hand. "How much can he stand and survive for two weeks?"

"I wouldn't push it over 500 rads, sir. Not if you want him to live until the detonation."

When Stern finally spoke, his voice was a knife blade. "In one week, Hess, you will stand in the dock before a war crimes tribunal in Jerusalem."

Hess laughed. "Yes? Well, you might be interested to know that your friend Hauer and his young Jewish companion are now in a Pretoria police cell. And General Jaap Steyn is chasing a school of red herrings at the request of my Pretoria office."

"You will be manacled," Stern went on stubbornly. "Israeli schoolchildren will file past your cell and spit in your face. History will judge you as it did your master, as one more tragic gangster with an inferiority complex—"

"Swine!" Hess shrieked. "When your skin turns black and begins to drop off, you will regret your words!"

"Don't let him provoke you, sir," Smuts said evenly. "In ten days time, Israel will be a dead island in a sea of Arabs."

"Yes," Hess rasped. "What do you think of that, Jew?"

"I think you should plead guilty," Stern retorted. "It will shorten the time you have to stand in shame before the world's cameras."

Enraged, Hess stabbed a button on his wheelchair and wheeled away toward the door. "Give him 500 rads! *Now!*"

Jürgen Luhr's hysterical laugh was cut short by a sharp knock at the door. A gray-uniformed soldier stepped in, saluted Hess, then turned to Smuts. "The radar shows one aircraft approaching, sir. Twenty kilometers out. It responded properly to the codes."

Hess smiled. "Our Libyan friends have arrived to take possession of their new toy."

"I should get up to the tower, sir," Smuts said.

"No, finish here first. I want this Jew to get his 500 rads today."

Smuts frowned. "I should be with you when you meet the Libyans. Lieutenant Luhr can finish here. The machine is set. All he need do is press the button."

Hess paused. "Very well."

"Fifty more exposures," Smuts told Luhr.

"*Jawohl*," Luhr replied, his eyes exultant.

After Smuts rolled Hess out, Luhr swaggered over to the table and leaned over Stern. "Are you enjoying this, you filthy—"

Stern spat into Luhr's open mouth. The German gagged, raised his fist high over Stern's neck, then dropped it shaking to his side. He reached up, took hold of the X-ray tube-housing and brought its barrel to within an inch of Stern's groin. Then he hurried behind the lead shield and peered through the thick bubble window.

"Let's see if we can burn your balls off, Jew," he snarled. He pressed the trigger.

6:04 P.M. *The Northern Transvaal*

The South African-built Armscor AC-200 armored car swerved off of the last road east of Giyani and crashed down onto hard veld. Six huge wheels hurled the long, wedge-shaped hull over berms and trenches at forty miles per hour—the speed of a mildly agitated rhinoceros. Machine guns bristled from the Armscor's steel hide, giving the low-slung fighting vehicle the look of a tank designed for a war on the moon. Inside, Dieter Hauer checked his watch. The hell-for-leather journey from Pretoria had taken three hours, and they still had twenty kilometers of punishing, trackless terrain to cover before they reached Horn House. He estimated they would find it about dusk—the worst possible time. It would still be light enough for the defenders to see them coming, but too dark for accurate small-arms fire by his assault team. He had tried to keep his mind off Hans's plight during the trip; he'd spent most of the ride conferring quietly with General Steyn. By concentrating on tactics, he had almost managed to ignore the fact that with Stern and the missing pages now in his custody, Hess had no reason to keep Hans and Ilse alive any longer.

The scene inside the Armscor comforted Hauer, though it would have terrified most civilians. Ever since Giyani, his team had worn their black Kevlar helmets and anti-riot respirators. These sophisticated gas masks concealed the entire face, giving their wearers the insectile look of Hollywood movie aliens. Every man also wore a full suit of black body armor. Made of Kevlar composite material fortified by ceramic tile inserts, these suits would stop not only pistol rounds and shrapnel, but high-velocity armor-piercing bullets.

Hauer could scarcely tell the men apart. He knew that General Steyn sat beside him on the metal bench seat, and that one of the men sitting across from him was Gadi Abrams. Captain Barnard was up front in the shotgun seat. The driver and the other two men were members of South Africa's elite counterterror (CT) commando unit, making up the five-man force Hauer had originally requested. All the rifles save Hauer's were South African. Gadi did not mind this, as the South African R-5 assault rifle was merely a carbine style variant of the Israeli Galil. Hauer carried the long, graceful sniper rifle he had requested from General Steyn— the Austrian-built Steyr-Mannlicher SSG.69. On the floor lay an assortment of weapons from grenades to combat shotguns.

He wrenched his respirator aside. "Stern said to expect a strong defense!" he shouted. "And I think he knows what he's talking about."

General Steyn pulled his own buglike mask off, revealing his perpetually red face. "He does, Captain. You're the one who insisted on one vehicle and five men. I would have hit this place with an airborne division!"

"And seen this corner of your country vaporized," Hauer reminded him. "What about land mines, General? Aren't they popular down here?"

"Very. We have so many unpaved roads that mines are the weapon of choice. The bottom of this vehicle is designed to deflect mine blasts upward and away, but a sustained series of hits—one large minefield, say—and we've bought it." General Steyn grinned. "I may be getting up in age, but I don't fancy a hot fragment in the balls!"

Hauer laughed. The closeness of the sound inside the respirator gave him a brief flush. Wearing a full suit of body armor was disorienting. It insulated a man from lethal projectiles, but it also isolated him from the men around him. Staring through his bubble eyeholes, Hauer wondered about the South African CT troops. General Steyn had vouched for their loyalty, but Hauer didn't count that for much. Not when one of the general's own staff officers had been on Phoenix's payroll. Hauer would have given his pension for a German GSG-9 assault team to replace the South Africans. He'd have few doubts about success then. But it was no use wishing. *You fight with what you have.*

He wondered if Jonas Stern calculated the same way. He could imagine the dilemma the Israeli was struggling with now—*if* Stern was still alive. If it came to a choice between detonating a nuclear weapon on South African soil or letting it be captured by Arab fanatics sworn to destroy Israel, Hauer knew Stern would not hesitate to turn this corner of South Africa into a radioactive wasteland. If the choice were between Germany and South Africa, he knew he would do the same. He only prayed it wouldn't come to that.

Across the narrow aisle, the South Africans sat like Sphinxes behind their black masks. Hauer finally discerned the smoldering gaze of Gadi Abrams through the bubble eyes of one respirator. Hauer stared back, trying to read the message in the Israeli's dark eyes. The best he could come up with was, *"I trust only you and me, and I'm not too sure about you,"* before the young commando turned away.

Hauer felt exactly the same.

6:11 P.M. Horn House

This time Smuts did not meet the Libyans on the runway. He waited in the relative security of the reception hall with his master. *If they don't like being met by a kaffir,* he thought, *to hell with them.* Hess sat in his wheelchair beside Smuts, wearing a gray suit-jacket and black eyepatch. He had once again assumed the role of Alfred Horn. Smuts peered through a window as his Zulu driver goosed the Range Rover up the final crescent of the drive. When the Libyan delegation climbed out, Smuts immediately noticed the ratio of four bodyguards to two negotiators. On the last trip, he recalled, that ratio had been reversed. He also noted the conspicuous absence of Major Ilyas Karami.

Smuts had expected something like this, and despite Hess's optimism, he had prepared for treachery. He had two marksmen waiting in the corridors on either side of the reception hall, and he had reinforcements on the way. This morning, when Major Graaff had called to report that he had taken Dieter Hauer into custody, Smuts had requested a contingent of NIS men to bolster his own force. Graaff had enthusiastically agreed. Smuts hoped they would arrive soon. He took a last look at his marksmen, then opened the great teak door and stepped back.

Wearing flowing white robes, Prime Minister Jalloud swept into the hall and threw his arms wide in greeting. "Herr Horn!" he exclaimed. "The historic day has come! Allah has brought us here safely. May He smile upon our business!"

Hess nodded curtly. "*Guten Abend,* Herr Prime Minister."

Dr. Sabri and the four bodyguards stepped over the threshold.

"Where is Major Karami?" Smuts asked. "I had hoped to see him again."

Jalloud smiled. "I'm afraid Major Karami was called away at the last moment to attend to pressing military matters."

I'll bet he was, Smuts thought wryly, flexing his fists to channel off tension. "Sorry to hear it."

"Would anyone like refreshments?" Hess asked. "It is a long flight from Tripoli."

"I'm afraid Our Leader has forbidden any delay, Herr Horn," Jalloud said softly. "He awaits our return with the utmost anticipation."

"To business then. I assume you wish Dr. Sabri to verify the weapon's operational readiness before we load it?"

"If we might so impose," Jalloud said timidly.

In that instant, inexplicably, Smuts decided that if trouble was coming, Prime Minister Jalloud knew nothing about it. The Afrikaner signaled his marksmen by touching his right eyebrow with his right hand. He intended to trigger any treachery long before the Libyans gained access to the basement complex.

"With all respect, Mr. Prime Minister," he said, "I must

ask that your bodyguards wait here. We allow no firearms in the basement."

Jalloud looked uncomfortable. "But Our Leader provided these men to assist with the loading of the weapon."

"The bomb weighs more than a thousand kilograms," Smuts replied. "It must be loaded mechanically. In fact, I have my doubts about your jet's ability to carry both the weapon and passengers. I had assumed you would bring a cargo plane."

"I see," Jalloud said slowly, wondering why no one in Tripoli had thought of this. *Or perhaps,* he thought with a shiver, *someone did.* "By all means," he said. He turned to the bodyguards. "You will wait here while Dr. Sabri checks the weapon."

Taken aback by this request, the soldiers hesitated. Their orders had been to wait until they gained access to the basement before carrying out their mission. But the Afrikaner had forced their hand. Simultaneously reaching the same conclusion, Major Karami's four assassins raised their Uzis as one.

Their faces showed even more surprise than Prime Minister Jalloud's when Smuts's concealed marksmen opened fire with their R-5 assault rifles. The gray-clad Afrikaners emptied their clips into the line of assassins from eight meters away, blowing all four backward against the great teak door.

"The elevator!" Smuts shouted. "Everyone get inside! *Move!"*

While Hess's wheelchair whirred toward the open elevator, Prime Minister Jalloud and Dr. Sabri shouted frantic Arabic and crawled along behind him. Jalloud took a bullet in the left arm, but in his panic he barely felt it. Smuts had looked back to make sure that Hess was safe inside the elevator when a stunned Libyan sat up with a wild cry and let off a long burst of bullets in his direction.

"Body armor!" Smuts shouted. "Head shots only!"

Bullets ricocheted through the marble-floored reception hall. One Libyan took Smuts's advice before the Afrikaners did; his teflon-coated 9mm slugs exploded the head of one of Smuts's marksmen like a cantaloupe. The surviving Afrikaner avenged this loss, then scurried to shelter behind a large rosewood chiffonier against the far wall. Another Libyan darted outside to use the doorway as a firing position. Two seconds later he staggered back into the great hall, blood spurting from his throat. Smuts's Zulu driver appeared in the doorway with a long hunting knife in his hand. The Zulu moved quickly to another downed Arab, dispatched him with his knife, then fell to a long burst from the surviving Libyan assassin. Smuts's marksman knocked down the last Libyan as Smuts himself hustled Jalloud and the dazed physicist into the cubicle where Hess waited.

"Stay here!" Smuts ordered his marksman. "I'll reinforce you soon."

The elevator door slid shut. Ten seconds later, the last Libyan to fall opened his eyes, brought up his Uzi and fired a sustained burst from the floor. Two slugs struck the Afrikaner guard in the head, killing him instantly. Groaning in agony, Major Karami's last surviving assassin began crawling toward the elevator.

From Hans and Ilse's bedroom the skirmish in the reception hall sounded like the Battle of the Bulge. When the firing stopped, Hans shoved open the door.

"Where do we go?" he asked. "Should we try to get out? They're probably guarding the main doors."

Ilse poked her head outside the door. "There's nowhere to run, I told you! We've only got one chance! Stern!"

Hans could think of no better plan. "All right," he said. "But stay *behind* me, understand?"

Another burst of machine gun fire rattled in the reception hall. "Behind you," Ilse murmured, wondering where Smuts might be holding Stern.

Keeping close to the wall, they started down the corridor, away from the sound of the gunfire.

High in the observatory tower, Pieter Smuts searched the airstrip through a pair of powerful Zeiss field glasses. Dusk was falling fast. He saw the wreckage of the JetRangers shot down last night spread out over the eastern end of the runway. In the midst of the debris sat Hess's own Lear, scorched black and missing most of its tail. There was a single guard standing beneath the Libyan Learjet. No one else. Where was the main body of the assault force? Where was Major Karami?

Behind Smuts, Hess nodded restlessly in his wheelchair. He was trying desperately to fathom the reason for the Libyan soldiers' attempt to kill their prime minister. Jalloud himself sat propped against a bank of satellite receivers, moaning from the pain of his shattered arm. Shaking in fear, Dr. Sabri ministered to him as best he could.

"No sign of Karami yet," Smuts said, pulling the field glasses away from his eyes. "But it will be dark soon. That's when he'll come."

"Who?" Hess murmured, still dazed by the suddenness of the attack.

"Yes," Jalloud groaned. "It is Karami. It must be."

Smuts glanced at the Vulcan gun. A trim young Afrikaner sat in the firing cage, his alert eyes checking the fearsome weapon's night-vision system. Three more gray-clad South Africans manned the radar and communications gear.

"*Why?*" Hess cried indignantly. "Has Qaddafi gone mad?"

Smuts chuckled quietly. "He always has been. We knew this was a risk. We needed more time."

"Sir," interrupted a radar controller, "I show one aircraft approaching from the north. He's very close. He must have been flying ten feet off the veld!"

Smuts pressed a button on his console. "Attention unidentified aircraft," he said tersely. "You have entered restricted airspace. Turn back now or you will be fired upon. Repeat, turn or be fired upon."

"It must be the Air Zimbabwe jet," said the radar man. "An hour ago I marked him as a civil airliner bound for Jo'burg. He must have sneaked off his flight path after he went into the ground clutter."

Smuts waved his hand to the Vulcan gunner. The Afrikaner donned his targeting goggles and depressed two foot pedals. With a deep hydraulic hum the entire turret rotated to face the airstrip.

Inside the approaching Yak-42, Major Ilyas Karami stood behind the anxious pilot and listened indifferently to Smuts's flint-edged threats.

"Do they have anti-aircraft guns, Major?" the pilot asked.

"Shut up!" Karami snapped. "You know what to say."

The pilot picked up his mike. "This is Air Zimbabwe Flight 132," he said in a quavering voice. "We are in distress. We have an avionics malfunction. Do you read?"

"Major Karami," crackled Smuts's voice. "This is your final warning. Turn back now or be shot out of the sky."

"Your mother fucks goats!" Karami bellowed.

"He knows who you are!" cried the pilot. "The mission's been compromised! We're unarmed! We must turn back!"

Suddenly a brilliant line of tracer fire flashed up through the gray clouds. It passed high over the nose of the jet, then swung back and forth, searching out the airborne intruder.

"Allah protect us!" the pilot wailed, instinctively beginning an evasive maneuver. He had flown MiG fighters in combat, but to sit helpless in an unarmed airliner was a new and terrifying experience for him.

Karami pulled a pistol from his hip holster and laid the barrel against the pilot's temple. "Land this whore!" he shouted. "Now!"

"*Where?*" shrieked the pilot.

"I see the flares!" the copilot yelled. "Dive!"

Steeling his nerves, the pilot banked sharply and headed down toward a line of flares laid by Jalloud's "bodyguards." It would be a belly-flop landing, but he didn't care. Never in his life had he wanted so badly to get on the ground.

Smuts cursed as he saw the chain of green starbursts light up the center line of the runway. *"Shoot out the flares!"* he screamed. "They can't land without them!"

"My goggles are going crazy!" the gunner protested. "I can't see a bloody thing!"

"Take them off! *Shoot!*"

The roar of the Vulcan blotted out everything. Hess covered his ears and shouted something, but no one heard him. The gunner made a valiant effort to extinguish the flares, but only succeeded in knocking a few out of line. The main effect of the Vulcan was to rip the surface of the newly laid asphalt to pieces.

Suddenly Hess gasped in horror. Dropping out of the sky like a great prehistoric bird was the Libyan Yak-42. It roared past the turret in profile as it fell earthward.

"There they are!" Smuts yelled. *"Fire! Fire!"*

The gunner depressed his trigger. Scarlet tracer rounds arced from the Vulcan's flaming barrels, reaching out for the black apparition . . .

Suddenly the turret's elevator door hissed open. Smuts turned in disbelief, then dived protectively across Hess's wheelchair.

Inside the elevator—propped on the floor with his back

against the wall—was the surviving Libyan assassin. He screamed a curse, raised his Uzi and fired. Bullets sprayed wildly throughout the confined space, hammering the polycarbonate windows and tearing through the faceplates of sensitive electronic gear. One of the South African technicians took a round in the back of the head and fell dead over his console. The radar technician managed to draw his pistol and get off three shots before a ricochet caught him in the neck.

And then there was silence. The Libyan had run out of ammunition. Smuts heaved himself off of Hess, picked up the dead radar man's pistol, and shot the Libyan twice through the face. It took him three more seconds to realize the true significance of the silence. The Vulcan had stopped firing! When Smuts whirled he saw why. His gunner had been blinded by flying glass. Worse, the Vulcan's electronic targeting system had been damaged beyond repair!

"The prime minister has been hit again!" Dr. Sabri cried.

Smuts took no notice of the physicist. He darted to the broad window. The Libyan jet had landed safely! Through his field glasses he watched fifty commandos spill onto the tarmac. He forced himself to stay calm. Soon the Libyans would be at the edge of the shallow bowl that surrounded the house. *Inside the killing zone.* He dropped his field glasses and jerked the bleeding gunner from the Vulcan's operating chair, then climbed in himself. He put his eyes to the visual aiming goggles and scanned the airstrip. Beneath a wide door in the rear of the Yak-42 he saw Arabs lowering some type of artillery piece from the plane by means of winches. Smuts grinned like a demon and opened fire. The armor-piercing bullets streaked across the Wash and raced toward the plane.

But just as the tracer beam reached the laboring Arabs, Smuts released the trigger. Destroying the jet might not be the smartest option in these circumstances, he realized. With no means of escape, the Libyans might fight twice as fiercely to take the house. As he watched the Arabs beneath the plane, Smuts noticed something sitting about ten meters behind the Yak-42's tail. It was a pickup truck. *What the hell is that for?* he wondered. Then he knew. They'd brought the truck to tow the big gun and to haul their stolen bomb from the house to the plane! Smuts jammed his thumb down on the Vulcan's trigger. It took longer than normal to acquire the Toyota using visual aiming only, but once he did, the uranium-tipped slugs chewed the Toyota into scrap metal in seconds. The gas tank fireballed and set aflame three Libyans beneath the plane.

Smuts climbed out of the Vulcan and went to the panel of switches that controlled his Claymore mines. His only real worry was the heavy gun. He would wait until the soldiers got it away from the plane; then he would destroy men and machine together. He pressed a button on the console and spoke crisply: "Bunker gunners, prepare to fire at will." He turned to Hess. "We'd better raise the shields, sir. We can't risk letting even one man get into the basement complex."

"The prime minister is dead!" howled Dr. Sabri from the floor.

Hess rolled his wheelchair over to the bloodied mound of robes lying near the base of the Vulcan. Prime Minister Jalloud—minus the lower part of his face—stared blankly upward at the steel roof of the turret. Two of the Libyan's bullets had found him.

"The shields, sir," Smuts repeated, reaching for the appropriate button.

"Wait!" Hess ordered. "Frau Apfel is still in the outer triangle."

Smuts grimaced with forbearance. "As are Lieutenant Luhr, Linah, the medical staff, the rest of the servants, and the Jew. Sir, we cannot afford to wait."

The old man's frantic eyes searched the closed-circuit television monitors above their heads. Although the cameras showed most of the outer rooms, he saw no sign of Ilse. "But . . . Pieter, she saved my life! If we shut her outside—"

"The Libyans will never reach the house," Smuts assured him, his voice taut. "But we *must* raise the shields, just in case."

"Very well," Hess said thickly. "Raise the shields."

Smuts pressed the button. Throughout Horn House, black anodized metal shields rose up from the floor, blocking every door, staircase, and window leading from the outer wings to the central complex. The Afrikaner sighed with satisfaction.

Suddenly an explosion rocked the turret. Leaping to the window in alarm, Smuts heard the distinctive *crump* of a mortar. Seconds later a round fell just short of the outer wall of the house. Two more crashed through the roof of the west wing. Horn House was on fire. As if urged forward by the flames, twenty Libyan commandos started across the killing zone at a fast run.

"Damn you, Karami!" Smuts shouted. He climbed back into the Vulcan and opened up on the Libyan mortar positions. He quickly silenced one, but a replacement immediately took its place. After forty seconds of continuous firing, the Vulcan's drum magazine ran out. Smuts screamed at one of his soldiers: "Hurry, man! Load the fucking gun!"

While the Libyan machine guns chattered and the mortar shells rained down on the outer walls, Smuts scanned the dark rim of the bowl. Just as he started to look away from the horizon, he saw the help he had desperately hoped for. A hundred meters southeast of the Libyans, a squat black shape stood silhouetted against the lesser shadow of the falling night. A pair of halogen headlamps winked once, twice, then died. The black shape crept slowly forward, hesitated again.

By God, that's Graaff, Smuts thought with elation. "It's Major Graaff!" he cried. "He made it!" Smuts hammered his fists against the Vulcan in triumph. If he knew Graaff, that armored car was only the spearhead of a veritable army!

"Drum loaded!" shouted the man beneath the Vulcan.

Smuts fired a celebratory burst into the darkening sky, then he opened up on the Libyans with a vengeance.

CHAPTER FORTY-THREE

Poised on the ridge above Smuts's killing zone, Hauer watched the burst of spectacular tracer fire lance up into the sky from the observatory turret.

"That's it!" he shouted. "They think Major Graaff sent us! Go!"

"Wait!" General Steyn called to the Armscor's driver. "Look at that tracer fire, Hauer. That's a rotary cannon. This vehicle's tough, but they could blow us to pieces in seconds with that gun."

Hauer ripped his respirator aside. "General, you gave me tactical command of this operation!"

"I'm sorry, but I can't let you sacrifice my men without any hope of success."

"They think we're here to *help* them! We've got a clear path to the house!"

General Steyn shook his head. "We need reinforcements."

Hauer stared in disbelief. He had come too far to be stopped here by one man's lack of nerve. He struggled to keep his voice steady. "General, my only son is down there. And the longer we wait, the greater the chance that he will be executed. If I must, I'll go down there alone and on foot."

"You won't have to, Captain."

Gadi Abrams's pledge was punctuated by the *chunk* of his assault rifle being cocked. He did not point it at anyone, but the threat was plain enough. General Steyn's hand moved toward the pistol at his hip. Gadi ripped his gas mask off and gave the general a look of open contempt.

"Israel fights," he said quietly. "Germany fights. What of South Africa?"

General Steyn's red face whitened. He knew he was being manipulated, but in front of his men the Israeli's challenge was simply too personal to ignore. He leaned forward into the driver's compartment and shouted, "Over the top!"

Hans and Ilse dashed down the smoky corridor with towels held over their faces. Horn House was burning, and the inner complex was sealed against them. They had searched nearly every room in the outer triangle of the house, yet they had seen no sign of Stern. Only panicked servants and their children. Hans carried an attaché case in his right hand; they had brought it from Horn's study.

"Hurry!" Ilse called. "It's the only room we haven't checked!"

As they neared the hospital unit, she wondered why she had skipped it before. But she knew: the nauseating memory of being strapped to the X-ray table had simply been too horrible to face again. Now she had no choice. She felt a jolt of terror as she eased open the infirmary door. The room was dark, but the smell of alcohol hit her immediately. Signaling Hans to follow, she crept through the shadows toward the interior doors. A crack of light shone beneath one of them. Halfway to the door, she froze. The sound had stopped her. The terrifying buzz cut short by the low, metallic *clang*. Ilse closed her eyes in remembered terror, then opened them again. She padded over to a countertop and felt her way along it. "Here," she whispered, closing her hand around the base of a heavy microscope.

Hans set down the briefcase and took the scope.

Ilse turned the doorknob as quietly as she could. As she pushed on the metal door, the sound came again. Buzz . . . *clang*. In the eerie amber glow of the X-ray machine's dials Ilse saw a blond man standing with his back to her. He was peering through the thick bubble window in the lead radiation screen.

"Are your balls getting warm yet, Jew?" the man called. He cackled wildly.

Ilse gasped.

The figure whirled.

"You," Hans murmured.

Luhr wore his police uniform, the green trousers tucked into his spit-polished boots. He looked first at Hans, then at Ilse. He laughed derisively. "You stubborn *Arschloch*. Don't you know when to quit?" He dropped the cable trigger. "This time Funk isn't here to stop me."

"He's the one, Hans," Ilse said hoarsely. "The one who cut the policeman's throat in Berlin."

"That's right," Luhr said with a laugh. "Just like slaughtering a fucking pig."

"Steuben," said Hans, his voice trembling. He felt his throat constrict with unspeakable hatred. He looked down at the microscope in his hand, then let it crash to the floor.

"Frau Apfel?" cried a weak voice. *"Is that you?"*

Ilse darted around the lead shield. Jonas Stern lay pale and bloodied beneath the leather straps that had bound her just two days ago. "Hans!" she cried. "Help me!"

Hans heard nothing. He watched Luhr's lips tighten into a thin, pale line as he dropped his shoulders like a boxer and moved out from the X-ray machine. Hans's nerves tingled like live wires. Luhr feinted with his right hand and kicked Hans high in the chest. Hans took the blow, staggered, steadied himself. Luhr jabbed with his left hand. Hans did nothing to block it. He felt his right cheek tear, but he ignored the pain. A crashing roundhouse struck him on the side of the head. He absorbed the shock, but this time he raised his fists and moved forward. Backpedaling away, Luhr fired off a right that drilled into Hans's eye socket. Hans roared in pain, but he shook the tears out of his eyes and lunged blindly forward.

As Luhr pivoted to evade him, he felt his back collide with the faceplate of the X-ray machine. At that instant Hans lashed out. His fist moved from his side to the bridge of Luhr's nose without seeming to cross the space between. One moment Luhr's face was pale with fury, the next it was covered in blood. Hans had broken his nose. Luhr screamed in agony, then tried to bull his way out of the corner. Hans stood him up against the machine and hit him three times fast in the solar plexus. Luhr sank to the floor. Hans tasted blood in his mouth. He picked up the heavy microscope and held it high above his head. His arm shivered from the weight. One blow would crush Luhr's skull like an eggshell.

"This is for Weiss," he muttered.

"Wait!" rasped a male voice.

Hans turned slowly, the microscope still high above his head. He saw a tall, wiry man wearing sweat-soaked trousers and an undershirt leaning unsteadily on Ilse's shoulder.

"Not that way," said Stern, his voice strangely flat.

Luhr lay gulping for air at Hans's feet. Slowly he got onto

all fours. Hans kicked him in the stomach, then turned back and stared at the tanned stranger. The beaked nose ... the weathered, hawklike face. "I've seen you," Hans said.

"Yes, Sergeant," Stern replied. "You have. Now pick that man up and put him on the table."

"We don't have time for this!" Ilse cried. "The house is burning! We have to find a way through those shields! A few exposures won't even hurt him!"

"Put that animal on the table!"

Hans stunned Luhr with a kick to the head, then he hoisted him onto his shoulder and hauled him around to the X-ray table. As soon as he dumped him there, Ilse strapped him down with the leather restraints.

"Get out!" Stern barked. "Both of you!"

Hans watched fascinated as the Israeli lifted the broken microscope from the floor and smashed it down onto the cable trigger Luhr had dropped.

"Shut off the power," Stern commanded.

Ilse found the ON/OFF switch and flipped it. Stern fiddled with the tangled mess in his hands for a few moments, then dropped it and stepped up to the bubble window in the shield.

"Turn the power back on."

Ilse obeyed. The entire room seemed to vibrate for four seconds; then it went still. Luhr's scream of terror rent the acrid air. Again the X-ray unit fired. The indescribable *buzz* ... *clang* chilled Ilse's heart. Stern had permanently closed the circuit in the cable trigger. The X-ray tube would continue to fire, recharge, and fire again until someone finally shut off the power or a fuse burned out. Luhr shrieked like a man trapped in a pit of snakes.

Hans looked up at Stern's lined face. He saw nothing written there. Not satisfaction, not hatred. Nothing at all.

"Let's go," said Stern, pulling his eyes away from Luhr's struggling body.

Ilse held up the black briefcase Hans had been carrying. "We've got the Spandau papers. We found them in Horn's study. The other book, too."

"The Zinoviev notebook?"

Ilse nodded. "Everything."

"Good girl." Stern grabbed her arm and hustled her into the hall. Hans backed slowly out of the room, his eyes still glued to the bubble window in the lead shield. The X-ray machine continued to fire in four-second intervals.

Four hundred meters of open ground separated the ridge of the bowl from Horn House. The Armscor had covered barely a hundred when a fierce hammering assaulted Hauer's ears. They were taking fire from the Libyan machine-gun positions on the ridge behind them. Captain Barnard was sitting in the Armscor's shotgun seat. Hauer grabbed his shoulder.

"Can you raise the tower on that radio, Captain?"

"I can try."

"Do it! Tell them to give us cover!"

Pulling off his helmet and respirator, Barnard began working through the frequencies on the radio. Hauer glanced back into the crew compartment. At the Armscor's firing slits, the black-clad team of commandos worked their R5 carbines like men on an assembly line. One man's head and shoulders were thrust into the tiny turret mounted atop the Armscor; he swiveled the .30 caliber machine gun between the Libyan positions with deadly accuracy. Yet Libyan bullets still pounded the vehicle's armor. Hauer turned again and watched Horn House growing larger in the Armscor's reinforced windshield: 250 meters and closing.

Suddenly an alien voice began speaking inside the vehicle. *Phoenix to Graaff . . . Phoenix to Graaff . . . Do you read?* The tension in Pieter Smuts's voice was like a cable stretched near to breaking. *Phoenix to Graaff! Where are your reinforcements?*

"Answer him!" Hauer told Captain Barnard. "Tell him Graaff's manning our turret gun!"

Hauer looked out at the house again: 160 meters. He gave Barnard an encouraging punch on the shoulder; then he ducked back into the crew compartment to confer with General Steyn.

The instant Hauer left the compartment, the driver lashed out with his elbow and struck Captain Barnard in the side of the head. The Armscor lurched to a halt 140 meters from Horn House. Hauer flew forward and crashed against a steel bulkhead; only his helmet prevented him from cracking his skull. The driver snatched up the radio microphone and began transmitting rapidly in Afrikaans:

"Armscor to Phoenix! Armscor to Phoenix! It's a trick! Trap! Trap! Major Graaff isn't here . . ."

Dazed, Hauer lunged back into the driver's compartment. He did not understand Afrikaans, but he recognized a warning. Taking hold of the driver's head, he wrenched with all his might, hoping to snap the man's cervical vertebrae. The driver went suddenly stiff, then limp.

"Take the wheel!" Hauer shouted at Captain Barnard. While Hauer dragged the driver back into the crew compartment, Captain Barnard scrambled into the driver's seat and wrestled the Armscor into gear. The vehicle lurched forward, back, then began rolling toward the house again.

Hauer laid the senseless driver against the Armscor's side hatch and tore off his own respirator. *"Another traitor!"* he yelled to General Steyn.

General Steyn ripped off his gas mask. His face was flushed with anger and disbelief. At his feet the traitor squirmed and flung his arms upward. In a fit of rage Gadi kicked open the Armscor's side hatch and shoved the driver out onto the veld. By the time Gadi shut the hatch, a Libyan machine gunner had riddled the man's body with .30 caliber slugs.

The Armscor shivered as another Libyan machine gunner locked onto the tail of the armored car. Hauer grabbed General Steyn's arm. "I don't know if the tower heard that warning, but—"

The sudden, steel-ripping roar of the Vulcan obliterated both Hauer's voice and the rattle of the Libyan machine guns.

Hauer leapt up to a firing slit. His stomach rolled as he watched the blazing tracer line march toward the nose of the Armscor. He had seen similar guns on American tank-killing planes on maneuvers in Germany. The rotary guns mounted in their stubby snouts spewed out 5000 depleted-uranium slugs per minute—enough to turn a T-72 tank into a burning hulk in seconds.

Captain Barnard swerved to avoid the oncoming tracer beam, but the Vulcan gunner simply adjusted his fire. Barnard screamed as the shells churned up the earth directly in front of the Armscor. Then suddenly—miraculously—the fiery stream of death winked out.

"He's jammed!" Hauer shouted. *"Go! Go!"*

The Armscor surged forward. Like a hailstorm from hell,

slugs pounded the vehicle from every side as Smuts's bunker gunners opened up from their concealed positions. Hauer peered out through a gun port, trying to pinpoint the source of the fire.

"Bunkers!" he shouted. "They're dug into the hill!"

From a slit on the Armscor's right side, Gadi fired his R5 assault rifle in careful, three-round bursts, aiming for the muzzle flashes of the bunker guns. *"Momser!"* he shouted, but no one heard him. The noise inside the Armscor had reached a deafening level. Hauer was leaning into the driver's compartment to urge Captain Barnard forward when Pieter Smuts detonated the first string of Claymore mines.

Two Claymores exploded directly beneath the Armscor, hurling the eighteen tons of hardened steel into the air like a child's toy. The vehicle tottered on its three right wheels, then crashed back onto all six and continued toward the house. Another string of Claymores exploded in front of the Armscor; hundreds of steel balls scythed into its hull, shattering the polycarbonate windshield. Captain Barnard screamed in pain, but the Armscor kept rolling.

Hauer's mind raced: they still had more than a hundred meters to cover. The mines could be handled, but not under the fire of the tower gun. If the gunner cleared his weapon in the next thirty seconds, they didn't stand a chance. The Vulcan had to be silenced.

"Stop!" he roared. "Turn this thing sideways and stop!"

Captain Barnard—not enthusiastic about hitting any more mines himself—gladly obeyed. Hauer turned back to General Steyn and his men. "Pour it in! I'm going out!"

One of the masked men jumped down from a firing slit, ripped off his respirator and grabbed Hauer's arm. It was Gadi. "If you go out there, you're dead!" he yelled.

Hauer jerked his arm free. "Just keep those bunker guns off me!"

While Gadi stared, Hauer snatched up his sniper rifle and unlatched the Armscor's side hatch. The full din of battle filled the vehicle. Holding the Steyr-Mannlicher close against his body, Hauer took a deep breath, and leaped outside.

He hit the ground hard and rolled beneath the huge vehicle, praying no one had seen him. He got to one knee. There was almost enough room for him to stand beneath the Armscor's undercarriage. The six giant wheels provided a wall from behind which he could fire in relative safety. Bracing his right knee behind one of the giant tires, he raised the Steyr to his shoulder and sighted in on the tower. The last light of dusk had almost gone. He had no night-vision scope, but the standard Kahles-Helios ZF69 optical scope was excellent. Even in near darkness it brought the tower in nicely.

When Hauer saw the turret in detail, he groaned. At 120 meters, accuracy wasn't the problem. With the Steyr, he could fire ten bullets into a sixteen-inch circle from six times that distance. The problem was the "glass" he saw forming part of the turret's circular wall. It would undoubtedly be made of transparent composite armor. Through the scope he searched for a weakness suited to his weapon. *The turret rotates,* he realized, noticing the huge gears mounted beneath the observatory dome. *But I can't damage those gears.* Twelve seconds later Hauer spotted his chance. Just where the Vulcan's six barrels protruded from the "glass," a narrow port had been cut so that the gun could be traversed vertically. Hauer felt the hair on the back of his neck rise. He could see men working frantically to clear the jammed weapon.

He laid his cross hairs on the tiny port and chambered a round into the breech. The Steyr accepted a ten-round magazine, but like most sniper rifles it was bolt-action. He would get one perfect chance, then nine snap shots. He took a deep breath and pressed his body into the huge tire that shielded him. He felt the reassuring weight of the rifle on his shoulder, the wooden stock cool and familiar against his stubbled cheek. The sound of the battle grew dim and distant as he focused on his target, melding his eye with the tiny crack between the Vulcan's barrels and the armored glass. In his mind, the coin-sized target expanded into a saucer, then a dinner plate ... His finger settled firmly on the trigger. *Squeeze* ...

The instant before Hauer fired, a blast of flame erupted from the Vulcan's spinning barrels. Tracer rounds arced out toward the rim of the bowl. The turret began to rotate ...

He felt his shot disintegrating. His shoulder twitched, his stomach heaved in sudden confusion. All around he heard the desperate rattle of guns firing at the moving turret, all to no avail. The dazzling beam marched from position to position, silencing one gun after another. He felt a sudden surge of hope. The gunner was ignoring the Armscor! *He thinks we're out of the fight! Because we're not moving, he thinks his bunker guns stopped us!* Hauer searched swiftly for a shot. With the turret rotating, hitting the tiny gun port was out of the question. Instead he picked a spot a few centimeters to the left of the Vulcan's barrel—the spot he estimated the gunner would be sitting behind.

He fired.

Nothing happened. His bullet struck the very millimeter of glass he had aimed for, but the transparent armor was simply too strong. How many perfect shots would it take to drill through the polycarbonate? Like an automaton Hauer worked the bolt-action rifle, tracking his moving target. *Fire! Eject shell, close bolt, fire!* The transparent wall shuddered as Hauer's slugs relentlessly hammered the same single square of armor. Six shots . . . seven . . . eight . . . *Fire! Eject shell, close bolt, fire!* He jerked out the empty magazine and loaded his spare.

Around him the battle raged on. The Vulcan whined, the bunker guns chattered, the hull of the armored car rattled like a tin can in a hailstorm. He smelled the burning phosphorus of tracer rounds as they streaked across the field in brilliant, lethal arcs. Suddenly, with a strange shiver, Hauer sensed the Vulcan's tracer beam stagger somewhere off to his right. He jerked his eye away from the scope and scanned the dark field. *Christ!* The gunner had spotted his muzzle flashes! His mouth went dry as the Vulcan's angle of fire lowered toward him.

Every fiber of his being screamed, *"Run!"* He shut his eyes against the fear, then forced himself to open them again and put his right eye back to the scope. *Somewhere up there,* he thought fiercely, *is the man who is trying to kill me.* He could feel the Vulcan's slugs hitting the ground, thousands in each burst, like the first shuddering waves of an earthquake. The roar seemed to swallow up the very air. And the *light* . . . it was mesmerizing, like some lunatic laser beam.

The tracer beam slowed as it neared the Armscor. Smuts wanted to be sure he did not miss. In that moment of hesitation Hauer steadied his twitching muscles, fixed his eye upon the tiny square of armored glass he had spent his first magazine against, and opened fire.

Pieter Smuts found his mark first. In the first two seconds of contact, the Vulcan slammed two hundred shells into the

Armscor's tail, shearing off a quarter-ton of hardened steel armor. The vehicle shuddered like a great wounded beast; black smoke poured into the air. Suddenly the Armscor's turbocharged V-8 diesel roared to life. In a last frantic bid for survival Captain Barnard floored the accelerator. The armored car bolted forward like a wild bronco, leaping out of the Vulcan's line of fire and leaving Hauer exposed on the ground.

Stunned, kneeling alone on the dark plain, Hauer raised his rifle and pressed his eye to the scope. Dirt showered over him as the Vulcan's bullets thundered after the Armscor just meters away. *There is nothing here,* said a voice in his brain, *nothing but you and the man behind that gun . . .*

He fired.

His bullet starred the glass.

He fired again.

The tracer beam jinked away from the Armscor and moved back toward him. Too late Smuts had realized where the real danger lay.

With the Vulcan gun thundering down upon him, Dieter Hauer actually closed his eyes as he fired his last shot. The tracer beam stuttered, flashed again . . . winked out.

The spell was broken. Hauer scrambled to his feet and dashed after the Armscor. Gadi Abrams dragged him back through the hatch.

"You crazy German bastard!"

The Armscor was filling rapidly with oily black smoke. "Everybody shoot!" Hauer shouted. "Clear a path through the mines! Detonate everything in our path!"

One Claymore exploded harmlessly nearby, but no more. The Armscor had reached the section of ground where Burton's Colombians had been slaughtered the night before. The mines here had been spent, no replacements laid. The Armscor roared forward and reached Horn House in twenty seconds flat.

Captain Barnard pulled the vehicle across the main entrance like a barricade. Instantly two South African CT troops thrust shotguns through the ports and blasted the hinges off the teakwood door. When Hauer shoved open the side hatch, he was staring straight into the marble reception hall where Major Karami's assassins lay dead.

"Move out!" he shouted.

"Wait!" General Steyn was up in the driver's compart-

ment, leaning over Captain Barnard. Hauer remembered the young man had taken some glass in the face when the windshield shattered, but as he peered over the general's beefy shoulder he realized that Captain Barnard was suffering from a mortal wound.

"Where is it, son?" General Steyn asked softly.

"My chest . . . sir."

Carefully the general probed the young man's torso.

"I thought he was wearing a vest," Hauer said quietly.

General Steyn pulled a bloodstained hand from beneath Barnard's right arm. "There's a splinter of polycarbonate sticking out of him," he whispered. "Right where the vest stops at the underarm. God only knows how deep it went in." He turned back to Captain Barnard. "Can you move, lad?"

The young man tried to smile, then coughed in agony. "It feels like the damned thing is buried in my heart. Like a sword . . . swear to God. Go on."

General Steyn's neck flushed red. "Nonsense, lad, you're coming with us."

"Don't move me, sir," Captain Barnard gurgled. "Please don't."

General Steyn looked ready to twist off the head of the man who had caused this pain. Setting his mouth in a grim line, he drew a .45 caliber pistol from Captain Barnard's belt and placed it carefully in the young man's hand. "If it gets too bad," he said tersely, "you know what to do." The general swallowed the lump in his throat. "I'll be back for you, Barnard. You have my solemn word. Stand fast."

General Steyn turned and squeezed his broad shoulders back through the door of the driver's compartment. His bluff face was swollen with emotion. He looked hard into Hauer's eyes. "If it's a war they want," he said, his voice trembling, "then it's a bloody war they'll get." He drew his own pistol and jerked back the slide.

"Into the house, lads!"

Pieter Smuts staggered away from the Vulcan and wiped the blood out of his eyes with his shirtsleeve. A dozen slivers of armored glass had been driven into his face by Hauer's slugs. He crouched beside Hess's wheelchair.

"They've breached the outer walls, sir. I don't know

who's inside that armored car, but they must be friends of the Jew."

Hess grimaced. "Who could it be but Captain Hauer?" he wheezed. "I told you never to underestimate an old German soldier. Hauer obviously outsmarted Major Graaff! *Damn* the man! A German! A German attacking *me!*"

"We can still stop them, sir."

"How?"

"If I order our bunker gunners to cease firing, the Libyans will advance and kill anyone left alive outside the shields."

"True," Hess said thoughtfully. "But then the Libyans will be inside the house."

"But not inside the *shields*. Not near you—not near the weapons."

Hess hesitated, realizing that the order would mean certain death for Ilse, Linah, and all of the servants. "Do it," he said finally.

Smuts pressed a button on his console and issued the order. Outside, the rattle of the bunker guns stuttered, then died.

In the eerie silence, Major Ilyas Karami ordered three quarters of his remaining commando force down the slope. The rest he held back to transport the howitzer. The battle was not yet over, and he did not intend to lose it through overconfidence. The prize was too great.

Alan Burton rolled back over the lip of the Wash and slid down the muddy wall into darkness. Juan Diaz lay half-buried in the mud-and-bramble shelter Burton had built at the bottom of the ravine. Diaz's wounds had developed an unpleasant odor, and his eyes were pale yellow slits. Burton leaned close to his ear.

"I've got our return tickets, lad. Can you make it?"

"*Sí,*" Diaz whispered.

"There's a big jet up there, an airliner, but it's too heavily guarded. There is also a lovely little Lear that looks like a bloody Turkish brothel on the inside. That's our bird."

Grunting in pain, the little Cuban heaved himself to his knees, pushing away Burton's helping hand. "Let's go, English," he rasped, forcing a grin. "Not enough *señoritas* on this beach."

It took the two men ten minutes to climb out of the Wash and cover the eighty meters to the Libyan Learjet. Burton had to carry Diaz the last third of the way. Instead of putting the Cuban on board the jet, however, Burton trudged to the edge of the asphalt runway and dropped him there. Diaz yelped as the pain of his wounds hit him.

"Sorry, sport," Burton panted. "But this is the safest spot for the time being."

"What?" Diaz exclaimed, finally guessing Burton's intent. "But the plane is right there!"

"Sorry, lad. I told you if I got half a chance I'd have another go at the house. When those rug-peddlers started shooting, they gave me just that. From my point of view, sport, unless I do the job I was sent here to do, that jet isn't an escape route for me. It's just a taxi back to purgatory."

Diaz muttered a stream of Cuban profanity.

"Come along now, Juan boy. Crawl into that brush over there. Wouldn't want those blighters over there to catch you out here alone." Burton pointed up the runway to where Major Karami and his men struggled in the dusk. "Cut your balls off with a bloody scimitar, they would."

When Diaz had settled himself in the tall grass, Burton said, "I know you can reach that jet on your own, sport. I wouldn't want you to leave without me. You wouldn't do that, would you?"

The Cuban pulled a wry face. "Yesterday I would have," he admitted. "But last night you saved my life, English. *Cubano* don't forget that, eh? You go play hero. Diaz be here when you get back."

Burton took a last look the Lear—his solitary means of escape—then he tossed Diaz his wristwatch and gave him a roguish grin. "If I'm not back in forty minutes, sport, it's *bon voyage* to you with my best wishes."

Diaz shook his head and lay back in the scrub grass. Burton unslung his submachine gun and started back toward Horn House.

Hauer charged out of the Armscor and into the marble reception hall with the South Africans on his heels. Gadi brought up the rear. The young Israeli ran straight to the corpses.

"Arabs!" he called. "All but two, and I don't recognize them."

"Look," said General Steyn, pointing to the rectangular black shield blocking the main elevator. "That must be the way to the gun tower."

"And the bomb," Gadi murmured.

Two CT soldiers aimed their shotguns at the shield.

"Captain!" called a voice from the shadows to their right.

Hauer felt his heart thump. Peering across the great entrance hall, he spied a figure against the darkness of a corridor to his right. It was Hans.

"Gadi!" called a hoarse voice.

"Uncle? Where are you?"

Stern stepped into the brighter light of the reception hall. Hans and Ilse stood in the shadows behind him.

"Jonas!" bellowed General Steyn. "You've got some bloody explaining to do!"

Gadi started across the floor, but Stern signaled him to hold back. Hauer watched in puzzlement as Hans slipped out of the corridor and raced around the edge of the great hall like a runner circling a track. When he skidded to a stop, Hauer drew back in shock. Hans's hair, face, and clothing were covered with blood. He looked like he had dived on a grenade.

"Hans! What happened? Were you shot?"

"No time to explain!" Only the whites of Hans's eyes showed through the blood. "We're dead unless we can get through those shields. We've got a plan, but I can't explain it now. I want you to find two rooms with windows facing the inner part of the house. There are cameras in some rooms, not in others. Find a room without a camera. If my plan works, the shields should come down for a few moments—just long enough for you to get through. Skirt the wall when you go—there's a camera by that elevator."

Hans squeezed Hauer's arm hard; then he sprinted back toward Stern. Hauer looked questioningly at Gadi. The young Israeli shrugged and started toward the hallway on their left. Hauer and the South Africans followed.

High in the turret, Pieter Smuts watched Major Karami's commandos charge across the bowl. In a matter of minutes Hauer and his men would be slaughtered. Smuts smiled. His protective shields probably had claw marks on them by now.

It was a pity about Linah, of course, but servants were replaceable.

"Pieter!" Hess cried.

When Smuts whirled, he saw his horrified master pointing at one of the closed-circuit TV monitors. Ilse Apfel filled the screen. Her face and clothing were smeared with blood, and she held an Uzi submachine gun in her hands. She screamed silently at the monitor for help. Then she turned away from the camera and fired a burst from the Uzi.

"That's the elevator camera!" Hess cried. "Open the audio link!"

Instantly the sound of gunfire filled the turret. Ilse turned back toward the camera and screamed. *"In the name of God, help us! They're going to kill us! Herr Horn, please! My husband is wounded!"*

At that moment Hans staggered backward into the camera's field of view and fired a burst from an Uzi he had seized from a dead Libyan. He too was covered in blood. Both the blood and the Uzis had been provided by Major Karami's dead assassins. Hans and Ilse had rolled in the bloody pools of the reception hall until they looked like walking casualties.

"For God's sake, Pieter!" Hess pleaded. "Those are Germans down there!"

Smuts shook his head angrily. "We can't risk it, sir. Hauer and his men could already be inside the house."

"Can you drop only the elevator shield?"

"No, sir. It's all or none. That's the way they're designed."

"Then drop them all for five seconds!"

Smuts clenched his fists. Like most Germans, his master could be infuriatingly sentimental. In the same way a man who sent millions to the ovens could love dogs, Smuts thought. For the first time since he began serving Hess, the Afrikaner felt mutiny in his heart. "I think it's a trick, sir! I see no Arabs!"

Ilse whirled back to the camera, her blue eyes wild with terror. *"In the name of God, Herr Horn, save me! Save my baby!"*

Hess's knuckles went white on the arms of his wheelchair. "I don't see Hauer anywhere," he said quietly, his eyes scanning the other monitors.

"Not all the bedrooms have cameras!"

Hess's face contorted with rage. "Those are *Germans* dying down there, Pieter! She saved my life last night!"

"But—"

"Do it!"

The Afrikaner slammed his right fist down on the console.

CHAPTER FORTY-FOUR

Gadi swung himself through the bedroom window even before the black shield had fully retracted. Hauer leaped after him and landed on the cobblestones of a small courtyard. To his right he saw the South African CT troops helping General Steyn to his feet.

"We've got to find my uncle!" Gadi cried.

General Steyn pointed to a large wooden door across the courtyard and gave a circular flick of his wrist. The shotgun-armed CT troops blew the hinges off the door. Silently they sprinted through the opening and somersaulted into defensive positions, the others close behind them.

Hauer was the last man through. Just before he stepped over the threshold, he realized that the firing outside the house had stopped. He puzzled over this for a moment, then forgot it as he followed Gadi and the South Africans down a short corridor and into a huge, windowless room. Several large crates were stacked in the middle of the floor. A forklift had been parked in front of a door in the far wall.

Suddenly, from a hallway to Hauer's right, Stern and Ilse came running into the room. Sensing danger, Hauer waved them back, but before he could call out, two men wearing *Wehrmacht* gray uniforms rose up from behind the forklift and opened fire with automatic weapons. Stern dived to the floor, pulling Ilse down with him. Gadi returned fire. As the bullets flew, Hans came pelting out of the corridor, skidded, then backpedaled into the hall.

"Ilse!" he shouted. "Crawl back here!"

Ilse looked back, but Stern had thrown himself on top of her. Hauer and General Steyn scrambled back into the hall behind them. The South African CT troops reacted differently. The highly trained commandos considered their

Kevlar body armor an offensive weapon. While one soldier fired covering bursts, the other loaded a tear-gas canister into his shotgun and fired at the forklift. Stinging vapor fogged the far side of the room. Without even waiting to hear a cough the South Africans charged, firing as they ran.

"Clear! Clear!" came a shout in Afrikaans.

"That's it!" said General Steyn. "Let's go!"

At the forklift, Hauer hugged Hans and Ilse fiercely, but there was no time to speak. At their feet lay the bodies of Smuts's men, cut to pieces by the South African commandos. The CT troops had already secured the stairwell beyond the door. The steel steps led both up and down. Leaning out over the rail, Hauer looked up and counted six flights of stairs that ended on a wide landing three floors above. Below, the stairs disappeared into darkness.

"The bomb's downstairs," said Stern. "A hundred meters down. That's our objective."

"But the enemy's up *there*," Hauer argued, pointing with his sniper rifle.

"They don't matter," said Stern. "*He* doesn't matter."

"Who?" asked General Steyn. "Horn?"

Hauer cut his eyes at Stern. "If we don't neutralize that tower, we won't be able to do a damned thing about your bomb even if we find it."

Stern laughed softly. "How long do you think those shields will hold those Arabs back, Hauer? Five minutes? Ten? Horn will probably lower them himself, so that the Arabs can kill us for him."

"Scheisse!" Hauer cursed. "That's why the firing stopped! They're already coming, Stern. We've got to get control of that turret gun. You can do what you want, but I'm taking the South Africans with me."

Without hesitation Stern and Gadi started down the stairs. Hauer, General Steyn, and the South Africans started up, with Hans and Ilse bringing up the rear. On the top-floor landing Hauer put his ear against the green metal door and listened. He thought he heard voices on the other side, but he couldn't be sure. Backing away, he saw the South Africans preparing to blow down this door just as they had the one in the courtyard. He signaled them to wait. Taking hold of the aluminum knob, he applied a very slight circular pressure.

The knob turned.

He glanced back at the South Africans, nodded toward the door, held up a fist, and shook his head. The CT troops got the message: no grenades. Hauer licked his dry lips beneath his respirator. Then he raised his leg and kicked open the door.

Five men—Hess, Smuts, and three of Smuts's security troops—looked up in stunned surprise. After one frozen moment, Smuts's men made the mistake of going for their guns. General Steyn's troops instantly killed all three with shotgun blasts. Smuts himself did not resist. He stepped calmly away from the observation window and set down his field glasses.

No one seemed to know what to say. General Steyn stepped from behind Hauer and looked down at the wizened old man in the wheelchair. "Thomas Horn," he said rather pompously, "in the name of the Republic of South Africa, I place you under arrest."

Still wearing his black eyepatch, Hess looked up with contempt.

The general cleared his throat. "You *are* Thomas Horn?"

"I am *not*," Hess said with disdain. "I am Rudolf Hess. And you, General, are a traitor to your nation and to your race."

General Steyn's mouth fell open. "You're who?"

"Ignore him, General," Hauer snapped. "He's mad as a sewer rat." Hauer turned to Smuts. "Why aren't you firing on the Arabs?"

Smuts wiped his still-bleeding face on his sleeve and smirked.

"They'll kill you too," Hauer pointed out.

"Probably," Smuts conceded. "But they might not."

Hauer moved to the bullet-starred polycarbonate wall and looked out. Half the Libyan commandos had already crossed the bowl, and more were coming—black phantoms gliding across the moonlit earth. Hauer looked back and studied the cage that controlled the Vulcan gun. "General Steyn, can your men operate that gun?"

At a nod from the general, one of the black-suited South Africans pulled off his gas mask, climbed into the cage, and opened fire. The noise was shattering. The gunner knocked down a dozen Libyans in less than twenty seconds. When Smuts's bunker gunners saw the Vulcan resume firing, they assumed that their chief had gone back over to the offensive, and they added their machine guns to the fray.

Pieter Smuts eased his hand toward the console that controlled the shields on the ground floor.

"Touch that and you're dead," Hauer warned.

Smuts's hand lingered over the switch until Hauer backed him off with a flick of his rifle. The Vulcan thundered on, vomiting shells and flame into the darkness.

"Listen to me!" Hess said, struggling to make himself heard. "You ..." He pointed to Hauer. "You're *German.* In the name of the Fatherland, *join* me!" The old man looked around in sudden confusion. "Where is Frau Apfel?"

As if on cue, Ilse stepped through the door. Hans had held her outside until he was certain the skirmish in the turret had ended. "*She* understands!" Hess wailed. "You should all join—"

At that instant the first shell from Major Karami's howitzer struck the tower. The explosion rocked the entire structure on its foundations.

"*Everyone out!*" Hauer shouted. "*Move!*"

Pieter Smuts darted across the room, lifted Hess out of his wheelchair, and carried him bodily into the stairwell. Everyone else hurried after them. Only the South African manning the Vulcan remained in the turret, probing for the howitzer through the smoke below. The group had reached the second-floor landing when the second howitzer shell tore through the turret window and exploded, incinerating man and machinery in a blinding fireball. Stunned by the explosion above, everyone looked to Hauer for instructions.

"Follow him!" Hauer shouted, pointing down at Smuts. Even with Hess clinging to his neck, the Afrikaner had already managed to reach the ground floor. General Steyn and his men started after them, but Hans and Ilse hung back. Hans grabbed Hauer's arm. "Come with us!" he begged. "You'll die here!"

Hauer pointed through a narrow slit-window on the second-floor landing. With the Vulcan out of action, a strong Libyan force had begun charging toward the burning house. And more dangerous, the big howitzer was actually being towed across the bowl under human power. Its progress was slow but steady.

"Find Stern," Hauer told Hans. "There's nothing you can do here. The basement is the only safe place now. I'll buy you all the time I can. Hurry!"

When Hans hesitated, Hauer shoved him down the stairs.

Hauer felt a startling surge of emotion when Ilse stood up on her toes, threw her arms around his neck, and kissed him on the cheek. She drew back and looked into his eyes.

"Thank you for coming for us," she said. "You are a good father." She smiled once, squeezed Hauer's arm, then took Hans's hand and hurried down the steel steps into the darkness.

Hauer smashed the narrow window with the butt of his sniper rifle and thrust the long barrel through. He rolled his shoulders once, took a deep breath, and put his eye to the scope. The Libyan infantry were the closest targets, but he ignored them. He had to slow down the artillery piece. He lined up the reticle, laid his forefinger against the Steyr's trigger, and squeezed.

He knocked down four men in eight seconds. Down on the ground, the big howitzer slowed, then stopped as the men towing it scrambled for cover. Hauer began searching out the infantry, hearing as he did a calm voice in his head: *Running target, fifty meters . . . fire! Eject shell, close bolt, fire!* As he picked off the commandos one by one, he wondered how long he had before the howitzer team pinpointed his muzzle flashes and decided to redecorate the second level of the tower with a 105mm shell.

Alan Burton lay prone on the rim of the bowl, watching the Libyans cross the killing zone. He had seen the howitzer destroy the rotating gun turret, and he had almost decided to try to cross the bowl himself when he saw the Libyans falling to Hauer's rifle. *At least somebody up there knows what he's doing,* Burton thought with admiration. Clearly he would have to find an alternate route into the house.

The renewed chatter of the bunker guns gave him the idea. He peered through the darkness at the nearest one, a concrete pillbox dug into the shallow slope forty meters to his right. All he could see was a narrow horizontal slit with a flashing machine gun barrel protruding from it. *The bunkers serve the tower,* he thought. *They're permanent installations. So how are they supplied? From the surface? No . . . from the house. But how?*

"Tunnels," he said aloud. "Bloody tunnels."

Crouching low, Burton crab-walked around the rim of the bowl until he lay directly over the concrete bunker. Then he pulled three grenades from his web belt and laid them on the grass beside him. The machine gun beneath him fired sporadically, searching out targets in the gloom. Pulling the pin on the first grenade, Burton swung himself down, lobbed it through the narrow firing slit, and rolled back up onto the lip of the bowl.

The explosion shook the ground beneath him. The machine gun fell silent. Gray smoke poured from the firing slit. Grabbing the other two grenades, Burton dropped down in front of the bunker. One meter below the slit he noticed a padlocked steel handle set in the bunker's grass-covered face. *Escape hatch,* he thought. Arming another grenade, he jammed it against the lock and hopped back onto the roof of the bunker.

The blast tore the hatch right off its hinges. Covering his nose and mouth with his shirtfront, Burton disappeared through the smoking hatch like a rabbit down its hole.

Hauer's lungs were on fire. He had just flung himself down the twenty flights of stairs to the basement complex, thanking God with every step that he had run out of ammunition before the howitzer gunners spotted him. Now he worked his way through almost total darkness toward the voices he heard at the far end of the dark laboratory. When he finally reached open space, he saw eight people standing in front of a shining silver wall with great doors set in its face. Someone was speaking English very loudly, but Hauer didn't recognize the voice. When he was only five meters from the group, he finally saw what held center stage.

Lying prone on a wheeled cart like truncated guided missiles were three bulbous, metal-finned cylinders. Ominous and black, they seemed to hold everyone away by some invisible repulsive force. No one had noticed Hauer yet, so he hesitated, trying to gauge exactly what was happening.

Jonas Stern stood with his back to the glinting storage vault, speaking in low, urgent tones to General Steyn, who faced him across the bomb cart. Gadi stood on Stern's left, an assault rifle hanging loosely in his right hand. The two surviving South African CT soldiers, still masked and helmeted, stood directly behind General Steyn. Smuts had propped Hess against a nearby wall, his wasted legs splayed out before him. Hans and Ilse stood arm in arm beside Dr. Sabri.

Hauer slung his empty rifle over his shoulder, strode

through the semicircle and interposed himself between Stern and General Steyn.

"Captain Hauer!" said General Steyn. He jabbed a finger at Stern. "Do you know what this madman wants to do? He's talking about *detonating* one of these weapons!"

Hauer had already guessed as much. What he could not understand was why Stern had told General Steyn about his plan at all. Perhaps the South Africans had surprised the Israelis in the process of arming the bombs. Hauer looked at Smuts and pointed to one of the bombs. "Exactly what are we looking at here?"

When Smuts did not respond, Dr. Sabri said, "You are looking at three fully operational nuclear weapons, sir."

Hauer studied the bespectacled young Arab. "And you are . . . ?"

"He's a Libyan physicist," Gadi said irritably. "We've established that already."

"Hauer," Stern said evenly, "the situation is hopeless. You know that as well as I, and General Steyn knows it better than both of us. There is no way out of this building. In a matter of minutes the Libyans will break through. When they do, Israel is lost. Unless—"

"Unless you blow the northern half of South Africa to hell?" General Steyn bellowed.

Ilse's voice rose above the others. "How much time do we have? I haven't heard any explosions for a few minutes."

Hauer rubbed his chin with the back of his hand. "I think some of the Arabs are already inside, but they won't be able to breach those shields with light weapons. The main force is trying to drag their big gun across that bowl. Three hundred meters. Plus, our armored car is blocking the door to the house. I'd say we have fifteen to twenty minutes before we have to fight."

"Thank you, Captain," said Stern. His voice softened as he spoke to General Steyn. "Jaap, the damage from these weapons might be far less than you imagine. Dr. Sabri, what are these bombs capable of?"

The young Libyan answered in a shaky voice. "I've only examined one of the weapons closely. It's a forty-kiloton bomb. That's a fairly low yield by today's standards, though it's twice the size of the Hiroshima bomb. If it were detonated as it was designed to be—in an air burst—the results would be catastrophic. But here . . . I would guess we're about a hundred meters underground. The walls look like re-inforced concrete, that's good." He frowned. "Such things are difficult to predict, but if only the one bomb exploded, the result could be similar to a medium-sized underground nuclear test. If, however, the other weapons detonated with the first—and if they are of the same approximate size—the explosion might blow upward and break through the surface. Where we are standing would be the epicenter of a large cra-ter. As for the above-ground effects, estimating blast radius and such, my rough guess would be . . . perhaps five kilome-ters? The radiation is the real problem. But if the wind is right, the whole cloud might drift right out to sea."

"Or it *might* drift south and kill everyone in Pretoria and Johannesburg!" General Steyn exploded.

Hans stepped tentatively forward. "You said you brought an armored car with you. Is there some way we could sneak the bombs out of here?"

Hauer shook his head. "Even if we could fight our way up to the vehicle, we'd never get the bombs up to it. God only knows how much they weigh."

"Sixteen hundred and fifty kilograms each," Dr. Sabri vol-unteered.

"There it is," said Stern with a note of finality. "The bombs cannot be gotten safely away. That leaves only one option."

"That's ridiculous!" roared General Steyn. "All we have to do is find a way out of here ourselves! We can leave the bombs right where they are. As soon as we reach a phone, I can call Durban airbase. The air force can shoot these Arab pirates down before they even leave our airspace!"

This suggestion found immediate favor in the group. But while General Steyn expanded on his idea, Gadi Abrams eased slowly across the room to where Hans and Ilse stood listening.

When the general finished speaking, Stern put his foot on the nearest bomb, laid an elbow across his knee, and leaned toward the South African. General Steyn stared back with the tenacity of a bulldog. Behind him, his masked soldiers stood with their shotguns at the ready.

"Jaap," Stern said softly. "I simply cannot allow these weapons to fall into Libyan hands. Not even for an hour. The risks are simply too great."

General Steyn raised his right hand. The gesture had a distinctly military quality to it, and it brought an immediate response. Both South African commandos pointed their shotguns at Stern. Their futuristic garb gave them the look of hostile aliens, and their command over the group was total.

Or almost total. At the moment they brought their guns to bear, Gadi swung the barrel of his assault rifle up from behind Ilse and fired from the hip.

Ilse screamed.

Gadi's accuracy was startling. Fully aware that the South Africans wore body armor, he fired two consecutive bursts straight through the black gas masks, killing both men instantly. General Steyn groped for the pistol at his belt. Gadi put one round through the general's left shoulder, spinning him around and knocking him to the floor. Then he darted back into position behind Stern and pointed his carbine at the rest of the group.

Dr. Sabri's face had gone white. Smuts was grinning. Ilse was still screaming, but Stern shouted above her: *"Everyone stay calm! He had no choice!"*

"No choice!" Hans cried. "He murdered them!"

General Steyn struggled slowly to his feet, his face flushed with pain and outrage. Hauer had already relieved him of his pistol. "You will pay for this, Jonas," he vowed. "Israel will pay! And you know South Africa can make it pay!"

"Yes," Stern acknowledged. "The problem is, some of you were already planning to make us pay."

"A few fanatics!" General Steyn spat. "You've gone too far!"

Stern spoke in a monotone. "We are talking about the survival of Israel, Jaap. If these weapons explode here in the Transvaal, it will be a disaster, to be sure. But if only *one* of these bombs were to explode over Israel, our tiny state would cease to exist, and the entire world might be sucked into the vortex of war. It's a devil's choice, but it's that simple. Tragedy versus a worldwide holocaust."

There was a high-pitched cackle from the far wall. *"An excellent choice of words, Jew!"* Even in his helpless position, Rudolf Hess wore an expression of triumph. "A holocaust is exactly what is going to happen! Just as the Führer planned! Even if you could persuade these cowards to allow you to detonate the weapons, you don't have the knowledge to do it. I have won!"

Gadi Abrams pointed his R5 at Hess's face.

"No, Gadi!" Stern cried. "God, I wanted so badly to take him back to Israel for trial! To see him forced to tell the world his vile story. To tell what he knows about the British."

"I'll tell you now," Hess coughed. "You'll all be dead within minutes, anyway. I might as well entertain you while we wait for Major Karami."

"Shut up!" Stern snapped in German. "No one cares anymore!"

"Let him talk," Hauer said. "If we're going to die, I want to know why. I want to know what this Nazi bastard had planned for Germany."

Hess smiled defiantly. "I think I'll keep that to myself, Captain. But I will tell you about the British."

Hans stepped forward. "Maybe there *is* another way out of here, Captain. Why don't we search the lab?"

Pieter Smuts laughed dryly. "Sorry, Sergeant. One way in, one way out. That's the best security there is. You're going to die where you stand."

"You'll die before I do," Hans shot back.

Ilse reached out and squeezed Hans's arm. "I want to hear Hess's story, Hans. I want to know why an innocent man rotted in Spandau all those years, and why the Allies kept silent about it. My grandfather came here to find those answers. He thought they were very important. I want to learn them, if I can."

Hess signaled for Smuts to set him up straighter. The gesture silenced everyone in the room. In spite of the Libyan commandos who would soon hammer through the protective shields above, in spite of the incomprehensible danger that lay between them all like coals delivered up from hell, every person in the basement crowded silently around the old man propped against the steel wall.

"The Jew knows most of it already," Hess rasped. "What he doesn't know—what nobody knows—is what *my* part of the mission was. For so long the furor has focused on my flight to Scotland. The simple truth is that my flight was only a small part of the plan." Hess's voice gained strength. "Our goal was to replace the government of England. No one in England wanted another war, yet any idiot could see that Churchill would never make peace with the Führer. So, the answer was simple—get rid of Churchill. The Americans and the Soviet Union did the same thing many times after the war. Coup d'état is the fashionable term, yes? The Führer was always years ahead of his time." Hess scratched at a wisp of beard on his chin. "It makes me laugh now, all that rot about how the valiant British saved the world from Hitler. Ha! There were *dozens* of powerful Englishmen ready to throw Churchill out and put a right-thinking man in Downing Street. And I don't mean radicals. They were lords and ladies, members of Parliament, knights of the realm. They understood that the only way to stop communism was to ally England with the Reich. So they tried it! They got word to the Führer that if Churchill and his gang could be got out, they had men ready to step in. If the king could be eliminated, they could fill his shoes also. Of course the Führer agreed immediately. While he made arrangements to have Churchill and the king liquidated, his English friends prepared to fill the coming power vacuum. Windsor was to take his younger brother's place on the throne."

Hess's voice gained strength. "It was to happen on the tenth of May—the anniversary of our victorious attack on Western Europe. My mission was simple. The Englishmen behind the coup demanded absolute proof that the Führer would live up to his end of the bargain—that he would actually make peace with Britain, cease the terror bombing of London and so forth." Hess's eyes glazed with lost glory. "So the Führer asked Rudi—his faithful deputy and lifelong friend—to be his emissary to his British friends!"

"But why was your double sent?" Ilse asked.

Hess smiled cagily. "British Intelligence learned that I was planning to fly to Britain. They had informers everywhere. They expected me to land near Dungavel Castle—which was my original plan—but two weeks before my flight, Reinhard Heydrich discovered that MI-5 knew about the Dungavel meeting. Rather than cancel it, however, Heydrich simply changed the actual rendezvous to the beach opposite Holy Island." Hess nodded admiringly. "It was Heydrich's idea to send my double on to Dungavel. To act as if nothing had changed, you see! The double's mission was to dupe MI-5 into believing they had captured me, but *just long enough for me to complete my real mission.* It was never intended that he do what he did!"

"But you *didn't* complete your mission," Hauer pointed out. "Why not?"

Hess sighed. "Because by the time I jumped out of the plane over Holy Island, MI-5 had found out about that rendezvous as well. Another informer had betrayed us. When I landed—several hundred meters off target, by the way—I heard shooting. I quickly realized that something had gone wrong. When I moved closer to the firing, I saw that British agents had already stormed the rendezvous site—which consisted of a half-dozen autos parked on a shingle of beach. There was a gun battle between some MI-5 operatives and my contacts." Hess grimaced as if at some private pain. "It was there I received the wound that eventually took my eye. A stray bullet." He shrugged. "My part of the mission had failed. I knew the name of a German agent who maintained a radio link to Occupied France from a nearby coastal village, and I made my way to his house on a stolen motorbike. The rest is unimportant."

"But what of the plan to kill Churchill?" Ilse asked.

Hess looked tired now. "Ask the Jew."

Stern cast Hess a disparaging look. "It actually might have worked," he said, "but for a confused Englishman who came to his senses just in time to thwart the assassination. If my guess is right, the only man to escape from that part of the mission—a Russian named Zinoviev—fled to the same German agent Hess did." Stern looked at Hess. "Isn't that right? Isn't that where the two of you met?"

Hess smiled distantly.

"Zinoviev never went back to Germany as his journal claimed, did he?"

Hess chuckled.

"And in spite of your eye wound," Stern guessed, "the two of you escaped together to South America, and finally ended up here." Stern's eyes flashed as he looked at Hess. "Zinoviev tried to warn us, you know. In 1967. He must have realized then how mad you were."

Hess flung out a scarecrow-thin arm. "Zinoviev was *weak!* All he cared about in the end was his precious Mother Russia! Holy Russia. He was practically a religious fanatic by 1967." Hess sighed. "We found out about that warning, though, didn't we, Pieter? And dear Vasili had to meet his maker a bit earlier than even he wanted to."

"Why didn't *you* return to Germany?" Hauer asked.

Hess looked genuinely sad. "I was confused. It was never even considered that things could turn out as badly as they had. You must understand: I had long accepted in my mind that by May eleventh I would have succeeded in my mission or I would be dead. Yet I had failed, and I was still alive. It seemed foolish to kill myself at that point. And stranger still, Churchill's government had chosen to believe—publicly at least—that my double was, in fact, me. Day after day, hiding on the coast, I listened to reports of my capture while Zinoviev tended my eye. And then came the news from Germany—from the Führer himself—that I was mad. I had suggested he say that if the worst happened, but it was un-nerving all the same! The pronouncement told me how things stood. The Führer had assumed that either I had com-mitted suicide as planned or the British had indeed captured me. His only option was to discredit me publicly. It was the most difficult moment of his life, I am sure. Not only had he lost his most faithful friend, but he now faced the impossible situation we had sought to avoid in the first place! With the failure of my mission, war on two fronts was inevitable."

Hess took a deep breath. His face was pale and sweating. "Nine days later, I managed to get a message to the Führer. I told him what had happened, that I was alive, and asked for instructions." Hess's face steeled with resolve. "I men-tioned nothing of my wound, and I offered to do what cow-ardice had not let me do on May tenth—take my own life. Hitler's reply came two weeks later. First, he awarded both myself and Helmut the Grand Cross. As a foreign national, Zinoviev received only the Iron Cross. Then came my or-ders: I was to sail to Brazil, and there administer a massive network of assets and companies that the Führer had moved for safety to South America. The coming two-front war had sobered him. At this time he was still of sound mind, and he knew the chances for ultimate victory were problematical. The Führer was surrounded by traitors; Himmler plotted ceaselessly to take his place. Some of the Party's top bank-ers had already fled Germany. Hitler wanted—he *needed*— someone he could trust outside the country, preparing a place for him should his position become untenable." Hess's face glowed with pride. "*I* was that man! When the time came, Zinoviev killed the agent who had hidden us, and he and I traveled to South America. Just as Alfred Horn had be-come Rudolf Hess to the world, I became Alfred Horn. Zinoviev served as my lieutenant and bodyguard until we emigrated to South Africa." Hess looked up at Smuts. "And Pieter assumed that position after I arrived."

"There's one question you haven't answered," Stern said, recalling Professor Natterman and his obsession with the Hess mystery. "Was the Duke of Windsor really a traitor?"

Hess mopped his forehead. "Who knows? Windsor was a fool. He just wanted to be king again."

"Yes, but did he *knowingly* conspire with the Nazis to regain the throne? That's what I want to know."

"It never came to the test!" Hess snapped. "Don't you understand, Jew? It was a setup! A double-cross from the very beginning. They *used* us. Me, Windsor . . . even the Führer. British Intelligence discovered their own bloody traitors and played them back against us! They *lured* me to England, damn them. Of *course* Windsor conspired with us! Would he really have assumed the throne as Hitler's vassal? Would he have stolen the throne from his murdered brother? No one will ever know!" Hess shook his head in desolation. "Lies . . . all lies. Letting us hope for peace with England until it was too late . . ."

Hess's head swayed oddly on his neck. He seemed to have forgotten his audience. "Bormann," he murmured. "Ilse always knew. Abandoning the Führer in his hour of need!" Smuts tried to calm Hess, but the old Nazi slapped the Afrikaner across the face. "Bormann terrorized my family! My own wife! He tried to evict my Ilse from our house! Thank God Himmler stopped him!"

"My God," Ilse murmured. "No wonder he had a fixation on me."

Hess's eye came clear again. "The swine paid for his impudence! In 1950 I saw him hanged with piano wire by members of the ODESSA! I have the film in my study!"

"Enough!" Stern cried, stepping in front of Hess. "Everyone, stand back! The time has come to bring down the curtain on this farce. Dr. Sabri, prepare the weapon for detonation."

"Wait!" Hans cried, springing up to Stern. "Listen to me! To hell with Hess! To hell with the Nazis! I understand your love for Israel, but not everyone here is a Jew. I am German. General Steyn is South African. We want to *live*. Does that make us cowards? If it does, I'm a coward! Look at my wife. She's pregnant, you understand? We want our child to live! What right have you to take that away from us?"

"The right of the greater good," Stern said softly. "I'm sorry, Sergeant."

"You're sorry? Do you plan to murder everyone who doesn't agree with you?" Hans pointed to the South Africans Gadi had shot. "How are you different than the Nazis?"

Stern looked at Ilse. His face softened momentarily, but he quickly turned away. "Captain Hauer," he said tersely, "do you believe I am wrong about what must be done here?"

With a strange sense of fatalism Hauer looked down at the dead South Africans. He looked at General Steyn, bleeding steadily from his shoulder and heaving for breath. He looked at Hans, his own son, his face flushed with passion for life, his innocent fervor mirrored in his wife's beautiful eyes. He looked at Hess, cadaverous and gray, a living anachronism sitting aloof on the floor beneath his Afrikaner protector. And finally at Stern. Hauer had known the old Israeli less than a day, yet he felt closer to him than he did to many men he had known all his life. *Stern is no fanatic,* he thought. *He's a realist. He's seen enough of the world to know that giving fate one chance to beat you is one chance too many. Or perhaps he's just my kind of fanatic.* Hauer didn't want to die. But what choice was there? To fight their way out was impossible. With all eyes in the room turned to him, he stepped toward Hans and Ilse with a heavy heart. Yet before he could speak, an unfamiliar voice shouted from somewhere in the dark jungle of laboratory equipment behind them:

"Hullo the house! Hullo! White flag and truce!"

Gadi jerked his rifle toward the sound.

Hauer spun to face the darkness, but he saw nothing. "Call off your dog, Stern! That's a British accent!"

"That doesn't make me feel any better!" Stern retorted. "All right, Gadi," he said finally. "Stand down."

After the young Israeli lowered his weapon, a sandy-haired man of medium height rose from beneath a soapstone lab table. He was wearing tattered commando gear, and his left hand held a well-oiled MP-5 submachine gun. "Hullo," he said. "In a bit of a pinch, are we?"

"Who the devil are you?" General Steyn croaked.

"How did you get in?" asked Hauer. "That's the question."

"Name's Burton, sport. Ex-major in the British Army,

lately soldier for pay. And how I got here is too long a story to tell."

"Have the shields been lowered?" Stern asked, afraid that the Libyans might already have penetrated into the inner complex.

"Don't know about any shields. I came in through a bunker. There's tunnels running to every one of 'em and they all intersect right here."

"Are you serious?" Hauer cried. "The Arabs didn't see you?"

"Those camel humpers? Not bloody likely."

"But what's past the bunkers? Is there any way to get truly *out* of here? Away from this place?"

"It just so happens," said Burton, "that I've got my own personal Learjet and pilot waiting outside."

Hauer's mouth fell open.

Hans and Ilse ran to the Englishman. "We've got to get out of here!" Ilse cried. "Now! The Arabs will break through any minute!"

"Boarding in five minutes," Burton said jauntily. "One carry-on bag per person, please."

CHAPTER FORTY-FIVE

General Steyn threw his good arm over Hauer's shoulder, believing that Burton's revelation of an escape route had resolved de facto all the argument that had gone before. Ilse barely had time to snatch up Hess's black briefcase before Hans pulled her across the room toward the Englishman. Dr. Sabri also moved cautiously in that direction.

Yet Stern and Gadi did not move. They stood with their backs against the gleaming steel storage vault, staring watchfully at the excited group gathering around the British mercenary. Hauer laid his hand on General Steyn's pistol. He understood only too well what was passing through the minds of the Israelis.

"Gadi," Stern said sharply.

With his rifle braced on his hip, the young Israeli marched past Hauer, grabbed Dr. Sabri by the sleeve and pulled him back to where the three bombs waited on their carts. He kicked the Libyan behind the knee, dropping him to the floor, then shoved him down over the bomb in the middle of the cart.

"Open it," Stern commanded.

"Wh-what?" the Libyan stammered.

"Open the weapon!"

"I need tools."

Gadi swung his rifle around on Smuts.

"We don't keep any down here," Smuts lied.

Gadi fired a slug into the wall beside the Afrikaner's head. Smuts didn't flinch, but after a face-saving moment he stepped over to a drawer and pulled out a metal tool kit. He carried it to the Libyan, then returned to Hess's side.

General Steyn watched all this in disbelief. "What are you

doing now, Jonas? Our problem is solved! As soon as we take off, I can radio the air force from this man's plane!"

Stern looked up from where Dr. Sabri worked on the bomb. "This changes only two things," he said quietly. "First, you people now have a chance to get clear. And second, Hess can go with you."

Pieter Smuts stiffened.

Stern touched Gadi's sleeve. "Hess is your responsibility. You'll take him out with the others."

The young Israeli's face wilted like a little boy's, then it hardened to stone. "I shall stay behind, Uncle," he said solemnly. "You should be the one who takes Hess to Israel."

Stern shook his head impatiently. "You—"

"I say there," Burton cut in. "You're not talking about setting off these bombs. I've seen enough conventional weapons to know an unconventional one when I see it. Even if we manage to get airborne, the blast wave from one of those would knock us right out of the sky."

Stern crouched beside Dr. Sabri, who had just gotten the cover plate off the bomb's arming system. "What's the minimum safe distance for the aircraft that delivers this weapon?"

Dr. Sabri looked up at Stern with wild eyes. "There's no way to know! If the explosion breaks through the surface . . . Five . . . perhaps six kilometers?"

Stern rose to his feet. "If you all leave now," he said loudly, "you should be able to reach minimum safe distance before the Libyans break through the shields. I suggest you get moving."

Hauer jabbed a finger toward the bomb cart. "Stern, that thing must have some kind of timing mechanism. Why not set it for thirty minutes and get out with the rest of us?"

Gadi's face lit up. "Uncle, that's it!"

Stern shook his head. "In fifteen minutes the Libyans will be inside this room. They're almost certain to have someone with them who would know how to stop the timer." Stern pulled Dr. Sabri to his feet. "What kind of detonator does this weapon have? *Is* there a timing mechanism?"

"A timer, yes! But not the kind you imagine. This is an air-burst weapon. It's meant to be exploded above ground. Once armed, its clock begins at a preprogrammed atmospheric pressure level."

"How long does the clock run?"

"This one is set for twelve seconds. But I could set it for much longer!"

Gadi jammed the barrel of his R5 into the terrified Libyan's stomach. "How do we know he's telling us the truth about the detonator? What if you stay behind and the bomb doesn't explode? You'll have thrown your life away for nothing!"

Stern turned to Sabri. "Show me how the detonator works. Be quick!"

While the Libyan bent over the bomb casing, Hauer stepped up to Stern. "Do you *want* to throw your life away, Stern? You have a real alternative now. General Steyn is right—the South African air force can easily shoot down the Libyans when they try to leave the country."

Stern smiled wryly. "And if someone in the South African air force doesn't *want* to shoot them down?"

"Sir?" said Dr. Sabri, looking up from the weapon.

Hauer looked down. In the Libyan's hands, held as gingerly as if they were coiled vipers, were four tricolored wires that led from a small aperture in the bomb casing. Two exposed copper wire ends glinted in the fluorescent light.

"Touch these together," Dr. Sabri said hoarsely, "and the bomb will think it has reached the preprogrammed altitude. The timing mechanism will run its course, and the detonator will explode. A few nanoseconds later, nuclear fission will be initiated."

There was dead silence in the room.

"Must the wires remain connected during the timer's entire run?" Stern asked.

The Libyan nodded.

Before anyone could stop him, Stern seized the two wires, wrapped them together, and closed them in his fist.

Ilse screamed.

Alan Burton dived under a soapstone lab table, as if it could somehow protect him from a nuclear blast. Hauer and Gadi froze, mesmerized by Stern's insane act. But no one reacted with the abject terror of Dr. Sabri. Shrieking wildly, the Libyan grabbed Stern's wrists and tried desperately to separate the two wires. But despite the great age difference between the two men, Sabri failed. After what Stern judged to be nine seconds—long enough for everyone in the room to stare death in the face—he jerked the two wires apart.

"I think he's telling the truth, Gadi."

Dr. Sabri fell to his knees and peered into the bomb's access panel. "There are only two seconds left on the clock! In the name of Allah, do not let the wires touch again!"

"Not until you're all safely away," Stern promised.

Hauer half-smiled. "Or until the Libyans break into this complex. Right, Stern?"

"You'd better hurry," Stern said tersely.

Gadi laid a hand on his shoulder. "Uncle, please do not sacrifice yourself. I am a soldier. I should be the one."

"I am a soldier too." Stern sighed deeply. "An old one. But it doesn't matter. I'm dead already."

"What?"

"I've already been exposed to enough radiation today to kill me. And if not enough to kill me, at least enough to make what little that remains of my life quite unpleasant." Stern rubbed his eyes and sighed. "I can barely see you now, Gadi. Everything has a halo."

"What are you talking about?" Gadi cried.

"It's true," Ilse interjected. "They did the same to me. Or they pretended to."

Gadi looked mystified.

Against the wall, Pieter Smuts shifted his body slightly away from Hess.

"X-rays, Gadi," Stern explained. "The same way I confirmed that Horn was actually Hess. They strapped me down and dosed me with X-rays for two hours."

The young commando blinked. "*What?* Who did that to you? Who!"

At that moment Smuts nodded almost imperceptibly. Rudolf Hess slid silently to the floor.

"That man there!" Ilse shouted, pointing to Smuts.

As her accusing finger went up, the Afrikaner whipped up a Beretta automatic he had slipped from an ankle holster and aimed it at the two Israelis. No one had thought to search him; now he had both Stern and Gadi in his sights. From ten feet he could not miss.

With a short cry Gadi knocked Stern down with his left hand and jerked up his carbine with his right.

The two men fired at the same instant.

Outside the front entrance of Horn House, one of Major Karami's commandos leaned into the empty driver's compartment of the Armscor and saw that the ignition keys had been removed. He craned his neck around the seats just in time to see Captain Barnard's bloody face appear out of the gloom like a ghost. It was the last thing the Libyan would ever see. Barnard's bullet struck him right between the eyes.

Hearing the shot, two more Libyans leaped through the Armscor's doors. Captain Barnard shot them both through the head. Struggling to breathe through the blood in his throat, the South African thrust his pistol through the shattered windshield and fired wildly at the Libyans grouped around the howitzer.

"Hold your positions!" Major Karami shouted.

The 105mm howitzer stood only twenty meters from the Armscor. Two of Captain Barnard's bullets struck the barrel of the big gun, sending several Libyans scurrying for cover, but Major Karami stood still as stone.

"Hold your positions!" he roared. "Set elevation and blow that pile of shit out of my way!"

For an artillery piece the shot was point blank. Everyone opened their mouths and put both hands over their ears. Major Karami raised one brown hand high, then dropped it.

"Fire!"

Pieter Smuts's bullet struck Gadi square in the center of the chest. The Israeli flew backward and knocked Stern down. Gadi had fired a burst, but only one round struck the Afrikaner, splintering his left wrist in a spray of blood and bone. Before either man could move again, the exploding howitzer shell shook the ceiling of the basement like a thunderclap.

"They're coming!" Hans shouted.

Hauer saw the subsequent action in slow motion. Smuts steadied his pistol for a second shot. Gadi—who had been saved by his body armor—struggled to his feet. Hauer shouted a warning to Smuts, but the Afrikaner fired anyway. His second shot tore through Gadi's unprotected right thigh. As Hauer heard the second howitzer shell explode above them, he raised General Steyn's pistol, pointed it at Smuts and fired four times.

His bullets nailed the Afrikaner to the wall. Smuts hung there a moment, wide-eyed, then dropped like a sack across his master's crippled legs.

"Pieter!" Hess cried. "My God, no!"

Another explosion shuddered through the house.

"It's now or bloody never!" Burton shouted. He took a last look at Hess on the floor, then he turned and ran.

"Everyone out!" Stern ordered. *"Now! Go!"*

Hauer hustled General Steyn toward the dark laboratory aisles that led to the tunnels, but the wounded general collapsed after ten steps. Hauer started dragging him; Hans came back to help. Dr. Sabri glanced fearfully at Gadi, then darted after the others.

"May I come with you, sir?" he asked Hauer.

Hauer shoved the Libyan down the aisle, then turned back to Stern. "Give us every goddamn second you can, Stern! These people deserve to live! Keep your fanatic nephew with you and hold them off as long as you can!"

"Don't worry, you Kraut bastard!" Gadi yelled back, gripping his bleeding thigh. "I'm staying! I'll kill every Arab up there!"

"No, Gadi!" Stern insisted. "You're going with them! You must get Hess out!"

"I'm staying with you!" Gadi pointed his assault rifle at the old Nazi. *"Go to hell, you Nazi bastard!"*

Stern grabbed his arm. "Stop! You *must* take Hess to Israel! Pick him up, Gadi! Pick him up and carry him out of here! Carry him all the way to Jerusalem! He'll hang soon enough!"

Hauer and the others had paused halfway to the tunnel. All eyes were riveted on the surreal drama taking place in the pool of fluorescent light before the silver storage vault. Even facing their own deaths, those who wanted so desperately to live could not tear their eyes away from two men so ready to die without fear or regret. Another explosion rattled the glassware in the lab.

"The Englishman's gone!" Hans shouted. "Let's *go!*"

Dr. Sabri broke and ran. Hans shoved Ilse after the Libyan.

Stern squatted astride the bomb and picked up the stripped detonator wires.

"Mother of God," Hauer murmured, backing toward the shadows.

Gadi stubbornly took up a firing position behind Stern. Stern turned around and gazed into the young commando's burning eyes. His voice cracked with emotion. "In the name of Abraham, Gadi, take Hess to Israel. That is not an order.

It is a sacred charge on the souls of your ancestors. Leave me a gun and *get Hess out!*"

A tear streaked the young Israeli's face. With shaking hands he laid his rifle against the bomb casing and crossed to where Hess lay. Favoring his good leg, he crouched down, caught the old man under the arms, and lifted. Hess immediately began to struggle. Gadi punched him in the side of the head. Then he heaved the wasted body over his shoulder.

"Yes!" Stern cried. "Get him out!"

Quivering beneath his hundred-pound load, the wounded Israeli staggered after Hauer and Hans. Yet after only four short steps his savaged thigh muscle gave way. He crashed to the floor, screaming in agony. Hess fell on top of him. Gadi clenched his jaws shut and rolled the old man off. Then, with his bloody thigh twitching uncontrollably, he struggled to his feet again. Again he hoisted Hess to his shoulder and tried to walk. He gasped with each step, fighting the searing fire in his leg. Like a boxer knocked senseless but still on his feet, he reeled backward toward Stern.

"No, Gadi!" Stern barked. "The other way! Forward!"

The young commando tottered a moment, then collapsed. Hess hit the floor hard this time and didn't move. Sobbing with rage and pain, Gadi got to his knees and tried once more to lift the old man. He summoned every ounce of strength he had left, but Smuts's bullet had done too much damage.

"I can't do it, Uncle! I'll never get him through the tunnel!"

"Hauer!" Stern shouted. *"Come back and help the boy!"*

"Yes!" Gadi called. "Help me, Captain!"

Hauer's answer flared out of the darkness. "Hess can go to hell! I'm saving General Steyn! You just hold those Arabs back as long as you can!"

"You owe it to us!" Stern shouted. "For Munich! Yes, I know you were there! Come back, Hauer! For the Jews you let die!"

"Let it go, Stern! That war is over!"

"Leave him, Gadi," Stern cried angrily. "Frau Apfel has the Zinoviev book and the Spandau papers. That's all the proof you need. Those papers alone indict the British."

"Then I'm staying with you!"

"No. You must get that evidence to Israel!"

"The others can do it."

"A *Jew*, Gadi. A Jew must do it. To be sure."

Gadi looked wildly at his uncle for a moment, then he made his decision. He stripped the guns from the South Africans he had killed and laid them at Stern's feet. "Kill as many as you can, Uncle. I will get your papers to Jerusalem."

Stern smiled. "I know you will, my boy. Now go." He hugged Gadi's face to his own. *"Shalom."*

"*Shalom,* Uncle." Gadi choked back a sob. "No Jew will ever forget you."

"Go," Stern commanded. "My time has come."

Dragging his bleeding leg behind him, Gadi picked up his rifle and went.

The barrel of Major Karami's howitzer now protruded through the shattered front door of Horn House. Karami watched the leader of his search detail race into the reception hall.

"We find only corpses and servants in the house, Major!"

Karami smiled. "Clear the house."

Taking a last look at the black shield blocking the elevator, the Libyan major squeezed between the door frame and the gun carriage and took up a position behind the howitzer. He remembered the elevator from his first visit, and he knew that at the bottom of its deep shaft lay Horn's basement storage facility. And inside that basement—a sword worthy of Mohammed himself!

"Fire!" he shouted.

Alan Burton had been waiting in the darkness beside the bunker for a full minute when Dr. Sabri poked his head through the jagged hatch.

"Come on, then!" he snapped as he pulled the Libyan out. "I heard you speaking Arabic back there, sport. You with these blighters out here?"

"No, sir! Those men are assassins! They murdered my prime minister!"

Before Burton could reply, Ilse squirmed out of the black hole. She explained that Hauer and Hans were still struggling through the tunnel with General Steyn. Burton looked anxiously at his watch. "We can't wait any longer," he said. "You'd better follow me."

He turned and trotted toward the airstrip. Dr. Sabri followed, but Ilse hung back, clinging tightly to Hess's briefcase. After thirty agonizing seconds, General Steyn's head appeared, his face a bloodless mask of shock and confusion. While Hauer and Hans pushed from behind, Ilse pulled. Hans followed the general through the hatch, and finally Hauer wriggled through. Ilse hugged Hans fiercely, sandwiching Hess's briefcase between them. Only Gadi had not yet appeared.

"Come on," Hauer said harshly. "Either he makes it or he doesn't."

Jonas Stern squatted silently on his cylinder of Armageddon and waited for the Libyans to come. Holding the stripped wires like talismans, he surveyed the shadows around him. He was king in a world of corpses. At his feet lay the South African counterterror troops, their futuristic gas masks lethally punctured by Gadi's bullets. Behind them, splayed out on his back like a broken doll, Pieter Smuts lay in a spreading pool of blood. Only Rudolf Hess remained alive. Too crippled by arthritis to drag his frail body to safety, the old Nazi had managed to struggle into a sitting position against the wall to Stern's left. His eyepatch had slipped off. Now a scarred, empty socket stared at Stern.

Stern listened for the slightest sound from the far end of the lab. He heard nothing. He looked curiously at Hess. Here was the man who had brought them all to this place. *Hess . . .* The name carried Stern back to a youth so torn by fear, loss, and pain that he remembered only the ceaseless throb of grief. He had survived the cruelest war that ever scourged the earth, and near him now lay one of the men who had unleashed it upon the world. Strangely, he felt no personal hatred for the bag of brittle bones—only a detached curiosity, a desire to know if there had ever been some *reason* for what was done.

"Hess," he said softly.

The old Nazi's good eye fluttered open. "What do you want, Jew?"

"Tell me something. Have you ever come to understand what Hitler did? The obscenity of it? The inhumanity?"

Hess looked away.

"Tell me," Stern insisted. "I want to know *why.* Why the Holocaust? Why murder thousands of children? What was it that made Hitler hate us so? Fear? What did the Jews ever do to him? Or to you?"

Hess looked back at Stern. Another explosion rocked the ceiling above them, but Stern saw only Hess. A dark fire had come into the withered Nazi's solitary eye, a blind, animal hatred so removed from the community of man that Stern felt driven to cross the room and crush the skull that contained it. It was a blindness that could not see murder, a deafness that could not hear the screams of children, a muteness that could speak only through violence. *Why did I even ask?* he thought hopelessly. *It's like asking a bully why he drowns a cat . . . or a father why he molests his infant child . . . and hoping for some reason one could understand. There is no reason!* Stern lifted an R-5 assault rifle from the floor and brought its barrel to bear on Hess's crippled body. The old Nazi's watery eye showed no fear.

"You want to kill me, Jew?" he said softly. "You can kill me. But you cannot kill what I lived for. Captain Hauer said Phoenix will be wiped out. But he is wrong. What united the men of Phoenix exists everywhere. In Germany. South America. In the Soviet Union. The United States and Britain. Everywhere. All governments know about our groups, but they do nothing. The press calls them ultra-right organizations. A few members go to jail now and then, so what? Why are they tolerated? Because deep down, people *understand* these movements. They express something every civilized man feels—the justified fear of anarchy, of *racial destruction.* They know that one day the great struggle will come . . . the struggle against the *Schwarze* and Asian and the Jew—"

"Didn't you hear what I said this afternoon!" Stern cried. "The Jews don't want to destroy anyone! That's the difference between us and you. We have the power to vaporize our enemies, yet we choose not to."

Hess smirked. "I'll tell you what that tells me, Jew. It tells me that your race is weak. The Jew is clever enough to *build* atomic weapons, but he lacks the moral courage to *use* what he has created."

"You're mad," Stern said quietly.

Hess chuckled. "Don't deceive yourself. There are individuals in Israel who want to use their nuclear weapons. That is why your nation must be obliterated."

With a profound emptiness, Stern dropped his rifle to the

floor and turned away. Seeing this, Hess heaved himself away from the wall and began dragging himself slowly toward Stern.

"You'll have to kill me, Jew."

Sweating and grunting in the darkness of the airstrip, Hans and Hauer lifted General Steyn through the main door of the Libyan Learjet. Ilse and Dr. Sabri were already aboard. After laying the general on a pile of carpets at the rear of the cabin, Hauer leaned out of the plane to speak to Alan Burton.

The Englishman had disappeared. Peering into the darkness further up the runway, Hauer saw the Libyan Yak-42. Several guards patrolled beneath the big airliner, but as yet they had not spied the activity around the Lear. "Burton!" Hauer called into the darkness. "There's no pilot in here!"

Hearing a scuffle of footsteps at the edge of the runway, Hauer raised his pistol.

"Help me get him in!" said Burton.

"My God," Hauer breathed, spying Diaz's blood-soaked shirt. He slid beneath the Cuban's shoulder and struggled up the jet's three steps. It took both him and Burton to get Diaz to the Lear's cockpit. Hauer looked down at the Cuban's face. "He's unconscious!"

"Just resting his eyes," said Burton. "He's a tough little bugger." The Englishman slapped Diaz on the cheek. "Aren't you, sport?"

The Cuban's head lolled forward in something close to a nod.

"Jesus," Hauer muttered.

As Hans pulled the Lear's step-door closed, someone grabbed it from outside and tried to pull it down. *"Captain!"* he shouted.

Hauer darted back to the cabin, kicked the step-door down, and shoved General Steyn's pistol through the door. Gadi Abrams stood there gasping for breath, his left trouser leg soaked with blood. Hauer pulled the Israeli into the plane and secured the door.

"Ready!" Hans shouted forward.

In the cockpit, Burton strapped Diaz into the pilot's chair. Everyone else hunkered down in the passenger cabin. Ilse did her best to comfort General Steyn, who lay with his head propped on a small pillow. Hess's briefcase lay on the floor at Ilse's feet.

"Can that man fly?" she asked worriedly.

"If he wants to live," Gadi groaned as he tied a pillowcase around his torn thigh.

Hans ducked his head and walked up to the cockpit partition. Over Hauer's shoulder he saw Burton sitting in the copilot's seat, massaging Diaz's ashen face. "Can he do it?" Hans asked quietly.

Hauer shrugged. "He's trying."

Diaz's hands floated forward and hit several switches. The cockpit lights came on. Hans felt a soft thrumming in the jet's hull. Burton glanced up at Hauer.

"Those camel humpers will come running when they hear the engines, mate. Can you handle them?"

Hauer moved back into the cabin and lifted a Libyan Uzi from the floor. Hans pulled open the rear door for him.

"Put your hand in the back of my pants," said Hauer. Then, with only Hans to keep him from falling, he leaned out and drew a bead on the black figures beneath the Libyan airliner.

Suddenly General Steyn sat up and shouted, "Can't! Can't let Stern . . . detonate! He'll kill thousands . . . *millions!*"

Ilse tried to calm the South African, but he would not be comforted.

"Shut him up!" Gadi snapped from the floor.

Hans glared back at the Israeli. "You shut up, you fucking fanatic!"

"Everyone be quiet," Ilse begged. *"Please."*

The Lear shuddered once, then lurched forward. Through the open hatch Hans heard distant shouts of alarm. Hauer's Uzi barked three times in quick succession. Hans thought he saw two Libyans fall, but in the darkness it was hard to tell.

"Secure that hatch!" Burton shouted from the cockpit.

Hauer fired twice more, then he pulled the steps up into the Lear's belly. The sleek jet gathered speed rapidly. Through a side window Hans saw the Yak-42 flash past. Diaz pushed the engines to their limit. Everyone in the cabin clung fearfully to whatever he could.

Hauer struggled up to the cockpit and looked out through the windshield. He saw only darkness ahead. Gripping the back of Diaz's seat, he heard the Cuban muttering a prayer. He said a silent one himself. Suddenly Diaz pulled back hard on the stick, and with a sickening *boom* the Lear tore itself from the earth's grasp. The dark veld fell away beneath them.

They were airborne.

CHAPTER FORTY-SIX

Stern peered into the darkness at the far end of the lab. Hess lay motionless beside him. The old Nazi had dragged himself too close, and Stern had clubbed him with the butt of his rifle. He looked dead. Three silent minutes had passed since the last explosion. Then—just seconds ago—Stern thought he had heard a furtive shuffle from the shadows.

There . . . again. He recognized the sound now: the stealthy rustle of soldiers maneuvering into position.

"Herr Horn!" called a voice from the darkness. "*Guten Abend!* This is Major Ilyas Karami! I have come to take delivery of my weapon!"

Squatting behind the bomb with the stripped wires in his hands, Stern leaned his cheek against the cool metal.

"Herr Horn!" Karami shouted. "There is no need for more men to die! We want the same thing, don't we? The destruction of Israel!"

Stern glanced at his watch. He reluctantly set the detonator wires aside and picked up one of the rifles Gadi had left him.

"Herr Horn!" Karami cried. "I know you are there!"

Stern stared down at the exposed detonator wires. They were blurred now. The radiation had done its work. *I could touch them together now,* he thought, *and end the whole mad game. But the others will barely be airborne by now, if they've reached the plane at all. Gadi . . . Hauer . . . Frau Apfel . . . the Spandau papers . . .*

Stern pulled back the bolt on the R-5 and pointed it into the darkness.

"If you do not answer," Karami shouted, "I shall be forced to order my men forward!"

Stern rose to one knee and depressed the R-5's trigger.

The muzzle flashes seared his damaged eyes as he strafed the far end of the dark lab. He fired until the clip ran out, then picked up another rifle. His ears were ringing like fire bells.

Someone moaned in agony.

A deep voice screamed Arabic in the darkness: "Don't shoot back!"

He doesn't want his men to hit the bombs, Stern realized. *That might buy me a few more—*

Stern froze. Through the groans of the wounded he could hear the rustle of the Libyans edging forward through the unfamiliar darkness. They were coming. Fighting an almost irresistible urge to thrust the wires together, he cocked the second R-5, rose up, and opened fire.

The Lear was at seventeen thousand feet and still climbing. Diaz had pointed the sleek jet dead-east, toward Mozambique and the Indian Ocean. It streaked upward like a bullet, passing four hundred miles per hour. Alan Burton sat in the cockpit beside Diaz and did his best to keep the Cuban conscious, while behind them a violent argument raged in the passenger cabin.

Gadi Abrams wanted Hess's briefcase. He meant to obey his uncle's last wish, and that meant taking the papers to Israel himself. The briefcase lay beside Ilse, who was ministering to General Steyn at the rear of the cabin.

"It is my duty and my right!" the Israeli repeated. "Hess was a Nazi and his mission was directed at the Jews!"

Hauer stood up from his seat beside Hans and placed himself between Gadi and Ilse. "Take it easy," he said. "The Holocaust doesn't give you the right to take possession of every scrap of history relating to the Nazis. The papers deal first and foremost with Germans. We should be the ones to—"

"You'll bury them forever!" Gadi accused.

Hauer shook his head. "You idiot. Those papers don't hurt Germany, they hurt Britain."

"This is ridiculous!" Hans snapped. "We could all die at any moment! If you want to argue about who owns the Spandau papers, it's me. I found them, so just shut up. Ilse will keep them until we're safely away from here."

"When will that be?" Ilse asked Dr. Sabri.

"I'm not sure," the Libyan replied. "It depends on how

fast we are moving. We could be nearing the minimum safe distance point now."

"Listen to me!" Gadi interrupted. "You may have found the Spandau papers, but Hess gave the Zinoviev book to my uncle."

"In the belief that he was my grandfather," Ilse reminded him.

Gadi wobbled uncertainly on his wounded leg. Fearing he might lose consciousness, he raised his R-5 threateningly. "Tell Frau Apfel to pass the case to me, Captain. Or I will be forced to take it."

"Put that down!" Hauer bellowed. "If you fire in here you'll kill us all!" He took a step toward the commando.

"Stop!" Gadi warned, jabbing his rifle forward.

With the mesmerizing stare he had used on the Russian KGB officer all the way back at Spandau Prison, Hauer took one more step, then pinioned Gadi's wrist with a grip of iron.

"Let go!" Gadi cried, his face white with rage. The muzzle of the R-5 was an inch from Hauer's left eye.

"Drop it," Hauer said quietly.

"Let's all calm down, shall we?"

Alan Burton had spoken quietly from the cockpit door, but his MP-5 submachine gun put steel in his words. "Let the nice lad go, Captain," he said. "So he can drop his weapon."

"He won't drop it."

"I think he will," said the Englishman. "This is a pressurized cabin, Captain. If he fires that rifle in here, he will kill us all—himself included—and the papers will be destroyed. My weapon, on the other hand, holds teflon-coated bullets. They explode before they pass through a human body. A rather handy innovation. Our Israeli friend probably knows all about it."

Hauer loosened his grip.

"And I must tell you, gentlemen," Burton added, "I rarely miss what I aim at."

Hauer let go. Gadi reluctantly let his R-5 fall to the cabin floor.

"None of you need worry about the papers anyway," said Burton, "because I am taking that briefcase with me."

Hauer and Gadi gaped at the Englishman. Burton grinned. "You didn't think I was down in that basement on vacation, did you? I was sent to do a job. To kill a man. And after hearing what was said down there, I finally realized who that man was. Bloody Rudolf Hess! That's the reason London used me in the first place. I'm a mercenary, I'm totally deniable." Burton smiled engagingly. "I'd like to thank you all for doing my job for me. When I first heard Hess's name back in that basement, I was in quite a quandary. I needed to kill the old Nazi to fulfill my contract, but I was outgunned. Still, it worked out for the best, after all. That old fanatic we left behind is going to incinerate Hess along with everything else down there." Burton raised an eyebrow. "And *that* brings us to the papers—the only loose end that could interfere with my final payment. I'll just take that case, love, if you don't mind."

"But the British government will bury the papers!" Gadi cried.

Burton shrugged. "Not my problem, sport."

Gadi leaned down toward his rifle.

Burton whipped his MP-5 toward the Israeli. "Don't be a fool, lad."

"I can't believe it," Gadi murmured. "After all this time . . . all the killing. The British government will just wipe it all out again. They've been covering up this story for almost fifty years. You *can't* do this. Israel will pay you anything for those papers! Anything! What . . . what were you to be paid for killing Hess?"

Burton smiled sadly. "Sorry, lad. Repatriation to England is my price, and Israel can't meet it."

"Forget the papers," Hauer told Gadi. "Don't you understand? You think you're going to unveil some grand conspiracy to the world? The damned world doesn't care."

"You're wrong!" said Gadi, his eyes burning.

"I wish I was. Oh, the Jews care, of course. It's one more thing they can hold up to the world and say, 'Look here, you're all guilty!' I'm sure some British bluebloods are quivering in their slippers. But the rest of the world doesn't give two shits if Hess was in bed with the Duke of Windsor. The story would sell a lot of magazines and TV commercials, but that's all. Don't you get it? The people who matter *already know the story.* You think the Russians didn't know about the double in Spandau? About Hitler's plan? You think the Americans didn't know? Do you know how many Nazis were shielded by Western governments after the war? *Hundreds.*"

"This is different!" Gadi cried. "Hess was part of Hitler's inner circle!"

"It's no different," Hauer insisted. "Look where we had to come to get Hess. He lived in a fortress. Remember the Union Building in Pretoria? Hess had informers in the highest levels of this government. Where do you think he got those nuclear weapons? He was a *billionaire*—part of the military infrastructure of a world power."

"If the British knew about Hess all along," Hans interjected, "why did they wait so long to kill him?"

Hauer turned to Burton. "When did you receive your contract to kill Alfred Horn?"

The Englishman shrugged. "About eight weeks ago. He was a tough man to get close to."

Hauer nodded thoughtfully. "And Hess's double was murdered just five weeks ago. It seems to me that the British decided very recently that all traces of Hess's true mission had to be wiped out. Obviously they were afraid of something. Maybe they thought something like the Spandau diary was about to surface. That the real story was about to break after all those years."

Hans was shaking his head. "But in the basement Hess said that British Intelligence had *lured* him to Britain to trick Hitler. That would make the British heroes. Why would they suppress that story?"

Hauer smiled. "Hess said MI-5 learned the identities of British traitors and played them back against Germany. That's a very different thing. British *Intelligence* did a heroic thing, yes. But that doesn't excuse the treason of the Englishmen MI-5 used against Hitler. For fifty years British Intelligence has been forced to hide English heroism to conceal English villainy. From what Hess said back there, probably royal treason as well."

Even Alan Burton looked intrigued by the mystery he had unknowingly been a part of. "But that doesn't answer the question. Why wouldn't they have liquidated Hess years ago?"

Hauer shrugged. "Each held the other's secret. The same secret. And each, for different reasons, feared exposure of the truth. It was a standoff—Hess versus British Intelligence." Hauer looked thoughtful. "But I can't believe the secret was held only by those two. I wouldn't be surprised if Israeli Intelligence knows who Horn really is. He used the very name his double gave when he parachuted into Scotland. How long would it take the Mossad to figure that one out? A week? Yet the story has never been made public. If what Stern said about Israeli/South African nuclear agreements is true, I can see how the Israelis might have let him live. Hess left Germany in the spring of 'forty-one, and most of the atrocities weren't committed until much later."

"That's not true!" Gadi argued.

"It is," Ilse said softly. "My grandfather told me that the real crimes against humanity didn't happen until after Hess left Germany."

"That's obscene!" Gadi shouted. "You're crazy!"

"This is all terribly interesting," Burton cut in, "but I'm not much on history." He turned to Ilse. "Let's have that case, love."

"Take it!" Ilse cried. She hurled the briefcase at the Englishman.

Gadi tried to intercept it, but his wounded thigh prevented him. The case landed at Burton's feet. "Would you get that for me, Captain?" he said to Hauer, keeping his gun trained on Gadi.

Hauer knelt and retrieved the case.

"Open it."

The case was not locked. Hauer opened it and glanced inside. A thin smile touched the corners of his mouth.

Gadi snatched the case. Burton made no move to stop him. The young Israeli threw the case to the floor. *"Where are the papers!"* he demanded, his eyes on Ilse.

Ilse glared from one man to the other. "Those papers have caused enough pain! They should have been buried with the rubble of Spandau! The whole sick business should be allowed to die!"

Gadi put his face in his hands. "Oh God . . . no."

Ilse raised her chin defiantly and pointed toward the tail of the Lear. "Yes," she said. "They're back there."

"In the tail?" Burton asked hopefully.

"In hell."

Stern had shot three Libyans already, but he couldn't hold out much longer. If the Libyans rushed him, he might be hit before he could detonate the weapon. He simply couldn't afford to buy the Lear any more time. Crouching low, he laid his rifle gently on the floor and took one of the bright copper wires in each hand.

"I want to talk!" cried a voice from the shadows.

"It's too late for talk!" Stern shouted back, the first verbal response he had given the Libyans.

"Why do you fight me, Herr Horn?" Karami asked. "Listen, please. I know who you are. Deputy Führer Rudolf Hess, yes? You visited Tripoli in 1937, I believe. You have seen my people, sir. We have the same goal, you and I—the destruction of the Jews. I was wrong to attack you, perhaps, but I need *all* the weapons you have here. Speak to me, please! Let me finish the job your Führer gave to the Mufti of Jerusalem! Please, Herr Hess. I do not understand your position!"

Stern laughed silently. "Come forward, Major. You'll understand soon enough."

Karami considered this. "All right," he said at length. "I'm coming! I am unarmed!"

Crouched behind the bomb casing, Stern watched the tall, black-mustached Arab step from the darkness, his hands raised above his head. His onyx eyes blazed with fierce passion.

"Herr Horn?" Karami asked, puzzled.

Stern raised a hand and pointed to the motionless heap lying just in front of the bomb cart. "There," he said.

Karami's eyes searched the gloom until they settled on Hess. "Who is behind there?" he asked. "Mr. Smuts? What happened here?"

"Allah took a hand in things," Stern said.

For the first time, Karami noticed the masked corpses of the South African commandos. Not far away he saw the body of Pieter Smuts. Then his black eyes lifted, drawn by the gleaming cylinders behind which Stern waited.

"So there are three," he said, his voice shallow. "I knew there had to be more. I *knew* it."

Stern waited in silence. In spite of what the X-rays had done to him, he felt strangely awed by the knowledge that his life was now measured in seconds. His mouth felt dry as sawdust.

"If Hess is dead," Major Karami wondered aloud, "and Mr. Smuts is dead ... who are you?"

Stern poked his head above the bomb casing. Then,

slowly, he raised his hands. The exposed copper wires glinted in the dim light.

With a weight like a cancer in his stomach, Ilyas Karami comprehended what the wires meant. "What do you want?" he asked hoarsely. "Do you want gold? Drugs? Diamonds? For these weapons, my master will grant you a kingdom!"

Stern crouched lower. He prayed to God the Learjet was well away by now.

"Why do you consider this mad thing?" Karami asked, genuinely puzzled. "You want to die? You want to be a martyr? Martyrdom is for the sons of Allah, my friend, not good Christians. For rescuing these weapons you will be a hero in my nation! Come out from there and let me make you the richest man in the world! Come out and tell me who you are."

Stern laughed. The sound was brittle as a voice from the grave. "We're both martyrs, Major. Isn't it funny how that works out?" His face hardened. "I'll see you in the afterlife, my Arab friend. *Shalom.*"

In one terrible instant Ilyas Karami realized that the man facing him across his coveted weapons was a Jew. From the hot core of his being he screamed a curse of pure hatred at his lifelong enemy, at the same time jerking out the pistol he had hidden in the belt behind his back.

But at that moment Hess jerked up from the floor and clutched at the wires in Stern's hands. *"Deutschland!"* he shrieked. *"Deutschland über Alles!"*

Stern swatted the skeletal arms aside, wrapped the two bare wires together, and clenched them in his fist. He smiled sadly, then closed his eyes.

Karami emptied his pistol as fast as his finger could pull the trigger, but Hess's still-struggling body shielded Stern from the first bullets. The old Nazi danced horribly in midair, and by the time a slug found Stern it was too late.

In the blink of an eye, darkness turned to noon. Even with the nose cone of the Learjet pointed away from the blast, the flash blinded everyone inside. Diaz lost control of the aircraft. It pitched over into a screaming, spinning dive, hurtling earthward at over five hundred miles per hour.

In the cabin, people slammed into each other in the terror of flashblindness. General Steyn screamed in pain.

Hauer half-fell past Burton into the cockpit. "Straighten up!" he screamed. *"Level out!"*

The Lear's engines whined insanely as the plane plummeted earthward. Hauer grabbed the Cuban's wounded shoulder and squeezed maniacally. *"Level out, damn you! The blast wave's coming! The blast wave!"*

Somehow Diaz managed to pull out of the dive. He had almost succeeded in stabilizing the Lear when the blast wave hit. The solid wall of superheated air tossed the tiny jet like a wave throws a surfboard, pitching it up and forward, then dropping it into a trough of dead air. Hauer felt a sudden nausea, as if hydroplaning a car around a curve, then just as suddenly the feeling passed. He heard Diaz cursing furiously from the cockpit as he wrestled with the controls.

"Is anyone hurt!" Hauer shouted. His vision was slowly returning.

"I can't see!" someone moaned.

"Holy Mother of God," General Steyn mumbled. "He did it! *Stern actually did it!*"

"I can't see anything!" someone cried. "Help me!"

"The blindness will pass!" Dr. Sabri shouted from the floor. "We were lucky! It could have been twice that bad!"

"The papers!" Gadi muttered, his voice cracking. "The Spandau papers are gone! Jonas is dead! *Where is that German bitch?*"

With Ilse now the object of all his rage and frustration, the Israeli scrabbled blindly across the cabin floor in search of his rifle. Hauer had finally had enough. When Gadi's hand closed around Ilse's ankle, Hauer lifted the rifle from beneath the Israeli's sightless eyes and struck him on the side of the head with its stock. Gadi collapsed in a heap. Quickly Hauer collected every weapon he could find—beginning with Burton's MP-5—and piled them all behind some pillows at the back of the cabin. Then he took Hans's hand and led him over to Ilse.

"It's all right," he said. "Just keep your eyes closed for a minute."

Ilse's arms went around Hauer's neck as well as Hans's. "We're alive," she said softly. "My God, we're alive." She opened her eyes. Tears of relief welled up in them and ran down her cheeks. A smile started across her face; then she pulled up her hand and covered her mouth. "Stern," she said haltingly. "Herr Stern . . . he's dead."

As Hauer held Hans and Ilse in his arms, he thought about that. He suspected that the old Israeli would have called the trade more than fair. The mystery of Rudolf Hess would probably remain "unsolved" forever—or at least until the British government opened its secret vaults—but Stern had never cared much about that. What mattered was that the State of Israel had received a new lease on life. A gift from one of its youngest fathers, and eldest sons.

EPILOGUE

(WASHINGTON)—At 8:47 P.M. Eastern Standard Time last night, a National Weather Office RORSAT 6 meteorological satellite recorded an intense flash and heat bloom over the northeastern corner of the Republic of South Africa. Weather Office analysts report that the event was consistent with data resulting from a large underground nuclear blast. The Weather Office recorded many such events over the Soviet Union during the 1960s, and believes its opinion to be accurate.

Both the National Reconnaissance Office and the Pentagon have refused to comment, but it is believed that this incident confirms the existence of a secret nuclear weapons arsenal in South Africa. A similar event was photographed over the Indian Ocean off the South African coast in 1984. Weather Office analysts do not have the equipment required to measure the release of radiation into the atmosphere, but they suggest that, with the prevailing winds over the northern Transvaal yesterday, any such radiation would likely have been blown out over the Indian Ocean.

Several international environmental groups have expressed outrage over the test. National Weather Office analysts place the probable nuclear test site less than 20 miles from the Kruger National Park, one of the richest preserves for wildlife on the African continent. The environmental organization Greenpeace intends to file complaints with both the International Atomic Energy Agency and the United Nations, but the activist group expects that "little will be done."

The White House has issued no statement on the event, and government officials in Pretoria and Capetown have bluntly refused to grant interviews, calling the charges alarmist and unfounded. A National Weather Office analyst who refuses to be named gave this comment: "Tell the South Africans, 'Welcome to the Club.'"

(WEST BERLIN-API)—At 4:00 A.M. Central European Time yesterday, an elite counterterror unit consisting of GSG-9 commandos working in concert with the U.S. Army stormed a Friedrichstrasse police station and cleared it of hostile elements. U.S. Army Colonel Godfrey Rose, the American commander on the scene, stated that a hostage situation had been going on for some time without the knowledge of the press. The terrorists inside the station had not demanded media coverage, Rose said, and it was felt that premature press involvement "could have impeded the rapid resolution of what was not a critical, but rather an unpleasant situation."

API has no further information on the terrorists who took over Abschnitt 53, but the West Berlin mayor's office has indicated that several West Berlin police hostages died in the assault. Among them was Wilhelm Funk, the prefect of West Berlin police. Funk, along with his fellow officers, will be buried on Friday with full police honors. Colonel Rose, who had worked extensively with Funk in the past, called his death "a loss that will be deeply felt, but is best put behind us." The funeral service at the Wilmersdorf cemetery is expected to draw thousands of loyal West Germans.

Minutes of the Special Inter-Allied Intelligence Conference on Disposition of the Phoenix Case. Schloss Bellevue, West Berlin

[Present: (US) Colonel Godfrey Rose, Chief of Military Intelligence, West Berlin; US Undersecretary of State John Taylor/ (USSR) Colonel Ivan Kosov; Grigori Zemenek, Chairman of KGB/ (UK) Sir Neville Shaw, Director General MI-5; Peter Billingsley, Special Counsel to Her Majesty/ (FRG) Senator Karl Hofer, Aide to the Chancellor; Hans-Dietrich Müller, Director of Operations for the BND (West German Intelligence) Meeting chaired by Undersecretary Taylor]

Following passage excerpted from the questioning of Julius K. Schneider, Kripo Detective First Grade:

[Taylor] Detective Schneider, is it your opinion, then, that the Russians will carry through with their purge of those Stasi officers who are listed on Captain Hauer's list?

[Zemenek] I strenuously object, Mr. Undersecretary! I have assured this council that all appropriate measures are being taken.

[Taylor] Then you should have no objection to Herr Schneider answering the question.

[Schneider] I believe the Russians will vigorously pursue such a purge. (pause) It's the political members of Phoenix I worry about, sir, on both sides of the Wall. I doubt that Captain Hauer's list contained a full—

[Müller] Objection! There is no evidence whatsoever that the Phoenix cult has influence in the political hierarchy of the Federal Republic! If there is such evidence, our Russian comrades should force the Stasi to open their infamous blackmail files, so that we may see who is vulnerable to coercion.

[Hofer] I do not think that will be necessary, gentlemen. The Chancellor has full confidence that our colleagues in the BND can root out whatever remains of this atavistic, but entirely anomalous reversion to the Nazi period of Germany's history.

[unintelligible grumbling on all sides]

[Taylor] Gentlemen, I understand the ramifications of the Phoenix matter. What I'm having difficulty accepting is that Rudolf Hess actually survived the war and lived until just a few days ago. The man would have been over ninety years old.

[Rose] (laughter) Ever watch the *Today* show, Mr. Undersecretary?

[Taylor] I don't follow you, Colonel.

[Rose] Every morning Willard Scott flashes up pictures of people having their birthdays. Every picture he puts up is of someone over a hundred years old. Hell, Prisoner Number Seven only died six weeks ago!

[Billingsley] (clears throat) Gentlemen, I am loath to waste Detective Schneider's valuable time with trivialities. If I may, I would like to return to the question of the Hess material. The security of the Spandau papers, the Zinoviev papers, and other related artifacts. Her Majesty's government is most concerned to know that all such material is now in the possession of the United States government, particularly, in Colonel Rose's Military Intelligence office here in West Berlin. Detective Schneider?

[Schneider] Sir?

[Billingsley] Is it your opinion that all tangible evidence of Rudolf Hess's actual mission in 1941 has now been suppressed? That no physical artifacts remain?

[Schneider] Artifacts?

[Billingsley] Photocopies, photographs, tapes, et cetera?

[Schneider] (lengthy pause) To the best of my knowledge, that is true.

[Shaw] Frankly, I'm much more concerned about the Russian promise. For the record, I want us all to be absolutely clear on that. In exchange for the list of Phoenix members compiled by Captain Hauer, the Soviet government will drop all public pursuit of the Rudolf Hess case.

[Kosov] (burst of unintelligible Russian)

[Zemenek] Colonel Kosov! I apologize, gentlemen. Yes, that is the agreement. My signature carries the weight of the Politburo.

[Billingsley] Thank you, Mr. Chairman. And we are agreed, then—unanimously—that the Israeli government will not be informed of the contents of any of these documents?

[Rose] From what we've learned about the secret Israeli/South African nuclear agreements, and the involvement of Rudolf Hess, I doubt the Israelis would make the story public even if they knew.

[sounds of agreement]

[Taylor] Well, then, gentlemen. If we've finished with Detective Schneider, may I suggest that we adjourn for lunch? We can resume at two P.M.

[Abstract concluded]

1:45 P.M. Martin Luther Hospital: British Sector, West Berlin

Professor Natterman looked up in surprise from his hospital bed. Framed in the doorway was the huge, hatted figure of the Kripo detective whom Natterman had last seen killing a Russian in a South African hotel room. Natterman shook his head to clear the fog of pain medication.

"Guten Abend, Professor," Schneider said.

Natterman nodded.

"You look worse than you did in South Africa."

"Infection," Natterman explained. "By the time I reached a hospital here in Germany, sepsis had set in. They say I'll be cured in two weeks or so."

Schneider smiled. "Good for you." He removed his hat and overcoat and stepped closer to the hospital bed. "You know, Professor, I just came from a meeting where a lot of Allied officials asked me a lot of questions about the Hess case."

Natterman looked suddenly wary.

"They wanted to know if any evidence of the truth remained. If there were any photocopies, tapes, anything like that. You know? When I thought about it, I did seem to remember some photographs Captain Hauer had in the hotel room. Or negatives."

Natterman lay still as a stone.

Schneider sniffed the hospital air with distaste. "I hate these places," he said. "Whenever I come, people I know seem to die." He laid an arm on Natterman's shoulder. "I told those bureaucrats nothing survived. To hell with them, you know?"

Natterman said nothing.

"But I've been thinking," Schneider went on, "about what should happen to evidence like that. *If* it really existed, of course. Should it be trumpeted in the press, or in a book? Rehashed for the millionth time like all the other Nazi history? Or should it be buried, like the Allies want it to be?"

After a long silence, Natterman said, "I've been doing some thinking too, Detective. I've decided that the decision should not be up to us. To Germans."

Schneider nodded slowly.

"Help me out of bed," Natterman said suddenly.

"What? The doctors said I couldn't visit you more than ten minutes. You can't get up."

Natterman's face contorted in pain as he pulled something from beneath his bedclothes. An envelope. "I've got something I need to deliver," he said. "And I want to make sure you take it where I want it to go. So, help me up."

"How do we get past the doctors?"

"You're a policeman, aren't you?"

Schneider put on his hat and overcoat, then lifted the old man out of bed as if he were a child.

* * *

At the Wilmersdorf post office, Schneider took a final glance at Natterman as he walked into the building. The old historian's face, framed in the open window of the taxi, was flushed by the freezing wind.

Inside the post office, Schneider withdrew Natterman's envelope from his coat pocket. When he saw the address scrawled on the paper, he smiled. Schneider suspected it had taken a great act of sacrifice on the professor's part to give up what this envelope contained. *If* it contained what Schneider thought it did. Unable to resist the temptation, Schneider took a small knife from his pocket, slit open the envelope, and looked inside.

He saw several strips of black-and-white photographic negatives. He held one up to the light. He saw what could only be Latin. The Spandau papers. The envelope also contained a note, written on a piece of hospital notepaper. It said:

> *To whom it may concern:*
>
> *I imagine your superiors will know what to do with these. The German who wrote these words wanted his story told, but it is for your people to decide what is best.*
>
> *Signed,*
>
> *A good German*

Schneider folded the paper and slipped it back into the envelope. Then, ignoring a long line, he stepped up to the postal counter. The clerk made an extremely rude face and motioned for him to move to the back of the line. Schneider pulled out his wallet, threw a banknote on the counter, and showed the clerk his Kripo ID.

"Polizei," he grunted. "Give me some tape."

The clerk handed Schneider a tape dispenser. Schneider carefully resealed the envelope; then he shoved it across to the clerk. "You make sure this gets where it's going," he said. "And no slip-ups. It's Polizei business."

The clerk snatched the envelope and stuffed it behind his counter. He acted annoyed, but Schneider could tell he'd gotten the message. Schneider pulled his coat collar around his big neck and ambled out into the freezing Berlin wind.

He nodded to Professor Natterman; then he grinned. He felt better now.

Inside the post office, the clerk jerked the envelope out of its slot and read the address.

Israeli Ambassador
c/o Israeli Embassy
5300 Bonn 2 Simrock Allee #2
Bonn, Germany

The return address was the same.

"Jews in the damned police department," the clerk muttered. "What the hell is happening to this country?"